SAN FRANCISCO

*Four Romances Blossom
in the City by the Bay*

Kristin
BILLERBECK

Published by Barbour Publishing, Inc., P.O. Box 719, Uhrichsville, Ohio 44683, www.barbourbooks.com

Our mission is to publish and distribute inspirational products offering exceptional value and biblical encouragement to the masses.

Member of the
Evangelical Christian
Publishers Association

Printed in the United States of America.
5 4 3

Dear Readers,

California offers everything a person could want: beaches, mountains, redwoods, and one of the most beautiful cities in the world: San Francisco. I'm the third generation of my family to be raised in the San Francisco Bay Area. I went to the same high school as my parents. In other words? I love California. My dad blessed me with a love for its history, and I have traveled in nearly every part of this wonderful, diverse state.

In a world where the news is filled with bad stories of California, I hope this book offers a small taste of my world—a few of the things that make this state rock!

Currently, I live in the Gold Country with my husband, a coach at a Christian school, and our four children. Now, rather than the beach, we take little jaunts to Tahoe to hike, golf, and mountain bike. An entirely new California for me, but still one of wonder and beauty. Blessings to you.

Kristin Billerbeck

Grace in Action

To Arin, an amazing and godly woman who inspires me daily.

Chapter 1

"Mom, can we go get the InCharge CD tonight? It's brand-new." Josh Brawlins flashed his irresistible smile, made even more charming by his two missing front teeth.

"Josh, we can't go out tonight. You have homework, and besides, we haven't the money for such things right now." Grace flipped a hamburger, searing it against the pan. "I just started this job. Things will be better when our steady paycheck starts again."

"Aw, Mom!"

"You know, I remember the days when you begged for more Barney videos. They had *those* for free at the library."

"Mo–om!" Josh whined as though he'd never heard anything so ridiculous. "Everyone at school has the new CD. Plee–ase!"

"Why don't you ask someone to borrow it?" Grace forced a smile as she put the finishing touches on their hamburger buns. "Is that enough mustard for you?" She placed the dish on the table in front of her young son, hoping to change the subject. Her son being a pauper among princes infuriated her and only caused her to harbor more resentment toward his father. What kind of man abandoned his boy? Especially Josh, who seemed to radiate joy from his very soul.

"Hamburgers, again?" Josh crinkled his nose.

"Yes, hamburgers, again." Grace wrangled her feet free from the torture of her high heels. Sensing her son's disappointment, she grasped his chin, pulling his dark brown eyes to hers. "Maybe you can ask for the new record at Christmas."

"Mom, records are from the Dark Ages. We have CDs now." He pulled free and grimaced at his dinner.

"Oh yes, the Dark Ages where I came from. I forgot."

"Mom?" The innocence returned to his voice, crushing the teenager that lurked within his six-year-old body.

"Yes, Josh."

"You know, we have the smallest house in the whole neighborhood. It's not even a real house. It's a guesthouse next to a real house. My friends call our house 'the rental.' "

Grace swallowed hard, slamming her plate on the table. *When did kids get so sophisticated? When did children begin practicing the latest dance steps at five years old? When did they notice and compare everything, including how many bathrooms one had?* Grace pondered the thoughts before answering Josh gently.

7

"We do live in a rental, Josh. That means we pay money to someone to live in his house. We're very lucky to live in this neighborhood. You're getting the finest education the public system has to offer." She sucked in a deep breath. Most kids in Josh's class had more spending money in their pockets than Grace had for the month.

"Yeah, but why do we live in a rental? Why don't we have a fancy car that smells like new shoes? Or a house with two doors in the front, like everyone else? Colton says it's because we got no daddy here."

"We have no daddy," she corrected. "Josh, sometimes families are just different. Our family is different. We have each other." Grace looked into his sad, brown eyes and tousled his sandy locks.

How long could she keep up this charade of living in the exclusive Los Altos Hills without a penny to her name? She hoped forever. At least until Josh got to college. Humiliating as it might be, she'd gladly be embarrassed every day of her life for Josh to have an education. He might not have the latest sneakers, but he'd leave with the same education. She smiled smugly. A little shame wouldn't hurt Josh—not in the long run—but it pained her now.

Josh fingered his fork until it flopped on the floor with a clang. "Mom, Jackson said my shoes were his brother's. That ain't true, right, Mom?"

Her eyes slammed shut, and she forced the lump in her throat down. She'd never planned to be a single mother. It wasn't right her son had to bear this burden! "Josh, would you please just eat your hamburger?"

"Don't cry, Mom. I'm sorry. I'm sorry. Did I say something bad?"

"No, Josh. You didn't say anything bad. It's good you have questions. Always ask questions, Josh. That's how we learn."

"That's what Fireman Mike says, too."

Grace choked on her bite of hamburger. It went down like a rock. "I don't want you talking to that man. He's a nut, you understand?"

"Mom, he's not a nut. He's Miss Jensen's boyfriend, you know."

"Josh, where do you hear such things?"

"He comes to the school all the time, and Miss Jensen gets all funny around him." Josh covered his broken smile, giggling until he had to shove his hamburger back into his mouth.

"I don't want you talking to him, even when Miss Jensen is around."

"You just don't like him 'cuz he goes to church," Josh spat.

"I don't want him filling your head with stories. That's why I don't like him."

"He says Jesus is real, Mom. He told me—"

"I don't want to hear what he told you. God never helped us, Josh. We've done it all on our own. Don't forget it. If you want to live in a big mansion like Mr. Traps, you work hard in school."

Josh looked to the ceiling. "Naw, I don't want a big house like Mr. Traps. Then you gotta have people cleaning it and stuff. I want a little house, but I want two front doors. Oh, and a big stereo so I can play my InCharge really loud." Josh stood and whirled about as though starring in his own rock video.

"Then we'd best get to your homework. Finish up."

"I wish you liked Fireman Mike, Mom. You should at least meet him. He's really cool. He has this big truck. He said it's midnight blue. I couldn't tell you because I never stayed up that late, but it's dark, all right."

"Clear your plate, okay, honey? Here's your homework sheet. It's counting—your favorite."

"Mom, Fireman Mike likes cool music, too. He—"

"Josh, what is the deal? Why are you so enamored with this fireman?" Grace dropped her hamburger, her appetite now completely gone.

"Because I knew you'd say no on InCharge, and Mike said he'd buy it for me."

Grace's eyes slid shut with a great sigh. "Joshua Blake Brawlins, we do not take charity. We are not destitute."

"It's not that, Mom. It's a present. He's bringing it over tonight."

"What? Joshua, get in your room. You know better than to give our address to strangers."

"Mo—om! He'll be here any minute. After dinner, he said."

"Get in your room, Josh."

Josh scampered to his room and slammed the door with vengeance. Grace rubbed her throbbing temples. The doorbell rang.

"Who is it?" Grace asked.

"Michael Kingston." He paused. "Fireman Mike."

Grace could hear the smile in his voice, and she mumbled under her breath that Josh was going to pay for this one. Opening the door, she nearly fell backward at the sight. A wall of a man filled her doorway. Well over six feet, he looked like a weightlifter. *One of those men who has more brawn than brains,* she thought wryly. Still, it wasn't the vision she was expecting. She thought all zealots wore short-sleeved, button-up shirts and carried a Bible. Fireman Mike obviously carried something heavier than Bibles.

"Look, I don't know what Josh told you, but—"

The wall raised a solid hand. "He told me he wanted the new InCharge CD, and I got it for him."

"Why?" She eyed him warily.

"Well—" he stammered, holding out the CD.

Grace ignored the gift, crossing her arms. "Because you thought we couldn't afford it?"

"Yes, actually." Mike made no apologies for his appearance at her door. He didn't try to pretend he was here for anything other than charity. For some reason, Grace looked at him with new eyes. Interested eyes. What kind of single man concerned himself with a poor kid? It wasn't natural.

"Maybe I don't want my son listening to that garbage. Did you think of that?"

He listened intently, but apparently didn't buy her story. "I grew up without a father. My mother didn't have the money for—well, for extras." Mike's blue eyes clouded. "I thought maybe I could help. I don't want anything in return. I promise." He thrust the CD toward her again. "You can throw it away if you want, but I promised Josh, and I wanted to fulfill my promise."

Grace looked to the floor. Calculations tumbled through her head. How could she afford something like this for Josh? Oh sure, he didn't need it, but Grace knew its importance to her son. She knew this CD was just one more dividing line between her son and the other children. Another stamp, *the poor kid*, across his forehead.

"I can afford five dollars a week. I would have it paid off in a month."

"I don't want your money, Mrs. Brawlins. I want Josh to be happy. This is not like everything else on the playground, Mrs. Brawlins. Music speaks to Josh, and I really felt the desire to get it for him."

"He doesn't need this, you know."

"Of course I do. Just like I didn't need the skateboard someone once bought me, but it changed my life."

Grace laughed. "A skateboard changed your life?"

"Not the skateboard. The man who gave it to me."

"Mr. Kingston—"

"Call me Mike."

"Mike, I really do appreciate what you're trying to do, but I don't want you filling Josh's head with fairy tales from church." Grace felt a pang of guilt at the denial of her childhood faith, but she forced it away. "Josh has had to deal with enough in his short lifetime. I don't want him living with false hope."

"But you do want him living without hope." The wall's deep blue eyes narrowed. He wore a rugged pair of torn Levi's and a stretched, navy T-shirt—or was it midnight blue, like his truck?

"I don't mean you any offense, Mike. But Josh's dad isn't coming to rescue him and neither is any invisible god, so I'd appreciate it if you left the matter alone."

"I'm sorry about your husband. I really am, and I'm not trying to be anything more than a friend to Josh." Mike looked her straight in the eye. "People will always let us down, but God won't. I believe that with my whole heart, Mrs. Brawlins, because I've seen it with my own two eyes."

This guy just didn't give up. *Enough with the heavenly realms already.* Sometimes she wished she'd never heard about the Bible. Right now, she wished she could childishly cover her ears and remove all of the doubt. This was how she was raising Josh, not under harsh law or a bunch of rules, but with love and encouragement. Why couldn't people understand it was her choice? Maybe part of it had to do with the fact that it was the opposite choice her mother would have made, but she wouldn't think about that now.

"It's Miss Brawlins, not Missus. It never was Missus. Does that shock you?" She eyed him harshly, seeing if her words sent his morally upright body to trembling, but he remained steadfast.

"I'm sorry. I didn't know, Miss Brawlins. I'll remember that."

Grace clenched her teeth. For some reason, it bothered her that he wasn't annoyed. "Josh is very vulnerable right now. I'd really appreciate it if you didn't fill his head with your beliefs. He doesn't have a man in his life, and he really respects what you say—"

"Maybe there's a reason for that." Josh splayed his fingers across the doorjamb.

She looked into the sincere blue eyes; the strong facial features were enough to weaken her resolve, but she held firm. "I'm raising my son on solid ground."

"You're raising him on sand."

"What?" Grace questioned.

"Nothing, Miss Brawlins. You're right. Josh is your son, and it's your business to guide him." He held out the CD again, and Grace ignored it. "I can't help but feel a kinship to him. He reminds me so much of myself as a young boy. I don't want anything from you or Josh. I just want him to know I'm here if he needs someone."

"*I'm* here, Mr. Kingston. He's my responsibility." Grace began to close the door.

"Wait!" He stuck the CD through the crack. "It's not like I'm buying you groceries, Miss Brawlins. Please, don't be so proud. It's just a CD. It doesn't mean anything. I know my mom wouldn't have had the money for it. That's all. Besides, every other kid at Los Altos Elementary had it yesterday. I just want Josh to feel he belongs."

Grace opened the door a little wider and blinked her tears away. "Thank you," she managed. She grasped the CD and looked into the wall's brilliant blue eyes. They were the color of exquisite cornflower sapphires. She didn't see pity or even pride in his gaze, simply concern. Mike turned and headed toward his truck, and with a roar of the engine, he was gone. Grace's heart pounded, and she wondered at her feelings. Why should it bother her that a total stranger just drove off?

Josh came running toward her, a bundle of energy. "Is that it? Is that it? Give it to me!"

"Joshua Brawlins, where are your manners?" Grace held the gift high above her head. "Now, since I have your attention, this CD is available to you when your homework is finished each evening. It doesn't go on until you've finished. Do you understand?"

"Yeah, Mom!" Josh jumped up and down, trying to reach the coveted music. "I told you Fireman Mike was cool."

"Yes, you did." Grace had to agree, handing him the present. Josh was off like a skittering squirrel. Mike Kingston was definitely cool. The question was, how big a threat was he to their way of life?

She sighed aloud. It would do her no good to fight the virtuous fireman. Josh thought highly of the guy, and as long as he was supervised when with him, what harm could he do?

~

"Well, she let him take it." Mike settled into the driver's seat and looked to Emily Jensen, his girlfriend of two months and Josh's teacher. "I'm glad she let him take it. I wish I could let her know that I really don't want anything from her. She appeared a bit suspicious."

"I think it's great what you're doing, Mike. She *ought* to appreciate it. I mean, why wouldn't she?" Emily's voice carried a tinge of disapproval.

"Because she's been taught she has to do everything on her own, that's why. You have no idea what it did to my mom." Mike shook his head, remembering. "Miss Brawlins was never married to Josh's dad, and who knows if she's ever been able to trust anyone." Mike watched the quiet little house with melancholy.

"Great. Another out-of-wedlock mom—just what I need to deal with in the classroom every day. Single moms aren't doing me any favors as a teacher. Is it too much to ask that people get married before they bear children?"

Mike let out a short laugh. "It might help to remember behind every single mother is a father who didn't do his part."

"Women get themselves into those situations, Mike."

"I'm sure Josh's mom would have taken your opinion into consideration if she knew she was going to be abandoned." Mike tried to keep the anger from his voice. "We all make mistakes, Emily."

It was so easy to judge, so to stand outside and blame—but he'd been there. As if it were yesterday, he remembered his mother clinging to his father as the burly man tried to shake her from his large frame. The last picture he'd ever have of his father. And the echo. The fury of the slamming door as his mother sobbed.

Emily frowned. "Mike, I didn't mean—"

"Let's just drop it."

"I only meant I've dealt with Miss Brawlins. She's not exactly the warmest woman in the world. I can't imagine her appreciating much of anything, much less a favor from a stranger. I just think your charity might be better spent elsewhere."

"It's not about if she appreciates me, Emily. It's about Josh. The boy doesn't know how to play football, basketball, or even soccer. All the kids at school are friends from outside activities and play dates. Tell me how the kid is supposed to make any friends or be successful if he doesn't have the simple boyhood pleasure of sports or an invitation to any parties." Mike shook his head.

Emily stared at him, her mouth agape. She snapped it shut. "I don't know, but quite frankly, I don't think it concerns you. Lots of boys don't play sports." Emily shrugged. "I don't mean to sound coldhearted, but just because you grew up without a father, it doesn't mean you're responsible for every fatherless boy out there."

"It's different with Josh." Mike wondered at his own words. Why was it different for Josh? Probably because Mike couldn't erase the boy's image from his mind. Josh was everything Mike had once been: tentative, clumsy, and starving for a father figure and male attention. Mike couldn't explain his feelings or motives, but he needed to be there for Josh. He felt it as intensely as he'd ever felt anything.

"Mike, they have programs for kids like Josh—after-school basketball leagues, Big Brothers, lots of things. I think you're taking this too personally. You have enough worries at the firehouse. Risking your life every day is not exactly a stress-free lifestyle. No one expects a single man to take on this role." Emily smiled at him, placing her hand on his.

Mike shook his head. "God does, or He wouldn't have sent me the heart I have for Josh. It's really easy for us to ignore the needs we see around us, Emily, but I don't think I can just let this one go."

Emily pulled her hand away abruptly and tightened her arms around her chest. "She'll just sue you for something ridiculous." She turned to stare out at the dark night. "I think it's great you bought Josh the CD, but leave the rest to God and to Josh's mother."

There was nothing hard-hearted or mean-spirited about Emily. She just obviously didn't agree with Mike's latest ministry.

Mike subconsciously clenched his jaw. "That's the way Christians seem to operate in this town. No one looks after anyone else or cares." Mumbling to himself more than speaking aloud, he softened his tone. "Church is just a consumer product where you pick the best programs rather than a heart for the Lord. Well, I expect more. Jesus expects more."

Chapter 2

Grace tucked Josh into bed, kissing his warm, round cheek. He was still a baby. *Her baby.* Josh still giggled at childish cartoons, built towers with blocks when he thought no one was watching, and made car noises with his Hot Wheels on the bathtub ledge. Yet, he also studied the InCharge videos that came on during cartoon commercials and practiced the dance moves in the mirror. When had *image* become a part of his little life?

She shook her head and wiped away her tears, wishing she could hold him back. "You are so cool, Josh. If you only saw yourself as I see you. You wouldn't have to prove a thing." She rubbed her sleeping child's forehead. "Your father missed the best thing he could have ever been a part of." *Probably the only thing he ever did right,* she added silently.

The telephone broke her reverie, and she pulled it off the hook before it woke Josh. "Hello."

"Gracie?"

"Lyle?" Grace's stomach turned, and she fell against the kitchen wall at the sound of her past. "How did you get this number?"

"I heard you were working for Holmby and Falk. I got your number from one of the secretaries."

Grace tried to still her trembling hands. "If you'd called my lawyer, I'm sure he could have helped you." She lowered her voice. "Does this mean you plan to help support your son?" Grace's heart pounded like a steel pole driver.

She heard Lyle take in a deep breath of air and give an exasperated sigh into the phone. "This again? After six years, that's all you have to say to me? Listen, Gracie, I didn't call about that illegitimate kid of yours. I thought we had that squared away. I'm back in town, and I thought—"

Grace had to keep herself from becoming sick. One night. If she could take back one night in her life. *No.* She forced away the thought, shaking her head. *Then there would be no Josh without that one night.* For all her mistakes, all her sins, she was still blessed. Allowed to be called a mother when she deserved nothing so gracious.

She'd known better. Raised in a Christian home, she'd been taught right, but this man. . .this charming snake of a man said so many beautiful words. He wrapped around her with his pretty talk until she became constricted. How could she know he would bite her like a cobra, draining her of romantic emotions for good?

"I don't want to hear what you thought, Lyle. I'm not quite so naïve anymore.

14

I'm not interested in seeing you. Ever. Unless you're ready to talk about financially contributing to your son's education."

"It's no use holding a grudge, Gracie. We were younger, more passionate. I guess I got carried away thinking about the past, coming back here. I transferred from the Chicago office. If you don't want to see me, you don't want to see me, but let's not start this again."

"The only thing I want to see from you is money for our son." She heard Lyle talking to someone in business tone, and her hands began to sweat. "You don't even have to see us. You can simply deposit it in an account for his college." She tried to keep the desperation from her voice. "I think I've been more than fair."

"Unless you have DNA evidence that kid is mine, you'll never see a dime from me. It was a mistake to call. You're still as whiny as ever." The phone slammed in her ear.

She looked at the handset for a moment and placed it back in the cradle. "It's your loss, Lyle. I'll raise this fine boy and work three jobs if I have to, just to prove you had nothing to do with his greatness." She would never submit Josh to a demeaning test to prove that snake was his father. They were better off alone.

"Mom?" Josh rubbed his brown eyes, squinting to avoid the kitchen light. "Who was that?"

"It was no one, and I mean that from the bottom of my heart." Grace grimaced and took her son into an embrace, squeezing as tight as she could.

"Mom, you're smooshing me."

"That's because you are the most smooshable, lovable, gorgeous little kid any mother has a right to call her son." She loved moments like this, when Josh would let her baby him just a little bit. The stress of the phone call evaporated in her son's hug.

"I'm sorry about the CD, Mom."

"I know." She nodded.

"I have an idea for us," he said brightly. "I want to talk it over with you."

Grace glanced at the clock. "It's a little late for discussions, Josh. Can we talk about it in the morning?"

"Well, yeah, but. . .I just wanted you to know I think you should marry Fireman Mike. He'd make a way cool dad, and then we wouldn't have to live in the rental."

Grace laughed, thinking a fireman's salary was probably not much better than hers. "I bet he would make a cool dad, Josh. But don't you think Miss Jensen might have something to say about that?"

Josh shrugged. "She can find a new boyfriend."

Grace lifted her eyebrows. "But I can't?"

Josh crossed his arms. "You'd probably pick some doofus who wore a business suit and walked around with a cell phone in his ear. Like the kids at school. Their dads. I don't want *that* kind of dad." Josh wrinkled his face in disgust. "Yuck."

15

Grace had to snicker. That's exactly who she had picked, and look how it had turned out. Too bad she didn't have Josh's discernment when she was twenty-one years old.

"So Josh—if I can't get you Fireman Mike as a dad, what is it about him you like?" Grace crossed her arms. "You know, just for reference sake."

"Well." He bit his lip, bringing a finger to his mouth. "He has to be strong so we can play sports, and the other kids gotta want him as a dad so they can be jealous."

"Anything else?"

"He should like cool music and drive a cool car. Not one of those fancy SUVs with the classical music and news blaring. A real car, like a truck."

Grace nodded. "Okay, I think I got it. Cool, muscular, and with a truck. Now get to bed. It's nine o'clock."

"Really, Mom, I'm serious."

Grace bent down, looking her son directly in his bright eyes. "Son, there's a good chance we might never have a dad in our house. We have to make the best of it, okay?" There was a very good chance, for Grace would never trust herself to select a man. Clearly, it was a skill that eluded her.

Josh nodded, looking resigned. "Night, Mom."

"Good night, sweetheart. I'm sorry the phone woke you."

"That's okay, Mom. You're the bestest ever." Josh kissed her on the cheek and scrambled back to bed.

The phone rang again, and Grace reluctantly answered it. "Hello." She swallowed hard, waiting for the voice to respond. Knowing it might be *him* again.

"Miss Brawlins?" A low voice with a hint of friendliness replied, and Grace released her breath.

"Fireman Mike?"

"Yes. Listen, Miss Jensen gave me an earful on the way home, and I think I might have made a mistake giving Josh that CD without you knowing about it. I'm really sorry if I offended you. It wasn't my intention."

Grace blinked a few times. Was this a man showing humility? She narrowed her eyes. What could he possibly want from her? She'd never heard a man apologize unless he had an ulterior motive. "Right, well, is that all?" Grace stammered.

"Miss Brawlins, that's all. I just wanted to say I was sorry."

Grace instantly thought of Josh's request for a father and wondered at the man on the other end of the line. Although he was incredibly large in size with hulking shoulders and massive biceps, she could not believe the gentleness she heard in his voice. He mystified her. She chose to change her tone for Josh's sake. There was no sense pushing away the only man who showed interest in her son.

"We appreciate it, Fireman Mike." Grace paused. "I'm sorry, I don't remember your real name all of a sudden."

He laughed, and she followed suit at her treatment of his name—as if he was a public television character. "It's Mike Kingston. Michael when I'm formal, which I never am."

"Well, Mr. Kingston. You really made Josh's day, and I'll be sure to get you the money as soon as I can."

"Miss Brawlins—"

"We're not destitute, Mr. Kingston. We're not on the welfare rolls yet, and we have a nice roof over our heads so—"

"But there's no money for extras."

"What?"

"There's no money for extras like CDs or designer shoes. Am I right?"

"Mr. Kingston, I don't think that's any of your business. We are not Los Altos's charity case, and we are certainly not yours."

"No, you're not. I work with the charity cases during the Marines' Toys for Tots drive. You have it far better than many."

"What are you trying to say, Mr. Kingston? I'm afraid I don't follow you."

"I like Josh. He's a good kid, and I just wanted to do something nice for him. I'm not trying to make you look bad. I promise."

"Why Josh?" She leaned against the kitchen wall, waiting for his answer.

"Because one day I saw this little boy sitting on the playground alone, and I started talking to him. He told me all about his awesome mom, his love of everything InCharge, and just generally stole my heart. It was like stepping back twenty-five years. He's just the kind of kid you want to be around."

"I agree."

"I'm not trying to take anything from you, Miss Brawlins. I'm just trying to be some type of male role model for your son. I know it's not something you asked for, but can't you appreciate it for Josh's sake? Miss Jensen is always with us. I'm never alone with him, if that's what you're worried about. And Josh likes me. We have some sort of connection."

Grace bit her lips to hold back her cry. She liked him, too, as much as it pained her. Any man who saw the special warmth in Josh could not be all bad, and Josh did need a role model.

"Miss Brawlins, you still there?"

"Uh-huh, I'm here." Grace didn't know how to tell him, she wanted Josh to spend time with him. The request wouldn't form on her lips.

"Come to church with us on Sunday and see. Josh is interested in things of the Lord. He's a very perceptive child."

The back of Grace's neck bristled. "No. Look, you might be a great role model for my son, being a fireman and all, but no religion. Okay?"

"It's not religion, Miss Brawlins. It's faith. Josh asked me about it. I never brought it up."

"Josh asked you about religion?"

"He asked me about God, yes. I told him what the Bible says."

"When did he ask you about God?" Grace had never heard Josh mention any interest in the heavenly realms. The fact that he'd discussed it with a stranger made her heart quicken.

"About two months ago when we met on the playground. He wanted to know if his grandpa was in heaven."

Grace moaned. "His grandpa is in Modesto."

"What?"

"Never mind. Look, I don't mind if you spend time with Josh. I'd actually appreciate it." The words came easy now that she wished to avoid a different topic. "Just no church, okay?"

"Agreed. Can I take you both to dinner Sunday, then?"

Grace's hand flew to her chest. "What?"

"I'd ask Miss Jensen along, but I think being Josh's teacher, she might make him a little uncomfortable. What do you say? Just a simple dinner. . .Chili's?"

Instinctively, Grace smoothed the back of her hair. This was too close to a date for her comfort. "No, no. I don't think so."

"I just want you to be comfortable with me, Miss Brawlins. For Josh's sake?"

Grace shivered. Was there suddenly a chill in the room? "We'll see."

"Oooh," Fireman Mike clicked his tongue. "I know what that means. When my mom said that, it was a nice way of saying no. Plee—ase—that's what I used to whine to my mom. Of course I was a lot cuter back then."

I doubt that, Grace thought to herself. "Very well, dinner. For Josh's sake."

"I hope I won't be *that* bad of company. But you can endure me for one meal."

Grace doubted Fireman Mike would be anything other than charming, and that's what scared her silly. "Good night, Mr. Kingston."

"Mike."

"Good night, Mike."

"See you Sunday."

Grace hung up the phone, a wide smile breaking across her face. "Sunday." She sighed.

Chapter 3

Mike's head jerked up at the sound of the alarm, and his heart pounded against his chest. The adrenaline rush—it was as fresh today as it was ten years ago when he started training. Every time the bell sounded, his heart started that powerful beat, making him feel like Superman. Adrenaline was his friend. It fought the fear. It pushed away thoughts of flames and tragedies and allowed him to focus on his mission.

Mike raced to the truck and got in while the crew followed suit. After they drove a block or two, he flipped the switch, and a wail of sirens and lights animated the massive, red engine. He listened to the call on his earphones: Los Altos Elementary. Josh and Miss Jensen's school. He pushed away his fearful thoughts. He muttered his usual prayer; only this one was more insistent.

"Punch it!" Mike yelled, and Kyle did just that.

As the engine pulled in, all the children and teachers were lined up neatly on the grass. He breathed a sigh of relief at the sight. He sniffed the air. It was absent of smoke, and there were no flames in sight. He looked at his partner, Jared, and they nodded in a silent acknowledgment.

As though guided automatically, the firemen searched the school thoroughly. Mike scanned his quarters with a skilled eye and nose and returned to meet his partners. A simple nod from all the men in uniform led their captain to the principal.

"All's clear. You can send the children back in," the captain announced.

The principal motioned to his teachers, and the giggling parade of children started.

Mike's attention rested on the principal, who held Josh by the back of his striped shirt. Josh had great tears rolling down his cheeks, and Mike forced down his own emotions.

"Is there a problem?" Mike asked the principal.

"This is the boy who pulled the fire alarm. He's coming with me, and we're calling his parents." The principal's eyes were narrowed and his scowl ready. Clearly, this was a man who knew how to intimidate six-year-olds. "I'm sorry to have caused the department any trouble." He grimaced at an obviously frightened Josh.

Josh looked up at Mike with a pleading expression.

"Would you mind if I had a word with the boy?" Mike asked. "Sometimes the uniform can show the importance of playing pranks."

"Be my guest." The principal released Josh with a slight push.

Mike held Josh's trembling shoulders, and the rush of emotion came pouring out of the child. Racking sobs shook Josh's little frame. "Not yet, Josh. Not yet. You just wait until we're out of earshot, okay?" Mike whispered.

Josh nodded, sniffling.

Mike walked him over to the playground and sat him on a platform. "What's this all about, partner? You didn't pull that alarm, did you?"

Josh nodded again.

Mike's shoulders slumped. "Josh, you know better. As firemen, we think someone's hurt when we hear an alarm. I've seen a lot of people hurt. It's not something to tease about. Do you understand that?"

Again the little bobbing head agreed.

"So why would you have pulled the alarm?"

Josh looked around him, then finally directly at Mike. "My fifth-grade student buddy, John, told me to do it."

"You know better than to do what other kids tell you when it's a bad thing. That's no excuse."

Josh sniffled. "He said he'd beat me up if I was too chicken, and he'd tell his teacher he didn't want to be my buddy in class. He said I was a worm and made fun of my pants. I don't like him." Josh looked to the wood chips that lined the playground. "I told Miss Jensen I didn't want to be his buddy. He's always yelling at me and stuff."

"You know he can't beat you up at school, and now you're going to be in trouble with the principal. Do you see that this was not a smart thing to do?" Mike gently patted Josh's back. "From now on, you tell Miss Jensen if someone threatens you. Don't try and handle it yourself."

Josh shook his head. "He's mean, Fireman Mike. He acts all sugarlike to Miss Jensen. She'll just think I'm a baby, too."

"No one thinks you're a baby. Come on, I'll go with you to meet with Mr. Walker."

"Are they going to call my mom?"

"I think so, sport. It's a pretty serious offense to pull a fire alarm when there's no fire."

"I'm sorry, Fireman Mike. I didn't mean to scare nobody. Are you mad at me, too?"

"I'm disappointed you listened to that older kid, but I'm not angry with you, Josh. Let's go see what Mr. Walker has to say." They walked to Mr. Walker's office. The building's brightly decorated walls and modern office equipment belied its tender shape.

Most alarm systems were now equipped with fire alarm annunciators to show if there was a fire and in which zone. He looked to the wall in disgust. This one had probably been installed when the school was built. Of course the wealthy parents of Los Altos had provided everything else a private school might acquire. The walls might crumble around them, but they'd be painted in the latest fashionable color.

"Mr. Walker?" Mike stuck his head into the man's office. "Josh Brawlins is here, and he has an apology."

Josh looked up at Mike before speaking. "I'm sorry, Mr. Walker. Someone told me to pull the red handle, and I did it. I knew it was wrong."

Mike nodded proudly at Josh, clutching the little boy's shoulder.

Mr. Walker looked sternly over his glasses. "Well, son, I've called your mother. She should be here soon."

Mike saw Josh start to shiver again, and he winked. "It's okay, buddy," he whispered.

"Please don't make my mom come here, Mr. Walker. She just got this new job, and she told me she can't afford to be away from it."

Mr. Walker laughed. "Well, that's a new one."

Mike failed to see any humor in the situation and spoke up for Josh. "Josh just has his mother, Mr. Walker. Her job is very important to them."

"Well, then Josh shouldn't pull fire alarms and call the fire department here. Isn't that right?"

Josh nodded. "Yes, sir."

"As a fireman, I must agree, but I also think we need to look at Josh's age and his accomplices."

"Thank you for your help, Mr. . . ."

"Kingston."

"Yes, well, I appreciate your trying to scare our young friend into not doing this again. I'll handle it from here."

Mike nodded, taking one last look at Josh. "Of course, Mr. Walker." He couldn't resist a final blow. "It might be wise to talk to the district and update that alarm system. If there were a real fire, we would have had to sniff it out. Antiquated systems can harm children."

"Yes, well, thank you. I'll be sure to speak to the taxpayers about it."

Mike shook his head. "See ya, Josh. You hang tough." Mike offered a thumbs-up sign as he exited.

His fellow crew waited in place with all their earphones and equipment ready for departure. Mike quickened his step when he saw Grace Brawlins get out of her car. He looked at his engine, then back at her. He held up a finger to the other firemen and jogged toward the young mother.

"Miss Brawlins."

"Oh, Mr. Kingston, is everything okay?" Grace's pretty blue eyes sparkled under the sunlight, and he suddenly forgot the words at his lips. Grace Brawlins was a portrait of beauty. She had a small ruby-colored mouth, a turned-up nose, and the most flawless skin he'd ever seen. His mouth went dry as he scanned her delicate facial features.

"Mike?"

He gulped. "Everything's fine. Apparently, Josh's older buddy at school dared him to do it, so Josh pulled the fire alarm."

Grace's eyes flashed. "What? I told them I wanted him to get a new buddy. That kid was scaring Josh. Is his name John?"

"That's what Josh said. Go easy on him. He's really scared."

"Thank you, Mr. Kingston. But it's not Josh who you need to worry about. It's your girlfriend and Mr. Walker." Grace straightened her shoulders, and her heels clicked in a determined march toward the office.

Mike watched her walk away, mesmerized by her tiny figure and the fierce mother lion who lurked within such a gorgeous package. He shook such thoughts from his head. Proverbs thirty-one described true beauty, and it was not available just on the outside according to God. His crew honked the engine horn and startled Mike back into the moment. He jogged toward the engine.

~

Grace Brawlins could barely contain her anger. Her teeth threatened to grind themselves away, and she shook so it was hard to stay upright on her weakened legs.

"I'm here to see Mr. Walker," she told the secretary, who scrambled into an office and whispered something. Mr. Walker held her son by the scruff of the neck. "I'd appreciate it if you'd remove your hands from my son."

He did so without hesitation. "Mrs. Brawlins, if you'll please come into my office."

Grace followed the man and grabbed Josh's hand, squeezing it tightly. "Mr. Walker, I'd appreciate it if Josh would be allowed to go back to class. I'd prefer to speak with you alone."

He nodded. "Tell Mrs. Hanson to get you a pass and run back to class."

Josh scrambled like a cat avoiding an oncoming vehicle, and Grace was left alone with Mr. Walker. Small in stature, he wore nearly invisible eyeglasses with almost no frames to hold them in place. He dressed like the wealthy parents his school served: a pressed pair of slacks with a button-up shirt, a tie, and no jacket. Standard for the Silicon Valley.

"Mrs. Brawlins—"

"Miss Brawlins," she corrected.

"Yes, well, Josh hasn't been in my office before today, but I have heard from Miss Jensen that he can be a problem. A bit on the whiny side, wanting to be coddled and the like." He removed his rimless glasses, setting them on his oversized, metal desk. "This is a very serious issue with the fire alarm. It's a five hundred dollar fine and a mandatory day of suspension."

Grace stood, setting her outstretched arm on the desk. "You listen to me, Mr. Walker: I understand about rules, I understand about fines, and I know Josh has some issues, but let me tell you something. I told you a month ago, in writing, that

22

I did not want that child, John Taylor, near my boy. I told you that he was a bully, scaring my son and introducing him to culture I don't want him knowing about—Japanese cartoons with sexual overtones and more." She drew in a deep breath. "I want my son held accountable for his behavior, but at the same time, I want this school held accountable for its own. You have a responsibility to protect my son, and judging by today, you did not."

He cleared his throat. "Yes, well. John Taylor is from one of the finest families in Los Altos Hills. Clearly, I don't think *he's* the problem. John Taylor did not pull the fire alarm; your son did."

Grace clenched her teeth, speaking through them. "Just because John Taylor's parents donate large sums of money to this school does not make him a good kid, Mr. Walker. I can tell you stories about that boy that would make your hair stand on end." Grace sat back down and held her breath a moment to calm down. "The fact remains, I told you—in writing—to protect my son from that boy, and I don't think you have. This buddy system you've enacted is a bad idea, and if I have to prove it in court, I will."

The mention of court clearly got his attention. Mr. Walker visibly gulped and broke into a smile. "Now, Miss Brawlins, let's not be rash. We both have Josh's best interest at heart."

"I certainly hope so, Mr. Walker. The fine should be paid. I have no objections to that. He broke the law, and there are consequences. Of course it's not an amount I have handy, but I will do my best to pay it quickly." Grace sat back in her chair crossing her arms. "However, I do not want that boy allowed within twenty-five feet of my son, and I will do whatever it takes to make sure that happens. If it requires a court order, so be it."

"Miss Brawlins, I'd have no problem upholding such an arrangement if I thought it was warranted, but John Taylor is a good student and respected in this school."

"By whom?"

"Pardon me?"

"Who respects this child? Is it his teachers? The kids on the playground? Who?" Grace bent in, anxious to hear any answer. She knew the only people who had any interest in being around this bully were the fund-raisers at the school. John's parents' money bought him a lot of leeway.

"Why. . .everyone," he stammered.

"I doubt that, Mr. Walker. Besides, Josh is not a child who dislikes kids easily. It doesn't matter if I'm right or not—it only matters that I've made my demands known. There is nothing I would consider hard about keeping my son away from a fifth-grader. They have separate playgrounds, so I think it should be easily managed during school time."

Mr. Walker sighed. "Very well, Miss Brawlins. And consider the fine paid, but the day of suspension will still have to be served."

Grace smiled and shook the man's hand. "Thank you, Mr. Walker. I hope we won't meet again in such a way, but I love my son, and I want him protected at school. That's my highest priority."

"I understand."

And, Grace thought, perhaps he did.

~

Grace pulled up to their cottage, and Josh leaped out of the car and ran toward the front door. Although still February, an early spring had brought a bounty of wildflowers, and the yard was an exquisite masterpiece of color. She sniffed the lavender and rosemary and immediately forgot the day's troubles.

She opened the door, and Josh scrambled into his room. Grace dropped her bag on the sofa. She'd missed a day of work already, after only one week on the job. She sighed deeply and fell to the couch, kicking off her heels. "What a day."

Josh came to her side, holding out his new CD as a sacrifice. "Here, Mom. I'm really sorry. Are you going to lose your job?"

"Come here." Grace patted the seat next to her. "You go play the CD and enjoy yourself for a while, okay?"

"But, Mom, I pulled the fire alarm. Even Fireman Mike is mad at me."

"He's not mad at you, sweetheart. We're both disappointed. We know you know better, but even the best of us make mistakes. Go play your CD. You've had a hard day as it is."

"Mom?" Josh's wide brown eyes met hers.

"Yes, honey."

"I'm scared to go back to school."

Grace tried to hide her concern. "Why?"

"Because John said if I told anyone he told me to pull the fire alarm, he'd have us kicked out of town."

"Josh, we live in America. It's a free country, although you'd never know it with the price of housing." She looked to her confused son. "No one can kick us out of town, honey." *They can make our lives miserable,* Grace thought, *but they can't kick us out.* "John is not going to be allowed to come near you anymore. I promise."

"Mo–om! What did you do? He's going to kill me now."

"Don't use that word. He's not going to touch you, do you understand?"

"I'm not going back to school!" Josh ran to his bedroom and slammed the door. Grace flinched at the noise.

"Oh, Lord, if You're up there, why must You test us so? Can't You give my kid a break? Or does he have to pay for my sin for the rest of his life, too?" Grace pinched the bridge of her nose, hoping to still the stress she harbored beneath the surface. She let out a short laugh. "Now I'm talking to God. Is there anything more absurd?" Pressing her lips together, Grace flicked on the television and immersed herself in a mindless talk show.

The phone rang, and she ignored it, figuring it was a telemarketer. "Trust me, my zip code has nothing to do with my bank account. You've got the wrong number." But her answering machine came on, and a familiar voice left a message.

"Miss Brawlins? It's Mike Kingston. Fireman Mike. Listen, I know Josh has a mandatory day of suspension tomorrow, and I was just wondering if you two would like—"

Grace picked up the phone. "Mike?"

"Hi."

"Isn't it illegal for you to socialize with fire alarm felons?"

Mike laughed. "Listen, I got the impression Josh was a little upset with me today. I'd like to make it up to him."

"Mr. Kingston, I appreciate your interest in my son, but this is really my problem. We'll manage tomorrow."

Mike cleared his throat. "You've got a son who's afraid of his own shadow. He hasn't got many friends, and he hates school. I've been there, and I want to help. Why won't you toss away that pride and let me help Josh?"

Grace bristled at his accurate, yet searing, description of her son. "We'll handle it."

"I'm sure you will, but why not see if I can help? Someone who's been there, Miss Brawlins—I'm offering you the voice of experience."

His sincere tone caused Grace to question herself, but for only a moment. "Quite frankly, I don't trust your motives."

"My motives? What do you think they could be? Every day I face tragedy and death on my job. I've learned that the quality of life is not measured by one's bank account or by one's stellar education. Your son is hurting, Grace, and I think I can help. Please let me, if not for Josh's sake, for my own."

Grace swallowed the lump in her throat. Letting this stranger help her meant giving up her dreams of full independence. It meant showing Lyle, should he come around, that she couldn't, in fact, do this alone.

"I—"

Mike cut her off. "I'll pick you both up tomorrow at eight. Dress casually." He hung up, and she stared into the phone in disbelief.

"Allowing a man to walk over me is exactly how I got myself into this mess, Mr. Kingston." But only an insistent tone on the line answered her.

Chapter 4

What do you mean, you're spending the day with them?" Emily Jensen blinked rapidly, and her face was contorted in an unnatural shape. Mike had never seen her so upset, and he lifted his eyebrows in surprise.

"Josh is on forced suspension, and I thought I'd use the day to let Miss Brawlins get to know me." He shrugged, not understanding what had gotten Emily so riled.

Emily let out an unnatural, forceful sigh. "Josh Brawlins is on suspension, Mike. He's not supposed to have a day at an amusement park. He is supposed to be at home, thinking about what he did."

"We're not going to any amusement park, and what Josh did was what any six-year-old would do when threatened by a fifth-grader. Miss Brawlins said she made it known she didn't want Josh around that kid."

"Well, guess what, Mike? We have fifth-grade buddies at Los Altos Elementary. It's not the school's fault Josh can't get along with anyone." Emily crossed her arms, and her brows were lowered in a frightful scowl. "I can't separate the child from everyone because he's afraid to look anyone in the eye. If he needs special help, he shouldn't be in my classroom!"

"Emily, you're Josh's teacher. How can you possibly think that about that sweet kid? He's never anything but respectful, and he scrambles to please."

"If that kid is so sweet, tell me why he doesn't have any friends. Did you ever think of that in your quest to make me a villain?"

Mike's hand raked through his hair. "I'm doing no such thing, Emily. You know that in your heart. Josh dresses in everyone's hand-me-downs in a school where being color-coordinated seems to outrank scholarly pursuits." Mike could feel the blood rushing to his face, and he clenched his hands to try and relieve some of his anger. "You are a Christian woman, Emily, and a kindergarten teacher to boot. I don't see how you cannot love that kid. He's just got a charm all his own."

"I love all my kids, I'll have you know." Emily's nostrils flared. "Josh is just different. It has nothing to do with his being poor, and I resent that you would say such a thing to me."

Mike studied Emily's apartment, trying to get his mind away from this all-out battle they were engaged in. Although only a tiny studio for one, the apartment was decorated lavishly. Emily had set a candlelit dinner in the center of the room on a card table covered by a lace tablecloth. Her futon, which served as both her sofa and bed, was off to the side, covered with an elaborate, lavender floral print. The plates and silverware were lined up to Martha Stewart–perfection, and Mike wondered if he would be able to swallow anything past the angry lump in his throat.

"I'm sorry, Emily. I didn't mean to accuse you of anything. I just think Miss Brawlins's suggestion that John Taylor not be allowed around Josh was not asking too much. After all, Grace knows her son better than any of you."

"Grace?" Emily bit her lip. "You're calling this woman, an unmarried, single mother—and a non-Christian, I might add—by her first name? Did you ever stop to think what your witness might be here, Mike? Hanging around with a heathen single mother and her son is just asking for trouble." Emily turned her back on him, taking out something from the oven. Something that smelled burned. She dropped the pan with a clatter. "I thought your faith was stronger than this. You're missionary dating now?"

Mike focused on the charred meat as she removed the foil. What a fitting sight, because it summed up their dating relationship pretty accurately. It was over. Still, he felt the need to defend himself.

"I am a man of prayer, Emily. I listen to God when He speaks, and I feel called to help that boy. I've asked you time and time again to let me bring him along on our outings, and you've repeatedly turned me down. I don't see what choice I have."

"I take care of children all week. The last thing I want to do is go on a date with them." Emily flipped her brown hair back, looking at the blackened meat and bursting into tears. She blinked her large, tear-filled eyes at him, and he embraced her, patting her back.

"God is calling me, Emily," he whispered into her ear. "If you can't cooperate with me now, you won't cooperate with me later. I'm a firefighter, but I'm a missionary first."

She clutched him tightly. "I never said I wouldn't cooperate. I only said I don't think it's appropriate for you to be involved in this ministry. It doesn't look right."

"Maybe not, but there's something about Josh that has grabbed me by the collar and won't let go. I can't ignore that, Emily. I can't."

"Why must you have Miss Brawlins with you? Don't you care what the appearance of that says?"

Mike looked down at Emily's soiled face. Sadly, he thought she cared little of what his being with Grace looked like to the world. She cared about what it looked like to her, his girlfriend. He supposed he couldn't blame her. Grace Brawlins was an incomparable beauty, but it was only superficial. Skin-deep. Couldn't Emily see Grace didn't possess the inner beauty he coveted in a wife?

He rubbed her cheek. "Of course I care about my witness, but I care about that little boy having a man in his life, and I care that I feel called by God to be that man."

Emily stamped her foot and pulled away. "What happens if Grace, as you call her, meets some guy and tosses you out of Josh's life anyway? What then?"

"Then I suppose God will lead me when the time comes."

Emily growled in frustration. "You might as well go." She shoved the pan against the stovetop with an obnoxious clang. "There's no dinner here, and there's no reason to stay. You've made your choice."

Mike looked at the dinner, then back at her, but she wouldn't face him. "Please, don't take this out on Josh when he comes back to school. I'm not trying to be difficult. I'm only trying to be there for a little boy who needs someone."

Emily turned to him and pointed a manicured finger in his chest. "You just go be the Christian you say you need to be, and leave me out of it. You go take a kid, who is supposed to be on forced suspension, out for a really fun day. I'll be happy to teach the little monster when he comes back to my world with no consequences for his irresponsible behavior."

Mike blinked away his shock. He'd never seen such venom in Emily and could scarcely believe she possessed it. His mother always said he was clueless with women. Judging by Emily's ugliness, he was starting to believe it.

"I'm sorry you feel that way." Mike grabbed his jacket and walked out the door. Emily could be heard banging pots until he shut the door to his truck.

"That was pleasant." He scratched the back of his head, wondering how he might have handled things differently.

As he drove home, he noticed the lights on at the station house and drove in, parking in the employee lot. The crew was all hovered around the exercise equipment, spurring each other on and shouting up a storm about which of them was weakest. Several dumbbells were lined up to prove each individual's manhood. Mike laughed. *If only women were this easy.* With guys, you knew the game, and you competed. With women, you had to second-guess everything that tumbled from your mouth. It was usually too late by then.

"I notice you have this competition when the real winner isn't around to prove himself," Mike quipped, flexing his biceps.

A collective shout of boos and hisses went up, and Mike broke into laughter.

"I think the fact that you had a date and you're here at eight o'clock proves that theory wrong." Jared looked at his watch and lifted his eyebrows. "Well?"

Mike shrugged. "Another one bites the dust."

Jared placed his arm around Mike, and they walked outside. Being dumped was off-limits for banter. Most of the firehouse was married, and girlfriends and possible wives were treated with the utmost respect. The men had seen far too much loss for anything but a healthy love and admiration for relationship.

"Sorry, bud," Jared said when they reached the pepper tree customarily used for such private conversations.

Mike shrugged. "It's no big deal." But inside, it felt like one. Mike was thirty-three and facing facts that he might never be married. Maybe God thought of him as a Paul, the kind better off not being married.

"What happened?"

"You know that kid?"

"Josh?"

"Yeah. I'm spending a little too much time with him for Emily's liking."

Jared smiled and raised an eyebrow. "Too much time with Josh or his mother? I saw her yesterday at the school, remember?"

"I haven't spent *any* time with her, yet."

"A fireman knows better than to play with fire."

"You think that's what I'm doing?"

"Don't know, man." Jared looked him in the eye. "I know you're a man of prayer, so I can only pray you're in His will."

"I don't think Emily has a heart for ministry."

"Maybe Emily doesn't have a heart for *your* ministry. That's something different altogether."

"Wonder if there's a woman out there who does."

"Sure there is, and maybe it's Emily. Your timing might just be off."

Mike nodded. Sure, maybe that was it. His timing was off. He was trying to force something into happening instead of waiting on the Lord.

"Thanks, Jared."

Jared looked away. "This pepper tree just gets bigger and bigger, huh?"

"Yeah." Mike looked up. "I have to run. I'm picking up Grace and Josh in the morning."

"I'll pray for you, buddy."

"Thanks." Mike got back into his truck and drove off, the roar of his engine offering a comforting arm around him.

~

Grace looked at her bills and tossed them on the table. How would she ever cover the five-hundred-dollar fine? She could barely pay her electric bill. Regardless of what Principal Walker said, she wasn't about to be a charity case. If there was a fine, there was a fine, and it would have to be paid. She made herself a cup of coffee and sat down with the newspaper. Avoidance felt good for the moment.

She lifted the society page and nearly spit out her coffee at a picture of Lyle Covington smiling, gazing lovingly at a beautiful blond. The headline read, DEFENSE ATTORNEY LYLE COVINGTON TO MARRY STAR REAL ESTATE AGENT LILY HAMPTON. Grace's breath left her. How dare he! How dare he go on with his life and start another family without paying for the one he already had. And what was that phone call about? A last hurrah? Well, Grace would give him a last hurrah, and it would come in the form of a child support payment.

Grace looked up the number and dialed her boss, banging the number out with ferocity. "Mr. Falk? It's Grace Brawlins."

"Grace? Is everything all right?"

Grace breathed deeply. "Well, actually, no, Mr. Falk, it's not. I hate to bother you at home, but I have some private business I'd like to discuss with you. On a professional level."

"Go ahead. Janice? Could you shut my door?"

Grace heard the door close at the other end of the phone, and she began. "Mr. Falk, I want you to know that I am committed to my job as a legal assistant. I know I haven't worked for you for all that long, but I'm good at what I do, and I plan to be there a long time."

"Wonderful."

"That being said, I'll be out of the office tomorrow. My son has been suspended for pulling a fire alarm at school."

"Oh dear," the older man said. There wasn't a hint of judgment in his voice. Having raised four children himself, he was probably very familiar with such antics. "I'm sorry, Grace. I realize you are still in the probationary period at Falk and Lawton, but I think I can trust you. If you must take a day off for your son, you must. I'm a pretty good judge of character, and I know you have it."

"Thank you, sir. The other concern I have is a bit more of a personal nature. I want to hire the firm to represent me in a paternity case."

Mr. Falk did not react, and for that Grace was grateful.

"Josh's father is about to marry. He's never taken responsibility for the child, and I haven't wanted to press it, but Josh deserves to be supported by his father."

"Are you willing to have a DNA test done?"

Grace paused, closing her eyes. "I doubt I have a choice. Mr. Falk, this man is a prominent lawyer. I was young and naïve—not that it excuses my behavior— but now, he is ready to get married and probably start a family of his own. I can't have Josh always being the poor kid, while this man's other children enjoy country club memberships. It's just not right."

Mr. Falk took in a deep breath and boisterously let it out. "What's his name?"

"Lyle Covington."

"The defense lawyer?"

"The same."

"I have to ask this, Grace: Are you sure he's the father?"

"There is absolutely no question. None whatsoever. He is Josh's father." The words tumbled out of her with urgency. She'd never admitted paternity, not even on Josh's birth certificate; but studying her bills, she knew this was the time. Josh had suffered long enough. He wouldn't have to know what the blood test was for, only that he needed to have blood drawn.

"Are you sure this just isn't about revenge as Mr. Covington gets married?" There was gentleness in the question.

"I wouldn't call it revenge, Mr. Falk. It's about justice. He just can't go and start a new family and leave a trail of fatherless children. He just can't. He practices law, and he ought to be made to uphold it. He took the bar to do so."

"Very well, Grace. I'll take a deposition as soon as you return to the office."

Grace sat up straight, willing herself to be brave. "I'm hoping you'll be able to reduce your fees a tad. Perhaps—"

"Grace, I don't want you to worry about my fees. This is not normally the type of work I do. I know you understand that. But I wish to make a moral statement with this case, and I'm taking it on pro bono."

"No, no. I don't want to ask that."

"You didn't ask. If you're better able to care for your son, you'll make a far better employee, Grace. I have my own selfish reasons."

Grace thought Mr. Falk was anything but selfish in his undertaking. She'd seen him running his prayer meetings in the morning. Maybe some Christians really did live like good people. Mr. Falk seemed to. Maybe Mike Kingston did, as well. She forced the thought from her head. Believing in people was exactly what put her in this situation. She wouldn't make that mistake again. For Josh's sake.

"Thank you, Mr. Falk. Thank you."

"Wait and see how we do before you thank me, Grace. I'll see you on Thursday."

"Yes, sir. And if there's anything you need me to do from home. . ."

"Just enjoy your son and keep him away from the fire alarms," he said jokingly.

"I will, sir."

"Good-bye, Grace."

Grace hung up the phone and cried at Mr. Falk's kindness. Searching Lyle's eyes in the photo, she shook her head. His fiancée looked like the type who would make Lyle happy. Even in the grainy newspaper shot, Grace could see she wore far too much makeup and was too buxom to be real. Although Miss Hampton's hands weren't shown, Grace had little doubt her nails were red, long, and clawlike.

"I imagine you think you've made quite a catch, Miss Hampton, when in reality, you should run for your life." Grace dropped the paper back to the table and went to check on Josh.

Josh's angelic eyes were closed in sleep, and his lips were curved into a sweet smile. Grace laughed, thinking about the InCharge songs or cartoon humor he might be dreaming about. Or maybe it was the following day with Fireman Mike that made him grin so big in his sleep.

Grace felt her heart beat at the thought. Something was different about that man. Although he was built like a wall and blessed with those sapphire blue eyes that reached out to people, he dated the mousy, little Miss Jensen. She was a sweet woman, kind in nature, but she was certainly nothing to look at. That fact startled Grace. She hadn't met any men who didn't just want an elegant package, someone to impress the boys at the club. Those blue eyes would turn any woman's attention in a room, so what was Mike Kingston looking for in a wife?

Or did he want a wife? Maybe he was like Lyle had been. Maybe he just wanted a woman for companionship—a woman to be there when it was convenient—certainly not all the time. Grace rubbed Josh's hair and wished with all her heart Lyle's child support would start soon. Embarrassing though it was to bare her soul to Mr. Falk, Josh would hopefully be the better for it.

"It's time we stopped living hand-to-mouth, Josh. You deserve better."

She rose and closed his door behind her, lamenting the empty house and how lonely it felt once Josh was asleep. This should be her time to do as she wished, but there was nothing she wanted to do. She had no hobbies, no great passion in life, so again she flicked on the television and tried not to daydream about a handsome fireman coming to her rescue.

Chapter 5

Josh chattered away like an eager chipmunk that had too many nuts to carry. Grace listened to the incessant talk until the words were so rushed, they could not be separated to make any sense.

"Josh," Grace finally said. "Please, just eat your breakfast. Fireman Mike will be here soon, I promise."

"This is the best day ever, Mom!" He looked down at his cereal, whirling it around with his spoon. "Sorry. I know I'm supposed to be in trouble." His eyes brightened, and he continued, "Do you think we could go to the zoo? What about a baseball game? The Giants play today. Or maybe we could ride bikes at the park. Do you think Fireman Mike has a bike? Hey, Mom, what about hiking up to the old farm? Do you think he'd like that? I wonder if he plays football, too. He looks like a wrestling star. I wonder if he ever wrestled."

"Josh!" Grace clutched her head. "Give it a rest, bud." Josh quietly removed his bowl from the table and set it in the sink. When he turned, his disappointed frown crushed Grace. "I'm sorry, Josh. I know you're excited. It's just that Mommy's coffee isn't ready, so I'm not awake enough to be excited yet. Give me five minutes, okay?"

He kissed her cheek. "I like you better after your coffee, Mom."

Who doesn't? Brown liquid, rich in scent, filled the pot. She waited alongside the machine, knowing exactly when there was enough for a cup. As if a bell rang, Grace grabbed the pot and filled her cup. She sniffed it, clutching the mug like a long-lost friend. The doorbell rang, and she longingly opened her mouth before setting the cup back on the counter.

"Good timing," Grace quipped.

She opened the door, and although she tried to be mad, there was something about Mike Kingston's face that prevented it. His dark hair was still damp; his face, clean shaven; and his sapphire eyes, brilliant. Something about him always appeared to be smiling, even when his face was missing a grin.

"Good morning," she offered.

His eyebrows lifted. "Are you ready for our big day?"

"You are far too chipper this morning, Mr. Kingston. I take it you got your coffee."

"Don't drink the stuff."

Grace rolled her eyes. Was there anything this scout did that might be considered habitual? Josh jumped around like a pogo stick and offered a plethora of ideas for the muscular fireman. Mike held up a firm hand, and Josh immediately halted.

Grace crossed her arms in amazement. "I wish I possessed that skill."

"Now, we have a lot to accomplish in one day, Mr. Joshua Brawlins. It is not every day one gets to play hooky from school." Mike looked to her. "With your mother's approval, of course." He winked, and Grace was mesmerized by the action. Bent over Josh, he had their full attention. Something about him just commanded it.

"What are we going to do, Mike?" Josh began to jump again.

"Well, first, we are going to the Monterey Bay Aquarium!"

Grace felt her smile leave, and she shook her head. "Josh, go get your coat."

Josh ran toward his bedroom like a rocket, and Grace approached the wall of a man. His expression softened at her advance, and she noticed again how his eyes smiled even when his mouth didn't. She blinked quickly, trying to remember what she was so upset about, and it finally bubbled up.

"Mr. Kingston, I cannot afford the Monterey Bay Aquarium, and I would appreciate it if you'd stick within our budget today. I'm more than happy to have you come along for Josh's sake, but we need to stay reasonable. Josh can't go thinking I have that kind of money to do such things all the time."

He held up tickets. "Free." He shrugged. "I saved somebody's cat, and they bought me a year's subscription to the aquarium. I'm a member. We'll just have to pay for Josh's ticket."

Grace began to protest when she realized he'd given her nothing to work with. Then, she remembered Miss Jensen. "What about your girlfriend? How does she feel about my using her ticket?"

Mike looked to the floor and put the tickets back in his wallet. "I have no girlfriend. Miss Jensen decided she was better off on her own."

Grace bit her lip. "Oh, I'm sorry." Their gazes met in understanding. Two people who felt the pain of being left. "Truly, I am."

He nodded. "Thanks."

"I'm sure you'll meet someone else at church." She smiled, hoping she'd said the right thing.

"I'll wait on God. He knows who's best."

She chose not to comment, and Josh came back into the room with three jackets. "I've got my raincoat, in case it rains, a windbreaker, in case it's windy, and a ski jacket, in case it's cold."

Grace looked out the window. "Josh, it is seventy degrees already. Go put your jackets away."

"But you just told me—"

"I was wrong. Let's go."

Josh dropped the jackets on the couch and scrambled out to Mike's truck. It was a gorgeous deep blue, darker than his eyes and far less sparkly, but it had room for six and a backseat for Josh.

"Let me just get his booster seat," Grace said.

Mike looked at her, then to Josh's small frame, and nodded. Although six, Josh was no bigger than the average four-year-old. She thought holding him back a year in school would make a difference, but he was still one of the smallest in his class. No wonder he seemed to worship this great big man with the gentle eyes.

Grace pulled the booster from her car, and Mike took it from her, setting it in the center of the backseat for Josh. The truck still had that divine new-car smell. Grace had never owned a new car, and there was something so luxurious about sitting in one.

"I like your truck. It's so comfortable." She ran her hand along the smooth leather.

"I bought it in December. Miss Jensen was embarrassed to be seen in my old jalopy." He laughed, but Grace stiffened. Thinking back to Lyle and his perfect car, she knew a decent vehicle had nothing to do with the interior of a man. If Emily had a lick of sense, she wouldn't have let Mike go.

They rode for a long time in silence, except for Josh pointing excitedly at every new sight they passed.

~

Cannery Row, made famous in Steinbeck's book, was still quaint. Its old sardine canneries were now transformed into gift shops and fine seafood restaurants. The aquarium stood like a mighty fortress on the edge of Monterey Bay, its gray color blending into the bold colors of the brown craggy rocks and deep blue waters. The air was fresh and whipped around her in gales. The slight scent of seaweed permeated the scene.

Grace took out her wallet, but Mike pushed it away. "I'm buying."

"No," she insisted. "It's enough you drove us here and had a ticket for me. We're not—" Grace cut her speech short when she saw an older woman staring at her. Something about the look in the woman's eye made Grace step back. Mike went forward and paid for Josh's ticket, and Grace looked to the woman expectantly.

"Let him pay, my dear," she whispered. "A man must be allowed to care for a woman. It makes them feel more like a man. It's nice to see chivalry isn't dead, and I'd hang on to him if I were you." She patted her gray hair and trotted off on the arm of a man—a man who'd obviously been her husband for a very long time.

"Grace?" Mike stood at the doorway with Josh, waiting with the door opened. "We're ready."

She nodded. "Of course." She ventured a look back at the married woman and received a wink and a smile.

Wandering through several exhibits, Josh oohed and ahhed over the sea otters, marveled at the diver in the enormous kelp bed tank, and dropped to his knees, stunned by the shark exhibit.

"Look at that big one, Mom! How do they keep them from eating the fish in the tank?"

A volunteer in a red jacket came closer to them. "We keep the inhabitants of the tank slightly overfed. They are usually too full to think about eating their neighbors, but every once in a while. . .well, a shark is still a shark."

"Cool!" Josh said. "Maybe we'll see him eat one."

The volunteer laughed. "You can come back for their feeding at three."

"Can we, Mom?"

"I suppose, if we're still here. We wouldn't want to miss that, now would we, Mike?"

"I have something better planned," he said mysteriously. "Something way better."

Josh's eyes grew wide. "What?"

"You'll just have to wait and see. Let's go pet the bat rays." Mike waggled his eyebrows.

The bat ray tank was filled with skimming, black, winged objects which maneuvered eerily, like birds in flight. Joshua reached out his hand, and Grace tried to grab it back when Mike caught her hand and shook his head. He didn't let go immediately, and she looked into his blue eyes. Whatever he saw in her, he didn't want to see, because he pitched her hand like a bad piece of fruit.

She swallowed hard and concentrated on Josh again. He had reached for a bat ray and crinkled his nose. "Ewww. It's really slimy, Mom. Touch one."

"I don't think so, Josh." She tried to laugh it off, but the lump in her throat would not be swallowed. "Mike, would you keep an eye on Josh for a minute? I'm going to find the rest room."

"Sure." He nodded.

Grace tore open the doors to the outside patio and breathed in the moist sea air. Seagulls cawed, sea lions barked, and the waves lapped up against the pillars of the building, a symphony of soothing sounds. Yet Grace found no comfort in the beauty around her. She could only think about Mike Kingston's searing rejection. Touching her hand disgusted him, as it would most Christians. She was bruised goods, forever tainted in the eyes of "good people" for her sinful choice to have her son alone.

Mike could see the innocence in her son, the helpless victim needing a father figure, but he could not understand her mistake. It was too much for Christians. It had been too much for her own parents to accept. Why should she expect anything more from a religious firefighter?

She tried to blink away her tears, but they pounded against her cheeks relentlessly, like the waves below. She thought about Lyle and his healthy check. She laughed at her innocence, thinking he meant it for baby clothes. She clasped her eyes, avoiding the reminder of what he'd truly meant by giving her the money. To this day, it stabbed her in the heart to think of his intentions.

First her parents, and now Mike—righteous Christians in her life reminded her she would never be good enough, never worthy to start a new life. Christians seemed to be everywhere, surrounding her 'til she thought she might choke on them.

"Grace?" Mike stood behind her, the brightness of the sun lighting him. He gulped at the sight of her, and she whisked away her tears with the back of her hand.

"I came out for air. Where's Josh?"

"He's right there, watching the otters lunch in the little inlet."

Grace scanned the benches and found him joyously watching the animals.

"He's having a good time." Grace grinned at the sight of her carefree son.

"I wish I could say the same for you."

She couldn't find words, so she just looked away, focusing on the same otter that held her son's rapt attention.

Mike looked out at the horizon. "I wasn't prepared for what I felt back there. I'm sorry."

Grace lifted her eyes to his, amazed he'd understood what had bothered her. "I understand."

"No, I don't think you do."

"You're a saint. A saint must find another saint. It's in that Bible of yours. I know."

"How do you know?"

"I grew up in a Christian home. I know all about your rules."

His shoulders slumped. "I'm sorry no one's ever shown you Christ's love, Grace. It's not about the rules."

Grace laughed. "Apparently, it is. I can name you quite a few people who would be more than happy to tell you how I fail as a saint."

"I'm sorry, Grace. Truthfully, they don't sound like anyone I want to know. Do we have time for one more adventure this afternoon, or have I ruined it?"

"I think we should be heading back. We're still ninety minutes or so from home."

"Ple—ase!" He clasped his hands together against his chiseled chin, and if there were a woman alive who could resist the request, Grace would love to meet her and shake her hand.

"All right. What did you have in mind?"

"How brave are you?"

She crossed her arms. "Not very. I don't rush into burning buildings for a living; I sit in front of a computer. Does that give you an indication?"

"Ah, you'll be a pro. Think how you can impress Josh."

"Impress Josh with what?"

"That's the surprise. Come on, let's move." He placed his hand at the small of her back but quickly removed it when she flinched.

~

They all piled into the truck as if they'd been doing so forever. Josh buckled his seat belt, and the adults followed suit. The sun along Monterey Bay sparkled like pure gold on the whitecaps in the water. Sea lions frolicked everywhere along the shore, and an occasional otter would make Josh squeal with excitement.

Five minutes later, they arrived at a public beach, and Grace breathed a sigh of relief. "Shoo." She hopped out of the truck, helping Josh out, when her smile abruptly disappeared. Before her were several kayaks on a rack with a red sign reading KAYAKS FOR RENT. She looked from the waves crashing on the sand, to the little plastic boats, and back at Mike. She simply shook her head.

"Come on; it will be fun." Mike gave her that wide-eyed look again, and she had to admit, it was no less charming than the first time.

"Yeah, Mom, cool! Can we?"

"Josh, look at the size of those swells. We have no experience in one of these things, and we're not going to jeopardize our lives for a cheap thrill." She pulled Mike by his elbow. "Mike, I do not appreciate being the bad guy here. I never agreed to let my son ride in a flimsy boat on Monterey Bay. I agreed to take him to an educational museum. I understand your desire to make a man out of him, but I'd like him to live to see his manhood."

"Grace, there's nothing to worry about. We'll be in wet suits and life jackets. If we tip, we just climb back in. We'll rent a kayak for three and put Josh right in the center, between us. I'll be in the back, and I'll see everything that happens."

He exuded confidence, but Grace had only to look at the surf again to know she was firm. "No."

"Let me take Josh, then, in a kayak for two. Grace, he'll have a blast, and I wouldn't let anything happen to either of you."

Grace looked to her son. He'd never had the opportunity to camp or do anything remotely so rugged. She nibbled at her lip and took in Mike's brawny arms. Surely, he could fish out wispy, little Josh if something happened. But no, what if something did happen?

"Can you swim?" she finally asked.

"Grace." He crossed his arms, showing the full power of his biceps. "I am a firefighter. I rescue people for a living. Of course I can swim, and under dire circumstances, too."

"Will you promise me Josh will be fine?"

"Scout's honor." He lifted three fingers.

"I'm coming, too. There's no way you're going out there while I'm powerless on the shore." She could kick herself for giving in, but if Josh was going to stretch his wings, she needed to let him lift off the ground.

Mike smiled with his whole handsome face. "Great!"

Somehow, Grace wouldn't have described what she felt as great. She believed *fear* was a better term.

Chapter 6

Mike paid for the kayak, and he looked to Grace, surprised she didn't argue about money. *I guess she figured I could pay for this harebrained scheme.* With narrowed eyes, she watched the whole transaction, as if heading before a firing squad. . .with him as her executioner. She apparently didn't want to pay for the privilege. Mike had to hide his grin. For all her protests, Josh's enthusiasm kept her from voicing her further objections.

As a final insult, the man behind the counter asked for her weight. Mike offered a sheepish smile, but it didn't appear to work. Grace released her wrath. "Is there a reason you need to know my weight?" she finally asked, cocking her head.

"The wet suits are calibrated by weight, ma'am. I can guess if you don't want to tell me," the employee said. Mike fought a smile at the suggestion. Certainly, she'd find that no more appealing. Mike wasn't sure what she worried about. She had a wispy figure, like her son, only she was curved in all the right places. He chastised himself for noticing, but he was a single man, and he certainly wasn't blind.

Grace's eyebrows lifted. "I'd rather you not guess."

The man scanned her quickly, anyway. Mike shut his eyes, preparing for an onslaught of words, but the employee had obviously done this before. "Probably an extra-small. Up to 120 pounds?"

Grace broke into a smile. "Well, I'm five-foot-eight, so I'm closer to 124."

Mike let out his breath. Fitted properly in their wet suits, they made their way toward the boat and their lesson. Josh bounced about like an out-of-control rubber ball and even looked the part in his black neoprene suit.

"Josh." Mike held his small shoulder to plant him steady. Looking into his big brown eyes, Mike knelt down. "I know you're really excited to go on the kayak, but we have to listen to the lesson now. You need to know what to do to help us out and what to do if you get into trouble. This is important, so I want you to act very seriously."

Josh nodded, blinking rapidly. "Okay, Fireman Mike. Will we see a whale? Or sharks?"

Grace's eyes grew large.

"Probably not, buddy. We're on the bay, not the open ocean. We'll see some sea otters, though. You like them." Mike did not add that sharks teemed below, but the kayak would be on the surface. Sharks had very little interest in people, and most big enough to do any damage would be out in the open waters. Still, it was information he kept close to his breast.

After a lesson, which Grace panted through most of, they carried the three-man kayak down to the shore. Waves nibbled at their feet, and Grace turned around as if to run before looking at Josh and relenting by showing him how to get into the kayak. Mike couldn't help but admire the love she showed that boy. Her small frame was shivering from fear, but she put Josh's desires before her own. She helped him into the middle station and climbed to the front.

"I guess we're ready." Her voice shook.

Mike held the boat at shore while they positioned themselves, then climbed into the last seat. "Row!"

Frantically, the pair, looking like the two stooges themselves, tried to get the kayak straight. Mike had to laugh. He could easily maneuver the vessel on his own, but what would be the fun of that? Grace caught on fairly quickly, and soon they were past the whitecaps and into the blue swells. As the water got deeper and darker beneath them, he could hear Grace moaning in her terror while Josh shouted an endless chorus of "cool!"

With the two of them rowing in tandem, the boat sliced through the water quickly, and they came to the end of the wharf. "Turn!"

Grace froze at his order and lifted her oar from the water. "Am I okay?" she asked without turning.

"You're fine. We'll go into this inlet and let Josh see the otters feeding."

Grace nodded gently, clearly too nervous to make any rash movement. He chuckled to himself. Once the kayak was in shallow, calm water, her shoulders visibly relaxed, and she turned to face him.

"Are we done now?"

"No way, Mom. This is cool. Did you see those huge sea lions?"

"Oh, I saw them all right—after I smelled them. Ick." Grace turned around and crinkled her nose in the most charming way. "You know, I never thought of a sea lion as threatening, but when they dive in with a great splash, and you don't know where they'll bob up, they might as well be a treacherous sea monster. I'll gladly give them back their turf."

Grace wore one of Mike's old baseball caps to keep the sun from her eyes, and Mike sat mesmerized by the panoramic picture before him. This is how he imagined his life. Out on the open water, adventuring with his family, taking in one of the most picturesque spots God saw fit to create. He took a photograph in his mind, scanning all the details before him.

Grace's profile resembled a classic painting. Her skin, without a hint of makeup, bordered on perfection, and her wide gray-blue eyes held all the innocence of a child. With a name like Grace, he wondered what had happened to harden her so. He knew Josh's father had something to do with it, but he didn't dare ask. Had she been loose in younger days? Had an affair with a married man?

He forced such thoughts away. Judgment was exactly why Grace wouldn't speak of faith, or religion, as she sharply called it. If she ever cared to tell him, she would. Otherwise, Mike would focus on loving Joshua and Grace for who they were, not only as potential Christians. For them, he was only a clanging gong.

Rubbing the sand from his palm, he placed a hand in the water to clear away the grains. A flash of silver blinded him. He pulled his hand from the bay. The boat rocked, and Grace and Josh screamed. Mike steadied the kayak with his weight and looked to his two frightened passengers.

"What was that?" Grace asked.

Mike laughed out loud. "It was a fish. A really big fish. I guess my dive watch attracted him, and he thought he might lunch on my fingers."

Grace clutched her heart, but soon broke into a giggle. "A fish? Oh, I'm far too jumpy. All those tales of sharks you've been telling Josh have this mom in a panic."

"You're doing wonderfully. I've never seen anyone take to the oars so naturally."

Her expression softened, and she freed her hair from the baseball cap in a glimmer of gold. "Really?"

Mike swallowed hard and looked toward the rocks. "Look at those sea lions over there, Josh." He pointed toward the shore, aware of her steady gaze upon him. Flirting seemed beyond Grace's world. She wasn't flirting with him; she simply engaged people with her presence. *Careful, buddy*, he reminded himself. Bringing her back into his view, he straightened his shoulders to appear unaffected by her beauty.

He thought of his girlfriend, now his ex-girlfriend. A relationship wasn't based on physical attraction. Perhaps he needed to call Emily tonight. He should at least apologize for his feeble attempts at explaining himself. Perhaps he hadn't given it enough of a chance.

"Mike, it's getting late. Do you think we should be rowing back about now?" Grace turned her head and faced him. Her cheekbones appeared almost carved into a sweet heart shape, and he cast his gaze away. *Now I'm noticing cheekbones?*

"Yes, I suppose we should. We'll get some dinner and drive back. My stomach is a little queasy after that burger for lunch."

"I saw a McDonald's right across the street!" Josh announced.

"Oh no. When I say we're going out to dinner, Josh, I mean somewhere the meal doesn't come with a toy, okay?"

Grace laughed. "I don't think Josh has been to the kind of restaurant that doesn't serve value meals."

"Tonight, he's going to try seafood."

Josh shook his head violently. "No way! I don't want to eat a slimy fish. I want a hamburger."

"You can have a hamburger after you try some of our fish," Grace chastised. "And I'm getting dinner. I won't hear any arguments."

Mike nodded. "Fair enough. It's too bad I don't have a place to cook, though. I'm quite a fine chef."

"I thought that was a myth about firemen. A wives' tale, you might say."

"You thought wrong. I bet my comrades could outserve the best of your house-wife friends." Mike put his hand on his hip.

"Well, sure, you guys don't have kids at your feet, yelling if the meal takes longer than twelve minutes to prepare." Grace's lips curled into a smile. "Besides, I don't have any housewife friends. There's something about the married types. They don't care for us single types."

"We have a great singles' group at our church," Mike offered before remembering her thoughts on church.

Grace's smile disintegrated. "Ah, you forget I wear a brand." She nodded toward Josh. Deciding it was a conversation best left unstated, Mike turned the kayak around and headed back toward the shore.

Once in the vicinity of the surf, he ordered them to row vehemently straight through the waves. Soon, the kayak grounded into the sand. Grace quickly hopped out and grasped Josh, getting him to the shore. Her oar plopped into the water, and she bent to fish it out. Just then, a rogue wave came up from behind, hurling her face first into the shallow waves. She bobbed up quickly, spitting the saltwater from her mouth and pushing soaked tendrils from her face. She looked at him expectantly.

"Your leash was loose." He held up an empty oar wrap and shrugged.

Feeling her knotted hair, she fit his cap back on her head. "McDonald's, here we come!"

～

Grace felt like a wet rat. After she'd shimmied out of her wet suit, she was still cov-ered in a light film of salt and sand. Still, nothing could wipe the ear-to-ear grin from Josh's face, so it had all been worth it. Trying to get a brush through her tan-gled web of hair, she sported nominal success and finally gave up, throwing her makeup bag back into her purse. Her appearance mattered little to the bulky fire-man, anyway. Her soul turned him off. *Doesn't matter,* she thought to herself. *The likes of Michael Kingston wouldn't be seen with the woman at the well.*

She pictured little Emily Jensen—the petite kindergarten teacher with the gentle, pure nature. If there was only a way Grace could transport herself back in time, to get married first and build a proper home for Josh. Why hadn't she thought things through, gone with her first instinct, and fled from temptation?

She opened the door, and Josh and Mike waited for her with matching smiles. "Dinner! Dinner!" they chanted together.

She propped her fist on her hip. "It's about time both of you learned a lady is worth waiting for."

"I agree." Mike's eyes met hers, and he quickly looked away. "Let's go, sport. Our feast awaits."

After a short drive back to Cannery Row, they picked a quaint, family-friendly seafood restaurant. Grace's mouth watered at the delectable menu. Shrimp, halibut, crab. . .she licked her lips at such a decision. She usually just had to contemplate if she wanted fries with her order.

The prices on the menu caused her heart to beat quickly. She hoped her credit card would allow for this meal. She looked to Mike, who sat beside Josh, telling him about all the fish they might try. He caught her looking at him, and she worried he would know how her breathing increased in fear over the bill.

As if his God gave him some type of sign, he dropped his menu. "You know, I think I recognize this restaurant's logo from something. He leaned forward, grasping his black wallet, and took out his aquarium tickets, scanning them. "Well, look at that. There's a coupon for half off dinner here. I knew I remembered that logo from somewhere." He tossed the ticket on the table.

Grace wanted to reach over and kiss him. She released a breath and watched Josh's hair sway in the breeze. She lifted her menu again with relief, studying her choices with renewed faith.

"Josh, I really want you to try some seafood." Mike leaned over, showing Josh the menu. This one didn't have pictures, so Josh took Mike's word. "We'll just let you eat the bread and nibble off our plates. Hamburgers are nine dollars here, and I could buy you a good part of a cow for that. We'll do ice cream after dinner. Okay?"

Josh happily agreed because Mike suggested it. Grace had little doubt if Mike suggested Josh eat the tire from his truck for dinner, Josh would have acquiesced.

The waitress came, asking about drink orders, and Grace rejoiced in the fact that Mike didn't drink. Grace also declined, and they each ordered a soda. She ordered a pasta salad for dinner, without the luxury or cost of seafood, and Mike ordered the affordable special: baked salmon. Looking at the prices, she noticed he selected the other least expensive meal on the menu.

"Well, are we ready?" Mike said after their meals were finished and cleared away by the server.

"Yes." Grace opened the leather wallet to find the bill and marveled at the actual outcome. It was barely more than a fast food tab. She smiled gratefully at Mike, and he winked at her. "Thank you."

Mike shrugged. "For what? Eating a great meal with a beautiful woman and her son? Anytime." He laughed. For the moment, he'd forgotten she was Grace Brawlins, single mother, former Christian; and she basked in the moment.

After dinner, Josh slumped forward, asleep in his car seat for the long drive home. Grace tried to fill the awkward silence. "I never thought I'd enjoy kayaking."

"I didn't know you did enjoy it." He turned and grinned. Somehow she knew she'd remember that smile against the backdrop of the fading Monterey Bay forever.

"I did, Mike. Really. I don't understand why you've taken such an interest in Josh, but I do appreciate it."

"How can you question me? Your son has an awesome little personality. He just makes people want to be around him." He looked forward, and she watched his profile with interest. He had a masculine nose, strong, but not too obvious. A thin, open smile always showed his perfect, white teeth. He might have starred in toothpaste commercials if he weren't saving cats for his day job.

"Mike, you have a lot going for you. You have no responsibilities other than your job; you're not bad to look at." She looked out the window when she said this. "And taking on a kid with Josh's issues is just admirable. Especially for a religious type."

"What is it you have against Christians, anyway?"

She contemplated the question. What didn't she have against them was a better question. Deciding he deserved honesty, she went on, "I wasn't always this way. I tried to take Josh to church a couple times when he was young. I could have used the support."

"But?"

"But there was no Sunday school class for me because they didn't consider me appropriate in a singles' class when I had a child, and the young marrieds didn't want me to tempt their husbands." Grace shrugged. "So eventually I just stayed home."

"I'm sorry that happened to you."

And Grace thought he truly was.

"A deaconess was sent to my house to counsel me for my past sins. God may have forgiven me, but His people didn't. My childhood experiences weren't distant memories, but all too real in the church. I didn't return, and they didn't call me. I figured I'd been right all along. If you don't have your perfection card punched and your floral dress on Sunday morning, don't show up. That's the way it is, huh?"

"You can't judge God by His people—at least not all of the time."

"Then what's the point?"

"To get to know God, Grace. That's the point." He took a hand from the steering wheel for emphasis.

"God knows where I am if He wants me." Grace shrugged.

"He does want you, Grace. And He wants Josh, too." Mike shook his head. His chest heaved up and down. "If you're interested, go to the Bible, not people. People will always let you down. I'm sure I will if you give me long enough."

"Did you let Miss Jensen down?"

"Pretty much."

"Well, Fireman Mike, you Christians have some type of club I just don't understand, and quite frankly, I don't want to be a part of it. How long did you date Emily?" She moved to safer waters, where she wouldn't have to answer any more uncomfortable questions. She'd lost her Christian club card long ago, and there was no going back.

"Emily and I dated for two months. Just before Christmas, I met Josh when I'd helped her after school. Josh was always hovering like a bee around her door."

Grace frowned. "He was supposed to be in day care."

"The day care lets them out on the schoolyard when school finishes. Josh just wanted a little extra attention, no big deal."

Grace looked to her hands, clasped so tightly her knuckles were white. "Josh didn't have any friends." It was a statement, not a question.

"He's a slow bloomer, Grace. He'll find his way."

"Will he?" She looked back to her sleeping son. His mouth dangled open, and he breathed loudly.

"He'll bloom. I know it, as sure as I know how to rescue a cat from a tree."

"He's never done anything like today, Mike." Grace smiled from her heart. "He was captain of our kayak."

"Is that a thank-you?"

"It is," she admitted. "You'll make a fine dad someday. I think you should call Emily again. Maybe you two will work it out."

The traffic slowed, and Mike turned toward her. "Maybe we will."

She sucked in a deep breath. "She's a fool if she doesn't." *A big fool.*

Chapter 7

The door closed, and the lights went on in the Brawlinses' home. Mike rested his head on his steering wheel. Why did this feel so right? He had no claim to this small family, no reason to feel drawn to them. They weren't his responsibility. He looked up to the heavens, searching for an answer.

Why couldn't he make things work with a good Christian woman like Emily? His heart raced at the burden he felt for the Brawlins family. Grace's innocent eyes and full lips sent his heart racing. So much so, he had to avoid her direct gaze, like the sun. He laughed at his romantic notion. He'd just been dumped by Emily. Catching his breath, Mike realized that must be it. He just felt his loneliness. The fact was, nobody waited for him at the end of each day.

He looked at the cottage again and shook his head. Grace wasn't a Christian, and no matter how he might desire it, there were no guarantees. With Grace's anger toward religion in general, it was almost ensured she would never believe. He forced the thought away, yet reality bubbled to the surface. How many men had fallen away while trying to convert a woman? He mentally counted the ones he knew.

His cell phone jolted him from his mind's wanderings. "Hello. Mike Kingston."

"Mike? It's Emily."

Her name should have caused him a reaction, but it didn't. Only mild curiosity as to why she called. That much occurred when a new telemarketer broke into his dinner. "Hi, Emily."

She stammered to find words. He hadn't made it easy for her. "I've had some time to think about Josh and his mother."

"And?"

"I'm sorry about Josh—what I said, I mean. He's a nice kid. I shouldn't have faulted you for spending the day with them." She hesitated a bit. "How was your day, by the way?"

"It was long but worth it. Josh had a great time."

"What about Miss Brawlins?" Her tone irritated him, but he knew accountability would do him good, even if he resented it.

"She had a good time, too, I believe. But then with Josh so happy, it would have been hard for her to be disappointed."

"I bet."

Mike let out an annoyed sigh. "I offered to spend time with Josh and *you*, if you'll remember correctly. That was my preference."

"It wasn't my preference, Mike. I've talked with Jared at the station house. He agrees with me."

"About what?" Mike snapped.

"That you have no business witnessing to a single woman. Jared agrees."

"He said that?"

"He didn't have to," Emily said.

"You said it for him?" Mike took in a deep breath, held it for five seconds, and released it to calm down. "Emily, if you'll ask Miss Brawlins to church, I'll continue to see Josh on my own. I don't think Grace would have any objections to that now."

"Are you really that naïve?"

Mike sat back in his truck. "Yeah, maybe I am." He loosened the shirt around his collar. Suddenly, his truck felt stifling. Rolling down the window, he squelched the desire to run, to get away from this noose Emily wanted to place gently about his neck. "I have training in Los Angeles next week. I'll be gone. Maybe you could ask Grace then."

"Maybe I could," she said coldly. "What are you training for?"

"Radioactive emergencies. It's put on by the Department of Energy, and with California's electricity crisis, we're trying to be proactive in the department."

"I'm glad your career is still important to you."

"Yes, it is. I'm on early in the morning, so if that's all you have for me."

"I'm praying for you," Emily practically shouted.

"Thanks," he said absently and started his truck to head for home. If second thoughts ever haunted him, they were long gone now. Emily's heart felt hard to him. Hard and bitter, just the way Grace felt all Christians were. Mike sniffed aloud. He hadn't been on the other side of Christianity. Maybe Grace had a point.

～

Although worn out and achy from kayaking, Grace returned to work Thursday. She had a skip to her walk, and her coffee tasted richer than usual. Brushing powder on her skin, she noticed her tanned face didn't speak of a miserable day with Josh on suspension. *Thank goodness I told Mr. Falk the truth about my absence.* Grace thought she practically glowed.

Up and ready with a seashell for show-and-tell, Josh sat on the sofa, watching cartoons, and dutifully waited for Grace to finish her coffee. She kissed him good-bye in the house, as she always did to prevent his mortification at school, and they drove the familiar route.

～

Her office, set in the center of venture capital firms, actually relaxed her. The familiar trickling waterfalls and elaborate water gardens gave peace and serenity to her. It was one of the reasons she'd taken this job as a paralegal for an arbitration specialist.

Mr. Falk smiled as she entered. "Good morning, Grace. How was your day with Josh?"

"Great."

"I have some time this morning, if you're ready for your deposition."

"Now?"

"No time like the present." He opened a hand toward the conference room, and Grace entered, her heart pounding in her ears. "You won't have time to get nervous this way."

"Want to bet?"

He turned on the tape recorder that sat ready in the center of the table and took out his notes. "When did you first meet Lyle Covington?"

"When I was twenty-one and fresh out of college. I was a legal intern at his father's firm." Grace fidgeted in her chair. If she didn't like this line of questioning, she knew it could only get worse. She drew in a deep breath, trying to separate herself from the questions.

"When did you begin to see Mr. Covington on a social level?"

This felt like telling her grandfather secrets, and she thought she might hyperventilate. She took another deep breath. "We often went out to lunch and even dinner after long days at the office. Then, there was a Christmas party in 1994."

"How long did your relationship last?" He looked at her over his glasses, then finally looked back to his notes.

"Maybe six months." She crossed her legs.

"When did it end?"

"After the Christmas party. I drank this great-tasting fizzy soda." Grace grappled with her hands. "It was actually champagne, and I wasn't quite myself by the end of the evening." She looked into Mr. Falk's furrowed brows. "I wasn't used to alcohol. I went home to Lyle's apartment with him."

"Did he force you back to his apartment?"

"No." Grace shook her head. "If you know Mr. Covington, he's quite charming, and he doesn't have need to force people into anything. They willingly consent."

"Did you—"

Grace cut him off. "Yes. We consummated the relationship that night." She clutched her hair, twirling it nervously.

"And then?" Mr. Falk's eyebrows lifted.

"Nothing. He had all he wanted, and he lost interest. When he found out about Josh, he gave me a check and the name of a doctor who performs—" Grace stopped. "A doctor who kills babies. His father fired me for lewd behavior, and Lyle shipped off to Boston for a lawyers' master's program to help the firm bolster its case law clientele."

"Have you spoken with him since?"

Grace nodded. "Twice. Once when I had Josh." Grace looked at the window and focused on the waterfall. "He was the most beautiful baby I'd ever seen, Mr. Falk. I instantly fell in love, and I was naïve enough to believe Lyle would, too. I called him to tell him his son was born. He hung up on me."

"And the second time?"

"He just called this week. I saw in the paper he was getting married. He either called for a last fling or to be sure I wouldn't make any waves. I don't know which."

"Grace, I'm sorry, but I must ask this because Lyle's attorneys will most certainly bring it up."

"My personal life." Grace let out a short, uncomfortable laugh.

"He will most likely make you out to be a woman of loose character. It's a standard practice in such cases—anything that helps to put off the actual court-ordered demand for a paternity test."

"That Christmas party was my personal life, Mr. Falk."

"Are you certain?"

"Absolutely. God gave me Josh when I didn't deserve him. I wasn't going to give Him any reason to take him away."

Mr. Falk leaned back. "Grace?" He shook his head. "God doesn't work that way."

"Oh yes. I know all about His punishment to fit the crime. Justice in God's world is not one I would mess with again. If that fear helps me in the courtroom, so be it." Grace stood. "Are we done for the day? I don't think I can take more now."

"We're done, Grace." Mr. Falk wore a frown unlike any she'd seen on his usually smiling face. In fact, Grace thought he looked capable of crying. She bolted for the door, rushed to the bathroom, and splashed cold water on her face. She felt ill but forced the feeling away.

"This is for Josh," she told the mirror. "So Josh won't have to wear hand-me-downs and sneakers that are too big for him. So kids won't make fun of him and giggle behind his back. Don't be selfish, Grace!" She had the sudden urge to call Fireman Mike and pour out her aching heart. Grace didn't know how she would manage keeping a smile on her face during her days in court. It was bound to get ugly. For the first time in Josh's six years, she wished she could call her parents.

Lyle was not one to part with money easily and certainly not for the likes of her, a "guttersnipe," as he'd once called her. The fact that he was marrying only made things worse. Grace braced for defeat. Her name was about to be dragged to the lowest parts of the sewer system. Lyle wasn't about to admit his fling with a paltry legal assistant resulted in a child, and she knew he wouldn't let Josh stand in the way of his future.

~

Mike wandered the aisles of the grocery store while his comrades stood in line at the espresso shop at the front of the store. He gathered the ingredients for dinner, hoping they'd make it through the line without a call. The fresh scent of sourdough bread permeated the air, challenging anyone to leave the store without a loaf.

He dropped a package of chicken into a basket on top of the fresh seasonings and headed toward the checkout. A car alarm wailed in the parking lot, echoing through the store each time the door opened. Jared waved from the Starbucks' line, and Mike relented to the powerful call of bread, running back to the bakery for a loaf. Squeezing the still-warm bread, it collapsed easily between his grasp. *Perfect*, he thought.

"You through feeling the bread?" Jared stood beside him. "You need a girl-friend, man." He laughed, slapping Mike on the back.

"Speaking of which, what did you say to Emily last night?"

"She's just worried about you, Mike. Says you spent the whole day with that single mom."

"And her son."

"So what's going on?"

"Nothing more than was going on yesterday. Josh needs me, Jared. I told Emily what she might do at school to make things easier on the kid. She hasn't taken any of my advice, nor has she listened to Grace's suggestions for Josh. It's just easier to believe he's a troublesome kid than to try and lift him out of it."

"You sound awfully passionate about this kid. Don't you think you're overly involved?"

"Maybe I am, but what's the harm in that? You know where my faith is. You want to hold me accountable? Hold me accountable, but don't fall for Emily's fake concern. It's nothing more than paltry jealousy."

"Mike, what are you talking about? Emily is about as sweet as they come."

"Emily is sweet as long as things go her way. Have you discovered that about her? Because I have, Jared, and I'm just not interested in playing her games any-more. Emily's not even concerned about my life so much as she's concerned about hers. It's fine that we're not together, but it's not fine if I'm with someone else."

"She's just concerned. You are spending a lot of time with a non-Christian."

"No." Mike shook his head while Jared sipped his iced coffee. "Don't buy it. If Emily were concerned, she'd listen to a parent's requests."

"You ain't the kid's father. She's got a right to be concerned. I understand you want to help out, but how far can you take it?"

Mike clenched his jaw. "I don't know, but I'm sick of hearing from Christians about how the unsaved aren't my problem. They're your problem, too. Ever heard of the Great Commission? What would happen if we all just sat idly by, waiting for the most convenient witnessing opportunity to wander our way?"

Jared shrugged.

"Oh, look, there's one now. She's wearing a cross. Why don't you go tell her about Jesus. She looks easy."

"Come on, Mike. This isn't like you. What's going on?"

"Truthfully? No woman has ever made me feel like Grace Brawlins. When she blinks her blue eyes at me, I'm captivated. I want to do anything I can to make her life special, to make her feel loved."

Jared scratched the back of his head. "This is serious."

"I feel like I've known her for a lifetime. I've never let my emotions get to me like this. I'm a rational thinker."

Jared laughed. "Women can take any resemblance of rationality we have and twist it to their will. When we're under their spell, it's magical." He clicked his tongue. "But Grace isn't a Christian, Mike, and I will hold you accountable for that. Whatever you're feeling may not be from the Lord."

"I'm sure it probably isn't, and that's what I hate. How can I love her, show her Christ's love, without getting in too deep?"

"Maybe you can't." Jared shrugged.

Mike whipped the basket over his elbow and strutted toward the register. Something made him stop, and he turned to see a man drop his groceries. They landed with a clatter at his feet. The sound of breaking glass echoed in the cereal aisle. Just as the man clutched his chest, Mike dropped his own basket, sprinting to the man's side before he fell to the ground.

"My arm!" the man groaned before suddenly losing consciousness. Jared was at Mike's side in a second, calling for backup and supplies. Mike gently lowered the well-dressed man to the floor, checking his vital signs and scrutinizing his color, going into action naturally, like a bodyguard for a great politician.

Finely groomed with expensive shoes and aftershave, the older man appeared strong and healthy. Devoid of a wedding ring, Mike wondered if the man had a family. Did anyone care that he was having heart failure in the middle of the cereal aisle? Mike blinked. *Would anyone care if I did?* The man's chest ceased its natural rise and fall, and Mike loosened the man's silk tie. He listened for respiration but heard nothing. The man's ankles were thick and fluid-filled.

Mike started resuscitation, with Jared counting off the seconds. Though either one of them could have done this in their sleep, there was something comforting about the sound of the numbers.

As natural as saving a life was, it never became routine. One couldn't help but think about the life this person lived. Would he get another chance? Had he made peace with his family? Only God knew those answers in the midst of procedure, and neither Mike nor his comrades ever lost respect for that.

"I've got a pulse!" Mike called, relieved he wouldn't have to shock the heart. "You're going to be all right," he said gently. Whispering assurance was a vital part of recovery. He checked the pulse again. Although it was weak, it was steady. The man's eyes fluttered open, focusing on Mike.

"Thank you," he croaked.

"You fight. That's thanks enough for me." Mike squeezed the man's hand and felt a lump in his throat rise. Compared to life and death, everything else paled.

An ambulance arrived shortly, taking over and transporting the man to the local hospital only two minutes away. Mike thought the man had a good chance for recovery.

Mike picked up his groceries, putting them back into the basket. Everything seemed in order, except the bread, which lunged out of its protective paper coating.

Kyle Meinrich, a fellow comrade and captain, slapped him on the back. "Good work today."

Jared agreed. "Do you know who that was?"

Mike finished up his silent prayer. "Who?"

"Travis Mann," they said in unison.

"He started Mann Graphics," Jared said, naming the biggest local producer of Hollywood movie effects.

"Then a lot of people care what happens to him." Mike smiled, happy the man wouldn't be alone as he recovered.

"What?" Kyle asked.

"When I saw he didn't have a ring, I wondered if anyone cared that he was here in the store having a cardiac arrest. You know, a wife, children."

Kyle took him aside. "Mike, your value doesn't come from how many people show up at your funeral. Since when did you start being so morbid?"

Since no one really cares if I die, Mike thought. He focused on his captain's piercing gaze. "How is it morbid to think how my work will affect others?"

"Mike, I think you need some time off."

Mike's eyes flashed. He'd heard this speech before, and it was never a good thing for the recipient. "I'm going to the Department of Energy training next week."

"No." Kyle fingered his black collar. "I mean a real vacation, complete with relaxation and peace from the rescue business."

"I'll take one when I get back. The men are all off for their kids' spring break. I'll go after that."

"You've been taking on too many people's shifts. I don't want you trading for the next six months. Do you understand?"

"But, Captain, the men need the weekends with their families. I don't care. I don't have anywhere to be."

"I'm writing it up to make it official, and I've got my eye on you." Kyle's cheek clinched, and Mike felt duly reprimanded.

Jared came beside him, putting an arm around him. "He's right, you know."

"You think I'm going crazy, too?"

"I think it's hard not to go crazy in this job. We've seen death in the worst ways possible. How do you not think about that?"

"By concentrating on the afterlife and praying they made a decision for Christ," Mike offered.

"Perfectly spoken by someone who keeps forgetting to live his own life."

"Just because Emily dropped me does not mean my life is over. I've been dumped before, you know. Lots of times."

"Yes, but now you're taking on this family you barely know. You're sacrificing Emily Jensen for them, and you're playing with fire by escorting a gorgeous blond

52

under the guise that her son needs a role model. I know Mike Kingston knows better than this."

"I don't feel crazy. Why is everyone treating me that way?" Mike carried the groceries with Jared at his side.

"You think what happened to your father will happen to you, but you can't know that." Jared paid for the groceries. "And you can't force things to be different."

"Want to bet?" Mike clenched his teeth. "Just watch me."

Chapter 8

Mike walked the pale green hallway, scanning the numbers along each room. Kyle had taken him off duty for the next three days, as though he were some type of mental case. Mike still shook his head at the thought. He could feel the angst of Jim Barrow, a father who would miss an important Little League game over this suspension. Mike shoved his hand in his pocket and finally found room 304.

He peeked into the room and saw the patient sleeping peacefully. No visitors sat in the chairs, only a bodyguard at the door. Mike flashed his badge and a smile and was nodded through the door. Entry accomplished. He couldn't help but smile. In Silicon Valley, high-tech gurus were the rock stars of yesterday.

He sat in the hard chair alongside the bed and watched the patient's chest rise and fall steadily. Mike leaned back in the chair and waited. Within five minutes, the man's eyes blinked open, and he smiled.

"Well, if it isn't the last face I thought I'd ever see. Does that mean I'm dying again?"

Mike laughed. "I'm glad you got another crack at this life."

"Serves me right for doing my own shopping. I can never find anyone who knows how to pick the right apple." He held his hand in the air, like the evil stepmother in *Sleeping Beauty*. Mike could almost hear the cackle. "They have to have a crown. Is that too hard to understand? Crown equals sugar." He held up his hands, his fingers tensed in a clutch.

Mike tried to force away his surprise. If the man got this tense over his apples, no doubt he was ripe for a heart attack. "Maybe you could get a picture. Sometimes it's easier to translate what we mean in pictures."

"Did you come for your reward?" He raised an eyebrow.

"I did, and I've received it in full. You're alive and well."

Travis Mann gave a derisive laugh. "I'm worth more to you that way, I would imagine."

Mike stood and brushed off his sleeve. "Well, Mr. Mann, it might interest you to know, I cannot accept payment for doing my job." Mike guiltily remembered the aquarium tickets. He should never have taken them. This was just the kind of instance where gratitude might hurt his reputation. "If you care to bake me an apple pie, I can accept that." He squared his shoulders and walked toward the door. "Or if you wish to donate something to the fire staff, that's all right, but I won't be able to accept your cash gift." Mike chuckled.

"Wait a minute." Mr. Mann's eyes narrowed, and he scrutinized Mike from head to toe. "No need to get uptight. I didn't mean anything by my words. I'm a businessman, Mr.—"

"Mike Kingston." He walked toward Travis's extended hand and shook it.

"I just assume everyone else is a businessman, too. I forget there are some of you soft hearts still left in the world. Some of you who just want to do good and move on."

"Be thankful there are." Mike winked.

"Touché." Travis fiddled with his tubing, trying to wrestle free of its grip upon him. "What about a dinner invitation? Can you accept that?"

Mike shrugged. "It doesn't appear that we have anything in common, Mr. Mann. I came by to see that you were all right, that's all. You don't owe me a thing."

"I disagree." Travis shook his head. "I owe you the rest of my life, as do my children."

"You owe that to God. Just make yourself worthy of His gift."

"I married a young woman recently. She's twenty-six."

Mike forced his widened eyes to look away.

"I know what you're thinking, Mike Kingston. I hope you're not a gambling man because that poker face of yours is bad, indeed." He opened the drawer beside him and pulled out some papers. "I'm sixty-four, in case you haven't mentally calculated yet."

"How old are your children? If you don't mind my asking."

"Twenty-eight and thirty-three."

Mike nodded, trying to appear unfazed, when he actually wanted to throttle the man. He looked at Travis's elegant, silver hair and the crimson silk robe worn as though he were royalty. The sight of the man sent a wave of sickness through Mike's already tight stomach. A twenty-six-year-old could be his granddaughter.

"Well, I'm glad you'll make the most of your time." Mike turned on his heel.

"Now wait a minute." Travis opened the folder on his lap. "This here's my will. My wife was quite thrilled it hadn't been updated after our marriage."

Mike held up his palm. "Mr. Mann, I am really glad you've made it, but this is none of my business, and if you knew my history, you probably wouldn't be sharing it with me."

"Nonsense. I'm sharing it with me, because you didn't just save my life, you saved my children's inheritance. How long have I been in here, Mr. Kingston?"

"Since yesterday, sir."

"And it turns out my little wife has already been to see her lawyer." Travis shook his head, his heart clearly bent on revenge. "I've rewritten the will, and I'd like you to witness it, Mr. Kingston. Since you're here, I think it's quite hysterical that such a good-looking young man should sign my wife's financial demise. She seems to have an eye for the poor, brawny types. Well, she's not going to live on my quarter."

"I'd rather not sign any such thing, Mr. Mann. I'm sure you have a few family members or friends who warned you about this woman *before* you married her."

"As a matter of fact, I did."

"I'm just glad your children aren't going to pay the price for your temporary foolishness for the rest of their days. They deserve the inheritance." *I'm sure it's the only part of you they want anymore,* Mike added to himself. He felt his jaw twitch.

"You certainly speak your mind for not knowing me from Adam."

Mike had already crossed the line; there was no sense retreating now. "I think the fact that your children are older than your wife speaks for itself, Mr. Mann."

"Prejudices, prejudices. I thought she was madly in love with me." Travis shrugged. "I'm young for my age. I still ski, keep fit, look good for my age. Why wouldn't I believe she was in love with me?"

"Did you ever ask yourself if you were a poor man, would she still love you?"

"No, I never did. Successful men are attractive to women, Mr. Kingston. That's why the older ones can still get the young gals."

Mike couldn't hold back his laughter. "Is that what you think? You, who started one of the most successful companies in the country, do you really believe that the success is what attracts these women? Not the money?" Mike slapped his leg, unable to maintain his mirth.

"Success and money go hand in hand, Mr. Kingston. I'm glad this is so hilarious to you, but it's the end of my marriage. Do you find that funny?" Travis's steely gray eyes met Mike's, and all humor left.

"No, I don't find that the least bit funny. I guess I'm just shocked you're surprised. What did you expect to have in common with this woman?"

"I want to ski, I want to mountain climb. How many old ladies my age would be able to do all that?"

"I bet there are quite a few. Did you ever bother looking for one?" *I know my father didn't.*

"You're an upstart, you know that?"

At the first hint of anger in Travis's voice, Mike got nervous. He didn't want to upset the man in any way, and when the heartbeat beeps quickened, Mike knew he'd made a mistake in coming. "Mr. Mann, I don't mean you any disrespect. You've accomplished a lot in your lifetime, and you deserve to be rewarded for that. I let my own history cloud my opinion. I'm sorry."

Mr. Mann's face relaxed. "No need to apologize, Mr. Kingston. I respect you for saying your piece. It's not many who will tell me what they really think. I like that in a man."

Mike thrust his hand forward. "It was a pleasure to meet you, sir. I'm glad you're all right."

"You ever need a job, you come see me."

"Thanks, Mr. Mann, but I'm happy in my current one. Take care of yourself, and write your will first. . .before the next marriage."

Travis laughed heartily. "Will do."

Mike walked out of the hospital room and leaned against the wall, chastising himself for not sharing the Lord with a man who so desperately needed Him. He said a prayer for Travis Mann and waved good-bye to the security guard.

~

Grace finished the day's work, sorted through her paperwork, and locked her desk. She waved to Mr. Falk as she exited. Her stomach swirled at the sight of the older man. It didn't feel right, having her boss know so much about her personal life. But what choice was there? She and Josh lived in one of the most expensive areas in the country with only Grace's small salary to support them. There had to be more for him. She would see to it that Lyle Covington didn't buy one more sports car on her son's money.

The trickle of the atrium waterfall instantly soothed her, and she smelled the sweet scent of grassy hills that bordered the office. She closed her eyes and just let the peace wash over her. Just one moment when she had no worries, nothing on her mind, just her senses filled by the beauty around her. She savored it.

She opened her eyes and faced her broken-down Ford in the parking lot. The peace was shattered. The short, scenic drive to Josh's school lost its beauty in the bumper-to-bumper traffic she encountered with her car sputtering the entire way.

Josh waited at the school, his little fingers curled through the chain-link fence, his knuckles white, as though he'd been there for some time. Grace's heart cinched. How she envied the mothers who picked their children up when school ended. She slammed the door on her Ford and sprinted to the fence, where she took his hands in her own.

"I missed you today, Josh."

He blinked rapidly, and she tried to ignore the red in his eyes. "Can we go now?"

"Of course we can. We have to go by the grocery store. I'm out of lunchmeat."

"Aw, Mom, I'm tired. Can't we just go home? I'll eat peanut butter tomorrow."

"Okay, buddy." She unlatched the gate and went toward the portable building to sign her son out. The college students who worked there were stretched out on the sofas while children ran about wildly. They sat upright at the sign of Grace. She tried to still her angry breathing. She scribbled her name, grabbed Josh's backpack, then Josh's hand, and left without a word.

"If we go to the grocery store, can I get some ice cream?"

Grace looked down at his large, brown eyes. The melancholy borne there wouldn't be erased with any amount of ice cream. Grace got into her car, and despair washed over her in a rush. Leaning against the steering wheel, she couldn't fight the tears any longer. Though she was her son's only protector, she was utterly powerless to defend him during the day. She gritted her teeth and raged against Lyle and his selfishness.

"I'm sorry, Mommy. I don't want any ice cream. Peanut butter is good."

Grace whacked the steering wheel. "No, honey. It's not you. We'll get you some ice cream at the store. We'll get something good for dinner, too. Whatever you want."

"I want a Lunchable. With a soda."

"No soda before bed. You'll be up all night, but you can pick a Lunchable with a different drink." Grace pulled her Ford between two luxury sedans. She could just see the horror in the owners' eyes when they came back to the lot. She stifled a giggle.

"Mom, there's Fireman Mike!" Josh shot out of the backseat and laid on the horn. Grace tried to sink into the seat, but Josh waved vigorously. Fireman Mike had, indeed, seen them, as had everyone else in the shopping center.

He approached the car. Grace caught her breath. She'd forgotten since yesterday just how handsome he was, and she questioned fate for running into him. Being seen by Mike Kingston at the end of such an emotional day was like going on the Oprah show on the worst hair day of your life.

"Hi, Grace! Hey, Josh! What are you two up to?"

"Grocery shopping." Josh crinkled his nose. "What are you doing?"

"Well, I'm living in a typical bachelor pad today. My milk is sour, and my lettuce is wilting, so here I am. How was your day, Grace?" He opened the door for her and extended his hand to help her up.

Inwardly, Grace cringed at the ripped upholstery and faded dashboard after riding in Mike's elegant truck a few days before. "I've had better."

"Me, too. Let's just say I'm glad I had the fun of our adventure to live on today."

Grace stared into his eyes, his laugh lines worn into the edges. The ever-chipper Christian had disappeared behind a pained expression.

"I'm sorry your day was bad, Mike." Instinctively, she grasped for his hand, and he clutched hers in return. There were no sudden movements, no disgust apparent in his grip.

"Thank you." Mike took his hand and placed it on Josh's shoulders. "What about you, sport? How was your day?"

"Stupid. I told the kids I spent yesterday with you at the aquarium and kayaking, and they didn't believe me. They said I lied and that I just was pretending 'cuz I got no daddy."

"You tell them I had no daddy, either, Josh. That's what we have in common."

"Did you ever get a daddy?" Josh asked.

Grace nearly fainted against the car. She hoped Josh wasn't about to ask the gorgeous fireman if he'd like to apply for the position. "Josh! That's none of our business."

Mike bent over. "The truth of the matter is, I always had a father, but I never had a daddy. Now I have God, and He's the best daddy ever."

Grace couldn't even be mad at him for going against her wishes on religion.

58

Mike meant no harm. It was obvious he only wanted to help Josh. Maybe he would benefit from some of the social programs at Mike's church. If the kids saw him with Mike, maybe they might be more inclined to include him at school. "I don't mind if you take Josh on Sunday, if you're free."

Mike blinked several times before speaking. "Really?"

"Really."

"Was your mommy nice?" Josh asked.

"She was the best." Mike stood tall, meeting Grace's eyes again. "Well, maybe the second best."

Josh took both their hands, connecting them together in a shared bond of love for a precious little boy. They embarked on a grocery shopping adventure that Grace found herself hoping would never end.

Chapter 9

"Hello?" Grace dropped the groceries on the table, breathing audibly as she answered the phone.

"Miss Brawlins?"

"Yes, who is this?"

"It's Emily Jensen, Josh's teacher."

Grace's heart sank. "Oh, Miss Jensen, is Josh in trouble?"

"No, no, nothing like that. This call is of a personal nature. I hope you don't mind. Is this a good time?"

Grace tried to concentrate in her confusion while she watched Josh get himself his Lunchable and set himself down for a less-than-healthy dinner. "Sure. What can I do for you, Miss Jensen?"

"I wanted to invite you to church this Sunday. Well, you and Josh."

Grace felt more riddled with questions than before. What was this sudden interest in her getting religion that everyone seemed to have? Now, Miss Jensen, too. And what about church and state? Was this woman allowed to invite her to church? Wasn't that going against the Constitution or something?

Grace finally found her tongue. "Fireman Mike already asked Josh to church this Sunday. He said he has the day off before leaving for his new training in Los Angeles. I was actually thinking of going with the two of them." Grace thought she heard Miss Jensen's breath catch, and she found herself rattling off an excuse. "I think it might be good for Josh, you know, to have the two of us there."

"We'll be going together, Miss Brawlins. Mike and I. I was calling to invite you with us."

Grace watched Josh, trying to avoid the feelings churning within her. *Jealousy.* Red hot, boiling jealousy. Plain and simple, that's what she felt. An emotion not present within her since she'd found out Lyle was seeing other women at the office before his father could ship him off to his master's.

"That's very kind of you, Miss Jensen, but I am confident Josh will be in good hands with the two of you."

"Great. You'll have a nice morning to yourself then. Maybe you can treat yourself and a friend to brunch."

"Yes, that sounds nice," Grace pretended, lowering herself into a chair. She didn't have the money to enjoy a brunch out, with or without a friend. She'd probably spend her Sunday morning alone, curled up on the couch with a cooking show, lamenting why she ever gave up precious time with Josh to these strangers.

"Did Mike say what time he'd be picking up Josh? I'll probably just meet him at your house and save him a trip to pick me up."

"He said he'd come at nine."

"You're sure you won't come with us? We usually have a late breakfast or lunch following the service." It wasn't a question. It was more of a statement. "We'll probably get back about one thirty."

"You know, Miss Jensen, I only get my son nights and weekends; that's a long time for me to be away from him. Maybe—"

"Nonsense. The break will do you good. Mike is always talking about how tired you look. This will give you a chance to rest."

Grace stretched the phone cord to the small mirror at the back door. Taking a forefinger, she pulled her under-eye area, studying the bags. She did look awfully sallow, but it had been a trying day. Didn't Mike understand that? "Well, since it's just this once, I suppose one thirty will be all right."

"That's right. Just this once. Maybe Josh will get to be a little friendlier with some of the kids attending. That would help him in my class, as well."

Grace felt the sting of the comment as though it were a slap across her cheek. "Yes, that would be nice."

"Well, I guess I'll see you Sunday morning. I'll take your address down at the school."

Grace hung up the phone and stared at Josh. His Lunchable stood, a wreckage of plastic and paper, the foodstuff all devoured. "I guess that was pretty good, huh?"

"You're the best, Mom. I'll eat my string beans tomorrow, I promise."

Grace laughed. "I'll remind you tomorrow that you said that."

"I know."

"That was your teacher on the phone. She's going to go with you and Fireman Mike to church this weekend." *The perfect little family.* Grace swallowed hard, forcing back the sick pangs of envy she felt.

"Aw, why? Why is she coming with us? I don't want her coming with us, with her sickening sweet voice." Josh broke into a falsetto, " 'Why, Mike. What a wonderful surprise!' It's really disgusting."

"Where did you learn that word?"

"From the girls at school. I showed them this bug, and they all said that word. But it was really cool, not disgusting. Girls don't know." Josh plopped onto the sofa, crossing his arms.

Grace kissed Josh's head. "Where's your homework?"

"No homework tonight."

Grace breathed a sigh of relief. Homework for a kindergartner was ridiculous, but she tried to be supportive, knowing Josh could only benefit from keeping up with the wealthy set at Los Altos Elementary.

"Can I call Fireman Mike?"

"What for? You just saw him at the grocery store."

"No reason." Josh's brown eyes opened wide, giving every indication he wasn't telling her the truth.

"Fireman Mike has enough to do tonight. You'll see him on Sunday."

"Oh, all right. You like him, right, Mom?"

"Of course I do. He's been very kind to us, and we had a nice time kayaking and at the aquarium."

"No. I mean *like* him. He makes you all funny like Miss Jensen, and I think we need him more. I am going to tell him so."

Grace clutched her pounding heart. "You'll do no such thing, Joshua Blake Brawlins. These ideas of yours are nice, but they are only your imagination. Fireman Mike will marry someone else, maybe Miss Jensen, and have a nice family of his own. We are our family, Josh. I'm sorry Mommy made it that way, but that's the way it is. Go ahead and watch *Rugrats*. I'll be in as soon as I fix myself something to eat and get these groceries put away."

"All right, but you're prettier than her, Mom. Way prettier."

Grace stifled her giggle. "Thank you, Joshua. You made my night." Unpacking the milk and orange juice, Grace couldn't help but hope Mike agreed with her son.

~

Mike cut up a little cilantro and topped his Chinese chicken salad with the garnish. He took a whiff of the spicy Mexican parsley and inhaled. "Mmm, this is living." The phone rang and broke his reverie.

"Michael Kingston speaking."

"Mike, it's Emily."

The sweetness in her voice reeked of apology, and Mike found himself not in the mood. Emily's heart for his ministry was cold as ice, and suddenly he felt the same way about her. "How are you, Emily? Things going well at school?" He forced his friendliness. He still hadn't forgotten their heated words.

"I did what you asked me to."

"What do you mean?"

"I asked Grace to church."

Mike's hardened emotions softened. "You did? Emily, that's great. What did she say?"

"She wasn't really interested. I think Miss Brawlins has a little animosity toward God."

Mike raked his hair back. How he wished he might help Grace's heart to open toward God. "It has something to do with her parents, though I'm not sure what. Somehow, she's been very hurt by God's people."

"Well, regardless, we can't sow a seed when she doesn't have ears to hear. Shake off our sandals, you know? I told her I'd meet you at her house with Josh, so she wouldn't have any worries on Sunday."

"Great!" Mike let out a deep sigh. "Maybe we can talk her into going with us on Sunday when we see her."

"Sure, sure." Emily cleared her throat. "Listen, can we do lunch after Sunday school? I feel like we haven't connected at all, you know?"

Mike couldn't explain his hesitation, but he stalled for time, unsure why he regretted the idea of spending time with Emily. . .sweet kindergarten teacher Emily, a Christian since childhood. Why would he rather be with a single mother who didn't know Jesus?

"With Josh, of course," Emily clarified.

"Right. Sure, if it's okay with Grace, I'm sure that would be fine. You'll get to spend some more time with him and see why he's such an awesome little boy. Grace has done an incredible job raising him on her own, especially without calling on the Lord. Think how much easier life would be for her if she only cast her cares on the Lord and resorted to prayer instead of her own will."

"I think if you saw a little more of Josh Brawlins, you might rethink her perfection. The kid has a severe social problem. He has no friends, Mike."

"Maybe it's Los Altos Elementary that has the social problem." Mike clenched his teeth but released them after inhaling a deep breath.

"Mike," Emily said gently, "Joshua is a charming little boy. I'm not denying that. And sure, for a single mother with questionable morals, Grace does a fine job, but Josh is not without problems. He puts on a careful face for you. He's looking for a father, Mike, and I just don't want you to raise his hopes."

Mike felt a stab of guilt. Was he doing that? Raising a little boy's hopes only to crush them in the future? "You're probably right, Emily. I will be careful."

"I've got a full lesson plan tomorrow. I'd best hit the hay a little early."

"Okay, Emily. Thanks for calling, and thanks for calling Grace. Maybe she'll come with us next time."

Mike's gourmet salad sat before him, the freshly roasted chicken from the grocery wafting its scent throughout the whole kitchen. Suddenly and without explanation, he'd lost his appetite. He grabbed his Bible and began reading, looking for solace in the scriptures.

~

Grace tucked Josh into bed and kissed his forehead. "Bad day today, huh? Let's hope tomorrow is better."

"Why don't we pray it will be better?"

Grace sat back. "Josh," she said quietly, "I know Fireman Mike is a neat man, and I know he believes in God." Grace wished there was some way to avoid the conversation, but their differences were bound to come out sooner or later. "That's okay for Fireman Mike, honey, but I think we need to concentrate on tangible things. Do you know what that means?"

Josh shook his head, his eyes wide. "No."

"It means that we depend on things we can see and touch." Grace clapped her hands in the air. "Wishing for things is fine, but expecting them and believing some big, invisible god in the sky is going to get them for us is just not healthy. We have to work for things to make them happen."

"Wishing is just wishing, Mom. You wish for something, maybe it will happen, maybe it won't, but praying for something is telling God."

"Josh, I don't believe God is there for me. I'm sorry, buddy. I know that's hard for you to hear."

"I do. And I'm praying for Fireman Mike to be my daddy."

Grace was startled to hear her son's words. She had never mentioned God other than to tell Josh how most people based their view on an Almighty in the sky and told stories from an old book about who this God was. Where did he get such ideas? Mike simply hadn't spent that much time with him.

"Fireman Mike is not going to be your daddy, Josh." Grace brushed her son's bangs away from his eyes. "You need a haircut." Mentally, she calculated where she would get the eight dollars she'd need for that.

"All you have to do is ask Jesus into your heart. That's what Mike says. Why can't you do that, Mom? Then he could marry you, and I could have a father, and Miss Jensen could find someone else—someone not as nice as Mike because she doesn't deserve him."

Grace got up from the bed, bending to pick up Legos and assorted toys that littered Josh's bedroom. "That's not for us to decide. I'm not asking Jesus or anyone else into my heart, Josh. Maybe church on Sunday isn't such a good idea for you."

Josh shook his palms, sitting upright. "No, Mom. I'm sorry. I want to go on Sunday, please? Some of the kids in after-school care will be there, and I told them I was coming. If I don't go, they won't believe Fireman Mike and me is friends. They'll laugh at me again."

Grace wondered if Josh had been born differently, into a wealthy family with two parents, if he would have been the popular, cool kid instead of the skinny, fearful child he was. "I'll let you go on Sunday because I promised, but no more, Joshua. Fireman Mike needs to go about his business, and we need to move on. We are not getting him as a daddy, and he needs to spend time finding himself a wife or getting engaged to Miss Jensen."

"You'd just let him marry Miss Jensen?" Joshua pointed at her accusingly. "She'll be mean to him, Mom, like she's mean to some of the kids at school. Then, she's all sugary around the principal and Fireman Mike." Josh puckered his lips, imitating kissing sounds. "All you have to do is pray to Jesus. Mike told me!"

"Stop it, Joshua!" Grace felt her voice rising, and she could tell by Josh's reaction, it had, indeed, reached a higher pitch. She stopped and counted to ten. "Go to sleep." Grace clicked off the light and shut the door.

Josh shouted after her, "Well, I'm gonna keep asking Jesus. You can't stop me, and you can't stop God!"

Grace closed her eyes and fell backward against the wall, sliding down until she reached the cold tile floor. She gripped her hair and pulled as tightly as she could, until pain seared through her scalp. "My mother has something to do with this. I don't know how, but that woman will haunt me with her cold, callous religion until the day I die."

Grace sat directly across from the utility room. Dirty laundry covered the floor, and Grace rose, knowing it had to get done. Josh had nothing to wear to school. She started the washer and poured discount detergent into the machine, then added Joshua's jeans and broadcloth, button-up shirts. All his clothes were the finest designer labels. She didn't know where they'd come from. Someone had left them on the doorstep, but she wasn't about to thumb her nose at good, sturdy clothes. The shirt she held in her hand probably cost thirty dollars or more, and it was barely worn. Tossing it into the washer, she closed the lid and headed to the kitchen.

Josh had gotten out of bed and sat at the kitchen table, his little fists holding up his chin. "I don't know why you're mad at God. He didn't get us into this mess."

Grace halted in the doorjamb. "What? I suppose you think I got us into this mess. Is that what you're trying to say?" Grace shook with anger—anger at herself for getting them into this, and anger at her son for figuring it out.

"Mike says God doesn't allow things to happen to His people that won't be good for them later."

"Mike certainly says a lot. When, pray tell, does he tell you all this valuable information?"

"When he comes to after-school care."

Grace went toward Josh, kneeling on the floor and placing her chin on the table at his eye level. "Mike comes to after-school care?"

"Not anymore." Josh had a tear in his eye. "He used to come and see Miss Jensen, and then he'd come to after-school care and see me for a while, but he doesn't come anymore. That's why I was so sad when you picked me up today."

"Josh, we just had a bad day all around. It will get better, I promise."

"I want to pray for it to get better."

"Josh—"

"Mom, I wondered about God, but you would never answer me. Fireman Mike did."

"Okay, Josh, if it makes you feel better, you pray. I'll hold your hand and close my eyes, and you pray, all right?"

Josh broke into a grin. "Cool." Josh clenched his eyes shut, and Grace watched him through an open eye, but he opened his again to make sure she followed suit. Grace clenched her own eyes shut.

"Go ahead." She sighed.

"Dear Jesus, my mom and I are having a really hard day. We don't want any more bad days, God. Could you give us a good day tomorrow? And could you make Mike my daddy? Amen."

Grace grimaced at his prayer but kissed his forehead, and he ran off to bed without another word. She hoped Mike would marry Miss Jensen quickly. It would squelch any false hopes in Josh. *And me, too*, she thought. She pictured Mike in his torn-at-the-knees jeans and his navy fire department T-shirt stretched over his muscular chest. She relived her joy as he held hands with Josh in the grocery store and ultimately with her. It was the life she imagined for herself—the one she would have been living if she hadn't angered God. She let out a deep sigh. Since when did she become such a daydreamer?

Chapter 10

Grace awoke with a start at the sound of the phone. She stumbled toward the kitchen, tripping over the basket of laundry she'd left in the hallway. "Hello." Her voice held fatigue. She clutched the phone with both hands. "Hello?"

"Grace?" An unfamiliar woman's voice answered. "This is Kathy Houston. Do you remember me?"

Grace's blurred vision focused on the clock. It was only 9:50 p.m., yet she felt like it was three in the morning. She rubbed her head. "Kathy." She processed the name a few times in her mind. "Yes, we were paralegals together a long time ago."

"Right. Listen, I'm sorry to call so late. It sounds like I woke you, but I wanted to warn you about something."

"Warn me?" Grace shook the sleep from her head.

"I got a call from someone at the old firm. I guess you have some type of suit going against Lyle Covington."

"Already?" Grace's breathing quickened. She had no idea the ball would begin rolling so quickly. She'd only just given her statement. *How on earth?* Mr. Falk wouldn't threaten her case, but who would? "I'm sorry, Kathy, you've thrown me a bit. I wasn't ready for this yet. I thought I'd have more time to prepare. We haven't filed suit yet."

"Grace, I think you remember how our old firm went after a case. That's why I called. I wanted to share what I knew so you could prepare against the machine. I'm not under any oath, and I certainly don't owe any Covington favors."

Grace clutched her stomach, hoping this was some kind of nightmare, but looking around at the pile of unfolded laundry, she knew things were exactly as she'd left them before sleep. "What did they ask you?"

"They're looking to harm your reputation. They wanted to know what I knew about your social life during your time at the firm."

Grace doubled over, feeling like she'd been punched. "Did you tell them anything?"

"I told them I remember you dating Lyle and no one else, but then I didn't see much of you socially. We were too busy with the hours at the firm."

Relief flooded her. "I didn't date anyone else, Kathy, just for the record." For some reason, she felt the need to justify herself to Kathy, to anyone who would listen now. She'd been quiet for too long, and Josh had suffered too much.

Kathy, as if reading her mind, continued. "Grace, I don't know if this is what

67

you need to hear right now, but who knows when I'd get the chance to tell you again? I think it might be important to your case."

Grace swallowed. "Do you have a child by Lyle?"

"Oh, heavens, no, Grace. It's nothing like that. It's just that Lyle tried to get me drunk at an office party once. I had been warned by others about him, and I feel really guilty that I never warned you, especially when I learned it eventually cost you your job."

"I knew better than to drink, Kathy. It was my own fault."

"I left the firm shortly after you did, but it always bothered me that I should have warned you." Kathy paused for a moment. "So if you're wondering why you're hearing from me out of the blue, it's because I feel God has given me another opportunity to make things right. I'm warning you now. He's a snake, Grace, and he'll do whatever he can to win this lawsuit. . .whatever it may be."

"He can't win it, Kathy. It's a paternity case, and once I get the court order for him to give DNA evidence, there will be no denying his role in my son's life." Grace squared her shoulders, finally confident in something.

"Be careful, Grace. He'll do whatever it takes to avoid that test. I have no doubt. He'll paint you as a harlot. He'll say you came after him because he is rich. He'll do whatever he can. I know just by the questions they're asking. Remember when we worked on discovery how ruthless the firm was?"

"I remember." Her stomach swirled.

"Grace, tell your lawyer I'm willing to testify that Lyle tried to get me drunk and take advantage of me, and I can probably find a few others who would testify to the same thing. I'll do what I can to help, and we'll force Lyle to take that test and own up to his responsibility."

"Why would you do this?"

"Because I'm a Christian and Christians tell the truth. I should have been more forthright seven years ago, then maybe none of this would have happened."

Another Christian. Grace closed her eyes and shook her head. They were like cockroaches, living under every corner and crevice, invading her thoughts and dreams. She pushed away thoughts of her childhood, romantic memories she'd probably embellished over the years due to loneliness. God didn't care anymore. He couldn't.

"I appreciate you calling, Kathy. It couldn't have been easy for you to admit that, but I don't blame you for keeping quiet. Not at all."

"Thank you, Grace. It's just like you to worry about my feelings when you're facing a mountain of trouble."

"Lyle's getting married, Kathy. That's why I'm doing this now. Our son wears hand-me-downs and goes to after-school care while I work my tail off to provide a home for him. It's just not right, and he is not going to start fresh with some cute little family without paying for the one he already has. Whether or not he wanted Josh, he's responsible for him."

Kathy's voice was clear and soft. "I'm glad you're fighting to establish paternity. It's vital that a man provides financially for the children he creates. But don't let it eat you alive, Grace. I'm sure you're a wonderful mother. You always had the gentlest nature. A lack of finances a child can always get over, but your son is lucky to have you as a mother. Don't forget that."

"Kathy, thank you." A lump formed in her throat. There wasn't a day that went by in which she wondered if she was doing right by Josh. The words of confidence inspired her. "I appreciate you calling out of the blue like this. I won't let Lyle sideswipe me again. I'm ready for the battle." Grace straightened against the wall. Suddenly, she felt as though her armor was ready.

"I'm praying for you, Grace, and I'm in the book if you need anything else. If you need someone to baby-sit or just talk to, please call."

"Thank you, Kathy. Good-bye." Grace placed the receiver back into its cradle. She stared at the phone a minute longer and steeled herself for the phone call she'd been dreading. Now was as good a time as any. Josh, fast asleep in the room, would be spared her emotions; and since Lyle had already started his inquisition, it seemed fair for Grace to hit them with the news first.

Carefully, she pressed each button, amazed at how time had done nothing to diminish the speed in which she dialed the number. She drew in a deep breath and braced herself against the wall.

"Hello." She heard the familiar voice, the judgment still apparent through thin, pursed lips. Grace could see them, the wrinkles probably now more set by the elder woman's anger. Grace almost hung up, and the harsh tone came back at her. "Hello. Listen, it's late here. You got something to say? Say it."

"Mom." She paused and drew in another breath. "Mom, it's Grace."

Silence greeted her, and Grace just waited. At some point, her mother would have to answer her or hang up. The silent game of cat-and-mouse continued until, finally, Harriet Brawlins spoke. "Are you in trouble again?"

"In a way, yes," Grace answered, almost defiantly.

"Well, your father and I are on a fixed income and—"

"Mom, have I ever asked you for money? Ever?"

"No, but it seems odd you should call out of the blue like this when we haven't spoken for seven years, and so late, too. I told your father one day you'd call, in trouble."

"Gracie?" Her father's voice came on the line, and Grace teared at the sound of his comforting voice.

"Daddy?"

"Gracie, what's the matter, honey? Do you need something? Is Joshua okay?"

Grace was startled at the use of Josh's name. She didn't think her parents even bothered to remember their grandchild's given name. "We're fine, Daddy. I just wanted to tell you both that I am going to court to prove Lyle, Josh's father, should be paying child support. I wanted you to know before anyone called. His firm might call asking questions."

"Your father lost his deaconship at the church over your behavior." Harriet's disappointment in Grace hadn't diminished a bit. "I suppose you didn't think about the wake you left behind."

"I'm sorry about that, Mom, but I thought church was in the business of forgiveness."

Her mother started to speak again, when her father's voice interrupted. "Just never mind about that, Harriet. Your daughter's on the phone. Let her talk."

"Anyway, I just wanted you to know that I didn't live a loose lifestyle, and no matter what Lyle tries to tell you, it's a lie. Joshua is his son, and he needs to support the child."

"You, who became pregnant out of wedlock, are going to tell me you didn't live a loose lifestyle?" Her mother let out that same haunting, rude cackle that brought every hateful feeling back.

Grace pursed her lips, trying with all her might to rein in the emotions that hovered in her throat. "I suppose you would have rather had me take that check from Lyle. Is that what you're saying, Mother? That Joshua would be better off dead because he didn't come into the world your way? That your life and your deaconship might have been spared if I'd taken matters into my own hands?" Grace shook with anger, and she wished she could reach through the phone and throttle her mother.

"Gracie!" Her father sounded horrified, and she heard him break into a sob. A heart-wrenching, gasping sob. Grace crumbled, hearing the awful sound of him crying out in his pain.

"You just won't be happy until everyone in your life does everything to your satisfaction, will you, Mother? Well, I've got news for you. Joshua is ten times better than I ever was. He's a delightful child who will probably be a doctor or an engineer or something equally successful, and I relish that you'll take no credit for his success. None." Grace sniffled relentlessly, trying to will her raining tears back. "Because you know what, Mom? I don't care if Josh is perfect. I just want him happy!"

"Stop it, both of you! Gracie, we're sorry. We're so sorry. We were wrong, and we miss you, darling. We want you to come back home. To come back to your faith."

Grace harbored a bitter laugh. "I don't want anything to do with your religion, and I don't want Josh to, either. Because when Josh lets me down, Dad, I'm going to take him in my arms and tell him it's okay—that I love him anyway."

Her father could barely speak. His voice broke in coughing sniffles with every attempt. "Oh, Gracie, we have let you down so." Harriet began to speak when she heard a new side of her husband. "Be quiet, Harriet. Get off the phone if you can't keep your judgment and hateful thoughts to yourself. We've pushed our daughter away long enough!" He coughed again and apparently tried to compose himself.

Grace waited patiently, wishing she could hug the man who meant so much to her.

"Daddy."

"Gracie, I remember when you were on my knee at seven. I remember when you asked Jesus into your heart, and I believe with all my heart He still dwells there, if only you'll apologize to Him. Tell Him you'll live your life for Him again. Please don't let our mistakes turn you against God."

"Dad, it's too late. I'm not that little girl anymore. She died when Josh was born."

"You are that little girl to God, Gracie. He'll take all your mistakes, all our mistakes when we own up to them. Don't you want Joshua to know that kind of forgiveness?"

"Joshua is doing just fine on his own strength, Dad."

"He's a nice little boy, Gracie. You've done well with him, but finish the job."

"How do you know anything about Josh, Dad? Maybe I've done a terrible job."

"I've seen you two together, Gracie. I've come down to the Bay Area a few times. I wanted to talk to you, to see you, but I was afraid. I let you down as a dad, and I didn't want to be reminded about that. I didn't want to see your anger vented toward me. I was a coward."

"You were here?" Grace fell against the wall.

"I love you, Gracie. I've been a fool, but that never stopped my love for you or for Josh. I left him clothes on your doorstep. Clothes and a few toys. Did you ever get them?"

Grace always thought those clothes were hand-me-downs, but thinking back, many had shrunk the first time she washed them. The clothes had always arrived just when she didn't know what she was going to do for shoes or jeans. She thought the wealthy of Los Altos had passed their expensive things to Josh. She should have known they wouldn't have thought twice of the resident single mother.

"The clothes have been great, Dad. I don't know how I would have made it without them sometimes."

"Can I meet him, Gracie? You don't have to tell him I'm his grandpa, but can I meet him?"

"Oh, Dad, really? You want to meet him?" Grace grabbed a towel from the laundry basket, then swiped her soaked cheeks.

Her mother harrumphed and hung up the phone. Both Grace and her father ignored the gesture.

"I've wasted seven years of his life, seven years of yours. Forgive me, Gracie. Forgive me." He sounded older, and Gracie wondered if he had aged so much in seven short years.

"I do forgive you, Dad." And she did, too. Everything within her longed to be in her father's arms again, to be his little princess and bask in his tales of Jesus and his prayers over her each evening. "I want Josh to know you as Grandpa, Dad."

"I'll earn the title from here on out. I don't want you to worry about this Lyle character, Gracie. I should have protected you seven years ago, and I don't intend to let him hurt my baby again. He'll pay for his son, as he should have done long ago. I'll sell the house if we need money for the lawsuit, but we will win, Gracie. Mark my words."

Grace relaxed at her father's will. She'd never known her father to lose any battle he set his mind to, and with his support, she would do it. And she wouldn't be alone. "Oh, I know we'll win, Dad."

"Gracie, think about what I said about the Lord. I've wasted six years of my grandson's life. I'd just be sick about it if I didn't know I could make it up in eternity with him."

She flinched. "I'll think about it, Dad, but if there is a God, where's He been?"

"The same place He always was. Where have *you* been? Make an appointment with your lawyer and let me know the day. I'll come down and meet with you, and then I'll finally meet my grandson."

"He looks a lot like you, Dad. He's got your brown eyes and everything."

"I'll talk with your mother before I come down."

"She's not going to come?" Grace bristled. She'd been given back her father. She didn't want her mother in the deal. That would ruin everything.

"No, I think it's best if she stays home this time. I'll be praying about the situation, as I have every day for the past seven years."

"I'll call you soon, Dad."

"Okay, honey."

Grace pushed the RESET button and hung up but let the phone dangle on its cord to the floor. She sank to her knees, crying out at God's relentless pursuit of her. She'd tried to ignore her childhood, ignore that she ever took part in Sunday school or a little childish prayer uttered at seven. But He wouldn't release her. As angry as Grace was at God's people, she couldn't deny she wanted that peace back. Not the legalism or her mother's cold, letter-of-the-law ways, but the comfort she'd once felt when she walked and talked with a heavenly Father daily.

She took several cleansing breaths and knew there was no escaping. If she continued one more day on her own, she was going to crack. She needed help, and God had sought her as His one lost lamb.

"Okay, God, I'm here. My dad says You have been here all along. I suppose that's true in some ways, but I sure have felt alone. I'm sorry You spoke and I never listened. Surrounding me with Christians at every turn lately was playing a little dirty, but I suppose I needed the wake-up. Please forgive me, Lord. Forgive me, and mark Josh for your kingdom. I'll take him to church every Sunday. I'll let him know all my father taught me, but love him, Lord. Call him to You." Grace looked up at the ceiling. "That's what You've been doing, isn't it? Calling my son to You? Using Fireman Mike, his teacher, the church. You've surrounded my son, too. Oh, Lord, now I truly understand what You gave up. I wouldn't part with Josh for anyone's sins, much less my mother's. But You did that. You gave Your Son, who was worthy, for us who aren't. Forgive me, Lord. Forgive me."

Grace sobbed with relief and overwhelming emotion deep into the night. She'd been welcomed back into two fathers' arms in one night. And for once, she felt loving arms around her instead of the cold judgment and wrath. Just like when she was a child, before she let anger toward her mother and hypocrites at the church taint her view of God.

Grace sat up, blinking. She would go to church on Sunday with Josh, Fireman Mike, and Miss Jensen. They could play family with someone else's child. She was reclaiming Josh once and for all.

Chapter 11

Mike closed the cover on his Bible and stood tall, stretching out his back. He rubbed his chin, confirming he had, indeed, shaved that morning. Satisfied that he was stubble-free, he moseyed into the kitchen and made himself a bowl of cereal. Usually on Sunday, he was excited to get on with the day, to worship, and be refilled for the week, but today wasn't a normal Sunday. He'd take a child to church this Sunday, a child whose mother feared the Lord's Word.

Grace's salvation weighed heavily on his soul, and he'd spent the morning in prayer for her. He prayed she would change her mind about attending service this morning, and mostly, he prayed God would speak to her. Something just seemed inappropriate about taking Josh and Emily, yet leaving Grace behind.

Dressed in his khaki slacks and tie, he straightened his collar and headed for his truck. What was this pressing emotion he felt about seeing Emily? They'd spent countless days at church together before. Mike worried he'd come to care far too much about Grace Brawlins, and it was affecting his chance for a real romance with a Christian woman. Why couldn't he desire the opportunity to be with Emily? To woo her and take it to the next level? What was it that held him back?

The drive was short and familiar. Arriving at Grace's cottage, he noticed the tulips lining the walkway were in full bloom. An array of color hit his senses, a testimony to her gentle care for the rented home. The house appeared storybook, and Mike marveled that no man was there to appreciate this perfectly kept home. Grace probably wanted it that way.

Thinking back to his overgrown lawn and unvacuumed carpet, he couldn't help but wish someone took care of him that way—not just as a housekeeper, but as a homemaker—someone who enjoyed making a house nice for the people who lived there. He shook the thought off and started up the walkway. Just as he approached the door, a horn broke his silent reverie.

He turned, and Emily waved. He stopped to wait for her. She scrambled out of the car, then tried to compose herself by smoothing her dress. She wore a straight floral skirt that blew elegantly in the wind. Her shoes, a soft periwinkle blue, matched perfectly. Still, her appearance didn't weaken his knees or his resolve. He prayed for the Lord to lead him—that he wasn't focusing on the impossible while passing the woman Jesus had for him.

"Hi!" Emily said brightly. Her face was carefully made up with a light shimmer of lip gloss and soft eye shadow to match her eyes. "What impeccable timing, huh?"

"Perfect," Mike said, but something didn't feel perfect. Something felt incredibly awkward. He thought back to the scorched dinner and her angry tantrum. She had a right to be upset. He was spending time with another woman, focusing on another family. Emily deserved better than that. He forced his guilt down. Perhaps it was time to start again.

"I hope Josh is ready. I don't think his mother was too keen on letting us have him for the day." Emily winked as though the two of them had conspired against Grace.

He took a deep breath. He was imagining things. Emily was a kind and sweet woman. She was not conspiring anything. He cleared his throat. "I prayed all morning Grace would join us."

Emily laughed, then covered her mouth with her manicured hand. "I'm sorry. It's just that I don't think Grace Brawlins will ever be interested in church. She has kind of a nasty attitude." Emily crinkled her nose. "But I'm glad you prayed, Mike."

He rang the doorbell, choosing to ignore the comment. Grace opened the door, wearing a smile that caused his heart to pound against his chest. Her blond hair was wrapped up into a barrette on top of her head, and tendrils hung in all the right ways, framing her heart-shaped face and flawless skin. Grace's blue eyes met his, and he forgot to speak. There was a softness to her, an innocence she couldn't feign. Her gorgeous lilac suit embraced her figure without being inappropriate, and Mike fell utterly speechless.

"Hey! Well, good morning," Grace finally said. "It's nice to see you both."

"You—you look beautiful," he finally stammered. From the corner of his eye, he could see Emily staring at him, but it wasn't his fault. The words had tumbled out of their own volition. He was lucky he didn't say, "I love you, Grace. I've never seen a woman who set my heart into overdrive like this. Marry me." He laughed at himself and his uncharacteristic loss of any cool he might possess.

"Yes, you do look nice, Miss Brawlins. Are you planning to do that quiet brunch we discussed?" Emily asked. "I bet if you go early, there won't be anyone in the restaurant."

Grace stood tall. "No, actually, I can't really afford to spend money on something so frivolous right now. I'm planning to come to church with the three of you and see what this is all about. It's been a long time."

Emily's smile faded, and Mike knew it best to refrain from further enthusiastic comments for Emily's sake. "We'd love to have you." He tried to stay monotone, when in actuality he wanted to scream from the rooftops, "This is the perfect woman for me, Lord. If she could only know You. Please, let her know You."

"Where's Josh? Usually, he's bouncing off the walls by now."

"He's drawing the two of you a picture. He said he had to finish it before we leave. Come on in for a minute." Grace stepped back and motioned them in. Her home smelled like fabric softener and lavender-scented candles with a touch of eucalyptus. He inhaled deeply but noted Emily glared at him, and he looked at some of the photographs around to avoid her gaze.

"Your furniture is just beautiful. I meant to comment on it before." Mike smoothed his hand along an elegant mahogany table with a marbled top.

"You've been here before?" Emily questioned.

"Yes, remember when I brought Josh the InCharge CD? You were with me, Emily." He decided to forgo the explanation of the day in Monterey out of sheer concern for his life.

"Oh, right," Emily said with a smirk.

Grace motioned for them to sit down. "You won't believe this, but all that furniture was bought at Goodwill and estate sales! I bought it for pennies and refinished it. Josh helped me a lot, and that furniture will last a lifetime now. They just don't make it that way any longer." Grace moved about the room gracefully, clearly proud of the humble abode she'd made into a showplace. "Some people are so careless about what they dispose of, but their loss is my gain." Her eyebrows lifted in her enthusiasm.

"Isn't it kind of gross, going through people's old stuff?" Emily wrinkled up her nose.

"Oh no. Josh and I love it, especially when you can get the history of who it belonged to. It's so much more exciting to have something that tells a story than something off a showroom floor." Grace started to sit, but stood back up. "Can I get you some water or anything? Coffee, Miss Jensen? I know the Boy Scout here doesn't drink it, but you might." Grace giggled, looking away from him in the most charming display he'd ever seen.

"No, no, thank you. I don't drink it, either." Emily's eyes flashed.

"Well, you two will never have to bleach your teeth, and you'll both stay much younger looking. I'll be haggard and visiting the dentist often, but I'll do so happily with my caffeine in hand." Grace held up her forefinger.

Josh came bounding out of the kitchen, trailing two papers behind him. "You're here! You're here!" His enthusiasm was that of a new puppy for its owner.

"We're here." Miss Jensen bent down and reached for her picture. "Who are these wonderful people you drew, Josh?"

"That's my mom and me and Fireman Mike."

"Who's this over here?" Emily traced her finger to the edge of the sheet.

"That's you, Miss Jensen."

Mike sucked in a deep breath. It was going to be a long, uncomfortable morning. "We should get going. Church is about to start."

The four of them drove in edgy silence to church, and Mike found himself locked in prayer for the duration. When they arrived at church, he thought it best to take Josh to Sunday school while the ladies found a seat. Emily readily agreed and carted Grace away toward the sanctuary.

"Josh, are you going to be okay in there?"

"Oh yeah, Mike." Josh balled up his fists on his wiry hips. "I'll be fine. I told the kids I was coming. They'll be happy to see me."

"Okay, buddy. We'll see you in about an hour and a half." Mike mussed the child's hair and made sure that all the kids saw him drop Josh off. A few kids enveloped Josh, and they ran off happily.

~

Grace marveled at the friendliness of the church. Everyone seemed to have a smile on his face, and she found herself thinking maybe something had changed in the Body since she'd been a part of it. People actually looked happy to be there—everyone except Emily Jensen. Grace felt for her. If she dated a man like Mike Kingston, she wouldn't want another woman within one hundred miles of him, either. She hoped to put the woman at ease.

"I haven't been to church for years. It's a perfect spring day to start again, don't you think?"

"Uh-huh," Emily said absently.

"Lunch is probably going to be a little long for Josh and me. Maybe you and Mike could drop us off after the service, or we could walk home, and you could have a nice lunch by yourselves."

Emily brightened for the first time that morning. "Yes, I can see where you'll be missing your time with Josh. That's probably a good idea. Mike is leaving for his training tomorrow. It will be a week before I see him again."

"Well, then, you'll definitely want to go without us third wheels. It was sweet of you both to include us this morning. I do appreciate the gesture." Since Grace couldn't think of another thing to say to Josh's teacher, they watched the people gathering after finding a seat on the aisle.

Many people introduced themselves, and Grace was shocked so many recognized her as a visitor. At her parents' church, she usually slipped into the back pew and never heard from a soul. She also noted people were dressed differently. Some wore suits and ties. Some wore nice jeans and button-up shirts. Grace's eyes were probably wide with her shock, and she read her bulletin to keep from staring.

"Josh is all set. He knew quite a few of the kids, and they ran off together." Mike's eyebrows lifted, and Grace could tell he was as pleased as she that Josh found some playmates. Mike sat beside Emily, and she took his hand. Grace looked away, avoiding the jealousy that lurked within. She would not come between a man and his girlfriend. Even though Mike said it was over, Grace would believe it when she saw it. Attending church and lunch together didn't exactly imply they were apart. She settled back into the pew and waited for the music to start.

The music was uplifting and easily transported Grace to tears. She closed her eyes and sang along, feeling the hot tears glide down her cheeks and not caring a bit. It felt as though she had never left the flock. The music washed over her soul like a tonic.

The pastor spoke on the prodigal son, and Grace smiled through her tears. It appeared God had a special message for her and her alone. After the message, Grace jumped up eagerly. "I'm going to get Josh. Where is he?"

"Grace, wait a minute. Do you want to talk to someone?" Mike asked.

Grace shook her head. "No, I want to go home and talk to Josh. I have a lot to tell him today."

"Are you sure?" Emily's face softened, and she showed legitimate concern.

Grace wanted to share her renewed faith, but this wasn't the time or place. The moment would arrive when Emily and Mike would know, but it wouldn't be today. She had to let her feelings sink in, let the emotions settle into reality before she told anyone.

Mike wanted to ask her. Everything in his face said so, and Grace met his eyes in understanding. *I want to tell you, but I don't want you to think it's a ploy for your affections. Emily is a nice, untainted woman. Make the most of starting fresh. You deserve it.* Grace looked to the floor, away from his sapphire eyes and what they did to her heart. Loneliness had become her continual companion, and she wouldn't play with a man's heart again—especially a man who belonged to another. The man would go on with his life, and she would be alone again. Josh deserved all of her, and that's what she intended to give him.

"Miss Jensen, thank you so much for asking Josh and me today. It means a lot to us." Grace took Emily's hand. "You are very kind, and I appreciate you thinking of us. It's been a long time since Josh and I attended a church. It's such a beautiful day that I think we'll walk home and enjoy it."

"I hope you'll come again." Emily looked her straight in the eye. "And I mean that."

"Mike, can you point me in the right direction for Josh?"

"I'll take you there." Mike looked down on the petite Emily. "You don't mind. Lunch can wait, right?"

"No, no, Mike. I'll find him. Just tell me where." He pointed to an outer building, and Grace nodded. "Have a nice lunch, you two. Thank you. Oh, and Mike, good luck at your training tomorrow."

~

Mike watched as Grace effortlessly strode toward the Sunday school building. What was it about that woman that attracted his attention so? It wasn't just her beauty. There was an inner sweetness she exuded. In anyone else, he might have thought it was the Holy Spirit pouring out of her, but Grace had told him how she felt about the Lord. He gulped, turning to see Emily staring up at him.

"I think church spoke to her," Emily commented.

"I think so," Mike said. "I prayed it would. I guess we shouldn't be so surprised."

"Did you still want to get lunch?" Emily twisted the toe of her shoe on the patio, and Mike put an arm around her.

"Of course I do. I'm sorry, Emily. I haven't been a very good friend to you lately. My mind has been occupied with Josh."

"It's all right, Mike. I think we both know this isn't going anywhere. We're friends." Emily shrugged. "That's good, isn't it?"

Mike squeezed his arm about her tighter. "It is good." But the pit of his stomach felt sick. Mike was approaching thirty-four without a serious relationship to his credit. What was wrong with him?

He saw Grace holding hands with Josh and the two of them smiling gaily. He bit his lip until it nearly bled. He wanted a family. Maybe that's why Grace appealed to him so. She'd already set up housekeeping: a sweet little cottage with flowers up the walk, a warm home with love and a child. All that was missing was a father. How easy it would have been to step into the role.

Mike sighed, forcing the romantic notions down. He needed to get away and think. The training would do him good. He had to get past these thoughts he wrestled with. Grace Brawlins had a complete life without him or the Lord. But how he prayed it would include them both.

"Earth to Mike." Emily waved her hand in front of his face. "You there?"

"Sorry." Mike laughed. "I think I've been off the job too long. My mind is starting to go. I need to get back to it." He clapped his hands and rubbed them together. "I need a good emergency to spark the old adrenaline."

"You've been off for a few days. Is something the matter?"

"The captain just thinks I've been getting a little too involved lately. He just saw some things. I reacted badly. It's nothing."

"I don't know how you can see some of the things you do on a daily basis and not be affected. You'd be a robot if you weren't." Emily pursed her lips. "Doesn't the captain see that? Emotions are a good thing."

Mike laughed. "Sometimes they are. Sometimes they aren't. Where are we going for lunch?"

"How about the Stratford Hotel? They've got a nice brunch, and we need to celebrate."

"We do? What are we celebrating?"

"We're celebrating that we're friends."

Mike's stomach lurched. "I'm not sure that's something to celebrate."

"Sure it is. Lots of people waste years figuring life out. We only took a few months. That's not bad, and maybe God has our perfect mates waiting out there for us. Maybe He's freeing us up for those special people." Emily laughed.

Mike saw Grace and Josh skip down the walk. Grace unclipped her barrette and let her locks cascade down her back. Mike's pulse quickened. "I sure hope so, Emily, but I'm leery."

"Cautiously optimistic. That sounds better." Emily took his hand, and they walked toward his truck. Grace looked back at them, offering both a smile and a wave.

Chapter 12

Grace had about a week of peace before the warfare started. Every time she answered the phone, she braced herself against a chair, preparing for the barrage of words each call might bring. Lawyers, witnesses, friends; some offering support, some threatening her with slander.

It never occurred to her that the battle might come to her front door, as well. Saturday morning began as any other. Grace cleaned and folded laundry while Josh played with his building set and Batman figurines. The doorbell rang.

"I'll get it!" Josh raced to answer the door, nearly knocking Grace over in the process. He swung it open and stepped back, his face puzzled. "Mom?"

Grace's mouth went dry. Josh's father filled the doorway, still handsome as ever. She used the back of the sofa to maintain her upright position. She felt faint when those dark, elusive eyes stared into hers.

He hadn't seen her yet, and it gave her a moment to compose herself. "Is your mom home?" He stared at Josh in a way that made Grace uncomfortable. . .as if he was trying to see any resemblance that might satisfy his sick curiosity.

"I'm here, Lyle." Grace stood tall, forcing her shoulders back. How hard it was to believe this weak-willed, dangerous man was Josh's father! Josh deserved so much better. What had she ever seen behind those dark eyes? Had she lost all discernment?

"Josh, you should get dressed. Fireman Mike will be home from his training by now and is on his way to get you for the zoo."

"Yes!" Josh pulled his upturned fist and bent elbow toward him. Then, he ran toward his bedroom, not giving Lyle Covington a second glance.

"I really wish you wouldn't come here again. Josh is very impressionable, and I'd like him kept ignorant of this situation."

Lyle disregarded her comment and stepped into the home, uninvited. Sitting on the couch and sprawling his arms out over the sofa's full back, he propped an expensively clad foot over his knee. "If you want me to pay for him, he's going to have to know *you* think I'm his daddy. You can't have it both ways, Gracie."

"You are not his daddy. You are his birth father, and you have a legal obligation to pay for him. The law says so." Grace lowered her voice. "Don't think that gives you any parental rights to him. If you really wanted to be a father to him, that would be one thing, but you just want to hurt me."

"Grace." He looked down, shaking his head. "Grace, I can just deny I ever knew about him." He shrugged, pressing his lips together. "Then I could request time with my son. . .maybe even custody?" One of his eyebrows lifted. He looked around the cottage. "I'm certainly in a better financial position to take the boy."

Grace laughed and crossed her arms. She remained standing. "Don't you dare threaten me. I'll only use it against you in court. Your discovery people aren't doing nearly the job they once did." She paced, feeling as though she was the prosecutor in trial, catching her guilty party in a web of lies. "Maybe your father should never have fired me. I wouldn't let something so big slip through the cracks." She clicked her tongue. "Sloppy, sloppy."

"Pardon me?" Lyle's dark eyes peered at her, as though he couldn't be trifled with.

Grace nearly burst into laughter. Once, she might have been so fearful of that look, but after raising a son by herself, she had nothing left to fear. Certainly not this weak man who hid behind his wallet and credentials.

"The check." Grace let one corner of her lips curve. "You wrote me a check, and the date on it just happens to coincide with the three-month mark of my pregnancy. Not only that, but you enclosed a note telling me what to do with that check. And here I thought it was for baby clothes."

She watched him swallow, and his jaw set. "All right. What do you want?"

"I want child support, just like the complaint says. I'm not going after back support, though I should." Grace checked to make sure Josh's door was shut. "You have a wonderful little boy in there who, thankfully, is nothing like you." She pointed at him. "Would you let your own child live hand-to-mouth any longer while you marry some society girl? While you travel around the world? Drive a fancy sports car? It's not right, Lyle."

"You never cashed that check," he said, obviously hoping to find out if she was bluffing. "There's no record of it. I checked." Again, a smug smile emerged.

"No, I never cashed it; but luckily, I did save it. I'm very sentimental that way, Lyle. In case you ever tried to come back in my life, I wanted to remember what you wished for your own child." Grace closed her eyes, shoving such evil thoughts away. *Praise God, Josh was safe.*

"I don't want to go to court with this mess. It will be public, and it will ruin my fiancée's wedding day." He crossed his arms. "Tell me what you want."

She looked at the contempt in his eyes. Lyle obviously blamed her completely for his having to complicate his neat little life with such ugly details. "I want a monthly settlement to cover private school for Josh and a college scholarship fund started that will mature when he's eighteen. I'll manage clothes and food on my own."

"Why private school? You live in one of the finest neighborhoods in California."

"I want Josh in Christian school from here on out. I have my reasons." Grace could list them extensively, but she didn't. She'd led Josh so astray. She wanted to start making up for lost time, and she felt Christian school was just one way to help ease the burden. At least he'd be with people who loved children rather than teenagers just trying to earn a buck after school.

"You'll keep this out of court if you get your money?"

"That money won't begin to harm your lifestyle or take anything away from your children when you decide to have them. I think it's fair, and it will give Josh the head start he needs."

"Fine." His jaw twitched. "Have your lawyer turn your requests in to my lawyer. I'll have something drawn up."

"*I'll* have something drawn up. I know the way your firm does business, remember?" Grace lifted a brow. "And remember, I'm far better at discovery than anyone you've got working there. Your father is far too cheap with his paralegals. When will you see how that costs you?"

"Why now, Grace? Why did you decide to come after me now? You've had plenty of time to make a case if you wanted money. Why ruin my wedding?"

"You think that's what this is about, don't you? Me ruining your life? Did you ever stop to think how you've harmed your son's life? How your playing around created a child? Not an inconvenience for your wedding date, but a real, living, precious child?"

"Spare me the right-to-life garbage, okay? Why now?"

"I've made a lot of mistakes in my life, Lyle." Grace sat down on the chair beside him and clasped her hands together. "I forgive you for your part in all this. I'm actually grateful to you for Josh. But how could I deny him what's rightfully his? He is already missing a father in his life; he shouldn't be continuously living in want, too."

"If you forgive me, why the lawsuit? Don't you know my firm is famous for such cases?"

"I filed the lawsuit before things changed in my life. I wouldn't have filed it today, though I still would have gone after the money. It's about consequences, Lyle. It's not right that the government should pay in grants for Josh to attend college, when you easily could write a check for what your son needs." Grace drew in a breath. "I'm giving you the chance to do things right. Look at it that way. He deserves better than I can provide for him by myself."

"You're not going to come after me when I get settled with my bride now, are you?"

Grace shook her head. "It's not about revenge. Maybe it started that way, Lyle, but it's about doing what's right. I won't interfere with your marriage. I'll even have it written in the agreement to show you. I hope you'll have a good life with her. Honestly. But you made a child. Regardless of what you wanted to happen, Josh happened."

"Okay, Grace." He slapped his thighs and rose from the couch. "You win. Send your agreement to the firm."

Josh came bounding out the door. "I got my InCharge shorts on, Mom.

82

Fireman Mike is going to think they are so cool."

Lyle watched his son and blinked several times. "InCharge, huh?"

"Yeah, they rock." Josh broke into a dance step, and Lyle snickered.

"He's a nice kid, Grace." Lyle left, and Grace watched through the window as he drove off in a pristine SUV. She heaved a deep breath and muttered a silent prayer. That was far better than she'd imagined. Perhaps she could trust in God again.

Fireman Mike swerved out of Lyle's way to get into the driveway. Looking back at the expensive car, Mike appeared melancholy. Grace's heart pounded at the sight of his familiar truck. She'd missed him so.

He got out, smiling. After seeing Lyle's slight frame, Mike looked muscular and unimaginably tall. Grace could make out the sapphire color in his eyes from where she stood, and her stomach flip-flopped. Josh ran past her toward him, and Mike lifted him in the air and spun him before setting him back down.

"Check out those shorts, dude!"

Mike slowly nodded in approval.

"Mom got them for me. Aren't they the best?"

"Just like your mom." Mike winked at her, and she looked away.

Her breath caught, and she pretended to sneeze to avoid being so moved by his simple gesture. She stepped out onto the walkway, relishing her giant tulips and the wash of color they provided. She concentrated on the pinks and yellows rather than dwell where she really wanted to focus.

"How was your hazard training?"

He came beside her, lightly touching her shoulder. "Are you talking to me or that tulip there?"

She turned to face him, but her stomach twisted and swirled, so she bent and rearranged the self-watering apparatus. "I was talking to you. The flowers don't usually answer." She nibbled nervously on her lip. Why couldn't she maintain her composure around this gorgeous wall of a man? Was she so shallow that she could be so easily affected by an incredible exterior?

"The training was good. Trying. I hope I'll never have to deal with such an emergency, but I'm prepared now. I just need to train the rest of the force, now that I'm back. Apparently, I'm the only one with an attention span long enough to withstand those cerebral training sessions, so they always send me." He caught a ball Josh threw at him. "I can read anything. A mind like a trap, my mom used to say." He laughed. "Well, you can buy all the intellectual excuses, or you can figure I'm single, and no one else wanted to go."

Grace checked her watch and stood. "So, what are you boys up to today?"

"The zoo. Josh says his monkey friends miss him."

Josh jumped at Mike, and they pretended to fight. "They're your friends!"

Grace laughed at her son's attempt at humor. "Well, I hope you both plan to visit the hippos because they take baths!"

"Mom!"

"Join us." Mike's smile disappeared, and he zeroed in on her eyes, unwilling to let her gaze go.

"I have laundry to do, the grass to mow, and groceries to buy. You guys have a great time." She thought about Emily Jensen and what she might think of the invitation, and guilt enveloped her. Emily was her son's teacher, and Grace knew what it felt like to be played like an instrument. She wouldn't succumb to Mike's natural charms. She needed to find herself, to get grounded in the Lord. She wasn't ready for any commitments until she knew her faith was solid again.

Mike was not so easily deterred. "The laundry can wait. I'll take you out to dinner, and the lawn will wait until next weekend when Josh and I can mow it."

"This is Josh's special time with you. I wouldn't want to—"

"Grace, it's been a week since I've seen you." He clutched the ball Josh threw at him. "A week since I've seen Josh," he corrected. "Josh only gets so much time with you. Come with us, unless you need the break."

Grace looked at him from the corner of her eyes. "When you say dinner, are you talking Big Mac?"

He laughed. "No, I think I could spring for a Whopper."

"Oh my, but you are a big spender."

"I'd treat you to lobster, but I have a feeling Josh would protest. How about Chili's?"

"Hmm," Grace pressed a finger to her chin, tapping it. "Chili's. You sure know how to woo a girl."

"Hey, some women appreciate a fine wine; you appreciate a restaurant with spill-proof drink cups."

Grace laughed. "Well, since I'm up against Bond himself, I guess I better agree. I am powerless to resist spill-proof cups." Grace shook her head and clicked her tongue. "I should have known you'd find the chink in my armor."

"Yes!" Josh's face crinkled, showing his missing front teeth.

"What about Emily? Will she be joining us?" Grace felt the need to remind him of his girlfriend. Grace didn't want to be known as a temptress, and yet it felt so wonderful to play family with Josh and Mike.

Mike sighed. "No, Emily and I have decided to concentrate on friendship." He tossed the sponge football toward Josh. "I hope that won't stop you from joining us at church tomorrow."

"Mom said we're going to go to church from now on, Mike! I can't wait to tell the kids."

Mike raised his eyebrows. "What's this about?"

"We'll talk about it later. I'm going to run and get my windbreaker. Sometimes it gets awfully cold in the city, even in the summer." Grace scrambled into the house, nearly hyperventilating. He was free. She fell into prayer as naturally as when she was a child.

Oh, Lord, You are enough, so why am I so tempted by this man of flesh and bones? I am not a good judge of character, Lord. You know that. I thought Lyle was sweet, caring, and considerate at one time, too. Remember? Today, Lyle didn't flinch at the sight of his own son. I want to believe Michael Kingston is different, that he is a true man of faith, but that's exactly why I cannot believe it. I must focus on You and what You can provide—not on a man. No man can take away my troubles and heal us, Lord. Only You.

Grace opened her eyes and went to the door. Mike and Josh were in the kitchen, fumbling about with things, and she followed the noise. "What's going on in here?"

"We're packing a picnic lunch, Mom. Mike said you'd like that. He said the zoo had lots of nice places to picnic." Josh dragged a chair to the sink to wash an apple.

"I'll get the cooler." Grace scrambled out of the kitchen. She just wasn't ready to deal with all the emotions Mike made her feel.

~

Mike watched Josh wash the apples, then dry them on his T-shirt. Tossing a towel his way, Mike raised an eyebrow, and Josh washed the apples again using the towel this time.

"So, how were you this week, bud? Did you take good care of your mom?"

"Yeah. She was kinda sad this week, though. Whenever I saw her, she was crying all the time. She told me it was happy tears, but she didn't look too happy to me."

Mike thought a moment, but his curiosity was getting the best of him. "Why did your mom say you could go to church now?"

Josh shrugged. "Don't know. She just said we were going from now on, and I was going to meet my grandpa soon."

"Your grandpa?"

"Yeah. I thought he was in heaven, but Mom said he was in Modesto, not heaven. I hope that means I'll get to meet my dad soon, too."

Mike stopped making the sandwiches and focused on Josh. "You've never met your father?"

Josh shook his head.

"My dad left my mom and me, too."

Mike thought, *How could anyone make such a choice?*

"Mom said he went away before I was born. She said that was okay because he wasn't very smart, or he wouldn't have left in the first place."

Mike forced back a laugh. "Your mom is right about that. I can't imagine having a better son than you, Josh."

"That's good. Because I been thinking you should be my dad." Josh placed the apples in a big paper bag and looked at him with wide eyes.

Mike took Josh's chin in his hands. "It's not that simple, buddy. I wish it were, but it's not. Maybe your mom will get married someday, and you'll have a step-father; but until then, I think we should keep spending time together."

Josh shook his head. "I don't want a stepfather. I want a real father. Mom would pick someone boring. Someone who wore a suit every day. Besides, she's not interested."

Mike thought about the nice-looking man who left the house in a costly SUV. Had *that man* been interviewing for the position? Dining the elegant Grace Brawlins while he was away? Mike already decided the man's car was far too expensive to let a little kid eat McDonald's in it. He hoped Grace realized that.

"She's not interested in what, buddy?"

"In getting married." Josh shrugged. "That's why I gotta find my own daddy."

"Josh." Mike sat beside the boy on a barstool. "You can't just make somebody your daddy. I wish you could, but you can't. Your mom gets to choose that."

"But she did already, and she said my daddy wasn't smart enough to stay. That's why I want you to change her mind about marrying and marry her. Or she might pick someone stupid again."

Mike laughed aloud. "What makes you think I have the ability to do that?"

"You told me with God, all things can happen. I prayed, and things are gonna happen. But you have to help. You already got her to agree to church. That's something."

The hope in Josh's eyes was something Mike couldn't bear to dash. He remembered those feelings like they were yesterday—yearning for someone to play ball with and teach him to ride a bike. Watching the other kids in the neighborhood run to their daddies after a long day's work. He prayed for strength. He had to show Josh that he would be there as much as possible but also that Grace Brawlins was another matter altogether.

"My dad left, and I never got another father, other than my heavenly One, Josh. Maybe you won't, either, but that doesn't mean—"

Josh shook his head wildly. "My mom's prettier than Miss Jensen."

Mike looked away, unwilling to answer such charges.

"She probably cooks better, too."

"Josh, there are things you are just too young to understand. Two people must love each other to be married, but they also must love the Lord together for it to work." Mike stopped at the sight of Grace in the doorway. His eyes widened. "I'm sorry, Grace. I know how you feel about my discussing religion with Josh, but—"

She held up a hand. "I think marriage is a discussion I should have with my son, Mike. It's personal, and I will handle it."

"The same way you handle religion?" asked Mike.

Grace's eyes narrowed. "Joshua, please go to your room."

"But—"

"Go!"

Josh scrambled from sight. A slamming door echoed a moment later.

"Michael Kingston, I do appreciate what you've done for my son. I don't know how I could live with myself if I thought of him in day care all day without your occasional visit. Don't think me ungrateful, but you're going to get married someday soon, and no woman is going to share you with Josh. That's just a fact of life. I will be left to pick up the pieces, so please don't lecture me on life lessons. I've more than earned my stripes."

"Grace." He stepped closer. "Why church? Why now?" He prayed it was because of him, that he had sparked something within her that made her yearn for the Holy Spirit.

She turned around, busying her hands with the cooler. He grasped them between his own. Her hands were soft and slender as though they'd never done a day's work, but he knew how ridiculous that was.

"I can't answer that. Not yet."

He looked down at her blue eyes. One of them held a tear. He caressed her face with his hand. "Please tell me, Grace." His heart pounded, and he prayed she'd tell him she'd entered into a relationship with Jesus, but she only blinked away her tears. "Grace?"

She snuggled against him, the warmth of her cheek against his racing heart. Her hair smelled of botanicals, and Mike combed his fingers through her hair, tangling them in her ponytail. He kissed the top of her head, and they held each other for a long time. How long he didn't know, but it felt like mere seconds. Josh opened his door, and the two of them quickly separated.

Chapter 13

It had been years since Grace had visited the zoo. She could hear the distant waves of the Pacific Ocean and feel the bite of the morning fog, but the sun peeked through the cypress trees, promising a brilliant day in San Francisco. It was early yet, and the crowds hadn't gathered. Josh ran ahead down the hill toward the hippos and big cats. Grace flushed red at the sight of her overly enthusiastic son.

"I don't get to do much of this kind of thing with him."

"Grace, you don't have to apologize. That's why I wanted to help, so Josh could do more of this kind of thing." Mike started to reach for her hand, but she pointed toward the lions, frustrating his effort. She saw the hurt in his eyes, and she wished she could tell him everything—how she'd given her life back to God. But her father would be in town soon. She wouldn't have him thinking Mike was like Lyle. If Mike was the right man for her, he would be there when her father left town.

"I'm glad you're helping us. It's made a world of difference to Josh. And me. You reminded me of some very important truths in this life."

"He says he'll be meeting his grandpa. Is that true?"

Grace nodded. "I called him to tell him about the lawsuit." She sucked in a quick breath, covering her mouth.

"The lawsuit?"

"I'm filing against Josh's father for child support." Grace watched as Mike's expression melted into a frown. "Well, actually I think we reached a settlement."

"His father?" Mike crossed his arms behind his back. "I guess I never thought about the fact that there was a father." He laughed a forced, confused laugh. "I can be pretty naïve sometimes. I just assumed he was out of the picture completely, like my own father was." He looked at Josh, then back to her, his expression pained.

"He is." Grace searched his face. "Lyle is out of the picture. He's getting married next month."

"Has Josh met him?"

"Today. That was him at the house, driving away when you came."

"I see."

"Mike, it's not what you're thinking."

Mike clicked his tongue. "I'm not thinking anything. It's none of my business." He shrugged. "Josh is pretty enamored with that lion over there. I think I'll go talk with him about it."

Grace sucked in a deep breath as she watched Mike's muscular frame as he walked away. She thought he'd be happy for them—happy that Josh's father would finally provide the much-needed financial support. But that's how people were, saying they'd forgive you when your sin was never far from their mind. A lion roared, waking her from her reverie.

Grace studied Mike. He'd lifted Josh up for a better view of an ostrich. Suddenly, her stomach swirled. Would Josh ever have a man who loved him like Mike? Was Mike interested in a woman with a past like hers? Loving her son was one thing, loving the mother who bore him illegitimately quite another.

She followed Mike, touching him lightly on the shoulder. "I'm using the money from Lyle to send Josh to a private Christian school. I got him entry into Calvary Academy, beginning in the fall."

Mike's eyes softened into a smile. "I'm so glad, Grace. Relieved, actually. Josh will flourish in that environment."

"The kids at Los Altos have been so unkind to him. I want him to be at a place where they appreciate and love him."

"Is that all?"

Grace focused on the lion behind the big, plate glass window. "Should there be more?"

"I just thought maybe, well, you know, the faith was a part of your decision."

Grace looked away from him.

"Most teachers love their kids. Emily certainly loves Josh."

Grace shook her head. "No, I don't think Emily does love Josh. I think she tolerates him because of you, but she doesn't see what's special about him. If she did, she wouldn't punish him for not fitting in or snub her nose at his out-of-style clothes."

"Grace, I can't believe that's true. Emily is a Christian."

"Mike, I mean you no ill will in this, but I've found that makes very little difference in the way some people act. I believe the Bible calls them a clanging gong."

He looked at his shoes. "The world is full of hypocrites, Grace. They are not just in the church."

"You're right, and I'm sorry if I offended you. You've never been a clanging gong to us, Mike. I know Emily means a lot to you, and I shouldn't have shared my opinion, harsh as it is. I need to learn to bite my tongue."

"No, no. If that's what you think, I'm in no position to judge. If you say Emily hasn't been that kind to Josh, I can't argue with you. You would know better."

"Someday, you'll be a father and understand. You'll know what it does to your soul when someone hurts your child—whether or not they meant to. Something just clicks in you."

His cheek flinched, and he crossed his arms. "So I suppose Josh will be seeing his father now."

She grabbed his arm, forcing his eyes to hers. "No. He doesn't want anything to do with Josh."

"How do you know that?"

"He's getting married to a high-society real estate agent. He doesn't have time for an unwanted kid in his life. The money is about fairness, Mike. I just don't want Josh to suffer while Lyle lives the stately life. That's all."

"Grace." He reached for her, cupping his hands around her cheeks. "Josh is not suffering. Not getting the latest InCharge CD is hardly suffering."

"Maybe not, but he's already without a father. I won't make it any more difficult than it has to be."

"So, will this make things simpler? The money?"

"Are you saying I shouldn't be going after child support?"

"Of course not. I don't know what I'm saying. I'm hardly the man to offer you advice, Grace." He dropped his hands to his side. "Forget I said anything."

"Cool, let's go see the zebra!" Josh pulled them both by the hands, forcing an end to their conversation.

~

Mike's mind wandered as Josh talked to him about the zebra. The child had a bevy of facts from an animal television show, and he relayed them endlessly. Grace seemed preoccupied as well, and he wished he hadn't pressed the subject. Why should it bother him if Grace went after child support? It was rightfully hers for bringing up Josh. He had no reason to deny her the proper support to raise her son. So why did it feel like a vise grip on his heart? He hated the fact that she asked another man for help, that Grace should be indebted to this Lyle character for the gift of Josh.

"Grace, I want us to go out to dinner." He looked around, unsure if he'd actually said the words aloud.

"Sure." Grace shrugged as though nothing was out of the ordinary. "When is your next day off? Josh—"

"No, not Josh. You and me. I want *us* to go out to dinner."

"Why?" Her soft gray-blue eyes clouded.

"I just want to finish a conversation with you. I don't know why." But he did know why. Something about her held his heart and wouldn't let go.

"I don't really have any type of baby-sitter, and—"

"Grace, do you feel at all what I do?" He held his hands out toward her, trying to stress his point, but not sure if she understood a word he said.

"I don't know if I feel anything, Mike. I'm a little numb."

"Do you," he halted, trying to find the words. *Do you feel this connection, this undeniable attraction for me? Or is it just me?* "Do you want to know me any better?"

"Of course I do. I can't tell you the stress relief I have felt just in having you care for Josh. Having someone else think he's as special as I do has meant the world to me." She smiled, an innocent sweet grin that told him nothing.

"Never mind."

"Yes! Yes, I want to know you better, Mike. I feel drawn to you. I thought it was the Lord at first. He has called me back to the flock, but it's not just that." She shook her head.

Mike felt as if he'd been struck in the stomach. He clutched it to force the queasiness away, checking the facts to make sure he'd heard correctly. "You are a Christian." He let out a deep sigh. "I thought I felt the Holy Spirit, but I thought it was my own desires, not reality." His fingers raked through his hair.

"It's reality, but it doesn't erase my past reality. My mistakes will always be readily obvious to anyone who cares to check."

Josh ran toward the giraffes. Mike turned to see a man taking pictures of them. At first, he thought it was the animals, but he noticed the man followed them. "Do you know that man, Grace?" Mike pointed, and the man turned. Mike sprinted toward him, and while the man began to run, Mike easily overtook him. He pulled the stranger around by the shoulder. "Who are you?"

The man cowered behind his raised arm. "Don't hurt me."

"I'm not going to hurt you. I rescue people. I don't harm people. Why are you taking photos of us?"

"I was taking a picture of the zebra. You just got in the way." The man was slight in stature, with dark brown eyes and a receding hairline.

"Did Josh's father send you?"

The man's brows furrowed. "Who?"

"Give me your business card."

"What?" The man shrugged. "I don't have a business card. I'm just taking pictures. Are you paranoid, man?"

Mike took out his billfold, flashing his badge. "I'm a firefighter. Who are you?"

Standing to his full stature, the little man balked. "I told you, I'm just a guy taking pictures."

Mike crossed his arms in front of him. "You will give me your business card, or I'll take you to the zoo offices, myself, and call the police. You were tailing us, and I want to know why. I've got a lot of friends on the force, and I think they're inclined to believe me if I say you're harassing me. I'm not inclined to lie."

"I'm not going anywhere with you. Leave me be." The photographer stood up straight, dusting off his black polyester pants.

"You see that kid there?"

"Yeah, he your son?"

"Can't you tell me?" Mike scrutinized his face.

"Listen, buddy, I'm not looking for any trouble." The man reached into his pocket and pulled out a card. "You just leave things be, and I'll do the same, okay?"

Mike scanned the card. *Gilbert Howard, Private Investigator*. "Who are you working for?"

"Listen, you got what you wanted. Let it go. I'm off the case, I promise." The man stuffed his camera into a case and turned to run. Mike watched him go.

"Mike, who was that?" Grace's eyes held fear. "Why did he want pictures of us?"

"He's no one. Don't worry, Grace. Everything's fine." But in his mind, he watched the slight man scamper into the distance, wondering what this Lyle character might be up to. He ground his teeth together. He wouldn't let anyone harm Grace or Josh.

"I'm sure we're just overreacting. We've been watching too many movies." Grace smiled and took Josh's hand.

Mike turned around and looked behind them again. Paranoid or not, he wasn't about to let another picture be snapped without knowing who wanted them photographed.

Chapter 14

A few months later

Monday morning greeted Grace like a new friend. The sun shone, and the rolling California hills began to turn from spring's rich green to their calming golden tone of summer. June was upon them. Grace stopped in the entry to her office building and listened to the trickling water of the natural fountain. Lush greenery over mossy rocks soothed her soul. Her mind drifted to Mike, their times together, and the way he showed such warmth for her and Josh.

She wondered if Mike would hold that same warm expression for her alone, though she'd never had the chance to find out. Their plans for that intimate dinner had come and gone several times. She flushed and turned her face up to the heat of the sun. Something always came up, and Josh always seemed to tag along. Would she and Mike ever get time to explore their feelings for one another?

Grace sniffed. *I suppose that's why romance should come before children.* She checked her watch. The fifteenth had finally arrived. Her father would come today, and the very thought sent her heart aflutter. How she missed him in her life! She prayed he would still be the same, that the years would not have taken their toll, and they might not have missed much. Thinking of Josh's years, she knew that simply wasn't possible.

"Miss Brawlins?" A few high-heel clicks on the cement alerted Grace to the tall blond. She looked familiar, but Grace couldn't place her.

"Do I know you?" Grace finally asked.

"I'm Lily Hampton. I'm Lyle's fiancée." The blond hitched her chin to the sky as though her statement was something to be proud of.

Grace wanted to answer, *And I'm the mother of his child. What can I do for you?* She stifled a giggle and answered more appropriately. "Can I help you? Did you want to sell me a house or something?"

"I hardly find this meeting funny, Miss Brawlins."

"I didn't know this was a meeting." Grace shrugged. "I'm just going to work. What you're doing here is beyond me." Grace flipped her hair in an exaggerated manner. "Usually, when there's a meeting, both parties are made aware of it—just a little tip between us girls."

"Listen. I didn't come here to have your trashy ways give me lessons in manners."

Grace stepped back, shocked anyone would behave so irrationally. "Quite frankly, I don't care what you came here for. If you have something to say to me, tell it to Lyle's lawyer. I'm sure I'll get the message." Grace turned and walked toward her office, but the woman followed her. Grace could hear the hollow clicks of the heels.

"Wait a minute. Wait a minute. I'm sorry. I didn't mean anything by that."

"You didn't mean I was trashy, or that you needed a lesson in manners? Because I'm thinking you do."

"Miss Brawlins, I just need to know something about Lyle. This is personal, and it's not anything a lawyer could answer."

Grace stopped in her tracks, studying the woman. Her confidence had clearly waned from the sophisticated engagement photo Grace had first seen. She looked a bit browbeaten and confused. "Miss Hampton, I haven't seen Lyle but once in seven years, so I'm sure I'm not the one to ask."

"He says this isn't his child, but that he's paying you off because you want so little. Is that true?" Lily Hampton's eyes narrowed. She obviously hoped for an answer Grace couldn't give her.

"He's your husband-to-be. I suppose his answer is your truth, but I'm no charity case, Miss Hampton. I was in law school when my son was born. I would have been a good lawyer, but I'm an excellent paralegal, instead."

"Listen, you don't look anything like I thought you would. You look younger, more innocent. I thought—"

Grace felt her expression soften. "I'm sure whatever Lyle says, he wants to protect you."

"Grace." Mr. Falk's steady, familiar voice broke her train of thought.

"Mr. Falk. Good morning." She heard her voice shake at the sight of her boss.

"I'd like to see you in my office immediately."

Grace nodded. "Of course sir." Grace looked back at the professional blond in front of her. The voluptuous figure made Grace feel lanky and childlike. Yet she wouldn't trade places with the woman for anything. For all Grace's faults, her mistake had taught her well. Men like Lyle Covington weren't worth their trouble.

"You have to go," Lily said.

"Yes, I do." Grace studied the red, clawlike nails. *Just like I imagined*, she thought to herself. "Lily, I have no intention of ruining your future. I only want what is rightfully Joshua's."

"You should have taken the check." Lily clicked her tongue and turned, but looked over her shoulder. "There's no reason Lyle should have to pay for the rest of his life because you couldn't take responsibility for yourself."

Grace felt the blood drain from her face, and she felt lightheaded with horror. How could anyone contain such evil behind a carefully designed, glamorous façade?

"We made a child." Grace crossed her arms, thankful her boss had reentered the office. "I don't kill my young. You're perfect for Lyle," Grace called after her. "Good luck. You'll need it." Grace stormed off to her office, holding back the tears she wanted to cry out of sheer anger. She breathed in deeply, the solitary trickle of the waterfall offering no peace whatsoever.

"I'm sorry, Mr. Falk. What did you need?" Grace braced herself against the doorjamb.

"There's a Michael Kingston on the phone. He says it's important."

Grace raced to the phone, clutching it tightly. "Mike?"

"Grace, first, it's nothing to worry about, so calm down." His answer caused her to release her breath. "It's actually good news."

"Oh, Mike, I could use some good news about now."

"You know the photographer who was taking our picture a few months back?"

"At the zoo. Sure. He really was filming us."

"Turns out, he was."

"Why? Did Lyle put him up to it?"

"No, actually, Lyle had nothing to do with it. He was following me, not you. Shortly before I met you or right around the time, I'm not sure, I saved a man after he had a heart attack in the grocery store."

"Oh, Mike, that's wonderful!"

"The photographer," Mike continued, "was hired by Travis Mann, the guy whose life I saved."

"Travis Mann, the computer guy?"

"Yes. He was apparently checking into my background to see if I was the type who might extort money from him."

"How sad. Why would anyone be so suspicious?"

"Unfortunately, I guess he has reason to be. I went to visit him in the hospital. I think that was a mistake. Anyway, he decided I was honest."

"So how did you find out who the photographer was?"

"Mr. Mann called the station house last night. I guess he was checking on my background before he did anything to repay me. I was just doing my job, so, of course I wouldn't accept a personal gift anyway."

"So what's the good news? You're keeping me in suspense."

"Well, Mr. Mann has donated five thousand dollars in new toys for the Christmas toy drive."

"It's June."

Mike chuckled. "Yes, but we collect toys all year round."

"That's wonderful, Mike. Just wonderful."

"He also bought us a new Jaws of Life. Our old tool was seventy-four pounds, and it's seen better days. Our new one is on the way. It's only forty pounds."

"You are full of good news today."

"Wait, here's the part where you come in. Mr. Mann also gave me and each of the guys an expensive gift certificate for a fancy restaurant."

"Wow, he's one grateful guy."

"So I thought we'd use my gift certificate together. I thought you could tell me which fork to use—you know, add a little class to my appearance."

Grace's stomach turned over. Was this the real date she'd dreamed of? She was afraid to ask. She closed her eyes and blurted, "What about Josh?"

"Emily said she'd watch him. We could go on Saturday night."

Grace felt the hair on the back of her neck rise. "I don't think so." Then another, more painful thought drifted into her head. "So you're still seeing Emily?"

"Grace." Mike laughed. "Of course I'm not seeing Emily." He cleared his throat. "I thought I was seeing you. But I'd like to spend a little time together—just the two of us."

Grace wanted nothing more, and at the same time the thought scared her to death. What if Mike and Grace had nothing to say to one another when they were alone? What if Mike and Grace had to be Mike, Josh, and Grace to work?

"My father is coming into town tonight," she announced.

"Grace?"

"I really need to get back to work. Mr. Falk has been more than patient with me this morning."

"There are guys at the station house with families, Grace. I'm sure they'd love to have Josh over for the evening, and he would have friends to play with. I know the guys are all CPR certified and good parents to boot. Please don't say no. You're making me think it's me, not Josh, who's the issue."

Grace looked at her desktop. It was covered with briefs and legal documents. She gnawed at her lip, hesitating in her answer. "Mike, it's not Josh. I know all your friends would be wonderful to him."

"Then it's me."

How could she tell him she wanted to spend time with him like nothing else but feared that would lead them closer to the end. She searched for words, but feared incriminating herself. The Christian community would react to such a handsome, eligible bachelor dating a single mother. Mike could have any beautiful, baggage-free woman he wanted, and maybe that was what Grace feared. Did she care enough to set him free?

"I have to be careful with Lyle checking into everything."

"Lyle can't expect you to have no social life, Grace. You've been on your own for nearly seven years. I think a dinner out is warranted."

"My son's reputation depends on how I behave, Mike. I just don't think it's a good idea to be seen alone together. Not yet, anyway." She bit her lip. It was a lie, and she knew it. Guilt trickled over her.

"Fine." Mike swallowed so she could hear it. "I guess I understand. These months were about Josh."

"Mike?" She heard a soft click. It was too late.

Grace bowed her head in anguish. *I can't toy with him like a kitten's ball of yarn. If it ends after the dinner, it ends, but I can't lie to him. What's wrong with me?*

"Grace? I need you in this meeting." Mr. Falk stood at the doorway. Grace looked to the phone. Her apology would have to wait.

~

"What's the matter, buddy?" Jared patted Mike on the back. "We're going to the grocery store. You about ready?"

"What is wrong with me, Jared? Do I have *sap* written on me somewhere?" Mike traced a finger over his forehead.

"What are you talking about?"

"I asked Grace to dinner with my certificate, but she doesn't want to be seen with me. I think she's probably just waiting to see if her son's father comes back to them." Mike slammed the phone in the cradle again for emphasis. "It's just like all the women around here. They all want someone with a billfold. A firefighter can't give them that kind of lifestyle. Not even with the occasional gift certificate," he snorted.

Jared sat on a weight bench, crossing his legs at the ankles. "That sounds a bit harsh, don't you think? Grace has given up a lot to raise her son right. You told me so, yourself. That doesn't sound like the kind of woman who's after a billfold. Besides, you two have spent a lot of time together. You just getting wind of this now?"

"You know, when she became a Christian, I just assumed that she was who God had for me. That's why I had been given a heart for Josh. It all made sense to me, but anytime I try to move it forward a bit, into another realm, you might say, she puts the brakes on me." Mike dipped his head. "I've had enough of this. I'm single. I'm going to stay that way. Women just make you crazy—especially when they look like Grace Brawlins."

Jared laughed. "Yeah, they do. As a married man of ten years, I can testify they definitely make you crazy. But I wouldn't trade mine for anything in this world."

Mike sighed. And wasn't it the truth? "So what now?"

"Now, you pray. You pray and you wait. You did that with Emily, right?"

Mike's eyebrows rose. "Um, yeah. . .and look how that turned out."

"Yeah, let's do. You found out that Emily Jensen goes to church every Sunday but doesn't really live out her faith. You found out that she was sweet to a fatherless little boy in front of you, but cruel when you weren't around. Is that the kind of woman you would have wanted for life?"

"Well, no, but—"

"But nothing, Mike. Anything worth having is worth fighting for. And especially praying for. When you go into a burning building because you know someone might be in it, why do you do it?"

Mike laughed. "That's a dumb question. Because someone's life might be at stake."

"And yet you put your life on the line, not really knowing if there's another life at stake or not. You go in on faith and experience."

"What's your point?"

"Part of being ready for marriage is God preparing your heart. If you're ready to toss Grace aside so easily, maybe you're not ready for the commitment of marriage."

"Does everything have to come so difficult? I would think if it's meant to be, it would be easy."

"Maybe. Maybe not." Jared shrugged. "It came easy for Jasmine and me at first, but we had our struggles after marriage." Jared stood up, roughly. "My point is this: Everything with value comes at a cost. Maybe that cost is later, maybe it's now; but you don't go into a burning building without a cost, and you don't enter into a Christian marriage without a little warfare." Squeezing Mike's shoulder, he continued. "So are you going to go into the building or stay out on the sidewalk, where it's safe?"

Jared walked away, leaving Mike to ponder and wrestle the thoughts. Grace felt worth every ounce of the trouble, but what if Lyle wanted back into her life? He'd just seen her that day of the zoo trip for the first time in seven years. Had he remembered how beautiful her oversized eyes were? Did he remember the porcelain smoothness of her skin? And what about Grace herself? Did she still see what she saw in Lyle all those years ago?

The alarm sounded, jolting Mike into action. He suited up, running for position in the truck. His comrades joined him, and they were all in place within seconds. The fire engine roared to life. Mike put his headset on and prepared for the code. A traffic accident, single car involved. Occupant trapped. Mike's stomach lurched.

Arriving at the scene, the vehicle rested on its roof, its hood wrinkled into an accordion and a woman outside what had been the driver's door. Her foot appeared lodged under the car. The men jumped out, and Mike went straight for the Jaws of Life. It looked like their old friend would get one last usage before retirement.

Jared assessed the situation. "Her foot is trapped beneath the brake pedal." The two men exchanged a glance, and they set the jaws to lift the vehicle from the woman. She was conscious but too numb to say anything. Even to scream. Mike whispered to her while he worked, hoping to keep her as calm as she appeared.

In less than a minute, they had the vehicle lifted, and the real work began. Firefighters covered the victim with a blanket to protect her and donned safety glasses. "This is going to be very loud. Stay calm and we'll have you out in a moment, but this sound is frightening. I know you've been through a lot, but we have to do this." Kyle continued to calm the woman while Mike and Jared prepared for the cutter.

The cutters were necessary to release her still-trapped foot, but the minute the machinery started, she shook violently, becoming aware of her situation. The cutter sounded like a chain saw, metal teeth running down a chalkboard—a grating, eerie sound that would never leave Mike, even if he never heard it again. The cutters sawed through the brake shaft quickly, and Jared gently pulled the woman's foot from the car.

A round of applause went up as they freed the woman. EMTs were standing by and placed the woman on a stretcher. Mike looked at her for the first time. She was petite and blond, and he thought about all the people who probably loved her. What would they say when they found out her life was saved by a simple piece of machinery? The ambulance doors closed, and she was whisked away to the nearest trauma room.

Jared stood beside Mike, shaking his head. The tangled metal before them brought a somber moment of thanksgiving. CHP officers scribbled notes and took measurements. The freeway had slowed to a single lane, and angry drivers lost a little of their rage when they saw the vehicle, a mass of twisted steel.

"The CHP says her car flipped six times," John said.

"I can't believe she's still with us." Jared shook his head again. "What a miracle."

Mike headed for the engine, climbing into his seat. Jared took his own.

"You got the shopping list?" Mike asked.

"You're not going to talk about that?"

"About what?"

"The accident."

"What do you want me to say?" Mike shrugged. They witnessed accidents like that at least once a day. This was the city, after all. What was Jared looking for? "Do you think I'm crazy, like Kyle did? I need more time off?"

"I want you to think about the price you paid today. Was it worth it to get the jaws for her?"

"What?" Mike's head spun in a thousand directions. "Of course it was worth it. What is up with you?"

"What if today was your last day with us? What if someone decided to avoid the roadblocks and barreled down the freeway while you tried to save that woman? How would you spend today if it was your last?" Jared was always such an intense friend, and for once, Mike didn't appreciate it. He felt trapped, as though he needed a set of Jaws of Life for himself.

He searched his mind for the answer, knowing full well Grace and Josh were the only people who came to his mind. They were his first thought every morning, his first prayer request each day. "She's worth the cost. Is that what you want to hear? I fell in love with her about the time I saw her marching into the principal's office with her blond hair flipping in her righteous anger for Josh." Mike smiled, looking down at his clasped hands. "What good will it do me?"

"The woman in that car could have been Grace. Are you going to take a chance and make a fool of yourself or let her slip away without knowing if she was worth fighting for?"

"I haven't decided yet."

Jared gave an exasperated snort. "So if you throw her into the arms of another wealthy Los Altos tycoon, will you feel the least bit responsible?"

"She won't agree to a simple dinner alone with me. These last few weeks, we've been inseparable, and yet, she's afraid to be alone with me. What would I do to her?"

"Love her. Give her something she wants but she's afraid of."

"What are you, Dr. Laura, all of a sudden?"

Jared pulled off his goggles, leaving a rim of grime around the edges. "Mike, I've known you a long time, and I have never seen a woman occupy so much of your mind or your time. Go get her! I'll have no respect for you until you do."

Mike gulped. Jared made it sound so easy, but would it be?

Chapter 15

G race dressed Josh in his Sunday suit, complete with a tie. She buttoned his top button and cinched the tie. "Now go brush your teeth. Grandpa will be so proud."

"Mom, why do we have to dress up for Grandpa? Isn't he nice?"

"He's very nice, but you've never met him. I want to make sure you look your best for your first impression." Grace brushed back Josh's bangs.

"How come he's coming today?"

"Mommy made a mistake a long time ago, and I haven't talked to your grandpa in a long time. I was wrong, and God didn't like all that silence. Tonight I get to tell your grandpa I'm sorry."

"Do I have a grandma?"

Grace bristled at the question. It was so much easier when Josh just cooed and accepted everything with a gummy smile. "Yes, you have a grandma, but she's not coming today."

"Why?"

"We'll ask Grandpa, okay? Maybe she wanted to wait to meet you. To hear all about you first."

"Or maybe she's still mad at you." Josh scampered off for his toothbrush, and Grace flopped on the sofa. She broke into laughter, wondering who raised this child.

The doorbell rang, and Grace froze. She felt her heart rise and fall with all the violence of a gun battle within her. She drew in several deep breaths, but nothing calmed her. She finally ran to the door and opened it roughly.

Her father appeared shorter, with more lines in his face—not the smile lines she remembered, but sagging, etched lines that drew his whole expression downward. His eyes were still the clear gray-blue she'd inherited, and they glistened behind his tears.

"Dad!" Grace crumbled into the outstretched arms of her father and held on as tightly as she could without hurting him. She finally pulled away, her newly made-up face now a streaky mess. She could taste the salt-laden makeup on her tongue.

"Gracie, how beautiful you've grown."

"I think I've just grown old, Dad." Grace laughed. "I feel that way."

He bowed his head, shaking it. "No, no, darling. You glow like a light. You must be very happy here."

"Josh has made me very happy, Dad. I can't wait for you to meet him." Grace shook her downcast head. "I can't believe I've been so stubborn and denied you of each other."

"We were all stubborn, bullheaded, and ridiculous, but that's in our past. Where is the boy?" Her father walked in slowly, and Grace noticed how his back was slightly stooped.

"Dad, are you okay?"

"Oh, all those years of hammering nails have just taken their toll on this old back. That's all."

"Sit down, Dad. I'll get Josh." Grace could see Josh peeking around the doorway, his brown eyes wide and curious. She placed her hand on his cheek. "You ready?"

Josh nodded. Grace's father had settled into the sofa, tapping his foot nervously. Grace took Josh by the shoulders and led him around to the front of the couch. Her father's mouth dangled, and his arms were outstretched.

"Joshua Blake Brawlins." George Brawlins croaked out the name. "You look just like your uncle." He squeezed his grandson into a tight embrace, while Josh crinkled his face, clearly enduring the show of emotion. "Doesn't he look like Georgie, Grace?" he asked, referring to Grace's brother.

"I guess he does, Dad." Grace smoothed some lint off the back of the sofa. "So, Dad, Mom didn't come with you?"

"No, Gracie, your mother hasn't been well."

Grace felt her breathing increase. She took shallow, jagged breaths. "What do you mean, not well?"

"She's just tired all the time and doesn't leave the house much." George looked back at his grandson. "But your grandmother sent something for you. Let me go get it."

Grace watched her father leave for his car with Joshua closely on his trail, and she knew her mother had done no such thing. Harriet Brawlins would never find it in her heart to give Grace's illegitimate son a gift. It went against everything the woman stood for.

George reentered with an enormous plastic bag from Toys 'R Us. The receipt floated onto the floor, and Grace picked it up. The receipt was from the local toy store, and Grace knew her father had once again tried to protect her from Mother's wrath.

"Dad, what is all that? Did you buy out the toy store?"

"I haven't had a grandson for six years. I have a lot of buying to do."

Grace put her arm around her father. "No, Dad. You being here is all the gift we needed."

The doorbell rang. "Who could that be?" Thoughts of Lyle drifted into her head. Would he ruin her reunion with her father?

George and Josh were frantically opening boxes and discarding paper about the room. The two of them hadn't even heard the door. Grace answered it, and

Mike's towering frame filled the doorway.

"Mike." She sighed with relief. "It's you. I thought you had to work until morning."

"I traded, against my chief's wishes, but it was important I come."

"I have my father here tonight."

Mike looked around her and offered a wave to her father, but George was blissfully tearing open packages with Josh. "It looks like I have a run for my affections." Mike looked down upon her, his blue eyes nearly melting her with their intensity.

Grace wanted to fall into his arms, to tell him no one could ever compete for her affections, but she squared her shoulders, holding steady. "Joshua will always love you, Mike, no matter who comes into his life."

"It wasn't Josh I was speaking of."

She swallowed audibly. "Mike, please don't play with my heart. I don't think I could bear it."

He cupped her cheek into his hands. "May lightning strike me if I should ever play with your affections, Grace. Joshua may have brought us together, but look at these last months, Grace. Are they really only about Josh? Or is there more between us?"

"Who's this, Grace? Bring your friend in." George interrupted them, and Grace forced herself to breathe, to come back into the moment. Her father was there, and she could hardly maintain her joy at having the only three men she ever loved in her home at the same time. It was too good to be true, and somehow Grace feared it would crumble around her feet.

"Grandpa! This is Fireman Mike."

George stood. "Ah, so this explains why the radio-controlled fire engine was such a hit."

"Dad!" Grace looked at the pile of boxes that now towered above Josh. "What did you do in that store?"

George laughed, standing to shake Mike's hand. "This is my only grandchild. Your brother may never settle down. I have a right to spoil Josh—isn't that right, Fireman Mike?"

"Absolutely, sir." The two men shook. "Grace has been counting the days until your arrival. I'm glad you came, Mr. Brawlins."

Grace's father brushed her cheek. "Me, too. Don't know what took me so long. This is my princess. She never walked anywhere. Danced everywhere she went. What a joy she's been." George looked as though he might cry again, and he coughed away the emotion. "I'm just a silly old man now, but she's still a princess."

"I agree," Mike said, and Grace felt warm.

She fanned herself a bit. "Does anyone want iced tea?"

~

"Grandpa, Mom said Grandma was waiting to meet me." Josh looked up with his huge brown eyes, looking for the approval Grace always wanted from her mother but never seemed to get. "Do you think she'll like me?"

Grace's anger flooded, and she could feel her face heat. She wouldn't have Josh search for something he'd never find in the coldhearted mother who abandoned Grace in her time of need.

George sat back down, patting his knee. To Grace's surprise, Josh readily went. She laughed to herself. Nothing like a bag of toys to gain a child's confidence. Grace only hoped George wouldn't be the once-a-year Santa and disappear.

"Grace, I'll help you get the tea." Mike took her hand, leading her into the kitchen. Grace's feet felt molded to the floor. She was so anxious to hear her father's answer. Was George Brawlins still answering for his wife who couldn't forgive their wayward daughter?

"Grace!" Mike's insistence finally caught her attention.

She followed him to the kitchen. Searching his face, she looked for something physically wrong with him, something that might tell her it was okay if he abandoned their family. She couldn't depend on a man for happiness, and she didn't. *The Lord is my shepherd. The Lord is my shepherd,* she reminded herself.

Mike turned, and she faced those sapphire eyes again. They would be her undoing. She braced herself against the countertop, letting him fumble through her kitchen for glasses and ice.

"Your father seems thrilled to be here."

"Uh-huh," Grace answered absently.

"What about you? Are you happy to see him?" Mike broke apart the ice in the trays.

Grace smiled. "He's still the same father I grew up with—the one who spoiled me rotten and loved me, no matter what."

"Grace, you have to forgive your mother."

Grace felt ashen as the blood flowed from her face. She met Mike's eyes in a challenge. "Oh no, I really don't."

"Grace, every day I am reminded how we only get one chance at this life. We can waste it being angry and bitter, or we can move on. You need to move on. If your mother chooses to lose out on Josh in her life, that's her loss, but you can't let her control you any longer."

"She'll hide behind her religion for a lifetime. She'll be too happy to tell me of my sins and where I've gone wrong. I don't need that in my life."

"Maybe not, but you don't need this resentment, either. This harms you, not her. She's done enough damage to herself. You don't have to punish her, Grace."

"Why would you care?"

Mike set the ice tray down and came toward her. She felt her heart pound under his gaze. "Because I love you, Grace. Or haven't you noticed?"

She shook her head. "No. No, you don't. You love Josh." She pushed him away at his chest, but he wouldn't be turned away. He enveloped her in a hug.

She felt his heart hammering as he pulled her against his chest, and she could barely breathe in her emotions. He whispered at her ear. "I watch people die nearly every day, Grace. I don't say things I don't mean, and I don't feel there's time to waste in this lifetime." He knelt down on one knee, holding her hands in his. "Grace Brawlins, I love you. Say you'll marry me and make me the happiest man on earth. I'll be a good father to Josh. I'll love him as my own, and the Lord willing, we'll give him siblings."

Grace pulled her hand away, clutching her heaving chest. She tried to keep her wits, to tell herself this was really happening, but it was too unbelievable. "We haven't even been on a date."

"Grace, we've been together constantly for months. What do you mean, we haven't had a date?"

"Alone. We haven't even been alone. What if Josh goes to his friend's house, and you find I'm not the woman you thought. What if—"

"Grace." He stood up, cupping her face into his large, masculine hands. "In every emergency since I met you, my mind is constantly reminded of you and Josh. I have more reason than ever to get home safely."

"Well, we do care, Mike."

"I could waste another year dating you because that's probably more appropriate by all accounts, but I don't want to waste that time, Grace. I don't want Josh to go any longer without a father, and more importantly, I don't want to go any longer without you."

Grace felt her whole frame shivering. This was too much for her. Her father spoke in the other room; the man she loved professed his love for her. When would the dream end? When would she wake to find none of this had really happened?

"I've been on my own so long. I don't know how to trust someone. I don't know how to live with someone else."

"We'll learn together." He reached into his windbreaker, pulling out a black velvet box. He bent to one knee again, opening the box. Inside twinkled a modest, brilliant-cut diamond, surrounded by tiny Ceylon sapphires—the color of Mike's eyes. She breathed deeply, first focusing on the ring, then on the love in Mike's expression. She looked around her, noticing the ice beside them was melting on the counter, and she reached for a piece, its chill telling her this was truly unfolding.

"Mike," she said breathlessly.

"Grace, will you do me the honor of becoming my wife and allowing me to adopt Joshua as my own?"

Grace tried to process the words over the sound of her pounding heart. "I haven't even kissed you." Grace shrugged. "What if there's no passion for us?" She suddenly giggled. She felt her heart race every time he looked at her. Was she even strong enough to withstand his kiss?

And with that, he stood, pressing his lips against hers. She melted into him, feeling passion to her toes. Her hair even tingled at the roots. He kept kissing her, and she returned it with a zealous desire, unlike anything she'd ever felt. She looked at the ring and relived his romantic notion of more children. There would be no ugly check, only the unrelenting joy she had felt forbidden to feel with Joshua.

"Well?" he asked again.

"Oh, Mike, really? You're sure about this?"

"I've never been more certain of anything in my life. Of course I planned to ask you all romantically at our fancy dinner out, but I couldn't wait. Looking at you tonight, I just couldn't wait. You are beautiful, Grace, and I want to be with you as soon as possible."

Grace let her head fall back, relishing the love she felt for this man, unable to comprehend that he loved her in return. She closed her eyes, wanting to remember everything about this moment. She felt her hair tickle her back, and she flinched as Mike placed a soft kiss on her exposed neck. Looking up at him, she met his lips again before pulling away.

"Yes, I'll marry you. I'd marry you tomorrow, if I could."

"Shh." He placed his forefinger at his lips. "Don't give me any ideas. You, my dear lady, are going to have a church wedding. We are going to declare our love and commitment before the entire congregation. Joshua is going to give you away, and I am going to accept you with bells on."

Grace started to giggle, covering her mouth. "I can't believe Josh got his prayer answered."

"His prayer?"

"When we first met and you told him about Jesus, he started praying for you to be his father. I told him how ridiculous the idea was, but—"

"But Josh knew God was bigger than what the two of us had in store."

"How will you explain to your friends that you're marrying a single mother? Will they hate me?"

"I work in a firehouse, Grace. My friends have seen so much tragedy, so much pain. . .they know when you find love, you reach out and grasp it with all your strength."

"Even if it's with someone who carries her sin on her sleeve."

"You've been forgiven, Grace. It's time you forgave yourself, or you are only the reincarnation of your mother. I was reading my Bible, and I found the perfect verse for you. I memorized it."

"Am I ready to hear this?"

"This is Jesus speaking about the sinful woman, 'You did not give me a kiss, but this woman, from the time I entered, has not stopped kissing my feet. You did not put oil on my head, but she has poured perfume on my feet. Therefore, I tell you, her many sins have been forgiven—for she loved much. But he who has been forgiven little loves little.' " Mike brushed her cheek with the back of his hand. "The only difference between your sin and someone else's is that yours is obvious because of Josh. Forgive yourself, Grace, and your mother, because she loves little."

Grace felt the tears glide down her cheeks. "I love you, Michael Kingston."

Suddenly, a piercing shriek invaded their happy moment. "It's my beeper." He grasped it, reading the message. "There's a fire, and the men need backup. I have to run."

"But Mike—"

"Wait to tell Josh, please. I want to be there when he finds out he gained a father and a grandfather in the same day."

"I love you," she called after him.

He came beside her, lifting her lips to his own. "I love you, too. Enjoy the time with your father, and make the most of it."

"I will, I promise."

Mike dashed through the living room. "Good-bye, Mr. Brawlins. A pleasure to meet you, sir. I have to run. Josh, take care of your mom, bud. I'll be back soon."

Grace held the sparkling diamond in her hand, closing the box and placing it in her pocket. It didn't feel right to put it on before they had officially sealed the deal.

With the roar of the truck, he was gone, leaving Grace somewhere between euphoria and overwhelming loss.

Chapter 16

Mike scratched his head, trying to figure out what happened. First, he went to support Grace with her father. To encourage her to forgive. Somehow, he'd spoiled his proposal and given her the ring in a clumsy, unromantic fashion—in her kitchen, no less. What woman wanted to be romanced in the kitchen?

He slapped his forehead. "And you wonder why you're still single," he said to his reflection in the rearview mirror. He could hear the whirl of the sirens in the distance. He knew this fire must be at least three alarms by the sheer number of engines on the case. His heart began to race, and thoughts of Grace soon disappeared behind the cloud of smoke in front of him.

Six ladder trucks surrounded an old hotel on Main Street. Adrenaline flowed freely now, and Mike ran to an engine and suited up. Jared waited for him. "I'm glad you made it. We're on together."

"Great. Anyone in the building?"

"We don't know," he said while running alongside Mike. "Someone over at the convenience store reported a woman went in a couple hours ago, but he doesn't know if she came out."

Mike looked up, flames licked the sky from the roof, and the crash of windows could be heard blowing out. The constant roar of ladder trucks and crews surrounding the building was deafening. At least 120 firefighters were in place, raining down a solid wall of water over the structure.

The captain looked at Jared, then to Mike. "Engine 6, you two are on tonight. We got report of a woman living on the second floor. I need you in there."

Mike instinctively looked up. The sun was beginning to diminish behind the mountain, and he knew darkness would envelop them within the building. The combination of smoke and darkness could be deadly. His heart began to pound with anticipation. To get in and out, with their occupant and all of them alive, that was his mission.

"Let's go!" Jared yelled in compliance, and the two of them, connected by radio and wearing oxygen tanks and special goggles, were off.

Mike muttered a prayer to himself. He waited for a team to ax through the door, and they stood back while heat and billowing smoke stormed at them. Then, along with Jared, he burst into the building.

"She's on the second floor, central," Captain Jackson said into the radio. "Engine 19 is on the infrared camera. You've got heavy smoke straight ahead. Veer right. The seat of the fire is on level three, at your left."

The eerie sound of his own breathing echoed in his mask. Their path had filled with dark, looming smoke, and Mike began to worry for the unknown woman on the second floor. So far, they hadn't seen any flames except for those lapping through the rooftop, but the smoke was thick and dark. Without goggles, Mike and Jared would have been completely blinded. Without a mask, probably confused and disoriented, possibly unconscious. He feared for the woman and knew their quest was growing more important by the second.

~

Grace could hear the wail of several fire engines, and she grew more fearful with each passing truck. Josh and his grandfather had opted out of dinner at a restaurant and were happily barbecuing hamburgers in the yard.

Josh scrambled in. "Mom, there's a lot of smoke coming from that fire. Is Fireman Mike okay? Can we call him?"

"There are a lot of firefighters out there. Mike is probably drinking a soda on the engine." Grace scrubbed the countertop with extra effort, trying to hide the terror she felt inside. Was this how life would be, married to a man who put his life on the line? Grace didn't know if her weak heart could stand it.

"Grace, I told Josh to come on inside. The smoke is awfully thick out here. Between me scorching these burgers and the fire, I don't know which is worse."

"Thanks, Dad."

"Mom, the fire isn't going to burn our house, is it?"

"No, Josh. The engines would be a lot closer if we were in any trouble. I'm sure whatever is going on, Mike has it under control."

"No fire is tougher than Mike, Mom. He's been in burning buildings and rescued people lots of times. That's why he's such a hero." Josh leaned with his elbows against the counter, trying to appear as cool as possible. "None of those other dads at school can say that."

"That's right, Josh. Mike is certainly a hero." Grace forced back her tears. Dicing vegetables for the salad, she hummed to herself, drowning the sound of sirens and running engines from her mind.

Her father came behind her, hamburgers in hand. Placing the dish on the counter, he placed his arm around her. "Your friend will be just fine, Grace."

"How did you know?" She faced him. George Brawlins knew things about her she never had to admit. Life with him had always been that way. "How did we let things come between us, Dad?"

He shook his head. "We had such high hopes for you, Gracie. We planned you'd be a high-powered lawyer or executive of some type. We never understood that God had something better for you."

Grace sniffed. "I can see where my being a single mother wouldn't be your idea of success." She watched Josh scamper to the radio-controlled fire engine, and the noise soon took away the opportunity for him to overhear. "It's hard, Dad.

I'm so exhausted when I come home from work, yet there's dinner to be made or groceries to be bought, homework, dishes, baths, then after a few hours' sleep, I get up and start all over again." She noticed her father's pained expression. "Oh, Dad, I'm not complaining. I'm just saying I know from the outside it must seem like a stupid thing to try and raise him alone. But his father didn't want him born, and I just felt like the only one who could truly protect him."

"It was your choice, Gracie. Your mother and I had no right to interfere. We should have helped you, not abandoned you. We were wrong." He bowed his head. "So wrong."

"I'm going to marry Mike, Dad."

"Your mother will come around. Maybe she'll come to the wedding."

"I'm going to call and invite her, Dad. I will eventually forgive her, and I hope she'll do the same." Another siren blasted past the house, and Grace slammed the knife to the counter. "Another one!"

"Mom, come here! The fire's on TV!" Josh sat on top of his new engine, watching the news. Huge flames burst from the top of a quaint, downtown hotel built at the turn of the century.

Grace searched the firefighters in the background, looking for Mike's jacket, praying to see "Kingston" scrawled across a yellow back. The newscaster came on, dressed in a jacket and tie.

"We're here at Main Street in downtown Los Altos. As you can see, there's a raging fire within this building that was currently empty while renovations took place." The camera angle zoomed in for a shot of the hot orange flames. "It is our understanding that firefighters are inside searching for a lone woman who is believed to be on the second floor."

"Oh, please, don't let it be Mike." Grace bit her lip nervously.

The newscaster shoved a microphone in a firefighter's face while he talked into a radio. Brusquely, the camera equipment was shoved away. "I'm working here. You mind?"

"I've got to get down there. Dad, can you watch Josh?"

"Gracie, it's illegal to go to a fire. There's nothing you can do."

"I can pray, Dad. I'll stay far away, I promise. I just want to see that he's out of the building." Grace grabbed her keys and shot through the door. She waited for her car to turn over, urging it several times, and raced to the scene. Police officers stood at the corner, turning people away. Grace ripped the engagement ring from her pocket, placing it on her left finger. She admired it for only a second, before parking the car haphazardly.

"Turn around, miss." The police officer halted her with his palm. "No spectators."

"My fiancé is a firefighter. I just want to stand here and pray. I won't pass. I promise."

He scanned her warily. Then her sparkling ring captured his attention. "It's unusual, but as long as you stay right here, I got nothing against it."

Some of the flames had ceased since she'd watched the television, and she thanked God for that. Still, she didn't know where Mike was. Why did she assume he was in the building? There were hundreds of firefighters on the scene. Surely, it wasn't him. Yet she prayed with all her might. Sinking to the roadside grass, she knelt, beseeching the Lord to deliver Mike back to her. She'd barely had a chance to tell Mike she loved him. Sure, she'd agreed to marry him, but did he know it was for him alone? Not for Josh to have a daddy?

Minutes seemed like hours, and it was then that she noticed the camera crew. Rushing across the street, but not past the protective line, she called out to the reporters.

"Hey there!" She raised a hand. "Are the firefighters out of the building?"

The reporter shook his head. "Not that we know of, but the chief hasn't got time for us, and they have no one on for media, so I couldn't tell you for sure. You know somebody in there?"

A helicopter hovered over them, and Grace had to scream her answer. "One of the firefighters just asked me to marry him tonight, then he got called away to respond to this fire."

The cameraman looked to the reporter, and Grace felt the pair drop something around her neck. Looking down, she saw it was a press badge. "Wait a minute, I can't go in there. I promised the officer."

"The fire's nearly under control, miss, and this makes a much better story."

Grace watched a woman carried from the building into an ambulance. The firefighter removed his mask, and Grace nearly fainted with joy. "Mike!" She ran toward him, and he wrapped her into a hug.

"Grace, what are you doing here?" He looked up at the building, and seeing the flames were under control, he removed his gloves, too. "The chief will have my head. I'm already in hot water." He embraced her. "Oh, who cares?" He kissed her quickly.

"I'm leaving. I don't want you in any trouble. I just wanted you to know that I love you, Mike! I've loved you for the longest time, and you're right. I don't want to wait anymore. Every day that passes is too long. We'll tell Josh today!"

He twirled her off her feet, covering her face in kisses. Then he stopped and lifted his helmet. "I'm getting married!"

A group of firemen hollered, and before Grace knew it, an important-looking man approached them. She stood tall, blinking rapidly, both from the smoke and her fear.

"Grace, this is Fire Chief Radson." Mike stood at attention. "Chief, this beautiful woman has just agreed to be my wife."

"Well, I'll be." The fire chief crossed his arms, clearly intent on letting them enjoy the moment.

A microphone jammed in her face, and she realized with embarrassment that their whole love scene had been caught on tape. *Film at eleven,* she thought.

"Is it true you just came from that burning building and this woman accepted your proposal?"

"Actually—" Mike began to clarify when the reporter cut him off. Clearly, their version was a better story.

"And is it true, miss, that you broke through a police barricade to profess your love to this hero?"

Grace giggled relentlessly, unable to control her emotions. "Yes, it is true. And I'd do it again for the love of this man. He's worth every river I might forge."

Mike kissed her again. "Hey, is that thing on?" he asked the cameraman, who nodded. "Joshua, you tell God a great big thank-you tonight. I'm going to get to be your daddy." Mike thrust a fist toward the sky. "Our prayers were answered, little guy!"

Grace kissed him again, snuggling against his smoky scent. "You are my hero."

"And you're mine, Grace."

They embraced and shared a passionate kiss. Grace flickered her ring finger for the camera.

The Landlord
Takes a Bride

To my mother, Kay Compani, who is
a. alive
b. kindhearted, and
c. fiercely loyal
(unlike many of the mothers in my books).
And to my aunt, Mary Bechtel, who is like a second mother.
A second good mother. Much love, Kristin

Chapter 1

Stefani Willems looked to the apricot orchards behind the new house. Only three trees remained now, but the ghosts of their lost companions danced in her memory. She shook her head to dislodge the thoughts. This was a day for rejoicing, not sadness. A new house in San Francisco's peninsula was nearly unheard of, but she'd struggled for the right and triumphed. "I did it," she said aloud to herself. "It's mine. They'll be so proud."

She breathed a huge, cleansing sigh. And dreamt of her new kitchen. She loved to cook gourmet meals for relaxation. *Where is that real estate agent? He's fifteen minutes late.*

George Daily, her real estate agent, pulled up with a screech in his European convertible. His comb-over hairstyle was in disarray from the wind, and he raked his stubby fingers through it as he approached her. His nervous smile alarmed her, and she felt her heart beat faster. *Oh, please, Lord, no. Don't let anything go wrong with this deal. You know what this house means to me.*

"Stefani," George said grimly, and she felt her head shake involuntarily.

Before he finished his sentence, an expensive-looking sport utility vehicle whirled into the driveway and stopped uncomfortably close to them. George and Stefani stood mesmerized by the tall, mysterious man in a cowboy hat who emerged. A cowboy hat in California. The shadow from his hat cast across his face, yet still the sea green of his eyes shone and met hers.

Throw this guy in with the deal, and I'll be set for life! He left her speechless. Everything about him exuded confidence. His dangerous stare pulled her in. She *knew* him. She'd never seen him before, but, inexplicably, she *knew* him. He aggressively reached over, grasped her hand, and shook it. Stefani felt a bolt of electricity rush up her arm.

She released his hand as though it were a hot iron.

"You must be Kate," he said in a deep, rich baritone. "This here's perfect. Just like we talked about."

She shook her head to correct him, but nothing happened. She still hadn't found her voice. She was still lost in the magnificent green of his eyes.

After a long, awkward silence, George finally intervened. "Mr. Savitch?" The rugged man nodded affirmatively. "This is Stefani Willems." George then turned to her and quietly added, "Mr. Savitch also put in a bid on the house. His was accepted."

Stefani felt her breath leave her. She looked to George for further explanation, but he conveniently avoided her gaze. Her perfect house: the right neighborhood, the separate rental unit for help with the mortgage, and, most of all, that heavenly, gourmet kitchen. Gone. *Gone! Swiped away by that gorgeous hunk of a man who will probably never use the kitchen. Not unless one of his harem can cook,* she thought viciously.

The stranger spoke, interrupting Stefani's dark thoughts. "I'm sorry, Miss Willems. I haven't seen the place, but if you like it, there be something to it." He tipped his hat as if that made up for his stealing her house. A lopsided grin emerged, and Stefani felt herself perused. His sea green eyes lingered on her legs for just a moment too long, and her anger built. If steam could have erupted from her ears, it would have. *Male chauvinist! To think I thought him handsome!* She chastised herself for being so shallow. Looks were fleeting. Didn't her grandmother always tell her that?

It was then she found her tongue. "You bought a house you've never seen?" she asked incredulously. His apologetic tone was wasted, his sympathy squandered. She could tell from his striking appearance that he was used to getting what he wanted. And right now, he obviously wanted to make her feel better about losing her dream house. *Impossible. An impossible feat.*

The cowboy continued. "I came from Colorado. I had to buy on faith so I'd have a place when I got here." He smiled that infuriating grin again, and Stefani's jaw clenched. Didn't this guy know that he'd just stolen the one material possession she'd ever cared about? He kept on talking his charming sweet talk, oblivious to her rising temper. "My agent said housing is quite difficult to find around here, especially a new development, what with land being so scarce." He had no idea just how scarce *this* land was. "Kate assured me this was the best neighborhood. I'd say I was right lucky to get this investment." He clicked his tongue, blatantly pleased with himself. His words only infuriated Stefani further.

"It's more than an investment, Mr. Savitch," she blustered. "This home is equipped with a gourmet stove in each unit, wood shutters, and a whirlpool bathtub in each master bathroom. It's a home designed for someone who can appreciate its superior qualities, not as an *investment*." Stefani felt like her child had just been offended.

"Well, I reckon it's all that, too, Miss Willems." He crossed his brawny arms and looked at the house casually, with a shrug. "So you have a key?" he asked George. "Let's see the place."

George fumbled with the real estate lock, and Stefani followed unwittingly, holding back her tears as she stepped onto the hand-laid Mexican tile floor she had selected. During the planning stages, she had befriended the builder and expressly asked for the special flesh-toned tile for the entryway. The sight of it now made her wince.

She watched the new buyer as he walked through the house. He judged all the options *she'd* selected. He opened every cabinet and checked each tiny flaw in the paint. It gave her hope. "What's the matter? Not what you'd thought it would be? You can always withdraw your offer; you're not in escrow yet." She smiled a counterfeit smile, and he looked at her with his brows furrowed. "This house doesn't seem to suit your tastes, anyway. Perhaps your agent might find you something more suitable."

"What's so special about this house, Miss Willems?"

"So you remember my name," she said coolly. "It's not something I can easily explain, but this property means a great deal to me."

"Is that so?" he replied evenly.

"Stefani, I think it's time we left Mr. Savitch alone in his new house." George grabbed her gently by the elbow, but she pulled away.

"I'm sure Mr. Savitch doesn't mind our being here, do you, Mr. Savitch?" She squared her shoulders and stared straight into those deep green eyes. No easy task. He had to be completely aware of his effect on women, and Stefani was determined she'd wouldn't fall victim to his charms. Superficial as they were. As her breathing quickened, she realized how difficult that might be. There was something so unnerving about people in real life that looked this good. They belonged on the movie screen or in the pages of a magazine, not here in real life.

Mr. Savitch gently lifted her arm onto his own, and Stefani shuddered that his touch affected her. "I don't mind at all, Miss Willems. Why don't you give me the grand tour?"

He looked down upon her from his perch. She guessed him to be over six feet tall, but with that ridiculous cowboy hat. . . At five-six, Stefani was fairly tall, but this man made her feel small in every sense of the word. She broke free and purposely walked him into the living room. She was reminded where each piece of her furniture would have gone. She wondered if he even *had* any furniture.

He wasn't married, she could tell. Not just because he was void of a ring, but because he didn't dress as if any woman had a part in selecting his wardrobe. Too masculine. Add to that the fact that he'd hired a female real estate agent, and he *had* to be single.

She inhaled deeply. "Crown molding throughout. You don't see that kind of workmanship in California too often." She pointed to the ceiling line, while he watched her curiously. "The builder is into details."

"Uh-huh, nice," he said absently, though she noticed his eyes never left her, and his arms remained crossed as he studied her.

She turned on her heel and leered at him, furious that he could be so indifferent about something that was so important to her. "Mr. Savitch, it's obvious you don't care about this house!" she accused. "Why don't you find something else? Something that suits your *bachelor* needs better. You know, maybe something where your stuffed animal heads might be more at home."

"Stefani!" George gasped. But Mr. Savitch only broke into a loud laugh, throwing his head back in sincere mirth.

"Miss Willems, I appreciate your concern about my *bachelor* needs, but I'm not much of a shopper. Besides, I like it. I think my animal heads will be right at home. You have excellent taste, Miss Willems."

"Stop calling me Miss Willems. My name is Stefani! I'm not your kindergarten teacher," she chastised, and his irrepressible, annoying grin appeared again.

"I don't want another house, Miss Willems. This one suits me just fine. I'm thinking the buffalo head will go right there." He held up his thumbs together and focused on a spot over the mantel. Stefani could only hope he was joking.

"I've lived in this area my entire life; I'll help you find another place." Her voice bordered on pleading, possibly pathetic. She had no room for pride. She wanted this house. At this point, she wasn't above groveling.

"I already have a real estate agent, and more importantly, I already have a house. Or at least I will in a few minutes." He checked his watch. "So I appreciate your offer, Miss Willems, but my answer is no," Mr. Savitch answered. "But I have to say I admire your persistence. You're a right pushy little thing." He smiled that infuriating grin again.

Stefani took in a quick breath to speak but could think of nothing to say. "Stefani, let's go. Your deposit is being refunded. I have a check at the office. We have no reason to bother Mr. Savitch further." George took her by the arm once again, but Stefani remained steadfast, looking to the stranger hopefully.

Stefani mustered up humility from deep within and took out a business card, handing it to the tall, handsome enemy. "If you change your mind, this is where I can be reached. My home phone is on the back, but I'm usually at work. I hope to hear from you." She smiled her sweetest smile and walked out the front door, clicking her heels on the beloved Mexican tile. George followed closely behind.

Stefani turned and stopped him in his tracks. "George, how could you? How could you let this house get away from me? You know what this land means to me!"

"Stefani, I have been trying to reach you since last night—and all morning. Your voice mail at work is full, you weren't home, you didn't answer any of my pages, and your secretary said you were out of the office until tomorrow. What was I supposed to do? I don't have the authority to make a more substantial offer without your approval or signature. You knew this deal was taking place today; if it was so important to you, why didn't you let someone know where you were?"

Stefani solemnly answered, "We had a power failure at the Sacramento site. All the computers were down, and I had to fly there last night. I just got back this morning." Stefani let out a muffled cry. *Of all the days to have a disaster at work, why did it have to be now?*

"Well, Stefani, Mr. Savitch's offer came in this morning, and I didn't have any authority to counter after his bid came across the wire. You know how Bay Area real estate is: You snooze, you lose."

"So that's it, I'm not the owner?" She tried to process the notion.

"I'm afraid not. Our offer was null and void because it expired before Mr. Savitch's came in." George shrugged. "Why don't we get an early dinner; we'll find something else soon." They both knew the statement was a lie. There was nothing else but this property. Nothing else that would prove to her parents she was successful. Nothing else that would keep her promise to her deceased grandmother. Her goal had slipped from her grasp into the hands of a handsome bachelor who didn't seem to care where he lived. The irony of it threatened to stifle her.

"Thanks for the dinner offer, but I couldn't eat a thing. I just want to get back to work and make this whole day just disappear." She definitely needed to pray about her situation. Her attitude toward Mr. Savitch was anything but Christian, and the truth was, Stefani was really angry with God.

George simply nodded in understanding. Obviously, he didn't want to pressure her for fear of losing a future sale. Stefani sulked to her car and hunkered down in the driver's seat, then sat looking at the house wistfully. *Why, God? I've finally given up the dream of marriage, a family, so why did You deny me this house? It's such a small thing in the scheme of this lifetime; I just don't understand. If I'm going to be an old maid, can't I at least be one in style?* She dropped her head to the steering wheel, but looked up at the unexpected sound of voices.

The bachelor's real estate agent had arrived. The pair walked the perimeter of the home. They talked of landscaping ideas and final finishing work. All details *she* should have been discussing with her agent.

Stefani wondered what Mr. Savitch did for a living. When he removed his hat, his hair was meticulously combed and his face clean-shaven, but he wore a tired chambray shirt around his broad chest with worn-out jeans on his long legs, with the beginnings of a hole in the knee apparent. The topper was the scuffed leather boots he wore. Stefani couldn't remember the last time that she'd seen a man wear boots in northern California. Or casual jeans, for that matter—and never without a braided belt and matching loafers. It simply wasn't done in the engineering world of Silicon Valley.

"He looks ridiculous," she mumbled, lying aloud to herself. He looked striking, just like a spiffed-up, rugged, rodeo hero. A real rodeo hero, not the phony urban cowboy type. And she knew it; she just couldn't stand to admit it. It was bad enough he'd taken her house. Couldn't he at least have been ugly? Petty and small as it sounded, it would have made her feel better. She gave one last look at the house, then at the tall, gorgeous enemy. She sighed aloud.

It wouldn't take him long to find a renter. Once prospective tenants got a look at him, they'd probably be throwing money his way. He noticed her staring and threw her a friendly wave. She grimaced and started her car. She meandered back to the office. Defeated.

When she returned to her cubicle, her coworkers had prepared a party with balloons and a cake that read, "Congratulations on your new home, Stefani!" She was utterly humiliated as she explained her loss and how it came about.

Her secretary and lifetime friend, Amy, smiled, obviously recognizing all was not right. Amy sweetly took Stefani aside and put an arm around her. "And we know that all things work together for good to them that love God."

Stefani forced a smile. There was nothing worse than having scripture quoted casually when you felt at your lowest. Stefani knew Amy didn't mean harm by it, but it annoyed her just the same. She didn't want to hear how she *should* feel, when she was so down. God *knew* what the land had meant to her.

He must have made a mistake. It was just salt in the wound to be reminded that she should feel grateful. She didn't feel grateful; she felt angry and ignored by God. *Why would He let that man—that savage in the cowboy boots—buy her house?* It was a complete mystery to her, one that would probably never be answered in this lifetime. She couldn't fathom ever looking back on this day and being glad for its outcome.

Chapter 2

John Savitch looked at the business card he held. *Stefani Willems, MIS Manager.* He had no idea what an MIS manager earned, but Stefani worked for a well-known company, and she obviously had the money to buy the duplex, so she must have reached a modicum of success. He scanned the card again, debating. It had been three days. Three days, and he couldn't erase her penetrating blue eyes from his memory. That pert nose or that exasperating, fake, doe-eyed smile when she thought she might change his mind.

Stefani's dark hair had been shaped into a short, serious cut. He imagined if she let it grow, she wouldn't appear so stern. But maybe MIS managers needed to be stern, for all he knew. Even with her serious haircut, she was darling. The type of woman who would forever be described as cute, no matter how old she got. She looked about twenty-four, but he guessed she had to be older than that to afford the duplex. He admired her spunk. For some odd reason, Stefani Willems wanted his house and badly. He couldn't help but want to know why.

She didn't think much of him. John knew better than to chase after some successful businesswoman with her mind set on material things. He was a simple farm boy at heart. Always would be, no matter how prosperous he became. Everything about Stefani's appearance screamed that work was her whole life: the conservative navy suit, the muted makeup, the haircut—and especially the dejection when she didn't get the duplex.

Just when he'd start to forget their meeting, he'd picture the sweet dimples, well worn into her naturally rosy cheeks. They belied her severe front and gave her true nature away. One thing was certain; he wanted to see more of *that* Stefani Willems. Even though he knew better.

I'm making a sound business decision, he reminded himself. *She's the only person I know here, and she can afford this.* Knowing full well that it was just a good excuse to call Stefani Willems, he inflated his chest with a deep breath and dialed the phone number on the card. To his surprise, she answered immediately, "This is Stefani."

"Miss Willems? It's John Savitch, the buyer for—"

"I know who you are, Mr. Savitch. What can I do for you? Have you decided against the duplex?" Hope resounded in her question.

"No, actually I have a proposition for you. Are you free for dinner tonight?"

121

She gave a long, annoyed sigh. "Mr. Savitch, your charms, while they may be irresistible to most women, are lost on me. If you need to start your harem here in California, perhaps you might start at the local singles' bar," she said sarcastically, but surprisingly she didn't hang up.

John stared at his receiver, unable to believe such a sweet little face with the innocent dimples could contain such a biting personality. He had thought her original reaction to him was just due to the shock of losing the house, but now he wondered. Had he been wrong about her? Maybe that spark he'd noticed between them was only in his overactive imagination.

He let out a short laugh. "Miss Willems, I have a legitimate business deal I'd like to discuss with you. While I'm sure you have men beating down your door for dates, that's not my sole intention. Are you available for dinner tonight? Trust me, you'll be safe," he added, possibly with more irritation than necessary. Everything that came out of her mouth was in sharp contrast to what he felt when he was with her—that feeling that they knew each other, understood one another.

"I can't leave the office until seven; I need to ensure that everything is online after a small issue we had here. Is a late dinner all right?" She sounded like she was doing *him* a favor.

John couldn't help his smile. "How's eight? I'll meet you at the restaurant of your choice." Her elegant navy suit wafted through his memory. No doubt she'd pick someplace that registered as a dining establishment.

"Eight o'clock. Stern's in Sunnyvale." Her voice had softened just the slightest bit. John hoped that tonight he'd get her to drop her cold front altogether.

"I'll be there," he promised and hung up the phone.

He dressed in a navy European suit with his yellow power tie. He checked his image in the hotel mirror before leaving. Satisfied, he stepped out of the elevator. The concierge stared strangely when John asked for directions to the restaurant. But the hotelier was used to seeing John in boots, so he was probably stunned by the dining choice. He hoped the meal would cost less than his suit.

After Miss Willems's reluctant acceptance, John arrived at the restaurant early so she'd have no excuses to miss their meeting. Doing Miss Stefani Willems a favor wouldn't be easy. Still, she had the ability to solve his problem, and he had the ability to solve hers, so their meeting made sense.

From the parking lot, the restaurant didn't look too fancy. It was an old, almost dilapidated redwood-sided building. The sign above the doorway had fallen off one side, so it hung ominously. He figured the restaurant must have been a hangout for locals like Stefani. It probably had wonderful food, but lacked the elitist environment.

Although he was in the heart of the city, the parking lot was filled with pickups. It was a welcome sight, but something told him it wasn't a good sign. For a moment, John was reminded of an old *Twilight Zone* episode. He opened the spring-action door, and it screeched painfully. Once inside, he burst into a hearty laugh. Loud bluegrass music emanated from every corner. The plank floor was covered wall-to-wall with sawdust, and neon signs illuminated the place. Over the music, a few patrons screamed their support for a would-be cowboy on the gyrating mechanical bull.

Couples whirled upon the dance floor. Full jean skirts and ruffled cotton tops flittered under the neon lights. Western attire ruled. John felt the judgmental stares and realized he looked ridiculous in his business suit and dress shoes. Stefani Willems certainly had a way of getting her point across.

Stefani entered the establishment and bit her lip, apparently to hold back her laughter. Scanning John, she obviously enjoyed her little joke. Her blue eyes sparkled with merriment. Despite her desperate attempts, her charming dimples kept appearing, and she finally let out her giggle at his expense. "I'm sorry." She covered her mouth with her slender, graceful hands to stifle her laughter. "I'm sorry."

"Go ahead, get it all out," he said stiffly.

"I just wanted you to feel comfortable," she explained, batting her eyelashes in mock innocence.

He wagged his finger at her. "Uh-huh, I'm sure my comfort level was the first thing on your mind. One day, the right man will ask you to wear jeans and a pair of boots and you're going to love it! Until then, we're out of here." He took her by the hand and led her to his car. Stefani's figure was made for jeans, he thought, as he eyed her small frame in a summer-white business suit. Her skirt was a couple of inches above her knees. Heaven help him, she had beautiful legs.

"Where are we going?" she demanded. She wriggled her hand free.

"We're going somewhere my suit will be appreciated. It isn't every day I dress up for a woman. And it isn't going to waste."

"I'm not riding in that!" she protested, as though the truck was beneath her. John had a feeling she'd never admit to liking anything about him. Something about that fact challenged him. Delighted him.

"You should have thought of that before you thought up this little scheme of yours, Miss Willems. If you wanted me to know you think I'm a hick, consider your message delivered. Now, do you want to hear my offer or not? Not that you deserve it."

"Yes, I want to hear it." She rolled her eyes.

"Then get in." He opened the door for her, and she climbed up, carefully ensuring she kept her legs as covered as possible. John shut the door behind her and got into the leather driver's seat. Country music blasted from the stereo when he started the car. From the corner of his eye, he saw she was rolling those big blue eyes again.

He turned off the stereo and hummed the theme song "Green Acres" just to annoy her.

"Where are we going?" she asked curtly, interrupting his song.

"I don't know. Where can you get a good side of ribs around here, the kind with lots of sauce?" He studied her white suit, and she smiled, despite herself. "Glad to see you can still smile, Miss Willems. Do you always get up on the wrong side of the bed?"

"I don't like it when things don't go the way I planned," she explained.

"I can see that."

"You want me to apologize, don't you?" Her blue eyes thinned.

He shrugged. "Nope. Not unless you want to. Far be it from me to make a spoiled child behave properly when she isn't mine."

"Spoiled child? I'll have you know I haven't been spoiled a day in my life."

"Maybe that's because you don't allow people to spoil you," he responded evenly.

She crossed her arms. "I don't want to be spoiled."

"Everyone wants to be spoiled once in a while."

She looked up at him, and he thought he saw a tear, but she blinked it away quickly and turned toward the window. Silence hung between them until they arrived at a small French restaurant. John had interviewed for his California job there. It was slightly too romantic for either occasion, but he didn't know of anything else, so that left few options.

He drove into the parking lot of the quaint little bistro. He looked around at all the foreign luxury cars and figured his suit was safe here. He watched the surprise in her eyes when she noted the restaurant. She obviously was familiar with it.

"This place is expensive," she said flatly. She might have been concerned for him, but her tone told him she didn't want to be embarrassed if his credit card was rejected.

"Us country bumpkins can afford to splurge once in a while." The corners of his mouth curved. "We can even spoil our friends when the occasion allows." He helped her from the car, and they walked the short distance to the entrance.

"That duplex isn't cheap; you'd have a lot more financial freedom if you decided not to buy. I could purchase half the duplex; you could buy dinner. What do you think?"

"You are relentless." He turned his attention to the maitre d' as they entered the quiet, candlelit restaurant. "Two for dinner, please."

"Yes, sir." The Frenchman led them to a cozy table in the corner.

John was pleased with the romantic ambiance. *It's been too long since I've had a date.* Too bad Stefani had no reason to call it a date. She perused him, studied his suit, then looked at his face once again.

She appeared accustomed to such restaurants, and why not? Clearly she was an elegant woman, well dressed and educated. Still, something about her told him she had worked hard for that image. While John could hold his own in the manners department, he would have preferred the slab of ribs he'd referred to earlier.

She covered her lap with the linen napkin and spoke. "So, this proposition you have for me?" she asked pointedly, her blue eyes blazing.

"Can we order first? I prefer discussing business on a full stomach. I'm not such bad company, you know?"

"I'm sure you're not, but I'm without a place to live soon, so I'm afraid that's my priority. To be more direct, your house is my priority."

John was rankled; he held up his hands, signaling defeat. "It's a building—four walls. How could you possibly be so attached to an object? Did you ever stop to think I might be an exceptionally nice guy and you're missing out on a great evening?" He tossed the linen napkin on the table in disgust.

"You seem pretty attached to the duplex yourself, Mr. Savitch. Enough to out-bid me and buy it out from under my nose." She sat back in her chair, crossing her arms. Other patrons were starting to stare. They looked like an old, antagonistic couple rather than two people on a first date. But of course it wasn't a date. Stefani had made that perfectly clear.

"I made an offer fair and square. It's not my fault you don't keep in touch with your real estate agent." *What am I doing? I'm starting to sound just like her!* He sucked in a deep breath and said a quick prayer for his even temper to return. "Look, Miss Willems, I didn't come here to argue with you. Let's enjoy a nice dinner together. Surely, you can put up with me for one meal. I won't bother ordering a soufflé for dessert." He let the corner of his mouth turn, and he noticed her dimples had appeared in full for the first time since their acquaintance.

Her dimples were gorgeous, the perfect accompaniment to her sweet, rosy cheeks and sparkling, wide eyes. Why on earth she chose to keep them under wraps for so long was beyond him. No matter what she thought of him, he felt her attraction. It was unstated, but undeniable. A force of chemistry unexplainable and bonding.

She looked up from her down-turned chin, and her long, black lashes batted coquettishly. Not consciously, though. Clearly she thought she appeared threatening, but her innocent features made her harsh nature almost comical.

"You're right, I'm sorry," she answered weakly. "We'll have a nice dinner." He noticed her eyes remained on his, and she scrutinized him—not in her standard, calculated way, but in a soft, thoughtful way. *What does she think of me? And why on earth does she care so much about a house?*

The waiter brought water and menus. Stefani grabbed the folder quickly; she clearly relished something to hide behind. She opened her menu wide and her features disappeared. When she didn't emerge for some time, he cleared his throat. "Do you speak French, Miss Willems?"

She dropped the menu to the table in defeat, letting out a long, deep sigh. "No."

"Would you like some suggestions?" he asked gently.

"I'm sure the waiter can help me." Stefani squared her shoulders, but then grimaced nervously, her self-confidence clearly waning. "I like chicken," she said meekly. "Do they have chicken on this menu?"

He put his hand to hers and noticed she jumped. "I know the perfect dish."

The waiter returned, putting on his best airs to make patrons feel intimidated. John wished he knew of another restaurant, but since he didn't, he used his best French to order their meals. The waiter glared at John as though the American accent was more than the server could bear. John folded the menus and handed them back, concentrating on Stefani.

"Thank you," she said, her voice barely above a whisper.

"The restaurant may be expensive, but the attitude is included at no extra charge." He laughed out loud and she joined him. The waiter gave them a cold stare, which only made them laugh again.

"I'm sorry I took you to the sawdust palace. I didn't mean to be uncivilized. I was just angry. Childish. . . Anyway, I'm sorry. I'm mad at my situation, and I took it out on you."

"The fact is that place is right up my alley. Ain't nothing wrong with a good night of cowboy music, and don't you roll those pretty blue eyes at me, princess. You give it a shot before you knock it." He cleared his throat. "So what is an MIS manager?" John asked innocently.

"An MIS manager is someone who reports to the vice president with data on all information systems infrastructure and its components."

"That's kind of vague. You want to help me out here?"

"I coordinate the equipment needs for all the departments. I help them decide which computer systems will work best and eliminate the ones that don't work well."

"Ahh."

"And what is it you do, Mr. Savitch? You own a suit; I suppose that's a good sign." She leaned in, setting her elbow on the table.

"Do you always say whatever you're thinking?" He met her blue eyes with his own and challenged her. She looked away quickly. He loved that she said what she thought. It was refreshing. Stefani Willems had more in common with him than she thought. Neither of them pulled any punches.

"As a matter of fact, I do say what I'm thinking," she said with an apologetic tone. "No sense in playing games. It's dishonest and annoying as far as I'm concerned." She shrugged. "It's just the way I am. I don't want to offend you, but that house is very special to me and—and I want to live there."

He saw her eyes glisten with moisture. The sight of true sentiment brought out his most tender feelings. Glory, she was beautiful—and too busy with her agenda to ever notice. If she had noticed, she wouldn't have chopped away all her hair. He wanted to tell her, whisper in her delicate ear that there was more to life than houses. More to life than business, but he swallowed hard and sat up straight.

"Stefani," he whispered. Her eyes snapped to his once again with the intimacy of her first name. *She had noticed.* "Stefani, I want you to rent the other half of the duplex. I know it's not the same as owning it, but if that's what you truly want, to *live* there, I'm giving you the opportunity. And if I decide to sell, you'll get the first option to buy."

Her head nodded up and down in slow motion. "Yes." It came out as a mere breath, and John wished he might kiss her soft, full lips at the delicious word. Something was definitely happening between them. He could tell she didn't want to acknowledge it, but it was there just the same.

Chapter 3

Boxes were strewn about the new house. Stacked, full, and everywhere. A constant reminder of all she had to do. *I thought I worked all the time, but apparently I had a little time for shopping.* Friends from church had moved her things to the new house in various pickups and vans. After a quick lunch of pizza and soda, everyone had slowly gone home, and Stefani was left alone to unpack.

The flower-box kitchen window held a perfect view of John's half of the house. She slowly made her way to the window. The professional movers had finished at John's house, too, and his open garage was filled to capacity. Stefani sighed at the seemingly endless amount of work and began taking out her dishes, one by one, rinsing them in the sink.

John emerged from his garage with a newspaper, a chaise lounge, and a tall glass filled with iced tea. He wore sunglasses, a T-shirt that framed his muscular chest, and a pair of athletic shorts. His long, powerful legs caught Stefani's attention, and she felt herself gulp when he turned and caught her gawking at him. He waved casually and motioned for her to come outside. He pulled out his chaise in their shared driveway and made himself comfortable. "He's just going to sit there," she stated to herself.

For the life of her, she didn't know why, but she wiped her hands on a towel and went outside. Perhaps it was her own guilt for treating him so badly. She stood over him, sheltering her eyes from the sun. "Don't you have to unpack? You're just going to sit here?" she asked incredulously.

"Why not? This is my favorite time of day. Right before the sun goes down and the cool, evening breeze from the bay comes inland. It's too good to miss. We don't have this moist air back home." He took a deep, audible breath. "Smell that air. It's something to be experienced. Join me; I'll get another tea and a lounger." He started to get up, and she pushed his shoulder back down.

"Don't bother. I can't lounge; I've got an entire house to put away! And so do you."

He shrugged. "This sunset will only happen once. God will never make one exactly like it again." He lifted his tea glass toward the reddish-orange sun on the horizon behind the mountains.

She wondered if he was a believer or just making light of God's creation. His lackadaisical attitude appalled her, but Lord help her, she desired to relax like that. To sit and sip tea with him until the sun came up again. If only she knew how to relax. John Savitch captivated her, even though she knew his type was off-limits. His laziness would only serve in her favor. She'd get the house back quicker. "I—I can't, thanks. My friends all went home, and I've got a million things to do."

"It'll all be there tomorrow," he encouraged. "Sit with me."

"I've got church tomorrow."

"Ah, so you're a churchgoing woman." He took a long drink from his glass. Mortified by her earlier behavior, especially taking him to the sawdust-ridden country café, she was now embarrassed to admit her faith—and she should be. She hadn't acted like a churchgoing woman.

"I am a Christian, although there are times I don't act like it. What about you?" she asked tentatively, swallowing hard. If he wasn't a Christian, she'd done nothing to further her faith with him.

"Born again in 1978," he stated with conviction.

"Seventy-eight? How old are you? I'm sorry, that was rude. I'm not always obnoxious." *Just whenever I open my mouth.*

"The word *obnoxious* never crossed my mind. I like a woman who says what she thinks. For the record, I'm thirty-five. Does that make me too old? Too young? What?" he asked. She had a feeling his question was a leading one.

"Are you asking how old I am?"

"Heavens, no. A gentleman would never ask that."

"Good, but I'm thirty-two." She felt herself smile. Upon learning he was a Christian, Stefani suddenly felt worse for the treatment. It didn't show her Christianity in the most positive light.

John stood and motioned for her to sit in his chaise lounge. She pointed back at her house. All the things she had to do. . . Against her better judgment, she sat down, anyway. He grabbed another chair from the garage and sat beside her. His head was slightly behind her, and she had a full view of his long, muscular legs once again—this time in close proximity. *Whatever he does to keep in shape, it sure works.*

She wasn't the type to gawk at men, but John Savitch wasn't just any man physically. Cowboys weren't her type; she liked men in business suits. But the fact remained: This guy would look good in full waders.

She stopped herself, remembering not only was this her landlord, but the man who held her dream house within his reach. Christian or not, he didn't seem like the marrying type. Stefani's mother had warned her about handsome men, and it was the one piece of advice Stefani had taken to heart. It didn't mean anything that she found him good-looking. It was just a fact.

John Savitch was nothing more than an attractive obstacle. And she'd find a way to remove it. A tiny sports car sputtered into the driveway. Stefani looked at

John apologetically. "I'm sorry, that's my secretary. I guess she came back to help." Stefani rose from the chaise lounge. "Thanks for the chair. I hope you enjoy the sunset."

"Your secretary must be committed to her boss," he replied. "Coming over on a Saturday and all."

"Oh no, we're friends first. We've known each other since school. She's only been my secretary for a year. I shouldn't have called her that. I'd better get back to work. Nice chatting with you. It looks like you could get busy yourself." She nodded toward the garage.

"When the sun disappears, I will." Even his voice was relaxed.

She rolled her eyes. That's why she liked businessmen; they were committed to getting things done. This guy had probably never even set a goal, much less achieved one.

"Amy, hi," Stefani called.

Amy ignored Stefani completely and held her hand out to John. "Hi, I'm Amy."

"Pleasure to meet you. I'm John Savitch. Tell Stefani to take a break and enjoy the sunset with me. I'll get you both some tea."

Amy turned, her blond hair flailing wildly. "We should enjoy the sunset, Stefani," she urged her friend through clenched teeth.

Stefani simply smiled and grabbed Amy by the hand, dragging her into the new house. "Come on, we've got work to do. Enjoy the view, John."

"I will," he said as he watched her walk away.

Once inside the house, Amy went straight to the kitchen window. "How can you possibly think about working when you've got *him*," she sighed the last word, "in your driveway?"

"Amy, get away from the window. We're not in high school anymore."

"Are you kidding? I'd pay rent just for that view; forget this house. What does he do for a living? Must be something physical, judging by that body."

"Amy! Mind your manners. You're a Christian woman! You sound like you're at a singles' bar."

"Sorry, you're right, but I don't think I have ever seen one quite like him before. Is he a contractor? He built this house, right?"

"I have no idea what he does for a living, and I don't think he's going to tell me, either. He thinks I'm a snob. I'm sure whatever it is, he doesn't use his mind."

"You? A snob? Goodness, I wonder what ever gave him that idea. Stefani, you didn't show him your business attitude? Tell me you didn't." Stefani shifted uneasily on her feet, a guilty expression crossing her face. "Stefani! Look at him!" Amy pulled her over to the window and yanked her chin so Stefani was facing John Savitch's profile.

Oh my, but he does look good. "Looks aren't everything, Amy. Besides, he's not

130

my type. He usually dresses like a cowboy. Boots. . .the whole thing. I like businessmen, suits. . .a man who knows how to treat a woman. If Mama taught me one thing, it's that a man who looks *that* good can only mean trouble. Give me an accountant any day."

"Stefani, just because someone wears a suit, it doesn't make him a gentleman. Most women like men who look rugged, men that have a little muscle on them."

"Most women probably think John Savitch is the ultimate male, so they can have him. Personally, I don't want any man, but I especially don't want a cowboy. I want this house, and one day, when John decides to settle down with one of his little fillies, this house will be mine. Like it should have been in the first place." Stefani pulled away from Amy's grip to avoid looking at John's physique for a moment longer.

"So where does one sign up to be one of the fillies?" Amy winked, but her smile left when Stefani threw her a chastising glare. "All right, I'm just kidding. Besides, I'm sure he's not a Christian anyway."

"Actually, he is," Stefani relayed. "Said he was born again."

"If he's too good to be true, sign me up as an investigative reporter to find out the truth."

"Amy! Did you come to help or not?" Stefani threw her fists to her hips in mock anger. "You act as though you've never seen a man before. Just like when we were in high school."

"Oh, chill out, I'm just kidding. You saw him first, so you have dibs. Even if you don't realize you want them yet. Come on, let's start upstairs and get your bedroom ready. I imagine those legs look pretty good from up there." They both broke into a giggle and climbed the stairs with boxes in hand. "What do you have in here?" Amy complained.

The two women laughed like schoolgirls as they put Stefani's clothes away. The sun dropped, and Amy sighed with disappointment to find John long gone from the driveway when she was ready to leave. "Ah, well, I suppose I'll be seeing more of him if he's going to be your landlord."

"Don't call him that. Someday I will own this house, and John Savitch will be nothing but a memory to it."

"Right, Stef, I'm sure he's just going to move out of his *house* because you want it. It must be nice, living in that little fantasy world you've made for yourself." Amy laughed at her own joke. "See you tomorrow at church. Do you want me to pick you up?"

"Nah, I'll want to get back home quickly so I can finish unpacking. I'll see you there. Thanks for all your help."

"No problem." Amy pulled out of the driveway and called from her open window. "And be nice to your landlord or it may be *you* that's the memory around here. Staple that mouth shut if you have to."

As Stefani turned to go back in the house, she noticed orange and red flames bursting within John's darkened kitchen. Frantic and acting on pure adrenaline, she ran to her garage and grabbed the fire extinguisher that came with the house. She broke the kitchen window with the back end of the extinguisher and pointed the black hose at a burner on the stove, which was submerged in a small, yet full flame. A loud fizzle sounded. Within a matter of seconds, the blaze was gone and replaced with a white, sudsy mess. Stefani rushed into the unlocked back door to ensure she'd gotten the entire fire. John stood beside her, clapping slowly. "Bravo."

Stefani was indignant. "What are you doing? That's a gourmet stove! Do you have any idea how much that thing cost? Certainly, you're bright enough to take care of this house!" Stefani shook her head, exasperated that anyone could be so careless.

"Stefani, I know you're prone to saying what you think, but *that* was uncalled for." His voice held none of his usual masculine charm.

"You're setting my stove on fire, and you're going to tell me I'm rude?"

"It's *my* stove, Stefani."

"I picked it out," she shot back. Reality slapped her. It was *his* stove and *his* house and *his* idiot mistake. And it wasn't hers to worry about, *yet*. She tried to recover a shred of dignity. "Regardless of whose stove it is, I don't think setting fire to it is a good idea either way. Give it a few days maybe." She held her chin high. "You haven't even had time to let the insurance take effect," she mumbled under her breath, casting a sideways glance at the broken window and fire extinguisher residue.

"I tried to light the pilot light and, apparently, the gas was running too long. I would have handled it, Stefani. I was a volunteer firefighter before I finished college."

"You went to college?" She hadn't meant to sound indignant, but that's exactly how it came out.

"Yeah, believe it or not, we have a few of them in Colorado. Us hicks gotta get educated." His sarcastic tone told her he was still angry. "We even have a city or two out there. But, I kin understand you city folks wouldn't know nuthin' about that," he replied in a fake drawl.

Stefani turned on her heels. She faced him with all her venom. "It wouldn't kill you to say 'thank you.' "

"Thank you?" he shouted. "For what? Breaking my window? Dousing my stove? Or for coming into my house and calling me stupid?" He held his hands open toward her, like she owed him an apology.

"I didn't call you stupid." Stefani was shocked at his accusation. She'd said nothing. She'd thought it, but she'd said nothing of the kind. She actually had congratulated herself for showing restraint.

"You might as well have called me stupid. What is it that frustrates you so much about me, Stefani?"

That you're gorgeous, you own my house, you're a cowboy, and I still find you incredibly attractive. "Nothing. You could have set the houses on fire!" she added. "In case you have forgotten, I live next door."

"I didn't set the houses on fire," he reminded her.

"Thanks to me." She held up the extinguisher.

"I'm glad to know I have an expert in fire prevention living next door. Why are you so angry at the world, Stefani?"

"I'm not angry at the world." *Just you.*

He motioned to the coffeemaker on the opposite counter. "Do you want a cup of coffee?" His tone wasn't necessarily inviting, but it was the least she could do after she'd put her foot in her mouth yet again. When would she ever learn to control her outbursts? Getting on John's bad side would serve no purpose at all.

"Coffee sounds great." She remembered the verse she knew so well about even the fool being thought wise when quiet. If only she could live it. Offending him would get her nowhere. Why did she have such a difficult time remembering such a simple task?

Stefani walked into the living room and stopped in her tracks at the sight of the furniture. Inside the elegantly traditional Mediterranean home, he'd placed a sofa that defied explanation. At one time it was obviously a bright turquoise floral print, but from its many years of use, it had become a pallid blue. Only a few specks of turquoise remained: elements of past grandeur, reminders of days long gone.

He'd placed the atrocity in the center of the room, even though it had no back on it whatsoever. Just a big hole that showed its sofa guts. Just like a sample on a showroom floor. He might have at least put it up against the wall or thrown something over it. Stefani searched for a pleasant comment, but nothing came. She snapped her gaping mouth shut.

John brought out a cup of coffee and with it the dreaded words she feared: "Have a seat."

As much as she wanted to keep quiet, her mouth resisted. "Why on earth would you move that thing across two states?"

"You know how long that sofa's been with me?"

"Please don't tell me you were *born* on it," Stefani cracked.

"Sit down. I had it cleaned just before I moved. I promise. And I've only had it since college."

She sat down with her coffee. "Well, it's comfortable and, when you're sitting in it, you don't have to look at it." She fidgeted into the back of the couch, and he sat down beside her.

"*I've* only had it since college, but it was a hand-me-down from a friend that got it at a secondhand store."

"Why do I not find that the least bit surprising?"

"This couch is ten feet long. It's hard to find a sofa this long anymore, and when you're as tall as I am, that's important."

"You just bought a duplex worth a small fortune, but you can't afford a new couch?"

"I just bought a duplex worth a small fortune," he repeated, "so, no, I can't. Well, I probably could if I raised the rent next door." He smiled and hid behind his coffee cup.

"Very funny. If this place is such a stretch for you, you might consider something more affordable," she suggested, but he saw right through her ruse. His friendly manner turned. His smiling eyes disappeared.

"Stefani, you can think of me as your enemy forever, but it won't change your situation. God didn't give you this house for a reason, so stop blaming me. I don't know what His reason is, but I imagine someday you will. Until that day, be thankful for what you have."

He put his mug down with a bang on the coffee table. She'd made him angry again. With her characteristic, say-anything style, she was used to offending people. But with John it bothered her. Perhaps because he was so difficult to offend. Stefani actually went out of her way to do it. It didn't speak well of her, and she didn't like that feeling one bit. She felt like her mother.

"I am thankful for what I have, but I still want this house. I'm sorry, but I just can't see any reason God would deny me this house. Do you know how long I worked for this? Only to have it stolen from me at the last possible minute? Do you have any idea how frustrating that is?"

His eyes softened. "I'm sure it is, but maybe God wants to give you something else, something better. And the house is not gone; you're living in it. The fact that you can afford to live in one of the best areas in one of America's most expensive real estate markets shows just how spoiled you are." John took the coffee cup from her and went to the kitchen. Apparently, their conversation was over. Stefani stood abruptly.

"You think I'm spoiled?" she called after him, squaring her shoulders. "Well, cowboy, I've worked hard for everything I have. Why shouldn't I have this house? No one gave me a thing!"

He walked purposely from the kitchen and wrapped her up in an unexpected embrace. Stefani felt like a rag doll in his arms, and she didn't know how to react. He nudged her chin upward with his thumb, forcing her to look into the depths of his eyes. She heard herself whimper.

His eyes flickered. "God never promised us happiness. He promised to take care of us. . .to meet our *needs*. And I'd say your needs are more than met. The happiness factor is up to you," he whispered forcefully, as he held her in his arms firmly.

She was face-to-face with those green eyes. Any hope of normalcy was lost. All her anger, her frustration seemed to disappear and transform into hope. The armored exterior she wore was stripped away in his warmth—by the deep, inexplicable awareness they had for one another.

He spoke again, still whispering. "You've got a lot of friends; I saw them helping you today, so I know you're capable of holding that tongue of yours. Could you at least try to be civil to me? To get your mind off your housing agenda for one minute?"

Even close up, she failed to find a flaw in him. She nodded slowly, unable to let out her breath. She closed her eyes, unwilling to stare into those green eyes a moment longer. *I don't like cowboys. I don't like cowboys,* she reminded herself. His grip tightened on her arms, and he pulled her into a kiss. She melted into it, becoming painfully aware that she'd never been kissed like this before. His kiss was unfaltering, confident, and it made her knees buckle.

He held her jaw gently, and she went forward toward his kiss. Perhaps she'd been wrong about cowboys. She'd certainly been wrong about John. He pulled away and her lips remained puckered, desperately wanting another kiss, but he straightened his back and dropped his arms.

"That's better," he commented before he started emptying a nearby moving box.

"Better than what?" she asked in confusion.

"Better than your mouth constantly berating me. I'm glad to know it has other attributes." He smiled assuredly. If she weren't so numbed, she would have slapped him. He continued to put things away, completely ignoring her presence. *After he just kissed me. . .like that!* Stefani stood motionless. Obviously, the kiss had meant nothing to him; it was just a way to shut her up.

Apparently, kissing women casually came easy to him. The idea sickened her. John Savitch had her house, and now he had something else: a portion of her heart. She wished she could take that kiss back to show him he meant nothing to her. Unfortunately, her body still clamored for another kiss—denying how she *should* feel.

She huffed a desperate, short sigh and ran to her house, utterly humiliated. He'd proved his point: She was weak, and he'd won the house for a reason. Well, she wouldn't let him get the better of her again. She was stronger willed than he was, and she'd prove it. She'd spent a lifetime studying the reasons to keep away from a man like him. Now it was time to put what she'd learned to good use.

Chapter 4

Stefani wrestled all night with her pillow; she socked it a few times in frustration. How had she let it happen? A kiss, to a man she barely knew. A man who stood in her way. She had always been in complete control of her emotions. How on earth could a cowboy manage to tear away the guard she'd carefully managed her entire life? It had just been a long time since she'd kissed a man, she reasoned. But it only made John's fiery kiss more vivid. She had *never* been kissed like that before.

With melancholy, she figured John probably had a lot of practice. She stared at her reflection in the mirror. *Will any man ever make me feel like that again?*

"Life isn't about feelings," she reminded herself. "Look how far your mother got on feelings."

Stefani resolved to get off to church early to avoid seeing John. If she couldn't avoid her own emotions, she could at least avoid him. The longer she didn't have to set eyes on John Savitch, the better. She dressed in her finest suit: a raspberry-toned ensemble with a conservative hemline and collared neckline. She stepped in front of the full-length mirror and sneered. *Has my haircut always been this way?* It was decidedly masculine. Boyish. Why hadn't she noticed before? Her bright blue eyes were lost in the haircut's severity.

"Blech!" she said to the mirror. *Vanity!* She threw down her brush in disgust, grabbed her Bible, and headed toward the garage.

She opened the garage door and nearly jumped out of her skin. John stood in the driveway, waiting with arms crossed, embracing a worn Bible. He wore a dark brown brushed leather jacket, jeans without kneeholes, and his clearly polished boots. She guessed he was trying to dress up.

He called out to her: "You own a pair of jeans, princess?"

"Yes?" she asked cautiously. "But I'm on my way to church; it *is* Sunday. Why do you ask?"

"Go grab your jeans. I want to show you something after church," he ordered.

"After church?"

"I'm tagging along. Since you didn't invite me, I'm inviting myself. I don't have a home church yet, so I'm sure you wouldn't mind if I tried yours." He shoved his hands into his leather jacket, tucked his Bible under his arm, and nodded at the brown duffel bag hanging on his shoulder.

"Actually, you're not really dressed for my church. It might be better if—"

"I'll be fine. Go get a pair of jeans and a sweater. Oh, and some shoes you can walk in, preferably boots." He motioned toward her heels and got into her car. He settled into her passenger seat.

Stefani leaned over the opened car window. "John, I don't *own* boots and there are hundreds of churches in the area. Wouldn't you be more comfortable at another one? I mean, we already live right next to one another."

"Don't they teach the Bible at your church?"

"Well, yes."

"Then that's as good a place as any to start. Did you want to take my car?" he asked, pointing back toward his own garage.

She sighed heavily. "No." She couldn't deny taking him to church. That bordered on unchristian. "But after church, I'm bringing you right home. I have a million things to do today. And throwing on a pair of jeans for anything, other than unpacking, is not on my agenda."

"I have something I want to show you. It's very special to me. Come on, it's Sunday. You're not supposed to be working today, anyway." He had her there.

Stefani suddenly reasoned whatever was so special to him might hold the key to his moving. Without further argument, she ran upstairs and grabbed a pair of jeans and a baby blue sweater. *He hasn't lived on the peninsula very long; perhaps he bought in a rush. Maybe there is a special place. . .* She could just casually look up listed homes and later mention an available house on the market. Her mind rambled with the possibilities. She picked up her running shoes in the garage and settled herself behind the steering wheel.

She glared at him. "You're accustomed to getting what you want, aren't you?" She broke into a knowing smile. *But so am I.*

"Hey, the Christian thing to do would have been to invite me to church. Especially after you kissed me like that last night." He riffled through her CDs and selected one, taking it out of its case.

Her smile disappeared. "Kissed you! John Savitch, you are incorrigible!"

He shrugged. "It's okay, I forgive you. I have that effect on women." He broke into a wide grin to show he was teasing, and despite herself, she wanted to kiss him again. *And on a Sunday!*

John's suave disposition managed to give the distinct impression she was the only woman in the world. Deep down, she knew men like him fell for gorgeous, flirtatious women. The kind that knew the right things to say at the right time. . . Attractive cowboys didn't fall for serious business types with trouble maintaining proper decorum in social situations. John was not falling for her. He was simply toying with her emotions.

"I'm taking you to church this morning because it's my Christian duty to help get you started church shopping, but after this, you're on your own." She tried to sound firm, knowing that if she didn't put a stop to his incessant flirting, he'd only break her heart. Strong willed or not, she wasn't made of stone.

"Well, thanks for performing your Christian duty."

"Speaking of which, don't you have a suit you could wear? My church is pretty formal." She leaned against the steering wheel, offering him one last chance to change.

"I've got my best boots on; what more do you want? This is what everyone wears to church where I come from. At least I shined my boots." He lifted up a foot, then sat back into her passenger seat, showing he had no intention of changing his clothes. "Besides, how do I know you won't screech out of here and leave me?"

He had a point.

When they arrived at church, Stefani had never felt so popular. Every unattached woman she knew, whether casually or intimately, suddenly became a lot friendlier. Their interest in her landlord was more than obvious. She had to admit it: Her church wasn't exactly teeming with available Christian men. John seemed oblivious to the attention, and for that Stefani was thankful.

That is, until they were stopped in the foyer by a familiar face and a low, throaty voice. "Stefani, hi. I heard you moved. Who's this?" Rachel Cummings was one of the most beautiful women at the church, and she knew it. She had red hair, green eyes, and a figure that seemed to come naturally. Stefani had to work out constantly to maintain a slim frame.

Rachel was one of those women whose eyes sparkled with intention, and she always knew the right thing to say. The kind who had very few female friends because she dripped of something unspoken and brazen—the kind whose faith was always questioned by other women.

Rachel snuggled up to John easily, like a cat would to a cat-hater, completely ignoring Stefani's presence. Stefani felt her own claws come out, and she realized she was actually feeling possessive of her handsome landlord. Stefani cleared her throat and made the introductions without ceremony or inflection. "Rachel, this is John Savitch, my landlord. John Savitch, Rachel Cummings."

"John," Rachel purred. "So nice to meet you. Stefani has told me all about you. Haven't you, Stefani?" she asked with raised eyebrows. Rachel tossed her red hair, and Stefani felt the swinging strand cross her cheek with a quick sting. Rachel held her head cocked, looking up with her big green eyes and luscious, long eyelashes. Stefani inwardly wondered how many coats of mascara it took.

"Rachel, it's such a pleasure to meet you," John said in an exaggerated drawl. "Stefani hadn't mentioned you, but it's so nice to meet you. Any friend of Stefani's is a friend of mine, right, hon?" He slapped her back lightly and she coughed.

"Anything you say, pardner. When you get a job, maybe you and Rachel could get together sometime." Stefani grinned.

"There's no hurry. My welfare checks don't run out for a few months now, darling," John answered slyly.

Rachel gave a half smile while John took Stefani's arm and led her away from the church's beauty queen.

"Are you through?" Stefani asked him. "Welfare? Really, John."

"You jealous?" He smiled.

"Not in the least bit. As a matter of fact, I was just thinking you two deserved each other. Want her phone number?" Stefani asked sarcastically.

"Oh, you wound me so. No thanks; I don't like redheads. I'm partial to brunettes. Brunettes with darling dimples and an agenda they can't seem to forget about." John lowered his hand into her own and gave it a quick squeeze. "Call me a glutton for punishment."

She grimaced as they sat down in the pew and began to sing the first hymns of the morning. Stefani fidgeted throughout the sermon, which went completely over her head. She couldn't help but notice the attention they were attracting together. After the service ended, John pulled Stefani into the foyer before they had time to speak to anyone.

"Don't you want to meet the pastor?" Stefani asked.

"I can meet him anytime. Come on, I have a surprise for you. Go change into your jeans."

She did as she was told and emerged to find John waiting in his standard, rugged jeans and scuffed-up boots. "That's better." He clicked his tongue. "You were made for jeans, princess. I hope to see you in them more often." Again, he took her by the arm with all the chivalry of an English gentleman. "Yep, we'll have to get you some boots."

"I like heels," she replied curtly.

Once in her car, he led her up into the hills and down several winding tree-lined roads before they came to a long asphalt driveway. Stefani had lived on the peninsula her entire life and had never seen the road taken. The car wound around the trees, and she had to admit the parklike setting was incredibly serene.

"Park the car over there." He pointed to a white fence where several horses grazed in the distance.

She parked her car amid the dust and coughed dramatically as she emerged from the car, waving her hand in front of her. "Now will you tell me why we're here?" Stefani had never heard such quiet. Even in their suburban neighborhood, this kind of peace was unheard of. Everything was perfectly still. A distant whinny from a horse only soothed her frayed nerves. She took a deep breath and inhaled the rich eucalyptus scent that surrounded her. As much as she hated to admit it, it was beautiful. One thing was certain: John Savitch knew how to relax.

"I wanted you to meet Kayla," John answered, and Stefani's peace was suddenly shattered.

Stefani looked at him like he'd just stepped out of a UFO. "You brought me out here to meet your girlfriend?"

"Not my girlfriend, my horse; Kayla's Pride and Joy. Kayla for short."

"Who's Kayla named after?" Stefani inquired uneasily.

"The gal who named the horse, I suppose." He shrugged.

"You didn't name your own horse?"

"The horse is named by the breeders. She's registered."

"For what, china? Is she getting married?"

"She's registered with the American Quarter Horse Association. Hang on a minute." He briefly disappeared into a stable and came out leading a magnificent horse by a ring and tether. "*This* is Kayla," he said proudly, beaming like a brand-new papa.

Stefani stepped back and gulped, "S–she's big."

"And the reason I don't own a better couch," he joked. "This beauty cost me a bundle. You want a ride?"

Stefani's eyes grew wide. "No way. She looks like a racehorse. I've never even been on a pony, and quite frankly, I don't plan to get on one anytime soon." Stefani started to walk closer to her car. She was scared to death of large animals. A fact she chose to keep to herself.

He laughed at her. "Not a ride on Kayla; she's still young. Just three years old. She's still being trained. I'll get one of the gentle stable mares for you, and we can ride together. Come on, it will be fun. Kayla needs the exercise."

"John, I still have an entire house to unpack." She looked back at him.

"Sunday is a day of rest. You would waste this gorgeous day unpacking?" He held up his hand to the blue sky.

"Resting and horseback riding are completely different things for me," she explained as she opened her car door. He pulled the horse and came toward her, sidling the oversized animal beside her, and she shivered.

"Look at those big brown eyes. You could refuse a face like this?" He patted Kayla on the short, wide nose and used his hip to shut the car door.

Stefani looked at the huge eyes on the mare. The horse was beautiful, truly noble in stature. Stefani didn't know anything about horses, but she knew this horse was special to John. If John wanted to be closer to his horse and the country lifestyle he'd left behind, Kayla was the answer. Suddenly, she realized she needed to get over her fear. Her plan would take time and probably a few horseback rides, but John's interest in her house might evaporate for Kayla.

"Will you show me what to do? If I ride?" Stefani stammered, unwilling to believe she was going to get on a horse.

140

"Of course. And I'll be right beside you. These horses are gentle, so you won't be in any trouble. I promise." His warm grin won her over.

"All right then."

He threw a saddle on a gray horse. "The saddle maintains your balance, but you'll want to stay above the mount's center of balance. Here." He cupped his hand and Stefani shot up onto the horse. She gripped the nub that he'd called a "pommel" tightly. "Sit up straight. . .shoulders back. That's it. Okay, now you'll want to keep a light, steady hand on the reins. Too tight and you'll hurt the horse. Too loose and you may lose control. Understood?"

Soon, Stefani was riding high on a steady, gray horse. Next to John's fine mount, her horse looked a bit worn by time and DNA, but Stefani was too tense to care. She felt so high and vulnerable on the huge beast. Every muscle in her body was clenched. John spoke more directions at her, but she was too frightened to take her eyes off the horse's back. She simply nodded quick, short nods.

When she became the slightest bit confident, she clasped the pommel tightly and looked around. The horse trail was incredible with sweeping views of the valley. Huge oaks dotted the path before them, and the trail ahead disappeared into a redwood forest. "Stefani, there's a view of the ocean from that ridge up there. Do you want to ride there?"

Stefani's head bobbed up and down swiftly, her jaw so tight she couldn't have answered him with words if she tried. He came beside her and spoke softly, his deep voice coming through loud and clear. "You're doing wonderfully, Stef; I'm so proud of you." She felt herself smile. She was proud of herself, but hearing it from John made her downright giddy. She was actually doing something new, something fresh and exciting, even adventurous.

They continued their slow pace and, once at the top of the ridge, John pulled his horse to a halt. Without any command on her part, Stefani's horse stopped as well. John dismounted and allowed his horse to graze. He came to help Stefani down, and she went willingly into his upraised arms. Her knees buckled under her, and she grabbed tighter to John's muscular frame. "Whoa, my muscles are toast."

"They'll get stronger." He smiled down at her.

Such tranquility was like a dream. She closed her eyes, trying to snap a picture within her mind. There was something magical about being surrounded by his protective arms and quietly overlooking the beautiful ocean view.

"You're a born cowgirl. And here I've been calling you 'princess.' I ought to be ashamed of myself." John winked at her when she finally opened her eyes. "I didn't think you were such an athlete, but you've done so well being on that horse all afternoon."

"I like her." Stefani looked to the horse. "She just knows I have no idea what I'm doing."

John let out a short laugh. "Ah, but you will. You're just a born country gal living in the city." He kept his grip upon her, and she didn't even try to break free of it. Her knees were too weak on their own. She snuggled her cheek alongside his chest before pulling away.

"Country girls drive horses and wear boots; I drive a coupe and wear heels. My rubber legs ought to tell you that."

"It's what's in your heart that matters. I think you're a country girl at heart. Those dimples prove it; they've been with us all day. I never see them in the city." He stroked her face with his rugged hand, then bent down with the obvious intention of kissing her, but she broke free of his embrace. She couldn't let *that* happen again. He was toying with her, and she was falling for it, hook, line, and sinker.

"I've never seen the ocean from up here, and I've lived here all my life," she said brightly as she stared over the ridge, avoiding eye contact.

"Is something the matter, Stefani?"

"No," she replied innocently. She tried to catch her breath and focused intently on the distant ocean. Her plans weren't working at all. She had hoped John would be so enamored with his day that all thoughts of the duplex would dissipate from his head, but instead it was Stefani who couldn't remember where she lived. "I think we should head back. I've got a lot of work to do on the house."

"Fine, Stefani, and you're right. We both have a lot of work to do, and I appreciate what a good sport you've been. Come on." He clasped his hands as a makeshift ladder and hoisted her up to her gray mare.

They rode back at a leisurely pace, taking in all the scenery. All too soon, for Stefani's liking, the stables came into view. Without warning, the horse bolted and began trotting at a pace that was beyond her abilities or comfort level. A full gallop soon had Stefani holding onto the reins for dear life.

"He—elp!" she wailed as she bent at the waist and hugged the horse's back and neck. The horse just seemed to go faster, and the tighter she gripped, the quicker the ground seemed to rush past her.

"Pull the reins!" John called after her. She could hear his horse pick up speed and soon he was beside her. "Pull the reins, Stefani!" She wanted to, but then she would have to sit up, and she was too afraid to pull away from the comfort of the horse's back. "Stefani. Hang on the reins in your hands and sit up."

Before she had any time to react, they were back at the stables and the horse stopped on its own volition, ending up at the feed bin. Stefani's labored breath and fresh tears couldn't be hidden. Embarrassed, she lashed out. "Thanks for the rescue," she said, haughtily dusting herself off.

He laughed. "Sorry, Stefani, but if you believe you were in any real danger for that forty-yard sprint on that tired old animal, then there's nothing I can say to make you feel any better." He fiddled with his horse's reins, then walked off with both horses into the stables.

Stefani was provoked by his casual attitude. *I might have been killed.* She mumbled continuously under her breath as she walked back to the car. "It wouldn't bother the cowboy; *you* grew up on horses. Riding your fancy, well-trained race-horse, while you leave me to that beast that just wants his oats. This is not a sport; it's just a big, hairy dog that acts on its own wild volition!" John hadn't heard a word of her tirade, but her grumbling soothed her frayed nerves.

Chapter 5

Stefani hadn't spoken the entire route home from the ranch. She sat stoic, with arms crossed, and let her body language do the talking. John hated to end the day on a sour note. They'd shared such an idyllic time enjoying his favorite thing in the world, and he'd seen a glimmer of that side of her she kept so carefully hidden. He wished he hadn't teased her. She'd been an avid horsewoman the whole day. He knew how much she wanted to organize her new home instead of going riding; he should have given her more credit. But it was too late to take it back now.

Monday morning, he watched her from the kitchen window overlooking their shared driveway. She looked the picture of vogue in her sapphire suit; it highlighted her long, shapely legs. She picked up the newspaper, threw him a wicked glance, and got into her car, slamming the door. She was absolutely exasperating, but he was captured, regardless. Stefani had an unspoken charm that mystified him.

Remembering her genuine sweetness and those dimples, he knew why. There were the unguarded moments when he'd capture a hint of the woman who had kissed him with genuine passion. It was all the encouragement he needed. Stefani wanted so desperately to hide her emotions; he almost felt sorry for her. He sought the innocent creature who showed herself so rarely, instead of the composed, often-times rude persona she hid behind. Stefani pulled out of the driveway in her midnight blue coupe and avoided waving, grimacing at him, instead.

John gulped down half a cup of coffee at the kitchen window and tossed the remainder into the sink. His partner, Tom Owens, honked in the driveway, and John grabbed his denim jacket and dashed for the door. Tom greeted him. "Hey, I like the new place. Looks kinda fancy for your tastes. You got a new gal you're trying to impress?" Tom leaned toward the steering wheel, gazing upward at the Mediterranean home.

"Nah, but I had to spend the money from the sale of the ranch, otherwise I'd give it all to the government. And working for the government, boy, they know just what you've got." They both laughed. "Besides, the only woman I've met here in California who interests me, uh. . .let's just say she's not exactly captivated by my charm. But she does love my house, so I suppose it has its benefits." John smirked.

144

"So. . .what? You're worried she'll marry you for your house?"

"Ha! No, I'm more worried she'll kill me for it." He laughed again and nodded toward the other half of the duplex. "She lives there; she's my renter." He clicked his tongue. "Cutest thing you ever did see, but, boy, when she sets her mind to something, she has a one-track mind."

"She'll come around."

"Where are we headed today?" John changed the subject. Stefani wasn't just any lady; she was the kind of woman a man thought about marriage for. She was competent, innocent, and needed a good dose of humble pie. John knew just the person to give it to her.

"We're going to Atlas Semiconductors," Tom relayed.

"*The* Atlas Semiconductors?" John asked cautiously.

"The one and only. It's one of our toxic Superfund sites. Last time we were out, they had a toxicity plume nearly six thousand feet long and five hundred feet deep." Tom shook his head in disgust. "If they haven't cleaned up their act by now, we're going after them. And nothing would give me greater pleasure." Tom acted like a bounty hunter who would finally get his white whale.

"Atlas is where Stefani, my renter, works," John said slowly, trying to grasp the latest information. He picked up the clipboard containing all the scientific data last gathered and gasped. "This is pathetic. They've got trichloroethylene levels of twenty-two thousand parts per billion, and look at this, dichloroethylene levels of thirty-eight thousand. Absolute poison. There's no way the drinking water could go unscathed with numbers like these." John reread the figures to make sure he had the numbers right.

"Yeah, and they just keep getting away with it. This time, though, they've got you on the case, John. No one in the EPA has a better reputation than you have for legally bringing these miscreants down. We will have no choice but to act, no matter what the big lobbyists in Washington do. It does my heart proud."

John shook his head in disgust. "Don't have *too* much faith in my abilities. I've just learned to take it slow and catch them by surprise. Their lobbyists just don't have time to act when I'm on the case."

"Welcome to corporate America, John. Just follow the money trail and you'll get to what stinks."

"*This,*" he held up the clipboard, "is why I became an environmental scientist. You grow up in a place like Colorado, you just don't want to let big business destroy the land for profit." John was seething; Stefani was working in a poison mill. He knew she had no idea what was going on underneath her. Likely, very few of the employees did.

Suddenly, he felt like a masked avenger. His future report could save Stefani from drinking contaminated coffee from the water cooler or from taking a leisurely stroll along the polluted walkway surrounding her office. He had the distinct pleasure of going after major polluters, but he'd also be there for Stefani. Maybe, just maybe, she might warm up to him if she knew he truly cared for her welfare—if he managed to stop Atlas from poisoning her further.

John and Tom pulled into the corporate driveway with their measuring devices and sterilized tubes for gathering soil and water samples. As they got out of the rented pickup, they were greeted by Atlas's company security. The man in the blue Atlas uniform held up a palm. "No unauthorized vehicles allowed on the property. You'll have to turn around now."

"Environmental Protection Agency," John announced as he held up his badge with conviction. The security man backed away quickly. "We have a report of continued pollutants on the property," John continued, his voice slightly lower to command respect.

"Sorry. Sorry," the officer repeated. He got back into his truck sheepishly and drove off, leaving them to their work. John knew they needed to work quickly. Of course corporations had no legal right to bother the EPA, but company security could make things more difficult. Partners for only a month, John and Tom had already learned to use their time wisely to get crucial samples. It was such a stupid dance they played, considering that the EPA was there to protect the security guards and others from toxic chemicals, but it was part of the game, nonetheless.

Within ten minutes they had the samples they needed and were off before the security guard returned. If company officials escorted them, the numbers would be decidedly more in the company's favor. The fact was that corporate officials knew where their toxicity plumes were and knew where to steer the EPA away from them, but still keep them on the property. The result was an unrealistic reading. "Let's get back to the lab." John and Tom ran for the truck and squealed out of the parking lot before any of the "officials" could steer them away.

He hoped that after analyzing the samples, he would get the opportunity to stop Atlas Semiconductors and, thus, win Stefani's approval. He inhaled, sticking out his chest proudly.

~

Stefani worked feverishly to get the latest software programs installed for the accounting department. Atlas Semiconductors was having a banner year; no doubt her stock would soon show the reward of her efforts. If she made the kind of money she hoped to, perhaps she could make an outrageous offer to John for the house. The kind he couldn't refuse.

If she could just learn to hold her tongue a little longer, he'd want to give her the desire of her heart. Stefani could turn on the charm if she had to, and for that duplex, she obviously had to. She would prove to her mother that success came to those who worked for it. And she didn't need a man to make her dreams come true.

Amy came running into her office, breathless and flushed. "Stefani, I just saw your landlord out on the running trail!"

Stefani continued to enter her information into the computer in front of her, trying to appear unfazed by Amy's announcement. "Really? I wonder what he was doing there."

"Why are you such a snob? You're worried he's in construction, aren't you? I know how your mind works."

"It's not that I'm a snob, Amy. I just like professional men; it's just my preference. It doesn't make me a snob just because I don't want some urban cowboy as my beau." Stefani bit her lip nervously; no accountant had ever kissed her like John had.

"Suit yourself." Amy slapped her knee, laughing. "Get it? *Suit* yourself. You like businessmen, get it?"

"I get it, Amy. It's just not that funny." Stefani smirked.

"I think you're afraid he might not be interested."

Stefani let out a short laugh. "Amy, when was the last time you saw me worried about what *any* man thought?"

"That's not necessarily something to be proud of, Stefani! When is the last time you had a date? No, wait, a better question. . .when's the last time you had a *second* date?" Amy asked with arms crossed.

Stefani swallowed hard at the question. Amy was right; Stefani wasn't exactly bride material. She always ended up discussing logistics of MIS protocol and boring the guy to death or saying something she regretted. Added to that, she didn't have the opportunity to meet many men, since most of them worked for her. Her dating life *was* pathetic.

"When was the last time I *wanted* a second date with any of those guys? Look, Amy, I have high standards, I admit that. And most likely, no man will ever live up to them, and I'll be an old maid. But better an old maid than to lose everything to a man because of my *feelings*."

"Stefani, listen to you. You sound so hard-hearted. I know you're not that way. I think Mr. Landlord might see through that hard shell of yours, too."

"I kissed him," Stefani said quietly.

"You what?"

"I kissed him. Well, he kissed me. Well, it wasn't so much a kiss as him trying to shut me up. I said something."

"My, what a surprise. You said something?"

"And I also went horseback riding with him. But only because I thought he might want to move because of it," Stefani admitted.

"You know, the frightening thing is, that statement actually makes sense to me. I've been hanging around with you for too long. You thought if you found something he liked, horses, for example, you'd find a reason for him to move. Am I right?"

Stefani crinkled her nose and nodded.

"No offense here, friend. But you're starting to sound like your mother." Amy's words slapped her with the sting of a whip.

"I'm *not* like my mother!"

"Stefani, I know you're not, but you're starting to do things that resemble her greatly. You have a good heart and you love the Lord. But please, stop protecting yourself so much. Getting hurt once in a while helps us grow; it's part of the plan. Have fun with John. Relax. Get to know him; you might find out you like him. Or that men aren't the enemy."

"You don't think I've been hurt enough?"

"Ah, Stef. Pray about it, okay? Listen, the gang from church is going to the Christian music house for coffee tonight. You want to come?"

Stefani was still reeling from the comparison to her mother. "Nah. I would, but I think I'm going to be here late tonight. I have to get this program up and running for accounting."

"Come on, lattes and good music. That new band that performed at church last month is playing. Summer will be over soon, and it's going to start getting dark before we leave work; that's so depressing. Let's have some fun while we can. I miss my best friend; it seems like she's always lost in some computer somewhere."

"Thanks, Amy, I appreciate the offer. . .maybe this weekend. I still have unpacking to do and it's my running night."

"Can't you put that schedule of yours aside for one night? It wouldn't kill you. Maybe you could invite John to come with us."

"No! John and I are just acquaintances. Business partners, you might say. The kiss was a fluke. It will never happen again."

"It might if you want it to." Amy smiled.

"Well, I don't want it to."

"I've said my piece, Stefani. I like John and I think he might be good for you. Don't throw him out with the others because of words a dotty old woman told you once."

Stefani felt her throat get tight. "Amy, if I let go of my goal and John disappears like the rest of the men in my life, I've got nothing."

Amy came and sat beside her. "That's not true, Stef. You've always got the Lord and me. I'm not going anywhere. I just wish you'd learn to fly, just a little bit. So let's say, just for the sake of argument, John is just a little fling of a couple dates. Someone you spend time with, go to the movies with, cook for, horseback ride with. . . It's a friendship, and friendships grow us, Stefani. Your grandmother was wrong. I know you've heard it a million times from me, but someday maybe you'll have ears for it."

Stefani shook her head. "After my goal is met. If it's meant to be, it will be there after I own the property."

Amy let out a long, deep sigh. "I want to be in your wedding someday. I don't want you to grow old alone just because you missed the boat."

"Oh, Amy, I don't think I'm cut out for marriage." Stefani's chin dropped.

"Nonsense. You're just feeling sorry for yourself."

"No, I'm being realistic. I'm thirty-two years old, and all the Christian men out there seem to want some young, sweet thing that hangs on every word they say. Lord knows I don't qualify for *that!* Someday I'll have my grandparents' farmland back, and I can enjoy my life *without* a man."

"I'm sure you enjoy your life without a man. My question is, Why would you want to when John Savitch is right next door? If I had a neighbor that looked like him, I wouldn't be so anxious about his moving. If you change your mind about the coffee house, buzz me."

"I will. Have fun tonight and tell the gang I said hi." Stefani smiled widely, thrilled the conversation about John was over. Just the mere mention of his name made her stomach turn over with anxiety. Regardless of her convictions, Stefani was succumbing to the charm of a cowboy. It was getting harder to maintain the cold front when she relished the thought of seeing him at the end of the day.

"I'll tell everyone you said hi." Amy winked and went back to her cubicle.

~

Stefani arrived home late. John was in the driveway, potting plants in the soil around the perimeter of the peach stamped-concrete walkway. She got out of her car, leaving it in the driveway, and rushed to his side. She stared at the ghastly collection of plants he'd selected, her mouth dangling.

"What are you doing? You're not going to plant those? They don't go with the whole Mediterranean theme of the home." She lifted her arms in expression. "I had pictured queen palms, azaleas, maybe a few crape myrtles. These plants don't match the apricot orchards, they're off center, there's no height to them, you're missing scale. . . I could go on and on." She pointed at the empty plastic containers piled neatly beside his handiwork. "They're. . .they're ugly plants, John," she said plainly.

He smiled. "Welcome home, Stefani. These are drought-resistant plants. Made for the dry, California summers," he stated with conviction. "I won't be accused of using too much precious California water when I use half the commodity as our neighbors." He continued to plant, using his wide, square fingers to press the soil around a sad-looking juniper. "Conservation is key to maintaining God's creation amid this high population."

Stefani's train of thought disappeared. "What are those awful plastic things in the ground?"

"They're milk jugs." He wiped his brow with the back of his hand, and Stefani noticed his hands were covered with mud.

"Why are they in the dirt? Are you trying to get milk from the soil? Or is this some cowboy secret I should know?"

He let out a short laugh. "You fill the jugs with water and turn them over in the dirt. They act as a slow drip system for the plants. No hoses or wasted water necessary," he stated proudly.

"You mean you're going to leave them like that? Not only do I get ugly plants, but I'm supposed to look at garbage, too?" Stefani threw her hand to her hip. "Don't I get some say in the landscaping? It's my home, too, and you're polluting the view with this. . .this garbage."

"It's not garbage. It's recycling, and if more people did it, we'd be in a lot better place. Besides, when the plants grow, they'll be hidden." John wiped the dirt from his hands and stood to his full height.

Stefani rolled her eyes. "Well, at least the winters will be garbage free. They will. . .won't they?"

"In the winter, we put funnels in the jugs and catch the rainwater under the rain gutters." John's eyes sparkled, and Stefani got the distinct impression he enjoyed baiting her.

"You're determined to have us be the laughingstock of the neighborhood, aren't you? You actually like the fact that our home looks like it's in the Sahara."

"No, but I'm determined to set a good example for young people that recycling is a way of life."

"We have politically correct plants? Is that what you're telling me? If you knew what this place looked like thirty years ago, you wouldn't be filling it with desert scrub." Stefani turned and walked purposely to her duplex, annoyed such a conversation had even taken place.

"How do you know what this place looked like thirty years ago?" He clapped away the excess dirt from his knees.

Stefani covered her mouth with her hand. How did that slip out? Now she'd lost a bargaining chip; he'd know just how much the house meant to her. The first rule of negotiating was being able to walk away. She recovered after a brief silence. "I can just imagine what it must have been like, that's all. They say it used to be fruit orchards here—everywhere." She started to walk again, but was thwarted by his deep voice.

"Stefani, are you lying? Because you're a terrible liar. Did you know your cheeks turn red when you lie?"

Stefani put her hands to her cheeks and felt their warmth. Her big mouth!

150

She searched his eyes; they seemed to be waiting for an answer. She wasn't lying, really, she just wasn't relaying the whole truth. Suddenly, her conscience kicked in. "Okay, okay. This was my grandparents' farm. I grew up here on this very land in an old clapboard farmhouse that sat about where our duplex is now. Those apricot trees in the back are the last remaining vestige of my family's legacy."

"Your family's all gone?" he asked, and she noted the sincere concern in his brow.

"No, they're not *gone*." She shook her head. "They just couldn't afford the taxes on the land anymore. Farming's not a lucrative business here in Silicon Valley. They sold out and moved to Sacramento, where it's a little more affordable."

"So why not move to Sacramento yourself?" he asked innocently. "If you miss them so much. It's only two hours away."

"You wouldn't understand."

"Try me."

She considered it, but then retreated. "Let's just say I'm where I belong." She was determined to fulfill the promise she'd made to her grandmother before the loving old woman had gone to be with the Lord. She needed to get the land back in her family. That goal was quickly slipping away because of John Savitch.

John reached out to her, but then pulled his hand back, noticing the dirt. "Do you want to come with me to ride Kayla tonight? We can take old Nelly out for an evening stroll. I bet we could even watch the sunset over the ocean on the ridge. You could tell me about the plants you'd like for the house." His eyes were bright with enthusiasm.

The last thing Stefani wanted was for the bachelor to feel sorry for her. "No, I don't think so. I need to jog tonight. Thanks for the offer, but I still feel like I'm riding Nelly." She rubbed her behind.

"I wish there was something I could say to make things better about the house."

"You could say it's for sale." She was beating a dead horse.

"Stefani, you know owning this house won't change anything."

"That's easy to say when you own it, John. But I suppose I know that deep down," she answered despondently.

He walked closer. "I don't know why God said no, Stefani, but I do know He sees the whole picture." He tried to get her attention, but she ignored him until he used the clean back of his hand to nudge her chin up toward his penetrating green eyes.

"So you've said." She crossed her arms and rolled her eyes. She knew she wasn't going to own the house just yet, but she didn't want to be lectured by the cowboy as to why. Even if he was right, she wasn't ready to admit defeat, especially not to him.

"You don't believe that God is keeping this house from you for a reason."

"I worked hard for my money. I can afford this house, and the only thing I see standing in my way is *you*." That wasn't true, but for some reason it felt good to say.

"Then you are misled, Stefani. I'm here for a reason. I own this house and live here for a reason—with *you* as my renter." He pointed his dirt-caked forefinger at her. "I'm not sure what that reason is, but instead of taking your vengeance out on me, why don't you pray? Ask God why He didn't give you this house and wait for His answer. But please leave me out of the loop. It's between you and God. It's not my problem and I'm tired of suffering your wrath."

Stefani felt like she'd been slugged. She hadn't realized just how much her agenda had affected John, but his anger certainly got her attention. The very idea that she had harmed him, in any way, hurt her. It was something her mother would do. *That's exactly what Amy said! Am I becoming like my mother?* She ran to her front door, ending the conversation abruptly.

~

Days passed and John had stayed mysteriously out of sight. He didn't wave from his kitchen window each morning, he didn't garden in the evening, and he didn't barbecue on his front porch. His absence made Stefani anxious.

Friday evening, the doorbell rang. Stefani was just on her way out to jog, but sighed audibly when she saw John on the porch. For as much as she missed his presence, she wasn't ready to face him yet, either. She turned her back to the door, debating. The last thing she wanted to hear was another lecture on why he owned the house instead of her.

Her guilt played a part in it. She hadn't prayed about it; she'd been too angry. Besides, praying meant doing what John asked of her, and her defiant attitude simply refused to let him control her. John was a man with no emotional attachments to the area or the house. He could afford to go elsewhere and put an end to this whole thing, so why didn't he?

She *knew* why, of course; people just didn't buy houses, then leave. Home ownership meant permanence, and that bothered Stefani to no end. As much as she'd missed John, when she opened the door, her old bulldog self was upon her.

"Yes?" Stefani barked. John was silent; he seemed prepared for her coldness, actually expecting it. Suddenly, he picked her up easily and tossed her over his shoulder like a sack of potatoes. She flailed her arms, bashing him in the back, but she felt like a mere child upon his broad shoulders. "What do you think you're doing? Put me down, you. . .you caveman!"

"Stefani, why can't you just admit we're pretty good together? We have a lot of fun," he explained calmly as he walked toward his side of the duplex. "You're like the second grader who keeps pulling my hair. These running pants look great on you, by the way," he commented, and Stefani thought she could actually hear his smile.

"You are such a male chauvinist. Put me down! You throw me a bone like picking out a few plants for the house, and I'm supposed to be grateful! Put me down!" she wailed again.

Without further struggle, he placed her gently on her feet in the middle of the driveway and smiled at her smugly. She gave him a look reserved for her most heated arguments, crossing her arms angrily.

"Stefani, would you like to have dinner with me?"

Stefani's mouth dangled aimlessly. "Why do you insist on tormenting me?" She straightened out the legs of her pants. "And why would I want to have dinner with someone who treats me like. . .like a bag of grain?"

"The lady doth protest too much, methinks," he said through a grin.

"What?"

"Shakespeare in *Hamlet*, remember?"

"What on earth are you talking about?"

"Okay, if not Shakespeare, then Dr. Seuss. You don't like green eggs and ham."

"It's been a long time since I read Shakespeare, and I don't know Dr. Seuss, so you'll have to refresh my memory if you're trying to make some point." Stefani crossed her arms again, waiting for his answer.

"The guy in Dr. Seuss. He didn't want to eat green eggs and ham at all, remember? But when he *tried* green eggs and ham, he liked them. I think if you'd give this old cowboy a chance and forget this house for five minutes, you'd like me. We had a great time on the horses, and I think we have more in common than you think. We both live in the same place, for example. You just need to get out of those suits more often and into your jeans and relax, that's all. You are a born cowgirl, and you'd enjoy it if you'd just let your hair down once in a while."

Stefani instinctively touched her boyish haircut at his comment. Tiny laugh lines were starting to appear next to his eyes, and Stefani couldn't remember marveling at anyone being so good-looking. She wanted his house, but right now she wanted him more. She loved his gentle manner, and, heaven help her, she may have even liked *him*. But she'd watched her mother toil a lifetime after a lazy father; she wouldn't end up the same way. Why was she being tempted by a handsome day laborer? God knew Stefani needed someone with the same goals she had, didn't He?

"Have dinner with me. Just one dinner." He smiled a lopsided grin, and Stefani marveled at the strong line of his chin, oblivious to his question.

Chapter 6

Stefani stood silent in thought for some time, contemplating the dinner invitation and trying to fight the conflicting feelings welling within her. Lifelong conviction or not, this cowboy was undeniably attractive, and the thought of jogging alone versus a quiet dinner with him suddenly paled in importance.

Her answer surprised both of them. "You're right, cowboy, I owe you. Not only will I have dinner with you, I'll *make* you dinner tonight." She shut her door behind her and led him to his house before she had time to change her mind.

"Should I be afraid? You're being awfully nice to me." He pulled her to a stop, and she pulled harder to get him walking again.

"I'm a gourmet cook; it's my hobby. Why shouldn't we have dinner together tonight?" *It doesn't mean anything*, she added silently.

"Yes, why not? But should I be afraid? You're not going to poison me or anything, right?" John's eyes narrowed suspiciously.

"I've just decided to be more neighborly. That's all. This is your house, and this is my way of acknowledging that fact. No strings attached, no ulterior motives, and no hidden agenda. You've told me you'll sell to me if and when the time comes and I'm satisfied with that." *For now.*

"What should we have for dinner? Should I go to the grocery store?" he asked as they entered his kitchen. He rubbed his hands together in eagerness.

"That depends. What do you have in the fridge?" Stefani opened his refrigerator without an invitation and riffled through the contents. She came up with potatoes, an onion, a chicken breast, and two soft drinks. "This is it?" She held up the contents.

"I haven't shopped."

"Since when, 1958?" She giggled and held his hand to show she didn't mean any harm. "I'm teasing. We'll have a fine dinner. There's some fresh rosemary growing wild in the back; do you have flour?"

"I do!" he answered, his eyes wide in enthusiasm.

"Then I have an idea."

Again, John tried to start the stove, and the burner burst into a small flame. Stefani jumped back, and John immediately tossed baking soda on the element to put out the fire. He leaned on the counter and looked closely at the stove. "No wonder. There's a small leak right here."

Stefani remembered how uncivil she'd been when the stove caught on fire the first time. She'd just assumed John was inept. It never occurred to her the brand-new stove may not have been installed correctly.

"Let's go to my house. The stove works fine there. Until you get that thing fixed, I'd say it's off-limits, but judging by your refrigerator contents, that shouldn't be a problem," Stefani suggested.

"We'll go to your place on one condition. You said you could make a dinner out of those ingredients, and that's all you can use. You've got me intrigued. Considering that's what I usually have around the house, I might be able to learn something useful."

"Deal." She grinned.

Stefani whipped up a simple but elegant meal of Italian gnocchi in rosemary and olive oil, topped with grilled chicken. John moaned with pleasure at each bite. "This is fabulous. How'd a city girl like you learn how to cook like this?"

"I wasn't always a city girl, John. Remember, this used to be an orchard, and my Italian grandparents used gnocchi as a staple. Gnocchi is so cheap to make and it feeds so many, it's the Italian rice. Just equal parts flour and potatoes and a perfect starchy pasta is yours for pennies. Now, of course it's a gourmet delicacy in the Italian trattorias, but we with Italian heritage know better. We also know what it does to our waistlines." She patted her tummy, then reached for the dishes to clear them.

John took the floral patterned dishes from her hands and stood before her. Stefani froze, fearing the magnetism between them. He must have sensed her discomfort because he pulled away. "You never cease to surprise me, Stefani. Thank you for dinner."

Stefani turned from him and looked into the bottom of her stainless steel sink. She needed to just get this over with, to apologize and be done with John for good. "John, I'm sorry I've been so rude." She tried to explain her actions, though she knew that didn't excuse her behavior. "I have always worked with this one goal in mind, that this property would be in my family again. That *I* would be the one to make enough to pay the taxes and take care of the remaining orchard trees. Even if the orchard is long gone and there are just a few trees. I don't expect you to understand, but I'm a very determined person."

"No kidding."

"When it didn't happen according to my plan, I just didn't know what God wanted me to do with this life. I took it out on you and I'm sorry." She looked over her shoulder into his eyes, which seemed to understand.

"Stefani, you are forgiven. Thank you for telling me and thank you for dinner. I'd better be going."

So soon? "You're welcome."

"I'm glad to hear you prayed about the situation," he said calmly. Stefani fidgeted uncomfortably. She hadn't prayed about the house, and she was still seething even if she was able to control her outward emotions. Her face flushed red. "Are you busy tomorrow night?" he asked.

"Saturday night? Uh, no. Did you want me to cook again?"

"Well, I would, but I'd rather treat you to a restaurant. It will give you a break and return the kind favor of this beautiful dinner."

"John, I don't know."

"I just want to take you to dinner and then to see Kayla in the rodeo," he explained. "No strings attached, as you say. Just two friends getting together for a good rodeo."

"You're in the rodeo?" she asked incredulously.

"No, *I'm* not. Kayla, my horse, is; she's performing in the barrel race tomorrow night. The women do the barrel racing; that's what Kayla's been trained for, and she's very good at it. I'd love for you to see what you could do on a horse, eventually."

"I have no idea what barrel racing is, so maybe you should find somebody else. Somebody who would appreciate the rodeo. I wouldn't want to waste the ticket. I'm still a city girl at heart, remember?" she offered as an excuse. She wanted to spare his feelings, because there was no way anything could develop from this relationship. Stefani had watched her mother toil a lifetime for the handsome man she loved. Stefani would never fall for someone who wasn't as driven as she.

"Oh, come on, Stefani, you said you had nothing else to do. And I don't want somebody else to come with me. I want *you*," he said directly.

Stefani forgot to breathe for a moment as she stared into the depth of his green eyes. His statement, although meant to be purely innocuous, was filled with a passion that caused her blood to heat. "What does one *wear* to a rodeo?"

He grinned knowingly at her. "I think you can probably guess that a dream date with me would include jeans and a pair of boots. The French restaurant was a fluke, and it probably won't be repeated too soon. I prefer ordering in English. Meat loaf and potatoes."

"A date? This is a date? I thought you said it was two friends getting together."

"Well, yes, two friends on a date. Unless you have some type of rule against dating your landlord."

"No, I, uh. . .no. Jeans and a pair of boots. Got it." *Oh, how do I get myself into these situations?*

"Thank you for the dinner," he whispered in a low growl, coming toward her with the wall that made up his chest. Stefani tried to react, to steel herself against his obvious intention, but it was of little use; she wanted his kiss desperately. She closed her eyes and prepared for it, but he left a small peck on her cheek and said good night. By the time she realized what had happened and opened her eyes, she was watching his back. The door slammed and she jumped.

~

Stefani spent her Saturday morning shopping for a pair of boots and trying to ignore the high school thrill she felt about her upcoming date. It was just two friends, she kept telling herself. She checked all the department stores and couldn't find a pair of boots. Clearly, it was a fad that had seen its day. She didn't want to stand out as a city girl, so she looked up western wear in the phone book. Shock registered when she found there was such a store in the high-tech Silicon Valley. She clambered into her car and dashed to the store, still questioning the effort for a man who had stolen her heart's desire and life's goal in one fell swoop.

She crinkled her nose at the tacky storefront when she arrived. The walls were lined with barn-type, rough-planked wood, and boots in every color and style imaginable hung from every nook and cranny. "I can't believe I'm doing this." She ran her hand through her hair, tempted to walk back out and forget this ridiculous charade. John liked a woman in boots; it was the least she could do for this one night. After that, she'd let him know she was only interested in a business relationship with him. When he wanted to sell the house, fine. Otherwise, she was strictly his tenant.

A salesman approached her wearing what appeared to be painted-on jeans hugging his too-thin frame. He topped it with an oversized cowboy hat, which might have tipped him over from the sheer weight of it. "May I help you, ma'am?" he asked, tipping his hat. Stefani looked around her, wondering if she was still in California. She felt like she'd just stepped into Texas. Or at least what she thought might be Texas since she'd never been there.

"I'm looking for a pair of boots," she stated, followed by a long sigh.

"Fer ridin', fer dancin', fer what?" he asked.

"Uh, I don't know. Wearing, I guess." She bit her lower lip. "No, wait, for riding," she clarified.

"Right this way, little lady."

The salesman personified all the preconceived ideas she'd formed about cowboys: not too bright, poor dressers, and living in a time no longer present. *This is definitely a mistake.*

"We've got ostrich or alligator boots; does that interest you?" He tipped his hat again. "They are all the rage this year."

"Yes, I saw them lined up all over town," Stefani snapped.

"Beg yer pardon?"

"Nothing." Stefani couldn't help her grimace. "Just regular leather, cow leather," she clarified. "Cow leather would be just fine. Thanks." She forced a smile. The salesman held out an arm and motioned to a chair near the corner. She took her leather loafer off and the salesman helped her from the seat.

"You'll want to stand for your fitting," he informed her.

"Of course." She nodded and stood.

He brought a bevy of boxes down from the wall. Stefani worried this was going to take all day. She checked her watch and sucked in a deep breath. "Don't worry." The salesman smiled, noting her apprehension. "Once we get you started, it won't take long. Now the instep will feel tight at first and that's what you want, because once it's worn in, you won't ever want to take them off. They'll feel like a second skin." His drawl magically disappeared.

Stefani tried on quite a few pairs before deciding on a white and light beige suede combination. She couldn't imagine where she'd ever wear them again, but she nodded at the salesman. "These are fine. I like them," she stated, as much to convince herself as the salesman.

"Would you like to wear them now?" he asked.

"Uh, no, just wrap them, that'll be fine."

She heard the cash register ring and the salesman smiled. "That will be one hundred sixty-three dollars and fifty cents," he said cheerfully.

"One hundred—" she began in disbelief, then snapped her mouth shut.

"These are genuine buckskin, lined—"

She held up a palm. "Spare me the details; that's all Greek to me, anyway." She handed her debit card over with reserve. This was going to be an expensive date. In the parking lot, she hoped that John's rider for Kayla wore the same sized shoe. "I hope someone will get some use out of these things," she muttered to herself as she threw the bag into her car.

Stefani dressed in her jeans and a linen shirt in a cocoa color that complemented her new boots perfectly. She sized herself up in the mirror, turning to get each angle. As much as she hated to admit it, the boots looked good. They emphasized the length of her legs and made her figure look quite pleasing. If she'd only bought a hat to cover up her lack of hair, she'd be set.

Her crisp, ironed shirt was probably missing some fringe or something, but for a first attempt, Stefani thought she might actually blend in at the rodeo. The doorbell rang, and Stefani felt the butterflies in her stomach flutter into her chest.

It had been a long time since she'd had a date. And this was the first one she'd been excited about since. . .she couldn't remember when. She opened the door and nearly swooned at the sight of John. He wore a black shirt and his standard jeans with scuffed black boots. He was rugged and beautiful all at the same time. Stefani felt herself smile shyly, embarrassed he might read her thoughts.

"Stefani, you look absolutely gorgeous." John's eyes rested on her boots.

"I am so honored you'd put a pair of boots on for me. They look like they were made for you."

"At this price, they should have been," Stefani said sarcastically, then bit her lip, praying for God's help in holding her tongue. There was a thin line between being herself and being offensive. Stefani vowed to try to be sweet for one night.

John's gaze lingered on her boots, then came to her eyes. "Well, whatever they cost, they were worth it," he confided, while nodding his head. He held out his hand, and Stefani took it readily. "My lady, your chariot awaits."

Stefani climbed into the SUV and inhaled the rich smell of leather mixed with John's lingering scent of musk cologne. It was a magical combination that sent her head spinning. John stepped in and turned on the ignition, a calming classical CD played, and Stefani looked at John questioningly. *Who is this man?* At first, she'd sized him up as some hick, but there were things about her first assessment that conflicted deeply. First of all, why had he chosen to live in the city? And how did he afford the expensive duplex, car, and horse, but still wear a workingman's clothes to work? And finally, the one that hit her the hardest: Why did it matter what he did for a living? She loved being with him, loved the way he stood up for himself, and loved the way he seemed to take control, even with Stefani's independent personality.

"Stefani, everything okay? You look a little lost."

"Everything's fine. I was just thinking about work. I'm excited about the rodeo. It's my first," she added, as though she needed to relay such information.

"I think you'll like it. It's not for the faint of heart, and I have a feeling that you'll stand up to it." He winked and backed out of the driveway.

Stefani could only take his comment as a compliment. After a quiet dinner in a small coffee shop, they arrived at the large Cow Palace where the event would take place. An air of excitement emanated from the parking lot. Huge pickups filled the lot, and giant searchlights crisscrossed in the night sky, announcing the big event.

John took her hand, and Stefani felt princesslike, as though she belonged in a fairy tale. Clearly, he was handsomer than any cowboy she'd seen, and she felt proud to be on his arm. They entered the Cow Palace, and the air was thick with a dry, brown dust making visibility difficult. The stench from the animals nearly bowled Stefani over, and suddenly, the romance of the magical night dissipated with the overwhelming smell.

She covered her nose with her hand and tried to be as discreet as possible.

"You'll get used to it," John announced, yelling over the loud whoops of the crowd and the booming sound system.

"I don't want to get used to it; this is awful. They need a big spray can of air freshener or something."

John's expression dropped. "Are you saying you don't want to stay?"

"No, no, I don't want to leave." She grasped his hand tighter, and her eyes said she was sorry. She'd bite her tongue if she had to, but she was going to enjoy this night. Calf roping was taking place in the ring, and dust flew as men on horses dashed from a gate and worked together to surround a calf and rope it. Stefani had seen the looped rope on television, but she would have never believed it was real. She found herself yelling in her excitement and watching the timed scores with anticipation. "Go! Get him! Faster!" she shouted, surprising herself. She'd crinkle her eyes shut, peering through one barely opened eye as each calf fell, then she'd holler like a coyote.

John sat up straight in his seat when the barrel riding started. "This is Kayla's event. Justine Hastings is the rider. Oh, Lord, let her do well," he muttered. His excitement was obvious; his green eyes had a sparkle in them she'd never seen. He was like a kid who had just gotten his first bike. "Here comes the first rider!"

After a loud horn, a horse raced into the arena at full speed and headed directly for one of three barrels in the ring. The racer rode a cloverleaf pattern around the barrels, getting so close she actually tottered two of the barrels; but none of them fell over, and John said that was a successful ride. Stefani held her breath until each rider finished, fretting over each barrel. Her hands were in tight fists from the suspense.

When Kayla's turn to ride came, Stefani lost interest in the horse and instead focused on the beautiful blond who rode her. Her hair was long; and unlike the other riders, she didn't have it tightened or clasped. It just fell luxuriously around her shoulders. Stefani watched John's expression, looking for some sign of his attraction for the young, avid horsewoman; but John's eyes never left Kayla. His fists were tightened and he said nothing. On the third barrel, Kayla dropped the barrel, and Stefani felt guilty she wasn't upset at the failure. Justine was disqualified. "I'm sorry, John." Stefani touched his arm, and he clasped her hand in his own.

"Thanks, Stefani. Kayla's young; it's not her time yet. I didn't expect much more than this," John emphasized. "Justine gets too excited still. She's got to learn not to cut it so tightly and stay calm."

"The rider looks pretty upset about dropping the barrels," Stefani commented, hoping he'd give her an indication of who Justine was to him.

"She ought to be. She rode lazy. She knows better. Well, it's her reputation at stake."

"Reputation? She looked like she was going pretty fast; dropping a barrel could happen to anyone."

"You've got to be more than fast in the barrel race. She knows that. It's precision." He looked at her, and she felt his eyes warm her to the core. His expression changed. His intense green eyes and his strong jawline were all that existed. "May I kiss you, Stefani?"

She only nodded her response, and he placed a soft, warm kiss on her lips. Not enough to be offensive in a crowd, just enough to make her realize she was falling in love with this cowboy. It probably wasn't the last time she'd wear those boots.

Chapter 7

John got called to work first thing Sunday morning. The lab readings he'd done on Stefani's company were at an all-time high toxicity level. It was time to make his move. Atlas Semiconductors was going to pay this time. John paced within his kitchen; he felt like such a traitor. What would Stefani say when she knew her company wasn't business as usual? These things took time, but there was no doubt in his mind: The Silicon Valley site of Atlas Semiconductors was going to be shut down—perhaps permanently. How on earth was he going to tell Stefani what he did for a living? It was bad enough he'd taken the house she so desired. Now, her job might be in jeopardy as well. He sighed. Had he known the toxicity was that high, he would have told Stefani right away. But she'd thought he was a country bumpkin, and he enjoyed baiting her for her own pride. Now, the joke was on him.

Stefani knocked on the back door wearing a lovely sapphire blue dress to match her eyes and a smile as wide as could be. Their evening at the rodeo had been a pleasant one, and she had obviously enjoyed it as much as he had. The sparkle in her eyes said it all.

"Good morning, John," she whispered coquettishly, clearly putting her harsh nature behind them. John relished the sight of her childish dimples in full view, knowing she finally trusted him. He cringed, acknowledging he'd let her down again. The house seemed like a nonissue for her now, but what would she do when she found out about her job? "Have you ever seen a more perfect day to worship?"

"Good morning, sunshine. Did you sleep well?"

"I did," she answered dreamily, and John was tempted right then and there to take her in his arms. But he couldn't; he needed to make his intentions clear and his occupation known. "Ready for church?" she asked.

"Actually, I can't go today, Stefani. I got called in to work on an emergency, so it seems I won't make it. But say a prayer for me, okay?" *I'm going to need it.*

Stefani's eyes fell to the floor, and her dimples faded. "Yeah, sure."

"Stefani, this has nothing to do with you. I have to work today. Something very important came up."

"Do you get paid overtime to work on Sunday?" she asked innocently.

"No, it's just something I have to do every now and then."

"Okay, so I'll see you later tonight."

162

"I'm looking forward to it." He closed the door slowly and beat himself up for misleading her. He should have told her he wasn't building some structure over the weekend. Should have told her he was an environmental scientist who had serious business. *Lord, how can I be so deceitful? Leading her to believe I'm some simple cowboy straight from the ranch, instead of the man who may put her out of work...*

He watched her walk despondently to her car and wave good-bye. He smiled and returned the wave and got into his SUV. Once at the lab, John rubbed his throbbing temples over the data before him. Beginning procedures for shutting down a company was tedious work, riddled with facts and lawyer speak. He set about getting all the paperwork ready for the law to take over and came home tired and annoyed.

He cupped his hand over the back of his strained neck and walked to his back door when he heard a small voice call him from outside the garage door. "John?"

He looked outside and saw the redheaded woman from Stefani's church who had flirted with him. She held a brown grocery bag and a ready smile. Her head was downcast, and her big green eyes blinked exaggeratedly. "Are you looking for Stefani?" he asked.

"No, actually, I was looking for you. You didn't come to church today, and I thought maybe you hadn't been properly welcomed into the church. I brought dinner to make," she said confidently. "I'm Rachel. Rachel Cummings, remember?" she added in her light tone. "Stefani's friend?"

"Sure, I remember." *Just what I need.*

"I told Stefani I'd come by tonight. She said you like home-cooked meals, so I thought I might help out. I guess you had to work all day."

John had a pretty good idea Rachel's landing on his doorstep was her own doing, not Stefani's, but he didn't know how to remedy the situation without calling her a liar.

"I have to feed my horse tonight," he offered by way of excuse. He clicked his tongue as though that was it. His answer.

"You have a horse?" she continued.

"A buckskin mare," he answered proudly. "She's a barrel racer, and it's my night to brush her down and make sure the ranch fed her properly. So I really appreciate the offer, but—"

"I'd love to see her," she replied hastily. "I love horses. Is there somewhere I can put this stuff down?" She lifted a perfectly manicured hand from the grocery bag and tossed her long red curls. Although she wore jeans and a simple tailored T-shirt, her makeup was more fitting for a night out at a dance club. Bright red lipstick dotted her light complexion, and her eyelashes were as black as night.

John hesitated before answering, looking to Stefani's front door to see if she might come out and rescue him. "Sure, come on in." He led her to the kitchen, and she began putting the groceries away as though she knew where everything went.

"I hope you like steak and mushrooms," she said happily.

"Rachel, I'm a little pressed for time. I've been working all day, and I've got to get to Kayla, my horse, before sundown."

"We've got plenty of time before the sun goes down. Did you want me to start dinner first or did you want to take me to see Kayla first?"

John couldn't stand pushy women. Independent, self-assured, confident, that was all fine, but pushy was just annoying. And with the mood he was in, he didn't have much patience. "Look, Rachel—"

"Oh, look, there's Stefani." Rachel pointed out the kitchen window to where Stefani stood in the driveway in her running pants, breathing hard.

Stefani checked her watch and turned off her timer, then bent over, resting her hands upon her knees to catch her breath after her nightly run. John watched her do the same thing every evening, and it invigorated him. Her tiny, shapely frame stopped in exactly the same spot every night, so oblivious to everything around her except the familiarity of her routine. She was beautiful, even fresh from an athletic sprint, her short haircut delightfully coiffed in a sweatband. It was messy and darling all at once.

John closed his eyes momentarily when Stefani turned. He watched with agony as Stefani's smile disappeared when she noticed Rachel Cummings in his kitchen. He felt the instant loss of trust that he'd worked so hard for. Why had he allowed this conniving beauty to come between him and the woman he wanted? He didn't deserve the trust anyway, at least not until he told her the truth about his job. This was probably his just desserts.

"I better go say hi; I'll be right back." Rachel bounced outside, and John followed slowly. He splayed his hand against the door frame and tried to show Stefani he was innocent. "Stefani. Oh, Stefani, hi!" Rachel called.

"Hi, Rachel, how are you?"

"I'm fine. You look pretty worn out. Is it really necessary for you to get all sweaty like that to keep skinny? What a shame."

John's teeth clenched. "Stefani's in fantastic shape. The one time I ran with her, I had trouble keeping up," he offered, hoping to quell a rising flame.

"Now, John, I can't believe that," Rachel purred, then directed her attention back to Stefani. "John and I are having dinner. Then he's taking me to see his horse, Kayla."

John's eyes fell shut again. "Rachel stopped by when I got home from work." *Uninvited*, he added silently.

"That's great. Well, you two enjoy yourselves." Stefani walked toward her duplex and gave a quick glance over her shoulder.

"Rachel, will you excuse me?"

"John, I—no, fine, you go ahead, I'll get dinner started."

"You know what? I'm really sorry, but Stefani and I had plans for tonight. So if you don't mind, I'd just as soon we not do dinner tonight."

"But—"

"Look, I don't want to be rude, but I had plans tonight."

"Well, maybe we could reschedule," she offered with honeyed sweetness.

Just then, Stefani's garage door opened, and she backed out in her sporty coupe. She had all the windows rolled down, and her still glistening face was weary from her run. She failed to look at either of them and squealed out of the driveway, offering a wave from her window.

"Well, whatever your plans are, it looks like they're canceled. Now, I won't take no for an answer, John. It's my Christian duty to make sure you're welcomed into our church. I'd do it for anybody."

John walked into the kitchen and grappled with the ingredients Rachel had strewn about in his kitchen. "I'm flattered, really I am," he paused, handing her the grocery bag, "but—"

"I bought these steaks and they shouldn't go to waste. They were expensive. Let me just cook them for you. You can feed your horse alone if it makes you feel better. Far be it from me to intrude."

John finally relented, wondering how he would ever make Stefani believe he didn't invite every beautiful woman to meet Kayla. "Fine. Why don't you hand me the lettuce? I'll make the salad," he offered, worrying idle hands would only make his precarious situation worse. The faster this ended, the better.

Rachel tried in vain to appear like she knew what she was doing in the kitchen. It was obvious she spent very little time at the stove, and she kept smiling that exasperating grin when she thought he might be on to her game. "It's been so long since I grilled a steak," she said after opening the oven door and plumes of smoke came billowing out. Since he'd had it repaired, he knew that the billows of smoke had nothing to do with the stove.

John's eyebrows lifted and he nodded. "Are these mushrooms for the salad?"

"No, I'm going to sauté them. Do you have any olive oil?" she asked.

"I do, just bought it yesterday." John reached up into the cupboard and brought down an enormous bottle of extra virgin olive oil, one that would probably last him a lifetime, if such things kept. "Stefani says you shouldn't be without this stuff."

"And she's right. It's a cook's best friend," Rachel answered knowingly.

Then I imagine you two are casual acquaintances, John thought through his smile. Rachel took the bottle from him and poured half the contents into a frying pan while John snapped his awed mouth shut. After a quick rinse in the sink, she dropped the full-sized mushroom caps into the pan. The poor vegetables floated wildly amid the excess oil. As the contents began to heat and sputter, tiny drops of oil splattered everywhere in the kitchen, and the mushrooms twisted and writhed in their greasy death.

John watched Rachel bite her lip nervously when she added onions and the grease droplets increased. "Ouch!" she yelped. He turned the burner down and looked at her hand, which was red from the fresh hot grease burning her thumb.

"Here, put some ice on that. I'll finish the vegetables." He got out a coffee can from under the sink and poured the excess oil into it. Then he finished with the vegetables, while Rachel sat on a nearby kitchen stool. Despite his efforts, any vitamins or minerals had been drowned out by the olive oil, and it still looked anything but appetizing.

"I'm sorry; I don't know what's come over me," Rachel whined apologetically as she held her thumb under a bag of ice. "Nervous maybe."

John smiled, feeling sorry for Rachel. She was clearly trying to impress him, and although he wasn't the least bit interested, it was no reason to be rude. It was a fine line between encouraging her affections and treating her compassionately.

When dinner was finally on the table, only the oil dripping from the mushrooms moistened the charred steak. "Dear Lord, we thank You for Rachel's special effort on the meal and ask for Your blessing upon it and the hands that prepared it. In Jesus' name. Amen." John took his first bite, while Rachel watched expectantly. He smiled while he chewed, and chewed, and chewed some more.

"How is it?" she asked.

"Well done, just like I like it," he lied, hoping to spare her feelings. Thinking back to Stefani's gourmet meal from potatoes and flour, John couldn't help but compare the terrible meal made with the grocer's finest ingredients. It wasn't the cooking; it was simply the fact that Stefani was so accomplished, so competent in all she set her mind to. No wonder it bothered her so much to lose the house. Everything she had worked for, Stefani had accomplished with the exception of the duplex. His duplex.

Rachel left all the dishes piled on the sink because her thumb hurt too much when she dropped it into the hot water. John didn't care; he was just thankful his politeness could come to an end. "Well, I really appreciate dinner, but as I've said, I've got to get to Kayla, my horse."

"Of course; we had a deal." She stopped in the doorway, expectantly.

"Well, thanks again." Just then Stefani whizzed into the driveway. She glared at them both and drove into her garage, shutting the great door behind her.

"Good night," John said without further delay and jogged to Stefani's doorstep. He rang continuously until she finally answered. "Stefani, before you go getting angry with me, you should know I've never seen Rachel before or since you introduced us at church. Her coming over here was her idea, and I had no idea she'd be here."

"I know." Stefani shrugged. "Come on in." She opened the door wider.

"What do you mean, you know?" John put a fist to his hip and glared.

"She does that for all the new men at church. She wants first dibs on them, I suppose. So you want to come in?" she asked casually.

"Stefani, if you knew all this, why didn't you warn me? Why didn't you stick around and show her we are—"

"Yes, we are what, John?"

He ignored her question. "So if you weren't jealous, where did you go before taking time to shower?" He looked down at her, his eyebrows lowered in expectation.

"I had to rush to the drugstore. I thought you might be needing these." She held up a roll of antacids and turned to run down the hallway, giggling like a child all the way.

"Oh no, you don't. Get back here!" He chased after her and caught her in the dining room doorway. Catching her up in an embrace, the laughter suddenly died, and her natural beauty silenced him. Her blue eyes shone with delight, and her full dimples slowly disappeared, revealing that she was as caught in the moment as he was. Her skin was flawless and her gentle, full lips a natural pink.

"Don't, John. Come on, I need a shower." She pretended to struggle, but she never left his arms, and his grasp inexplicably tightened.

How could he do this? He was falling in love with her, and when she found out he'd taken her house *and* her job away. . . Soon, there would be no sweet dimples, no laughter, and worst of all, no trust in her sparkling blue eyes. *Why didn't I tell her what I do for a living before it was too late?*

"I've got to go feed Kayla," he said abruptly and turned, leaving her and her confused expression alone.

Chapter 8

Stefani finally fell to her knees in prayer. *What is happening to me?* She was falling for John, regardless of what he did for a living. All the preparation and nagging her mother had given her were pointless against how John made her *feel*. Although she'd tried many times, she just couldn't bring herself to ask him what he did for a job. *Am I such a snob that I can't handle the answer?*

She looked to the heavens, praying for an answer. "Dear Lord, John is everything I thought I ever wanted in a man. Sweet-tempered, godly, self-sufficient, but, Lord, I don't want to repeat the sins of my mother. He's too handsome, Lord, he's not a businessman, and he works with his hands. He's everything my grandmother warned me about. I promised my grandmother, Lord. I promised her I wouldn't let a man come before my goal. I'm waiting on the house, Lord, but please, help me see Your plan in this. Help me focus on my goal and not on John Savitch. This house should belong to me, but I *have* to do it alone. It's what I promised my grandmother. Give me the strength, Lord!"

As if things weren't bad enough, Stefani's mother was coming to visit. She groaned aloud at the thought. Stefani hadn't explained she was living on the old family orchard. What would her mother say when she saw the beautiful Mediterranean duplex that had replaced the old clapboard farmhouse? The land Stefani had vowed to own, in the hands of the handsome John Savitch. She cringed. Although her mother didn't know about Stefani's vow to her grandmother, Stefani still felt like a failure, and somehow she knew her mother would point that out. Her mother would arrive with some sort of agenda. Gladys *never* visited her daughter without invoking some type of crisis. Stefani braced for it, whatever it was this time.

The doorbell rang, and Stefani combed her hair nervously with her fingers and instinctively straightened her back. "Mom!" She took her mother into an embrace, and her mother stiffened at the show of affection. She pulled away quickly.

"That church allows you enough money to live in a place like this." Gladys let out a small snort.

"Mother, the church doesn't require any money from me. The Bible asks that I tithe ten percent to Him. Since God has allowed me all this, how could I *not* give a mere ten percent?" Stefani changed the subject. "Do you want to see the house?"

168

"I'm seeing it, ain't I?" Gladys Lencioni set her bags in the foyer with a thunder. "First, you change your name to my parents' name! Lencioni ain't good enough for you, then you buy this monstrosity from the enemy. It's just like you; you always was too good for us."

"Mom, we had to sell the house because the taxes were too high. The man who bought it was very nice; he had nothing to do with our woes."

"You don't remember. You were too young, and you always did look at things through rose-colored glasses instead of how they really were."

"Come see the rest of the house, Mom." Stefani wanted to clarify she was only renting, but what good would that do with her mother's bias so blatant?

"Child, we had a simple life, never had need of any of this fancy housing or a new name! Of course you were right about my spelling, Stefani. Schooling wasn't important on the orchard, but you could have changed that to the right spelling, and I wouldn't have cared."

Sure, she says that now. Gladys's small but robust body wandered into each room, letting out a short, annoyed sigh with each sight. "You always did think you were above your roots. We buy you an education and you leave us high and dry."

"Mother, the name Willems is just easier for me at work. People have an easier time with it. It's not a reflection on you or Dad. Well, what do you think of me living on Nana and Papa Willems's old orchard? Isn't it neat how the family stayed on the land?" Stefani asked enthusiastically. "Like we were pioneers or something and it's our destiny."

"Except they didn't stay on the land. We sold the land, and now look at it with all these fancy new townhouses nobody can afford. Can't make an honest wage anymore. No, you have to build computers and stuff nobody has need of. You grow quality food like apricots, and they throw you off the land."

"Mama, they didn't throw you off the land until it stopped producing fruit and we couldn't pay the taxes." *And it wouldn't have stopped if Dad had worked the land.*

"There were years of fruit left in them trees. Life just got too complicated around here."

"Mama, I made homemade ravioli for dinner." Stefani hoped a well-made dinner might change her mother's attitude, but she remained doubtful. "I invited my landlord for dinner. John Savitch is his name. He's a cowboy, and he owns a beautiful horse that's in the rodeo." She felt like she was talking to a sulking child.

"How does a cowboy make a living here? You're gonna support him, too? Him and that church of yours? Seems like you're going to have to make more and more money. Your father always took care of his family."

Since when? "Mama, John owns this house. He makes a decent living, I promise. And we're just friends, so please don't go asking him about grandchildren, all right?"

Her mother grumbled something under her breath, and Stefani carried her mother's bags upstairs and into the guest room. Once there, she leaned against the door frame and stifled her tears. *How am I ever going to get through these two weeks?*

The doorbell broke into her thoughts, and she silently thanked God for John's availability for dinner. It would take off a little of the pressure of being with her mother alone. Her dad usually came along and helped curtail her mother's nagging, but Dad hadn't been able to come this time. Stefani had to wonder why and prayed it wasn't her mother's dramatic pause before she announced some big news. Gladys rarely came to town, but when she did, it was either to nag Stefani about a husband or announce some distant relative had died. Stefani and Amy had jokingly called her mother the grim reaper since Gladys's appearance usually meant someone's death.

Stefani raced down the steps, and her eyes lit up at the sight of John. His cowboy gear was gone, and he wore his gorgeous navy suit and carried two bouquets of yellow roses. "I can smell that dinner from my place. I probably would have showed up with or without an invitation."

"It's portobello mushroom and sun-dried tomato ravioli." Stefani smiled at him.

Stefani's mother glared from around the kitchen entryway, sizing John up without any thought of decorum or discretion.

"Mrs. Willems?"

"Lencioni. Mrs. Lencioni. Stefani's too good for our name," she answered bitterly.

Stefani gave a nervous grin. "Come on in, John. Dinner will be ready soon. This is my mother, Gladys Lencioni. Mom, this is John Savitch."

"I thought you were a cowboy," Gladys replied suspiciously.

"I am. Would you like to see my registration card with the American Quarter Horse Association?" He grabbed for his wallet, and Stefani bit back her smile.

"I have to stir the sauce." Stefani lifted her eyebrows at John, wishing him luck. John may handle a thousand pounds of horseflesh with ease, but he had yet to meet her mother.

"You didn't add enough basil and you got too much marjoram in it," Gladys barked as she walked past her. "I can smell it. Doesn't smell right."

John cut Gladys off. "Did you teach Stefani to cook, Mrs. Lencioni? She's unrivaled around these parts. She cooks for the church members when they have babies and bakes cakes for the neighbors. She's very popular around here," he said proudly.

"My mama taught me that a way to a man's heart was through his stomach. But never met a man who'd eat this fancy stuff Stefani dishes up. Stefani's papa likes meat in his ravioli, none of this fancy whatever-you-call-it she sticks in there. Beef. What's wrong with simple beef?"

"I like everything Stefani cooks." John threw her a knowing smile, and suddenly, Stefani was sorry she'd involved him in this fiasco. There was no pleasing her mother, and she pitied John for his futile attempts. She whisked the sauce too violently, trying to ignore the conversation around her.

"If you like this, then you ain't never had a proper meat and potatoes meal made for you." Gladys put a hand to her wide hips. "I'll make you *dinner* one night."

John was unswayed. "My mama used to fry us up big, aged steaks on the ranch. One for my dad, my sister, and me. Mmm, mmm, that was living. She'd cover it in onions and fresh-ground pepper; I thought I'd never taste the likes of it again. Then, Stefani made us steaks one night after riding horses, and I couldn't remember what Ma's ever tasted like." He put an arm around Stefani while she chopped cucumbers for the salad. Stefani thought she'd fall into him, his strength was so comforting. Every part of her was tensed and nervous, but his solid arm helped her relax—helped her remember her mother's visit was only temporary.

Gladys harrumphed. She walked past Stefani and added spices to the sauce, physically moving Stefani out of her way. "She still can't make her grandmother's sauce right."

"Mrs. Lencioni, it was good of you to teach Stefani to cook. A lot of women her age have no idea what to do in the kitchen. I can certainly testify to that," he mumbled, and Stefani grinned.

Gladys stopped stirring the sauce and looked at John, first warily, then happily. "Well, thank you, young man. It's nice to be appreciated that way. Has Stefani made her gnocchi for you yet? All the farmers' wives used to try to duplicate our gnocchi, but they could never get the consistency right. I believe Stefani could do that in her sleep. She's a right quick learner when she sets her mind to something."

Stefani was stunned. It was the first nice thing Stefani could ever remember her mother saying about her. "She *has* made her gnocchi and, do you know, I'd never heard of it," John said with a special kind of stupid in his answer. He was playing the village idiot, and her mother was relishing it. *Oh, I love him.* She loved him! The thought startled her, but at the same time, she knew it might be true. She was falling for John Savitch, and she didn't want him to ever move from her life. No matter what her grandmother said.

"Shall we eat?" Stefani asked abruptly, hoping to change her train of thought.

"Of course. Mrs. Lencioni, you sit at the head of the table here." John pulled out her chair and placed the linen napkin across her lap as she sat down. "Stefani's guest of honor should sit in the place of honor."

"Call me Gladys, John. I'm not that old." She smiled broadly at him, and Stefani just shook her head. No wonder she'd fallen for John. If he could work his wiles on Gladys Lencioni, Stefani was powerless against him.

"Gladys, I would love for you to come out tomorrow morning after church and see my horse. Kayla is going to be a champion barrel racer someday. It's the perfect time for you to see her because she is dappling right now." John sat down next to Gladys and looked intently into the older woman's eyes. Stefani felt invisible for a moment, but she knew John was just trying to keep her mother's attention off of her.

"Dappling?" Gladys asked.

"Yes, she's a buckskin mare. She has this wonderful deerlike coat. It's a beautiful golden brown color; you've never seen anything like it. She has black socks and a black mane and tail. In the summer, her coat lightens, and she gets these beautiful blond spots on her golden coat. She's just one of the prettiest horses you've ever seen."

"Church? You go to church, young man?" Gladys asked, her eyes thinning. Not a mention of the fact they'd been discussing horses.

"Uh-huh. I go to Stefani's church. Why do you ask?" John asked nonchalantly.

"And you own this duplex?" she asked rudely, her pudgy hand resting, once again, on her hip.

"I don't understand. What does going to church have to do with my house?" John looked to Stefani questioningly.

"My mother thinks that the church is just after our money. She doesn't believe in God," Stefani stated plainly.

"Oh, Gladys, no. Really?" John asked with the utmost sincerity and melancholy in his voice.

For a moment, Stefani thought her mother actually looked uncomfortable, and she felt the tiniest bit of compassion. Something Stefani thought she had lost long ago.

"God never did anything for my family. We struggled with this land and we had to sell it—if there is a God, He just watched it happen." Gladys looked straight at John, challenging him to give her an answer. Stefani had gotten into this same argument many a time and never arrived at an understanding. Her mother's heart was hardened. Hardened and bitter.

Still, John persisted. "Gladys, God doesn't promise us an easy life. He promises to take care of our needs. You've never wanted for anything." John studied her mother, and Stefani waited with bated breath, hoping her mother wouldn't lash out, her usual reaction.

"No thanks to that God of yours. I'm surprised such a bright young man would believe in God. Did you go to college? You know Stefani went to Stanford, earned her own scholarships and everything."

"Stefani, I didn't know that. How wonderful. Well, you see right there, Gladys, God's done a pretty good job of looking after Stefani since you and Mr. Lencioni left the area. And Stefani's had the finest education available. I think if God was going to dupe someone, it wouldn't be a smart cookie like your daughter."

"Stefani can take care of herself. She always has been like that. Very independent and determined and smart as a whip. The teachers used to rave about her when she was a child."

Stefani sat down slowly, unable to finish serving. She had never heard her mother say something positive about her, and John had gotten her to say almost nothing but since he arrived. Still, it was probably just her way of avoiding the subject of God.

"I know, Stefani is very intelligent." John put his hand on Stefani's, and she tried to still her trembling fingers.

John sensed her nervousness and picked up the serving spoon and began placing portions on each plate. "Salad, Gladys?"

"Please," she answered politely.

"You know Stefani almost bought this house. That's how we met." John filled up their iced tea glasses and sat back down.

"Stefani couldn't afford this house," she declared with a laugh. *That* was the mother she knew.

"Of course she could, Gladys. Stefani has one of the highest paying jobs in Silicon Valley. She's an MIS manager," he said confidently.

"Is that why you're interested in her?" Gladys remarked. Stefani's breath left her. She could take no more.

"Excuse me." Stefani screeched her chair as she got up. She tossed her linen napkin carelessly on the table.

Stefani scrambled up the stairs and quietly shut her bedroom door behind her. She flopped onto her green wrought-iron bed and cried into her floral pillow. *Why did I say yes when Mother asked to visit?* She knew it could only spell trouble. Stefani had only just learned she was in love with John Savitch, and her mother would destroy that, too.

Stefani's love for the rugged cowboy would go unrequited, just like her feelings for all her past boyfriends had. Once Gladys Lencioni showed them what a loser Stefani was underneath her confident business persona, they were gone. Run off by her mother's callous portrayal of Stefani. Fearful that Stefani might turn out like her mother. And now, John would be next. Stefani would not only lose his friendship, but her home as well. She had known better than to get involved with a good-looking cowboy. It was her own fault.

Stefani tried to pull herself together and go back downstairs, but every time she lifted herself from the bed, she just flopped back down again. Broken. *How can I explain my absence to John?* Leaving was the worst course of action. *Why couldn't I just have held it together a little longer?* She didn't want to face John again.

He'd probably made a fast exit anyway. Excuses were common responses to Gladys Lencioni's biting personality.

The longer she waited, the worse the situation seemed. She felt trapped in her own home. A small knock sounded on her door, and Stefani wiped away her tears with the back of her hand. She sucked in a deep breath and prepared to meet her mother.

Opening the door, she saw John, and the tenderness in his green eyes softened her immediately. "Your dinner's getting cold," he said gently.

Stefani dropped her face into her hands. "I can't go back down there, John. She hates me. I'm sorry I left you with her, but I just didn't know what else to do. I'm surprised you're even still here. Usually, people meet my mother and run the other direction."

"Stefani." He took her by the hand and placed her on the settee by the window, where he then sat next to her. "There is nothing your mother could say that would change my feelings for you. I'm falling in love with you, Stefani Willems or Lencioni, whatever your name is."

Stefani closed her eyes and listened to the words ring again and again in her ears. She dropped her head onto John's shoulder and cuddled herself next to his collarbone, where she could hear the steady beat of his heart. It was quick and steady and so very comforting.

"Your mom has agreed to apologize. Why don't you come downstairs and eat that beautiful dessert you made? My mouth has been watering all through dinner. Come on, I'll make the coffee."

"I'm sor—"

"None of that. It's all over. Let's go downstairs and eat that dessert. I promised I'd take your mom to see Kayla while you're in church tomorrow morning."

"John, you didn't have to do that. I can stay home from church tomorrow. You've done more than enough."

"No, I think it will be good for you to get your worship time in while she's here. I invited your mom to church with us, but she's afraid they'll take her wallet, I think." He let out a short laugh and stood, holding out his hand to help her up. "Come on, let's get downstairs before my reputation is ruined. I'm not usually inclined to invite myself into ladies' bedrooms."

"Well, I'm glad to hear that." Stefani stood and John pulled her close.

"But while we do have a little privacy, I might as well take advantage of it." He kissed her while he held her jaw in his hands. His grasp was firm and gentle and his kiss held definite intention. Stefani felt herself shiver, but it was over too soon and he let her go. "Okay. That's enough of that. *This* is not a good idea." He pulled her out of her room by the hand, and they descended the staircase together. "I think there might be kryptonite in there; I suddenly feel weak," he joked.

"Thank you, John."

He smiled, then his voice echoed through the home, "Gladys, slice the tiramisu, the chef has returned."

"Stefani makes the best tiramisu you ever had, John. Learned it from her grandmother, and she makes it the real way, soaked in espresso with genuine mascarpone cheese, none of these cheap imitations they use in the Italian restaurants today. That stuff just tastes like cheap whipped cream." Gladys took John by the arm. "Now you just sit down and take a load off. Tall man like yourself needs a break after a long day."

Stefani knew that was the closest she would come to an apology from her mother, but it was enough. John had put out yet another fire, but Stefani was still mortified that he'd witnessed Gladys's behavior at its finest. Still, the evening would go on, and Stefani had managed to come out of her room without tears. *Blessed heavenly Father, thank You for this man,* she thought as she watched him with her mother. He had her mother laughing and telling stories of the old neighborhood while Stefani watched with both awe and delight.

He was truly gifted with charm and incredible good looks. She sat wondering how it was that he was still single at his age. What dark secret did he harbor that kept the women at bay?

He was falling in love with *her*—plain Stefani Willems. She played his words over and over again in her head after he'd gone home. She touched her bedroom wall, knowing he was just on the other side of it. "John, I think I love you," she whispered to the wall while she ran her fingers lightly down its surface. "And I don't care if you dig ditches for a living. It doesn't matter."

Stefani fell asleep with a smile on her face as she dreamed of the man with those sea green eyes and the rugged physique. Not one thought of her mother crept into her precious dreams.

Chapter 9

He'll never marry you if that's what you're thinking," Stefani's mom quipped as she tackled the kitchen counter with a sponge. "Men like John don't marry; they just play with hearts. You need to find yourself a nice little accountant and settle down. I've been waiting a long time for grandchildren, and if you wait much longer, there won't be any."

The sun shone brightly into the kitchen, canceling out the darkness and doom Stefani's mother seemed to predict. "Mother, I'm thirty-two and I have a good job and a nice house; I'm not thinking about marriage. Can't you just be happy for me?"

"That's what all unmarried women say," Gladys continued. "That, and they're just waiting for the right man to come along. Humph."

"Mom, you didn't marry until you were thirty-four, and in that day, you were considered middle-aged. You've heard the old adage, 'Marry in haste, repent at leisure,' " Stefani shot back, embarrassed by her rising temper.

"I had plenty of opportunities to marry earlier, missy. I know men, my dear. I lived with your father for thirty-five years! And while John Savitch is as charming and handsome as they come, he's not the type that marries. He has too many interests as it is. There's that horse of his, which, while it is beautiful, I have to admit I don't get the infatuation. It's just a big dog that eats him out of house and home. And who knows what he does for a job? A man that charming doesn't work hard for a living, that's for sure. It's probably something illegal."

"Mother! That's enough. John would never do something illegal. He's a good, Christian man." Stefani bit her lip nervously, as was her habit whenever she got defensive. Although she trusted John, she really was starting to wonder about his profession. She knew he made good money, but she was no closer to finding out what he did every day. She thought about asking him, but it seemed to her that if he had wanted to tell her, he would have done so by now. And she had to admit, she hadn't exactly made it easy for him with all her rude "cowboy" comments. *No. I won't let my mother's paranoia get to me. I don't need to second-guess everything just because my mother told me to.*

Her mother continued, trying to goad her into questioning John. "The churchgoing ones are the ones you have to watch out for. Sinners on Saturday night, in the front pew Sunday morning." Gladys shook her head, and Stefani just rolled her eyes.

176

"Mom, what is it you have against the church? You haven't been in one for twenty-five years, so I fail to see how you know all about it."

"Don't you talk to me that way, young lady. I know all about the church." She stopped scrubbing and wagged a stubby finger at Stefani. Gladys began nodding her head continuously while she talked. "This young woman used to live right on the corner over there. Well, her husband used to beat her every day with a stick. And do you know that woman went to church like clockwork every morning? Every morning, she'd cart her two kids up the street so she could listen to some preacher tell her to come back home and be a good, submissive wife. All the church is about is male dominance. Male dominance and money."

"Mother, that is ridiculous."

"You tell that to Fanny Reilly." Gladys pointed again, then threw her sponge into the sink. "That poor woman went to that preacher and told him about her husband. Told him that man of hers drank and hit her with a stick. And do you know what that preacher told her?"

"I can't imagine," Stefani answered, rolling her eyes again.

"He told her to go home and be a good wife, then he'd stop drinking and everything would be okay. 'Divorce is wrong,' he'd say and then let that poor family go back and get beaten again. Don't you tell me I don't know about the church. I know all I want to know."

"Mother, they didn't understand alcoholism back then like they do now. And you can't blame the church for people's sins. People *sin*, Mom. It's a fact of life, and it has been since Eve held out that apple for Adam to bite into."

"I lived a right fine life, young lady. You can't call me a sinner. You mind your manners."

"Mother, everyone's a sinner. If you ever thought evil about someone, you're a sinner. If you ever said the Lord's name in vain, you're a sinner. And you've done that three times since breakfast! If you ever dishonored your parents or Dad's parents, you're a sinner. How can you tell me such baloney?"

"Well, I still say that boy won't marry you," Gladys snapped back. It was her favorite ploy. If she was losing a battle, she just changed the subject.

"Mom, I have everything I want now," Stefani explained. "Do you know I am the highest paid female at my company?"

"Well, I still don't have any grandchildren."

"That's what *you* want, Mom."

"Of course I want that. It's my time in life to spoil a grandbaby. Since you're an only child, that leaves little room for somebody else to make me a grandma."

Stefani couldn't imagine. Gladys Lencioni had never spoiled anything in her life, except maybe a jar of apricots one season. The thought of a poor, helpless baby against her mother infuriated Stefani. If she ever did have a baby, she didn't want it near Gladys Lencioni. She would protect that baby with everything she had. Her baby would never believe that if she didn't grow up to be perfect, she wasn't worthy. Her baby would be loved. Loved like no other. She'd never allow her child into that unhealthy atmosphere without her protection.

What am I thinking? Yes, John had said he may be falling in love with her, but that could have been as a Christian brother trying to help her when she was in need. Stefani didn't know his intentions, and she had learned early in life that relying on others for happiness would only lead to pain. You have to make your own happiness.

"Mother, could we please change the subject? I'm not having any babies. It requires a husband, something you will notice I don't have."

"Fine," she said shortly. "So what are we doing today? I've been milling about this big house all week by myself. I'm ready to get out. You know three of our original apricot trees are still there? They needed a good pruning and a little tender care, but I took care of it today."

"Mom, you shouldn't wear yourself out. John thought you might enjoy a stroll across the Golden Gate Bridge today. Do you think you're up for it?"

"With all the foreigners? I don't think so."

"Mom, John planned a special day for us in San Francisco. It would mean a lot to me if you went without complaining."

"Complain? When do *I* complain?"

"Complain is probably too strong of a word. Mom, let's just try to enjoy ourselves today. We'll have a nice crab lunch on the wharf and act like tourists ourselves, okay?"

"Your uncle Louie used to crack crabs for a living. Wasn't a soul that was faster. *Snap, snap, snap* and the whole crab right there on your plate ready to eat." Gladys snapped her fingers. "Not so much as a shell in sight."

John's SUV roared with anticipation, and Gladys stepped up into the front seat. Stefani had to admit how thankful she was for John's nearly constant companionship during her mother's visit. Without it, she didn't know how long she would have lasted without losing her temper with her mother. But, so far, she had managed to pray through all the little quips and underhanded remarks effectively and hadn't said anything she regretted.

"Is there a reason this truck has to be so far off the ground? Nearly breaks my hip to get into it. You know us older folks don't have the strong bones you young people have. Fragile. That's what they are after a lifetime of living. Fragile. Someday you'll find out."

"Do you need some help getting in? It's a four-wheel drive, Mrs. Lencioni; it has to be high off the ground to get through the snow and the mud."

"It doesn't snow here," she answered flatly.

"I'm from Colorado and it does snow there. Besides, I'll head up to Tahoe as much as possible to ski this winter."

Gladys turned around and faced Stefani in the backseat. "So he's a *skier*, too. You sure seem to have a lot of free time on your hands and a lot of hobbies. My husband never did have time for hobbies, didn't have time to play with a big animal like a horse. When we had a horse, it worked for its dinner, just like we had to."

John sounded defensive for the first time. "Kayla has the potential to earn upwards of hundreds of thousands when she gets strong. She's from excellent lineage, and her days as a champion barrel racer are close. I'll recover my expenses, don't you worry."

"I'm not worried. Fine man like yourself obviously has the ability to make money *somehow*," she said, her voice tinged with insinuation.

"Stefani, where do you want to go first, the wharf or the Golden Gate Bridge?"

"The fog has cleared already; let's go to the bridge. We'll have a nice, brisk walk. Hopefully, we'll get there before all the tour buses."

"Perfect idea," John replied.

John parked in the lot near the famous San Francisco landmark, and the trio became silent as they took in the view. There wasn't a cloud in the sky, a rarity in the city by the bay. The magnificent brick red suspension bridge was a monument to man's accomplishments. Its peaks were well in the air, their brilliant orange highlighted against the clear sky. The sparkling blue ocean glimmered with hope against the backdrop of magnificent mountains. Stefani couldn't imagine a more magnificent view.

"It's breathtaking," Stefani sighed. "Mom, have you ever done this?"

"In all my years on the orchard, I never did this. We just never had time," Gladys remarked. "If there's one thing I always wanted to do in this lifetime, it was walk across that incredible bridge," she said so wistfully that Stefani watched her curiously. It wasn't like her mother to say such dreamy things. Stefani smiled in satisfaction.

"Too bad Dad can't join us. This is going to be a day to remember."

"Well, you know your father. He's probably got three different morning papers spread out all over the living room with a Western playing loud on the TV. He'd view this as foolishness. Just wasted energy."

"I don't know, Mom; he might like it. There's nothing like being a tourist in your hometown. It adds an air of excitement being with all those people seeing it for the first time."

"Well, let's see if I can get across it, and maybe next time your father will join us."

The threesome gathered at the opening of the bridge and were nearly bowled over by the strong winds. The brisk, chilly sea breeze from the Pacific Ocean prompted them all to go back and get their coats. They started again, and Stefani thrilled at the grin her mother wore for the entire span of the bridge. Even when the older woman started to breathe heavily, she never let out a complaint or a gripe.

Tourists were everywhere, snapping pictures and speaking in several languages. Stefani took out her own camera and told her mother and John to pose. They both wore big smiles while they said "cheese," then Stefani traded places, and they each shot her picture with the other. Once they reached the other side, Gladys was weary and her smile was beginning to fade.

"Gladys, why don't you let me run back and get the car," John suggested.

"No, no. I can do it," she answered breathlessly.

"Mom, we know you can do it. John is just probably thinking of your stamina for the whole day. We still want to have lunch on the wharf and maybe a little shopping. We just don't want you to use up all your energy so early in the day."

"Very well, you don't have to twist my arm. I'll sit and wait." They found a bench at the park and sat down. "I'm an old woman; there's no shame in that."

John waved them a farewell and started a slow sprint back across the bridge. Stefani crossed her arms while she enjoyed the view, taking in all the sailboats and huge tankers that filled the busy bay. She couldn't think of a thing to say to her mother, so she just watched the boats and the people walking in the park.

"Stefani?"

"Yeah, Mom?"

"Stefani, there's something I want to tell you."

Oh no. Who died? "What is it, Mom?" Stefani pried her eyes from the tourists and looked at her mother. Her face was haggard and pale, not the robust woman Stefani remembered growing up with. Although Gladys had been here a week, as Stefani looked at her mother under the bright sunlight, she realized it was the first time she had *really* looked at her. Her mom was getting on in years, but Stefani hadn't noticed how old she looked this visit.

"Stefani, I'm really proud of you."

Stefani waited for the other shoe to fall and crush her in the process. "Mom, what brought this on?" Stefani was uncomfortable. This newfound appreciation of Stefani was eerie and frightening. And obviously not what Gladys had to say.

"Stefani, there's no easy way to say this, so I'm just going to blurt it out. I have cancer."

"Mom, no!" Stefani felt herself go white as the blood drained from her face. A sick feeling covered her. Of all the reasons. . . Stefani would have never guessed her mother's health. Gladys simply seemed too mean to ever get sick. Illness seemed to hold no power over her. Stefani checked her attitude, finally comprehending the scope of what she'd been told. For once, her mother's crisis was genuine. "Mom, so are you in chemotherapy? Radiation? What?"

"I'm not doing any of that stuff." Gladys let her hand cut through the air sharply.

"Why, Mom? Did they say it was inoperable?"

"Stefani, those doctors just tear you up with all their poisons and machines. I don't want to go that way. I would just as soon go peacefully. I'm not going to fight it. If death comes, I'm prepared to meet it."

Stefani softened for the first time since her mother's visit. Gladys wouldn't fight because she had no hope. And she had no hope because she didn't have Jesus. Stefani said a silent prayer. "Good, Mom, don't fight it; that's just what the devil would want you to do. He'd want you to give up. Just submit to him and go willingly."

"Stefani Lencioni, don't you talk to me that way. I ain't going to no devil, and none of your religious talk is gonna convince me otherwise. I lived a good life, Miss Willems! I took care of your father like a good wife should, and I always saw that you were raised right. I found the money to pay for your housing so you could go to Stanford. My daughter! You went to Stanford University because your father and me sacrificed. We saved and scrimped so you'd have a better life than we did. So don't go spouting your *going to the devil* garbage at me."

Stefani closed her eyes in prayer right there. Again. What could she possibly tell her mother? Gladys was closed to anything Stefani had to say, and she'd go to her deathbed the martyr she wanted to be. Unless God intervened. *Please, God. I can't think of anything else to pray. Please.*

Stefani knew she needed to love her mother—to free herself of the anger and judgment she clung to and just love her mother. Not just be polite and roll her eyes behind her back, but truly *love* her mother. . .to see her through God's eyes: as a broken child, hurting and victimized by a harsh world.

"Mom, I want you to fight the cancer. Tell me what the doctor told you."

"He said I probably have ovarian cancer, but he can't be sure until he cuts me open. I've been having a lot of stomach problems, not able to keep food down. . . I thought it was indigestion."

Ovarian cancer. It sounded so ominous, so deadly.

"Mom, I'll come stay with you. I want you to have the surgery."

"Why?" Gladys crossed her arms. "There's no guarantees."

Stefani called on God for the next words. "Because I love you, Mom, and I want you to live as long as possible. I want you to know how much God loves you. How much I love you," she choked out.

Gladys said nothing, but she was deep in thought. Stefani took that as a positive sign. When they arrived at Fisherman's Wharf with nary a word, John watched them both suspiciously. He told innocent cowboy stories of his days on the ranch. It was lighthearted and unimportant, but it broke the silence and kept their minds occupied.

Chapter 10

John breathed a sigh of relief. Stefani's mother had finally left. Gladys brought out a side of Stefani that John would not have believed existed. Stefani second-guessed her every decision, bit her nails nervously, and, worst of all, kept her precious dimples hidden completely. If there ever was a smile, it was counterfeit. Nothing was good enough for Gladys Lencioni. After two weeks of watching Stefani suffer, trying to live up to sheer perfection, John was ready to send Gladys home via parcel post.

Something had snapped in Stefani after their day in San Francisco. He didn't know what had caused it, and she wouldn't discuss it. But something had definitely jolted her security. The spunk and fire that made her "Stefani" was gone. He should have been awed by her uncanny self-control, by her ability to bite her tongue, even when Gladys purposely baited her, but he was sobered by her behavior. He wondered where his feisty beloved had disappeared to.

"Well, she's gone," John said from their driveway as he waved good-bye to Gladys.

"But her legacy remains," Stefani said cryptically as she turned to her side of the duplex. "I'll see you on Saturday night. Is that still okay?"

"I wouldn't miss it for the world. I'm honored you asked me."

"Wear your suit, please?"

"Stefani, I won't embarrass you," John said evenly. She smiled. He traced her dimples gently, thrilled for the chance to touch her again. To see her dimples and that smile that lit up his world. . .

"I know you won't. I can't believe I ever thought that you would."

John hadn't told Stefani about his profession. She had been so preoccupied with Gladys, the time never seemed right. Still, guilt prevailed. John had been working away on the legal means to get Atlas Semiconductors shut down. The courts worked slowly, and he wished he could tell Stefani without endangering his building case against Atlas. He tried to remind himself he was acting in her best interest. Any information she had could be held against her in future motions. The more naive she was, the safer her job would be in the future.

The days were shorter now as were their evening rides on Kayla and Nelly. As Stefani's company celebrated its record earnings, John promised to attend the party as her date.

John dressed in a black tuxedo and straightened the bow tie. It was too tight for his neck, and he fiddled with it, trying to loosen it. Staring at his reflection, he paused. *I must be in love. I didn't think any woman could get me into a monkey suit without the occasion of my wedding.* But here he stood, wildly uncomfortable in his tux and dress shoes—all for the occasion of Atlas Semiconductors' success. The irony of attending a prosperity event for one of the Silicon Valley's largest polluters was not lost on the environmental scientist.

He picked up the pale pink roses from his countertop and pulled his car out into the driveway. He rang Stefani's bell, and when she opened the door, his legs felt weak at the sight of her. "Stefani, you are absolutely stunning. These flowers would hardly do you justice." He held up the bouquet and smiled.

Her dimples appeared in full, and her rosy cheeks were luminous against her long, soft pink gown, which had an empire waist and no sleeves. She wore long white gloves and a sapphire pendant that was the exact color and shimmer of her eyes. Her hair had quickly grown out to make her appear more feminine. The bob she now wore was both stylish and businesslike. Now that her natural beauty wasn't hindered by the severe haircut, her dimples looked more at home on her sweet face.

"Thank you; I hope I don't get seasick," Stefani answered the compliment. "You look—let's just say I'm honored you would lose the boots for a night."

John held up a hand. "Enough said. I'm blushing. Shall we?"

Stefani took his outstretched hand, and he handed her the bouquet. He felt like he was reliving his prom as he watched her gently arrange the flowers in a vase of water. Only tonight he didn't have to borrow his mom's car, and his date was far more attractive. They spoke easily as they drove to the port of San Francisco, laughing and thoroughly enjoying one another's company. It was just like getting together with a best friend; they easily fell into step together. John felt like a wolf in sheep's clothing, entering the den of the enemy.

Atlas Semiconductors' grand extravaganza was nothing more than an expensive ploy. A scheme to show the world, and especially the stockholders, all was well. John knew the truth. And by tonight, so would Stefani. He promised himself, work ethics aside, that he couldn't deceive the woman he loved any longer.

Once at the covered dock, they lined up among the revelers in their black ties and evening gowns. An air of excitement emanated from the crowd, and within minutes they were boarding the private luxury liner for an elegant tour of San Francisco Bay. A loud horn sounded, and they were off, cruising the rugged surf of bay waters. The city lights were magical. As they went under the Bay Bridge, the clock tower onshore rang out to them like a beacon in the night. John felt hope. Stefani would understand his dilemma, he reasoned. *She had to.*

"Look at the Golden Gate Bridge tonight. Your mother would love this view," John commented. Stefani bit her lip again. *What's going on with Stefani? She seemed so on edge.*

"Yes, she would, wouldn't she?" Stefani replied sadly. She changed her tone immediately, plunging into a new topic. "*This* is heaven on earth." Stefani cuddled her back into his arms as they leaned on the railing, taking in all the sights. The great triangle-shaped skyscraper was the centerpiece of the city, and the tallest, a nearby building, was lit up like a Christmas tree. "I can breathe the air of Union Square and just see the interior of my favorite stores decorated for the holidays." She giggled.

"Stefani, that's sea air, not shopping air," he chastised.

"Whatever. I bet you can't buy boots like mine in San Francisco, though."

"If you could buy them here, *you'd* find them," John quipped, wrapping his arms around her waist even tighter. "My little shopper."

Suddenly, she turned to face him, childlike delight in her face. "Don't you love the soothing feeling of the boat rocking? I feel like a baby being rocked to sleep with your gentle arms wrapped around me."

"Honestly? No, it makes me a little ill." He turned her back around, and she nestled into his chest.

"Oh, come on, big cowboy like yourself. Former rodeo star—I've seen all your trophies in the living room, and I think riding a bucking bull has to be a little harsh on one's stomach. This is nothing; quit being a baby."

"You don't have time to be sick on a bull; it's over before the fear subsides enough to get sick to your stomach. Then you just have to worry about getting out of the way!" He cuddled her just the slightest bit tighter, thrilled to be with the woman of his dreams. *Alone.* Although he still preferred her in boots along the peninsula ridge, he was happy to share in her corporate world tonight. To see another side of her that she'd kept compartmentalized in her ordered world.

Stefani shrugged. "So I have a guy question. Why do men save their trophies? I mean, a guy could get a trophy in the third grade for a spelling bee, and it still holds a place of honor in his house. Why is that?"

John threw back his head in laughter. "I don't know, Stefani. I don't know."

"But it's true, isn't it? It's some kind of rite of passage we women just don't get. I mean, I got a trophy for figure skating in the sixth grade, but I don't have any idea where it is. But you know where all yours are, I'd be willing to bet. It's true, right?"

"I suppose it is, my dear."

"I saw your rodeo trophies next to the *floral couch*."

"Are you making fun of my sofa again?"

"*Moi?* Never! I'm appalled you would ask such a thing. After all, if you want to keep something that might be mistaken for garbage in your house, that is completely your business. I suppose you'll get married someday and all those trophies will slowly disappear."

"A dire prediction, Miss Willems."

"What's dire? The idea of getting rid of your trophies or getting married?"

"The trophies, of course. I think I'd make a right fine husband." *As soon as you accept my proposal.*

The captain soon announced that dinner would be served shortly, and the partygoers milled about toward the tables. The boat turned at the Golden Gate Bridge and took a tour of the inlet near Tiburon, an expensive tourist area in the north bay, then back to the San Francisco side once again. John and Stefani found their way to the table with their placards and enjoyed an expensive Italian water together.

"We're sitting at the head table?" John crinkled his nose distastefully.

"It's reserved for executives and board members; that's us." Stefani shrugged.

John became decidedly more uncomfortable, hoping he wouldn't be recognized. It wasn't that he had a problem facing these wicked men, who put profit before people, but doing so on Stefani's arm made him feel like an absolute heel. He certainly didn't want Stefani held accountable for his actions. An environmental scientist working for the Environmental Protection Agency was no friend of big business. And certainly no friend to Atlas Semiconductors. If he didn't act soon, he'd be no friend to Stefani, as well.

"I ordered you a steak," Stefani whispered as they sat down.

"Oh." John sounded disappointed.

"I thought you loved steaks. It was either that or salmon, and you just didn't seem like the salmon type to me. Do they have salmon in Colorado?"

"Yes, Stefani, we have salmon. You just forget I've had a Stefani's grilled steak and onions. Certainly, no San Francisco chef could ever duplicate such a feast." He winked at her.

"I don't know, you've had Rachel Cummings's steak, too." She let out a small giggle. John was reminded of the unappetizing charred beef made by the church flirt. "I'm sorry, that was rude." Her dimples soon appeared again, showing she had no real remorse.

"No comment, but I think I'll take one of those antacids if you have one. Suddenly I don't feel so well." The combination of the swaying of the boat and not being able to see the shore from his seated position made John too aware of his motion sickness.

Suddenly, John noticed the security guard that John and Tom had encountered when they collected soil and water samples. John instantly became self-conscious, wondering how he might avoid the man, but at six-foot-two, seated at the head table with the company's beautiful MIS manager, he doubted he could remain unseen for long. Hopefully, enough time had passed, and he wouldn't be recognized.

"Miss Willems, I'm glad you could make it." A stern voice broke into John's fears, and he forced his eyes from the security guard.

"Hello, Mr. Travers," Stefani replied professionally, then she turned to John. He eyed the older man carefully. There was something about the distinguished-looking gentleman John didn't like. Something eerily familiar. . . "Mr. Travers, I'd like you to meet my friend. This is John Savitch."

"Pleasure to meet you, young man. Savitch, that sounds familiar. What do you do with yourself during the day?"

Stefani stared at him expectantly as John remained speechless. He still hadn't told Stefani what he did for a living yet. And now just didn't seem like the time.

"Mr. Travers is the CEO and president of Atlas Semiconductors," Stefani explained, trying to break the uncomfortable silence, as well as let John know that this was her boss. John didn't need the prodding or the explanation; he knew all about Mr. Travers. He could tell by the condescending attitude, the air of eliteness, and the smug smile.

"Is that so, Mr. Travers. CEO?" John answered. *Travers.* The man responsible for a toxicity plume that seeped five hundred feet into the ground. . . The man who knowingly allowed his employees to dump toxic waste with the expressed arrogance he wouldn't get caught—or at least held accountable. What was the most frustrating about the man's name was the fact that it wasn't the first time John had run across it. John had closed down another plant in Colorado that bore Travers's name on the CEO plate. He prayed Travers wouldn't recognize him. Not yet anyway.

"It takes patience and drive to achieve success in this Silicon Valley," Mr. Travers boasted. "If you're going to court our little Stefani here, you're going to have to have some of that drive. She's quite a go-getter. She has what it takes." He winked.

"I invest in rodeo horses," John blurted without lying. Of course he did invest in Kayla, but it was hardly a profitable business. Yet.

"Interesting. Is there much of a market for that type of thing around here?" The CEO lifted his glass, and John's stomach turned at the stench of the strong, golden amber liquid.

"Not really," John said coolly.

The CEO had had enough of John's small talk. *Thank goodness.* Then, Travers's eyes flickered and narrowed. "John Savitch," he said slowly with malice. "John Savitch from Colorado? Stefani Willems, have you lost your mind?"

"Wh–what?" Stefani stuttered.

Travers whispered through gritted teeth. "I'm going upstairs and I'm telling the captain to stop this boat. You and your date, Miss Willems, will exit without incident, or you'll be looking for a new job come Monday. Do you understand?"

"Well, no, I don't," Stefani answered with the sweetest inflection of innocence. John felt like the worst type of heel.

"I knew I'd seen that face before. Stefani, you get this. . .this *gentleman* off my boat immediately, do you understand me?"

She looked at the plank floor. Travers disappeared, and it wasn't long before they felt the boat turn. "Maybe we'd better go up on deck," John suggested.

"What on earth is going on?" Stefani pleaded. "John, how do you and Mr. Travers know one another?"

"Let's just get off the boat. I'll explain it all to you when we're away from all these investors. No sense upsetting Mr. Travers any more than we already have."

"We? I didn't do a thing. It seemed to be *you* who upset him," Stefani remarked quietly.

The boat soon came to a sudden halt, and the couple could hear the roar of the crowd inside as they worried over the dinner cruise suddenly stopping. Mr. Travers saw to their exit personally, his big, burly security guard alongside him. Stefani's blue eyes were wide with fright as they were dropped on a cold, dark, abandoned pier in the middle of the San Francisco night. The Bay Bridge stood looming above them, the noise of the traffic silenced by the howling ocean winds that swept through the Golden Gate, leaving their bitter, moist chill with the lone couple.

John watched Stefani with a sense of wonder. She was so beautiful in her sleek, pale pink gown. Sophisticated and pure, all at the same time. Her blue eyes were awash with confusion, and she fingered the back of her long, elegant neck self-consciously. Her beauty made his knees feel weak. Things were about to change and he dreaded it.

Stefani Willems did not trust people easily. She had trusted him, and before he knew it, that trust had evaporated. Gone like the elegance of the night. They stood on the filthy pier, John in his tuxedo and Stefani in her designer gown with the smell of tar and diesel overwhelming their senses. Suddenly, Stefani reached out, her pink satin wrap draped gracefully over the elbows of the long white gloves hugging her shapely arms. She threw her head back and looked to the stars and turned in a dreamy circle. "This night is incredible!" she yelled to the sky.

"Stefani, I don't know what to say. I should have warned you about going tonight. Travers and I have dealt with each other in the past and—"

"Shhh!" She put her gloved forefinger to her full, soft lips and shook her head. "I don't want to know. I want to be blissfully ignorant. I want to believe that it's no accident we're on this empty pier alone tonight, under the stars without a bunch of business people yakking at me about stock numbers and projections. Without any-one to interrupt our time together. . . Not my mother, not Mr. Travers, not Rachel or anyone else, just you and me. I want to believe that God put us together so we could have a romantic evening away from our house, away from my work, and away from everything that interferes with the way I feel about you."

"Stefani, don't you even want to know why we're here?"

"No, no, I don't. . .I want you to kiss me. I want to finish this night as I imagined it would be. With the man I—with the man I care for."

"Oh, Stefani, I love you, but I have to tell you."

"Shhh!" She came toward him and snuggled into his chest, laying her head on his collarbone. "Tell me you love me again. I don't care about the rest. Not tonight."

"I love you, Stefani."

"John, you are so wonderful. Whoever you are. Whatever you do."

He looked into her eyes, and they sparkled with joy. How could he tell her? How could he ruin her faith in him? And yet he knew he must. If he had any decency at all, he had to tell her why she was being punished for his past.

"I know I made fun of you for being blue-collar when we met. I hope you're not embarrassed to tell me what you do. Because it doesn't matter. . .and anything I said to the contrary was just from a spoiled woman who didn't get her way. I don't care if you dig ditches for a living."

He stepped back toward her. "Actually, Stefani, I do dig ditches for a living. But I do a lot more than that."

"Did you not finish a job for Travers? He's very detail-oriented."

"Uh, no, I finished the job on Travers. That's why he dislikes me so much. I'm an—"

"No!" She pulled away and held up her palms. "Don't tell me. Kiss me."

"Stefani, I—" Before he knew what happened, Stefani's soft lips were on his own. He melted into the kiss, completely forgetting the topic at hand. He pulled her shivering body closer to him and kissed her as he'd never kissed another woman. "I love you, Stefani." Then, he held her shoulders and looked into her eyes. "Your job is in jeopardy."

"Because of you?" she asked quietly.

"Well, because of what I do."

"So what you're trying to tell me is that both my job and my house may soon belong to you?"

"Maybe, but my heart only belongs to you, Stefani. That's all that matters."

"Tomorrow is Sunday. A day of forgiveness and worship. I want to worship God without any malice or misunderstanding in my heart. Do me a favor. Tell me Monday. On Monday you can tell me what it is you do and, hopefully, I'll understand. But I need to pray beforehand. I need to go to God, so if you don't mind, just let me enjoy this night under the stars. I'm dressed like a princess, and I'm in one of the most beautiful cities in the world with a handsome rodeo star; let me drink it all in."

"You're sure?"

"Kiss me, cowboy."

"You got it, princess."

188

Chapter 11

Sunday morning Stefani's reality hit her like a wave from the choppy bay. Her mother was seriously ill, her job was in peril, and it looked like she would never meet her goal of owning the duplex. Nothing seemed to bother her as much as her mother's cancer. Guilt plagued Stefani for the lack of love she'd showed Gladys during the recent visit and well before. Stefani prayed and beseeched the Lord for His hand upon her mother, but to everyone else, including John, she remained silent on the subject. She didn't want anyone to judge her for past sins.

Gladys Lencioni was a hard, bitter woman, and the cancer had done nothing to change that. The only thing that had changed for Stefani's mother was her fighting spirit. And that scared Stefani more than the cancer. Stefani couldn't remember when her mother approached anything without a battle. Now that Gladys finally had a worthy opponent, she had just given up. Guilt raged through Stefani. If only she'd been a better Christian, if only she'd stayed in Sacramento, if only she'd kept her family name, maybe her mother wouldn't be sick. She knew it wasn't the truth, but it plagued her, nonetheless.

Stefani felt wiped out after her prayers and momentarily thought of calling in sick to work. She reasoned her process of combining all the data centers into one central location wouldn't wait, so she scrambled to finish dressing. She trudged to work, hoping to put her problems away and replace them with work's minor inconveniences—knowing that Bob Travers was not going to be happy to see her.

Amy met her at the doorway of her office. "Hi. Bet you never thought you'd see me at work earlier than you."

"I had a rough morning. What brings you in with the chickens?" Stefani asked, flopping her briefcase on her desk.

"I wanted to hear all the details of the big party cruise on Saturday night. Since I, ahem, wasn't invited, I knew you could tell me who danced on the tabletops and who said something out of line to a shareholder." Amy waggled her eyebrows. "You know, the good stuff."

"Amy, you ought to know me better than that. If there was anything to gossip about, I wouldn't have noticed it or repeated it. I had one purpose for that evening: to mingle with some key investors and, oh yeah, a luxurious evening with a gorgeous cowboy." Stefani clicked her tongue. "*That* was icing on the cake."

"Ooh, this sounds good. Much better than who got drunk," Amy said. "Tell me all about it. What did he wear? Was he a good dancer? Did he kiss you? I told you you'd fall for him."

"Let's just say, I think I could get used to being around John Savitch more often. He's a true gentleman." She thought about mentioning getting kicked off the boat in the middle of the cruise, but she figured that news would get around quickly enough without her mentioning it.

"It's the legs," Amy shrugged. "I knew you wouldn't be able to resist them for long. I told you there was something about a cowboy."

"Amy, he's not a piece of meat for consumption, he's a gentleman. . .who just happens to be a former bull-riding champion," she boasted. "Did you ever think you'd see me with someone who once rode bucking bulls for a living? Do you know he actually charmed my mother?"

"That's actually kind of frightening. If your mom didn't chew John up and spit him out, I'd worry if he was real or not."

"Amy, please don't say that." Stefani closed her eyes, painfully recalling all the harsh things she had said about her mother over the years. Of course whenever Gladys came to town, she proved them with a vengeance, but still Stefani was racked with emotion. Amy knew exactly how Stefani felt about her mother. It was no secret; Stefani had miserably failed in the "honoring her mother" department.

"I'm sorry, Stef. But when did you get so sensitive about your mother? I can't recall anything nice coming out of your mouth about her."

"'*Thou shalt honor thy father and thy mother.*' I guess I never took that verse to heart before. My mother is getting on in years, Amy. I guess that makes me a little more aware of trying to look past her ways. She's not a Christian, so why should I expect her to act like one?"

"That's true. I never thought about it like that." Amy looked decidedly uncomfortable. She grappled with Stefani's scarf. "Stefani, don't walk around with this guilt. I've heard your mother say some pretty awful things to you over the years. Tell her the gospel, but don't be filled with shame over it. Simply treat her with the respect she deserves as your mother. Okay?"

Stefani grabbed Amy and pulled her all the way into her private office, where she shut the door behind them. "She has cancer, Amy. Ovarian cancer." Amy gasped. "Her doctor wants her to have a surgery to determine the extent of it, then possibly follow up with chemo. She was having all these stomach problems. She thought maybe she had an ulcer or something, but apparently not." Stefani began to cry for the first time. She loved her mother. Stefani had been so busy battling for her freedom from Gladys that she'd never taken the time to appreciate all her mother had done right.

"When's the operation? I can cover things here for you; you need to go be with her." Amy held her at the shoulders, beseeching her for a commitment.

"She's not having the operation. She says they're not going to piece her apart, and if God's really up there, He can take her whole." Stefani's tears began to flow freely, her shoulders vibrating with sobs. Amy came to her and swept her up in a hug. Stefani just kept crying, using her silk scarf as a handkerchief. "Amy, what do I do? She won't listen to me. She has *never* listened to me."

Amy helped wipe her tears away with a tissue. "This is going to sound kind of rote, but I guess you have to trust God on this one."

"Why can't God let me know what to say or how to act? If I go home and try to take care of her, she'll know something's up. She'll know I think she's going to die because I've never wanted to go back since I left for college. Being in that house with my mother screaming and my dad lounging. . .doing nothing while that ramshackle house falls apart around them. I can't take it, Amy."

"God doesn't want *you* to handle it; He wants to handle it. Stefani, remember when you didn't get the duplex?"

"Of course how could I forget it? You threw me that stupid party, and I had to tell everyone I failed publicly." Stefani laughed through her tears. "Thanks a lot, by the way."

"Hey, what are friends for?" Amy laughed with her. "But do you remember how you thought that it was the end of the world?"

"Yes." Stefani sniffled. "It was."

"Well, life went on, didn't it? And it sounds like you're getting to know your landlord pretty well. I would say God made you a fine trade," Amy encouraged.

"No, Amy, I failed. And worst of all, I failed my grandmother. After I promised her. I don't want to let down my mom, too."

"How can you let down someone who isn't even alive anymore? Stefani, I've never understood your fascination with that land. I can't imagine how any plot of ground could be so important."

"That land belonged to my mom's parents. My grandparents. And before that, it belonged to their parents. Nana and Papa begged Mom not to marry my dad. They told her he was just a lazy slouch, that he'd never amount to anything. But my dad was handsome and the pride of the farmlands. He had an athlete's body and a smile that could light up the neighborhood. My mother couldn't help herself."

"So your mom married the man she loved," Amy said dreamily.

"And look what happened. My dad was never the worker my grandfather was. My dad lost the farm for them, the only home they'd ever known. Just like Grandma predicted. I told my grandmother that I would never let that happen to me. That I would own that land again, by myself, and I wouldn't let any man sidetrack me from success."

"And now that your mother's life is in jeopardy, does any of that matter? Your parents have a fine house in Sacramento. Success is not merely financial. Haven't you learned anything since becoming a Christian?"

"Yes, I've learned let your 'yes' be yes and your 'no' be no. I made my grandmother an oath."

"The Bible says not to make any oaths."

"Well, I did make an oath and I intend to keep it. My mother's illness only means my time is running out. I promised to get that land back. And I'm going to do it *before* anything happens to my mother," Stefani said with conviction.

Amy had a look of horror on her face. "No, Stefani. No one cares about that land but you! It's a stupid goal and your grandmother's dead. God said NO!" she shouted the last word.

"No, God said 'not yet.' I want that land to belong to my mother again. So she'll know God loves her. If she sees God gives us the desires of our heart, maybe she'll believe. I'm going to ask John. Not for the whole house, just my side of it."

"Only God can change your mother's heart. You would hurt your relationship with John to keep a promise to someone who isn't even here to see it?"

"I'm not going to hurt my relationship with John. I'm just going to ask him to sell me the house—at least my half of it. If he loves me like he says he does, he'll do it," Stefani said simply. *It's such a basic, natural plan.*

"Why don't you just marry him if you want the house so badly? That would be a nice perk, and you'd have the whole house and a nice-looking husband, too."

"I can't marry him for it. I promised my grandmother I'd do it on my own. Besides, he hasn't asked me, and I wouldn't say yes for a house. What kind of woman do you take me for?"

"One whose pride and goals have superseded her thought process. John Savitch cares about you, Stefani Willems. Do not destroy what you two have for some inane promise you made your grandmother. You are not responsible for that goal."

"I thought you were trying to make me feel better," Stefani chastised, as she wiped her cheek with the back of her hand.

"I'm trying to show you that your ways don't always work. God's ways do. If you go about this in your own way, you're going to lose John *and* the house."

"Stop preaching at me," Stefani lashed.

A light rapping on the door interrupted their conversation. Amy opened the door a small crack, then opened it wider. John stood in the doorway, then rushed to Stefani when he saw her condition. "Stefani, what's the matter? Did Mr. Travers say something to you?" he asked.

"No, it's nothing like that. What are you doing here?" she asked suspiciously. Stefani was overcome by his appearance. She tried to wipe away any remnants of her tears.

John's voice was low and serious. "We never had that conversation about my job, and I think it's important that you know what I do before it's too late." John crossed his brawny arms in front of his muscular chest. His navy T-shirt, worn tan boots, and faded jeans told her she probably wasn't going to like what he did for a living. *Just like my father,* she thought. *Remember what Nana said; don't let your emotions get the best of you. No matter how good he looks. Remember it. Oh, but how I love him.*

Amy stepped between them. "John, this probably isn't the best time. Stefani has had some really tough news."

"About your job?" John inquired.

"No, nothing like that."

"Stefani's mom has cancer," Amy blurted, and Stefani threw her an angry stare. He'd seen how she treated her mother. She didn't want him to think she was without compassion. If only she'd known earlier during her mother's visit. Looking at his deep green eyes, Stefani felt the butterflies rise in her stomach. No man was capable of making her feel the way that John did. Her grandmother had to know, she had to understand the power of attraction. That's why Nana warned her so vigilantly. But did Nana understand the power of love? Stefani *loved* John. Did that change anything? Or was it just her mother's weakness repeating itself in the next generation?

"Amy, would you excuse us please?" John held out his arm for Amy to leave. Stefani nodded to her friend, and Amy left the office. John shut the door behind her. He sat her in her contoured desk chair behind the great mahogany desk. "How long have you known about your mother?"

Stefani was too weak to lie. "Since that day on the Golden Gate Bridge. She told me when you went to get the car." Stefani wiped her eyes again on her white scarf, which was now covered in black mascara. She tossed it carelessly onto her desk.

"And what's her prognosis?" John asked.

"She doesn't know. But the doctor did say she needed surgery and possibly a chemotherapy follow-up. None of that matters because she won't do any of it. She hates doctors and thinks garlic is the cure for everything," Stefani said bitterly.

"Stefani, we're going to convince her to get treatment."

"We? John, this isn't your problem. I appreciate your concern, but I'll handle it."

"Just like you handled the house?"

Stefani felt stung. A fresh reminder of her failure—that he'd won. *Well, you won the battle, but I plan to win the war.* "Just please leave. I said I can handle this and I can. Just like I can handle my *own* house. I didn't need your rescue then and I don't need it now. This is none of your business."

"You know I didn't mean it like that. This *is* my business. I love you, and I'm not going to let the woman I love go through this trial without being at her side. So clear your weekend; we're going up to Sacramento to talk with your mother," he said flatly. "Why are you being so stubborn? Wasn't it just two nights ago that we ate in a run-down diner with you dressed as the belle of the ball? Did I imagine that?"

She felt hurt momentarily, then regained that stubborn pride and squared her shoulders. "That has nothing to do with this. You're not going to Sacramento with me."

"I am."

"And what if I say no?" Stefani threw her hands to her hips. She'd gotten along fine up until now; she wasn't going to start relying on a man now. Her mother needed her, and Stefani would rise to the occasion, just like she always did. He didn't respond right away, and she pressed him, challenging him. "And— if I say no?"

"Then you'd better find another place to live, Stefani." He opened the door to leave. "I'm not playing games with you, Stefani. Accepting help may not be your strong suit, but it's time you got used to it. Sharing isn't about life on just your terms. Understand?"

She couldn't say any more. She couldn't believe a man who had treated her so gently and kissed her so warmly could possibly be so brash. He clearly wanted to be in control of her, and Stefani would fight him for all she was worth. She'd prove to him that she didn't need him or anybody else.

John looked back at her, but she just turned her eyes away, too angry to let him see how much his threat bothered her. *I'll find a new place to live all right. Right after I get back from Sacramento. Alone. And one day, I will own that duplex.* She'd been sidetracked by John Savitch long enough.

John strode purposely from her office.

Amy walked to the doorway shaking her hand. "Szzzzz. What's got him so hot under the collar?"

"Just when you think you have found a man that's different from all the rest, the *real* man rears his ugly head and tries to take over. They all just want to control you, take over your whole life, so you'll be indebted to them and reliant on them, like some weak little Cinderella. I told you I was better off single, Amy! Why didn't I just leave it at that?" Stefani slammed the door to her office and paced the length of her desk, while she mumbled angrily to herself.

Amy opened the door and peeked in. "Stefani, I may not know John all that well, but he hardly seems the type to want to control you." Amy's face wrinkled in suggestion. "And I hate to remind you, but this isn't the only man you've claimed was trying to control you. All of the others just wanted a commitment from you. Is John any different?"

"Whose side are you on?"

"I'm on your side, Stefani. Which is why I'm telling you that I don't think John is trying to control you. I think he's probably trying to do what's best for you."

"Yes, I know," Stefani said shortly. "That doesn't make him perfect."

"All right, Stef. I'm going to give you the benefit of the doubt. What did he do?"

"He thinks he's going to Sacramento with me to talk to my mom about treatment for her cancer. Can you imagine the mortification on my mother's face if she knew that John knows about her disease?"

Amy stood with her mouth agape, a slow nod forming. "And?"

"What do you mean, 'and'? My mother is sick with cancer, and it's my job to convince her that God cares about her life, that He doesn't want her to perish, especially eternally. Can you give me any reason why John should have any part in that conversation?"

"I can give you three. One, you have absolutely no patience with your mother. John would help keep you calm while you talked to her: a sense of normalcy. Two, John can speak with your father on a level you can't. And three, I think this is too big a battle for you to fight on your own. And I can't go with you because I need to make sure this place doesn't fall apart while you're gone."

"But who does he think he is? I haven't asked for his help. He just wants to barrel over me like one of his horses in the rodeo." Stefani crossed her arms violently.

"You haven't asked for help because you never ask for help. You just take everything you can handle and a little bit more, then you become obsessed with it and lock out all the people who care about you. Well, good for John. You won't ask for help, so he's forcing it. Alleluia! It's about time someone got your number."

"He's not going with me," Stefani maintained.

"Then, I think you're going to have a hard time convincing him to sell you half his house," Amy barked.

Chapter 12

I'm glad you changed your mind about my accompanying you," John said through a smug smile as he drove his SUV down the long, straight rural roadway. *You'd think he was going home.* He had his cowboy hat on, presumably to accompany his standard jeans and thoroughly scuffed boots. Stefani rolled her eyes. *The cowboy has returned.* And so had her animosity toward him.

"I hadn't realized I had changed my mind," Stefani mumbled. "You weren't invited, or need I remind you of that?"

"Just think how boring this ride would be with no one to talk to. Nothing but flatlands for miles around." His free hand moved with expression.

"I like it. It gives me time to think," she spouted, hoping he'd get the hint and just leave her alone.

"What are you thinking about?" he asked after a few minutes, his inflection entirely too happy.

"I'm thinking about my mother, John. She's not an easy woman to sway. Once she gets an opinion, she generally sticks with it."

"Who does *that* sound like?" he muttered under his breath.

"I beg your pardon?"

"I said, 'Who does that sound like?' Stefani. The reason you and your mom don't get along is because you are so much alike."

"I am *nothing* like my mother. How dare you say that?"

"Stefani, I know you think my coming along was a bad idea, but I'm going to tell you why I'm here. First of all, you're nicer to her when I'm around. You and your mother have a very destructive pattern of behavior. She nags, and you generally run out of the room, say something nasty under your breath, or yell. I'd hardly call that behavior honoring, and it certainly won't change your mother's mind. Your mother has lived her entire life with a set of ideals she believes in, and you have not respected that. Now, we know she's wrong; she doesn't believe in God's Word and there's no compromising there. But, Stefani, if you would just work with her, showing her respect for what she wants, she might not be so cantankerous. She might see more grace.

"She's lashing out at you because you won't say what she needs to hear. She wants to know you love her and that you appreciate all she did for you, even if it was done with a poor attitude most of the time. Rising above your humanity is what Christianity is all about. You keep falling into your old patterns because you're not going to God first."

Stefani turned and stared at John. "Is that your version of the five-cent psychologist? My mother knows I love her, John. It's just not something we go around spouting in my house. I've never heard my parents say it."

"I know," he answered sadly. "And that's criminal. I love you, Stefani."

Stefani remained silent, unable to get the words out. She wanted them to come, but they wouldn't; she held them tight in the pit of her stomach. She was too angry, too lost in her own struggle for independence. He wanted to crush her, and she wouldn't let it happen. She held tightly to her grandmother's warning: Never let a man get in the way of what you really want. And she really wanted that house. To fulfill her goal.

They drove up to her parents' small ranchette on an acre of dry flatland. Her father hadn't bothered to landscape or plant any crops, so the house carried an abandoned look to it. Retirement took on an added meaning with her father, and it suited him. By the looks of the worn paint and dead lawn, it seemed to suit him *too* well. "This is it. Home sweet home. Sheesh, it looks like the Addams Family lives here."

They both laughed before John inserted the voice of reason. "Stefani, that's enough. We're here to edify, remember?" John tried painfully to keep a straight face, but he burst into another hearty laugh.

Stefani opened the screen door, and the top hinge fell loose, leaving the door to dangle in an odd, diagonal position. They both erupted into laughter again. Stefani's mother came to the door wearing an old tan floral apron. "What's so funny?" Gladys snapped.

"Mom, the screen door is falling off the hinges. This place looks like something out of an old horror movie."

"Well, tell your father. What he's got to read three newspapers a day for, I'll never know. This house could fall down around him for all he cares. What are you doing here, anyway?"

John intervened. "I've got my tools with me. Why don't I let you get settled, Stefani, and I'll fix the door."

Stefani grabbed his arm. "Don't leave me alone yet," she whispered through gritted teeth.

"You didn't even want me to come, Stefani. Remember?"

"Before you fix the door, come meet my father." Stefani was glad John was so strong: She was going to need him to lean on this weekend. Whether she wanted to admit it or not, she was thankful he'd insisted on coming. The sight of her parents reminded her how difficult the weekend was going to be. She still wouldn't allow John to control her, but she would be happy to lean on him for the weekend.

"Of course I can't wait to meet your father." John's roguish jawline broke into a warm smile, and Stefani took his hand into her shivering one.

"Dad?" she asked, while she picked up pieces of newspaper strewn across the couch and onto the floor. "Dad?" she said a little louder, trying to be heard over the blaring television set. "DAD!" she yelled at the top of her lungs.

Finally, her father looked up slowly. He flicked his glasses down lower on his nose and glared at John's tall frame. Her dad let his eyes roam freely down the length of John, then back up to the steely green eyes Stefani loved so. His gaze came to rest on Stefani. "I thought you didn't like cowboys. How long you been telling me you wouldn't marry somebody that knew how to work the land? He looks like he knows how to work the land."

"Dad, please!" Stefani pleaded with her eyes, beseeching her father to be quiet. "This is my friend." She felt like she was back at her high school sweetheart dance all over again. Her dad embarrassed that poor boy and scared him off for good. Luckily, John was already familiar with her mother, so he couldn't possibly have imagined her father was much different. "This is John Savitch. He's my landlord. John, this is my father, Bert Lencioni."

"Nice to meet you, Mr. Lencioni." John leaned over and reached out a hand. Bert just nodded in response and picked up his newspaper.

"Aw, call me Bert," he mumbled from behind the paper. "No sense in fancy titles around here. Gladys! Gladys!" he yelled until her mom came back into the room. "Get Stefani and her friend something to eat. Look at her." He peered over the newsprint. "Our daughter's so thin a bird could pick her up and fly off with her. And a big guy like John must need some sustenance after a long drive. Get them some food," he barked as he shifted the paper to straighten it.

"I've got a roast in the oven, but it won't be ready for another hour. Come on, I have a meat loaf left over from last night." Gladys started toward the kitchen and turned around when she realized no one was following her. "Get in here! John! Stefani!" she shouted. Stefani couldn't help but laugh. She hadn't told her parents she was coming, and yet, she knew her mother would have enough food to feed an entire house full of guests. No matter how tight the budget was, Stefani's family had always eaten well. For all her faults, Gladys Lencioni took pride in her duties as a wife and mother. Gladys had always thought feeding someone until they were ready to pop was a prime component of mothering.

They followed meekly, with John obviously forcing back his grin. "I love meat loaf, Mrs. Lencioni."

"Stop fawning!" Stefani whispered.

"You've never had my meat loaf. You may think you've had meat loaf, John, but you haven't lived until you try Nana Lencioni's recipe." She sighed deeply. "Nana Lencioni has a nice ring to it, doesn't it, Stefani?"

"Yes, Mother, it does. And I was just thinking about getting a puppy."

Gladys clicked her tongue. "John, what about you, do you want children?"

John shifted uncomfortably in his seat while Stefani grinned like the Cheshire cat. "Uh, I want a wife first," John answered carefully.

"Well, what are you waiting for? You do the asking, so ask!" Gladys stood with her hand on her hip as though John might actually pop the question in her kitchen with her gray eyes boring a hole through him.

Stefani couldn't help it; she burst into a loud laugh. She was beyond being embarrassed by her mother's outlandish comments. "Mother! John's hungry. He's probably saving his proposal until *after* he's been fed." Stefani giggled. "I've heard men never ask women to marry them on an empty stomach."

Gladys took a couple of slices of meat loaf, placed them over two big lumps of mashed potatoes, and smothered them in a rich jelled gravy. When it came out of the microwave, the entire house smelled heavenly. She placed the plate and a tall glass of milk in front of John like he was a child. She stood and waited, hand on her hip, for him to taste the meal. He bowed his head to pray, and she tapped her foot impatiently, anxious for her forthcoming compliment.

He shoved a mouthful in and stopped chewing as he savored the flavors. Stefani laughed at the sight of him, relishing the meal with all his expressions. One thing was for sure: She'd come by her culinary talents honestly. Gladys Lencioni could cook.

"I have never tasted anything like this. Stefani, do you have this recipe?"

Gladys intervened. "Of course she does. It's her grandmother's specialty. You can feed an entire house for pennies on that meal. And it sticks to the ribs, too. None of this waking up hungry with this meat loaf." Gladys remained at his side, watching him chew.

"John, do you know how much fat that meal has in it?" Stefani asked. "Of course it tastes good."

"Do you think after tasting this I care?" He winked, and Stefani felt her heart react to the stunning sea green eyes gazing at her. Just when she started to think of John Savitch as her best friend, he looked at her that way. A way she couldn't exactly describe but felt to her core.

Stefani forced the thoughts of a romantic relationship out of her mind. "Mom, these meals aren't good for you. You need to start eating more fruits and vegetables and sticking to a low-fat diet. I could easily help you pare this down in the calories department, and it would still taste good."

"Shhh!" She held up her finger to Stefani and bowed down over her. "Your father doesn't know about the cancer, and I don't want him worrying over such things, so you keep your low-fat recipes to yourself. A man works his entire life, he deserves to have a decent meal on the table at night. Low-fat, my eye."

"Mom, what do you mean Dad doesn't know? How can you keep something like this from him?"

"Your father will only worry. No sense in worrying him over nothing." Gladys went about folding her dish towels into neater rectangles than they already were, nervously looking for something to keep her hands busy.

"Mom, ovarian cancer is not *nothing*. You need to get treatment as soon as possible, and you need to tell Dad! If you don't, I will."

"Is that what you came up here for? To pester me? And I don't appreciate you saying that word in front of our guest. Stefani Mary Lucia Lencioni, you will not tell your father anything. The man's got enough on his mind." Gladys pointed her index finger in her daughter's face. "The chicken coop is falling apart, the screen door is off its hinges, and the oven door needs to be fixed."

"Mom, the chicken coop is not comparable to your health. And if you don't get help, you could die. Mom, you're not ready to die; you haven't made peace with God and you haven't admitted you're a sinner. And if you think I'm just going to drop this because it makes you uncomfortable, you've got another thing coming! You finally have something to fight, so fight it!"

"Shhh, your father will hear you."

"Mom, I could let off dynamite in here and he wouldn't hear me. He's got the horse races on."

"Stefani!" Gladys sat down and broke into a whisper. "Everybody's got to die of something."

Stefani felt John squeeze her hand under the table. Instantly, she was calmer. "Mom," she said gently, "who is going to take care of Dad if you go? Who's going to cook for him, clean this place? Iron his T-shirts? You can't freeze his meals for the rest of his days."

The fight left Gladys. Clearly, it was something she hadn't thought about before.

"I'm going to fix the door while you ladies talk." John excused himself.

"Mom, Dad doesn't know how to boil water. What do you think would happen to him without you?" Stefani pleaded. Gladys's eyes filled with tears. "I'll tell him if you want me to, Mom. But you've got to fight. For Daddy."

"I don't want to lose this fight," Gladys admitted.

"Then we need to pray, Mom. Because with Jesus in your life, you won't lose. You'll only gain eternal life. But God may have healing in your future; we have to focus on that."

"Does everything have to come back to your religion?"

"I'm sorry, Mom, but for me, it does. Please fight this. For Daddy."

With closed eyes, Gladys nodded affirmatively. "I'll tell him after you leave, and I'll call the doctor on Monday."

After she helped her mother clean up the kitchen, Stefani grabbed a sweater and headed for the front porch. A dingy, lime green lawn chair stood outside the front door just where it had once been at the old clapboard house. The chair was made of heavy-duty rubber cording, but it had weathered many years outdoors, and it soothed her to rest in it. She viewed the vast farmlands that surrounded her parents' tiny plot of land. The cornstalks swayed calmly in the breeze, and John sat beside her.

"You all right?" John's low voice murmured. His soothing voice was like a cleansing to her heart; she needed his strength and his calmness. She grasped his hand like a lifeboat in a stormy sea.

"Mom's agreed to get the surgery. She'll tell Dad tomorrow."

"It's in God's hands, Stefani. We just need to pray."

"I think I should take a leave of absence from work. Come up here and take care of things for a while. If she wasn't cooking these five-course meals every night, it might make things easier on her."

"Stefani, she lives to make those meals for your father. You can't take her life away; you've got to allow her the freedom to go on as she sees fit. She'll need your help when she's home from the hospital."

"My family. No Ozzie and Harriet here, I'm afraid."

He held her hand, his green eyes wrinkled in a smile. "I'm going to get my tools and fix up the other things around here that need a little attention. Why don't you go spend time with your parents, and I'll stay out of the way for a while? I'm enjoying playing handyman. Everything at our house is so new, I feel useless there."

"I'll be sure Mom keeps her plastic milk jugs out of your sight, or you'll be growing them a new garden." Stefani laughed.

"Very funny."

"Thanks for being here, John. I really do appreciate it." It took all the humility she could muster. She wouldn't say she loved him, but she could certainly say she appreciated him.

"I'm happy for any excuse to be with the woman I love."

She kicked the dust on the porch with her foot, focusing on the dirt. "I'm still going to talk to Daddy. I think I'm going to tell him about Mom's condition. I'm worried my mother won't do it."

"Stefani, you promised—"

"I never promised, I implied. And I don't think she'll do it without a little prodding. She may have the best intentions, but her follow-through isn't that great. See ya." Stefani planted a friendly kiss on John's cheek and walked back into the house.

Stefani approached her father, and her mother came into the room, wiping her hands on a towel. "Stefani, what are you doing?"

"I'm sorry, Mom, but I have to do this. It's for your own good. Do you want to tell him first?"

"I don't believe you'll do it," Gladys challenged.

"Then you don't know me as well as you think you do, Mom. Dad, Mom has something she needs to tell you." Stefani looked to her mother, and if looks could kill, Stefani would be six feet under.

"Bert, I have cancer. Ovarian cancer," she said flatly and headed back into the kitchen. "I've got to get the roast."

Stefani's dad looked up, bewildered. He looked at Stefani for clarification, to see if he'd heard right. "She has what?" he asked.

"She has ovarian cancer, Dad. The doctors want to do exploratory surgery and follow up with chemo."

"Gladys? Get in here," Bert called, and Gladys returned from the kitchen, still glaring angrily at Stefani.

"Stefani says you need to get some medical help. That true?" he asked sternly.
"Yes."

"Then you're getting it. Whatever the doctor says."

"Bert, I was going to tell you. I just didn't want to be cut up—"

"And I don't want a dead wife," he interrupted. "When can we schedule this for?" Bert had placed his newspaper down on the brown shaggy carpet. It was the first time Stefani remembered him ever holding a conversation without the paper in front of him. "Is that why you're here, Stefani?"

"Yes, Dad."

"Good for you, honey. You did the right thing."

"Mom, I did a lot of research on the subject, and I brought some stuff I thought you'd find helpful." Stefani took the pamphlets and articles out of her briefcase and felt the overwhelming need to run. She didn't want to stay any longer. Her mother and father had serious matters to discuss, and Stefani felt very out of place. "I'm going to go."

They made no attempts to talk her out of leaving. Her father simply rose and kissed her forehead. "Thank you, honey. You're a good girl."

Stefani took in a deep breath and grabbed her briefcase. John had fixed the screen door by the time she got to it. "I think we can go now."

"I wanted to fix the chicken coop."

"My parents want to talk. It's awkward in there for me."

"Fine, let me fix it quick and we'll go home. We'll stop and have a nice, leisurely dinner on the way home."

"That'd be nice. John?"

"Yes?"

"Thank you."

202

"You're welcome, Stefani. I'd do it for all the women I love," he said as he winked.

"John, if I asked you another favor, would you do it for me?"

"Of course, Stefani."

"There's no polite way to say this, so I'm just going to blurt it out. Will you sell me the duplex? Not the whole thing, just half of it. My half." Stefani cringed. Was she relying on a man by asking for this favor? Or would this count for doing it herself? She prayed so. She prayed her grandmother would approve. The important thing was that her mother lived to see it. She would own the land her fun-loving father had let slip through his hands.

John studied her for a moment, carefully contemplating the question. "Yes, Stefani. In six months, if you still want to buy it, I'll sell it to you."

"Six months? John, if you're willing to sell it to me, why wait six months? I can pay cash for my half. I've been saving for years."

"You ought to know me well enough to know that I don't care much about money. I have my reasons. Six months and that's my final offer."

"Done," she relented.

203

Chapter 13

Stefani? Mr. Travers wants to see you in his office," Amy announced first thing that Monday morning.

"Now? I've got a million things to do. Is there any way you could reschedule it?"

"He sounds really angry, Stefani. You may want to hustle in there. I think it has something to do with you getting kicked off his yacht that night."

She sighed. *Of all the timing.* "Okay. Will you call Sacramento and see if they got the last mainframe computer up and running? I'm sure Mr. Travers will want a report later today." Gladys's illness had kept their thoughts well occupied, and Stefani remembered that she and John had never discussed their cruise again. She had a feeling she was going to wish they had. John's prediction that her job was in jeopardy replayed in her mind.

"Sure thing." Amy saluted as Stefani walked past her.

Mr. Travers's luxury office suite was at the top of the five-story building. It took a special elevator code to get the door to open on the suite level. She pressed her number in quickly. Her day planner and a pen with the company logo was all she'd had time to grab from her desk. She hoped he wouldn't quiz her on specific numbers regarding the data center move. With all that occupied her mind, she wasn't prepared for an impromptu report.

Once the doors to the penthouse office opened, Stefani faced a tropical aquarium that served as a barrier wall. Brightly colored yellow and blue fish swam in a luxury-wrapped environment that most *people* only dreamed of. The marble floors led around the aquatic wall and Stefani faced Mr. Travers's secretary, sitting at her threatening black lacquer desk. The older woman held up a finger and finished a phone conversation. Several coworkers sat in the black leather chairs to her left waiting for Mr. Travers's time. No one dared speak. The austerity of the office didn't allow for it. Every sound reverberated off the cold marble flooring.

The phone buzzed, and Mr. Travers's secretary spoke quietly into the receiver, then looked at Stefani. "Miss Willems, you may go in now."

Stefani prayed she was prepared for whatever lay in store for her. *Why didn't I press John to tell me more?* Mr. Travers stood as she entered his office, his hands extended toward her. His entire suite was surrounded in windows with a glorious view of the valley. "Sit down, Stefani. I'm just finishing up a call on the speakerphone. Yes, Jim, go ahead."

The voice boomed out of the phone. "So, as far as I see it, the stays have all been tapped out. They've been on this a lot longer than we have, Bob. This guy's not one to mess with."

"I don't want to hear that. Forget the excuses and keep on it." He pressed a button, then turned his attention to her. "We're not closed yet," he mumbled. "Stefani, you've been with us quite awhile now." He sat back on the edge of his desk and crossed his arms. He was a handsome man for his age, which she guessed to be near sixty. He was still well built and obviously stayed in shape.

"Yes, sir, I've been with Atlas since college. Ten years now."

"Ten years of good, solid service." He stood and walked back behind his desk. "Which is why I'm prepared to give you such a healthy severance package before you leave." He sat in the burgundy leather chair behind his great black desk.

"Severance package, sir?"

"It seems the Environmental Protection Agency is dogging us again. We're probably shutting down our Silicon Valley site," he said with a shrug. Simply. As though the office was closing early for a holiday. "I'm sure you could tell me a thing or two about the shutdown." His eyes narrowed as though he was waiting for her to relay some kind of information.

"But what about Sacramento, sir? I haven't gotten all the data systems in place there yet. The valley site is pertinent to this business." Stefani sat up on the edge of her seat. She had given her heart and soul to this job. Not to mention that she wasn't fully vested in the last stock options she'd received. Did he honestly expect her to just accept such a statement? "Mr. Travers, you can't fire me. I'm in the process of transferring the data centers to Sacramento," she reminded him. "There isn't anyone else who can finish the process without extensive training."

"Stefani, I'm not firing you."

"Phew." She leaned back again.

"I'm laying you off. There's a big difference. You'll get a severance package and a nice letter of recommendation. If I had wanted to fire you, you'd be gone already."

"Mr. Travers, you can't do this."

"Stefani, I have no choice. If I have to pay the fines the EPA might level against me, I'll be lucky to get out with the shirt on my back. You're one of the highest paid executives on your level. I'm sorry, Stefani, but Ken Donitch can do your job for half the price. And he's willing to go to Sacramento. Are you?"

Stefani thought about living near her parents permanently, and the mere idea sent a shiver through her. "I don't think so. But neither do I think Ken can do the job."

"Well, Stefani, he'll just have to. I don't know what I'm paying these lobbyists in Washington for, but obviously they're not going to see another dime from me until they call off the EPA dogs." He cursed under his breath, and Stefani turned away.

"Mr. Travers, I don't understand what the EPA has to do with *my* job. I work in the data center. Nothing I do is even remotely associated with the environment."

"Choices, Stefani. Everyone makes choices in life. Usually, women lead with their heart, which is why men rule the business world."

"Wh–what?" Stefani stammered.

He shoved a stack of papers in front of her. "These are the benefits packages for you to offer your staff."

"My staff?"

"You need to let them go before you leave."

"You want me to fire everyone before I leave?" Stefani was incredulous. If the company was in this kind of trouble, she failed to see how they could offer such generous packages at all. Clearly, something was fishy, and it wasn't the lobby aquarium.

"It's all in the contract. The layoffs are part of your severance contract." He shoved another stack of papers in front of her. "A year's salary, plus your latest bonus if you complete your duties here to our satisfaction."

"And my stock options?"

"Fully vested. It's all yours." Stefani watched him in awe. She had always admired Mr. Travers as a self-made man, but there wasn't an ounce of remorse in his eyes. They were dead. Lifeless. Hammered by years of living for greed. No mercy for his employees, only thoughts of himself. Then again, something wasn't quite right; she saw it in his pulsating forehead. She scanned the contract he'd thrust before her. Her eyes rested on the small print. "Said employee waives all rights. . .legal proceedings. . .and any and all future claims shall be settled in binding arbitration with the arbitrator of Atlas's choice."

Bob Travers had never given her anything she hadn't worked heart and soul for. To fully vest her stock options and give her that amount of money could only mean one thing. It wasn't going to be worth anything very soon.

"Mr. Travers, what's this clause about arbitration and lawsuits?"

"Standard legalese. It's to protect ourselves from frivolous lawsuits. You know how greedy people can be."

"Yes, I do," she answered with obvious intention.

"Every company must do it or there wouldn't be a company to protect." He handed her a pen, and she met his eyes. Mr. Travers looked nervous. *Too nervous,* she thought. She didn't break eye contact and noted that for the first time in her career, he broke away from her gaze. Something was corrupt, and Stefani was not going to play a part in it.

"I'm sorry, Mr. Travers, but I can't sign this."

"A year's salary, Stefani. You can't afford to walk away from that. You don't have a job, remember?" He let out a laugh, certain she wouldn't turn down the money, but Stefani could see the beads of sweat forming on his brow. "Am I making myself understood? You're unemployed in two weeks."

"I won't fire my staff, Mr. Travers."

"Lay them off, Stefani. Lay them off. There's no guilt in a layoff; it's beyond your control."

"If you want it done, you'll have to do it yourself. I won't do it. I quit."

"Miss Willems, you have spent your entire career with Atlas Semiconductors. You need my letter of recommendation."

"That is blackmail, Mr. Travers, and if I sign that paper, I basically sign away my rights. No deal." Stefani stood to leave, and Mr. Travers's demeanor softened.

"Miss Willems. This doesn't need to get ugly. I am offering you a more than fair settlement. You'll need a job, and I need you to let this staff go. You're the only one who knows their individual time with the company and how much they're entitled to with the layoff."

"Something isn't right here. I can't put my finger on it, but it doesn't feel right."

The hardened businessman erupted. The truth. Stefani knew she was about to hear it. "This man you brought on my yacht, Stefani." He opened a manila folder on his desk and held up a fuzzy picture of John. John in the soil with a glass vial.

"Yes," she admitted. "He was my date. He's also my landlord," she answered with a shrug. "I fail to see what my personal life has to do with this."

"Stefani, every one of our shareholders saw you with this man on my boat. This man is a renowned environmental scientist for the EPA. The man is trying to shut this company down. You brought a spy into our midst. You allowed him to collect data and probably shared inside information with him. If you don't sign this agreement, I am free to personally sue you for endangering this company's future profits. And I can't think of a shareholder who wouldn't back me up."

"John is a—" Stefani couldn't finish the sentence. The man she loved, the man who held her house in his hands. The man who said he'd sell it to her in six months. *Six months.* The truth hit her painfully. John *knew* she was losing her job. He knew she wouldn't be able to buy the house. Stefani rose. "You'll have to excuse me, Mr. Travers."

"Stefani, you've got three days to sign this agreement, or you'll be hearing from my lawyers."

Stefani scrambled for the door, leaving the paperwork where it lay. She had to get to John. She had to find out his version of the truth. There had to be a misunderstanding. John wasn't an environmental scientist, he was a. . .what? She didn't know. She was in love with a man whose occupation was a mystery to her.

How had this happened? How could I have been so trusting, so stupid? Her grandmother warned her about men throughout her entire childhood.

"Leave your keys with my secretary," Travers called after her.

Stefani took the elevator to her floor and found Amy. Stefani grabbed her secretary by the arms. "Amy, Amy! What was John doing that day you saw him here? Tell me again."

"He was fiddling in the dirt." Amy shrugged.

"Amy, did he have anything with him? Tools? Wood? Anything?"

"I didn't see anything, Stefani."

Just then two burly security guards got off the elevator. "I'm sorry, Miss Willems, we've been asked to escort you off the property," one of them said.

"But I need to get my things from the office."

"You may take only your handbag and personal keys. Your personal items including your briefcase will be returned to you shortly along with your last paycheck unless you reconsider Mr. Travers's offer."

Stefani was breathless, but she allowed the men to take her arm. They escorted her to her desk and searched her purse before handing it to her. Then one of them removed Atlas's keys from her key ring. Amy stood, dumbfounded but calm, as they pulled Stefani back into the elevator.

Amy gave her a thumbs-up sign, and Stefani watched as the elevator doors closed between them.

~

John sat at his kitchen table, analyzing lab data on the samples he'd taken the day before. He looked out the kitchen window and saw Stefani drive into the driveway at half past two. *This is it.* The moment he'd been dreading. And the moment he'd deserved for keeping his occupation a secret. He tossed his lab reports aside and dashed over to her house, hoping she was just coming home for a jog. John had told her that jogging alongside work wasn't a good idea. She had heeded his warnings. Of course John's reasons were environmental, but Stefani had thought they were regarding strangers. Regardless, she had listened and he hadn't pressed it.

Her top button was undone, and her shirt untucked from her tailored skirt. "Stefani, your job?"

"You know very well it's my job, John Savitch. How dare you take me to my office party when you knew. . .how dare you use me! All that help for my parents, fixing their chicken coop, charming my mother, it was all a lie!" Her lips began to tremble, and soon a single tear fell from her eye. "Did you think I'd thank you for saving me from buying this house? Because you knew I was about to lose my job?"

"I thought I was protecting you from toxic chemicals." It was a stretch trying to make half of the truth seem to be enough. He prayed for strength to set the record straight. "No, Stefani, that's not all of it. I wanted you to fall in love with *me*—as a cowboy, not an environmental scientist. You seemed so convinced you couldn't fall for a workingman. I wanted to show you I was worthy of you as a cowboy. Then, I just got farther and farther into my research, and then I realized it was too dangerous to tell you. I didn't want you held responsible, and I couldn't risk having you confront Travers before my report was finished. It was a mixture of consideration, professional responsibility, and cowardliness."

"With an emphasis on cowardliness. How dare you make that choice for me!"

"Did I make that choice? You seemed to be pretty content being in the dark about my occupation. You never insisted on knowing what I did; in fact, you didn't want to know. You didn't want to admit you were going out with a working-class man, so you never asked!"

Her expression acknowledged the truth in his statement.

"You're not going to blame this on me, John Savitch. My grandmother warned me never to get involved with a handsome man. I did just what she said I would; I justified your behavior because I wanted you. And now, my chances of meeting my goal are null and void. I have no job, no home. . . nothing all because of you."

"You have a home. You'll always have a home. That house is yours. With rent or without, Stefani."

"You must be kidding. Do you think I'd take anything from you after what you did? You wormed your way into my heart, playing this remarkable Christian man, and all the while you lied to my face."

"Stefani, I may not have acted Christlike, I admit that. But don't question my faith or my love toward you. I sinned, yes. But I did it to protect you. Knowing about a toxic plume has huge consequences for employees. People have been killed for it! Didn't you see that movie *Silkwood*?"

"Such drama! I suppose this is where I rush into your arms and praise you for rescuing me—fall at your feet and sob?"

"Oh, Stefani, no. This is where I beg you for your forgiveness for acting like such a pompous heel and for thinking I knew what was best when I wasn't acting in God's will. The fact is, neither of us have been acting in God's will or we wouldn't be in this mess."

"I have my mother to think about. I can't be worrying about this. . .this nonsense. Consider this my thirty-day notice." Stefani turned on her heel and headed for the house.

"Stefani, please talk to me. We need to talk about this."

"I have nothing more to say to you. You need to concentrate on finding a new renter."

"I love you, Stefani. I know that probably doesn't mean much at this juncture. But I do love you."

"You cowboys have an odd way of showing it."

Chapter 14

After a restless night, Stefani slept in Tuesday morning. It was so refreshing to sleep until the sun became so bright that it nudged her gently from her state. She opened her Bible and prayed for God's guidance in finding a new job. She actually felt excited at the possibility of a new challenge. She'd been at Atlas her entire career; surely there had to be more to life than this one company. More to life than work that bled you dry and fired you.

But just when she started to feel joy, the memory of John crushed any hope for her future. He was a stranger. A man she never knew. Tears flowed again, and the oddest thing happened. Stefani wanted to see John. She wanted to cry on his shoulder and share her pain with the man she loved. *Why? Why didn't I heed my grandmother's advice?* It was too late now. She loved the man.

She rolled out of bed and made herself a cup of strong coffee. She breathed the rich scent deeply and ran out to the driveway to get her newspaper. The sooner she got to the want ads and started distributing her résumé to headhunters and former colleagues, the better. She would devote herself to her job hunt and her mother. She wouldn't have time to think about him. John's newspaper was still in the driveway, as well, and Stefani sprinted back inside before she would chance seeing him.

She sat at the kitchen table with her coffee and unfolded the paper in shock. There on the front page was John's picture. She read the photo caption: "John Savitch, Leading EPA Scientist, Does It Again." The headline above it, in big black letters: ATLAS SEMICONDUCTORS SHUT DOWN; EPA CALLS IT A POISON MILL. And in smaller letters: WORKERS TURNED AWAY.

Stefani's breath left her, and she read the headline again and again, then lowered her eyes to the story:

> *John Savitch, a leading environmental scientist for the Environmental Protection Agency, has won a first for the people of Silicon Valley after a string of successful closings in his home state of Colorado. After following up a lead from unnamed sources, Savitch and his partner, Tom Owens, discovered a toxic plume six thousand feet wide and five hundred feet deep under the manufacturing plant of Atlas Semiconductors. Savitch is quoted as saying, "Travers actually told his employees he was going to put a workout fitness station on top of the very spot that recorded some of our highest readings."*

Stefani tossed her newspaper down. *How could he?* He had actually quoted her verbatim and never even told her what he did for a living. He had worked his way into her heart, all the while systematically shutting her out of a home and a job, and even possibly destroying her career reputation. Stefani paced her kitchen, panting with her anger. She mumbled to herself, letting out a stream of harsh words, hoping he might just overhear her. She should have let her staff go. It would have been easier coming from her. Travers must have thought they had more time. The EPA had obviously acted before Travers could.

Her heart dropped. She'd give anything to just make this all go away. She wished it was all a bad dream and she'd wake up. But every time she tried to start the day over, she opened her eyes to that newspaper. John's exasperatingly handsome face staring back at her, mocking her—mocking any semblance of love she had for him.

Why didn't it occur to me that he had a real job? Why was I so blind, so trusting, so. . .naive? She had thought him an uneducated cowboy, straight from the back roads of Colorado, but when she searched her memory, she knew she had only herself to blame. He'd been to college; he knew Shakespeare. He could name each of the brightest stars as they appeared in the evening sky upon the ridge. "How could you be so stupid, Stefani?" She whacked herself across the forehead. "How could you have been such a snob and be blinded by that fake cowboy charm?"

He was everything she had wanted in a man, except he was none of it, because it was all what she wanted to hear. He'd made her believe he was something she needed. He must have known the first day when he'd seen her name on her business card. That had to be the reason he called her to rent the duplex. She let her head fall onto the kitchen table with a bang.

The doorbell rang, and Stefani picked up the crumpled newspaper and marched to the door, her seething anger rising ever higher to a boiling point. She opened the door hard, and instead of a repentant John, it was Amy.

"What does John have to say about this?" She held up the paper.

"Nothing. He did it; he's an environmental scientist." Stefani was truly wounded. Here she was, alone and worse for the experience. "You told me friendship grows people; well, I trusted him. I did what you said, and look how far it got me. I'm jobless, boyfriendless, and soon, homeless."

"Stefani, it's a job. Who cares? They weren't paying us what we were worth anyway. This valley is teeming with jobs. It's not like we live in the middle of nowhere. We'll have a job by the end of the week. I'm sure John is just sick over this."

"How can you possibly defend him, Amy?"

"I'm not defending him; I'm just reminding you. It was you who didn't want to know what he did for a living. It was you who was embarrassed by his jeans and lack of education. If he didn't tell you what he did for a living, I can't help but think that was your doing, Stefani."

"I don't know why he kept his work a secret, Amy, but I'm about to find out. Make yourself at home. There's coffee on the counter." Stefani climbed up the stairs and threw on a pair of jeans and a T-shirt. She reached for her boots, then hesitated before grabbing her familiar loafers instead. She brushed a light spattering of powder on her face and climbed back down the stairs. "Will you be here when I get back, Amy?"

"Where am I gonna go?" Amy flopped on the couch and flipped on a talk show. "It's not like I have a job."

"Did you take the severance package?" Stefani asked.

"Of course everybody did," Amy answered.

"No. I didn't," Stefani admitted.

"Stefani, how do you expect to wait it out until you get a new job? The right job?"

"I'll just have to get one soon. I'll pray," she said simply. "I need to talk to John. I have a feeling he's waiting for me. His paper is gone, so he knows by now."

"You want me to come for moral support?"

"No, I can handle it."

She rang the bell, and he answered immediately.

"Good morning, Stefani." He opened the door wider, and Stefani avoided his gaze and walked in. She heard the door shut behind her, and she suddenly became fully aware of his presence. Aware of his athletic shorts and running T-shirt and even of his bare feet. Whenever Stefani was alone with John, she felt that magnetic pull between them, something absolutely invisible that felt like an elephant in the room no one could mention. The attraction between them was lethal, and it was the reason he and Stefani usually went to public places like the ranch for their dates. The intimacy of close proximity was embarrassing to them both; to have such a sizzling reaction and fight it without admitting it existed.

She felt it even now. Even when he may have been responsible for ruining her entire structured life. "I see you have today's paper," he continued.

"Congratulations, you're a hero." Stefani tossed the paper on his countertop as she headed for the dilapidated couch in the living room.

John followed her and his tone was biting. "Would you rather I left you to die an early death of cancer from working on top of dangerous levels of trichloroethylene?"

"Don't use your big words on me, cowboy. If you had wanted to impress me with your education, you should have done so a long time ago when I asked what you did for a living. Because right now, I'm not impressed."

"I wanted to prove to you that you were capable of loving someone, no matter what they did. But now, I'm not so sure you are," he added bitterly. She sat on the couch, but stood quickly when she realized she had far too much animosity to just sit still.

"You're going to blame ruining my life on the fact that I'm not emotionally tender? That I'm not a sweet-natured doormat?" she asked incredulously.

"Stefani, I have told you many times what you mean to me, how I love you, and I've never heard a smidgen of the sentiment returned. You've never said how you feel once, not when you kissed me, not when I said I loved you. The only response I ever got was: 'Can I buy my half of the duplex from you?' Was that the proof you needed from me?"

"After you've destroyed my life, you want me to admit I love you?"

"I didn't destroy your life; I may have saved it. Cancer obviously runs in your family, anyway. Working around toxic pollutants couldn't help."

"You leave my mother out of this; she has nothing to do with it."

"She has everything to do with it, Stefani. If you would tell her how much you love her instead of trying to take care of everything, you might break her hard shell. If you'd let God work instead of trying to plan every moment of your future, you might be surprised how He handles things."

John was just fighting dirty. "You're just trying to keep the subject off of *you*. *You*, John Savitch from Colorado, the man who single-handedly brought down a multimillion-dollar corporation. You, who put hundreds of people out of work today, and you, who lied to someone you supposedly loved to score some kind of career goal."

"Isn't that what you did to me? You have something to prove about this house. You used my love for you to get me to sell it to you."

"But your goal was more carefully planned, wasn't it, John?"

"You know me better than that. Mr. Travers had the opportunity to do things right when he came to California. He'd already lost one business in Colorado by cutting corners. You didn't know that, did you? This was his chance to make things right, but still he put the profit margin above any concern he had for you or any of his employees. If you think Bob Travers is your friend, you tell me why you didn't sign that little severance agreement he gave you?"

"How did you know I didn't sign that agreement?" Stefani fell to the couch, her astonished eyes wide with inquiry.

"Because his lawyers tried to hire me as Atlas's exclusive environmental consultant, that's how. That's where the newspaper got that quote they used by me today. From Bob Travers's lawyers."

"If you had *told* me what Mr. Travers was allowing to happen, I might have been able to fix things. I could at least have gotten the data center moved to Sacramento and saved more jobs. Why couldn't you trust me with the information you had?"

"It's my job, Stefani. I couldn't—"

Stefani stood. "You couldn't jeopardize *your* job, but my job? No problem. After all, you own the house, not me, so what do *I* need a paycheck for? I'm just a woman, is that it? I can go find some man to take care of me, get married, have a couple kids, and forget all about my high-powered job. Except that was never going to happen, John. But that was your plan all along, wasn't it? To bring down Stefani Willems and her prideful ways. Well, congratulations, John. You've done it. I bow before your feet. You've won." She bowed an exaggerated curtsy at the waist in royal fashion. "You are smarter, tougher, and more determined than I. I admit it. I bow down before the master."

"Stefani, stop it." John came to her and forced her eyes up to his. They were still so pure, their sea green making her want to dive into their depths. If she allowed herself to look much longer, she'd forget all about her pain, all about his lies. She saw love in those green eyes, concern like she'd never felt before, and she wanted to fall into his wide chest and weep with all that was within her. To rest in his strength. *John, I love you. I love you, I love you. How could you betray me?* She fell against his chest for a moment, breathing in the deep, earthy scent mixed with musk cologne. So familiar and so agonizing all at once. She never wanted to pull away, but it was now or never, and she willed herself from his arms.

Her tears came, any hope of hiding them now hopeless. "John, how could you?" she cried, while pulling away from him. "You had ample opportunity to tell me what you did. I was wrong when I said it didn't matter what you did. Because it does matter. I want my simple cowboy back, the blue-collar, considerate man of God I thought you were. I liked the cowboy better than the environmental scientist. A lot better." She reached for the door and shut it quietly behind her. Outside, the rain clouds were forming above with a light sprinkle coming down. She ran for shelter, covering her head. Summer was over and so was the love affair of her lifetime. She would never love again as long as she lived. She was certain of it.

Stefani didn't feel like facing Amy when she returned to her duplex, but Amy was on the edge of her seat, waiting for her return. "Well, I'm dying; what did he say?" She flipped off the television and leaned her elbow on the sofa arm.

"Nothing." Stefani shrugged. "Nothing we didn't already know. I'm going back to bed, Amy. Make yourself at home."

"Stefani."

"I don't want to talk about it. He doesn't have any excuses, Amy. He kept the truth from me, plain and simple, and we pay the price. End of story." Stefani clambered up the stairs and shut her bedroom door with a slam. Her Bible lay before her and she turned away from it. "God, how could You do this to me? You've left me here with nothing! Nothing, God! I've got an ill mother who thinks You're a figment of my imagination. No job and no money because You

214

told me not to sign that agreement. I gave You my heart and this is where You lead me? Father, I love John. I love him with everything that's in me, even though I know it's wrong. He's no different than any of the other men who lied to me and moved on. Those who said they wanted a career-oriented, educated woman, but couldn't handle it in the long run. . . Oh, Lord, I'm desperate. Why did You give me John at all, if he was just going to betray me? Make this all go away. Please. Give me a reason to understand what he did."

"You shall know the truth." She kept hearing that verse in her head. Except, she knew the truth, but it had only caused pain, not relief. What was God trying to tell her?

A knock sounded at her bedroom door. Opening it, she started to apologize. "Amy, I—" It was John, standing tall, firm, and confident in a gray business suit. His expression told her he wasn't going to walk away without saying his piece, and he leaned on the door frame with fingers laced around its edge. She looked up at the rugged fingers worn from work and play. "You apparently have something to say, so go ahead. Since you've managed to sweet-talk your way past Amy, you've gotten your way, but what else is new? My feelings seem to count little in the scheme of things."

"I'm going to ignore that, because I think if you search your heart, you know the truth, Stefani."

"And whose truth would that be?" Her fists went to her hips, and she tried to look as determined as he did.

"This," he pointed down at her, "is the Stefani Willems I first met. Snippy, immature, and vengeful. And personally, I don't want any part of *that* Stefani Willems."

The fire left her, and she was stunned silent. He thought she was snippy and vengeful? There was not much she could do with that information. "So what is it you want, John, if it's no part of me?"

"To give you these." She opened her palm, and he dropped a set of keys into it. "What's this?"

"It's a symbol. I will take care of you, if you'd let me. If you'd stop fighting me every step. It's my keys to your house. The place is yours as long as you want it."

"You want me to take charity from you?" Surely, things weren't that desperate.

"No, I want you to accept some help until you get back on your feet and a new job. I don't think you know what you're up against with Bob Travers. He's a spiteful man, Stefani, and he's not likely to let you run free with the information you have on his company." John's jaw was clenched and firm, and his gentleness seemed long gone. He was robotic in form, and it crushed her. His words may have offered her his assistance, but his stance told her it was his Christian duty, not from an overwhelming love for her.

But that's what I wanted, wasn't it? I didn't want to be dependent on any man. So how is today any different from yesterday? Because today, she was back to square one with the attractive cowboy from Colorado, right when they'd met. The arrogant, selfish, condescending. . .wonderful man she loved.

"Is that your plan, John? To be my knight in shining armor and come rescue me from my reckless life, the life *you've* turned into a battleground?" Why did her mouth ramble misery, when she willed it to be sweet and pure? Where was this awful division coming from?

His jaw flinched, but otherwise she saw no outward sign of anger. "No, Stefani," he said evenly. "I could never rescue you. You'd never allow it, even if you needed my help beyond reason, you'd never humble yourself to take it. This is not charity." He looked down at the keys. "This is my peace offering to leave on a good note. You'll find another job soon, and I'm going back to Colorado. I did give you first right of refusal on the house. Did I not? Get a job so you can buy it with that small fortune you've saved up."

Fear enveloped her. John leaving? *Oh, Lord, no.* Why couldn't she just tell him she loved him and that she couldn't imagine life without him? *I love you, John. Why can't I just say it?* Because it wouldn't come.

John continued. "I'm sorry for the pain I caused you, both directly and indirectly. I've repented of my silence many times, but now I offer it to you with my sincere apologies. I would never have hurt you intentionally, Stefani. I'd make it up to you if you'd only give me the chance." There was no joy in his serious eyes, his laugh lines were almost invisible, and his straight, sculpted jaw offered no sign of falling into his ready smile. "Tell your mom I'll be praying for her." He turned and started down the hallway.

"Wait. When will I see you?"

"I'll be out of town for a few days. I'm looking into buying a new horse."

"Do you want me to take care of Kayla while you're gone?" She thought this was the olive branch necessary, but he snubbed it.

"No. Her trainer's taking care of her. Thanks, though."

"John?" *Say it, Stefani, just say it. Three little words, just say them!* "Good-bye."

Where should she even start to pick up the pieces? With her mother? Her job? What was the priority? What did God want her to do?

Chapter 15

The duplex was lonely without John. Although Stefani had lived alone for nearly twelve years, fear gripped her at night with his side of the house dark and silent. She hadn't realized how much she'd come to rely on his safety checks and just knowing he was there. Ready to help at any sign of trouble. Of course they lived in one of the safest neighborhoods available, but being alone now troubled her deeply.

Stefani packed her things and prepared to be at her mother's side when Gladys came out of surgery. Gladys had asked that Stefani not be there beforehand, and Stefani had obliged. The long drive to Sacramento was a blur. She arrived at the hospital to find her father in the surgical waiting room. Bert had his three newspapers, but they were folded neatly beside him, his own burdens a priority.

"Stefani! Oh, honey, I'm so glad to see you."

"Hi, Dad. Heard anything yet?"

"No, the surgeon said it would be anywhere from forty-five minutes to four hours. She's been in there about two hours now."

"I've been praying for her, Daddy. God will provide."

"I hope so, honey. Your mama's a fighter, but the information the doctor gave us doesn't offer much hope—if it's bad."

Just then, the doctor came in. He removed his green surgical hat, revealing his bald head. He seemed totally bewildered. "Mr. Lencioni?"

"Yes?" Bert grasped his daughter's hand tightly.

"There's no cancer."

"Did you say no cancer? What about the sonograms? Her symptoms?"

"I can't explain it, Mr. Lencioni. I can only tell you what I know now. There's not a spot of cancer in your wife. She had all the symptoms of advanced ovarian cancer."

Bert sat down and wept with the news, holding his face in his hands. Stefani had never seen such a sight. She sat beside him, unsure of whether or not to intrude upon his overwhelming emotions. Stefani felt triumphant. She knew God had cured her mother. God had given her more time to share His love and awesome healing. It was the only explanation.

"Oh, Stefani, I can't believe it."

"I told you people were praying."

"My beautiful daughter. What a delight you are, spreading such sunshine about. Thank you for being here." He grasped her hand tightly.

"I wouldn't be anywhere else, Dad. I'm here to take care of you and Mom until she's up and around from surgery."

"What about your job?"

"I'm looking for work. Don't you worry; I'll be fine."

Stefani's father held a vigil over Gladys until she awoke. They whispered and giggled to one another, and Stefani left to give them their privacy. Their intimacy brought forth so many memories. So many times she dreamed of being loved by a man like her father. Gladys Lencioni was his princess. Bert didn't seem to mind her mother's obvious character flaws. When did that dream end? When did Stefani become so cynical about men?

The following day, Stefani finally got some time alone with her mother. Gladys was weary from the wear on her body and slept throughout the day. But just before dinner, Gladys awoke. "Stefani?" she croaked.

"Yes, Mom, it's me."

"Oh, Stefani, I'm so glad you're here. Did you hear about the cancer?"

"Yes, Mom, I am thrilled."

"That surgeon expected me to be riddled with the stuff, didn't he?"

"I think so, Mom."

"Where's your cowboy?"

"Mom, he's not *my* cowboy."

"Stefani?"

"John and I had a falling-out."

Gladys sat up, grimacing in pain as she moved. "What do you mean?"

"I mean we're through," Stefani said simply.

"Stefani Lencioni, it had better be the drugs I'm hearing."

"No, Mom, it's true. You didn't even like John."

"Who says I didn't like John?"

"You were always telling me that he didn't have a real job and explaining to me he was too good-looking to be useful."

"I always talk about your boyfriends that way."

"So, what's your point, Mom?"

"John's the only one that didn't run. Ain't he?"

"No, Mom, he didn't run, but that's because he was busy. Busy with his *real* work of putting me out of a job. He lied to us, Mom. He's no cowboy; he's a highly educated environmental scientist of all things. He works for the EPA, shutting down polluting businesses."

"He never lied to us, Stefani. All you had to do was look at his crazy work hours and his fancy house to know he had some important job. You just weren't looking."

"Mom," Stefani answered condescendingly, "that house belongs to us. It was our land, and he's only been the last obstacle in my way. I'm going to own that land again, Mom. And when I do, you and Daddy are going to come back and live there again."

"Stefani, I don't want to live back there again. And I certainly don't want an elegant house where I can't even work the fancy stove. What is all this about?"

"I know why you sold the land, Mom. Grandma Willems told me. I wouldn't trade Daddy for anything; he's been so loving and kind. But Mom, he was never a hard worker, and Grandma told me how his negligence led to the sale of your parents' farm."

"What?" Gladys rubbed her eyes. "What exactly did Grandma tell you?"

"She told me that when you met Daddy, you tossed all caution to the wind and married him against their will. Their only hope for you was to give him the farm. She said the apricot orchards needed hard work, but Daddy was always off doing what he wanted and never had time to care for the trees. So when the taxes increased and came due, you had to sell. But John is going to sell me the land, Mom. I'm going to own it again. I know we won't ever have the orchards again, but we will have the land again."

"Stefani, we don't want that land in our family. Whatever gave you that crazy notion?"

"What do you mean? Mom, God provided it. It's yours again as soon as I get a job; John said he'd sell it to me. You don't have to be brave with me. It's okay to admit Daddy lost it."

"Stefani, have you ever seen your father do something for himself that didn't involve you or me? Other than read the papers and watch television?"

Stefani contemplated before answering. "No."

"If he went fishing or to a ball game, did he ever go without you?"

"No."

"Think about it, Stefani, would your father have ever sold that land without a reason?"

"I don't understand."

"Your grandmother was a wonderful woman, but she had one very black blind spot when it came to your father."

"I promised her I'd get the land back, Mom. Without a man, and I will."

"Stefani, you are not responsible for an unreasonable request made by a senile old woman. Go back home and get your cowboy and forget about this nonsense."

"No, Mom, I promised."

"Do you remember when I told you that story of the neighbor who went to church every day? The one who came home to get beat every day because the preacher kept telling her that divorce was sinful?"

"The reason you hate the church? Of course I remember, Mom. It sickens my soul that you hold God responsible for man's sin."

"That wasn't a neighbor. That was your grandmother, your aunt, and me. Your grandfather used to beat us all with a belt until we were black and blue. Sometimes just because we didn't hang the wash out correctly. My father was a hard drinker and a hard worker. His expectations for your father were ridiculous. Of course Bert could never measure up. No one could have. But when your father came along, the beatings stopped immediately. Your father would have killed your grandfather if he'd laid a hand on us again. Sure, your papa wasn't the hardest worker, but that was his choice."

"But Grandma said—"

"Grandma said a lot of things, Stefani. Especially when she got older. I think she started to blur Bert with your grandfather. In the end, she just equated all men with the evil Grandfather inflicted on her. It broke my heart to see you living on that property again," Gladys admitted. "I thought that land was cursed. But now I see it brought you John, so I guess there is gold at the end of the rainbow."

"Grandma told me Daddy lost the farm because he was lazy."

"No, honey, Daddy sold the land to pay for your college expenses. We moved up here where it's cheaper so that you could afford Stanford's expenses."

"You bought that ramshackle house. . .so I could get an education?"

"We like that house, Stefani. Your father's getting on in years and keeping it up is just a bit much for him. If there's one thing I learned in this lifetime, it's that stuff don't matter none next to people. You were our priority, Stefani. Always have been. You were so smart. You deserved to go to Stanford. But we didn't sacrifice nothing, Stefani. That land was full of pain for me. If it weren't for your father, I could never have lived there as long as we did. Your father taught me to be content where I was."

Stefani forgot to breathe. "I've been working for nothing all these years. Everything I thought was true was just a lie. I wanted you to believe in God again, Mom. I thought if you knew that God took care of your needs—"

"Stefani, it's too late for me and God. I stopped needing Him a long time ago, when your father came along."

"No, Mom. Read the Bible again. You still have so much healing to do."

"If it makes you feel better, I'll read it, honey. Now you go home and make Papa some dinner. He'll be getting hungry soon."

"But, Mom—"

Gladys was swept away by sleep. Her tired lids fluttered closed.

~

Stefani stepped onto her parents' porch two days later and found the screen door in fine working order. John's gorgeous smile filled her heart. His legacy was everywhere around her parents' home. She missed him terribly. Her goals for the house were long gone—replaced by the real desire to have a man who loved her like Bert loved Gladys. *Who would have ever thought I would have desired something my mother held?*

Her mother's screeching voice met her at the porch. "What? You don't have to work?" The older woman appeared in the doorway. "Screen door works great and you should see the chicken coop. That's some handyman you got there."

"Hi, Mom." Stefani came toward her mother and wrapped her arms around the wide frame. "How are you feeling?" She took Gladys's free arm and helped her father get Gladys inside.

"Like somebody shot me full of holes. How should I feel?"

"Come on, Mom, let's get you into bed."

"What's wrong with you?"

"Mom, nothing's wrong."

"My daughter, who never takes a day off in her life, sits at the hospital, cooks for her father, then stays in the middle of a weekday to wait on me? Something's wrong. I thought I told you to go home and get that cowboy. It ain't every man that can fix a chicken coop."

"Come on, Mom, let's get you into bed. It seems your fighting spirit has returned."

"Don't get smart with me, young lady."

"Hi, Dad."

"Hi, honey. Did you get your mom's bed ready?" her dad asked.

"I sure did. She's all set. I moved the TV in there and everything."

"I can't be sitting around watching television." Gladys allowed Bert to help her into bed. "Bert, you roll that TV back out there and go watch the races. You're making me nervous hovering over me. Stefani and I will be fine." Bert smiled and did as he was told.

"Are you feeling any better?" Stefani asked, while she pulled up the covers over her mother.

"I feel tired," her mom admitted. Her mother was sweating from the taxing walk.

"Do you want something to eat?"

"Nothing you'd make. None of your fat-free, tasteless meals you make for health. Who wants to live if I get to eat cardboard for dinner?"

Stefani ignored the comment. "I'm glad you had the surgery. Don't you feel better knowing you're healed?"

"Your friend said I'd feel better knowing. Also said he'd be praying. He's a smart boy; I trust him." Gladys nodded.

"My friend?" Stefani inquired, her brow furrowed with confusion.

"John. He was here to fix the barn door last week. I fed him good while he was here, don't you worry. And he got enough fat to keep him going through the day."

"John was here? You mean when I brought him. . .right?" *Did her mother possibly say what she thought she said?*

Gladys picked at the bedspread. "No, he was here again before my surgery. He came by to fix that gate that's been opening on its own and letting the goats wander. He was on his way somewhere, said something about buying another one of them big dogs of his."

"You mean a horse?"

"I suppose. Your father just pointed him in the right direction. Nice boy. Anyway, he told me about his mom. Such a shame. You know he lost his mom when he was only ten to breast cancer?"

"He told you that?" Stefani actually felt hurt that John had shared his most intimate secret with her mother, but not with her. *Why had he come here? What could have been his motive? Did he just want to make sure my mom didn't suffer the same fate or was it something more? Is he the considerate, loving caretaker or the reckless liar who played with my future?* What did it matter? He was leaving California and Stefani, as well.

"Now, Stefani, you have a life of your own to lead. Your father won't have you sitting around, waiting on us." Gladys pulled her hand away.

"Mom, I don't have a job to go to, so don't worry. Just concentrate on getting better."

"And I'm supposed to worry about you, instead? No, Stefani, you go home and get a new job."

"Mom, I need some time to think. All the information you gave me this week is just so overwhelming. I'm not ready to work yet. I was focusing my entire career on getting that land. Now what do I have to work toward? Suddenly, my life seems so meaningless. I wish God would just tell me what to do."

Her mother broke her vocal ranting with her old-fashioned common sense. "You're not staying here, Stefani. You've got your own life back in the Bay Area. You're not going to give up your life to take care of us. We've got a good health plan, and I've frozen enough dinners to last your father a month. I want you to go back home. We'll get you some money, but John said he'd take care of the rent for a while."

"Mom, I want to stay, and I don't need any money."

"You're young and you've got your entire life waiting for you. I won't have you put it on hold to play nursemaid. Besides, you're not exactly the nursing kind;

that's why we sent you to business school."

"Mom, I *want* to be here."

"All the same, I want you to leave. You can pray for me if it makes you feel better. John says you've got a home as long as he's in California, so go back and get him, Stefani. I don't know what happened between you two, but it'll do no good to have you here and him there. Now go home and get married."

"John doesn't want to marry me, Mom, and he certainly never asked me. John was only using me to get information on my company to bring down the mighty Bob Travers."

"If you believe that, that Stanford education didn't do a thing for you. Go home, Stefani." Gladys pointed a stern finger at her daughter.

"John's not even home. He went back to Colorado, and I don't know when, or even if, he'll be back."

"He'll be back. You just get there first and make him his favorite dinner when he comes home. I don't know what you think he did to you. But men don't drive two hours out of their way to fix barn gates for people they hardly know. He loves you. Even your uneducated mama can see that."

"He loves God, and he was probably doing his Christian duty by fixing up around here."

"Go get him, Stefani. Do you think your father just came and asked me to marry him? I had to be available and know when to play hard-to-get. Well, you've played your games; now it's time to come clean and collect your husband."

"I'm not playing games. I'm a Christian woman, and the man that God chooses for me must become mine without any games. Games are dishonest." Stefani squared her shoulders.

"Well, fine, but I know a man sometimes needs a little push in the marriage department, and you're not getting any younger. It's time you stopped relying on that God business and started getting busy. Otherwise, I'll never have a grandchild. I don't understand it, Stefani. You're a fine-looking woman, so what is it you say to men that makes them run away?"

"Mom, have you heard a word I've said? Have you bothered to listen to anything I've come here to say today? I'm not getting married!" Stefani was ready to attack her mother further when she heard that tiny voice within her, not even a whisper, yet loud and clear.

"You shall know the truth."

What is the truth, Lord? I asked for prayer for my mother, for her healing, for her salvation, and she's still the same hard woman, Lord. You may have healed her cancer, but her heart is as hard as ever.

Stefani found her favorite lawn chair on the porch and opened her Bible. Philippians 2:3 was highlighted on the open page: "Do nothing out of selfish ambition or vain conceit, but in humility consider others better than yourselves." Stefani's sin hit her with the weight of a freight train. Everything she had worked for had been for her own glory, not for God's. She wanted the land to prove to her mother that God was real, but all it really proved was that Stefani had been so set on her own agenda, she'd never heard what God wanted.

John was right. Stefani *was* just like her mother: stubborn, strong-willed, and trying to be worthy. Worthy of acceptance by others, instead of God. She fell to her knees, begging God for forgiveness. *Lord in heaven, I have tried so hard. So hard to be who I thought You wanted me to be. But now I realize I was being what I thought people wanted me to be: successful, rich, independent. I tried it all on my own power. And here I sit, unemployed and lonely. You never cared about that house, but You used it to give me my true heart's desire: a man who loved me like my father loved my mother. Why didn't I hear You knocking? Why couldn't I see what You were trying to say to me? Oh, Lord, I have been so selfish, so vain, and so full of myself. Without You, I can do nothing. I admit that to You now and beg You to help me. I want to be on the right track. I want to do Your will. No matter what that is, Lord. In Jesus' name, I pray. Amen.*

She suddenly understood that God spoke in a whisper, and if she was going to hear Him, she needed to be still and listen. Her entire Christian walk had been based on what she could accomplish through God instead of what God could accomplish through her.

"You just gonna sit around here in one of your trances, waiting for opportunity to knock?" Gladys came out onto the porch.

"No, Mom, I'm going back home to find work. God's given me a peace about you and Dad handling your recovery alone. I'll leave tomorrow, but I'll be here if you need me. You just call anytime, okay?"

"Stefani Mary Lucia Lencioni—"

Stefani walked toward her, enveloping her in a hug. The older woman stiffened and cringed under the closeness. As Stefani held her mother, she praised God for His miraculous healing. Knowing if her mother was going to be saved, it was going to be God's doing, not Stefani's. "I love you, Mom. God will be with you. If you get scared, you look in the Bible I gave you. Read the Psalms; He will give you peace."

"Ahh!" Gladys tossed her hand again.

Chapter 16

S tefani's eyes were wide with anticipation when she returned to the duplex. She came around the last corner muttering a prayer, hoping John would have returned home by now and they might work things out. She wanted to share with him all that God had taught her and how wrong she'd been. John was right about her stupid pride and inane financial goals, and she couldn't wait to tell him so—and to humble herself as God had told her to do.

As their model Mediterranean home came into view, Stefani's shoulders slumped at the sight of several newspapers on John's doorstep. "John, please come home. I don't care if I have a future with you; I just want peace between us. I want to tell you I'm sorry for my pride and my arrogance," she said to the air.

Stefani unlocked her door and went directly to the answering machine, hoping her job search had proved more successful than her love life. By now, there should at least be a request for a job interview or two. She tossed her keys on the desk with a jingle and sat down, fighting disappointment when she noticed there were no messages at all. No job opportunities and no phone calls from John.

The afternoon sun filtered into her kitchen when a reflection shimmered across the wall. Stefani flew to the flower-box window and saw John's SUV pull into the driveway. Tears welled up in her eyes at the sight of him, and she flew to the front door.

Just as she leaped from her threshold, she noticed the elegant blond beside him. The woman was almost as tall as John, and her long, slender legs were tucked neatly into svelte jeans and cowboy boots. Her blond hair seemed to glisten in the afternoon sunlight that peeked through the trees, and her fresh complexion was porcelain in nature.

Stefani knew getting caught up in idle jealousy would serve no purpose. Being humble before John and admitting her love for him would never be easy, but if she had any shot at a life with him, it would be necessary. "I'm trusting in my own power again, Lord. Give me the strength."

Stefani ran upstairs and grabbed her cowboy boots. She wriggled into her jeans and pulled her boots on. She let her hair fall loosely, running her fingers through it to emphasize its fullness. She puckered her lips and applied lipstick, hoping the subtle color would give her the confidence she needed. She emerged from her house just in time to see John's taillights turning the corner. Her heart sank.

She mustered up all her courage, muttering a continuous prayer, and drove up to the stables, following John's car at a careful, unseen distance. He pulled into the stable parking lot and helped the stunning blond from the passenger seat. Stefani parked behind a tree and sucked in a deep breath. She looked to the heavens for support. "It's now or never, Lord. Give me the strength. He has to know how I feel. Even if he doesn't return the feelings and even if there's someone else. I owe it to him to say how I really felt all those times I kept my mouth quiet when I should have said I loved him."

The California autumn was well under way, but it was still sunny and the ground was moist from the previous day's rain. It was chilly under the canopy of trees flanking the muddy roads, and she shivered as she emerged from her little coupe. She sloshed her way through the mud and into the stables. To her chagrin, John and the mystery blond had disappeared. Stefani stopped in the doorway and noticed another blond, the young female rider from their night at the rodeo. She was brushing Kayla's mane.

"Hi," the young woman called before Stefani could retreat. She pulled the brush away from the horse and pointed it at Stefani. "You're John's friend, right? The one he brought to the rodeo that night."

"Uh—yes. Right," Stefani stammered.

"I knew he liked brunettes." She smiled and went back to brushing the horse.

Although the comment was meant as a compliment, the sting of jealousy touched Stefani. Seeing John with a blond that morning only compounded her pain. There were certainly no shortages of beautiful women in John's life. This young rider had long, flowing hair and sparkling, glacier blue eyes. Her face was perfectly proportioned, and she could have easily been a fashion model. Stefani hadn't realized just how gorgeous Kayla's rider was under the cowboy hat and rodeo dust. Self-doubt plagued Stefani, and she could think of no response. John now felt further away than ever. This woman only served as a vivid reminder that she'd blown it.

The blond spoke in her perky, schoolgirlish way. "I'm going to take Kayla out. You want to ride the ridge with me? The new horse is here, and you'd save me another ride if you'd exercise her with me. I heard you've gotten pretty good on a horse."

Stefani tried to put aside her jealousy and focus on why she was here. If she really wanted to humble herself before John, she had to support him if he'd moved on. His young rider obviously supported him regarding Stefani. "Sure, a ride would be nice. Maybe you can show me a few moves," Stefani suggested. "I was really impressed with your riding that night at the rodeo."

"I was terrible that night. I didn't even get a score! But sure, I could show you a few moves. John's new horse is fabulous. Fully trained. You should see how tightly she cuts, and boy, is she gentle. Like an old stable mare tucked in the body of a rodeo champion. This way you can tell Uncle John personally that his horses were exercised. I don't want him to think Kayla or this new one were neglected while he was gone. I don't think Uncle John quite trusts anyone else with his horses. Even if I did grow up around them."

"*Uncle* John?"

"Uh-huh, he's my mom's brother," she continued casually. "Didn't he tell you that?" she asked innocently. "Usually, he tells people right away so they don't think he's dating some young girl. He gets embarrassed to be seen with me. Go figure. He doesn't look all that old to me, and I say, let people think what they want."

"Uh, no, he failed to mention you were his niece."

"Probably because he was too concerned with my riding that night at the rodeo. He was right, though; it's always better to slow it down just a hair and go for the score than to knock a barrel down and lose any hope of winning by being disqualified. I'll be ready next time, though. It's so hard to fight the adrenaline when you're out there under the lights."

"John had mentioned he had a niece close by, but I never put the two together. He always calls *you* the trainer."

"That's because when it comes to the rodeo, your beau is all business." She laughed. "Winning is everything!" She lowered her voice and laughed. "He has no time for family connections. Oh yeah, your beau has rodeo in his veins. He lives, eats, and breathes it, even living in the city."

"John's my landlord, not my beau," Stefani corrected.

"Uh-huh," she replied. "What's wrong with Uncle John, anyway? He's downright attentive, if I do say so myself. *When* you can get his mind off the rodeo or him saving us from the evil polluters."

"Nothing's wrong with John. I just didn't want you to get the wrong impression, that's all," Stefani explained.

"John said you went to Stanford. That's why I'm here; I just transferred for my junior year, much to my mom's dismay. My mother didn't want me coming out to *dangerous* California by myself. She thinks all you people do out here is drive by and shoot." She let out a small laugh. "Uncle John had mercy on me. He told my mom he'd take a transfer he'd been offered out here and keep an eye on me."

"That was sweet of him."

"Of course Mom doesn't know about my barrel racing, but what does she expect when she hands me over to a former bull rider?" She laughed aloud.

"I'm sorry, I don't remember your name," Stefani said.

"Justine Hastings."

"Well, I guess it's just us gals today, Justine. I'm Stefani." Stefani threw a saddle over the beautiful new animal and patted the horse on her nose, hoping they'd be long gone before John returned to the stables. Stefani was looking forward to the ride and the chance to escape her apology to John for the moment. "So what do you think of Stanford?"

"It's great. Met the man of my dreams there. Trevor Dane. We're going to be married at the end of the school year."

"Oh," Stefani said wistfully. "It must be nice knowing your future at such a young age." They started up the ridge. They were barely on the trail when a deep voice resonated through the quiet.

"Stefani! Stefani, wait!" It was John. Stefani turned to see him running toward her, the stunning other blond beside him, waving at her.

The sight of him reminded her how completely unprepared she was to meet him. Without thinking, she bolted on the horse. "Yah!" Stefani kicked the horse's hindquarters and sped up the path toward the ridge. Stefani was barely out of sight when she realized how much harder it would be to see John after running away. *Why am I acting so stupid? Why couldn't I have just pretended to be happy for John—even if he'd brought some cowgirl home with him?*

Stefani finally felt the full weight of John's new attachment. Her tears flowed freely, and she sobbed aloud, knowing only the grazing cows and squirrels could hear. Even with God's help, she wasn't strong enough to face John. . .to humble herself before another woman. She clung to Justine's words. *Your beau. . . Your beau. . .* When Stefani reached the top of the ridge, she slowed the horse to a mere trot. There was no going back now. Humiliation had won over humility. She couldn't face him or his stunning new girlfriend. Stefani knew she paled in comparison to the lanky blond on John's arm.

She lifted her voice in prayer, "What now, Lord? What now?"

It wasn't long before she heard the galloping horse behind her and saw John quickly approaching on his horse, Kayla. Stefani was mortified. "Yah!" She sped up again and cut sharply up the hill to get away from him, but he was gaining on her. "Yah! Yah!" she yelled between frantic cries.

John appeared next to her, galloping at full speed. "Stop the horse, Stefani!" he yelled.

"NO!" She tried an even sharper cut she'd watched Justine perform at the rodeo, only to have the agile horse take her command too quickly for Stefani's apprentice riding skills. The horse turned on its tail, and the last thing Stefani remembered was hurling through the air toward the muddy green pasture. When she came to, John was hovering over her, his deep green eyes thinned in concern.

"Stefani?" he asked softly.

"Justine taught me a few moves." She laughed aloud, then groaned in pain.

"You may want to practice them a few more times." He grinned, his wide smile baring his perfectly formed teeth and creating the tiny lines beside his eyes.

He winked and she groaned again. "Stay still. Let's see whether anything's broken. Try moving one limb at a time, slowly," he urged. He watched as she carefully flexed one leg, then the other, then her wrists and elbows. "You fall very well. Gracefully, even; I was very impressed. Maybe barrel racing isn't your sport, but the bucking bronco might be."

"Is this supposed to make me feel better?" Stefani looked at the horse standing nearby grazing. "Look at her; she can't imagine why someone so incompetent would be riding her. She's mocking me!"

"They do that. You should see the bulls after they've just kicked you off. They're worse than the horses. I think the bulls actually laugh. I think I even heard one say, 'Take that, you loser,' once."

Stefani laughed again and reached for her side to ease the pain. "This is why I'm a city girl," she moaned aloud. "Now I'm positive that saddles should have seat belts." She tried to get up, but her stomach lurched and the world tilted, so she headed back toward flat ground.

"I don't know any city girl that rides a registered buckskin quarter horse and wears real cowgirl boots. You're a country girl; when are you going to admit it?" His eyes smiled again. He pressed above her abdomen, and she screeched in pain. "I think you may have broken a rib or two." He clicked his tongue. "That's painful."

"Tell me something I don't know."

"Do you know I love you?"

"You love me? What about all those things I said to you about Atlas Semiconductors? You're not still angry with me?"

"How could I stay angry at the woman I love? Stubborn as she is. I'm just as stubborn, you know. But I suppose I'll have to prove that."

She grinned, but her smile disappeared as John bent down over her. She felt his warm breath upon her cheek, then she was lost in his gentle kiss. She felt his hand caress her chin, and she lifted her head higher to get closer to him. His scent was like a warm, wonderful memory that washed over her powerfully. All her fears and anger dissipated within the strength of his kiss. There was a genuine honesty about it that left little room for doubt about his true nature. "Who's that beautiful blond you brought with you? You know, the one I just made a fool of myself over."

"So *that's* what your little chase was all about? Good. I was beginning to think I was in *real* trouble." He winked at her.

"Are you avoiding my question?" She tried to brush some of the mud from her jeans, but a thin layer was dried and caked on. The back of her arm was also covered in mud, and she realized what a sight she must have been. She gingerly rose to her knees, but any farther proved impossible because of her sore ribs.

Stefani whimpered and remained on her knees.

John knelt before her and wiped the mud from her hand before he took it. "Stefani, I do love you. I think I have from the moment you took me to that place with the mechanical bull and thought you were so funny." He laughed. "I know keeping my occupation a secret was wrong, but everything else I've done has been aboveboard. Scout's honor." He held up two fingers. "Will you believe me when I say you can trust me? What is it you want from me to prove that I am who I say I am?"

Stefani realized just how much damage her grandmother had unwittingly passed on when she heard the pain in John's voice. She had been raised to mistrust men. And she did. She had even questioned her own loving father. She believed he'd lost the farm, when it clearly made sense for her aging parents to sell the orchard to pay for her college expenses and begin their retirement. It was time to change—time to allow God to lead her. It was time to be loved and feel all that it offered: both the pain and extreme joy.

"John, I have been so unfair to you. You've given me every reason to trust you, but I *chose* to look at the one area that was questionable. And I never wanted an explanation about your job. I was afraid of what you might tell me. It's such a long story, but I was so wrong about workingmen."

"It was stupid to deceive you. I just didn't know how to tell you I was an EPA scientist. At first I was a little insulted by your attitude; I guess I just wanted you to admit you were attracted to a simple cowboy. I knew you felt the electricity in the room when we met that day in the duplex. It was undeniable. I wanted to prove to you that you could fall for a lowly cowboy, I guess to humble you. But then my feelings got in the way, and I wanted so much more from you. I wanted you to fall in love with *me*—not a job title or a bunch of credentials, but *me*. It became harder and then too risky to tell you the truth as I got closer to shutting down Atlas. I didn't want you to know how I had deceived you. And I didn't want you in any danger. I just didn't have any choice."

"I know that now, John. And, yes, I did fall in love with the cowboy. It's *you* I love. The man who charmed my mother and showed me that being vulnerable is part of being loved. . . The man who taught me how to ride a horse and kissed me with a fire I've never known. . . *That* kiss had nothing to do with your education. *Unless* you majored in chemistry," she added and smiled.

Gentle lines appeared next to John's eyes as he softly brushed the wisps of hair from her face. He let out a low growl and kissed her again. "*We* major in chemistry, Miss Willems. Now, before I get caught up in this moment, are you ready to meet my sister?"

"Your sister? That's who the blond is? Oh." Stefani groaned. "I feel like such an idiot. I can't go meet her. Not now. She'll think I'm such a loon, taking off on your horse like that."

"She has her own drama to worry about." He kissed Stefani's forehead and stood. "How's your side? Can you get up?" He lifted her gingerly to her feet, and she stood below him, locked in a loose, careful embrace. His wide, solid chest made up her entire view, and she clung to his steady warmth.

"Ahem. We better go."

"I'm sorry about your job."

She reached up and pressed a soft kiss to his warm lips. "What job?"

"That's my girl." He kissed her again. "Come meet my sister." He took her by both hands. "I want to show her the woman who's stolen my heart."

"Oh, John, she'll think I'm crazy, running off like that on the horse."

"You are crazy, Stefani. If you weren't, we would have nothing in common," he teased. "Well, you're going to have to meet her sometime. No time like the present. We'll just tell her you were excited to test-drive your engagement present."

"My engagement present?"

"The horse. I'm allowing you to name her, so we'll have to change her registration papers later. She's yours."

"You bought *me* a horse. That's where you went?"

"What kind of cowboy would I be if my wife didn't have a horse?"

"Wife? You certainly were sure of yourself when you left."

He dropped to his knee and held her hands in his. "Stefani Lencioni Willems, would you do me the honor of becoming my wife?"

The words she'd dreamt of for countless nights fell like a tropical rain upon her. She never thought she'd actually hear them. Certainly not from a man who made her weak in the knees. John was everything she'd envisioned and everything her grandmother warned her about. She looked down at her boots and knew she'd been captured. Lifting her lashes, she locked eyes with the rugged cowboy who exemplified all she'd once feared for her future: passion, submission, and a fiery attraction that felt dangerous, even illegal. She just stared into his eyes for a long time, taking in their obvious love for her and reeling at the idea that somebody loved *her* that way. She had never felt more special. "Yes," she managed.

"Yes?"

"Absolutely. Although my grandmother told me to find an accountant," she joked.

"An accountant, huh? Not a former bull rider?"

"I think I would have remembered if she had told me that."

"Well, one day you'll just have to explain to Grandma that God wrapped your husband in a different package."

"He certainly did." Stefani lifted her eyebrows.

"Oh, before I forget, I'm going to have the contractors come as soon as possible and make our duplexes into one happy home. We'll knock down the walls,

231

take out a kitchen, and put in a nursery or two. What do you think?"

"I don't care where we live as long as we're together."

"Stefani Lencioni Willems, you have made my life a living nightmare over that house. Now that it's finally yours, you're telling me you don't care?" His fists flew to his hips, and he gave her a threatening stare. "Did I miss something?"

"It's a woman's prerogative to change her mind." She shrugged.

"Dare I ask what brought this on?"

"It's a long story. I promised my grandmother I'd get the land back again, but Mom said that she didn't want it. It seems my grandmother was a little dotty by the end, and I was confused about my true heritage. So now it doesn't matter anymore." She shrugged again. "See, it's quite simple actually."

"Am I supposed to understand any of that?"

"No, you just need to know that I've finally made peace with God, and whatever He wills for us, I take happily. If it's the duplex, so be it."

"I was all prepared to make that house into your dream home."

"John, any house with you in it is my dream home. Whether it's on my family's old orchard or in Timbuktu. Come a little closer, cowboy."

"Anything you say, princess." John wrapped his arms around her carefully. She winced, and John gently helped her mount Kayla before him. They rode back to the stables with the new horse trailing behind them and the dwindling sun in the distance.

When they returned to the stables and dismounted, John's sister and Justine were hugging. John walked ahead with the horses, but Stefani followed, anxious to get to the comfort of her car. Her broken ribs ached with every step.

John tethered the horses to the fence and went toward his sister. "Justine and Angela, I'd like you to meet my fiancée, Stefani. Stefani, these charming ladies are my sister, Angela, and her daughter, Justine."

Stefani smiled and hugged both blonds, but moaned from their touch. Her body ached from her fall.

232

Epilogue

Stefani saw her beloved duplex in a whole new light. It felt strange. Like she was visited by an entirely new history, instead of the happy, created memories she had clung to for so long. Knowing her grandfather was an alcoholic and had abused his wife and children sent a shiver down her spine. So much more made sense now: her grandmother's unrelenting hatred for laziness, the constant pressure on Stefani to have her own money, and the old woman's unrealistic view of Stefani's father that had been etched in her mind. Stefani was ashamed that she had believed her grandmother without question.

Stefani had rediscovered herself by knowing the horrifying truth of the family's life on the orchards. How ironic that she'd worked so hard to purchase something for her mother that brought only sadness and bitter memories. God had shown her, in vivid color, the flaw of being self-reliant.

She cuddled next to the fire with a warm mug and waited for John. He'd been gone all day on errands. She prayed over the several job offers she had, and she took great pleasure in the fact that Bob Travers's illegal dealings had come to an end. Although her former boss had threatened to sue her personally and keep her from working, he had found himself being sued personally by the Environmental Protection Agency and facing a long list of criminal charges.

Gladys had continued to get well and was reading her Bible, and while she was making no further commitments at the time, she often had Bert reading it to her. No doubt her skeptical mother needed her husband's guidance, as well. She prayed that her future wedding would serve as an opportunity for her parents to hear that everyone is acceptable for redemption.

The doorbell rang, and Stefani jumped to meet her fiancé. John filled the doorway with a huge bouquet of pink roses, her favorite, and held out a tiny black velvet box. "John? What did you do?"

"Open it."

She pulled him in by the fire, and they stood beside its warmth. She looked at his green eyes, smiling in their excitement. She slowly opened the tiny box and a key fell into her lap. "You got me a key?" she asked, her confusion evident.

"It's the key to my heart."

She wondered if she should thank him for the charming token or pinch him for teasing her unmercifully. She liked his teasing, so she opted for a sweet, dimpled response: "John, you're so old-fashioned."

"And it's also the key to this great little ranch up in the redwoods by Kayla's pasture. I want you to see it before we buy it. It's perfect for a family. A big family."

"How big?" she asked tentatively.

"Well, we already have two horses. We can go from there."

He reached into his breast pocket and pulled out a diamond solitaire ring. "Is this what you were expecting?"

"John!" She couldn't believe her eyes. "It's kinda big!"

"Just like you imagined it would be." He grinned. "My sister told me women like gaudy rings. Is it gaudy enough for you?"

"It's disgusting!" she teased. She slipped it on her finger and watched the fiery lights play off its incredible color.

"So when can I make you mine? Do I have to wait for a big wedding?"

"I'm Italian; of course you have to wait for a big wedding. We'll have to find out when my uncle Vito is available to play the accordion. It will be great! The funky chicken on the accordion is a must for any decent Italian wedding," she teased and rewarded him with her dimpled smile.

"I can hardly wait," he said without inflection.

"I love you, John Savitch."

"It's about time you admitted that."

"It's way past time." She kissed her husband-to-be with genuine passion. The truth had finally set her free. God's truth.

"Do nothing out of selfish ambition or vain conceit, but in humility consider others better than yourselves" (Philippians 2:3).

Meet My Sister, Tess

To my brother, Gary Compani.
Life would never be the same without you.
You are such a blessing.

Chapter 1

Tess Ellison nervously checked her appearance in the small mirror next to the front door. She had left her full, dark brown tresses to dry on their own, and they had curled up into childish ringlets. "I can't believe people pay to have their hair permed. What a mess," she grumbled, lifting the mass into an oversized barrette to keep it off her face.

She noticed the reflection of her brother. He was sitting in his usual position before the blaring television set, carefully threading an ancient reel-to-reel tape player and watching the shiny brown ribbon as it escaped one rotating reel and entered the other. He would continue the procedure until the tape was completely wrapped around one of the reels. Then he would reverse the rotation and start the process again, mesmerized by the circular motion.

Seeing him so relaxed when she was so uptight exasperated her. "Robby, you need to get your shoes on. Clark will be here soon." He ignored her and began making clicking noises to drown her out. "Robby, if you don't get your shoes on, I'm leaving you here!" she screamed. Just then the doorbell rang, and Tess inhaled deeply before answering the door.

Clark Armstrong, Tess's fiancé, appeared in the door frame. His smile abruptly disappeared when he noticed Robby in the background. "What's *he* doing here?" Clark demanded, crossing his arms. "We had a date, Tess."

"I know, but Robby got kicked out of his group home yesterday. I tried to call you at work, but they said you were in court all day. He's here until I find him a new place." Tess knew Clark had little patience for her adult, developmentally disabled brother and even less for Tess's taking care of him. Tess hated being caught in the middle.

"He's a grown man. You can't drop your life every time he gets himself into trouble." Clark looked at her expectantly, then went on. "I put aside my work to be with you tonight. I've got cases ready to go to trial."

"He's autistic, Clark. You can't have the same expectations for him as for a normal adult. Where's your Christian compassion?"

Clark raised a palm. "Don't try to turn this on me. Sugarcoat your terms all you want, but your brother's retarded and needs to be in a home with professionals who can care for him. You've got to work to support yourself, and someday you will be raising our family. I'm not trying to be a villain here—I'm trying to do what's best for you in the long run." He stroked her cheek and walked past her into the living room. Robby soon noticed Clark's presence and rushed toward Tess's fiancé.

Robby was thrilled at the sight of someone new.

"Clark! Clark, why you wear suits? You like ties? You got a secretary, Clark?" Robby's burly frame approached and hugged the clean-cut lawyer with the force of a full-grown bear. The smaller Clark struggled to free himself, but Robby would have none of it. He only increased his grip and mussed Clark's carefully coiffured blond hair.

"Robby, stop it!" Clark yelled. "Tess, could you do something, please?" Robby eventually lost interest in the struggle and released the distraught man. Clark straightened out his suit and sighed repeatedly.

Tess shrugged. "He's just saying hello. He hasn't seen you in a while." Robby never did this to anyone but Clark.

"You have no control over him." Clark used his hand to smooth his hair into place while he glared at her expectantly.

"Of course I don't; he's thirty years old." Tess knew that wasn't exactly true; usually Robby minded well. But when Clark was around, Robby's behavior worsened. Something about Clark made her brother increasingly more enamored of him. "Look, let's just go somewhere casual for dinner and make the best of it," Tess suggested. "I'll get Kelly to watch him this weekend, and we can go out alone then. Okay?"

Robby was ecstatic at the prospect of going out to dinner and stepped into his black-leather zip-up boots without so much as a word from Tess. Robby gripped Clark's upper arm and spoke closely and, because Robby was slightly deaf, loudly. "I want to go to Rockin' Rolls; they got a jukebox."

Tess smiled, and Clark turned around to chastise her. "I fail to see the humor in this. I had reservations at Le Maison."

"I don't think Le Maison would welcome us tonight. Besides, I'm not exactly dressed for it." She spread out her arms and let her fiancé see her worn jeans and T-shirt. "I had to take the afternoon off to collect Robby's things from the home. I haven't had a chance to change or shower."

"All right, then, the burger palace it is." Clark shook his head and grinned, breaking away from Robby. "But Tess is my date, okay?" He took her arm and whispered, "I'm sorry I was so angry; it was just the timing. I wanted to discuss our wedding plans. We've only got six months to go, and a lot of details remain."

The countdown made Tess even more nervous. In only six months, she would be Mrs. Clark Armstrong. She hoped she was doing the right thing. She nodded and tried to appear excited about the wedding plans. She took Clark's arm, and the couple followed Robby to the car.

Because of Robby's girth, he elected to sit in the front seat of the sports car, so Tess climbed into the back, patting her fiancé's shoulder to help him control his rising blood pressure.

～

The restaurant was loud and boisterous: Children cried, the jukebox belted out tunes from the fifties, and waiters shouted food orders to the cooks behind the enormous steel counter.

The host came forward, and Robby immediately perked up. "What's your name?"

"Uh. . .Jim," the host replied, obviously uncomfortable with Robby's interest.

"Jim, meet my sister, Tess." Robby motioned toward her, and she smiled politely, the way she always did when Robby introduced her to everyone nearby.

"How ya doing?" Jim asked.

"Jim, you like Buddy Holly or Elvis?" Robby asked. He cocked his head and waited expectantly, moving closer to the host when the answer didn't come immediately.

Robby's speech was loud, fast, and slurred, and strangers often could not discern his words. Nearly always, they looked to Tess to decipher his questions. She either would do that or reprimand her brother, depending upon the situation.

"Robby, step back and let Jim work," Tess pleaded. "He likes Elvis," she added, answering for the host. Robby backed away, ready to find someone new. They sat in a family-style booth, with Tess seated across from her brother and Clark, who sat on the outside to keep Robby in his seat. The busboy delivered ice waters to the table.

"What's your name?" Robby asked, tossing aside his menu.

"Okay, Robby, no more questions," Tess said. "If you ask any more questions, we're going to have to leave. You need to let the people work."

"It's all right. My name is Michael," the busboy said as he placed the waters and silverware on the table.

"Michael, meet my sister, Tess," Robby said, gesturing proudly toward his sister.

Michael shook hands with Tess while Clark rolled his eyes. "Is this necessary?" Clark muttered. "I mean, do we have to meet absolutely everyone in the place? Because I think there might be some employees in the back we forgot to greet."

"You like my Buddy Holly glasses?" Robby inquired.

Michael nodded, and Tess shot her brother a threatening stare. Robby put up a hand, knowing his sister had reached her limit. "Okay, okay." He opened his menu and hid behind it while he assessed everyone in the restaurant.

"Robby, they have hamburgers, hot dogs, and fried shrimp. What do you want?" Tess questioned.

"Uh, I want a hamburger, french fries," Robby responded, lifting his hand to summon the waiter before Tess pulled his arm to the table.

Clark sank further into the red vinyl seat. He had removed his suit jacket and tie, but he still looked out of place in the nostalgic burger joint. Tess felt sorry for him; she herself had had a lifetime of dealing with Robby and his public escapades. Nothing surprised or embarrassed her anymore; it was just a way of life. Clark seemed to feel that everything Robby did was a direct reflection on him, and Tess had no idea how to alleviate her fiancé's uneasiness.

"I have to go to the bathroom," Robby broadcast loudly.

"Fine, Robby." Inwardly, Tess cringed at the announcement, but she turned to Clark. "Clark, do you mind?" she asked softly.

"Mind what?"

"Taking Robby to the bathroom. One time he got slugged for talking to someone in the bathroom." In truth, Tess never really knew if Robby needed to use the bathroom or not. Usually he just wanted to pose questions to bystanders, and since Tess couldn't enter the men's room, it was a perfect opportunity.

Clark threw his menu on the table. "Fine. I'll do it." He leaned in closely, whispering in Tess's ear. "You're pushing it now. Order me a veggie burger." He took Robby by the arm and handled several conversations Robby had along their route.

Tess sat sipping her Pepsi and tapping her foot to the music. Minutes passed. After the pair had been gone awhile, she allowed herself a flicker of hope; perhaps Clark was trying to accommodate Robby. Tess had hoped that as her fiancé spent more time with her brother, Clark would grow to understand Robby and be less annoyed by his idiosyncrasies. But the opposite seemed to be happening. Tess found her stress level rising every time her two men came into contact. She only felt uncomfortable with Robby when they were with Clark.

She dropped her head into her hands and muttered a heartfelt prayer. "Please, Lord, let Clark see the good in Robby."

Robby returned to the table with his spirits high, while Clark was clearly distraught. Suddenly Robby turned and bounded away, and Clark yelled in exasperation, "Robby, get back to this table—*now!*" Clark gestured sharply, as if he were directing a wayward puppy. When Robby ignored him, Clark slammed his hand on the table, causing the silverware to crash noisily.

Everyone in the restaurant glared at Clark. All could see that Robby was different, but a professional, educated man should know better.

Robby came back to the table tugging one of the most handsome men Tess had ever seen. It wasn't like her to notice good-looking men, but this one was hard to ignore. He was tall, raven-haired, and had blue eyes the color and clarity of a Sierra stream. Tess felt herself being drawn into their depths. His jawline was sharp, and his nose mirrored the perfection found in classical sculpture. His expression was open and inviting, and the crinkles beside his eyes and mouth promised a ready smile. He was attired simply: well-worn jeans and a Stanford sweatshirt.

Tess was mesmerized. Abruptly, she realized she was staring and dropped her eyes to the floor, but they were immediately drawn back to him.

"Meet my sister, Tess," Robby announced in typical fashion. Tess shyly looked the stranger in the eye, keeping her chin low. The thought that Robby should introduce her to more handsome men like this stranger entered her mind, but she immediately chastised herself. She was, after all, getting married in six months.

To her surprise, the man threw an arm around Robby and held out his other for a greeting. "Tess," he said. "What a pleasure to finally meet you. Robby has told me so much about you. He said you were beautiful, but I figured he was probably being kind since you are his sister."

Clark rolled his eyes again. Tess stood and felt tiny next to the tall man. She held out her hand, and he took it firmly. "It—it's nice to meet you," she said. "You know Robby?"

"I'm Robby's new social worker from the Bay Regional Center. I spend two afternoons a week with him. We come here all the time—great burgers." He slapped Robby's back gently. "I think all Robby cares about is the jukebox," he added.

Tess laughed, and the social worker's smiling eyes seemed to warm her. Tess heard Clark groan.

"The name's Greg Wheaton," he began again. "What a nice surprise. I was planning to call you tonight to discuss home options for Robby."

"Amen to that," Clark interjected.

"What?" Greg asked, and Tess turned to glare at her fiancé.

"Greg, this is my fiancé, Clark Armstrong."

Tess stepped out of his way, but Clark simply gave a half salute and muttered, "How ya doing?"

"Do you mind if I steal your fiancée for a moment, Clark? I'd like to discuss the case with her, since I have this unexpected opportunity."

"Be my guest," Clark replied sarcastically. "I was just enjoying the ambiance here anyway." Tess felt leaving Clark alone with Robby was exactly what Clark deserved for his childish behavior.

Outside the restaurant, a loudspeaker trumpeted Robby's music choices. Realizing Greg Wheaton was the type of man who must attract women like a magnet, Tess found it odd that he would be dining alone at Rockin' Rolls. *Does he have a wife waiting at home?* she wondered. She tried to fight what she was experiencing—a strange attraction that wouldn't let her take her eyes off of him. She knew he probably was used to being stared at due to his stunning good looks, but Tess also knew that staring wasn't proper. Try as she might, though, she didn't seem to be able to control her gaze.

"I apologize for interrupting your dinner," Greg began, "but as you know, your brother has been getting into some serious trouble lately. I've been dealing almost daily with the group home management throughout my entire two months on the job. They told me my next step would be to talk with you, but I assumed they'd let me know before they kicked him out. I'm sorry. I–I feel like I failed Robby."

Tess was stunned. Normally, social workers spoke legalese and covered themselves in all ways possible to avoid lawsuits and paperwork. Not so this man. She found herself being equally open with him.

"There's a young woman who has been in various programs with Robby since they were children," she said. "They are volatile together, and when she moved into the group home, I knew Robby's days were numbered. I'm not trying to blame her, but you'd think with their history, the county would know better than to place them in the same home. Don't they keep records? I mean, what's this constant parade of testing and questions if no one's going to look at the records?" Realizing she was allowing intense emotion into her voice, Tess paused to gather her thoughts.

"Don't be discouraged," Greg said kindly. "When you're dealing with someone like Robby, you have to take it one day at a time. I'm sure I'm not telling you anything new." His tone wasn't patronizing—it was gentle, concerned, sincere. She felt he really understood Robby, and that was a first among Robby's various social workers.

Tess found herself wishing Clark possessed a little compassion where Robby was concerned, but then realized it was due to Clark's stable personality that she thought he'd make an excellent husband.

"Look, I'd like to meet with you tomorrow and give you some of Robby's options for homes in the area. I assume you work. . . ."

"I do, but I'm willing to take the day off. When Robby's bus is late for his day program, I'm late for work. So my boss is as anxious as I am to get this resolved. Robby's been kicked out of three homes in the last two years. My boss is pretty understanding, but you can imagine that his satisfaction with me is really being put to the test."

"Do you mind if I ask what you do?"

"I'm an executive secretary at the Nob Hill Hotel in San Francisco. My boss is the general manager."

"That sounds exciting. I bet you get to meet a lot of interesting people."

"Oh, I do—Tony Bennett was there last week," Tess said enthusiastically.

Clark's friends were all so well educated, they failed to see the glamour in a secretarial position of any kind. So she was always reluctant to talk of it. During Tess's second year of college, her mother passed away, and Tess dropped out and took a secretarial position while she tended to her mother's estate settlement and her brother's care arrangements. It was a decision she never regretted, except when asked about her university education. People were well-meaning, but they always made her feel so stupid.

"I'm going to quit work and go back to school when I get married," she added.

"Why?" he asked innocently. "Is there something you'd rather do?" His gaze locked with hers, and she bit her lip self-consciously.

"I don't think so. I like being a secretary."

"Oh." He nodded, and Tess suddenly felt even more stupid than she did when around Clark's associates. "So, is tomorrow okay, then?" he continued.

"Uh. . .what time?" she asked.

"How's eight thirty? I thought you might let Robby stay home from his day program. We could spend the day out of his routine, discussing his needs. That would give me a better understanding of his independence skills. We could do something fun; maybe we could go roller skating in Golden Gate Park?"

"Roller skating?" she asked, astounded. "With Robby?"

"Why not?" He shrugged. "He'd love it, and what better way to meet the people of San Francisco?" He laughed, and she watched him curiously. He *knew* Robby.

She couldn't think of a reason to say no. "That sounds great. Robby will love it. I've been so busy lately, I haven't taken him out much," she admitted, a hint of guilt in her voice.

"Don't worry about Robby. I've had him out at least once a week. We've gone bowling, miniature golfing; we've been to the county fair. Hmm, let's see. . . . Where else have we been?" He put a finger to his chin.

"Never mind. I should have known better than to feel sorry for my brother." She shook her head. "You don't do business like other social workers Robby has had," she commented.

"I will take that as a compliment. Thank you."

"Tomorrow then." They shook hands, and Tess held on a bit longer than necessary before realizing that his touch moved her. She didn't like the way Greg Wheaton made her feel. Her feelings were getting the better of her. Tess was an expert at masking emotions, but for the first time in a long while, they threatened to overwhelm her. She felt sadness over the way Clark treated her brother with contempt, anger over the unfair removal of her brother from the group home, and something she couldn't quite describe with Greg Wheaton.

Greg broke into her thoughts. "Tomorrow I'll be the envy of San Francisco," he said jauntily. She felt a blush rise to her cheeks and was suddenly aware that Clark and her brother were waiting for her to return to the restaurant. Greg seemed to notice her sudden shyness. "I'm sorry; I didn't mean to embarrass you. Let's just say what I said was meant as a compliment to your fiancé, and we'll leave it at that." He nodded toward the booth where Clark and Robby sat.

"Sure," she said as her eyes self-consciously dropped to the sidewalk.

"Feel free to invite him along," Greg added.

"Who, Clark? Uh, thanks, but he doesn't miss a day at the office for anything."

She wrote down her address and phone number, and Greg waved good-bye to Robby and Clark. "See ya tomorrow, Robby!" he called.

As Tess expected, Clark was miserable when she returned to the table, anxious to discuss in detail his latest embarrassments. "Robby did the twist in front of the entire restaurant when the Chubby Checker song was played." Clark looked perturbed beyond measure, but after her pleasant conversation with Greg, a man who appreciated Robby's outgoing traits, she felt bolder than normal.

"Clark, you're a successful corporate attorney. Surely you can handle six minutes alone with my brother."

"That's not the point. This was to have been a date. I expected to sip a rich coffee over a French soufflé, not gulp down a greasy burger in this circus."

Tess wistfully watched the departing Greg through the window of the restaurant. How could two men see Robby so differently?

Chapter 2

Tess cried all night—deep, heart-wrenching sobs. The tears came unrestrained until she fell into a restless sleep. She credited her mood to the emotional evening and her exhaustion from making sure Robby's needs were met. She wept for her brother, for her strained engagement, and for all the opportunities of her life that were different because of her brother. She loved her brother, but life with him was so difficult; nothing was as simple as it might have been. Everyday events were just so much slower when you were introduced to everyone who crossed your path.

It seemed to Tess that the first time she'd actually felt rest in her life was when she was with Clark; that's what made him so appealing. All Clark had required of her was respect and an appreciation of his finer attributes, but somewhere along the line she started feeling his pressure to perform to his high expectations. If pressed, she would admit to loving her fiancé, but it wasn't the kind of love that could hurt her.

God had sustained her through the difficult times, but still, there was something so attractive about having a husband who could fulfill her desperate need for security. Her fiancé wasn't overly affectionate, and that suited Tess just fine. She had buried so many emotions in the past, and with Clark they were safely locked away. It seemed like the perfect partnership—a marriage grown from mutual respect and collective goals. But, once again, Robby had entered into the picture and had complicated things. Now Tess questioned whether or not Clark's even personality wasn't a little too even, a little too staid, and would it hold up to Robby's roller-coaster, thrill-ride life?

Tess overslept after her troubled night and emerged from the shower at the sound of the doorbell. Looking at her alarm clock, she knew it was too early for this to be the new social worker. She threw on her black lycra running pants and an oversized T-shirt and ran downstairs to answer the door. Her hair was a wet mass of mahogany-colored ringlets, so she threw it up in a towel. When she reached the front door, Robby was already there, entreating the poor messenger with a variety of questions.

Tess walked past Robby. "That's enough questions for now, Robby. I'll get you some breakfast in a minute." Tess opened the door wider. "May I help you?"

"Uh—delivery for Tess Ellison," he stammered, handing her a crystal vase full of red roses and baby's breath. "Sign here," he said quickly, obviously anxious to leave.

Tess signed sloppily with her free hand and closed the door. Turning around, she ran into her roommate, Kelly, who eyed the roses with a grin. "Uh-oh, what did Clark do now?"

"Robby went on our date with us last night," Tess commented.

"Oh," Kelly answered with understanding. "Did you make the coffee yet?"

"No, but it's all ready to go; just turn it on." Tess removed the small floral card from its envelope and read it as if she were reading directions for a small appliance.

"Are you ever going to tell him you don't like flowers?" Kelly yelled from the kitchen.

"Do you think it would make a difference?" Tess asked.

"No, but it might force him to be more creative. Maybe next time he could send you a good novel or an old Cary Grant movie. Something you actually care about."

Tess entered the kitchen, and the two women broke into a playful giggle. "Yeah, right," they said in unison.

"It's not that I don't like flowers, I just don't notice them." Tess shrugged as she placed the bouquet on the kitchen table. "Just remind me to throw them out before they smell, okay?"

"Gross." Kelly crinkled her nose.

"I know, I know. But I don't get the point of flowers; they just die. At least a plant lives."

"Not around you it doesn't," Kelly said, making a point of Tess's black thumb. "You are such a romantic. Does Clark know what a warped woman he's marrying?" Kelly removed the coffeepot and filled her cup with the rich, dark liquid.

"Clark knows I've been friends with you for twenty years; *that* ought to give him an indication I'm strange." Tess got a glass of orange juice out of the refrigerator and placed it in front of Robby while he munched microwaved bacon. She poured milk into his cereal bowl and pulled a coffee cup out for herself. She applied her makeup quickly right there in the kitchen and pulled her wild hair into a loose ponytail; several rebellious curls fell around her face.

"I gotta run. I have parent conferences tonight, so I'll be late. Tell Clark I said thanks for the flowers; I'll enjoy them. See ya, Rob." Kelly bounded down the steps and picked up her work basket filled with teaching supplies and lesson plans for the day. She was looking through the door's beveled glass when she said in surprise, "Hey, there's a guy coming up the walk who looks like that actor who plays Bond."

"Oh, that must be Robby's new social worker," Tess answered flatly, as though her previous meeting with him hadn't affected her in the least.

246

"You know this guy? I think my students can wait!" Kelly dropped her basket in its normal place by the door and settled into the couch with her coffee.

"Robby, are you all ready? Greg is here," Tess called, trying to ignore Kelly.

"Me?" Robby got up from the table, excitement filling his expression.

"Yes, Greg is taking us roller skating, so why don't you put on some sweatpants? It'll be cold until this afternoon."

Robby lumbered up to his bedroom while Tess threw on a sweatshirt that read "Ski Tahoe." She looked in the mirror by the sunlit entryway and noticed her eyes were red and puffy from crying.

"It doesn't matter what you look like—you're engaged, remember?" Kelly reminded her from the couch. "How do *I* look?" She puckered her lips, then broke into a familiar boisterous laugh.

"Terrible," Tess responded, deadpan. "So go to work before you cause more trouble."

"Not a chance," Kelly said, while her eyebrows went up and down. "I wouldn't miss this for the world. And no matter what you say, I *know* your type, Tess. You can play cool all you want. This guy gets to you." She then mumbled, "Although next to Clark, who wouldn't?"

Tess grimaced at her friend. Sometimes it was annoying having someone know you so well. Kelly knew Greg impressed Tess, and she was going to stay to see if Greg felt the same way. The whole idea infuriated Tess; she hated being so transparent.

She opened the door, and Greg stood holding the morning paper, his blue eyes sparkling in the sunshine. "Hi," he said, handing it to her.

"Hi. Thanks. Come in." She stepped back. "Would you like some coffee?"

"I'd love some. I can smell it out here." Greg wiped his feet on the mat and entered. "This place is really nice. Is it new?" He looked up toward the cathedral ceilings and let his eyes wander to the oversized window.

"It was new when I bought it about six years ago, after my mom's estate settled. It's not very big, but the amenities are nice. I love the trilevel arrangement—it just makes it feel bigger. That way, when Robby stays here, he's far enough away from my room that I don't have to hear 'La Bamba' all night."

Greg noticed Kelly sitting on the couch and leaned over, reaching out a hand. "Hi, Greg Wheaton."

"I'm sorry. Greg, this is my roommate, Kelly. We've been friends since kindergarten and she has a job to get to."

"Nice to meet you," Greg said sincerely.

"And you," Kelly responded. "Well, I'd better get to work. I don't want twenty unruly five-year-olds loose in my classroom." She stopped in front of Greg in the small foyer, and Tess cringed at the thought of what might come out of her roommate's mouth. Tess stood behind Greg and gave Kelly a threatening stare. "Tess hates flowers, so don't make her mad. Bye," she said brightly as she exited.

Greg just laughed. "What was all that about?"

"Nothing. When you've been friends as long as we have, half of our conversations don't make sense to anyone else. Have you eaten?"

"Yes, thank you. Where's Robby?"

"He's upstairs getting dressed," Tess called from the kitchen. "Do you like cream and sugar?"

"Just black, thanks."

She met him in the dining room and handed him a mug. "I didn't tell Robby until this morning because he would have been too excited to sleep."

"Speaking of sleep, it doesn't look like you got much last night. Are you sure you're up to this?" he asked. She nodded, embarrassed that he had noticed. "Look, I know it's difficult having your brother here, but we'll find something soon, I promise. And it will be something better." He grasped her hand, and again she felt a strange sensation.

Tess shook her head. "I'm used to being responsible for Robby. It'll be easier after I get married. I won't have to work, so I can spend more time making sure Robby's in the right programs. You know, constantly assessing and reassessing, the kind of thing I don't have time for now."

"I thought you liked your job," Greg commented innocently.

"I do. But Clark, my fiancé, says none of the vice president's wives work because they have a full-time job at home. He said that after I finish college, if I want to have a *real* job, that would be fine." She busied herself rinsing the breakfast dishes in the kitchen while Greg leaned against the door frame.

From his expression, she was sure Greg thought her shallow and probably dimwitted. But she knew she couldn't share the real reason she was marrying Clark. She tried to take the focus from herself. "Don't you believe in a woman staying home?"

Greg paused for a moment. "Sure, sure I do—especially if there are kids at home and you can afford it." He shrugged. "I guess you just didn't strike me as the corporate-wife type. No offense."

She smiled. "None taken."

He spoke quietly, intensely. "You seem very capable, Tess. I'm sure you'd be great at whatever you set your mind to doing."

Robby entered the kitchen and surrounded Greg with a pretend headlock. Greg placed his coffee on the table and wrestled back, turning the tables and grabbing Robby in a full, loose headlock. Robby broke into a contagious giggle, and Tess found herself analyzing how long it had been since she'd heard Robby laugh like that.

The men finished their fun, and the threesome walked to the guest parking lot of the complex. Greg unlocked his shiny new Volkswagen Beetle. "You drive a Bug?" Tess was astonished that any man would drive such a "fun" car. It seemed so at odds with her perceptions.

"I had a blue Bug in high school. It was my first love, and I guess you could say I never got over her." He smiled and held the door open for her. She started to climb into the backseat, but Greg took her by the arm and gently pulled her out. "Robby, you ride in the back. The first thing you need to learn, buddy, is that women always ride in the front. Understood?" He slapped Robby on the back in his rough, thoroughly masculine way.

"Understood," Robby grumbled, sliding into the backseat. He held a handful of cassette tapes and was disappointed that he wouldn't have free access to the stereo. "Greg, you like Chubby Checker or Jimmy Buffett?" Robby riffled through his cassettes and listed the oldies they might choose from.

"Tell you what. You pick, and I'll put the stereo on in back so I can talk with your sister."

"Okay. . .James Taylor," he decided, handing Greg the cassette.

Greg reached back over his shoulder and took the tape. "Great. He's one of my favorites." He slid the cassette into the stereo and turned the knob to switch the music to the back.

Tess watched, incredulous. "Did you notice the condition of my brother's tapes? Your car is brand new; are you sure—"

"Robby's been in this car about fifty times already. Any damage done to the stereo is already done. Besides, look at that smile." He nodded toward the backseat. "That's worth the price of a stereo, wouldn't you say?"

"No," Tess said.

Greg laughed out loud. "Different strokes, I suppose. It's just a car. My grandmother always said, 'Don't cry over anything that can't cry over you.' "

"Smart lady," Tess said quietly.

"She was my biggest fan and my sharpest critic. I only wish she'd lived to see me get married." He merged onto the freeway and avoided her gaze, concentrating on the traffic.

"Are you getting married?" Tess stammered, realizing too late that she sounded too interested.

"No, but I think my grandmother would have known if I picked the right woman. Now I'm on my own. Well, I've got Robby. Have you noticed how your brother has a sixth sense about people?"

"No."

Greg continued, not noticing Tess's discomfort. "I mean he doesn't take to certain people. Sure, he talks to everyone, but he doesn't *take* to everyone. Haven't you noticed that when people treat him poorly, he bugs them all the more? Not in his fun way, but in kind of a spiteful, annoying way."

That was just how Robby treated Clark, and the insinuation didn't set right with her. "Who? Who does he treat like that?" she asked angrily, trying to prove Greg wrong.

"Oh, I don't know. Let's see. . .Lyn, the woman who got him removed from his home, for one. He drives her absolutely crazy. You really haven't noticed that before?"

"This has nothing to do with Robby's present situation. Can we please talk about his living arrangements?" she demanded.

"Certainly. See that yellow folder on the floor there? That's a listing of all the homes that have openings right now. Robby's not qualified for all of them, but there are a few that I think he would do well in. I don't know how you feel about God, but there's a very good Christian home in the mix that I think would be perfect for Robby. Robby's a very spiritual person; he loves the Lord." Greg looked at her with his last statement, and Tess felt her mouth drop.

"I thought social workers weren't allowed to talk religion—thought you were all atheists." Tess glared at him, but he kept his eyes on the road.

"Where'd you get that idea? I am a Christian, and I couldn't do this job without Him." He pointed upward. "So, are all secretaries atheists?" he asked, a sparkle in his blue eyes as he turned toward her momentarily.

"Very funny. Tell me more about the Christian home."

"It's in Emerald Hills and run by a community church up there. One of their pastors had a son like Robby and found there were no quality homes where disabled adults could live semi-independent lives in a Christian environment. So he and his wife created one. There's a brochure in the folder, toward the back there." He reached over and began riffling through the papers. "I think it's green."

"Here it is," she answered, pulling out a trifold sheet. "Serenity Springs. It sounds like a cemetery." She scowled.

"They're caregivers, not marketing experts. Just read the brochure." He laughed, and she found herself smiling against her will.

"It sounds great. Is it coed? I'll probably just get him settled, then Lyn will move in."

"It is coed, but men and women are in separate buildings, not just separate bedrooms. They dine together and work together during chore times, but at seven they are required to be in their own building, unless there's a planned activity. And Diane, the woman who runs it, reads all of the reports thoroughly. So I don't think you'll have to worry about Lyn being admitted after Diane sees Robby's history. If you're interested, we can go visit this afternoon after skating."

"Greg—I mean, great." Tess turned around and saw Robby happily rocking

250

to his Walkman, which he had put on during the ride. Tess pressed a button and turned off the stereo.

After a forty-minute drive from Tess's Redwood Shores home, Greg pulled up to Golden Gate Park and found a parking place right next to the duck pond. He grinned. "The early bird gets parking in San Francisco."

Greg helped them both out of the car and opened the trunk. Two sets of rollerblades in luminous purple and black shimmered in the sunlight. Next to them was one pair of bulky, old-fashioned roller skates for Robby.

"I assume you rollerblade," he said to Tess, pulling out a small pair of skates.

"I do, but I think those are Cinderella's skates and I've got the ugly stepsister's feet." She held up the skates and opened the boot, looking for the size. Everything about Tess was tiny, except for her hair and feet. Her mother always said she looked like a puppy that hadn't quite grown into her paws and needed a good clipping. "Whose are these?" she asked.

"They're my sister's," Greg answered.

"She has awfully small feet. I'm afraid if I wear her skates, I might damage them."

"Those were hers when she was thirteen; she's sixteen now. They don't fit her anymore. You're so small, I assumed they'd fit you."

"Guess you never got a glimpse of my feet, huh?" She let out a short laugh.

"Sit down. If Prince Charming can make the glass slipper fit, I can make these fit." She sat down in the front seat and turned her legs outside the car. Greg pulled her socks up tightly, unlaced the skates, then gently slid them onto her feet. His touch against her foot brought back that feeling that was becoming familiar. He laced the skates as tightly as her foot would allow and helped her to her feet. "See? Nothing to it." They felt tight, but she wouldn't admit it. She'd wear Cinderella's slippers with a smile.

Robby sat on a nearby park bench while Greg outfitted him in skates and all the protective gear known to humankind. After everyone was equipped, Greg laced his own skates and they were off. Greg and Tess flanked Robby and helped him as he tried to stay upright. Robby had about as much grace as an elephant on ice skates, but he was anxious to get away from Greg and Tess and talk to the tourists that milled around the gardens. It wasn't long before Robby was confident enough to take off ahead of them, not needing them to grasp his arms any longer.

Their skates provided a speedy way around the lush grounds of the park. Robby seemed to enjoy having Tess and Greg behind him and began to skate faster and faster. But Robby hadn't yet learned to stop, and the couple realized this at precisely the same time. Greg and Tess stopped momentarily, then looked to one another with wide eyes. They leaned forward and began skating as fast as their legs would carry them. Meanwhile, Robby was gleefully hollering as he descended one of the park's infamous inclines.

"Robby, stop!" Greg yelled.

"Robby, roll your foot forward!" Tess screamed. Just then they noticed that Robby was closing in on a bystander who was intently gazing at a cherry tree. "Sir!" Tess yelled, trying to get the man's attention, but to no avail. She squeezed her eyes shut, unable to watch.

Robby straightened his arms out before him and ran headlong into the man, hanging onto him as he spun around to a stop. Tess opened her eyes. The shocked tourist just stared at Robby. "Are you okay?" he asked when they were both steadied.

"Yeah, yeah. What's your name?" Robby asked.

Greg and Tess skated up and apologized profusely. The man held up a hand. "No harm done. No problem," he said in a thick German accent.

"You talk funny. Where you born?" Robby asked.

"Austria," the man stated.

Robby inhaled excitedly, pointing to the man and looking to Tess. "Like Arnold!" Robby screamed.

"Yes." The man laughed. "Just like Arnold Schwarzenegger."

"What's your name?" Robby repeated.

"Einer," the man replied. "And the beautiful woman over there taking the picture, that is my wife, Petra."

Petra joined the small group. "Hello," she said.

"Hello," Greg replied. "I'm Greg Wheaton and these are my friends, Tess and Robby Ellison. I'm afraid Robby introduced himself to your husband a bit too forcefully."

"I saw that." Petra laughed. "That will teach him to not become so entranced by the trees. Next time he'll pay attention. Besides, I got a much more exciting picture than I would have of the tree alone." She held up her camera and they all laughed.

"You like Elvis?" Robby asked Petra. She looked confused, then turned toward Greg so he could decipher Robby's speech.

"He wants to know if you like Elvis Presley."

She nodded, "Yes, yes. We both like Elvis, don't we, Einer?"

"Everyone likes Elvis," he answered, his German accent cutting the words sharply.

The small group skated and walked, discussing everything from American politics to art. They sipped bad coffee and listened to a mediocre high school band in the park's shell-shaped amphitheater. By the end of the day, they had become fast friends, meeting other tourists from Japan, China, Italy, and the Philippines.

After the mini-concert, Greg turned toward Tess. "You look exhausted.

Maybe we should postpone our tour of the home today." Greg gently placed his hand on her shoulder.

Tess looked at her watch and saw that it was already four in the afternoon. Where had the day gone? The last thing she wanted to do was end the fun day, but she was almost too weary to get back to the car. Between missing a good night's rest and skating all day, Tess felt answering Greg's question might prove too tiring. Her mouth didn't want to move. "I think you're right about Serenity Springs, Greg. I hate to waste your time, though; I'll go visit Saturday by myself. You don't have to hold my hand."

They skated slowly toward his car. "Sit down." Greg pointed to a bench near his blue Bug, which Robby had already entered. Robby had fallen asleep in a matter of seconds, and Tess found herself wishing she could do the same. Greg carefully began removing her skates, and she felt her head beginning to wobble from weariness. But then he touched her, and she felt the electric tingle run through her body.

She found herself gazing at his handsome face. She closed her eyes and opened them again, only to find he was even more attractive after the brief respite. "Why did you do this?" she asked suspiciously.

"Unlace your skates?" he asked. "Because you looked too tired to reach them." He laughed, and the small crinkles around his blue eyes deepened.

His lighthearted treatment of her question only made her more suspicious.

"No, why did you take us skating today? I know your caseload doesn't allow you to waste this kind of time. . . ." She didn't know what kind of answer she expected. It would have been improper to tell her what she wanted to hear—that he wanted to be next to her. But logic seemed to fly out the window when she looked at him, and that alone made her uncomfortable.

He held her foot for a moment longer, then handed her a worn white running shoe. He remained in a crouch with his arms draped over his long legs. "I did it because Robby is my favorite client. And because last night in the restaurant, you looked like you needed to be reminded what a blessing he is." He sat beside her on the bench.

Tess fumbled with her shoe and concentrated on its faded canvas, avoiding the mesmerizing intensity of his eyes. "I *know* what a blessing Robby is!" she replied angrily. "But he's also a lot of work, and sometimes you get tired, Greg. When you are done with your caseload, you go home and it's all over." She swiped her hands together. "It's never over for me. I have to make sure Robby is with someone every moment of the day. So, I'm sorry if the romance of your viewpoint is lost on me."

"I don't know what you have against social workers, but you seem to think we're all out to get our clients."

"I just don't think you have the same level of responsibility I have. You can

253

concentrate on the positives in your clients because you're not with them every day. When they get kicked out of their day program, you don't have to skip work until they find a new one; you just write up the report and you're done. I'm worn out, Greg, and I'm only twenty-six. I've been looking out for my brother since I was seven. I've never even been away from him on a vacation. And I wonder what it's like to be free. Is that so awful?" She had never admitted that to anyone, and she was overcome by guilt after she'd said it.

"Is that why you're getting married?" His smooth baritone was soft and encouraging. Had he noticed that Tess was moved by him? That Clark seemed to fade into the background when she looked at him? Certainly she was capable of treating her fiancé with more respect, and she vowed to do so in the future. But had he noticed that she and Clark lacked what many young engaged couples had—a starry-eyed gaze.

Tess was tempted to tell Greg everything, but she knew telling him, telling anyone, would release a torrent of emotion that she'd carefully kept under control. *This is why I'm with Clark,* she reasoned; *he never asks such personal questions, and he certainly never analyzes simple comments. This guy is too analytical, too nosy, and just too intense.* She hated the way he seemed to reach into her and pull out feelings—feelings buried long ago.

"Of course that's not why I'm getting married," she said sharply. Did he wonder why she could so easily be under the spell of another man? Tess had wanted a prince to come rescue her, and Clark was ready, willing, and able. For a price.

"I didn't mean to imply anything. I just wondered. . .well, never mind." Greg stood and held his hand out to her. "I had a great time being international with you!" Tess was relieved that he had changed the subject, and they laughed together, remembering Robby's many crashes into people. He never did learn to stop on his own.

Tess tried to speak through her giggle; she covered her mouth self-consciously to relay her best memory of the day. "My favorite was the Japanese models. To see those beautiful, petite women holding big ol' Robby up while he played the invalid, and all the while he's enjoying the company of those gorgeous women, *that* was priceless!" Tess threw her head back, unable to contain her laughter.

His smile left. "That infectious laugh. *That* is why I brought you here today," he said seriously, the crinkles disappearing from his eyes. She felt herself swallow hard. "So you could remember the blessing of Robby," he said. Suddenly, she understood.

Chapter 3

Tess came home from skating to find three messages from Clark on her answering machine. The first was amiable and indicated concern about her absence from work. The second was insistent, requesting that she call back immediately, as he had made plans for the evening. And the third was heated, his voice edgy as he made clear his annoyance at being unable to reach her all day.

Before she had time to contemplate the final message, the phone rang again. "Hello," she said.

"Tess, where have you been? I've been worried sick. I even called Kelly at school looking for you. She didn't have any idea where you were. . ." Clark's voice was strained. Tess rolled her eyes over Kelly keeping her day with Robby a secret. Kelly never did like Clark, and apparently she saw Greg as a better option. Tess hadn't meant to be deceitful, but she had to smile at Kelly's secretive response.

"Robby and I met with Greg Wheaton today to discuss homes for Robby. Greg wanted to assess Robby's independence skills in public."

"And?"

"And I'm going to investigate a possibility on Saturday."

"Saturday? Tess, it's only Thursday. How long do you plan on having Robby live with you? It's hardly fair to Kelly," Clark reasoned. But Tess knew better than to think her fiancé was actually worried about her roommate's well-being. Kelly had grown up with Robby, too, and his presence didn't bother her.

"I can't take tomorrow off; my boss needs me back or his correspondence will be backed up for a week. Robby will be fine here until the end of the month." Tess was so ecstatic about her day, she couldn't wait to share it. "Oh, Clark, you should have seen Robby today in Golden Gate Park! He was on roller skates! I would never have had the guts to try that, but he did great. The best part was that he never learned to stop, and he just kept finding some innocent bystander to use as a backstop. Except I know he really could stop, because when a toddler walked in front of him, he had no problem stopping. It was such fun meeting everyone when they were still stunned by Robby's surprise attack." Tess smiled and shook her head. "Oh, and if we go to Austria—"

"You took a day off work to *play* in Golden Gate Park? Tess, how do you ever expect to be more than a secretary if you don't have a solid work commitment?"

Clark chastised, and the joy in Tess fled.

"Clark, I've been at the hotel for seven years. I've got four weeks of vacation saved up. . . ."

"Yes, but all the vacation and sick days you *have* taken have been for your brother's problems. You'd have a lot more time saved if you weren't trying to fix the messes he gets himself into. I want us to have a special honeymoon, Tess, so don't waste the days we have coming to us."

"But I still have four weeks! That's plenty of time for a honeymoon. I can't go for too long anyway—who would watch over Robby?"

"*Professionals,* people who should be doing their job in the first place. Honestly, think if I ran my law firm the way these bureaucrats run these homes. I'd be out of business." He suddenly switched topics. "Look, the vice president of sales is having a small get-together tonight. I need my beautiful fiancé to make me look good. Are you available?" he asked brightly, his earlier rebuke forgotten.

Tess looked down at her filthy sweatshirt and tired lycra pants. "Tonight? Kelly's got parent-teacher conferences tonight, and I don't think I can get a sitter on such short notice."

"Call around. They've got that social-worker thing that helps out, right? Anyway, I'll call you back in ten and give you the directions." Clark hung up, and she gazed at the phone in disbelief. Robby was sleeping on the sofa, a deafening snore emanating from him.

Tess sighed aloud and dialed Kelly's classroom. Her friend answered immediately.

"Kelly, why didn't you tell Clark where I was today?" Tess put a hand on her hip and tapped her foot, knowing she'd never get a straight answer from her roommate.

"Did I talk to Clark today? It's just been so busy, I—"

"Spare me the innocent routine. I know what you're thinking, and you can just forget it. I'm marrying Clark, and any fairy tales you have in that head of yours need to disappear."

"But he drives a Beetle, Tess! He looks like heaven on earth, and I know he's a Christian because he had a fish symbol on his car. Plus, doesn't he just seem to exude Holy Spirit joy? He seems like so much fun. And his name is Greg, your favorite Brady! It's a sign!"

"Do you want to date him?" Tess asked pointedly. "Because I could arrange it."

"I don't think he likes blonds. He seems to have an eye for the dark-haired Mediterranean type."

Tess changed the subject. "Can you watch Robby tonight?"

"Are you and Greg meeting over dinner to discuss Robby?" she cooed.

"No, Kelly, would you get your mind off him? Clark has a business get-together tonight."

"Oh," she groaned.

"Please," Tess begged. "I owe him one after last night. What time is your last conference?" She looked at her watch, thinking she'd better get into the shower fast. With her thick hair, drying time was a significant part of her shower routine.

"I can be there by seven if that's okay."

"That would be great. Thanks. I gotta run and get dressed."

"Yeah, yeah. I still think a business meeting with dreamy Greg sounds like more fun than dinner with a bunch of lawyers!"

"Give it a rest. I'm putting a chicken in the oven for you and Robby, so don't eat." Tess hung up the phone, locked the front door, and threw a light blanket over her slumbering brother before running upstairs to her bedroom to make herself presentable.

～

Tess drove to the city alone and pulled up to the San Francisco address she'd scribbled down on a scrap of paper. The host had hired valet parking, so she stepped out of her trusty old Honda and handed the keys to a red-jacketed young man. He disdainfully eyed the simple, ten-year-old sedan.

Stepping into the elevator, she checked her appearance in the mirrored wall. Her hair was elegantly set in a bun, with small wisps hanging along her long neck. She wore a short black cocktail dress with a cropped bolero jacket, and the length of pearls that Clark had given her for her birthday. Gazing at her reflection, she saw a completely different woman from the one that afternoon whose thin, lycra-outfitted legs contrasted with her overgrown-puppy feet in clunky skates. Tonight she looked. . .grown-up.

When she arrived on the penthouse level, the elevator opened to a gathering of about twenty-five people—all in their midthirties and all dressed in dark, classic clothing. She smiled as she speculated about how much they all must have paid to look alike. Suddenly she didn't feel grown-up at all, but like the little girl who had spent a carefree day skating around Golden Gate Park. Clark's strained, smiling face met her.

"Tess, I'm so glad you made it. This is my colleague, Jennifer Ness." A shapely blond stood beside Clark. She seemed very interested in Tess and didn't see the need to hide the fact. Tess felt herself being scrutinized and judged. She wondered if the woman could tell her dress was off the rack of the discount store, rather than one of the designer dresses Clark had bought for her.

She suddenly felt hot. It wasn't necessarily the examination itself that bothered her—she was used to that with Clark's friends. It was something else—it was as if Tess held something that Jennifer wanted. Tess looked at Clark; could Jennifer be interested in him? The thought threw her, for Clark was not someone Tess thought of as extremely interesting. He was just ordinary, nondescript Clark.

"What a pleasure to finally meet you, Tess," Jennifer cooed. "Clark goes on and on about you. I could hardly wait to see who had him so head over heels." She ran her hand along Clark's sleeve, and Tess smiled to hide her discomfort. Oddly enough, she didn't feel jealousy, just an increased desire to leave the stuffy party. She longed to breathe some of the cold, foggy air outside these walls.

Tess felt herself smile wider, and she spoke some appropriate response to Jennifer. She lifted a foot and flexed her ankle to relieve a dull ache; wearing heels after a long day skating was agony.

"What do you do, Tess?" the young blond inquired.

"I'm an executive secretary for Nob Hill Hotel," she rattled, waiting for the standard prodding about her education.

"Where did you—"

"I didn't finish college." Tess looked at the glittering diamond on her left hand unconsciously. *Here we go*, she thought.

"Oh," the other answered haughtily.

"Tess had family responsibilities during college; she had to drop out. She's planning to attend Berkeley this semester." Clark smiled down at her as though she were best of show at the American Kennel Club's annual event.

She wished she were home with an iced tea in her hand, her feet up on the coffee table, and an old *I Love Lucy* rerun on the television. She found herself looking at Clark in a new light, wondering if she could endure a lifetime of his company.

"Would you like a shrimp cocktail, Tess?" Clark placed his hand gallantly in the middle of her back, and she nodded. It had been hours since she'd eaten, and she was famished. Clark left the two women in search of the hors d'oeuvre table, while Jennifer continued to make conversation.

"So where did you two meet?" she asked before sipping her Italian water.

"At church," Tess replied, wishing Clark would return promptly.

"Church? I can't imagine Clark at church—I guess because I see him 'go for the throat' all day at work," Jennifer said, and Tess just nodded. "You know those lawyers."

"Are you a lawyer, too, Jennifer?"

"Oh no. I'm vice president of sales. This is my party, actually."

Tess thought the young woman looked far too young to be a vice president, but she could easily see the sales personality in her. "This is a beautiful place. You've got a fantastic view of the Golden Gate Bridge."

"Thank you. I understand you and Clark are looking at the penthouse up the block. Wouldn't that be an easy commute for you to the hotel? You could just hop on the cable car or walk, if you were up to the hills." Clark returned, and Jennifer directed her attention to him. "Clark, she's absolutely charming." For some reason, Tess felt it wasn't the compliment it was meant to be. "I'm so glad you could both make it tonight, especially since we might be neighbors. I need to check on dinner, but please make yourselves at home."

Clark handed Tess her shrimp cocktail glass and wore a pained expression as he rubbed the back of his neck. The moment Jennifer departed, Tess glared at Clark. "Why are you looking at penthouses?" Her voice was discreet, but Clark's scowl told her this was no place for such a discussion. But for some reason, she simply couldn't hold her tongue tonight. "Robby needs to remain in San Mateo County to stay in his day program, and I need to be close to him." Hadn't that been their agreement?

"Tess, Robby is not going to be around forever. We can't plan our lives around him," he whispered harshly, hoping he'd shut her up, but his comment had the opposite effect.

Tess stepped backward, her mouth wide with horror, and slowly her fingertips came to her mouth. She studied him for a moment, hoping to see a glimmer of sorrow, but there was nothing, only distress that their conversation might be noticed by his colleagues.

"Of all the cold-hearted, self-centered. . . Make my excuses." She turned to leave and felt his arm wrap around her waist.

"Tess, you can't leave before dinner. What would I say? Sit down and have a mineral water; we can discuss this later," he said firmly, never relinquishing his grip on her waist.

Her eyes were narrow with rage; she had to clench her teeth to keep from screaming at him for his callous remark. It was annoying that he had gone against their agreement, but to blatantly disregard her brother in hope that Robby might not live long was more than she could bear. Her small frame shook with anger, and it took every ounce of self-control within her to keep her emotions in check.

"Make my excuses or I'll make that scene you are so worried about."

He followed her into the elevator and held her hand so their argument might appear to be a moment alone together for two lovebirds. The elevator doors closed, and his affectionate facade quickly faded. "Tess, you know I didn't mean anything by that; I'm just being practical."

She took her forefinger and ground it into his chest. "I know you are extremely practical. That's one of the reasons I want to marry you, but sometimes, Clark. . .sometimes your 'practicality' is downright cold, and there's no excuse for that. I'm trying my best not to embarrass you in front of your coworkers, so let me go." She pointed at the elevator doors. "If I go back in there, I will not be able to live up to my part of the agreement, which, may I remind you, you broke by house hunting in San Francisco. You know I'm not given to tantrums."

"Tess, this isn't like you. Since when did you become a victim of your emotions? I know you are capable of going back in there, and I need you to do that." He fiddled with his tie, and she could see small beads of sweat taking shape on his forehead.

"Clark, I wouldn't do this to prove a point; you know me better than that. I *need* to leave. It's been a long day, and this evening has just gone from bad to worse." The elevator opened to the lobby, and she stood on her tiptoes and kissed his cheek. "I'll call you tomorrow." She left him alone in the elevator, his brow furrowed in confusion.

Chapter 4

Tess dragged herself up the steps of her condominium and plopped on the couch in exhaustion. Kelly was eating popcorn and correcting papers. "I told you you should have gone out with Greg," Kelly commented without looking up from her work.

"Not funny, Kelly. Not funny at all." Tess was in no mood to be teased, even if her friend was right.

"I didn't mean it to be funny. You're a secretary, Tess. Every time you come home from one of Clark's little get-togethers, you're miserable. Why do you want to go through life like that?" Kelly removed her glasses and dropped the binder sheet she held in her hand. "Those people value all the wrong things, Tess. Why would you want to join them?"

"I don't care about any of that. I just want to know Robby will be taken care of and that I'll have the time and money to ensure his care. I want to be certain no one will ever have power over us again. Marrying Clark puts me back in control—he understands my needs and I understand his."

"Sounds like you need to trust in God a little more and Clark a little less. You can't *ensure* your future, no matter whom you marry. That's Christianity 101. Where's your faith? God will only find another way to perfect your faith if you choose this marriage."

"Where's Robby?" Tess asked, changing the subject.

"Still sleeping. He woke up for dinner, then went straight up to bed. I guess roller skating wore him out."

"Me, too. I can't believe I have to go to work tomorrow. I feel like the walking wounded." Tess pulled her hair down from her tightly wrapped bun and threw off her heels, rubbing her tired feet. "See, with Clark this wouldn't be an issue," Tess said, inadvertently changing the subject back to her upcoming marriage.

"Tess!"

"You know what I went through with Robby as a child. Clark can ensure that no one can hurt us that way anymore. I'm marrying him because he's stable and he'll make a good, solid husband."

"Come on, Tess. It sounds like you're buying a used car. I haven't heard the word *love* once."

"He's good for me, Kelly. Just because I don't fawn over him doesn't mean

I don't love him. You don't get to see some of his better qualities. He's arranged my admission at Berkeley and paid for my books and tuition."

"That's because he doesn't want his wife to be a college dropout. Look, if you really love Clark, forget I said any of this. But if you're marrying him for a shot at security for you and Robby, give him up now. I beg you. Neither of you deserves that. Besides, I don't see what's so wrong with your life right now." Kelly shrugged. "You've got a great place here and a job you love, so I guess I'm missing what's eating you."

"You wouldn't understand," Tess answered cryptically.

"Try me."

Tess hesitated a moment, then decided to take a chance; perhaps Kelly would understand. "It's like what I did to Doug Marshall to get him back for all his teasing."

Kelly eyed her warily. "Doug was just a stupid kid who didn't know better when he hurt your brother. You were old enough to know better than to exact revenge!"

Tess ignored the reprimand. "See, marrying Clark is insurance that I'll be able to control Robby's environment. That he won't be in hurtful surroundings anymore. That the Doug Marshalls of the world won't get near him."

Kelly's mouth dropped open in shock. "Tess, please tell me this is a joke. You can't protect Robby from everyone that might hurt him, and you can't protect yourself, either. That's what I think your real motive is. I think you're marrying Clark because he's a nice guy, and you don't care all that much for him. Robby doesn't realize these people are teasing him anyway." Kelly slapped her palm to her head for emphasis.

She had nailed Tess's reasoning, and the bride-to-be clambered for a way out of the conversation. "I said you wouldn't understand." Tess stood up and began to unzip her dress.

"I understand perfectly, Tess. God gave you beauty; that's undeniable. But He didn't give it to you to use against people. You don't marry someone because he has something you want and he's willing to exchange it for your package! Marriage is hard enough with someone you love. Trust me, I know." Kelly's voice was tinged with sadness as she obviously recalled her own failed marriage.

"Clark is a gentleman. He will take care of me, and I'll take care of him. Just because we don't act on pure emotion, you think this marriage won't last. But marriages last because both people are committed to the sanctity of marriage, not just the person they're marrying. Clark and I both feel that way," Tess explained rationally. If she were being completely honest with her friend, though, she would have to admit that Clark had done things lately that had caused her both to question his motives and his Christianity.

"Fine. I'll say no more about it." Kelly held up a hand with her blue eyes downcast, hidden behind her hanging blond bob. "If you're determined to do this, I'll support you, but I will not stand up beside you unless you've proven to me you love Clark. You stood beside me on that altar when you knew I was making a mistake marrying George. You didn't do me any favors, did you?"

"No," Tess answered solemnly.

"Okay, then. You've got five months to prove this is the man you truly desire— with all your heart—to marry."

Tess nodded, struggling with how she could convince her best friend that a marriage without passionate romance would be best for her. She climbed the stairs without another word, her thoughts in turmoil.

She slept until half past seven and shot out of bed when she noticed the time—she had shut off the alarm nearly an hour before. She ran to Robby's room, but found his bed unmade and him gone. She flew downstairs and found him in the kitchen, with Kelly making him a breakfast of eggs and pancakes.

"Thank you, Kelly. I needed the extra sleep. What would I ever do without you?"

"Probably wilt away," Kelly teased.

"I'm sorry about last night," Tess said truthfully.

"I'm not. I just want you to be happy, Tess."

"I'll be late tonight. Robby's got a dance at the community center."

"So, I'll see you after the dance, around ten?" Kelly grinned. She was hinting at how Tess always danced with Robby's friends instead of coming home after dropping Robby off.

"Very funny. I'm not staying." Tess cut her hand through the air. "I don't care how many of Robby's friends ask me to dance or how sweet they are," she said, holding her chin high.

"You say that every time, but your heart always wins out. You can't bear to hurt anyone's feelings. So, I expect I'll see you around ten." Kelly grabbed her work basket and headed downstairs. "Bye, Robby. Have fun at the dance."

"Robby, hurry up and get dressed. Your bus will be here soon. And you need to shave and brush your teeth. Go on upstairs; I'll put your breakfast in a plastic bag." Tess cleared away the dishes in front of him, and he slowly climbed the stairs.

"I hate to brush my teeth," he screamed and bit his forefinger. "I not want to shave!" he wailed. He stopped on a stair and began to beat the wall with his free fist, keeping the finger of the other hand clenched in his teeth.

"Robby, stop it! Please, not today or you won't get to go to the dance." Tess nearly threw the dishes into the sink. She simply didn't have the patience for one of Robby's tantrums today. She was running late as it was, and after two short nights of sleep, her patience was long gone.

"I not want to shave!" he moaned, now holding onto the railing so he could kick the wall.

"Robby, either get dressed now or you will come home tonight instead of go to the dance. And there will be no television or music, either."

Robby began to whine in frustration, but he reluctantly climbed the stairs.

Tess could hear him in his room throwing things, but at least he was getting dressed. Tess closed her eyes and bent over the kitchen sink in defeat. Looking out the kitchen window, she cringed at the sight of Robby's bus parked in the drive, waiting. She caught the bus driver's eye with a wave and shook her head. The bus driver nodded, and Tess heard the bus's engine start up; the sound nearly made her cry. Robby hadn't made it; Tess would have to drive him herself. "Why?" she yelled in frustration, her hands over her head.

Tess threw on a pair of black slacks and a white polyester-blend shell with a red jacket. It was her standard "late" outfit because it never required ironing or nylons. She helped her brother brush his teeth and took the electric razor to his face haphazardly. When his appearance was satisfactory, she applied her makeup and hurried Robby into the car, taking along a handful of cassettes to appease him.

~

Five o'clock came quickly, and Tess dashed from her desk, waving to Klaus as she headed toward the garage. With traffic, it took her forty minutes to get to Robby's program, and she still had to get them dinner and help Robby into his tie and sport coat. They ate fast food in the community center parking lot, and she knotted his tie at precisely 6:30.

"Stop the clock! We did it!" Tess exulted.

Robby picked up his box of 45-rpm records to play on the old record player at the dance. "Tess, you like Elvis?" he asked excitedly.

"Not really, Robby. Do you have your name on all those records? You don't want to lose them." Looking into her brother's eager eyes, she suddenly felt guilty for being such a nag. Robby was so excited, and Tess's frantic scheduling was ruining his enjoyment.

"Let's goooo!" he whined impatiently.

Tess sighed and followed her brother to the doors. About seventy-five disabled adults milled around the old cinder block building, waiting anxiously for the music to start. Robby was out of her sight before she even signed him in. A Down's syndrome adult took his place as DJ. He quietly explained that this would be a tribute to the eighties, and music started pounding off the walls. The old record skipped soon after it was placed on the turntable, and the DJ ripped it off with a loud screech. It was soon replaced, but the dancers seemed oblivious to the change.

After signing Robby in, Tess turned to leave quickly. She was stopped by a burly, smiling young man in the doorway. "You want to dance?" Tess could tell by his hand motions and speech impediment that he was deaf as well as developmentally disabled. She always wondered why these children of His so often had health problems in addition to their lowered mental capacity. It would be one of the first questions she would ask God when given the opportunity. "You want to dance?" the young man repeated.

No, no, I don't, she thought. *I have a million things to do tonight without Robby in the house.*

"Sure," she said with a nod, wanting to kick herself because she knew she'd never get out the door now. Kelly was right—Tess couldn't say no to Robby's friends. They seemed to have such pure hearts and intentions. Whenever Tess was among them, she couldn't think of anything more important than sparing their feelings. So she danced for nearly an hour with different partners until the DJ took a break from his montage of music.

Tess's latest dance partner brought her a punch, and she explained that she was Robby's sister. The music soon started up again, and the DJ said, "Do the hustle," into his microphone, and the old seventies song began.

"This is before my time," Tess admitted. She was startled by a familiar voice behind her.

"Then let one of us old-timers teach you." She turned to see Greg Wheaton, an inviting smile on his devastatingly handsome face. "May I cut in?" he asked her partner.

"You g–go ahead, Mr. Wheaton. Y–you boogie," he stuttered.

"There's nothing to it," Greg said as he began sidestepping, adding a slight kick of his leg at the end. "Doot, doot, doot, dudoot, doot, doot, doot." His hands were clenched in tight fists, his elbows bent, and his shoulders bobbed dramatically to the disco beat. He bit his lower lip and closed his eyes, acting as though he was really feeling the music, but she could see his smile breaking through and a squinting eye watching her. At the appropriate moment, he opened his eyes and shouted, "Do the hustle!" pointing his finger into the air in true John Travolta style.

Tess threw back her head and laughed aloud. Seeing this Adonis lookalike doing the hustle so intently sent her into a giggling frenzy. He grabbed her and beckoned her to join him. She allowed him to pull her to the dance floor, as he grasped her waist and modeled the steps.

She quickly learned the hustle, and soon they were leading the entire group in the seventies dance craze. Everyone in the building, even those not dancing, would stop and shout, "Do the hustle!" with the lyrics. The DJ decided the dance was so much fun to watch, he played the song twice, and Tess added wild arm movements and exaggerated kicks, oblivious to everything but the dance. Her stomach ached from laughter, and she fell onto the bench, out of breath, when the dance finally ended.

"Not a child of the seventies, hah! You just never had the chance to boogie." He lifted his muscular arms high into the air. She laughed again, and her gaze unconsciously locked onto his. All time seemed to stop as she stood and approached him. He grasped her hands. Suddenly there was no music, no disabled adults; there was nothing in her world but Greg Wheaton. She thought he would kiss her—desired it with her whole being—but he dropped her hands and stepped back as if pulled away by an outside force.

"Do you want something to drink?" Greg asked suddenly. He didn't wait for the answer but walked across the room to the punch bowl. He returned with a plastic cup filled with unnaturally red punch. "When they play Glenn Miller's 'In the Mood,' then we can really swing." He held up a thumb and winked.

"Why are you here, anyway?" she asked. Robby had had over ten social workers in his lifetime, and Tess couldn't remember seeing any of them at one of his dances.

"Why are you so suspicious?" Greg inquired.

"I'm not suspicious, just curious."

"These are my clients. This is the fun part of my job—a chance to see them really enjoying themselves. It helps me to get closer to them when they see me in an unofficial capacity. Besides, where else can I boogie with a beautiful woman, teach her the hustle, sip Hawaiian Punch, and not spend a dime?"

"I'd say your options were limited." She felt a blush rise in her cheeks.

"Well, there you go."

Tess suddenly remembered she'd never called Clark after their disastrous date the night before and stood urgently. "Greg, I'm sorry. I need to make a phone call."

"Right outside the door there's a pay phone. You won't have much privacy, though." He pointed to all the dancers outside, trying to cool off in the evening air. "Do you want to use my cell phone in the car?" he asked, and she nodded eagerly. "Here are the keys. It's right outside under the tree."

"Thank you," she said gratefully, grabbing the keys and dashing down the steps.

Tess could smell Greg's spice aftershave lingering inside his Beetle. She inhaled deeply, and suddenly she was back in his arms, breathing in his sensuous cologne while dancing her heart out. *He even smells good. That man seems to affect every one of my senses.* She watched him for a moment through the open doors of the old building. He was holding hands with two developmentally disabled women, dancing a forties-era swing. He took turns dipping them, and the women delighted in his attention, each one clapping like a child when she rose from the dip. Truly, Greg had a way of making his partner feel like the belle of the ball.

Tess smiled to herself and dialed Clark's number. "Hello," he answered stiffly.

"Clark, I'm sorry I didn't get a chance to call you before now," Tess explained.

"I figured you were busy with work after two days off," he said, a hint of judgment in his voice. "So where are you now? Kelly said you took Robby to his dance."

"I'm still at the dance. Robby's friends kept asking me to dance, and I couldn't get away. Robby's social worker, Greg, is here, too. He taught everyone the hustle."

"Now there's a fad that needs a new life," Clark said sarcastically. "Listen, do you think Kelly could watch Robby tomorrow? I thought brunch might be nice."

"Clark, I'm sorry, but I have an appointment at Serenity Springs, the home where Robby might stay. Maybe we could go later and do lunch."

"No, no. You've got to get a place for Robby. That's your first priority. I made an appointment for next Friday night with the caterer I want to use for the wedding. They've done some beautiful work at our office. They did Jennifer's party last night. Didn't you think that was nice?"

Tess was tempted to reply she had no idea because, although famished, she'd never consumed a bite. "I—I just assumed we'd use the caterer from my hotel. What will my coworkers think?"

"Tess, of course if we had one of the chefs from Les Saisons cater the wedding, that would be fine, but to use the hotel's regular catering service is. . .well, my colleagues will all be there, and you know they have certain expectations."

"Clark, my hotel is world-renowned, one of San Francisco's most famous landmarks. I can't imagine anyone not being impressed with our catering—if that's what's important. Klaus would never let them do anything second-rate for me." Tess caught a faint whiff of Greg's masculine scent on his cellular phone and felt her eyes close as she breathed in deeply. *Why am I so attracted to Robby's social worker?* Greg was everything she didn't want in a man. For one thing, he stirred every emotion she owned. For another, he wasn't the stable, nonemotive, careful type she needed. She needed Clark, needed his meticulous planning and even keel to keep her steady.

"Tess?" Clark broke into her thoughts.

"I'm sorry. . .what?"

"You're preoccupied. I'll meet you Sunday after church, and we'll finalize all the wedding plans before we meet with the caterer next Friday. Good luck tomorrow."

"Thank you, Clark. Good-bye."

She pressed a button and sat back in the Bug's comfortable bucket seat. The car reminded her of her childhood, riding around in her mother's Beetle. She didn't know how long she sat there daydreaming before Greg rapped softly on the window.

"Everything okay?" he asked.

She nodded and opened the door. "Everything's fine. I was just remembering my mother's old navy blue Bug. They sure are different now. I bet they don't catch on fire anymore," she said jokingly.

"No, they don't. Just think of all the excitement I'm missing out on." He laughed, and she found herself studying his eyes in the orange glow from the lone streetlight. Even in the dim light, his eyes seemed to sparkle with a joy she'd never seen before in a man. Neither of them seemed comfortable with the obvious attraction that stirred between them. She tried to break the tension by stepping out of his car. "I'd better get Robby; it's time to go. I'm visiting Serenity Springs tomorrow."

"I hope you like it. Be sure to put Robby's name on the waiting list if you do."

"Waiting list? How long is the wait?" she asked cautiously, not previously aware there was such a list.

He shrugged. "Depends."

She felt like shaking him. "You're acting pretty casual about this, but I've got to find a place for Robby to live as soon as possible. He can't stay with me forever."

"Why not?" he asked seriously.

"Because I can't care for him every day. I've got to work. His social security checks don't begin to cover his costs, Greg. His medical copayments alone are enough to send me to the poorhouse!"

"Do you want me to pick you up in the morning and help you look? Perhaps my nudging might give you a better chance of admission."

"I suppose," she admitted, although she knew better than to answer affirmatively. The fact was, she'd spent far more time with Greg than she had with her fiancé the last few days. She just knew at that moment that she would have gone anywhere with him. Guilt struck her like a lightning bolt. "No, I can't tomorrow. I must find Robby a home," she said nervously.

"I know, Tess. That's what I'm talking about. I'm going to help you. I'll take you to the homes of my clients, and we'll find something tomorrow. I know the locations of all the homes; it would go faster with me."

"No," she heard herself say, although her conflicting emotions wanted to scream, *YES! Take care of me. Wrap me in those muscular arms and let me be lost in those blue eyes for a lifetime*. She didn't need to "go faster" anywhere with Greg Wheaton. She backed away from him, her hands in front of her like he had hurt her in some way.

The truth was, she couldn't remember when she'd had so much fun. There were no pretenses or appearances to keep up with Greg. He was just easy to be with, and that fact was making things very difficult, indeed.

He looked at her deliberately. "You don't want my help?"

"No, I don't. Clark will come with me, and we'll find something," she lied, trying to remind them both she was engaged. "I appreciate your concern and that you care so much about your job, but I can't rely on the county social worker for everything. I need to see what's out there and pray about it. So, I won't be needing your help. Besides, if you're anything like the others, you'll be gone within the year anyway." She handed him his keys and ran into the building.

She fought her way through the dancing couples and tapped her brother's shoulder. He was standing alongside the DJ, riffling through the records and making suggestions. "Robby, it's time to go. Get your jacket."

He whined and socked his leg, then put his finger into his mouth to bite it, but ended his tantrum before it began. "I'm thirsty," he said, forgetting his anger.

"I'll get some punch to go, but you need to get your jacket. We've got a big day tomorrow," she said with enthusiasm.

"I not want to go! I want to hear Buddy Holly again!" Robby protested.

"Robby, if we get home early enough, you can play your records when we get there," she said. "The dance will be over in five minutes anyway."

Tess sat in the car and waited while Robby talked to every person along his route to the car. She noticed Greg talking to some parents, and her heart lunged as she watched him. She prayed aloud, "Lord, I don't want to feel this way. I'm engaged to be married to a wonderful, successful man. I want to forget about Greg Wheaton and the way he makes me feel. Please, Lord, take this burden away. I'm marrying Clark—that's what you want, isn't it?" And for the first time since her engagement, she wondered.

And then she heard it, as clear as a bright summer day. *"Rest in Me."*

"What does that mean, Lord? You have provided Clark, so what does that mean?"

"Rest in Me."

Chapter 5

Saturday morning was as hectic as the rest of the week had been. By the time Tess had made her brother presentable by helping him shave and brush his teeth, it was nearly nine thirty.

Once in the car, she looked at the list Greg had given her on Thursday—the better options, in his opinion, were circled in red. Robby fiddled with the stereo while she studied the list. Only one of the five homes had an opening. Thinking optimistically, Tess went to that one first and was met by the young man who ran the home. He was strict and the home remarkably neat, *too* neat, she thought. Picturing her brother's giant record collection strewn all over his room, she knew Robby would never make it in such a structured environment. She politely told the man she didn't think Robby was right for the home. Judging by the man's careful analysis of Robby's files, she knew he agreed.

"I not want to live here," Robby said as they took the walkway to her car.

"I know, Robby. I wouldn't want to live there, either. Don't worry, we'll find something you like." But in her heart, she was greatly troubled by the first house, as though this were a harbinger of future failure. She could eventually set him up in a private home that she controlled, but until then she needed to find something suitable. They visited four homes, and Tess found something she disliked in each one.

She saved Serenity Springs for last. Knowing the Christian home was full, she figured her trip would be wasted. But after a fruitless day, she had little choice. Clearly, Robby was going to be with her for a while, so a waiting list was the least of her problems. She recoiled at the idea of explaining another unsuccessful search to Clark.

Tess drove up to Serenity Springs. The grounds were an image of pure peacefulness. Giant oak trees provided a huge canopy of shade over the vast, deep green lawns and sheltered the redwood-stained buildings. Serenity Springs was idyllic in its hilltop location, looking from a short distance away like a health spa for the wealthy. This was nothing like some of the seedy neighborhoods they'd visited. Some residents were gardening outside, while others played board games on picnic tables near the grass. She rang the doorbell and was met at the door by a middle-aged woman wearing gardening gloves and an old leather apron.

"May I help you?" she asked, a kind smile crossing her face.

"Yes, I'm Tess Ellison, and this is my brother, Robby. Greg Wheaton suggested we stop by and see if Serenity Springs might be right for Robby in the future. I called you yesterday."

"Please, come in." She stepped back and they walked in. Honey-colored hardwood floors were homey yet practical. Residents were milling about, each involved in an activity or job. No one was sitting idle, and the television was turned off. That was a big plus for Tess, who saw so many homes plop its residents in front of the television for half the day.

"This board is the activity chart." The woman pointed to a huge erasable chalkboard by the front door that had the name of each resident posted with a schedule of chores beside them. "Everyone here is expected to participate in making this into a home. Some obviously have more abilities than others, and we take that into account, but everyone can contribute in some fashion. Robby, what chores do you do at home now?" she asked, placing herself right in Robby's view. She obviously was used to dealing with disabled adults, but Tess knew Robby would never answer her.

Robby ignored the question as Tess guessed he would and meandered into the large meeting room. "I'm sorry, but Robby doesn't usually answer when he's spoken to first. You sort of have to let him come to you," Tess said apologetically.

"Quite all right, I understand the quirks," the woman said, smiling knowingly. "I'm Diane Laney, by the way." She removed her glove and held out a hand.

"Nice to meet you." Tess reached out and felt the dry, callused hand of the other woman. Her age was hard to calculate, but she appeared to be about sixty.

Tess soon heard Robby inhale excitedly from the adjoining room. "I can't believe it! I can't believe it!" Robby shouted, and Tess walked around the corner to make sure he was all right.

"Robby, what's—" And then she saw it—an old, fifties-era jukebox stood in the corner of the room opposite the television set. Tess was incredulous. "Oh, my, Robby loves music—especially from a jukebox." She knew of no way to explain to Diane just how much her brother enjoyed a jukebox.

"Residents can earn special coins for the jukebox by completing their jobs on time or by doing an exceptional job. Robby, would you like a coin?" Diane reached into her apron pocket and pulled out a tiny gold token.

"I can't believe it! I can't believe it!" Robby repeated, his huge frame jumping in excitement. Diane handed him the coin.

"Robby, what do you say?" Tess reminded.

"Thank you, thank you," he said absently while he went to make his selection. Diane continued her explanation without pause. "In addition to their chores, residents are expected to attend church and a weekly Bible study. This is a private Christian home, and we run it as such. There are no questionable movies or television shows allowed and nothing that we feel could jeopardize our residents' spiritual health. My son, John, is autistic."

"Robby was diagnosed autistic, but he really doesn't live in his own world like most autistics. He's one of those people who seem to fall through the cracks of the system. He loves music and movies and meeting people, but he also loves to watch things turn endlessly."

"Oh yes. The Laundromat is a favorite place of my son, John, too. John doesn't speak, though; he makes sounds to express himself, but he doesn't form words," Diane explained.

Although Robby's vivacious behavior sometimes drove her crazy, she was thankful he could express himself. Then Tess realized the irony of feeling sorry for Diane—it was what strangers did to Tess every day, but Tess knew having a developmentally disabled family member was just a way of life for both her and Diane.

"Diane, I don't know what to say; I just can't imagine a more perfect home for Robby. I can just feel the Lord's presence here. I know there are no openings, but I'm going to pray about this with all my heart because I feel God leading Robby here. I know he would be even happier here than in my home. I knew it the moment I walked in, even before the jukebox!" Tess found herself thinking this home was good enough for Robby to live permanently. *A private home paid for by Clark might not be necessary if this worked out,* she thought hopefully.

"I think Robby would do wonderfully here." Diane crossed her arms and smiled wistfully. "There's quite a range of ability levels here. Some hold full-time manufacturing jobs, and others are just capable of seeing to their daily needs, like my son."

"I see," Tess commented.

"We are at capacity, but only because we're short one full-time aide. It could be as long as a year before we have a space. We either need funding for the aide or one of our residents needs to move on—which isn't likely. They usually stay with us unless their parents move out of state." Diane's weathered face frowned. "It may look impossible now, but don't doubt God."

Tess nodded. "Even if it takes a year, I'm going to wait. I want Robby here. This is the only place that feels right for my brother. I can't explain that; I just know it's right." Tess was fully satisfied with her decision.

"Why don't you fill out the paperwork? Of course we'll need medical histories, records—you know the drill. And all of Robby's little idiosyncrasies that make him Robby, and adults from programs and elsewhere who he doesn't get along with, and why. But if we can get all that processed ahead of time, when an opening does come along, Robby can move right in." Diane brushed a graying strand of hair from her forehead.

"Wonderful." Tess filled out the paperwork on the spot. She was constantly being called upon to update Robby's files and probably could have done it in her sleep. She drove home happy, singing to her radio and tapping out the beat on her steering wheel.

Kelly greeted her at the door with wide eyes. "I'm so glad you're here. It's five o'clock; where have you been?"

"It was a longer process than I expected," Tess explained.

"I've got a date tonight and was worried you wouldn't be back with Robby, my date-o-meter." Kelly was dressed in an elegant navy dress that was conservative, yet cut close to her slender figure, showing off her shapely hips. Her blond bob was brushed into perfect order, and her blue eyes were highlighted with mascara and champagne-colored eye shadow. She turned and modeled for Tess.

"Wow, this guy must be special. Mascara even," Tess noted, and Kelly smiled.

"Seriously, where's Robby?" Kelly looked behind Tess and down the steps into the garage.

"He's sleeping, why?" Tess took off her sweater and hung it up in the closet.

"I told you why. I've got a date tonight. I need Robby's opinion." Kelly smoothed her dress and patted the bottom of her bob hairstyle.

"What is all this about Robby's sixth sense? Greg tried to give me that line yesterday."

"If you were smart, you'd listen to Greg. You just don't want to believe Robby's a good judge of character because you don't like what he says about Clark." Kelly turned her back to Tess and applied lipstick in the small mirror beside the front door.

"That's not true. Robby just decides quickly who he likes and who he doesn't; that doesn't qualify as a special sense in my opinion," Tess answered sharply.

"Even if he's always right?" Kelly opened the door to the garage and went down the steps. Tess could hear her trying to rouse Robby from his sleep. A few moments later, they both appeared—Kelly wearing a cat-that-swallowed-the-canary grin and Robby, groggy from sleep.

"So, where'd you meet this guy?" Tess asked as she sat on the sofa, kicking her shoes off.

"Here."

"He lives in the complex? I thought every man who lives here is married." Tess flipped on the television and began answering *Jeopardy* questions as she conversed. "Thomas Hardy!" she shouted at the television screen.

"No, he doesn't live here at the complex. He's Greg Wheaton's friend. His name is Ryan Scott."

"Greg Wheaton's friend?" Tess lost interest in *Jeopardy* at the mention of Greg's name, but continued answering questions so she didn't appear shaken. "This game is impossible," she sighed, silently wishing for more information about Kelly's date.

"Greg came by today with Robby's jacket. Said you left it at the dance." Kelly looked at her accusingly, as though Tess had done it on purpose. "He tried to call you, but you were gone all day, so he figured he'd leave it on the deck out front. But, luckily, I *was* here and just happened to see him and his friend, Ryan. Imagine— two gorgeous single men on my doorstep, after I'd changed out of my Saturday morning sweats and applied my makeup. Life just doesn't get any better than this."

"You met this guy today, and you're going out with him tonight? He'll think you have nothing better to do," Tess protested, not sure she liked the idea of Greg Wheaton's friend hanging around.

"I *didn't* have anything better. As it turned out, I'll be with a devastatingly handsome youth minister tonight. And by the way, if he can look good standing next to Greg Wheaton, he's something to see!

"Anyway," Kelly continued, "Ryan was given tickets to tonight's ballet by a church member, and they would have gone to waste. So we will have a perfectly elegant evening, whether you approve or not." Kelly pursed her lips.

Before Tess could reply, the doorbell chimed. Kelly opened the door, and her interest in the minister was apparent. "Hi, Ryan," she cooed. He was blond, rather short, by Tess's accounting, but well built and athletic. He looked like a football player. He was dressed in chocolate brown slacks and a coordinating hounds-tooth sport coat. His dashing appearance showed that he had taken pains to pre-pare for his date with Kelly.

Robby was immediately by Kelly's side at the prospect of meeting someone new. "What's your name?"

"Ryan Scott. What's yours?" he asked.

"Robby. Ryan, you like Frank Sinatra?"

"Sure, I guess so," he said with a shrug. "But I like Elvis better."

Robby inhaled excitedly, pointing at Kelly's date and looking at Tess. Kelly also turned to Tess, obviously for confirmation that Robby did, indeed, have a sixth sense about people. Tess was unwavering. "Lucky shot," she said.

"I beg your pardon?" Ryan asked.

"Come on in, Ryan. You don't need to stand on the porch." Kelly gently pulled him in by the hand.

"Greg warned me about you two." He wagged his finger. "Kelly, I thought we might go to Jake's for dinner before the ballet. Is that okay?"

Inwardly Tess felt her heart tug at the thought of having dinner at casual Jake's restaurant. Clark was forever taking her to places that had everything on the menu in a foreign language except the price. Tess always wondered why she wasn't expected to know what she was ordering, but she could know the cost.

"Jake's sounds great," Kelly said.

"You marry Kelly?" Robby asked.

Without a pause, Ryan answered, "Marriage is a big step. That's why people date, Robby."

"Oh," Robby answered, satisfied. Tess could have sworn he asked questions like that on purpose, just to see the reaction. She supposed most people would do the same if they could get away with it.

"I'll have her home early, Tess." Ryan winked, and Tess looked up in surprise at the mention of her name. "It's too bad we didn't know you were going to be home. I had five tickets originally—we could have doubled with you and Greg and Robby. We would have made a nice fivesome."

Tess swallowed hard at the mention of Greg.

Kelly giggled to alleviate the tension. "Oh no, Ryan. Tess is engaged to be married. You ought to meet Clark; he's charming," Kelly said sarcastically.

Ryan didn't notice the jab. "Oh, sorry, Tess," he said. "Greg didn't mention your fiancé. I wondered how two beautiful, godly women were still single. I guess I'm just lucky Kelly was free tonight. A little divine intervention never hurts." Ryan and Kelly looked at one another, and Tess doubted a rocket blast could have separated their gaze. He took Kelly's arm, and they left without a glance back.

The jingle of the phone broke Tess's concentration. "Hello."

"Tess, it's Clark. How did the search for Robby's new place go?" he asked tonelessly.

"Very well. I've found the perfect place for him. It's Christian, it's close to his program so he won't have to spend all day on the bus, and it's within my budget. The downside is that they may not have room for another year."

To her surprise, Clark didn't chastise her or comment on her unsatisfactory solution; he simply asked what the name of the home was.

"Serenity Springs in Emerald Hills."

"It sounds wonderful, Tess. Listen, I'm calling to let you know I can't make it to church with you tomorrow. I have unexpected business in Boston, and I'm flying out tomorrow evening. I need to run a few errands, get packed—you know."

"W–when will you be back?" she stammered. She wanted the protection and excuses a nearby fiancé provided her against her warring feelings.

"Don't worry. I'll be back before we meet with the caterer Friday night. You'll have to get used to my being gone, Tess. After we're married, you'll be spending a lot of time alone when I attend law conferences. You understand that."

"I thought we were going to discuss the caterer issue. Remember, I have my friends at the hotel to think about. I can't just—"

"Meeting with the caterer is not hiring him. But Tess, we can't have a second-class reception just to satisfy your friends. I'll leave the name of my hotel with my secretary. I'll see you when I get back. And don't worry, I'll take care of you."

Tess tossed the phone back into its cradle. "He's taking care of me, all right, but I sure don't have any say in the matter." She immediately ran an attitude check, remembering that Robby would be safe and her life would be significantly easier with a husband. *Even God rested,* she rationalized. "Robby, want some popcorn? There's an old Rudy Vallee movie on tonight." She headed toward the kitchen and patted her brother lovingly as she passed.

Chapter 6

Tuesday morning at the hotel was a blur of activity. Klaus had nonstop meetings, so Tess was left to manage her desk and her boss's, as well. She sighed as her phone rang, two lines at once.

"Good morning, Klaus Kilborn's office; can you hold?"

"Tess? It's Greg Wheaton." She nearly dropped the phone when she heard the richness of his deep voice.

"Greg, can you hold a moment? I've got another call." She slammed her finger on the button and tried to slow her breathing. *This is stupid; he is just Robby's social worker. Get a grip,* she told herself. "Good morning, Klaus Kilborn's office; can you hold?"

"Tess, this is Diane Laney from Serenity Springs. I won't keep you long. I just wanted to let you know we've had a miracle, and there's room for Robby. Funding for the new aide came through yesterday. Can you believe it?"

"No," Tess managed to stammer.

"Robby can move in Friday. Will that work for you?"

Diane's excitement was clear, but Tess was at a loss to feel anything. She had grown used to having her brother around, and even though she knew he'd be better off where he could exert some independence, the announcement that it could happen so soon threw her. "Diane, can I call you back? I've got Robby's social worker on the other line, and I'm so shocked about your news, I don't know what to think. I need a little time to let it sink in."

"No problem. I'll be here all afternoon. I'm just so excited, Tess, for John as well as Robby. He seems to have a certain kinship with Robby!"

Tess nervously picked up the other line. "Greg, are you still there?"

"I'm here, Tess," he said gently, and Tess felt her eyes close as she was lulled by his warm tone.

She opened her eyes quickly, answering in a businesslike manner, "What's the problem?"

"Robby had a little trouble at independence training today in the program. It's a long story and I won't bore you with the details while you're at work, but I've got him here with me at my home. I'm going to keep him for the rest of the day. He's watching television."

"Is anyone hurt?" Tess asked tentatively.

"No, Tess, it's nothing to worry yourself about. I just thought I'd do some paperwork here so you wouldn't have to miss more work. He's fine."

"Is he getting kicked out of the program?" She dropped her head into her hand, allowing loose curls to fall forward onto her desk. *Not again. Please God, not again. I can't miss any more work.*

"No, Tess, not this time. They say he's making progress, so they don't want to disrupt that, but we may have to rethink his independence skills. We may want to place him back in a full-time, supervised program."

"Greg, no. Robby was doing better, and I don't want to take a step back." Tess could hear her voice cracking, and she sat up straight in her chair, determined to get hold of herself.

"Look, Tess, I didn't call you to upset you. Everything is fine. Robby will be all right, and we'll discuss this later. He'll be fine with me for the day. Just take your time at work, and we'll meet afterward. How does Rockin' Rolls sound? That would give us time to talk while Robby plays the jukebox."

"Good idea. Thank you, Greg, I owe you one. This would not be a good day to bail on my boss." She surveyed the mountain of paperwork on her desktop.

"Seven at Rockin' Rolls, then. I'm looking forward to it," Greg said, and Tess thought she noticed a hint of design in his words. Perhaps she had just imagined it. She had promised herself not to meet with Greg personally until Clark returned, though, and breaking her vow made her uncomfortable.

She hung up the phone before she said something else she would regret. *Will life ever get any easier with Robby?* Just when she thought she had excellent news, Robby did something to blow it. And if he kept it up, Serenity Springs wouldn't take him, no matter how many aides they hired.

～

Greg and Robby were already at Rockin' Rolls when Tess arrived. Robby was interrogating the busboy, and Greg was happily chiming in, unconcerned that Robby might be bothering him. Tess laughed at the sight.

"Hi," Tess said as she slipped into the booth. Robby immediately asked to go to the jukebox, hoping to avert punishment for his behavior earlier in the day. "Go ahead," Tess agreed. "Here, these are all the quarters I have, so use them wisely." The quarters she'd dished out of her car's ashtray clanked as she dropped them onto the table.

"Yeah, yeah." Robby scooped up the change and dropped it into his pocket.

Tess put down her purse and settled into the seat. Greg smiled warmly at her. All of her questions seemed to fly out the window at the sight of him. His chiseled features contrasted sharply with his gentle nature, and Tess found herself wondering what kind of kisser he would be. Would he be strong and confident like he appeared or sweet and considerate like his personality? She shook the thought.

278

"Tess? What are you thinking about?" Greg cocked his head to the side, looking more like a rough-and-ready ranch hand than a social worker.

"Me? Oh, nothing," she answered too quickly. "What happened today?"

Greg gave the waiter their order, then looked back at Tess. "Do you want the good news or the bad first?"

Tess shrugged and crossed her arms. "Why don't you just give it to me all at once. It's not like I haven't heard it all before."

"Robby was supposed to learn how to take the bus by himself. His trainer told him what to do, how much money to give the driver, *and* told him he was not to talk to anyone on the bus."

Tess snickered. "Mission impossible."

She saw the laughter in his eyes, but he continued. "He got on the bus and took it for about a mile, but he got off about two miles before his stop."

Tess's eyes widened at the thought of her brother alone on a city bus. "Oh no!"

"Robby's trainer was following in her car, but she wanted to see what he would do next when he exited the bus on his own—to know what they would need to work on next time. She said he waited at the crosswalk and crossed the El Camino Real by himself, which he did very well, by the way."

"Great," Tess said sarcastically, "except he wasn't supposed to cross the El Camino Real!" Tess silently thanked the Lord that her brother had crossed the boulevard safely.

"So his trainer, Robin, made a U-turn and waited to see what he would do next. Robby sat down at the bus stop, talking to everyone on the bench, and eventually he had the entire bench to himself. He waited until the next bus came and got on, going in the opposite direction. He rode the bus south for about five miles, then Robin decided it was time to end his little game. She waited until the next stop, honked her horn, and approached the bus. When she got on, your brother was happily engaged in several conversations, gleefully oblivious to everything but his first shot at freedom."

Tess covered her mouth to suppress a laugh. "Then what?"

"So Robin said, 'Robby,' and your brother turned around with sheer horror on his face at the sight of her. Instantly, he began to cry, wailing, 'I'm loooost, I'm lost!' "

Greg and Tess began to laugh heartily. They would manage to stop, then they'd catch each other's eyes and start all over again. "What would my life be like without Robby's constant entertainment?"

"Probably pretty mundane," Greg responded.

"How am I going to punish him for this? I'm not going to be able to look him in the eye without laughing. The truth is, Greg, if we were watched as closely as Robby, we would look for a little freedom ourselves. Did anyone tell you about the time he locked his bus driver out of the bus?"

"Nope. I haven't heard this one," Greg said.

"He had a new bus driver, and you know how he always plays the invalid with people who don't know him?"

"Yes." Greg smiled.

"Well, he got this poor guy to help him off the bus, like Robby couldn't do it on his own. Then to help the guy, Robby manually closes the door behind him—and they are locked out. Meanwhile, the bus is running, and this poor driver has eight kids still on the bus. So the driver frantically enters through the emergency exit window and saves the day." Tess shook her head. "I think my brother has probably retired a few bus drivers. Come to think of it, I'll bet he's caused a lot of social workers to rethink their career choice, as well."

"What is it you have against social workers?" Greg crossed his arms. "I think we're a nice breed. We get paid next to nothing, are overloaded with cases, and are expected to work nights and weekends because of our love for the kids. I think we deserve more credit."

"It's nothing personal, Greg. It's just that most social workers think they know what's best for my brother by reading his label, *autistic*. Robby doesn't act like an average autistic, and it ruffles my feathers when they think they know what's best for him. Like I don't? I mean, who has raised him, them or me?"

"I don't think it's a reflection on you, Tess. It's just that most of us are so overworked. We want to accomplish the greatest good in the shortest time. That means we sometimes can make rash judgments. However, I think I have a pretty good handle on what makes Robby tick."

"I know you do. You're the first one who has ever appreciated Robby for the character he is. I needed to hear from someone who can appreciate his positives. It seems that Kelly, my roommate, and I are the only ones lately. Oh, and before I forget, I owe you a big thanks for getting him into Serenity Springs. You were sure right about that place."

Greg shook his head. "I didn't do anything to get Robby into Serenity Springs. I prayed about it, but. . ." He shrugged.

Tess couldn't hide her surprise. "He can move in Friday. Klaus gave me the day off to get things taken care of."

"Klaus sounds like a gift from above. Isn't it great how God always provides for our needs, even when they seem impossible?"

Tess looked down nervously at her hands, then back at Greg. "I suppose it is." She thought about how Clark was what she needed—a man who didn't invoke so many emotions, didn't fill her stomach with butterflies when she looked at him. Yes, Clark was a gift; so why was she having such a hard time remembering what he looked like?

"What are you getting your degree in? Did you tell me?" Greg asked.

"I'm getting my degree in literature at U.C. Berkeley."

The waiter placed their meals on the table. Robby grabbed his burger and went back to the jukebox.

"Good school. Quite a feat getting accepted there—congratulations. Also quite a commute. You really think you can work in San Francisco, cross the bridge, then return home at night? And what about Robby?" Greg eyed her warily. "That sounds like a lot of responsibility for someone *without* a Robby in her life."

"Are you asking about this as a friend or as a social worker?" Her eyes narrowed, and she studied him, trying to guess his motives.

"Both, I guess. You know, I think you are the most suspicious person I ever met!" he joked. But Tess knew there was truth in his statement. "I just think that sounds like a lot of work; you just got through telling me how much you like your job." He threw a french fry into his mouth.

"Well, my fiancé thinks it's important that I don't get pegged as 'just a secretary.' "

"I don't get what's wrong with being a secretary. It's a fine job if you enjoy it." He shrugged his muscular shoulders, and Tess felt herself being drawn to him. Greg seemed unaware of how he affected women. Tess had noticed that he attracted the attention of every woman that passed by, and she felt smug knowing she was the envy of all the women in the restaurant. "What's so important about a bachelor's degree?" he added.

"That's easy to say when you have your master's degree. It's not important. Let's talk about something else." She didn't like where the conversation was going.

Following dinner, Greg walked Tess and Robby to her car. He let Robby into the passenger side, then opened Tess's door, standing with his hand on the window frame. "Go easy on him. It was his first taste of real freedom, remember."

She felt herself smile flirtatiously. Suddenly Greg's strong hand was against her cheek. "You don't need a college degree to be intelligent, Tess." She was aware of his warm breath and longed for him to pull her into a kiss. His masculine scent seemed to overwhelm her, and she felt irresistibly drawn to him. *What am I doing? These are exactly the feelings that allow someone to hurt you. Pull away and request another social worker. Now! Before it's too late.*

"I have to go." It was a start. It wasn't the clean break she needed to make, but it was all she could muster while under his intense, blue-eyed gaze. She swore to herself that she would never let this happen again. She had to think; she had to pray. But most of all, she had to get away.

"I'll see you Friday," Greg said casually.

"F—Friday?"

"Yes—to help Robby get adjusted to his new home. You weren't planning to just drop him off, were you?"

"No, of course not. I just didn't think you. . ." Tess fumbled with her words.

"Didn't his last social worker help him into his last home?"

She nodded. *But his last social worker didn't look like James Bond!*

"Okay, then, I'll see you both Friday." He leaned into the window and said good-bye to Robby. Tess felt light-headed at the thought of him so close, his neck mere inches from her face. His aftershave made her tingle.

~

Arriving home, Tess saw to it that her brother got a bath, then she sat down to watch the news. She was exhausted from her long day. Her six thirty alarm would come awfully early the next morning. Rubbing her weary neck and shoulders, Tess thought Friday couldn't come soon enough.

Kelly came in a few minutes later and sat down next to Tess on the couch. "You look like something the cat dragged in," Kelly remarked.

"Thank you, just what I needed to hear. Another date with Ryan?" Tess asked.

"Uh-huh. We went to a Giants game. It was a playoff game, but the Giants lost, so that's it for the season." Kelly shrugged.

"Oh," Tess said evenly.

"Tess, you used to love baseball. What's the matter, the game's not good enough for Clark?"

"Would you cut it out?" Tess spat. "I'm sick of your harping on my fiancé. I think it's great you've got yourself a nice boyfriend, but leave mine out of this." She rose and started up the stairs.

"Stop!" Kelly ordered while wagging her finger. "Don't take another step. You're not going to bed on that note. Sit down." Kelly motioned toward the sofa, and Tess sauntered down the steps like an incensed teenager in trouble with her parents.

"Honestly, Tess, I don't know what you see in Clark. I think his faith is minimal at best; I don't see anything that points to fruit in his life; and I think he cares more about his image than about God. His obsession with your education disgusts me. And worst of all, he's boring! His idea of a good time is the symphony, and yours is a Steven Curtis Chapman concert. Help me, Tess. Help me understand why you are marrying this man. Do you want to live a separate life from your husband? Please enlighten me."

The phone rang, and Tess jumped to get it. *Saved by the bell.*

"Don't answer that," Kelly commanded.

"I have to; it might be about Robby. Hello."

"Tess, it's Clark. Sorry to call so late, but I tried to call earlier and no one was home. Is everything all right?"

"Everything's fine. Robby had trouble in the program today, and I had to pick him up from the social worker."

"It's a good thing he won't be living with you much longer. I'm beginning to worry about you—you looked positively ragged on Friday." Tess rolled her eyes at yet another remark about her worn appearance. "You're scheduled to start university next week, so I want to be sure you're saving up your strength."

"How did you know Robby wouldn't be living here?" Tess asked.

"I paid for the aide at Serenity Springs. That's what you said you wanted, right?"

Tess sat slowly, trying to digest the news.

"You did what?"

"Tess, we've got a wedding to plan, and you're beginning classes at one of the country's finest universities. It's time to start thinking about you. You're nearly twenty-seven, and you've been a mother to Robby too long." She couldn't answer. "Tess, trust me," he said firmly. "We had a deal, right?"

"Yes, Clark," she finally managed.

"See you Friday night. The caterer is going to make us a fine meal at my place. Dress nicely." The phone clicked. Tess stared at the phone, gingerly putting it into the base.

"Tess?" Kelly went to stand at her side.

"Clark got Robby into Serenity Springs," she said absently.

"Isn't that what you wanted?" Kelly wore a confused expression.

"I thought so," Tess said while she stared out the darkened window. But now she was indebted to Clark, a fact that lay heavy on her heart.

Chapter 7

G reg looked at the envelope in disbelief. He'd been waiting two years for an answer to his inquiry, and here it finally was. He took a deep breath and ripped open the envelope. He closed his eyes and shook his head. The job he'd anticipated since moving to California years earlier was finally his. He had always intended to practice social work in Oregon, his home state, but that dream had come to an abrupt end when he was fired for misconduct. "Misconduct, indeed," he grumbled aloud.

Now, finally, news that a former client had cleared him of all charges had arrived. He was free to return and practice with child protective services once again. Greg crumpled the letter and threw it angrily against the wall. "Why now, Lord? I've started a new life here in California. Why provide a way back to Oregon now? Back to the elementary-age kids I wanted to work with in the first place?" Greg threw his arms up in frustration. A knock on the door ended his heated prayer.

Greg opened the door brusquely. "What? Oh, sorry, Ryan. Come on in."

Ryan walked past him into the apartment, looking about the room. "Who you yelling at?" he asked, looking at Greg as though he were a few cards short of a full deck.

"God," Greg answered. "What are you doing here?"

"Nice to see you, too," Ryan said as he helped himself to a soda from the kitchen. "Want one?" He held up a Pepsi.

"Nah." Greg tossed his hand.

"So what are you yelling at God about? That pretty little roommate of Kelly's?" Ryan winked. "She's a beauty, all right."

"Is this how you act when you counsel church members?" Greg asked grimly.

"Sorry, bud, I was trying to lighten the mood," he said with compassion in his voice. "I didn't realize you were that upset. What's wrong?"

"I got a letter from the state of Oregon today. I've been reinstated; I can work with elementary kids again." He practically choked on the words, he was still so angry.

"That's great. So what's the problem?"

Greg paced the floor, his arms clasped behind his back. "Do you know how long it took me to get another job after those false charges? And, of course, they

284

wouldn't let me work with *normal* kids, as if my retarded clients are any less important! But the worst thing. . .the worst thing is that I'm good at working with the developmentally disabled. I love them, and I'm angry that God is throwing this decision at me right now—after I was reconciled to maybe doing this forever."

"I thought you wanted to go back to Oregon."

"Yeah, well, I'm worried about Robby and Tess," he reluctantly admitted.

"From what Kelly tells me, Tess is a little firecracker who doesn't need much looking after."

Greg shook his head. "She's going to marry someone who doesn't understand Robby. She thinks it's going to make life easier, but I know. . ." Greg dropped his head despondently.

"That's Tess's problem."

"I'm supposed to look out for my clients," Greg rationalized.

"Tess is not your client."

Tess Ellison was marrying a man she didn't love; he could feel it; and Greg wanted to know why. Against his better judgment, he *had* to know why.

～

Tess placed the last of Robby's bags in his bedroom at Serenity Springs. She stood up straight, stretching her back after all the unloading. "This is it, Robby. Like your new room?"

He nodded. "I like it! I put my record player here," he said, pointing, "and my tape player here, and my records right there." Robby had owned the same furniture since he was a child, and its familiarity always made his bedroom look the same, no matter where it was.

"Are you going to be good so you can play the jukebox?"

"Yeah, I be good."

Tess felt her eyes welling up. This was so much harder than she'd imagined. For some reason, all the other homes Robby had been in had felt temporary. Serenity Springs felt permanent. Since she was getting married, her relationship with Robby would probably never be the same again. She'd soon have a husband and probably a family of her own; somehow this saddened her deeply.

"You crying? Why you crying, Tess?" Robby asked while putting his bulky arm around her roughly.

She enveloped him in a solid hug. "Robby, I love you. And I'm going to miss you. You're my favorite person in the whole wide world."

"Yeah, I miss you. Can I go to the jukebox now?" he asked impatiently. She nodded. Only Robby could give up this poignant moment for a jukebox.

Tess plopped on the bed, smoothing out the dark green spread she had selected from a catalog. She'd placed Elvis posters and Buddy Holly memorabilia all over the walls, and the room seemed to shout Robby's name. "He's going to be happy here." She nodded while talking to herself. "It'll be just fine; life is about to get a lot easier," she choked out through her tears.

"Better not talk to yourself too much around here. It might get you committed." Greg's familiar voice held a hint of mirth, but she knew he understood her ambivalence.

Without thinking, she walked to him and snuggled into his outstretched arms. She held on tightly. He stroked her back softly, and she allowed a torrent of tears to come, not aware of how long she cried. Finally, she sniffled and pulled away. "I think I'm done now." She removed a balled-up tissue from her pocket and wiped her eyes. The tissue came away covered with black mascara, and Tess guessed she must look a sight. "Did you come for Robby or for me?" She laughed through her tears.

"Both," he replied kindly. "Let's go see how Robby's doing. It will make you feel better to see how he's getting along." He pulled out a clean tissue from the box on the bureau and finished wiping her eyes. She felt his tender thumb softly wipe away a lone tear on her cheek. He smiled down at her, and the intense blue of his eyes forced her gaze to the floor.

He led her to the activity room, where Robby was happily conversing, getting to know his new neighbors. The residents had made him a welcome cake and had taken up a collection, offering him a small satchel of jukebox coins. Their reception was hearty and, judging by Robby's wide smile, well appreciated.

Tess felt herself beginning to cry again; she grasped Greg's arm and led him outside. "This feels so different. This time I feel like I'm really relinquishing control, and I don't like it," Tess admitted. The oaks and pines surrounding the property filled her senses. It was nearly dusk, her favorite time of day, and the woodsy setting for Serenity Springs helped to alleviate a lot of her anguish.

"But Robby is ready for this, Tess. God wants you to give up the control; hand it over to Him." He sat down beneath an ancient oak tree and reached out his arm for her to join him. She dropped to her knees, then sat with her jeans-clad legs off to her side.

"I don't know how I'll manage without all the responsibilities." Tess felt like she was losing control of everything in her life. By allowing Clark to pay for the aide, Tess had given *him* control. Soon her own freedom would be meshed with Clark's plans.

"Is this the same woman who told me how desperately she needed a vacation?" He tipped her chin with his hand.

"One and the same," she admitted. "That was only true while it was unattainable."

"You start classes soon. You won't have time to miss Robby. Besides, I imagine he'll still be up to something that'll require a phone call now and then."

"My brother?" Tess put her hand to her heart in mock innocence. "I think you must have Robby confused with another one of your clients, Greg."

"I don't think so." He lifted his eyebrows and smiled at her from the side of his aristocratically structured face. "Just give it up to God. You've got your education to think about now. . .and your wedding," he added somberly.

"My wedding!" Her hand flew to her forehead. "Oh, Greg, I forgot about that catering meeting Clark set up. I've got to go, I—"

"I'll stay with Robby this evening and get him settled. Go plan your wedding, and we'll talk soon." He stood and helped her up.

Tess rushed to her car and looked down at her dust-covered figure. "Clark's going to kill me." She tried to brush away some of the dust on her jeans, but it was useless. She looked like she'd been doing hard labor for a week. She pulled her full mane out of its ponytail and let the mahogany tresses fall loosely down her back. Inside the car, she pulled the vanity mirror down and gasped.

She riffled through her cosmetics bag and pulled out her lipstick and powder compact. She did the best she could with her available tools, but Clark was still going to be sorely disappointed. Her mascara had run, covering her cheeks with coal black tracks. Her eyes were puffy from crying, and her nose was a bright shade of pink. She considered canceling, but knew that would probably upset Clark and his carefully arranged plans even further. She started the car and prayed for calm.

She drove the familiar route at the speed limit and prayed for green lights. Traffic in San Francisco was horrendous; it was Friday night, and all the plays and restaurants beckoned people from the peninsula. Tess parked in the spot Clark always left open for her in his garage and entered the luxurious lobby.

Once at Clark's apartment, she breathed deeply and braced for his reaction to her appearance. Tess's presentation was so important to Clark. He had purchased designer dresses and even had apparel delivered to her office. But Tess was so tiny, and the costly clothes were always somewhat too large. Tess thought she looked like a teenager in her mother's closet when she wore Clark's selections.

She knocked quietly, inwardly hoping their dinner was off.

He opened the door, dressed in an elegant, European-cut suit of navy blue, with a light sheen to it. He looked at her questioningly, and she explained before he had a chance to ask. "I'm so sorry. I've been moving boxes all day for Robby, and it was either this," she let her hands fly down her sides, "or cancel. I figured I'd let you make the call." She looked at him with wide eyes.

He took her hand and led her inside. "Come on in. This is the first evening we've had together in a long time. Under the candlelight, I won't even notice your clothes." Clark's small dining room table was draped in burgundy and gold lamé cloths with six candles in crystal candlesticks.

A middle-aged man wearing a tuxedo entered bearing food artfully arranged on a gold platter. He smiled at her and began arranging the plates. A masterpiece in gourmet delicacies lay before them: pâté, caviar, small squid in an aromatic brown sauce. Tess's squeamish stomach screamed for a hamburger. The waiter pointed to each entree and gave a detailed description, causing Tess's stomach to turn even more. He left her alone with Clark, and her fiancé collected a sample from each dish and placed it on her gold-rimmed plate.

Tess was mortified. She had worked all day long and wanted real food, not pricey samples. "Clark," she whispered, leaning in over the table, "I don't like any of this stuff, and I don't think my friends will, either. We need to have at least one chicken dish." She looked around as if her conversation were top secret and waited anxiously for his reply.

"We do, honey. We have quail." He pointed to one of the platters.

"Quail is not chicken, Clark. Quail is the state bird."

"All right, we'll have chicken," he relented. "Now try some of this; it's wonderful." He held a fork up to her mouth, and she swallowed quickly, grimacing at the awful aftertaste.

"Normal chicken. Not chicken dressed as something I can't pronounce or chicken hidden inside something."

"Fine. Normal chicken. Maybe you'd just like to order a big bucket from the Colonel," he teased.

She began to laugh. "I like the Colonel," she admitted through her giggle.

"I know you do." He shook his head. "It never ceases to amaze me that your little body stays that way." He cut up a piece of unidentifiable meat. "How is Robby's new place?"

It was the first time Clark had asked about her brother with legitimate concern in his voice, and Tess felt herself smile with satisfaction. She had been so harsh on Clark lately. He wasn't the emotional type—that's why she wanted to marry him in the first place. To fault him for being the way he was wouldn't be fair. *And I haven't been playing fair lately.* Her mind flew to Greg Wheaton, and Tess felt her back straighten as the thought made her uncomfortable.

"Robby's new place is great; he seems to love it. They have a jukebox, of all things, in the living room. Plus they have lots of scheduled activities during the evening. He has a list of chores that he's capable of doing." Tess pulled her chair away from the table to escape the odor that was sending her stomach into a frenzy.

"That's great." Clark ate like a truck driver, groaning with pleasure over each new dish he tasted.

"Robby seems happy, just like he is at my house. Since it's a Christian home, it seems to meet a need the others didn't."

"Speaking of Christianity, how would you feel if we got married at Grace Cathedral? It could accommodate a lot more people than our little church."

Clark's tone was casual, but Tess was aghast.

"Grace Cathedral? That seems a little grand for us, don't you think? Besides, I don't know if Pastor Hall would feel comfortable in someone else's church." Tess pictured the magnificent cathedral in the heart of San Francisco's Knob Hill. All of the city's elite society seemed to marry in the renowned sanctuary, but Tess wasn't sure she was up to the spectacle. It would be a dream come true to be married in such a place for many women, but it wasn't Tess's dream. "I just want a simple wedding."

"Tess, with your gorgeous figure and those enormous green eyes, you were born to be a bride. Where else could we get married that would do you justice?"

"I appreciate the compliments, but I just don't know. Robby is giving me away, and I don't want him to be out of place. He knows our church, he knows Pastor Hall—"

"Pastor Hall will still be there. I'll make sure of that." Clark patted her hand condescendingly, lifting it to gaze at the diamond solitaire she wore. "Are you sure you want Robby to give you away? He's going to talk to everyone on the aisle. It'll take you ten minutes just to get to the altar."

"I don't care if it takes me *twenty* minutes to get to the altar. Robby has been talking about this since the day we got engaged. It's his day, too, Clark! He'll never be married; this wedding is almost as much for him as it is for me."

"What if he doesn't follow Pastor Hall's directions?"

Tess wanted to answer that Robby never followed directions, so why should their wedding day be any different, but she refrained. "Then Pastor Hall will handle it. He knows how to deal with Robby."

"So Grace Cathedral is approved?"

"If, and only if, you can get Pastor Hall to agree to it."

"Consider it done," he said enthusiastically. "So, school next week."

"If all goes well with Robby."

"Honey, Robby is not going to be an issue anymore. He's at Serenity Springs, and it's time you stopped playing the mother hen and become the carefree young woman you should have been a long time ago. I'll handle Robby."

"I wouldn't call twelve units 'carefree,' but trust me, Clark, Robby will always be an issue. No home will ever take care of all his problems. I'm his legal guardian, and as such I will always have responsibilities for him."

"I'll take care of it." He grasped her hand and squeezed.

～

When Tess arrived home after her elegant meal, she was starving. She bolted into the kitchen and found Kelly and her date, Ryan, playing Scrabble on the kitchen table. Tess leaned over the table and examined the board. "So, who's winning?"

"He is, but only because he cheats," Kelly said sharply.

"I'm a pastor; I don't cheat!" He smiled. "I just use the bonus squares."

"He's inventing all these two-letter words and putting them on the triple score squares and wiping me out. Look at that, I spelled ODYSSEY, and he gets more points with AN." Kelly grimaced.

"Hey, it's not my fault you never learned to use the math part of the game." Ryan smiled and winked at Tess.

"Well, next time we're playing Trivial Pursuit with Tess. She will clean up the floor with you. She's got more useless facts stored up in that head of hers than you've got verses memorized." Kelly cupped her mouth and whispered loudly, "I think that's why her hair's so curly."

"Don't pick on me just because you're losing. She's a terrible loser, Ryan."

"By the way, there's pizza in the fridge," Kelly said without looking up from her game board.

"How do you know she's hungry?" Ryan crossed his arms and waited for the explanation. Longtime best friends, Kelly and Tess shared a bond that was beyond most people's understanding.

Kelly turned to Ryan. "She had a date with Clark. So Clark took her to some fancy restaurant. He ordered something for her, and she snubbed it, thinking she'd grab something on the way home, instead. But then she thought that, rather than waste money, she'd just come home and raid the fridge. Right?" Kelly looked up at her.

"Almost." Tess took out a bottled water and gulped it mightily. She looked at Ryan. "By the way, if you're coming to my wedding, you may want to eat beforehand. The caterer is a little, uh, what's the right word? Artsy. The caterer is artsy."

Ryan smirked, then placed a tile on the Scrabble board. He was disarmingly handsome, Tess thought, and together they looked like the perfect Barbie and Ken couple on top of a wedding cake. "So if this food is so awful, why don't you get another caterer?" Ryan asked innocently.

"Let's just say my husband-to-be is a connoisseur, and I appreciate the simple pleasures in life." Tess took another long drink from her bottle.

"As long as you have chicken— You're going to have chicken, aren't you?" Kelly whined.

"We are *definitely* going to have chicken," Tess answered.

"Ryan was just telling me he's taking his youth group up to Yosemite for a weekend in October. Are you interested in being a counselor?"

"Me?" Tess asked.

"We could be roomies," Kelly answered with a grin. "Ryan said he'd be willing to room with Robby, so your brother could go, too, if you would help out with the teenage girls."

"Really?" Tess looked to Ryan, her eyebrows lifted. The opportunity to take Robby to Yosemite seemed ideal.

"Greg says he's no trouble," Ryan said, and both Tess and Kelly giggled. "What did I say?"

"If Greg says he's no trouble, Ryan, then *Greg* can come along and be in charge of Robby." Kelly dropped her head, shaking it. "No trouble," she muttered. "Since when?"

"I'll ask Greg. If you two can come as counselors, he can come as social worker. Can't beat those credentials." Ryan placed two more tiles, and Kelly shouted in frustration.

"He wins with AT! I'm telling you, he cheats." Kelly stood and poured the tiles into the empty game box. "Game over," she declared.

Ryan said a quick good night, and Kelly walked him to the door, laughing about their evening of Scrabble. When Kelly came back into the kitchen, Tess had already cleaned away any sign of their evening together.

"Thanks for cleaning up." Kelly slapped her hand onto the countertop, leaning against it with her hip.

Tess turned quickly. "I can't go to Yosemite if Greg is coming; you know that. Robby can just stay at Serenity Springs. I thought it would be nice for Robby to see the waterfalls, but Greg's coming is out of the question."

"So why don't you ask Clark to come and help?" Kelly's eyes narrowed.

"Yeah, right."

"Tess, you won't be with Greg; you'll be with twelve teenaged girls, helping to keep them away from the twelve teenaged boys! Since when did you have a problem being around Robby's social workers? Seems like you were always on a first-name basis with them." Kelly paused a moment, lifting her brows suggestively. "Since they came in a package like Greg Wheaton?"

"It has nothing to do with that, Kelly. I'm engaged to be married. Only six more months, and we'll be dining on delicacies no one can pronounce at my wedding!"

"If you really love Clark, I don't see how a ministry for teenagers, with Greg Wheaton possibly in the vicinity, would threaten your marriage."

"Did I say threaten? It's just not appropriate," Tess clarified. "Greg's single; I'm single."

"Tess, we're all single; that's why we go together. You chaperone us; we'll chaperone you."

"Did I say I needed chaperoning?" Tess was really getting angry now.

"Being accountable is important, Tess. I'm agreeing with you."

Tess stopped her scrubbing and looked at her roommate. "Being accountable to Clark is important."

"I *never* worry about anything happening between you and Clark." Kelly tossed one lone potato chip into her mouth and left the kitchen.

Tess followed her. "Listen, I can't go gallivanting off to Yosemite anyway. I'll have homework, and I've got my wedding to plan. So neither Robby nor I can go, regardless of Greg Wheaton's plans—which mean nothing to me, by the way."

"Tess, you *have* to go," Kelly pleaded.

"Why?"

"Because if you don't go, I can't go, and if I can't go, they don't have enough chaperones and the trip is off."

Tess smirked. "That's a load of guilt for something I never planned to do in the first place."

"Come on, Tess. I want to see if I can do this ministry alongside Ryan, and we're dating, so it's not appropriate for us to go together without others there. I want to know if we might have a future together."

Tess knew she could never say no to Kelly's request. Kelly had always been there for Tess, and if Kelly had a chance at happiness, Tess had to support it. "I wouldn't miss it," she said quietly.

Kelly turned serious, her teasing manner abandoned. "I know being around Greg is hard for you, Tess. I see it when you're near him. He moves you. I think he makes the bells ring, and I *know* Clark doesn't. I've never even seen you kiss Clark, other than the noncommittal kind you'd give to a friend." Kelly looked at her suspiciously. "Marrying Clark won't protect you from getting hurt. I think taking the chance with someone you have real feelings for is more fulfilling than a lifetime of being safe." Kelly sat at the dining room table.

"Would you say that about your failed marriage?"

"Yes," Kelly said simply. "It was worth it, even though he left me for another woman."

"What?" Tess exploded. "I remember what you felt like! I remember the endless nights of tears and the quiet sobbing that filled our lives for nearly a year!"

"I didn't know Christ, Tess. I was acting on pure emotion when I married George. That's not enough to build a marriage on, any more than security alone is. If George hadn't left me, I might never have hurt deeply enough to find Jesus. And if I hadn't found Him, you might not have, either. God knew I'd make that mistake. So ask me again if it was worth it, and I will tell you yes, yes, yes!"

Tess listened eagerly. Kelly was making sense. Perhaps a marriage built on mutual goals wasn't the best foundation. Maybe being in love for a fleeting time was better than a lifetime of stability. For a moment, Tess felt hopeful. Then she thought of the money Clark had already invested in her and Robby, and her future seemed solidified.

Chapter 8

Greg flipped through his old files and found Robby's thick, worn manila folder filled with medical records, psychiatric records, and personal history. With Robby's new living arrangements, it was time to update his files. Instantly Greg's mind flew to Tess. It was clear Tess desired him as much as he did her, but whenever they got close to addressing the attraction, she would turn away, never giving him the chance to find out her real reason for marrying Clark, a man who obviously disliked her brother.

So, why? Why was this beautiful, headstrong woman ignoring her feelings and marrying a man who didn't appear to do much for her? Did she have some kind of loyalty for Clark he hadn't seen? They were almost never together, and when they were, Clark and Tess acted like business partners, not lovebirds. What was the glue that held them together?

He reread the former social worker's case notes handwritten after Robby's mother died.

Case Notes by Robert Gulfman, M.S.W.

May 15
  Tess will gain custodianship of Robby, per her mother's will. Father's whereabouts still unknown. I am concerned about Tess's present state of mind, as well as her age, and would suggest a psychological profile before final guardianship is granted.

May 21
  Tess Ellison has denied my request for a psychological profile, telling me to "Take a long hike off a short pier." She has quit college and is looking for work as a secretary to support herself and Robby. She has put their mother's home on the market to purchase a smaller place without a mortgage. She has applied for, and received, short-term government aid to bridge the gap until her mother's estate is settled. My request for her psychological profile was denied by the county (see enclosed report). To summarize, the report states Tess Ellison had shown wisdom and maturity in all of her actions pertaining to Robby and has exhibited the ability to care for him successfully.

293

Greg dropped the heavy file back onto his desk. "Well, that explains why she hates social workers," he said aloud.

Something about Tess Ellison held his heart, and he couldn't shake it. He told himself his interest was in the name of social work, but when he was near her, when he breathed her soft floral scent, he knew his pursuit had nothing to do with his job.

Greg's secretary appeared in the doorway. She leaned her shoulder against the frame and began to read from her steno pad. "Robby Ellison. . ."

"Yes?" Greg said, hoping this might be the clue he needed.

"He set off the fire alarm at program today."

"Did—"

"He set off the fire alarm, then while throwing a tantrum, broke his trainer's car window. They decided to suspend him and put him on a special bus to Serenity Springs, and he cracked the bus window."

"Is that it?"

"Isn't that enough?" his secretary said.

Greg rose, grabbing his sport coat from the back of his chair. "Was he hurt?"

"No, and neither was anyone else. He's back at Serenity Springs. Diane Laney called to say he is fine—no signs that anything is amiss."

With the last piece of information, Greg sat down again. "I'd better call his sister first, then." He shuffled through his Rolodex and pulled out Tess's elegant business card from the hotel. A gold-embossed "NH" dominated the card, and Tess's name and direct line were printed in small black script.

He dialed the number, and Tess answered immediately. "Klaus Kilborn's office, Tess speaking."

"Tess, it's Greg."

"Oh no," Tess groaned. "Not today. What did he do now?"

"Nice to hear your voice, too," he quipped.

"Sorry. I'm just stressed because I'm starting school tonight, and something told me I wouldn't make it to class. So give me the details. Why will I be staying home tonight?"

"Tess, he's at Serenity Springs; they'll handle Robby. I'm just calling because this particular problem may cost you some money, and I wanted to warn you."

Tess closed her eyes and let her head fall back. "How much money?" she asked tentatively.

"That depends on what price his program puts on a false fire alarm, his trainer's car window, and a county bus window."

"In one day?" she asked in disbelief.

"On an upnote, I've seen his trainer's car. It's a piece of junk, so that shouldn't cost too much."

They both started to laugh. "Stop it, Greg. Don't make me laugh. This isn't funny. Do you have any idea how many windows I've paid for in my young lifetime?"

Greg wanted to say no, but he'd love to count them over dinner. "Uh, two?" Greg guessed.

"I think it's closer to two hundred. I'm not even going to ask if he was hurt, because I know he wasn't. He never is—he just breaks windows with his fists without consequences."

"Ah, but there *will* be consequences. I'm going to talk to Diane Laney about suspending jukebox privileges."

"Oooh, you're good."

"So don't give it another thought. What class do you have tonight?"

"Geometry, and math never was my best subject," Tess whined.

"Geometry? Starting out a little heavy, huh?"

"It's the next of the required courses for those of us brain-dead in math. After that, I should be done with the technical portion of my education."

"If you need any help with the math, I'd be happy to help out. I have an undergraduate degree in architecture; it involved a lot of math." He cringed as the words escaped his mouth; he didn't need to be bragging about his own education.

"How did you get from architecture to social work?"

"I had a double major. It's a long, boring story; trust me. My university was sad to see me go—all that lost revenue." He let out a short laugh, and he was relieved to hear her laugh with him.

A loud knock interrupted his pleasant conversation, and Tess's fiancé stood in the doorway, his frame filling it. His eyes bore through Greg, and the social worker's lighthearted state of mind disappeared. "I need to run. He'll be fine. Talk with you soon." Greg abruptly hung up the phone and focused on Clark with wary eyes. "What can I do for you?" he asked, keeping his gaze locked with Clark's.

"You can stay away from my fiancée. I can make your life rather miserable if you choose to go your own route."

Greg picked up Robby's file and pounded the stack of paperwork, bringing order to it. "I am Robby's social worker; your fiancée is your business," Greg said, turning to file the reports.

Clark came and stood next to him. "Resign from this case, or I'll see to it that you are asked to resign."

Greg couldn't help himself—he laughed. "I see through your type, Armstrong. Let me just see how I do. Young lawyer looking for a wife heads to the singles' group of a church in search of a young innocent—not the type he usually dates, the kind he wants to marry. Enter Tess Ellison, a young woman in need of a break." Greg lifted his eyebrows for confirmation and could tell by the angry scowl on

Clark's face that he'd come close.

"Don't waste your psychobabble on me. You want to question someone's religion? Look at the type of man who deliberately courts another man's fiancée." Clark pointed his finger, and Greg remained stoic.

"That wasn't my intention. I'm sorry if it appears that way." Greg swiveled his chair around to his desk.

Clark whirled Greg's chair around by force and wagged his finger in Greg's face. "Listen to me. If you think I'm making idle threats, just try me. I want you off this case and away from my wife."

"To be. Your wife-to-be," Greg clarified. Greg stood to his full six feet two inches, looking menacingly over Clark. "Is that all? You can find your way out, I'm sure."

Clark walked away, stopping in the doorway and turning. "This isn't over." He pointed once again and knocked shoulders with Greg's questioning secretary as he left.

"Charming. Who was that?" she asked as she brought in his latest phone messages.

"No one of consequence," Greg said absently.

~

The lecture hall for her first class was a monstrosity of cement, open and cavernous inside, the kind of place that echoed naturally. The hall would have accommodated hundreds of students, but a small group of about forty students huddled toward the front. Tess took a seat in the center of the theater, sheepishly taking out her notepad and the used book she'd bought for the class. She felt out of place and restlessly fidgeted in her seat.

After a three-hour lecture, the last thing Tess wanted to do was go sit in her old sedan for the hour drive home, but she had little choice. Berkeley was not a place to hang out alone.

She entered her trusted Honda and tried the ignition; nothing happened. She tried again; still nothing. She looked at her watch and saw it was nine thirty. It would be ten thirty before she got home on the peninsula without car troubles. *Now what?*

She tried one last time, grabbed her purse, and ran toward an all-night pizza joint. She walked briskly by all the students, some of them working industriously on homework in the earsplitting environment and some laughing and chatting. She dialed Clark's number. His phone rang and rang until his answering machine finally came on. "You've reached the residence of Clark Armstrong. Please leave your name and number and I will most certainly return the call as soon as possible." *Beep.*

"Clark, it's Tess. My car won't start and I'm in Berkeley." She looked at her watch again. "It's 9:35. If you get this message soon, call me back at 555-2343. Thanks."

Tess hung up the phone and stared at it for a moment. She dialed home and there, too, listened to the recorded message of the answering machine. She pressed her code to hear any messages. Kelly had called to say she and Ryan were at a youth-group planning meeting, and she would be home by eleven. "Oh, Kelly, why tonight? You never go out on weeknights!"

Beginning to feel fear, she immediately thought of Greg Wheaton. He was in San Mateo, and it wouldn't take him that long to cross the San Mateo bridge. He would miss San Francisco traffic altogether, she reasoned. She took out his business card and dialed his home number scribbled on the back.

"Hello?" Greg answered on the second ring.

"Greg?" She sighed with relief at the sound of a live person.

"Tess, is that you?"

"Greg, I'm in Berkeley, and my car won't start. I'm afraid to ride on BART at this time of night, and I can't reach Clark or Kelly," she explained.

"I'll be right there. Where are you?"

"I'm at Popeye's Pizza, across from Sproul Hall. Do you know where that is?" she asked hopefully.

"I'll find it. In the meantime, stay put. Don't go back to your car, and don't leave the restaurant. Okay?"

"Don't worry. As I speak there's a purple-haired, mohawked kid trying to sell something outside the door." Tess shuddered. "I think I'll just sit down inside."

"I'm leaving now." Greg hung up, and Tess breathed a huge sigh of relief.

Greg arrived forty minutes later, and Tess was so shocked to see him, she checked her watch. "That was *fast.*"

"Gentlemen don't leave young ladies stranded in Berkeley longer than necessary," he explained. He picked up her books and took her hand firmly, protectively, and walked her to her car. He lifted the hood and laughed.

"What's the matter, is it just a loose wire?" Tess asked, feeling stupid that she'd called him all the way to Berkeley.

"No, Tess—someone stole your battery."

"Stole the car battery?" she repeated, astonished.

"Yup. Is it okay to leave it here overnight? Or do you want to have it towed somewhere?"

"I suppose it's not going anywhere. Besides, I'm too tired to think about it tonight anyway. I'll take care of it on my lunch hour." She shrugged.

"Get me the license plate number and your registration information, and I'll have a friend take care of it. He drives a tow truck."

She shook her head. "No, Greg, you've done plenty already. Driving out here was more than enough."

"Tess, it's ten at night. I'm not going to argue with you. Please get me the information."

They walked to his car a short distance away, and he opened the door for her.

"Where's Clark tonight?" he asked casually as he got behind the wheel.

"I don't know—probably working late. Look, I'm really sorry I had to call you. I'll pay for your gas." She crossed her arms.

"Tess, I wasn't insinuating anything. You're my friend. You can call me anytime you need help; you know that." She nodded and gave him a weak smile. Up until now, she had always thought it was his looks that moved her, but there was so much more. She felt she *knew* him and that he understood her. Looking at him, she realized she couldn't marry Clark, and that was troubling, indeed.

Chapter 9

Tess sat at the kitchen table, its entire surface covered by textbooks, spiral notebooks, and writing implements. She tried again to understand a geometry question and finally dropped her head to the table, crying in frustration.

"Tess?" Kelly's familiar voice was laced with worry. "Tess, what's the matter?"

Tess lifted her head off the table. "Nothing." She wiped her eyes with the back of her hand. "I just don't get this, Kelly. No matter how many times I read this stupid book, I don't understand geometry."

"Have you asked your professor?" Kelly set a glass of water in front of Tess.

"I tried staying after class, but he just put a hand up and told me to read the book."

"Tess, you're paying tuition to learn geometry from a capable professor—you can't let yourself be intimidated by him. He's there because you pay his salary."

"He's there because he's trying to sell multiple copies of this inane textbook he wrote; no one else would use it." She slammed the book shut.

"Tess, you look so worn out. I'm starting to see bags under your eyes. Is this worth it?"

Tess ran her fingers roughly through her mangled mass of curls. "I don't know, Kelly. I'm doing fine in all my other classes, but I just don't see how I'm going to pass this class. If I can just get through it, I'll be done with math." Tess rubbed her temples, trying to ease the headache that had plagued her intermittently for weeks.

"So drop it, and next quarter you can request a better professor," Kelly suggested. She opened the pantry and dragged out a large cooler. "I'm supposed to bring the makings for s'mores," she explained. "For our Yosemite weekend, remember?"

"Yes, I remember," Tess said cheerlessly.

"Why don't you leave Robby here, Tess? He'll be okay at the home for one weekend. You look like you could use the break."

Tess dropped her head, shaking it. "I can't go to Yosemite. I've got to study for this geometry exam. Besides, Robby's having trouble at Serenity Springs—they said he's been breaking things. Plus I promised Clark I'd attend some banquet for his bar association tomorrow night. I skipped my American history class to be home to study for geometry tonight."

"That's ridiculous. You're going to burn out," Kelly rebuked. "Besides, you promised."

"I know, but what if I don't pass? You said there were enough parents going."

"Just quit," Kelly said simply.

"Not on your life, Kelly. I'm going to be on the dean's list if it's the last thing I do."

"And it just may be."

The doorbell rang. "That must be Clark. He's going to help me with my geometry." Tess ran downstairs and opened the door.

"Tess? What is that you're wearing?" Clark's greeting sobered her immediately.

"I'm wearing shorts and a T-shirt, Clark. I didn't think I needed to put on my finest for you to help me with my homework."

"I thought we'd get dinner first." His eyes roamed up and down her body judgmentally.

"I'm not running for Miss America; I'm trying to pass a geometry exam."

He plowed through the door and headed toward her closed book on the table. "It helps if you open the book."

"This is not a subject to push," Kelly warned Clark quietly before Tess had reached the kitchen.

"You have your degree, Kelly," he answered rudely.

Kelly rolled her eyes. "I'll be upstairs packing."

The phone rang. "Hello."

"Tess, it's Greg Wheaton. Robby broke a crystal frame belonging to Diane Laney. It had her wedding picture in it, and he threw it across the living room when she told him he hadn't earned jukebox tokens."

"Tell Diane I'll be right there. She can call me directly, Greg. I'm sorry you were bothered."

"She called me because she's worried about his progress in the home, Tess. He's not through with his probationary period, and Diane wanted to discuss therapies that might help his behavior. Otherwise—"

"Greg, really? Is it that serious?"

"I'm afraid so, Tess."

"I'll be right there. Thanks again."

She hung up the phone and addressed Clark's angry frown. "I'm sorry, Clark. Robby's having some big troubles. I need to go to the home tonight." She felt so overwhelmed, she wanted to throw something herself. She had wanted to break off her engagement, but with Robby's home situation so precarious, she couldn't take the chance. She had promised her mother she'd keep Robby out of an institution, and she intended to do so, no matter what the cost.

"You're just going to drop the homework?" he asked impatiently.

"Do I have an option?"

"Tess, every time I come down here this Greg character calls you with another reason for you to go traipsing off. Your brother is coming between us, and I think it's time you made your choice."

"Choice? What choice? And what does Greg have to do with it? He's just the bearer of bad news."

"Greg wants to be more than a bearer of bad news, Tess. Really, are you so naive? Marriage means leaving the family and cleaving to your husband; that's the choice that every wife must make. This schedule of yours has you wiped out. You're losing your youthful glow, and you haven't even mentioned our wedding. I know you think I'm being cruel about your brother. But Tess, if you want to have a future, you need to give custody of your brother to the state. The professionals are equipped to handle these situations a lot more effectively than you are. When you are my wife, you'll have a flurry of responsibilities to keep you busy, even before we have children. Marriage is a huge commitment, Tess. I'm asking you to take a step toward me and away from your past."

Somehow she couldn't help but wonder if he was right. She had been supervising her brother's care for nearly seven years, and nothing had changed in his cycle of behavior problems. If anything, Robby was getting worse. *Could the state handle it better?* she wondered—for the first time, seriously.

"I've got to go. We can talk later." She threw on a pair of sweats over her shorts and added a sweatshirt.

Clark shook his head, following her with his eyes. "It's not a suggestion, Tess. Either you give custody to the state and give yourself to me, or you haven't made the commitment necessary to be my wife." He set his briefcase on the kitchen table and snapped open the locks, then withdrew a packet of typewritten information. "I've taken the liberty of having someone at my law firm draw up the necessary paperwork. All you have to do is sign the document and put it in the mailbox. My secretary even put postage on it."

Tess was incredulous. "Get out of here and take that with you! I can't take any more, Clark. This marriage is off!" She grabbed her keys and headed for her car. Her heart was beating a thousand times a second, and her breath was labored. She got into the driver's seat and slumped onto the steering wheel. "Lord, why are You doing this to me?" she screamed aloud. "You said I could rest in You, so why are you making things so difficult? Now I've ruined things with Clark, and if Robby gets thrown out of his home, I'll have no choice but to put him in an institution. How could You let me do something so stupid?"

Seeing Clark emerge from her condominium, she turned the ignition and raced out of the parking lot.

Tess broke the speed limit several times on her way to Serenity Springs. Once she arrived, she knocked impatiently at the door of the home. After being admitted, she hurried to her brother's room.

"Robby?" Tess entered his room. He was wearing headphones and playing his record player. She pulled off the headphones, and Robby glared at her. "Robby. . ." She tried to continue, but her crying choked her words.

"No cry, Sis. I be good. I be good." He patted her back and moved so she could sit down.

"Robby, you've broken a lot of things, and it's costing me a lot of money. If you continue to break people's stuff, they are going to make you live somewhere else. If you hurt people, they'll make you live in jail!" She prayed she was getting through to him. She didn't know why she used the argument of how much money he'd cost her. Money meant nothing to him. If given the choice of a five- or a ten-dollar bill, he'd choose the five because he liked the picture better. She hoped maybe the threat of jail meant something to him.

"I be good," he repeated.

"Do you want to live with me again?" she asked softly.

He shook his head. "No, I like it here!" He pointed to the floor where he stood.

"Robby, it's not enough to just like it; you've got to earn the right to stay here. You've got to respect people and their things. Would you like it if someone threw your record player across the room?" Tess knew her words were useless. Robby would just continue to agree and plead until she left, but none of it would sink in.

Greg came in silently and sat beside her, pulling up another chair. He never ceased to amaze her. Clark had had the opportunity to accompany her on this burdensome trip, but he'd chosen to go home to the safety of his expensive lifestyle. But Greg Wheaton never seemed afraid to step out onto a limb if he thought he could help in some way. Greg and Clark were as different as night and day. It was kind of humorous that she had seen life with Clark as the "secure" road.

Greg patted her back. "You all right?"

Robby put his headphones back on and went back to his music. "I'm not getting through to him, Greg. I don't know what to do next. He says he doesn't want to live with me."

"He loves it here. We've just got to learn what's causing these angry outbursts and teach him to curb the behavior."

She nodded. "But how?"

"We'll figure it out." He held out his hand to help her up. She took it, hugged her brother, and walked to her car alongside Greg, knowing her urgent visit had solved nothing. She was exactly where she'd been an hour ago, and Robby was an hour closer to getting kicked out of another home.

"I've hit bottom; there's nothing else I can do." Tess felt dejected, thinking

Clark had been right. Robby was better off with professionals—she just couldn't see it because she'd been in the same fruitless holding pattern for years.

"So now it's God's turn." Greg's gaze met hers, and this time she didn't look away. She took in the fullness of his gaze, desiring with her whole heart that Greg was right and Clark wrong. Tess didn't want to let down her mother—she wanted to keep Robby out of an institution. But the idea of marrying Clark to fulfill the promise now turned her stomach.

Tess nodded, and Greg shut her car door, waiting patiently until her car started and she was well down the long driveway.

Chapter 10

Tess descended the staircase gingerly, rubbing her eyes as she attempted to face the coming day. No flowers had arrived, so she assumed Clark had taken her seriously. She reached the kitchen, and Kelly laughed at her. "What happened to you?"

"Just once can't you tell me how beautiful I am?" Tess smirked.

"Uh, this morning? No." Kelly pulled a mug from the cabinet. "Sit down; I'll get you some coffee."

"Robby might be asked to leave Serenity Springs," Tess began, cradling her aching head.

"I heard." Kelly placed coffee and buttered toast in front of her.

"Thanks. How'd you hear about Robby?"

"Greg called late last night after you went to bed. He asked a favor of me."

"Greg did?" Tess's forehead was furrowed in confusion. "What kind of favor?"

"Not saying." Kelly went about her packing for Yosemite and loudly poured the ice chips into the cooler she'd packed with sodas and s'more makings the night before.

Tess was too tired to care, so she shrugged it off and sipped her coffee. "Mmm, nice and strong, just the way I need it."

"Go get dressed in jeans and a casual shirt," Kelly ordered. "And put on some makeup! Oh, and Clark called; he wants his ring back."

"Kelly, I have work today—I'll drop it by his office. And why is everyone suddenly so concerned with my looks? I'm a secretary, not a fashion model."

"We don't care about your looks; we care about how tired you are. And you don't have work today. I called Klaus. You're off for a week," Kelly said quickly, trying to slip it past her.

"Excuse me?"

"I'll explain it all later. Greg will be here soon, so go put some makeup on before you scare the daylights out of him. You may be beautiful, but with those bags you're sporting, you either need a full night's sleep or some concealer before he gets here. I'd opt for the makeup at this point."

"Kelly. . ." The doorbell rang, and Tess's eyes opened wide.

"That would be Greg," Kelly said coolly.

Tess hastened up the stairs, taking them two at a time. She threw on some concealer and foundation and pulled on a pair of jeans and a favorite baby pink sweater. She finished with a touch of mascara and blotted some pale pink lipstick onto her full lips, then raced back down the stairs.

Tess felt breathless at the sight of him. Kelly stood at the base of the stairs and whispered into Tess's ear, "Oh no, he doesn't do a thing for you."

"Greg, Robby's not getting thrown out yet, is he?" Tess came around the banister and headed toward Greg, who sat on the couch with a cup of coffee.

"No, no. I'm kidnapping you," Greg said calmly. "Well, you and Robby."

"What?" Tess smiled at the joke. She looked back at Kelly, hoping to be included in the gag.

"You're going to Yosemite with us. We're picking Robby up in...," he glanced at his watch, "about twenty minutes."

"No, Greg." She smiled sweetly. "I'm going to work. I don't know what Kelly and you are up to, but I have to work."

"No, you don't." He picked up the phone. "Would you like to confirm it with Klaus?"

She looked at Greg, then to Kelly, then back to Greg again. "What is this?" She felt like she was in the midst of a conspiracy.

Kelly came forward. "We're your friends, Tess. You're going to Yosemite; you're going to relax if it kills you, and you are going to have a time of deep prayer. As your friends, we're demanding it. And if you say no, I'll tell Greg what you did to your prom date."

She looked to Greg, and he nodded in agreement. Tess wanted to cry out that a weekend near Greg Wheaton was the last thing she needed. To be around the man that made her heart roar like a lion was no solution. Clark had asked her to make a choice between Robby and him, but when Robby's side included Greg, Tess found the scale decidedly tipped.

Her oath had seemed so simple since her feelings were so easily pushed down. Marrying Clark had been her solution, but with Greg in the picture, her emotions were becoming harder and harder to ignore. She reminded herself how she needed Clark's calm, his lack of emotions. Right now, she thirsted for it. She had better call him; perhaps she could apologize.

Greg picked up her things that Kelly had packed and walked toward the door. Kelly came forward and laid a kiss on Tess's cheek, then whispered in her ear, "You never convinced me about Clark, so maybe I can convince you about Greg."

Tess felt like she was walking into the dragon's lair when she looked at Greg. She had been so careful to stay away from men she could fall for. Why was she so weak now? God said she wouldn't be tempted beyond what she could bear, but spending a chaperoned weekend with a man who ignited her every passion was certainly going to push her to the limit.

Sensing her hesitancy, Greg tossed her duffel bag over his shoulder and picked her up like she was a child, cradling her in his muscular arms. "I can see you're tentative, so I'll make it easy for you. See? Now you had nothing to do with it." He didn't say another word until he gingerly placed her in the front seat of his car. "Just forget about your troubles and relax."

～

At Serenity Springs she found Robby in a trance over his record player. He looked up.

"Tess, you marry Greg?" he asked while Greg was conveniently at the car with Robby's bag.

"No, honey," Tess answered.

"I not like Clark," he mumbled to himself.

"Robby, what did you say?" Tess asked in shock. In all her years of dealing with Robby, she had never heard him outwardly say he disliked anyone. It was completely out of character, and she momentarily wondered if someone had set him up to it. When he answered her, Tess knew it was from Robby's heart alone.

"He not like Elvis, he not like Buddy Holly, he not even like Chuck Berry. And he not like me, either, Tess," Robby said.

She instantly thought of the emotional pain she and Robby had endured as children. When the kids at school had tormented him and laughed at his habits, she had always rushed to his aid. Even at the expense of her own image. The kids had laughed at her, too, taunting her with a refrain she could still hear. *Tess, Tess, life so hard; Daddy left the two retards.* Tears filled her eyes at the thought, but she forced them back. Robby had always seemed oblivious to the schoolchildren's taunts, so why did Robby notice Clark's?

"Robby, why do you say Clark doesn't like you? He likes you," she said, her tone questioning.

Robby began to spin a ribbon in the air, ignoring her question. Tess knew the conversation was over—that no matter what she asked, it would go unanswered. Robby had moved into his own world.

Greg came in with a wide smile. "Are we ready to go?"

Tess nodded.

～

After a long drive through the flat, barren farmlands of California, they arrived at Yosemite.

When they entered the valley, her jaw dropped at the spectacle. No matter how many times she'd seen Yosemite Valley, it was always like the first time. The dramatic waterfalls were extraordinary, even in the fall, and the Merced River that wandered lazily through the meadows was a sight to behold as it rolled over the granite rocks that intermittently jutted out of the water. Finally, they reached the campgrounds, and Tess stretched like a cat when she got out of the car.

"Tess, look up there," Greg said as he handed her a pair of binoculars and held them to her eyes. His touch made her unconcerned with the sights.

Robby was asleep in the car, and Tess thought it best not to wake him. She'd help Greg set up the tent first.

"Kelly and Ryan are bringing your tent," Greg said. "Robby will stay with me and a couple of the teenagers. You and Kelly will be together. We had enough parents come along that you two can have your own tent. Sound good?"

Tess breathed the heavy pine scent deeply. "It sounds positively wonderful," she said dreamily.

After they had finished setting up the tent, Greg opened her red duffel, where he retrieved her Bible. "This is from Kelly. She said to use it." He smiled. "Why don't you go have a quiet time before all the noise arrives. I'll keep an eye on Robby." He motioned toward the asphalt walkway that meandered through the park.

"I will, thanks." She took her Bible gratefully. It had been so long since she'd picked it up; it seemed like a lost friend. She was walking away from the campsite when she caught sight of Greg's blue Volkswagen; it was rocking back and forth as if it were a mere toy in a child's hand.

She ran closer to check on her brother and saw a huge brown bear rocking the car, trying to rip into the vehicle. The window by Robby was open slightly, and the bear was clawing at it. She heard her brother scream, then saw the bear break the window away. "Greg! Greg!" she screamed. Robby moved away from the bear just as the huge animal stuck its arm inside the window.

Greg rushed past her, pushing her. "Get back! Slowly," he commanded. But she stood firm, too afraid to move.

"Please, God, watch out for my precious Robby—and my precious Greg," she added quietly. Her body shivered with fear. She wanted to rush to her brother, but she obeyed Greg's command, trusting him fully.

Greg lifted his arms high into the air, approaching the bear. "Tess, go get some food, fast—anything!" The bear pulled its arm out of the car momentarily and looked questioningly at Greg. Tess sprinted with more energy than she thought herself capable of. She grabbed a bag of potato chips and a box of cookies and was back within seconds. Greg backed up slowly, still talking to the bear, keeping the animal's attention off the car and Robby. "Okay, Tess, slowly hand it over to me and walk backward to the campsite *slowly.*"

Tess did as she was told and watched as Greg frantically ripped open the cookies and chips and spread them out on the ground, leaving a trail away from the car. The bear dropped down on all fours and began devouring the junk food, forgetting the Volkswagen altogether.

"Go find a ranger!" Greg called out to Tess. He walked ever so slowly and carefully to the opposite side of his car, being sure to stay in the bear's line of sight. He unlocked the door and helped a stunned-silent Robby out of the vehicle.

"You got food in here, Robby?" Greg asked. Robby's wide eyes answered affirmatively. "Give it to me now!" Greg ordered, and Robby handed him a bag of beef jerky. Greg pulled back his arm and made a long pass of the bag. It landed with a plop on the other side of the bear, which eagerly dropped the cookies when it smelled the dried meat.

Greg pulled Robby away from the car and took him to the river's edge. "Wash your hands. You need to get that smell off of you." Without question or comment, Robby reached into the icy cold water and rinsed his hands and arms thoroughly.

The bear took its time eating the teenagers' treats before lumbering on across the parking lot. A park ranger's truck soon appeared, and Tess hopped out with two rangers, both sporting guns. Greg pointed for the rangers, and they took off after the bear. Tess rushed toward her brother. "Robby, Robby," she called as she ran. Robby was still too shocked for words. Tess just pulled him into her arms, her arms barely long enough to reach around his back. "I'm so sorry, honey! You can't have any food in the cars. I completely forgot about the jerky." She hugged her brother tightly, while he remained motionless.

"I'm sorry, Tess. I thought I took all the food out of the car." Greg obviously felt awful about not being careful. The flyer they'd been given warning them about the bears circled mockingly in the breeze, along with the empty cookie and chip bags.

Tess shook her head. "It's my fault. I bought him the beef jerky on our last stop. I never thought about it."

They heard a shot peel through the air, echoing eerily off the cavernous granite sheers.

Tess flinched. One of the rangers came running back to the truck. "We got her. She's tranquilized, thanks to you." The ranger sharply addressed Tess, while looking towards Robby as if to apply blame.

Greg watched as Tess's demeanor instantly changed; her warm nature was gone. By the look in her eye, Greg thought she might physically attack the ranger. "Yeah, well, I don't think too much of my handicapped brother being attacked, either! Or maybe you think we thought it might be fun to watch a retarded man get scared out of his wits by a bear," Tess shouted, her shoulders rocking defiantly. Greg grasped her hands, trying to calm her down, but Tess was back on the playground as a child, protecting her brother. "You animal lovers always seem to think your precious animals are more important than people." She pulled away from Greg and got right in the ranger's face. "Look at my brother!" she screamed. "He's just a child in a man's body!"

Greg watched as the ranger eyed Robby, noticing Robby's childlike state, and he saw the ranger's guilt take on an ashen look. Without a word, the ranger started up the truck and left, probably afraid to upset Tess more. The three of them wandered back to Greg's car to survey the damage. The car window had been smashed and jagged shards of glass protruded from the base. The window frame bent outward, like a twisted piece of tin.

Tess looked coolly at the car. "Great, another window to pay for." She dropped her head into her hands. "I'm sorry, Greg, it seems we're just a jinx." She took her brother's hand and started to walk away.

"You're not paying for the window. That was my fault. I never should have let Robby sleep in there alone. And you're not walking away from me after that outburst." He took her by both hands. "Do you want to tell me what it was all about?"

She yanked away. "Stupid animal lovers," she mumbled under her breath as she walked away.

"Is there a reason you ripped that poor ranger's head off? He may have been a jerk, but he didn't deserve that."

She turned. "Now *there's* the social worker I know." She took her brother by the hand again, and Greg winced at the accusation.

"Robby," Greg said, "Ryan just got here. Go say hi. He's got a music job for you." Greg praised God silently for Ryan's timely arrival. Maybe now he could get to the bottom of this. Robby started to walk away, excited at the prospect of new people.

"I'm not leaving my brother—he's still frightened half to death," Tess said as she followed Robby.

Greg grabbed her by both shoulders. "He's fine. Quit babying him. This is not going to ruin our weekend. It's bad enough the teenagers don't have any cookies." He smiled down at her, and for a moment he thought he saw her soften.

"I'm going for a walk. Robby can stay with you since you seem to know what's best for him." Tess stormed off angrily, and Greg was left to wonder how he might have handled her differently.

～

Tess wandered around the valley for a while, taking in the splendor of God's creation. Hearing the gentle sounds of the river and the roar of Yosemite Falls behind her, smelling the fresh, clean air, and seeing the majesty before her, Tess thought about how God had created all the senses to be used to worship Him.

She sat and flipped through her Bible—it had been so long since she'd even looked at it—and she read some of the highlighted passages. How could she have substituted geometry for the Word of God? She shook her head and began to pray. "Dear God, I thank You for leaving us with this awesome display of Your creative power. You are so wonderful, and I am so sorry that it's been so long since I told

You that. Please forgive me, Lord, especially my childish outburst over one of your creatures. Please tell me where to go from here. I have always thought You wanted me to marry Clark, but when I look at Greg, I don't see how I can. I love Greg, Lord—so much that it aches just to think of living without him. Lord, please help me fight the temptation. Help me to walk in Your paths."

Tess had prayed aloud. It was so heartfelt and crushing that she never thought to keep it quiet, but God had honored her privacy. No one roamed into her idyllic spot in the meadow by the deep green Merced River. She sat under an ancient pine, watching the golden grass of the meadow sway in the breeze.

She turned to the Gospel of Matthew and came upon a verse she had forgotten about, although it was highlighted in bright pink. At one time she could have quoted it, chapter and verse. "Come unto me, all ye that labor and are heavy laden, and I will give you rest."

She began to weep after reading the verse; it had been so long since she'd given any of her burdens to the Lord, and she had been carrying them all, buckling under the load. She knew God wanted to take her burdens away, and perhaps that meant Clark, as well. God wanted her to rely on Him, not a husband. But what about her promise to her mother? Her mother's dying request had been that Tess keep Robby out of an institution. With Robby's behavior and Tess's limited financial means, she could never be sure to do that without Clark's money. A social worker certainly didn't make enough money to help her. So her struggle continued.

She meditated and prayed for hours. As the sun began to fade, she closed her Bible and took in the sights once again.

"Tess?" Greg emerged from a pathway along the meadow. Despite the receding light, his blue eyes were bright as he smiled gently. "It's getting dark. Can I walk you back?" She smiled invitingly, and he went to her. "Did you have a good day?"

"I did. I'm sorry about that scene earlier. I'll apologize to the ranger," she said quietly.

"It's all right." He sat down beside her. "I just wish you'd tell me what's bothering you. I might be able to help."

"I wish you could, but I don't think you can. I made a promise, and I have to keep it, no matter what."

"Is that the reason you were marrying Clark?"

"Yes," she answered simply.

"Did you love him?" he questioned.

Tess opened her mouth to lie, and perhaps it was the Bible in her lap, but try as she might, the lie wouldn't come. "No."

Greg gently stroked her face, pausing to give her time to explain. "So, why?" he finally prodded. "And I'm not asking as a social worker." He grasped her hand,

and something in the action told her his feelings.

"It's a long story."

"I've got time." He stroked her cheek and reclined on the grass, propping his head with an elbow.

"It's one of those 'woe is me' things," she warned.

"I'm a social worker. I live for that stuff." He grinned.

"My father left when my mom was pregnant with me. He said he didn't want to raise two retards. Back then they didn't know if Robby's condition was genetic or not, so they just assumed the worst. My mother still loved him, even after she was left to raise two children by herself. I don't know if she was totally blind about him or if she really saw something no one else did.

"I thought he was dead until I got to school. Some of the kids had heard their mothers gossiping and told me what really happened to him. They said he was a drunk who left my mother because he thought she made mentally retarded children."

"Tess, I don't know what to say, other than you've got to let it go. Give it to God, sweetheart. He'll take it all away, and He will care for Robby like you or I never could." Greg tipped her chin and traced her jawline gently.

Tess felt such relief—for once she felt her tight stomach muscles start to relax. She relished finally being able to divulge her history that had been bottled up inside for so long. "They didn't integrate kids like Robby, like they do now. They were put in special classrooms in regular schools. At lunchtime I'd go out and see Robby playing with a top or something similar that spun around, and all these boys would be huddled around him, laughing at him." She felt her tears stinging hot as they ran down her cheeks. "Robby didn't seem to notice the taunts, but then they'd close in on him, making the circle tighter and tighter. Robby would hug his knees and start to hit himself because he felt so trapped. Then the kids would laugh all the harder because he was hitting himself. The teachers never did anything about it! Unless they sent my brother to the principal's office for hitting himself, it all went unpunished. Except *I* got sent to the office once for cussing at them."

"I still don't understand why you agreed to marry Clark," Greg said.

"I'm getting there. After school, these same boys would come to our neighborhood and watch our house like Robby was some freak show. They'd bring a snack and just sit across the street. I'd go out and yell at them, but my mom would just pull me inside, telling me to ignore it."

"So you feel like that when people taunt him?" Greg asked.

"Sure I do. Wouldn't you? I mean, I can't understand why people are so rude to him—it's like hurting a child. When I became a Christian, I took solace in the fact that they'd pay for the sins. I'm sorry, I know that doesn't sound very gracious."

"It's all right."

"When I got into high school, all the boys started treating me differently. My mom always said it was because I was growing up."

"Uh-huh."

"Sorry. I told you this was a long story." She felt so self-conscious talking about herself.

"Go ahead."

"I started noticing that when I looked a certain way, these boys would give me all this attention and a respect of sorts. And when I brought my brother places, they would treat him nicer, too, because they wanted to impress me. Doug, the lead bully who used to torture my brother every day, was right there with them, treating me all sugary sweet. The guy didn't have a clue that I held such a grudge against him.

"He saw how all the other guys wanted to date me, and being so incredibly full of himself, he thought he *deserved* me. He asked me to the junior prom, and I agreed to go with him. He actually showed up on my doorstep with a waiting limousine and a corsage. The same house he used to sit in front of to taunt Robby!"

"I'm afraid to ask what you did next," Greg admitted.

"I showed up at the door wearing jeans and tennis shoes and asked him what he was doing there." Tess shrugged.

"So why marry Clark?" Greg inquired again.

"Because Clark has the means to protect Robby, and my salary can't ensure that."

"No, but God can."

"That's not the only reason. I promised my mother Robby would never end up in an institution. Maybe after I get my degree, things will be different, but for now, I need Clark's resources to keep that promise."

"You mean his money."

"Whatever. Before you think me cold-hearted, you need to know that Clark doesn't love me any more than I love him. He just wants a pretty little ornament to help him climb the social ladder. I can turn on the charm when needed, so a partnership was born."

He looked at her in disbelief. "What about love?"

"What about it? It never got my mother anything but a lifetime of pain." Tess shrugged. "Love is fleeting. Clark and I have complementary goals."

"Love is not fleeting, Tess. 'Love never fails.' " He quoted the Bible verse in a quiet, moving tone, and Tess thought she might tell him then and there she loved him.

She squared her shoulders. "The Bible doesn't say anything about a woman loving her husband, only respecting him."

"And do you respect Clark?" He had her there.

312

"I need security for Robby; he wants a wife. Everyone's happy." Tess clapped her hands together.

"Except no one's happy," Greg responded.

"The Bible commands the husband to love his wife, but there's nothing about a woman having to love her husband," she repeated.

"What about the verse that says it's better to marry than to burn with passion?"

"It's talking about the man," Tess said flatly. But when Greg gazed at her, she lost all conviction. This man truly made her burn with passion, and her self-control was at its limit.

"Then why is it addressed to the unmarried and widows?" he asked.

"You're twisting it to confuse me," Tess accused.

"I'm doing no such thing. I'm asking you to look at it for what it says, not what you want it to say. Come on, it's getting dark." He lifted her from the grass and walked silently alongside her back to camp. And they walked into the sunset with Tess's childhood hauntings fully known.

Chapter 11

Tess and Greg returned to the hectic campsite amid a flurry of activities. Kelly was shredding lettuce violently when Tess approached her. "The ranger left this for you."

"What is it?"

"A ticket for three hundred dollars for feeding the bears."

Tess turned to Greg, stuffing the ticket in her jacket pocket. "I take it back; I'm not apologizing."

Greg held out his hand. "Give me the ticket, Tess."

Tess waved him away. "No. I'll just add it to my tab."

"Quit being a martyr. Is it so bad to accept someone's help once in a while? Or do you have to be in control at all times?" Greg stormed off toward Ryan, and Kelly crossed her arms, waiting for an explanation.

"What? I didn't do anything."

Kelly glared at her, shredding the lettuce with greater force. "Girls, could you excuse us a moment?" The two teenagers helping Kelly immediately left, thrilled to be released from the chore. "Tess, you'd try the patience of a saint. Let Greg help you with Robby. I don't understand why you're willing to accept help from Clark and not Greg. You don't have three hundred dollars—you could at least split the ticket with him. It was his fault as much as yours."

"I've got nothing to give Greg."

"Maybe he doesn't want anything. Maybe he just wants to be kind and Christian. Did you ever think you might be holding back a blessing from him?"

"I don't want anybody pitying Robby and me. Clark doesn't feel sorry for us."

"Clark doesn't feel anything," Kelly muttered.

"Well, maybe that's good."

"Tess, marriage is based on love and faith. You and Clark are lacking both. So what about Greg?"

"What about him?" Tess said, avoiding the inevitable.

"Tess, I've seen the way you look at him and the way he looks at you. Are you going to acknowledge that? Or are you going to make idiots of the both of us. I've heard your theory about a wife not being required to love her husband, but what about when she loves another man?"

"I don't love Greg. I barely know him!"

"You're kindred spirits, you and Greg. You know, I actually thought Clark was a nice guy at first, but the more I'm around him, the more I dislike him. His facade seems so put on, and when he's shaken, it comes down quickly."

"I'm too confused to make a decision," Tess said quietly.

"Good. That means you can ask God His opinion and quit relying on your own warped ideas." Kelly grinned.

Ryan came back from the rock wall and tossed a cherry tomato into his mouth. "Hey, girls, how goes kitchen duty?"

"Watch it, or you'll find out," Kelly warned. They smiled at one another, and Tess thought it probably wouldn't be long before she lost Kelly to marriage. She had believed she'd be the first to leave with Clark, but it was beginning to appear otherwise. Suddenly, she found herself wishing she'd met Greg earlier. Maybe things would be different. Regardless, Greg was a social worker and only doing his job, no matter what Tess felt.

Tess watched as Robby put his tapes into the teens' portable stereo and delighted in her brother being the center of attention. *If I had been a Christian earlier, would things have been easier for Robby?* she wondered. These kids were so different from the ones at her school; they cared about people and had given up their beloved popular music for the entire afternoon to make Robby happy.

She went and sat beside her brother. "How ya doing, Rob?"

"Good, good. I got work to do. I'm busy." He shook his hand at her, waving her away. "They need music," he explained. She took the hint and left, thrilled at his show of independence.

She wandered back toward Kelly. "I'm going to take a walk."

Tess walked around the campground slowly, marveling at the deer that fed in the meadow and the stillness of the gentle fall evening.

～

Greg watched Tess as she meandered through the meadow, dreamily taking in the sights. Her cavalier attitude made his jaw tense. He simply couldn't understand how childhood taunts had caused her to desire to marry outside of love. Even if her engagement was called off, how could he convince her that love and marriage go together?

Ryan came up behind him and joined him in watching Tess walk along the path in the distance. "Thinking about your job choice?"

"I asked her what her favorite book was; you know what she said?" Greg asked, ignoring Ryan's question.

"Hmm?"

"*The Count of Monte Cristo*. You know why? Because he gets revenge on everyone that ever hurt him."

"You're in over your head, Greg. Tess may be a fantastic woman, but she's carrying a lot of baggage. You're getting too involved, and if you don't watch out, you will get fired from this job for the same reason you did from your last one. Then there will be no job choice—only a damaged reputation and a useless education."

"That doesn't sound like a pastor talking. You think she should have married this guy she doesn't love?"

"You don't know she doesn't love him, you just assume it. If she seeks God, He'll take care of her. If she chooses to go her own way, she'll have to deal with the consequences." Ryan shrugged. "No sense in you losing your job because she's too foolish to listen."

"You'd write her off just like that?" Greg snapped his fingers.

"You're my friend; I'm trying to protect you. Tess is not your problem. Pray for her, help her with Robby, but don't get personally involved. Don't make the same mistake twice."

"You don't understand, Ryan. I love her, and she's not engaged anymore. I plan to wear her down with God's help."

"Kelly says she already has a thing against social workers. When she finds out your history, you're done for. Pray for her brother; that's what she needs." Ryan patted him on the back and headed back to a wild game of volleyball.

Greg watched as Tess bent to smell a stray wildflower rising up through the meadow grass. The last of the evening sun cast her wisp of a figure into silhouette; it was like a scene from a romantic calendar. And it felt like God's clear sign. *For I am fearfully and wonderfully made.* She wasn't someone to be abandoned but someone made by God for a purpose. Greg refused to believe that purpose was solely to care for her brother. She deserved to be loved, to be treasured.

~

The next morning Tess was invigorated by the crisp mountain air. Much to her dismay, Greg thought a walk sounded great. Tess, half angry at herself for revealing her pain to Greg and half mad at him for his trying to help her, tried to recruit Robby as a chaperone.

"I not want to go. The kids need me to play music," Robby said.

"Robby, it's too early to play music," Tess said. "You'll wake up the other campers. Come with us, then you can come back and play music."

"Nooo!" he whined and began to hit himself. He started to bite his already mangled forefinger and stomped his feet, wailing like a wounded animal.

"Robby, stop it," Tess demanded in a hushed voice. "Stop it, or Greg will take us home right now."

At that point Robby headed toward Greg with the express intention of hitting him. "Robby, no!" Tess got in between the two men and took a hard left hook to her right temple. It was the last thing she remembered before waking up in Greg's arms.

"Tess? Are you okay?" Greg held an ice pack to her head, and she groaned when she awoke to the pain.

"Where's Robby?" She sat up too quickly, and her woozy head fell back into Greg's arms.

"Tess, don't sit up yet, you'll black out again. Robby's fine. He's with Ryan, and they're taking a walk."

"What happened to him? Is he okay?"

"Tess, you just got punched by a 220-pound man. I think you're worried about the wrong participant in this fiasco." Greg smiled at her, and she giggled, sending a sharp pain through her head. She groaned again. "Here, I've got a couple of painkillers Ryan had in the first-aid kit. Do you think you're ready to swallow them?"

"Oh, Greg, Robby is moving backwards." The realization struck her like Robby's fist. She rubbed her throbbing temple.

Greg stroked her hair gently, bringing the cold compress to her temple. "I think I may have the answer to our problem with Robby's behavior, but I'll discuss that when you're a little more lucid."

"I'm lucid," Tess said enthusiastically.

"Here's some water, Tess—swallow those pills." Kelly stood over her, smiling. "And by the way, the next time you see somebody built like Greg about to get slugged, let him take the hit." Kelly winked, and Greg smiled at her.

"Smart gal, that Kelly," Greg commented.

"I'm sorry, Greg. I've never seen him hit anyone or come at someone so violently. He has always just hurt himself. I didn't want him to hit you."

"Thanks. I didn't want him to hit me, either. But Tess, you're half my size; next time let me handle it, okay?"

"You think I'm going to argue?" She laughed, then groaned again. She swallowed the pills Greg held in his gentle hand, then fell back into his chest, enjoying his warmth and nursing care.

Tess started to drift back to sleep, and Greg lifted her to her feet. "Come on, you can't go back to sleep." He shined a flashlight into her eyes, and she winced at the bright light.

"What are you doing?" she whined in agony, shutting her eyes tight.

"I'm making sure you don't have a concussion. You need to stay awake for the next four hours."

"I liked it better when you were just a hard pillow," she said, rubbing the side of her head. She felt dizzy and out of sorts, but mostly she was worried about her brother.

"Come on, let's walk."

"Where's Robby? I want to talk with him."

"Ryan took him to the park police station," Greg said casually.

"The police station! Greg, what are you talking about?" Tess was angry now, her pain secondary to the news of her brother's troubles.

"Tess, calm down and let me explain." Greg held her tightly as she wobbled in her confused state and did everything she could to avoid leaning on him.

"You sent my brother to the police? It was an accident!" she yelled, but she knew that was a lie.

"Tess, you have done everything within your power to help your brother. Now it's God's turn. I have prayed a great deal about Robby's situation, and I believe I have the answer, but you're going to have to trust me."

Trust him? She didn't trust anyone, much less a social worker. "Look, Greg, I appreciate your concern and all you've done for Robby and me, but I think this is my call. I've—"

"That is exactly why you're failing!" He pointed at her, and she tried to make sense of his accusation.

"Why? Why am I failing, Mr. Expert? Perhaps employing the mighty wisdom conferred with your master's degree, you can shed some light on poor, half-witted, college-dropout Tess Ellison."

"I've got more than a master's degree in social work, Tess. I've got the *Master's* degree." He pointed to the brilliant clear blue sky. "You haven't once stopped to ask God His opinion of Robby's situation, have you?"

She felt so awkward leaning on Greg when she so desperately wanted to pass on Robby's left hook where it should have landed in the first place. "Have you?" he asked again.

"No," she admitted, giving him a dirty look as though he were the cause of her sin.

"Well, Miss Ellison, I *have* asked God. I think He's given me a direction, and I'm following it. The first step is to make Robby responsible for his actions. When the serpent deceived Eve, did the serpent pay the price alone? No, Eve suffered her own consequences, and it's time Robby accepted his. He's like a spoiled child, Tess. He's been so long without a solid, unchanging set of rules that he's abandoned all order. And a 220-pound spoiled child is not very welcome in society."

"Are you saying I've been a terrible parent to him?" Tess felt tears coming on, but closed her eyes to will them away.

"Tess," he began, tipping her chin and gazing at her sympathetically with ocean blue eyes. "Tess, I'm not blaming you. In all my years of social work, I've never seen a young woman, or anyone else for that matter, who would take on the task you tackled alone. But that's the problem, Tess. Somewhere along the line you lost sight of God's plan and substituted your own. God wants you to have help, Tess. He doesn't want you to do it alone anymore, and that doesn't mean you are supposed to marry someone you don't love."

Tess began to relax. "So why is Robby with the police?"

"Because he hit you, Tess. He has to learn he can never lay a hand on someone else when he is frustrated. Ryan is arranging to have your brother remain in custody today. Ryan or I may have to stay there with him due to Robby's special circumstances, but Robby will pay for his actions this afternoon, Tess. It's the law, and he's not above it because he's developmentally disabled."

"But he never hit anyone before!" Tess pleaded.

"I hope this will teach him never to do it again."

"What if he likes being in jail? I mean, there probably will be someone to talk with all day, and that's like heaven to Robby."

"I'll make sure he doesn't. For one thing, it will be perfectly quiet—no records, no stereo, no conversation. Just a nice quiet day to think about what he did.

"Kelly's on her way. I'm going to leave you with her and see if Ryan needs any help at the station. Are you okay?" He steadied her against a large pine tree and stepped back, studying her.

"I'm fine. Why don't I come with you?" she asked hopefully.

"No," he said firmly. "Part of Robby's punishment is not knowing how you're faring. Are you going to trust me?"

She nodded. "I'll try."

"I guess that's all I can expect from you right now." He turned and walked away.

Kelly came and helped support Tess. "You okay?" she asked.

"I'm fine," Tess said in frustration.

Kelly's eyes followed Greg. "With looks like that, women must knock his door down constantly."

"I suppose they do," Tess agreed distractedly. "I'm going to take my Bible and walk out to the meadow."

"Tess, you could have a concussion. I'll get mine and come with you."

"No, Kelly, I'm a big girl, and I'll be right across the road there." She pointed. "Ryan and Greg are dealing with Robby, so you need to be here to help the parents with all these teenagers. I'll be fine. I'll stay close by, and Greg knows where to find me if you get worried."

"Oh, all right. But if Greg gets after me, you're going to explain that I tried to stop you." Kelly wagged her forefinger at her.

Tess held up two fingers. "Scouts' honor."

Kelly rolled her eyes. "Oh, I feel *so* much better."

Tess walked for about half a mile until she found the tranquil spot by the river in the shade of the timeless pines. She sat in a quiet place where she'd be protected from falling pinecones and opened her Bible. She was taking Greg's advice, even though it annoyed her that he might be right. She hadn't prayed about Robby, and she'd been ineffective.

"Trust in the Lord with all of thine heart; and lean not unto thine own understanding." At times like this, Tess wondered why God gave her understanding in the first place. If she couldn't be trusted to use it, why did she have it? She knew the answer to her rhetorical question, but still it frustrated her. Relying on God was so difficult when He didn't seem to act in her timing.

A brilliant flash caught her eye, and she looked down at the enormous diamond solitaire that sparkled in the sunlight. She yanked it from her finger and put it in the zippered compartment of her Bible cover.

Clark. *Oh, Lord,* she prayed, *I don't even want to see him again to give this ring back. Please, Lord, make a place for Robby and me. Without Clark's money, Robby will have to stay at Serenity Springs. And Lord, with Robby's behavior, that seems impossible. Lord, please don't abandon us. Please remember us and guide our paths. I don't know if we can make it on our own for much longer, Lord—Robby is failing so. Please strengthen us and allow us to do this on our own as we have for so long.*

She had convinced herself that life with Clark wouldn't be so bad, but now she knew differently. Life with Clark would have been a life-term sentence.

She fell asleep under the tree and woke to a startled scream. "Tess! Tess!" Her eyelids flew open, and she saw Greg running toward her, his muscular frame taking long, athletic strides.

She stood immediately. "Greg, what is it?"

He stopped beside her, not even out of breath after his sprint. "I—I thought you may have fallen asleep with a concussion, but you're fine." He tried to act cool after his frantic run, but couldn't quite pull it off. They both broke into laughter.

"No concussion, just lazy. You scared the daylights out of me."

Her laughter died, and their gazes locked. Suddenly even the beauty of Yosemite Valley seemed to fade away. There was only Greg Wheaton's deep, stunning blue eyes. She studied his rugged jawline and thought that God had never designed a more exquisite-looking man. In his worn plaid shirt wrapped loosely around his broad shoulders and muscular chest, he was the picture of rugged outdoor life. One would never guess he held a desk job, for his physique told a different story. If she concentrated on his looks, she seemed to forget all that was inside: the intelligence, wisdom, and discernment abiding there. She gazed at his chiseled features and felt only desire—a simple desire for his lips on hers.

She remembered wondering what kind of kisser he would be, strong and confident or gentle and sensuous? At that moment, in the afternoon sunlight, she knew she would find out. He reached for her, and she took his hand eagerly. He cupped her chin in his hand and pulled her close. He kissed her intensely, and it was everything she had imagined and more. Every thought that had run through her mind was gone; only Greg existed as he stirred a passion she thought would never touch her. She fell into his kiss blissfully.

At that point, Tess would have promised Greg Wheaton anything to spend her days with him. His kiss was sensuous, gentle, confident, *and* strong. Just like Greg himself. He let her go and looked at her for a moment. He roughly raked his fingers through his dark hair as though wondering if he may have made a mistake, then pulled her to him again, kissing her with renewed desire.

He stepped back and grasped her hands, never taking his eyes off hers. "No, this isn't right. You need to sever things with Clark completely," he said. "I'll be here."

She only nodded; words seemed unnecessary. Greg then kneeled, keeping his eyes unwaveringly upon her. "Sit with me for a while." He pulled her down beside him. "I don't ever want to forget this image. I've tried so hard to keep my eyes from boring a hole right through you. I want the opportunity to touch those luxurious curls and unlock the secrets of those green eyes of yours without worrying about being caught looking at another man's fiancée."

She looked away, embarrassed by his steady gaze. "Stop it," she said, flinging her long curls in front of her face to hide herself.

He brushed the wisps from her face and smiled.

Chapter 12

Following the long weekend at Yosemite, Tess felt refreshed enough to try her hand at geometry again. Something about the weekend, about Greg's belief in her, revived her and gave her a confidence she had all but lost. Greg stayed after their long drive home to help Tess ready herself for the big exam the following day. They refrained from kissing, and Greg informed her she was off limits until she'd given the ring back and made things permanent with Clark.

Tess had made them a quick spaghetti supper, then cleared the table so they could work at her math homework. She sat down and sighed. "I've been in the business world for seven years, Greg. I've never found a reason to memorize the Pythagorean theorem." She was so frustrated, she wanted to wing the book across the room at the sight of it. He came beside her, and she felt his warmth. Geometry was the last thing on her mind.

"And you probably won't find a reason to use it. But if you were an engineering major, you might look at it differently."

"I doubt it. I fail to see the point of geometry." *Especially now,* she thought.

"The properties of math are ultimately perfect, a way for us to look into God's design of the universe. Just as the Yosemite Valley is such a perfect example of His creation."

Tess shot him a doubtful look. "Uh-uh." She felt guilty at his mention of God when her mind was racing with worldly thoughts. She shook herself free of them and turned her chair slightly to avoid looking at him.

"Take *pi* for example."

"That inane number that goes on forever on my calculator and doesn't make a whip of sense." She rolled her eyes and waited for his boring explanation, hoping it would help her on the test. At least she was able to stare at his gorgeous blue eyes while he spoke.

"Pi is God's creation. He gave us certain numbers to help us figure things out; it's all part of His design."

She groaned. "I'm supposed to believe pi is God's gift? Now you're really pushing it."

"Watch." He traced the circle in her book and pointed to each of the properties he discussed. "If you take the diameter of a circle, that's the width, and multiply it by pi, you get the total area of space within the circle. It doesn't matter *how* the diameter changes, pi always works!" Tess looked as though he'd come from another planet. Undeterred, he continued. "Just think of how important that circle information would be to, say, a tire manufacturer."

As Greg traced the circles on her page again, a light came on in Tess's head. "You mean that's it? That's what geometry is used for?"

He held up his palms and sat back in the chair. "See? Nothing to it."

"You're amazing." She marveled at her new understanding. To think, if only her genius professor had bothered to explain the *point* of pi, she might have understood this concept weeks earlier.

"No, God's amazing," Greg corrected. "He invented this universal language called math."

Suddenly there was a knock on the door, and Tess heard Clark call through the door. "Tess, are you in there? Open up!"

"It's Clark," she said fearfully.

Greg stood. "Calm down. You knew this was coming, and you've got to make sure you sever the relationship properly and give him his ring back."

"I know, but I don't want to do this. Clark has a way of twisting things, and I always end up believing him." She grabbed Greg's wide shoulders. "Stay. Please stay or I'll forget."

"No, Tess. Just remember all your prayer this weekend. I have some clients to check on, but I'll call you later." He bent down and kissed her cheek. "You owe him a thorough explanation. The truth, Tess."

"I know," she mumbled while she scuffed her foot on the floor. She hated emotional scenes, and she prayed that Clark's staid, even demeanor would remain that way.

"Do you want me to wait in the car until he leaves?" Greg asked, showing his concern.

"No, Clark doesn't care about losing me, Greg. He cares that he lost. That's how he'll see it." She sighed again.

Clark banged on the door again. "Tess! I know you're in there!"

Greg opened the door. "Clark, nice to see you again."

"I can't say the same for you. Where's Tess?" Clark surveyed the condo. "Robby isn't here, is he?"

"No, he's back in his home," Greg stated calmly.

"Good. So what are you doing here?" he asked.

"Geometry."

"Oh," Clark grunted.

Greg walked out, and Clark marched in and crossed his arms. He wore a scowl, and his features were contorted in anger. "What is all this grief you're giving me, Tess? Where's your ring?" He looked down at her finger and shook his head.

"I have it here for you." She pulled it out of her mother's dining room hutch and handed it to him.

"Tess, we *are* getting married. Put this back on," he stated firmly, yet without emotion. "You are not going to embarrass me in front of my colleagues and friends; we had a deal."

"Clark, I'm not trying to embarrass you, but I don't love you the way a woman should love the man she marries," she stated plainly while she entered the kitchen, Clark following close behind. She closed her geometry book and began clearing away her study materials.

"Love has nothing to do with our arrangement. Look, Tess, I thought we understood one another. You were to marry me for protection and something for Robby I don't quite understand, and I was marrying you for your qualifications as a corporate wife. You're beautiful, intelligent, and just about the best organizer I ever met." He smiled as though he'd just given her the biggest compliment known to humankind. "Love just complicates things."

Tess stopped working and looked at him. He was so innocent in some ways; he honestly didn't understand that there was something wrong with their relationship. A few days ago, she felt the same way. "I don't want that kind of life anymore. I want to be in love with my husband."

"Why?" He started to hit her weak spots, and Tess stood straighter to brace for it. "So this love of your life can break your heart like your father did? Maybe run off and leave you with a couple of kids when he's tired of you? Do you doubt that I'll be there, that I'm a man of my word?" Clark scrutinized her with his hazel eyes. The intensity of his gaze weakened her resolve; she'd suddenly forgotten her convictions on love.

"No, I just want more," she answered sheepishly, "someone who makes my heart beat faster when I'm near him. Don't you want that, Clark?"

"It's because of this crazy social worker, isn't it? Tess, you don't belong with some touchy, feely, feminine man. You belong with a man who can control you, who knows what's right for you."

"Greg's not like that!" she shouted. "He's been there for me and Robby."

"With what, Tess, his *feelings?* I don't want to hurt you, but you're a gorgeous woman. Of course Greg Wheaton would be attracted to you, probably enough to help Robby more than his job requires. But don't forget, Tess, he's being paid to help you; I'm not." Clark sat at the dining room table and scrutinized her. "When Greg Wheaton has moved on in his career and has forgotten all about you and Robby, I'll still be here. I know it feels good to have someone around that ignites sparks, but Tess, that's not for you. You're a practical woman. You know better than to fall for this momentary rush that will one day be gone."

Tess was so confused. She thought she knew Greg, but suddenly she wasn't sure. Clark made so much sense, and he was right about Greg igniting sparks. Was he right about him moving on as well? She was attracted to Greg like no man before him, but was that enough to put Robby's future in jeopardy? Greg had made her no promises; he had just kissed her.

And she'd wanted that kiss so much; she wondered now if it hadn't been her who kissed *him*. Just because she desired him didn't mean he returned her feelings or that it went beyond a basic animal attraction. Her mother had always told her a man didn't equate physical affection with love. Clark's finances could take care of Robby's every need: a private home, a private program, the best health coverage. With Greg, all she had was emotion—just like in Kelly's failed marriage to George.

"Come here, Tess." Clark held out his arms, and she walked into his placid, robotic hug. "Robby needs to be cared for by someone who can afford to do it properly. A social worker doesn't have the kind of money or influence that I do."

She nodded into his chest, battling the feelings inside her. "But Clark, God spoke to me this weekend. He told me I needed to trust in Him," she said meekly.

"So trust in Him, Tess. No one's stopping you from going back to church or living a Christian lifestyle." He dropped his hands to his side, then touched her gently on the cheek. "I don't know what else to say, but obviously you haven't thought this through." He reached for the door. "I'll see you Friday after work—I have court all week. Are you going to be okay?"

"Uh. . .yeah, sure." She slumped onto the couch as he left, completely lost in her confusion. It never even occurred to her to pray—she was too caught up in her emotions.

Kelly came in later and saw her sitting without expression, staring at the television that was turned off. "Tess?"

"Hi, Kelly. Everyone get home okay?" she asked quietly.

"Everyone's fine. What's going on?" Kelly pointed to the television.

"Nothing. I was just thinking."

"About what?" Kelly sat down next to Tess. "Please tell me you're not reconsidering this marriage. I didn't buy the maid of honor dress yet, you know."

"You were supposed to buy it last month," Tess accused.

"I didn't buy it because I'm hoping you will see the mistake this marriage would be, Tess. I thought Greg made that clear to you this weekend."

"Fine. I'll pay for the dress." Tess flicked her hand toward her roommate.

"Tess, it's not the money. I don't want to stand up for you and Clark."

"Why, Kelly? Because he isn't the man *you* would pick for me? Well, it isn't your choice. I've got my brother to think about, too, you know. It's not just me."

"Clark hates your brother, Tess. I'm sorry to be so candid, but it's obvious to everyone but you. And if you think his money is going to make the difference, you've got a long, sorrowful life ahead of you."

"Clark doesn't hate my brother; he's just awkward around him. Have some sympathy for Clark; he's used to being around educated people all day. It's difficult for him to be around a grown man with a second-grade reading level."

"Then what kind of father do you think he'll be, Tess?" Kelly pulled her hair out of the sloppy ponytail she wore during the camping trip.

"Kelly, please don't do this to me. I'm so confused, and you're only making it worse. Greg is a wonderful man; I admit that. He's everything a woman dreams of, but he's not *real*, Kelly. He has no intention of making me any promises, and I have to go with what I know. I'll learn to love Clark." Tess felt her eyes welling up with tears, and she angrily wiped them away with the back of her hand. "Or better yet, I'll live without love—it'll be cleaner that way."

Kelly said no more. She took Tess into her arms and hugged her, crying with her.

Chapter 13

Greg settled into his seat and tried to concentrate on the test results before him that needed to be analyzed and entered into his clients' files. He tried to focus, but all he thought about was Tess Ellison. He remembered her confession and the childhood issues she still dealt with. He had his answer for Robby's therapy and had begun his quest for props as soon as he arrived home from Yosemite. If everything went as planned, he would implement Robby's program by Saturday, ending the likelihood that Robby would be thrown out of Serenity Springs and Tess's reasons for being tied to Clark.

Greg's private line rang, and he picked it up on the first ring. "Greg Wheaton here."

"Mr. Wheaton, it's Clark. Clark Armstrong, Tess's fiancé."

Greg felt his teeth clench as he pictured the arrogant, stuffed business suit that still claimed to be Tess's fiancé. He was tempted to tell Clark exactly what happened between Tess and himself over the weekend, but he would never harm her reputation. "What can I do for you, Mr. Armstrong?"

"It seems you've been filling my fiancée's head with all sorts of ideas, and I want it stopped," Clark commanded.

"Tess." Greg used her first name so as not to give Clark the pleasure of referring to her as Clark's fiancée. "Tess is her own woman. I assure you I do not control what she thinks. If she doesn't want to marry you, I can hardly blame her."

"Listen, you impudent. . .Tess *is* marrying me, and it's time you got that through your head. I don't think the county appreciates its social workers getting personally involved in clients' lives, and I don't think they'd take kindly to your kidnapping her, coming to help her with her homework, or any of the other means you've used to weasel your way into her life. I've already warned you once, and this is the last time."

Greg seethed at Clark's threat. Of course the man would resort to threats; what else could he do? A woman like Tess wouldn't be with him otherwise. "The police force doesn't take kindly to threats."

"Listen, Wheaton, stay away from Tess; you got that? You're not invited to the wedding, and trust me, it will take place."

"I can't avoid Tess. She is my client's custodian, and Robby has several issues that we're dealing with right now," Greg said smugly.

"She won't be his custodian for long; I've taken care of that. And I can take care of your career by simply writing up a lawsuit charging you with impropriety and sexual harassment of a confused young woman you've taken advantage of. Am I making myself clear?"

Greg shook with anger. He wanted to take Clark's face and beat his smug attitude against the wall. He stopped and took a deep breath, praying for God's peace to come upon him. "Mr. Armstrong, don't you think Tess deserves a man who loves her?" Greg tried reaching any heart that might dwell in Clark's chest, but he should have known better; the man was cold-hearted and cruel.

"Tess has a real man who doesn't break down and cry with her because her feelings might be hurt. Tess needs me, Wheaton, so leave it alone, or I'll make your life a living nightmare. Understand? Robby's not going to be Tess's responsibility for long anyway."

"What do you mean by that?" Of all Clark's threats, this one scared him most.

"I mean that Tess will have an entire household to run—her own family—she doesn't need to be running off to Serenity Springs every time you deem there's a problem."

"Are you suggesting I create Robby's issues?" Greg was astounded; his mouth hadn't quite closed since this conversation began.

"Tess is not your problem. Just leave Tess to me, got it?" Clark waited for an answer, but Greg refused to give him one.

Greg slammed down the phone and took several deep breaths, trying to calm himself. He was not a violent man, but with everything inside him, he wanted to take Clark down to the floor. To threaten a lawsuit to hold onto Tess was unconscionable, but Greg knew it was the only way the weak, manipulative lawyer would ever keep Tess. Greg had to do something, but what? Tess was old enough to decide whom she wanted to marry. Clark had made a firm offer of commitment. If Greg ever wanted to claim Tess as his own, it was clear he had to make a move toward permanence quickly.

~

On Friday afternoon, Greg paced the jewelry store with his hands clasped behind his back. He looked at a ring like Clark had purchased for Tess and knew he had no hopes of ever duplicating the giant diamond solitaire. When the jeweler returned from the back room, he held out what would appear to be a tiny chip of a diamond next to Tess's first ring. He glared at it, disappointed. "That's it, huh?"

"In your price range, yes. But it's a very beautiful stone. Look at it through this glass; it's nearly flawless. If you'd consider a more flawed stone, we could increase the size," the jeweler suggested.

"No, it has to be perfect. She's perfect for me, and her diamond has to be the same, even if it is tiny." He nodded with conviction. "I'll take it." He handed the man his credit card and watched as the large number appeared on the cash register. He took the black velvet box and tucked it into his pants pocket and headed toward the Nob Hill Hotel.

It was nearly five o'clock when Greg walked to Tess's desk and saw her intensely making keystrokes on her computer keyboard. Her dark brown curls glistened in the harsh office light, and he thought she looked just as beautiful behind her desk as she did in worn jeans at Yosemite. She possessed full red lips and lovely olive skin from her Mediterranean heritage.

Her slender fingers seemed to know the keyboard well, and it was then that he noticed her left hand was still free of an engagement ring. Greg stepped forward. "Tess?"

She looked up, and her breath seemed to leave her. "Greg? What on earth? Is Robby all right?" she asked frantically.

"He's fine. Tess, listen, I was wondering if we might have dinner tonight. I have something very important to talk with you about."

Tess shook her head. "I'm sorry, Greg."

"No. I should have phrased that differently. We *are* having dinner tonight. After tonight, you don't ever have to see me again, but I need to speak with you." He came around her desk and took her hand, helping her up from her chair.

"If it's about Robby, you can call me." She sat back down.

"I think you know it's not about Robby." He grasped her upper arms and lifted her to her feet again. He cupped her chin and kissed her with a vengeance. She seemed to weaken and kissed him back. Just then, her boss emerged from his office.

"Clark?" the tall man said in a German accent. "So this is him, eh? The one who doesn't think the Nob Hill Hotel would provide the best catering for its favorite executive secretary," he accused, his eyes narrowing.

Greg was speechless. He didn't know what to say. If he claimed to be Clark, things would be difficult for Tess if Klaus met the real Clark; and if he claimed to be himself, how would Tess look kissing a man so soon?

Thankfully, Tess took over. "Klaus, this is Greg," she said simply. No explanation, no excuses.

"Oh, good. You know this hotel is one of the best in San Francisco, you know this?" he asked curtly.

Greg smiled. "Everyone knows that. Tony Bennett stays here."

"This one I like," Klaus said, shaking Greg's hand firmly. "You two have dinner on me tonight at Les Saisons, no?"

Tess looked at Greg and smiled. "Yes." Greg grinned at hearing the word he hoped he'd hear again later that night.

Tess gathered her personal items, and they took the elevator to the elegant French restaurant named for the seasons. The maître d' greeted Tess by name and escorted them to the best table in the house, with a full view of the city lights and the Golden Gate Bridge. Greg couldn't help but think he might have spent another two hundred dollars on her ring, had he known dinner would be free. He didn't have much hope his proposal would be accepted this night anyway, but he was determined to make his offer, to let her know Clark was not her only option. God would have to take care of the rest.

The wine steward came and offered them a wine list. "I know you don't drink, my dear, but perhaps tonight's list may change your mind." He winked and handed Greg a leather folder.

"It means nothing to me, Ellie. It's all vinegar to me."

"Tsk, tsk. Such a beautiful woman but no wine sense. I've offered to teach her. . . ." He threw up his hands, looking to Greg.

Greg shrugged. "I'm afraid it's all vinegar to me, too."

"Oh." He tossed up his hands, disgusted with them both.

They laughed as they waited for their iced teas. The waiter told them he would start a soufflé for their dessert, and Tess eagerly nodded her head. "Yes, please. Raspberry." She grinned, licking her upper lip lusciously.

"Raspberry it is, my dear." The waiter took their menus and wandered off.

Greg was struck by how much love everyone at the hotel showed for Tess. She obviously had charmed them all as easily as she had charmed him, and he felt a distinct pleasure in being allowed to see her at work. She wore a childlike smile and took pleasure in each specialty brought to the table. The waiter brought her taste samples of all the specials on the evening's menu, and she delighted in everything, but asked for a detailed description of what was in each of the dishes.

"So, you enjoy French food?" Greg said, wondering how many times a year he could afford a meal like this.

She leaned in, whispering, "Actually, I'm partial to hamburgers, but I enjoy being spoiled by coworkers once in a while. They know I don't like strange foods, like quail or snails or anything else foreign. So they go easy on me." She winked. "This was very nice of Klaus."

"Klaus always tries to make sure I'm happy. I feel so protected here at the hotel, with all these wonderful people looking out for me. I guess that's why I'm skittish about leaving here. Although, I must tell you, I got a B-plus on my geometry exam! Can you believe it?" Tess's eyes lit up with the announcement.

"That's wonderful, Tess. Congratulations! I knew you could do it."

"I couldn't have done it without you, my pi hero!"

"Glad to have been of service." He smiled. As they brought out the salads, Tess examined the ingredients carefully, coming mere inches from the greens.

"Just making sure there are no questionable items floating around in my lettuce." She grinned.

"Tess, you gave Clark's ring back?" He hadn't meant to be so abrupt, but it came tumbling from his mouth. Her smile left, and the happy sparkle in her eyes seemed to dull.

"I gave it back, but I have to admit, I don't know if I did the right thing."

"Tess, of course you did. You don't love him."

"You're right about that," she said uncomfortably. "Greg, what if Robby gets thrown out of Serenity Springs? I don't have the money to keep him out of an institution."

It was now or never. If someone had told him he'd be asking a rebounding woman to marry him, he would have never believed the person. Everything in the rule book said to leave her alone, but he couldn't do it. He bent on one knee and came beside her in the chair.

"Tess Ellison, I love you. I want you to be my wife. I know I don't have the resources Clark does, but I'll love you forever and will be there for you, for you and Robby, for as long as God allows." He reached into his pocket and pulled out the simple diamond solitaire he'd purchased. The ring looked even smaller than he'd remembered, and he shifted on his knee self-consciously. "Tess, marry me. Shed the chains of a man you don't love and marry me."

Marry him? Oh yes, how she wanted to marry him. How she wanted to melt into his arms each and every night of their lives and wake up beside those deep blue eyes each and every morning. Tess had said she had no commitment from Greg Wheaton, but now she did, and with it, no excuses. He knelt below her with the most beautiful diamond she'd ever laid eyes upon. It was sweet and simple and she could tell by its bright, shimmering depth that the diamond was perfect. His choice made a glaring statement: that he cherished her enough to buy her the most perfect diamond he could afford.

She looked at him questioningly after looking away from the ring, uncertain if she had dreamt it or if he really had asked her to marry him. "Greg, I don't know what to say." *Yes, yes, yes!* her heart screamed, but then she remembered Robby.

"I *know* this is hard for you, Tess, and I'm not asking you to make a decision now. I just want you to know you have a choice. Agree to be my wife. I know my ring hardly compares to what Clark gave you, but I'll make up for it in every other way. I'll be there for you and Robby and promise to be there until death do us part."

Tess held Greg's face in her hands and leaned over to kiss him softly. "Greg, I can't." She spoke quietly, completely unaware of anything around her. "Not yet. I owe Clark so much money already; I need to get things settled first."

He shook his head, and his dark, wavy hair fell out of place. "None of that matters, Tess. You can't spend your life with someone because of debt. I'll find the money to pay Clark back. I'll get a night job. But don't marry him because you feel an obligation." She swept his hair back into place. Everything he said made sense.

When she looked at him, none of the details *did* matter, but she knew what awaited her. Come Monday, she'd listen to Clark's arguments, and she would know *he* was right. With Clark there was no feeling, so there was no expectation of fireworks that would last until their golden anniversary. And with Clark she'd have her education, her brother's needs would be met, and best of all, she would be free from worrying about anyone taking advantage of her and Robby again. Greg only offered her passion, and how long could that possibly last?

"Love is fleeting."

"God's love is not fleeting. You need to trust in *Him*, not me. Tess, I've prayed about this a great deal. This offer is not made lightly. It's a firm, solid offer that stands, even if you tell me no today. When you stop and listen to your heart, when you hear what Kelly, I, and God are all trying to tell you, you will be free to come back to me. No questions asked."

Tess was shaken by his confidence. He couldn't really believe that God wanted them to be married. He stood and returned to his seat. Their main course arrived, but Tess had lost interest in the food. She cut her apricot Cornish game hen into pieces and shoved them around on her plate.

"Tess, eat. I'm through, and there's no sense in letting this wonderful dinner go to waste." Greg cut up his peppercorn steak and concentrated on his plate.

"Greg, I—"

He held up his hand. "I don't want your excuses, Tess. I want your prayer. Keep praying about this, then give me your answer. I don't want to talk about it again tonight, okay?" His voice was cordial, but Tess was stumped.

She nodded. "Fine."

"On to our next item on the evening's agenda."

"You mean there's more?"

"Robby's therapy. It occurred to me that Robby listens for just so long, then he retreats into his own world. Am I right?"

Tess was still focused on their last conversation, and regrouping to talk about her brother threw her. "Uh, yeah, I guess that's true."

"So, when he retreats to that little world, what if we could send him the message about self-control *during* that down time?" Greg was remarkably enthusiastic, so much so that she had to wonder if she really had heard a marriage proposal from him earlier.

"I'm afraid I'm not following you."

"Before we left for Yosemite"—he avoided her eyes when he mentioned Yosemite—"I looked at some successful case histories for autistics who turned violent and stopped listening to directions. I learned that if they could be reminded while they were in their own retreat, they could maintain self-control. But for each of them that involved something different."

"So how would we do that?" Tess felt elated at the possibility that Robby might be able to advance again. She wanted so much for him to live a more independent life. Not just for his sake, but for her own sake, as well.

"Music," Greg said simply.

"Of course." It was so simple. Why hadn't Tess thought of it before?

"This music." He pulled a cassette from his pocket.

Tess looked around the table at his pocket. "What else do you have in those pockets?" She giggled and bit her bottom lip self-consciously.

"You'll find out," he answered cryptically. "This tape is a medley of oldies I had the church band put together. All the songs are personalized for Robby, and all will remind him of scripture and self-control."

"You did this for us?" Tess took the tape from him. She wanted to perch herself in his lap and smother him with kisses. She wanted Greg Wheaton as her husband with all of her being. But she knew she had to pray. Doing what she wanted only seemed to lead to trouble.

Greg pulled a Walkman from his suit coat pocket and fastened the headphones over her ears. He placed the tape in the machine, and she began to listen to the tune of "Jeremiah Was a Bullfrog." But she heard these lyrics:

Robby was a good man, he was a good friend of mine.
But Robby hit and threw things
And a new home he had to find.

She fast-forwarded to the next song and heard "Jesus Loves Me" with the name *Rob* inserted for the word *me*. The entire tape, a full half hour of music, went on to sing God's praises and to describe Robby's part in God's plan. It would allow Robby to hear God's truth when he was entrenched in his own impenetrable world. "This is going to work, Greg. I know it is."

"All we need to do now is pray."

Greg removed the headphones from her head. He combed his fingers through her tousled mane, and she felt his touch clear down to her toes. He leaned over and kissed her softly on the lips. "Like I said, my offer stands. Good night, Tess." He pulled out a single red rose from his interior jacket pocket and dropped it onto the table in front of her.

Tess watched him walk away, bewildered at his action. Who was this man who made an offer of marriage, helped her deal with her brother's needs, then just walked out of her life? She had so many questions for Greg, but there she was, alone in an elegant restaurant, with only a single red rose to prove to her that any of it had ever really happened.

She picked up the flower and sniffed it. Greg had removed all of the thorns.

It smelled divine, and she breathed deeply its sweet scent. As she placed it back on the table, she knew it was the one flower she would never part with. She would care for it, dry it, and keep it close to her heart.

After an hour of deep, heartfelt prayer and repentance, she dialed Clark's number at ten minutes past midnight. He answered groggily, "Hello, who is this?"

"Clark, it's Tess."

"Tess, do you know what time it is?"

"I do. This can't wait." She exhaled loudly and continued. "Clark, I'm not going to marry you. . .ever. I'm going to trust that the Lord will take care of Robby's needs and that my education will be completed if He sees fit. I know it's wrong to tell you this by phone, but Clark, I can't marry you or anyone else until God wills it."

"Tess, look, I know you've been going through a lot lately. And I know things have changed in our relationship. But how do you expect me to argue against this? I mean, you're telling me God's talking to you, and we're supposed to call off the wedding while you wait for Him to tell you something else." He sounded disgusted.

"Exactly," she said brightly. "I'm not crazy, Clark. God spoke to me, and I'm going to do what He says. God warned Cain before he murdered Abel, but Cain was too arrogant to listen. I can't make that same mistake, Clark."

He sighed loudly. "Who's going to pay Robby's bill at Serenity Springs? Or all the copayments for Stanford Hospital's heart division?"

"I don't know," she answered.

"Are you going to finish your degree?"

"I don't know that, either."

"If God tells you to jump off the Golden Gate Bridge, are you going to do it?" he asked condescendingly.

"He's just asking me to trust Him, and finally I do."

"Do you know what I've paid for—"

"God doesn't care about your money; He only cares about your heart. If you haven't given your money in reverence to Him, your gifts are worthless." She spoke gently and in love, but with a power she'd never felt with Clark.

"That's easy to say when you've taken my money for Robby's home, your education, uh, this wedding. . . ."

"Write up a bill, Clark. I'll pay back every cent. I had no right to take that money from a man who wasn't my husband."

"Tess, you haven't got that kind of money."

"I know I haven't got the money, but God does, and He'll find it for me. God says that where your treasure is, that's where your heart is. My heart was trusting in your money, and that was a sin. I had no right—"

"Tess, honey, it's late. You're talking nonsense, and I just don't want to hear it anymore. You don't want to marry me? Fine. It's your loss. I'm not going to beg you. There are a million women out there who would faint at the sound of my proposal. So I wish you the best, hon." He hung up with a loud click, and Tess felt free for the first time in years. She smiled upward, praising God for His conviction in her heart.

Chapter 14

Greg hadn't heard from Tess in more than a week. He had begun therapy with her brother and was pleasantly surprised to find that Robby was making great strides in his independence skills for such a short time. Robby had learned to care for his own grooming needs in the morning and no longer needed reminders to get dressed and shaved before his bus arrived.

Greg also noticed a certain peace had descended upon Robby, and the angry outbursts were fewer now. He still didn't have the skills he needed to take the bus by himself or to discipline his conversations with anyone and everyone, but Greg enjoyed that part of Robby, anyway.

Greg stepped out of Serenity Springs on a glorious November Saturday. The sweet song of birds filled the air, and he was struck by the developing fall colors. Although California isn't rich in autumn changes, the modest changes announcing the new season were not without merit. The liquidambars were a dazzling crimson, the oaks a burnished gold, and the sequoias wore their unfailing evergreen coat like a mantle.

Greg was enjoying the tranquillity when he was approached by an unfamiliar man wearing a suit. "Greg Wheaton?" the stranger said.

"Yes," he replied.

"This is for you—a summons and a restraining order. Good day." The stranger smiled and saluted, then walked away.

Greg stood under the old oak tree and ripped open the envelope. RESTRAINING ORDER, the note was headed. It read, "Greg Wheaton is hereby ordered not to come within 150 feet of Tess Ellison or her brother, Robby Ellison." Inside the paperwork was another envelope, which he ripped open. "Request for denial of custodianship. Tess Ellison has hereby requested custodianship of Robby Ellison be transferred to the State of California."

Greg dropped his head into his hand, then roughly pulled his hand through his hair. He shook his head and walked swiftly to his car, stepping hard with each stride. He would get to the bottom of this.

～

Greg arrived at Tess's doorstep and stopped for a moment, gathering his thoughts and trying to calm down. She opened the door and was the picture of loveliness. Her beautiful, full curls were in a cascading ponytail, and her face was natural and glowing, free of makeup. He almost forgot his purpose until he looked down at the crumpled papers he clutched in his hand. "What's this?" he asked, as he shoved the paperwork under her eyes.

She tried to look innocent, but Greg knew only one person could have signed her name to the papers he held. "Greg, I—"

"You're bringing sexual harassment charges against me? That's what this restraining order is about?" He threw it at her feet, and she bent slowly to pick it up and examined it as though she'd never seen it before. "How do you expect me to finish Robby's therapy if I can't go near him? Are you trying to get me fired?" he demanded. "What do you think the county's going to say to a restraining order by one of my clients? Especially with my history!"

"Greg, I–I—" she stuttered.

He cut her off. "You're transferring custodianship to the state. What happened to all your righteous anger toward social workers and their inability to properly care for your brother? All of a sudden we're saviors?" He held his arms up in the air.

"No, I signed that when—"

"So you *did* sign it. Did you pray about it like I asked, or did you think Clark's money could save you again?"

"It's not like that, Greg."

Her eyes were pleading, but Greg was beside himself with anger. This was exactly how he'd lost his job in Oregon.

"Tess, I think you should know something: Your father isn't dead." The words hit her like a brick, and he watched her cower and her breathing become labored. He could see her chest rising and falling heavily.

"M–my father. . ."

"He lives not twenty minutes from here," Greg said. "Your father has requested visitation with your brother—maybe eventually custodianship. This sure makes his case easier." Greg tossed the papers at her feet and stormed down the steps.

"Greg!" she called after him, but he only flipped his hand back toward her in a brush-off gesture.

Tess closed the door slowly and prayed for God's guidance. *Oh, Lord, what have I done?*

～

Kelly bounded down the steps eating a carrot. "Was that Greg?" she asked enthusiastically. "Did you tell him you wanted to marry him?"

"I never got the chance." Tess was in a trance and sat down robotically, trying to assimilate the news she'd just received. She couldn't believe Greg would just tell her about her father so casually, then she thought about what he'd been through with the restraining order. Clark had exacted his revenge against her, but

Greg was paying, too; however, it was Tess who was paying the ultimate price. Clark knew exactly what he was doing.

"Why not?"

"Clark put a restraining order out against Greg. Greg's been told to stay away from Robby and me."

Kelly looked out the window. "Well, he's not doing a very good job of it."

"I'm not kidding, Kelly. Robby is making excellent progress with Greg's therapy. Without it, he may go back to his violent ways soon, and if he does that, I don't have the money to fund another private home. I don't know how to reverse the damage from this restraining order, but I'd better find out."

Tess picked up the wrinkled paper from the carpet and studied the signature. Clark had carefully traced her signature from the custodianship order she had stupidly signed in a moment of weakness, after Yosemite. Everything Clark had done was due to her own foolishness and inability to trust in God. She had allowed all this to happen, and now Greg and Robby—the two men she loved most in the world—were suffering.

"My father's alive," Tess blurted out.

"Why would you think he was dead, Tess? He'd only be fifty years old."

"I guess it was just wishful thinking." Tess noticed her body was trembling. "I don't mean that; I'm just scared. Kelly, what am I going to do? I've made such a mess of things."

"First of all, you'd better get on the phone and call off the hounds," Kelly said seriously.

Tess dialed the police but was told she would need to call back on Monday to have the restraining order removed. When she told the attending officer that her name had been forged, he casually told her she'd need to fill out a report against Clark to stop the order. As far as her custodianship request, that would have to wait until her hearing. Tess slammed down the phone, sick over being thrust into a tangle of government red tape and court battles.

She called Greg's numbers, both home and office, but only got his answering machines. According to Diane Laney, Greg had been told to stay away from Serenity Springs and all of his clients there until his ordeal with Robby and the restraining order could be rectified. Tess grieved over the turmoil she'd brought into Greg's life.

Tess passed most of her weekend in prayer, pleading with God to save her from her own stupidity. Sunday night, she tried reaching Greg at his cell phone, only to have it ring endlessly, just as his other lines had. He'd turned off his answering machines. She picked up the phone again and dialed Clark.

"Clark Armstrong," he answered.

"Clark, it's Tess."

"Tess, how nice to hear from you," he said, goading her.

"How can you do this, Clark? You are trying to ruin an innocent man's career."

"Tess, Greg Wheaton is anything but innocent. I warned him to stay away from you, twice in fact, to stop filling your head with the ridiculous notion that you would be fine if you didn't marry me, but he didn't listen. He brazenly took you out to dinner the very next night and asked you to marry *him*. Anything Greg Wheaton gets, he deserves."

"How did you know that?" Tess was stunned and more than a little frightened at his knowledge of the proposal.

"Tess, I'm not a stupid man. You obviously think differently, but I take care of what's mine or at least what I thought was mine. Greg Wheaton broke his honor code as a social worker when he became personally involved with you. He has no concern or respect for me, and I'm only paying him back with his own medicine."

"Clark, if you're angry with me, take it out on me!"

"Tess," he said calmly, "the truth is, I'm happy to be rid of you. You're as loony as your brother. But if you think for one minute that I'm going to let the three of you ride off into the sunset, you don't know me very well."

"No, I certainly don't. I should have seen this coming. You sit in the front pew, but that hasn't done anything for your soul. I'll have to be sure Pastor Hall knows the truth, as well. I always thought you were too shy to share your testimony with me; now I know you just don't have one."

"Oh, you wound me so!"

"I know you were hoping for a spot on the deacon board this year. That would have been quite a feather in your political cap, wouldn't it? It's too bad you're going to be convicted of a felony for false filing of a restraining order and fraud for forging my name. Don't they disbar people for that?" she asked innocently, her mouth breaking into a grin.

"You really do think I'm daft, don't you? This is why you'll always be a secretary, Tess. I offered you a world of education, society at its finest, and you snubbed your nose at it. Well, Tess, a good lawyer knows how to cover his tracks. And trust me, I covered mine. By the time your crazy insinuations come out, you won't have the respect of any judge in this state. And Greg Wheaton, your witness, is a mere social worker in dubious standing with this county. Lawyers do not file lawsuits or restraining orders without their client's approval, Tess. You should know that." He cackled like something from an early horror movie.

"You're right, I should," she answered meekly. "I'm sorry to have bothered you. Please rethink this. I'm begging you, for your own sake as well as mine."

"I don't think so, Tess. When you call me a liar before the judge, he'll only laugh in your face. No judge in this state will ever believe an uneducated secretary over me, considering my record with the bar. Clark Armstrong has his reputation, my dear, and you have nothing."

"Good-bye, Clark. I'm so sorry things had to end this way."

She hung up the phone and shut off Robby's sturdy old tape recorder that she had attached to the speaker phone.

"High five!" Kelly shouted as she lifted her palm and slapped Tess's own in the air.

Tess slapped her hand over her heart and opened her eyes wide. "It's too bad I'm just a lowly secretary. I just don't know what I'd do without Clark's guidance." She used her best southern-belle dialect, and she and Kelly broke into laughter.

"I hate to say I told you so, Tess, but we *all* told you so."

"I know," Tess admitted. "But I wasn't listening to God, and I had to find out the hard way."

"You, my dear, are hardheaded. And listening to others is not your strong suit."

"I wish I had listened," Tess agreed sheepishly.

"I think this calls for a celebration. We don't have to eat squid at your wedding! Let's go get some ice cream."

"Since I don't have to fit into that wedding gown, I'm getting a banana split!"

Kelly grimaced. "Oh yes. . .one more sundae and, my goodness, you might have required a size three gown rather than a size two! Why, we couldn't have you waddling down the aisle like that!"

Tess was used to having fun poked at her by Kelly. Kelly had a beautiful, womanly figure, but Tess's figure was always compared to a teenager's.

"Pipe down," Tess responded. "I can't help being thin any more than I can do anything about these big gunboats I've got for feet!" Tess lifted up her bare foot and smiled. "Besides, I don't really feel like celebrating. I feel like tracking down Greg and begging him for forgiveness."

"Tess, I think you'd better just get this all straightened out with the police before you go bothering Greg. Clark may have hurt Greg's career badly. Even if none of what it says is true, the fact that Greg has been presented with a restraining order brought by one of his clients doesn't look good to the county. They've got to protect themselves. And Ryan told me Greg had problems at his last job that may not help his situation any."

Chapter 15

C hristmas was just around the corner, and Tess still hadn't been able to have the restraining order removed from Greg's record. The government's red tape, combined with Clark's legal expertise, had made voiding the order nearly impossible.

Robby didn't like the new social worker and avoided the poor man's every attempt at conversation. Although Robby was still doing well at Serenity Springs, the social worker was reporting that Robby's progress had slowed simply because he refused to speak to the social worker.

Tess spent an hour each morning in prayer, praising God and asking for deliverance from the situation she'd brought upon herself. She set up an appointment with Pastor Hall to discuss Clark's candidacy for the deacon board. The church's constitution allowed anyone to protest a potential deacon's nomination without consent or knowledge of the nominee. That way, if someone was hiding a secret sin that would render the person unfit for the job, the issue could be dealt with quietly, in private. Tess had nothing to hide. She called Clark and offered him the opportunity to be there and hear her protests against his approval.

The day after Tess's last final exam, she marched into Pastor Hall's office carrying her tape recorder and prepared to see Clark for the first time since their breakup. Clark showed up at the meeting in an elegant business suit; Jennifer Ness was on his arm.

Jennifer flashed a sideways grin at Tess and grasped Clark's arm a little tighter. "So you're really going through with this, Tess," Clark said with a mocking grin. "You, a person who hasn't been to church in six months, are going to sling dirt."

"I've been to church. I just haven't been to *this* church, Clark." Tess and Kelly had been attending Ryan's church since Tess's breakup. She would eventually return to her own church family, but first she needed to clear the air about Clark.

"Either way, Tess, I don't understand why you insist on trying to ruin my reputation just because I broke off our engagement," Clark remarked in mock innocence. At the same time, he casually lifted Jennifer's left hand, and Tess could see what had once been her diamond ring there. He'd apparently made short work of finding a new owner for it. Tess didn't address Clark's lie that he'd broken things off. Seeing Jennifer's worshipful fixation on Clark, Tess figured that's what Jennifer would always believe anyway.

"Tess, how nice to see you. We've missed you so much. Clark, I'm glad you could be here as well." Pastor Hall shook hands with both of them, then Clark introduced Jennifer. "Well, I'm sorry such unfortunate events bring us together, but please come in."

The three of them took a seat in the pastor's office, and the elderly gentleman spoke. "Tess, I understand you are protesting Clark's nomination for the deacon board, is that right?"

"Yes, Pastor." She clung tightly to the tape recorder in her lap and swallowed hard. Suddenly she was fearful of going through with her plan, but she said a short prayer. She needed to do this; Clark had broken the law and was in violation of his career oath as a lawyer. She wanted him to know she had the power to ruin his career but had chosen not to do so. She also had a responsibility to report Clark's conduct to the church, and she hoped Clark's guilt might lead him to repent. Clark was not practicing Christianity. Whether or not he'd ever made a true commitment, Tess didn't know, but he wasn't walking with God; he certainly was unfit for the church's deacon board.

"You realize, Tess, that Clark does not have to be present for you to present your objections," Pastor Hall said warmly, giving her an opportunity to back down.

"Yes, but I choose to be open about them." Tess sat up straight, still fidgeting with the machine she carried. From the corner of her eye, she could see Clark smugly smiling at his new fiancée as though he could beat any rap easily.

"Very well then. Clark, is there anything you want to say beforehand?" Pastor Hall looked at him, and Tess's eyes followed.

Clark stood dramatically, as if he were in court, and straightened his jacket. "Pastor Hall, Tess and I—well, you know our history. We were scheduled to be married in a few months, and unfortunately, I found out some things about Tess's lifestyle that forced me to reconsider and break off our engagement. I'm sure she'll tell a good story, but the fact remains that she is a jilted bride-to-be, and I hope her testimony will be taken with that information in mind."

"It's not a testimony, Clark. I'm simply giving Tess a forum to speak her mind about why you may not be a suitable candidate for the deacon board. Tess could have chosen to remain anonymous."

"Absolutely, you have a responsibility to hear her out. As it should be." Clark gave one nod of his chin and sat down, taking Jennifer's hand as he did so.

Tess suddenly wished she'd taken Kelly up on her offer to accompany Tess. Tess tried to ignore Clark's presence altogether. "First, I think it should be known that Clark and I were marrying because of a sort of business arrangement. I have repented of my sin in that agreement, and I assume he has done the same." Tess glanced at the couple, then turned back toward the pastor. "However, while we were engaged, I met another man and fell in love with him. This man was instrumental

342

in helping me return to God's family and also helped Robby to become more independent—capable of living on his own at Serenity Springs." Tess let out a long, deep sigh.

Pastor Hall smiled at news of Robby, and Clark shook his head, unable to believe Tess had shared that she had been unfaithful to him during their engagement. Tess knew Clark saw his case getting stronger and stronger. Pastor Hall spoke. "Tess, did you think about breaking things off with Clark before you became involved with this other man?"

Tess exhaled deeply. "At the time, neither of us really knew we were involved."

"I see. So your problem with Clark? He has, after all, found happiness with someone else. And while I may question the hastiness of it, obviously he's had his share of pain in this situation."

"*I* broke up with Clark, Pastor Hall. I tried to do it the moment I realized I was in love with this other man, but Clark made me believe I needed him. I was worried about Robby's well-being."

Clark jumped to his feet. "That's an outright lie," he nearly shouted.

Pastor Hall stood and helped Clark back to his seat. "Tess, I'm going to need more facts." He looked at her sympathetically. After all, Pastor Hall had known Tess since she was a child; she was not given to emotional outbursts, and her being in his office was decidedly out of character for her.

Tess stood and plugged in the tape recorder. Every sin and illegal act Clark had committed against her and Greg was heard by the group, and she watched Clark sink into his seat at his own final words, "No judge in this state will ever believe an uneducated secretary over me, considering my record with the bar. Clark Armstrong has his reputation, my dear, and you have nothing." Tess could tell by Pastor Hall's surprised expression that there was no doubt it was truly Clark on the recording.

She tried to appear contrite; after all, she took no pleasure in ruining Clark's reputation. But he had made the alternatives impossible. Pastor Hall looked to Clark, waiting for an explanation, but the eloquent lawyer was speechless. The pastor spoke. "I see. Well, Clark, it seems your own account of things backs up Tess's story."

"Her *created* tape recording is useless in a court of law." He gave a short laugh, looking to Jennifer for support, which she offered readily.

Pastor Hall spoke harshly. "This *isn't* a court of law, Clark, and you're forgetting—I've known Tess Ellison since she was a child." He pointed at Clark. "I watched her suffer when her mother died so young of cancer, and I watched her grow up fast when she was suddenly responsible for Robby. After hearing Tess's statement and that recording"—he pointed to the machine, then aimed his finger at Clark again—"I will back up anything she has to say in a court of law as her character witness. That tape may not be admissible in court, but my testimony about it is." Pastor Hall stood and, for the first time, Tess saw fear in Clark's eyes.

"You must be kidding. Can't you see she's a sick woman?"

"What I see is a very disturbed man. Anyone who would try to ruin Tess Ellison's chance at happiness after all she's been through is disturbed in the extreme. Now, if you are willing to undergo counseling and repent, I would be happy to see you in this office. Otherwise, I suggest you leave. Your nomination for the deacon board is officially revoked." Pastor Hall's angry words were unlike anything Tess had ever heard him say before.

Clark abruptly stood and stalked out, Jennifer in tow.

Clark waited for Tess outside the doors of the church. "All right, Tess. What do you want, money for your education, for your crazy brother, what?" He pulled his checkbook from his back pocket and waited.

"I want you to go to the police and admit you forged my name on that restraining order against Greg. Then I want you to admit I signed that release of custodianship under duress. Duress caused by *you.*" She crossed her arms and waited.

"If I do this, you won't go to the bar association?"

"Contrary to what you might think, Clark, I don't want to ruin you. I just want you to do what's right—do what you should have done in the first place."

Clark just stood there. "Fine. . .I'll do it," he finally replied. Jennifer's eyes widened. He might as well have said, "I lost," because that's what it meant to him.

"Today!" Tess demanded. "I want Greg's name cleared today."

"I'll do it today." He grabbed hold of Jennifer, and they strode quickly to his expensive sedan.

～

Tess arrived home after a leisurely prayer time at the park and called the county regional center to see if Greg's name had been cleared. A woman who introduced herself as his former manager fielded the call. She confirmed that Clark had been there and the problem had been taken care of, but she also explained that Greg had resigned the previous week amidst the turmoil. "If you know where we can reach him, let us know," his manager said before Tess hung up.

Tess frantically tried to reach Greg at every number she had for him, having to dial each number several times due to her nervous fingers. When she was unsuccessful, she called Ryan. He explained that Greg was taking a position in Oregon to be near his parents and younger sister. Tess's heart seemed to freeze at the news. She had to find Greg before he left.

Just as she was about to drive to his apartment, her phone rang. "Tess? This is Diane Laney. Honey, Robby's disappeared from the home, and he's taken my son with him."

"What do you mean disappeared?"

"He was outside with his new social worker, and the social worker went to get some paperwork from his car, and Robby left. Since John is missing, too, we're assuming they're together."

"Have you called the police?" Tess asked frantically.

"Yes. They're looking for them now. Apparently, they were spotted on a city bus, so the police are checking out leads to see where they might have gotten off."

Tess put a hand to her forehead in angry frustration. "Where should I go?" she asked herself out loud. Diane answered her.

"Anywhere you think Robby might have gone. Only leave your front door unlocked in case he comes home," Diane advised. "I talked to Greg, and he seems to think Robby could get where he wanted to go on the bus, if left to his own devices."

"You talked to Greg?" Tess's heartbeat quickened. "He's still in California?"

"He's leaving today, only right now he's out trying to find Robby and John."

"Diane, thank you. I'll let you know immediately if I hear anything, and you do the same, okay? Oh, and if Greg calls, please tell him not to leave California without calling me."

"You can count on it."

Tess grabbed her jean jacket and headed down the steps to the garage. She sped out of the condominium complex and drove straight to Rockin' Rolls. Cheap tinfoil Christmas decor was everywhere, and the entire restaurant seemed to blink on and off in multicolored lights. Tess looked toward the jukebox and saw Greg waiting patiently beside it.

"Greg!" she called desperately, breathing a deep sigh of relief. "Has Robby been here?" Greg's presence filled her with confusion. She wanted to run to him and tell him how much she'd missed him, to share her final grade in geometry, and most of all, to share another explosive kiss like the one at Yosemite.

He nodded coolly. "Tess."

She had been about to hug him, but his response stopped her cold. She tried to focus on the fact that he had not abandoned her and Robby. "Greg, thank you for looking for Robby."

"You would have found him, obviously. He'll be here; he just has to figure out the busses. But I suppose I should thank you for getting the restraining order lifted. My boss explained the situation."

"Then you know I didn't file the order against you," she said desperately, thrilled that he now understood she hadn't meant to hurt him. So why was he treating her this way? "Does that mean you'll testify for me at Robby's custody trial?"

"I talked with your father. He says he would never contest your rights to Robby, so you shouldn't have any problem." Tess cringed to hear again that her father actually existed.

"The hearing is next week. You'll be gone that soon?" Although she knew the answer to her question, she hoped he'd discuss his plans.

"I'm leaving today. In fact, now that you're here, I'll leave immediately. I have a flight to catch."

"No, please. I mean, we don't know he's going to show up here. You're just going to up and leave for Oregon?" she asked, hoping to stall him. Looking at his intense blue eyes, she wanted to ask if his "standing" offer of marriage was still good; but judging from his demeanor, she guessed it wasn't.

He nodded.

"But Greg, Robby and John are out there alone; we don't know for sure they'll come here. Why don't we leave your cell phone number and go look at the record shops?"

"Fine." He dropped his card with the manager and explained their situation. They were in Greg's Volkswagen before Tess knew what hit her.

"I'm sorry if I had anything to do with your decision to leave California—my troubles involving you and such." She stared at him, trying to goad him into a real conversation, but he was having none of it.

"Nah." He waved his hand. "It's a good job they offered me—near my home-town and my folks; I'll be working with elementary school kids. I have nothing to keep me here." He looked at her for the first time.

Tess felt tears coming on, but just then she saw Robby get off the bus. "There they are, Greg!"

Greg pulled the car over. He threw the door open and ran to Robby with Tess following closely behind. "Robby!"

Robby looked to Greg, then to Tess. "Greg, you marry my sister?" he asked, trying to take the focus from his own troubles.

Tess couldn't help herself; she looked at Greg hopefully, but his answer was tempered and unemotional. "No, Robby, I'm moving to Oregon, remember?"

"I want you to stay," Robby said, stepping next to Tess, blocking Greg's path.

"That's nice, Robby, but I've got a new job. You need to take care of your-self and listen to Diane and your new social worker, okay? I love you, bud." Greg hugged her brother fiercely, and for a moment, Tess saw the Greg she loved, the man she wanted as her husband. A glimmer of hope rose in her heart only to be dashed. "Take care, Tess." He turned and walked out of their life, leaving the three of them standing on the street.

Chapter 16

"All rise," the bailiff for Robby's custody hearing announced as the judge entered. Tess was dizzy with emotion, unable to form a word, much less defend her brother's custody.

Lord, please help me through this. I just don't know how I'm going to manage. . . .

The judge was an older woman. She opened the file folder before her and spoke to Tess. "You are Tess Ellison."

"Yes, Your Honor."

"I have read the files here as well as documented letters from your father, house manager Diane Laney, and Robby's social worker, Greg Wheaton. You hereby are granted custody in full." The judge hit her desk with the gavel, and it was over, all in the snap of a finger. Tess looked at the letter written by her father, the only indication she had that he existed.

Robby's new social worker tried to argue. "But Your Honor, I am Robby's new social worker and I—"

The judge cut him off with a swift strike of her gavel. "You haven't been on Robby's case long enough to make a recommendation. My judgment is for Tess Ellison." She rose and exited the room. Tess jumped up and hugged her brother excitedly.

~

As spring approached, Tess tried to put Greg Wheaton firmly in her past. Robby had graduated from his independence training and hadn't had a violent outburst since the musical tapes were made for him, a vivid reminder of Greg's legacy in their lives. Ryan saw to it that the band taped more songs for Robby, and the band seemed to enjoy their music ministry.

Easter Sunday was approaching quickly, and Tess had a renewed desire to celebrate the special day. Kelly attended church with Ryan, and Tess decided it was time she went back to her church home. Afterward, she planned a very special meal for Kelly, Ryan, Robby, and herself. Kelly arrived home and knew immediately where Tess's thoughts were. "Why don't you call Greg and wish him a happy Easter," Kelly suggested.

"Kelly, I don't have his number. He probably wouldn't even remember me."

"Men usually remember women they propose to."

Tess nodded. "I nearly destroyed his career, I turned down his marriage proposal, and I made a fool out of him with his boss. I'd say Greg has very few reasons to want to talk with me."

"Yeah. Well, I'm sure there are other fish in the sea who look like movie stars and have a heart of gold and have professed their love for you." Tess's gaze fell to the floor, and Kelly continued. "Meaning, so that's it? You're just giving up?"

"Well, I'm through feeling sorry for myself. By next Easter I'll be an official graduate of U.C. Berkeley; I have my best friend and her wonderful boyfriend here with me; and my brother is coming for Easter dinner. Life doesn't get much better." Tess dusted the excess flour off her hands and placed her berry pie in the oven.

The doorbell rang, and Tess bounded down the steps to answer it. "Happy Easter!"

"Happy Easter!" Ryan said as Tess opened the door. Robby stood at his side. Ryan handed Tess a beautiful centerpiece of spring flowers, then stepped forward and kissed her on the cheek. "Thank you for the invitation. It means the world to me." Studying his wide grin, Tess knew he meant it.

Robby walked past her without a greeting and headed straight for the television, which he turned to a music station.

Tess just laughed and shrugged it off. "Robby's annual celebration. Who wants iced tea?"

She removed her apron, which had been protecting the stylish, short spring dress that hugged her small figure. Kelly walked into the kitchen as Tess poured tea into the elegant glassware that had been handed down by her mother. Kelly's eyes opened wide in surprise. "You're wearing that dress for us? Don't tell me you actually shopped." Kelly's blue eyes watched her warily.

"I did. I bought new clothes that I liked and a few dresses for special occasions. Maybe a date or two," she said optimistically, although her heart sank with the words. Kelly smiled sweetly, rubbing her arm comfortingly.

"Dinner is served," Kelly announced as though she'd been slaving all day in the kitchen.

Everyone sat at the table, and Ryan tapped lightly on his crystal glass filled with carbonated fruit juice. "I have an announcement to make," he said as he stood again. Tess was puzzled. She looked at Kelly for a hint of what Ryan would say, but Kelly's expression gave nothing away.

"Oh, the blessing. . . ," Tess said aloud. She picked up her Bible and prepared to read about Christ's resurrection.

"Actually, Tess, if you could hold off on that for a moment, I have something else to bless." He touched her hand lightly. "I have asked Kelly to be my wife, and she has graciously accepted. We have a date set for May—next month—when she'll make me the happiest man on earth." He raised his glass high into the air. "A toast!" His blue eyes sparkled, and his wheat-colored hair, highlighted by the glow of several candles, seemed to brighten with his excitement. Kelly never took her gaze from his. She watched him intently, mesmerized by the man she so obviously loved.

Tess felt guilty for not experiencing the pure joy she should have felt for Kelly. But the knowledge that she would soon be alone, without the constant support of Kelly, left her divided in her feelings. "Here, here," Tess managed as she raised her tea. She wore a fabricated smile, but her heart was crying for her loss, which made her feel even more selfish. "I forgot the butter." Tess pushed back her chair with a scrape against the hardwood floor and headed for the kitchen. Unknowingly, she'd taken her Bible, which she still grasped in her hand.

Kelly was right behind her. "Tess, I should have told you, but I wanted you to be surprised. I'm sorry. You're not exactly at a place in your life where surprise engagements are happy news," she said somberly.

Tess turned toward her. "Kelly, please forgive me; this truly is wonderful news. I had a chance to marry the man God had ordained for me, and I threw the opportunity away." Tess shrugged. "If God wants me single, so be it. But I will not let my mistake ruin your happiness." She tried to be upbeat. "Now, do I get to pick out my own maid of honor gown?"

"Well, I kind of met this new friend who wanted to be maid of honor. . . ." Kelly couldn't go on; she broke into laughter.

Tess played along. "Oh, that's too bad. I'll have to dispose of her before I take my rightful place in the wedding, then."

They laughed together and fell into a hug. "Come back to the table; we haven't shared all our news yet."

Kelly and Tess returned to the others, and Tess plopped the butter plate in the center of the table. "Before we hear more exciting news from Kelly and Ryan, I'm going to say a blessing." Tess opened up her Bible, and out fell the dried red rose Greg had given her the night of his proposal. Kelly picked it up and placed it back in the Bible without another word.

"Dear Lord, we thank you for the chance to celebrate Your life and, ultimately, Your death and resurrection. You are the Way, the Truth, and the Light, and we praise Your holy name as we celebrate the union of my best friend and Ryan and this very special Easter. Please bless this meal and the company here tonight."

"Amen," they all said in unison, and Tess began passing the turkey platter.

Kelly said, "First of all, I want it known that Ryan knows I don't cook, so let it never be said I pulled the wool over his eyes. He thinks I'll learn, but I'm afraid Tess could probably testify otherwise."

Ryan spoke up. "The other news we have is that I will not be a pastor any longer with my church." Kelly put her hand over Ryan's, and he continued. "As you know, the church has very strong beliefs about divorce, and because Kelly has been divorced, I will not be able to continue being a pastor."

Tess sat back in her chair, angry for Ryan's sake. "Do they know the circumstances of Kelly's divorce? That she remained biblically pure the whole time?"

"Of course they do, but church bylaws state that a divorced woman is not to remarry, and they stand by their conviction. I don't expect them to change the rule for me. The good news is that I've been asked to remain on the church staff and begin a divorce-recovery program. With all the divorces in this country today, I see a deep need for the church, in God's grace, to embrace broken people and help them heal. I feel this is an opportunity, God's leading for us as a couple to develop a needed ministry. Right now there's no place in our church for older singles or divorced people; Kelly and I plan to change that." He looked to his fiancée lovingly.

Kelly confirmed his words. "A degree from seminary means nothing if you're not doing God's will. We believe this is where God wants Ryan, so please don't be angry, Tess." She looked imploringly at her friend. "Let's just enjoy this perfect dinner you've made."

As the evening drew to a close, Ryan gripped Tess's hand and slid a scrap of paper into it. "This is my Easter gift to you. It's Greg's phone number in Oregon. I hope you'll use it." He smiled with his eyes.

After everyone had left and Kelly had gone upstairs, Tess pulled the scrap of paper out of a drawer and gazed at Greg's name scribbled on it. It was just a little past ten—not too late to call him, she reasoned. Before she could lose her nerve, she quickly dialed his number.

"Hello." Instead of hearing Greg's soothing voice, she heard a young female. Perhaps Ryan had written down the wrong number. She wasn't sure what to say. "Hello?" the voice repeated. "Greg Wheaton's residence."

Tess quietly put down the receiver. So that was it; Greg had replaced her as easily as Clark had. Tess let out a deep sob.

～

"Who was that?" Greg asked as he walked into the kitchen.

"I don't know; they hung up. You'd think they could at least say happy Easter," Greg's sixteen-year-old sister answered. "Where does this go?" she asked as she dried a platter.

"Up there, Marie." He pointed to a cabinet over the sink. "So, how was your first Easter without Mom and Dad?"

"Pretty good. I missed Mom's Jell-O mold, but she promised to make it for me when they get back from Australia. Besides, I'm with my big brother, and that's the next best thing to having them here. He doesn't buy expensive presents for Easter like Mom and Dad do, but they'll take care of that, too."

"Sounds like you need a good sermon on the meaning of Easter."

"Hey, I know the true meaning of Easter, but I still like presents. So did you get me anything?" She pulled herself up and sat on the countertop.

"I'm single. Single men don't have to buy gifts; they wait until they get married, then their wives do it," Greg quipped with a smile.

"With an attitude like that, no wonder you're still single! I'm all alone; my mom and dad left me," she wailed dramatically, putting the back of her hand on her brow.

"All right, all right. I give in. Of course I got you something. Just a minute." Greg hurried off to the bedroom and could be heard rummaging in his closet.

Marie opened the utility drawer with her foot as she waited on the countertop. As she did, she noticed a black velvet box. Opening it, she saw the small diamond solitaire Greg had purchased for Tess, and her eyes widened in shock. "Greg?" she called.

"Yeah," he answered as he came out of his room carrying three store-wrapped gifts.

"I thought you said you didn't buy gifts. Who's this for?" She held the open box out toward him.

"For the woman I'm going to marry, whoever that is." He shrugged as casually as possible. The sight of the diamond made his stomach upset. *Tess. Was I right to just leave?* He'd been so angry for her waffling about marrying Clark, but looking at the ring, he knew his feelings for her hadn't diminished. He'd never given her the opportunity to say yes to his proposal. His own childish anger and foolish pride had prevented it.

"Greg Wheaton, you wouldn't ever spend this kind of money on nobody. I'm sixteen, not stupid." She held the ring out closer to him.

Greg wondered how it was that his sister seemed to have forgotten about her own gift and was now only interested in Tess's ring. He pushed the ring away. "I asked someone to marry me when I was in San Francisco, and before you go planning the wedding, she said no."

"Why didn't you take the ring back?"

Greg shrugged. "I don't know; pride maybe. There's something personal about that diamond; I picked it out for her myself, and I guess I just haven't reconciled to the fact that it has to go back." Greg somberly looked at the ring, with its small diamond that seemed made for Tess's elegant, feminine hand and slender fingers. He snapped the box shut and put it back in the drawer.

"Maybe that was her who just called," Marie said brightly.

For a moment Greg was hopeful. But then his pride came roaring back. "She doesn't have my number. Now, do you want your present or not?" he asked rudely.

"*Not.*" Marie hopped off the countertop. "I'm going to bed," she announced, then marched to her room and slammed the door.

Greg sighed aloud. "Happy Easter," he mumbled.

The phone rang again, and Greg picked it up eagerly. "Greg? It's Ryan."

"Happy Easter, buddy," Greg replied.

"You, too. Hey, I'm calling because Kelly and I are getting married in May."

"As in next month?" Greg asked.

"Yeah. I can't believe she said yes. Listen, there's going to be a few changes in my life. Kelly being divorced and all, I'm relinquishing my pastoral post and signing on as the new head of divorce recovery at the church."

Greg sat down slowly. "You're not going to be a pastor anymore? What about all those years in seminary?" He was dumbfounded. As long as Greg had known Ryan, he'd planned to be a pastor. Now he was going to give that all up to marry Kelly?

"I've prayed a lot about this, Greg. God doesn't care about my title; He cares about my ministry. I think I'd be more effective in this field right now. It's an important area, and I feel His calling."

Greg just shook his head, unable to answer.

"I'm calling because you're going to be my best man, of course. The wedding is May 9, so plan on being here that weekend. There's no rehearsal dinner because there's no money for one. Kelly and I just don't feel the need to spend all that money for one dinner when we can invest in the wedding, instead."

"Sounds fine by me."

"Listen, I'm also calling to warn you. I'm sure you've figured out that Tess will be Kelly's maid of honor. You two will be spending a lot of time together at the wedding."

Greg felt his heart beat faster at the sound of her name. Of course Tess would be there; why hadn't he thought of it before? "I'm a big boy." Greg's tone was flat, but his stomach was doing somersaults.

"Great. You and Tess are the reason Kelly and I met. If Robby hadn't left his jacket at the dance that night, this might never have happened."

Greg's mind flew to the dance, and he couldn't help but smile. He remembered Tess doing the hustle, her small limbs flailing. "I couldn't be happier for you, Ryan. Congratulations. You've got yourself a wonderful woman."

"I know. Listen, I've got one more confession to make. I gave Tess your phone number," Ryan said quietly.

"No big deal," Greg replied. Inwardly, he was deeply disappointed that she hadn't called.

"Okay. So we'll see you May 9."

"Absolutely," Greg replied enthusiastically. He pushed the button, breaking the connection. He was tempted to call Tess, but he glanced at his watch and knew it was too late. He hung up the phone and switched on the television set, his heart heavy.

Chapter 17

Greg checked his tie, straightening it in the mirror of the church dressing room. Then he helped Ryan straighten his. "How do I look?" Ryan asked nervously.

Greg shrugged. "Like a bridegroom."

"Good, then I'm ready." Ryan exhaled deeply. "How about you? Are you ready to see Tess?"

"Ready as I'll ever be." Greg tugged down his black tuxedo jacket and shook his arms to straighten his cuffs, looking in the mirror and avoiding Ryan's penetrating stare.

Ryan came up to him and looked at him in the mirror. "So, have you forgiven her for her part in messing up your job here?"

"Every time I think so, it rains again in Oregon, and I find myself blaming her because I'm not in California."

The organ music struck a chord. "There's your cue. I'm praying for you, Greg."

"I'm praying for you and Kelly. You've got yourself a beautiful bride there."

"And she was worth losing a job over, any job," Ryan stated calmly.

Greg nodded, thinking about how selfish he'd been about Tess. Ryan's life-long goal had been to be the youth minister of a large church and yet, when he decided to marry Kelly, he was forced to give up his post. He would no longer possess the title of pastor, which he had labored through seminary to achieve.

Greg's job change seemed like small potatoes next to the price Ryan paid. Not to mention the fact that once Tess got Clark to admit his lie, Greg had been told he was welcome to return to his job at the Bay Regional Center. But he was too angry and prideful to do it. What an idiot he'd been; it might be he and Tess getting married today if his pride hadn't sent him running to Oregon.

Greg stepped into the foyer and saw Tess for the first time in months. Her olive complexion seemed to glow a healthy pink, and her smile was joyful and genuine. Her abundance of hair was swept up in a romantic bun, with several locks of hair cascading around her gorgeous face. She wore a Victorian ivory lace dress with the slightest hint of pink to it. Her tiny figure was gently caressed by the gown, and Greg was breathless at the sight of her. He had forgotten his anger; all he wanted to do was sweep Tess into his arms and get on with their life together. But would she forgive him?

Greg walked to her and took her arm, placing it over his. Their eyes were drawn to one another, and Greg had to consciously focus on getting her to the altar to take her place as maid of honor. He was glad that the situation forced their silence, for he was at a loss for words. He left her and took his place next to Ryan as they all awaited Kelly's arrival, but he never took his gaze off her.

Kelly was a stunning bride, but Greg's eyes were repeatedly drawn to the most beautiful woman in the room—Tess. He saw Tess's eyes fill with tears at the sight of her best friend entering the auditorium, and Greg could see Tess wasn't the same woman who had always held her emotions so tightly in check. Tess pulled a lace handkerchief from her sleeve and patted her eyes, smiling at Kelly through her tears.

Throughout the ceremony, Greg watched Tess as she carefully tended to Kelly's needs. At the reception dinner, Tess was alongside Kelly while Greg sat beside Ryan. As soon as their meal was finished, the wedding couple excused themselves to go and greet their guests. Only two empty chairs divided them, and Greg stood, smoothed the wrinkles out of his jacket, and approached Tess.

"May I?" he asked her.

"Please," she answered, pulling the chair out for him. He sat, and she touched his hand, sending a shiver through him. "I'm so glad to see you. Praise God you were able to come."

"I wouldn't have missed it." He watched her for a moment and couldn't help but notice the warmth in her eyes. He wanted to kick himself for allowing the separation between them. "How have you been?" he asked.

"Fine, thanks. One more year of school and I'm finished. Since you got me past the rough part of geometry, it's gone quite well," she said, smiling proudly.

"Tess, that's wonderful."

"I took a small mortgage out on the condominium to pay my expenses and pay back Clark," she added sheepishly.

He nodded. "I'm proud of you. I think your mother would be, too."

"Yes, she's got two independent children now. We owe a lot of it to you, Greg. You'll never know what you did for me." Greg saw her tears. He leaned in as the tear fell down her cheek, next to her full red lips, and kissed it away, ever so gently. The tears began to fall more freely with his kiss, and he kissed her again. She stood up abruptly. "Excuse me."

Greg looked out at the large group of guests; he now sat at the head table alone. Again he'd blown it. Tess dashed from the room in a flash of flying lace, and Greg hid his face behind his palm, shaking his head. *When will I ever learn how to treat a lady?* He threw his linen napkin on the table and went outside looking for Tess.

The reception was being held at a country club that was conveniently located adjacent to the church. The club's luxuriously green golf course and grounds made the reception appear to be a lavish affair, but Greg was aware of the couple's small budget. Greg quickly spotted Tess where she stood staring into the green distance under an ancient oak tree. With the sun setting behind her, she looked glorious. He would have Tess for his wife, and he'd fight for the honor, if necessary.

He took off his jacket and walked over to her with purpose. "I'm sorry I kissed you in front of a room full of people. I had no right." To his astonishment, Tess ran to him, snuggling into his chest. She said nothing, just held him tightly. Afraid he would blow it again, he just hugged her, keeping his mouth shut.

Tess pulled away and just gazed at him with obvious love in her eyes, her face wet with tears. Her handkerchief had been soaked, so he removed his own from his tuxedo pocket and handed it to her. She wiped away her tears, and with it, the remainder of her makeup, but Greg thought she was still devastatingly beautiful.

"I didn't know they'd fired you, Greg. Why didn't you tell me?" she asked, and he could have kicked himself. Of course they wouldn't have told her he'd been asked to leave.

He shrugged. "The regional center had a hearing about my case, but I just bowed out and resigned like they wanted me to." He embraced her gingerly. "Will you accept my apology?"

"Yes," she answered.

"What you don't know, Tess, is that I was fired from an earlier job in Oregon, too. I had taken in a youngster when his stepfather beat him. The state said there wasn't enough evidence to remove him from the home, so I did it on my own. Unfortunately, the child, a ten-year-old, was more troubled than I knew. He told the agents of the state that I'd given him drugs."

Tess gasped. "Why would he do that?"

"Because he wanted to go back home. Kids don't know what normal is when they live in circumstances like that. The poor guy just wanted his mom. Had I been a better social worker and more mature, I would have understood that. I would have understood why the state sets protocol for those situations. That's why I ran back to Oregon. They cleared me of any wrongdoing there, so I took the easy route to avoid more trouble. Before they could fire me from my job here in California, I resigned to save my skin. The problem was, I hurt you in the process."

"Greg, why didn't you tell me?" Tess was more hurt that Greg had chosen to keep his pain a secret than in his actual running.

"I didn't want you to know about my past in Oregon. It was so sordid, even if most of it was untrue."

He kissed her softly. Tess felt Greg's hand in the middle of her back, and his touch moved her, causing her to recall all the old feelings she'd thought she had mastered. She loved him more now than ever. He looked down at her, and she melted under the intensity of his blue eyes. She saw the crystal blue of the rushing Sierra waters within them and remembered their embrace in Yosemite.

Gazing into his face, she saw the lines next to his lips that announced his ready smile. She took her finger and traced a line lightly.

"What are you doing?" he asked softly.

"Remembering," she answered.

"Remembering what?"

"Yosemite," she replied. She could tell by his smile that they were both remembering the same event at Yosemite—an unforgettable kiss. She grinned.

"Miss Ellison, if I didn't know better, I'd think you were trying to tempt me," he said playfully.

"Me?" She showed him her widest, most innocent eyes. "You know me better than that," she replied truthfully.

"So when do you want to do this again?" he asked.

"Kiss you?"

"No, have a wedding." He bowed on one knee. "Tess Ellison, I love you with all my heart, and I love Robby, too. Say you'll be my wife, and I'll do everything I can to protect you both." He held up the small engagement ring.

She kissed him again with all the feelings she'd been suppressing for the months that he'd been gone. This was the man she loved, the man she wanted to be with for the rest of her life, and he was offering himself to her again.

"I would like nothing more than to give myself to you—wholly and completely—as your wife," she responded.

"And I promise I will be the finest husband I can be, using the Bible as my guide. And I will love you and cherish you as Christ loves His church." Looking into his intense blue eyes, Tess believed him completely.

The couple walked arm and arm back into the reception. Robby was the first to greet them. "I told you. You marry my sister," Robby said with disgust, as though he'd known what they hadn't all along. He clicked his tongue and walked away, back to the disc jockey who played soft background music.

Tess laughed, then sucked in a deep breath at the thought that Greg Wheaton was going to be her husband. The reality hit her like an unexpected storm.

Tess kept her gaze firmly locked on Greg's stunning blue eyes as they rejoined the celebrants. The two of them enjoyed their time with friends and family until well into the night.

When the festivities finally ended, they said a tearful good-bye—Greg would be leaving for Oregon the following day. "I'll call you the minute I get in," he promised. He winked. "And then I'll be back for good."

"I know," she answered.

"I love you, Tess Ellison. I have your brother to thank for introducing us."

"Well, where were you?" She put her hands to her hips. "Robby introduced me to a lot of frogs first."

"That was so you could appreciate me when I came along." He lifted his eyebrows a few times. "Robby knew exactly what he was doing."

"Amen," she replied. She kissed him softly and waved as he drove away in his rental car. "Amen," she repeated as the red taillights faded in the distance.

Epilogue

It took her eleven minutes to get down the aisle with her brother—Tess kept track by the clock on the sanctuary wall. Pastor Hall then quickly began to make up for lost time. "We are gathered here today to join in marriage this man, Greg Wheaton, and this woman, Tess Ellison. Greg has written his own vows and asked to read them."

Tess's heart filled as she watched her beloved Greg tremble nervously as he took out a well-worn sheet of paper. "Tess, I love you, and I know the woman who has been so committed to making a home for Robby will be equally wonderful if we are entrusted with children of our own. I will now read from the book of Ruth. 'Intreat me not to leave thee, or to return from following after thee: for whither thou goest, I will go; and where thou lodgest, I will lodge: thy people shall be my people, and thy God my God: Where thou diest, will I die, and there will I be buried: the Lord do so to me, and more also, if ought but death part thee and me.' That's so you know I'll always be there for Robby."

Tess began to cry, her emotion and overwhelming love for Greg rising within her. Releasing her tears in front of the entire congregation, Tess knew God had healed her heart and brought her a man to share in its bounty.

Tess giggled as Greg slipped a slim gold band onto her finger. She repeated her vows with an enthusiasm born of the knowledge that she was marrying a man she trusted, a man she knew would be there for her and Robby. Robby was safe, and Tess was in love—the romantic, fireworks-in-the-heavens kind of love. Surely God had planned for this all along.

An Unbreakable Hope

To Aunt Mary
You are such an inspiration to everyone around you.
I love you more than I can say and appreciate all the
love you have shared with me and my children.
Now, fight for all it's worth! God is with you.

Chapter 1

"May I present to you for the first time, Mr. and Mrs. Mike Kingston." The preacher's voice boomed, and Emily Jensen winced. Kingston. She had practiced the name Emily Kingston in her journal many times, but that name now belonged to Grace. To Grace, Mike, and Josh Kingston. They were a family now.

Emily's heart clenched. Not for the loss of Mike, for that hurt had been shallow and over with months ago, but for the loss of her dreams. Again. It felt as though every time she reached for marriage and a family, the balloon of hope got more distant; the string floated farther away. Disappointment shimmied through her frame. The piteous glances of the other wedding guests bored through her. One more wedding where Emily wasn't the bride. What was wrong with that poor girl? Their eyes told her what they were thinking, and she felt her body slink down farther into the pew.

"I'm so sorry, dear." Mrs. Purcell rubbed Emily's shoulder as if they faced an open casket rather than a stunning bride and groom.

"What's to be sorry about, Mrs. Purcell? Aren't Grace and Mike the happiest couple you've seen in ages? And look at little Josh. A stonecutter couldn't wipe the smile from his face."

"I know, but, dear, it could have been you."

Tears threatened to spill once again, but Emily swallowed them whole. It wasn't about Mike. Anyone could see from the way he watched Grace that there was no substitute for that kind of love. Emily coveted it, yet it slipped through her hands like mercury again and again. She didn't want to be a man's second best, but would she ever be someone's first choice? The hope of such dreams was quickly fading with each birthday and failed relationship. It wasn't that she'd ever loved a man so thoroughly that her heart was broken in two; it was that no one had ever loved her, either. Not in the way that causes long-term emotion. She discreetly wiped her eyes.

Emily held the withered hands that reached out to her. "Mrs. Purcell, I'm very busy with teaching. My class and my Sunday school kids need me. God called some to remain single, and I guess I'm one of them. Like Paul, I will be content in all situations." Her tone was strong—so much so, she could almost believe herself. The truth was she'd never imagined being a parent to twenty schoolchildren without having one of her own. A husband to come home to and a child who looked up with wide eyes and called her Mommy, not Miss Jensen. She was angry at herself for not being content with the life God had blessed her with.

"That's the spirit, my dear. Those children love you, and you're a wonderful teacher." After a supplicating pat, Mrs. Purcell went to darken someone else's door with her words of doom. Emily breathed relief. The first test had been passed and no tears shed. So maybe a few had pooled, but not one had fallen. Indeed, now she felt a bit stronger.

She made her way toward the back of the church, where Mike and Grace stood with Josh, a testimony to the glow a real family presented. Grace's dress flowed elegantly to the floor, a spray of white silk. Blond tendrils hung in ringlets from a high-swept updo, and Grace's long, lean neck moved like that of a princess. That kind of beauty was rare, for Grace's beauty went beyond the exterior.

Emily moved toward them. "Grace, you are the most beautiful bride I've ever seen. Mike, you are one very lucky man."

Mike, in full fireman's dress uniform, kissed her cheek. "Thank you, Emily. I'm so glad you came today. It wouldn't have been the same without you here."

Josh, Grace's son, looked up and nodded. "You're still my favorite teacher even though I'm in second grade."

Emily winked. "Let's keep that our little secret, okay? I'll see you at the reception. You were a very good ring bearer. The best I've seen, in fact."

Emily hiked her shoulders back and walked resolutely toward the church event hall.

Test two completed. No tears shed.

The short walk across the open courtyard to the reception filled Emily with more confidence. Churchgoers and Mike's fellow firemen milled about, waiting for the reception line and photographs to be completed. Twinkling lights and floral sprays gave the old church hall a fresh feel, a romantic buzz. Emily could barely believe it was capable of such beauty. As she made her way toward the punch table, a handsome stranger handed her a glass.

"Thirsty?" he asked.

She felt her stomach tumble at the question. For a moment, she heard only silence as she stared into his eyes—eyes that accepted her into a world deemed off-limits. What she was feeling was akin to waking up in Wonderland. She felt like she had known this stranger her entire life, yet her mother would never let this kind of man near her.

Emily nodded and took the cup of red liquid.

"Do I know you?" she asked, feeling inept the moment the words escaped.

"You do now. Darin Black." The stranger's eyes were remarkable. Although they were a nondescript gray-green, the intensity that flared within them made them absolutely mesmerizing. His eyes extended some unmistakable compassion within him. She felt a sudden peace, completely forgetting she was at the wedding of an ex-boyfriend.

Darin's head was shaved bald, but from his eyebrows and stubble upon his head, Emily could see a natural light red shade. She felt her own eyes widen at the unexpected sight of an earring. Never in all her days had she known a man to wear an earring. She studied it a bit too long, and he commented.

"The earring?"

She choked back her punch. "Was I that obvious?" Emily looked around at all the well-dressed firemen and regular churchgoers, then back to the stranger. His suit was just a gray tweed sports coat over navy slacks, but the earring threw the whole look off for Emily. She pondered the statement the jewelry made before answering. Perhaps it should have mattered that he wore the earring, but it didn't. It only made her more curious about whom he was, why he was at Mike's wedding, and whether he knew her sordid tale. Realizing her long silence, she blurted, "I've never met a man with an earring before." She was tempted to ask if he was a gang member but quickly thought better of the idea. Emily Post would not have approved.

"Never met a man with an earring? What a sheltered life you've led." His smile was captivating. So much so, she almost forgot about the jewelry. But then her eyes were drawn back to the simple silver stud. There was something piratelike about it. Something attractive that she didn't want to admit to liking. It was too strange. Her mother certainly wouldn't approve. Maybe that explained Emily's fascination, but there was something in his eyes. It wasn't a feeling she recognized, but something familiar to her all the same.

She cleared her throat; it was probably best to avoid the subject of the earring. "How do you know the bride and groom?"

"Mike pulled me out of a gutter one night."

"I beg your pardon?"

"I had a sports car in my wilder days. Let me stress the word *had*. I crashed it against a tree. Mike was the attending fireman who pulled me out of the mangled steel. Been my good friend ever since."

Emily was subconsciously retreating from the shadow this man cast under the twinkling aura of tea lights. Fear wasn't what she felt; it was an intense curiosity, and that's what scared her. She'd never met anyone like him, much less in the church hall. Dangerous. He felt dangerous, so why did she want to know more? And why did she feel a security standing beside him?

"Mike led me to the Lord in the hospital, after I saw my life flash before my eyes and God called me from my stupidity." The corner of his mouth lifted, and he was obviously waiting for some semblance of a response.

"The Lord can do mighty things." Emily closed her eyes at her easy statement to his incredible testimony. What a hack she was.

"Amen."

"I grew up in the church." She supposed that probably needed no explanation. The floral dress with the lace collar and sheer lip gloss probably gave her away. She looked like she grew up in the church, and suddenly she felt herself fingering her collar, wishing she'd bought something more stylish for the wedding. Would it have killed her to buy a new outfit? Certainly not anything leather, but a trendy outfit from a store—maybe even nice slacks.

"What a blessing for you to grow up in the church. You should thank God for that every day." His enthusiasm wasn't forced, and he was shaking his head at the thought. "I'm so excited that my kids will be able to start better than I did. I can hardly wait to do family devotionals and teach them everything I can about the Lord. Not just the simple stories, mind you, like the flood or Jonah, but all of it. I want them to crave the Word."

She blinked rapidly, hoping he hadn't noticed how attractive she found him. He had kids. Children were just a ticket to Emily's heart; unfortunately for her, wives usually went with them.

"How many kids do you have?" She held her breath at his answer.

"Me?" He laughed. "I don't have any kids. I'm not married."

A spring rain of relief washed over Emily, but she couldn't have said why. This man reminded her of someone who was brave enough to preach on the street. To walk into a homeless shelter and feel perfectly comfortable. God had a man for her. A man carefully groomed in the church. The man her father prayed for every day during her childhood. And certainly that man didn't wear an earring or crash sports cars. Emily felt her breath leave her. Would that man make her heart pound like this one did?

"Well, I'm sure your family will be very fortunate when God brings children to you."

"Thank you."

Emily scanned the room for someone she knew, looking for an escape route. The best way to avoid temptation was to stay away from it. Even Mrs. Purcell would be a welcome reprieve. This man, handsome in a movie star way, unnerved her. He was too good-looking for his own good. Too intense for hers. His bold pronouncements of faith were something akin to a weekend revival in the South. Nothing like her reserved, quiet faith that lived its life out in consistency.

"It was very nice to meet you. Maybe I'll see you around church sometime."

"We haven't actually met." His outstretched hand extended toward her. "I've told you my name is Darin Black, but I haven't heard yours."

"Emily Jensen."

"*The* Emily Jensen?"

She swallowed hard. "What do you mean by that?" As if she didn't know.

"You're the one Mike used to see. Before he met Grace. You helped bring Grace around, right?"

Where was a plastic fern when she needed one? Emily wished she could crawl under the table and disappear. She'd passed the first two tests, but this one proved impossible. Tears began to sting her eyes. She blinked them away as fast as she could.

"You know, I'm thinking maybe I've outstayed my welcome here. I need to get my lesson plans ready for Monday, and Mike and Grace have plenty of guests to celebrate with them." Emily moved quickly for the door, but she could feel Darin Black behind her, even hear his steps. She quickened her pace but felt her hand grasped. She whirled around, tears now apparent upon her cheeks. "Please, Mr. Black. I'm sure you'll understand if I just want to go home. I'm very pleased for Grace and Mike, but the church knows our story, and you can imagine this is uncomfortable for me. Being the 'other woman' at a church wedding is hardly a good feeling."

His eyes met hers, and she lost all sight of the earring. There was only this gorgeous man peering down at her with compassion and concern. "Emily, you were never the other woman. I didn't mean it that way. Only that Mike raves about you because you helped Grace to find the Lord when he hadn't treated you as well. I'm an idiot. Forgive me."

She just shook her head. Words wouldn't come. Mike remembers me for my words to Grace? She wanted to shout, but she couldn't get past the lump in her throat for fear she'd start blubbering.

"Would you like to have dinner with me tonight? I'm not trying to hit on you. I just don't want to leave you with this bad impression, and I know this is a difficult night. This is going to sound very strange, but I feel like I know you. I want to know you better."

No, she said via gesture. "Home."

"Please, let's go get some dinner together. We can have church potluck anytime. Mrs. Purcell's chicken will still be rubbery." He laughed. "Here, wait. . . Pastor," and he pulled unwitting Pastor Fredericks toward them. "Tell Emily I'm a good guy. That I'm safe to be with and that I won't stick her with the bill."

Pastor Fredericks smiled at them both, and Emily swallowed the guilt she felt. *No, I'm not swallowing up another man with my black widow ways, Pastor Fredericks. I promise.*

"You're in good hands, Emily. Darin is an upstanding gentleman with a big heart for the Lord," he said. "Go enjoy your Friday evening. The excitement is over here. Mike and Grace are leaving tonight for Carmel, so they'll have to get a move on." He checked his watch. "They only have the weekend, then they're back to work and school for Josh. You two have a lot in common."

Emily looked up at the shaved head, the steely gray-green eyes and, of course, the earring. What she could have in common with such a man remained a mystery to her. But she trusted her pastor, and Darin did offer her an escape from the reception, where the deaconesses of the church had staged a pity party for her. They were coming toward her in a gaggle.

Pastor continued. "Emily, why don't you take him to that soup house you're always frequenting? Every time I go in there you're sitting there with a book. They're open late, and Darin can probably afford that." He winked at Darin.

She almost kissed him. So he could have left off the part about eating there alone with her book, but other than that, she wasn't ready for this night to end. She wasn't ready to ignore this connection she felt with a complete stranger. She'd feel safe at the soup house. The owners knew her and loved her. They started her order before she sat down. The Vietnamese soup house would be a perfect place to have a friendly dinner with this different kind of man. Her stomach was flipping, and she hoped she could find the control to eat.

"That's a wonderful idea, Pastor. It's up the street from here on Castro. Do you know the place?" she asked Darin.

"Sure." He nodded. "I'll meet you there so you don't have to drive with a stranger. Is that all right with you?"

His thoughtfulness nettled her, and she nodded in agreement. But her comfort gave way to trepidation in her car. What on earth was she doing? Meeting a strange man for dinner with Pastor's approval. It was so out of character for her, yet so exciting. What would her mother say? For the moment, she didn't care. The fluttering she felt in her stomach was new.

In the brightly lit restaurant, Darin studied Emily Jensen, her chocolate brown eyes rimmed in red. Her exterior was so simple in her plain dress, but Darin could see the depth within her soul. She may wear an easy churchgoing façade, but Darin believed he saw an explosive spark within, that glimmer of light that wanted to come out and dance before the Lord, but didn't know how—an untapped missionary's heart. He knew what she probably thought of him, but that didn't stop him from wanting to know her. She felt the immediate communion between them, too, or she wouldn't have been so tongue-tied.

"That was a nice wedding, don't you think?" Darin asked.

Emily nodded.

"So I hear you're a teacher."

Emily nodded again. "Yes, I taught Grace's son, Josh, last year."

"Do you like teaching?" *Come on, Emily, help me out here.* Darin tapped his foot, hoping to end this sudden uneasiness between them. No longer were they in the safety of their congregation. Now they were officially on a date, and Emily looked everywhere about the restaurant but at him.

"I love teaching the children. I teach on Sundays, as well. I have the second- and third-graders."

Emily still wouldn't look at him when she spoke, and his heart hurt at the reminder that he wasn't the type such an innocent would marry. She probably imagined he dated Camaro-driving, stiletto-heeled women. He winced at the thought of his former life. Emily's beauty went beyond her lovely dark hair and espresso eyes and into her innocent expression of love for the Lord. Darin wanted the chance to prove his past life was over, and he wanted to be worthy of such a pure woman. Would someone like Emily Jensen ever look his way?

He cleared his throat. "Since you're working in Sunday school maybe I'll see you. I just started work with the junior high ministry. I've been bringing some kids from the inner city. I work with them on Wednesdays, playing pickup basketball, then having a Bible study in a garage."

"I've never been to the inner city. What's it like?"

"I thought you grew up here."

"I did." Emily blinked, clearly not understanding his point.

"You grew up within a couple miles of East Palo Alto, and you've never been there?"

"My mother always warned me not to go there." Emily shrugged.

He leaned in, and she sat straight up in her chair. "Didn't that make you want to go there? To find out what was so bad about it? People are the same, only the circumstances are different."

She shook her head. "Of course that didn't make me want to go. It wasn't a good part of town. It still isn't a good part of town. What more do I need to know?"

"Emily, EPA is a ripe mission field. There are people there who live in absolute squalor yet know the Lord is with them always. Their joy in the Lord is like nothing you've ever seen here in Los Altos. It's practiced with abandon. These people know peace in all circumstances. Don't you think that's admirable?"

"Not if it means going where it's dangerous. I'm not really very adventurous. I like knowing my surroundings well."

Darin's heart sank at the shaky fear in Emily's voice. Didn't she know God would protect her? He probably should have kept his thoughts to himself, but he blurted, "Fear is the work of the evil one. God says not to be anxious for anything. That means when there are bullets flying in your neighborhood, you can rest in Him."

"There's a line between trusting the Lord and doing stupid things like going into a dangerous place and expecting Him to rescue me."

Her words pierced him. Their soup arrived, but Darin wasn't hungry. The vigor and life he thought he'd seen in Emily had quickly disappeared behind her love for safety. Darin's life was bold. From bungee jumping to street preaching, he lived dangerously. Where once it had been for the adrenaline rush, now it was for the sake of the gospel. After all, he'd almost been killed—anything after the crash was a gift from above. Darin prayed over the Vietnamese noodle soup, and they ate their meal in silence. Maybe this had been a mistake. It certainly wasn't an ideal first date. Darin peered at the golden liquid inside his bowl. *I'll never be a Christian in the proper church-sense of the word.*

Chapter 2

Emily arrived early as usual on Sunday and straightened the Sunday school lessons and cut out all the necessary shapes for the craft. She lined everything up into neat rows so the students could easily access their take-home study. She loved it when parents continued the study at home during the week. It brought her immense joy to know her work was helping young Christians become grounded.

"There," she said aloud at the sight of her perfectly organized table.

"Hi." Darin Black leaned against the doorjamb, his broad shoulders filling the entrance to the classroom. Emily swallowed over her nervousness. She noticed as she lined up the papers again that her hands trembled. The pirate had returned, and she was unprepared for her reaction. She giggled nervously, like one of her first-graders.

"Hi," she said quietly. "Are you working with the junior-highers today?"

"I am, but first I have some of their little brothers I brought with me from town. They'll be in your class. This is Nicholas." Darin brought forward a little boy who looked like an overgrown puppy who hadn't developed into his paws yet. "He's only in the second grade. He's just the size of your average high schooler." Darin mussed the boy's hair.

Nicholas had a wary look to his eyes, and they thinned at the sight of her, announcing his immediate defiance. Emily knew the look well from her years of teaching and looked forward to an eventful hour. She instantly felt thankful she taught in a nice part of town and didn't have to deal with this defiance on a regular basis. A few more of these kids, and her joy for teaching might dwindle quickly.

"And this," Darin added, "is Jason."

"The worm who cried when he left his mama," Nicholas said tauntingly.

"Hey!" Darin lifted the corner of Nicholas's shirt. "You mess with him, you mess with me. Got it?"

Emily flinched at the harsh words. Echoes of her childhood chilled her, but when she looked at Darin, he had a smile plastered on his face. He seemed almost serene, and both the boys laughed.

She tried to put the boys at ease immediately, knowing her organized classroom and the well-coiffed children probably made them feel uncomfortable.

They each wore a cartoon T-shirt that most kids wouldn't be allowed to own in the church. The chasm between the children saddened her. No wonder so many visitors stopped coming. She prayed, hoping she could find the connection to keep the boys interested.

"Nicholas and Jason, it's nice to have you in my class. Would you like to color until we get started?" She handed them each a coloring sheet.

"Whatever." Nicholas rolled his eyes and pushed past her to a desk, where he flopped into the seat. He cursed as he hit his knee on the top of the metal. Darin apologized with his eyes. "I'm not three. I don't color."

"I also have building toys," Emily offered. She liked to have cool things for the boys to do with their hands while they listened. She found it was far more effective than telling them to sit down countless times. So Legos were a regular feature in her classroom.

Jason said nothing but also ignored the coloring sheet. He crossed his arms over his chest. His hair hung over his eyes, hiding his true expression. Emily felt hopeless looking at him. The boy seemed to have no joy left in him. And although he wasn't more than eight, Legos were beyond childish to him. She pitied how fast these children had to grow up in the ghetto. Childhood never existed for them, judging by the hardness of their expressions or the coldness in their eyes.

She drew in a deep breath, and Darin said, "Don't take any of Nicholas's garbage. He needs this." With a wink implying collusion, he turned and walked toward the middle school class. A bevy of kids, including several giggling girls, followed him like the Pied Piper. Emily laughed at the sight, secretly wishing she could follow, as well.

She turned back to her class. In all the commotion of her new students, she hadn't noticed that everyone had been signed in and now sat around the room, staring at the two new children like new animals at the zoo.

"Well," Emily said. "For those of you who don't know me, I'm Miss Jensen, and today we're going to learn about Cain and Abel—two brothers who had two different hearts toward God."

Nicholas raised a hand.

"Yes, Nicholas."

"I have to go to the bathroom."

"My teacher's aide isn't here yet, so you'll have to wait a bit." She didn't trust the boy to come back, so she needed to make sure he was chaperoned.

Again the boy cursed and reiterated his need to visit the bathroom in a coarse way. Although he was only eight or so, he frightened Emily with his harshness, and he probably sensed it. She'd never met a boy so young who acted in such a raw way, and visions of violent news footage played in her head. She shook her wild imagination.

"Nicholas, I'm telling you, we don't talk like that at church. Whether you believe it or not, there is a God listening, and He is not pleased. You can try to make me mad, but I wouldn't test God."

"I'm shaking." By now, all the children were mesmerized. They'd probably never witnessed such insolence, and in all Emily's years of teaching, she was certain she hadn't.

Nicholas jumped up on the desk and started dancing. "Tell God to come get me then!"

Almost as soon as he lifted a foot, he slipped from the desk and the back of his head hit another. Emily rushed across the room to where Nicholas lay crying. She was thankful for the jagged sounds, knowing that Nicholas was not knocked unconscious. He'd pulled into a fetal position and was screaming like an angry toddler, kicking the surrounding desks.

"Nicholas, show me where it hurts." Emily cradled his head and felt the knot on the back of his skull. Where was her teaching help? She scanned the room of wide-eyed children and selected the most mature of her kids. "Rachel, would you go find Mrs. Kless and tell her I need help. Quickly."

Rachel nodded and ran from the room with obvious relief.

Emily soothed Nicholas with soft words and asked the rest of the children to pray for the boy's head. He wasn't badly hurt. His ego was far more bruised than his head, but it was the way he cried. The childishness within him scared Emily. She'd heard this kind of explosive crying before, when a broken soul let the pain ooze freely. Suddenly, she saw Nicholas in a whole new light—as a broken heart rather than a defiant child.

She had to focus. She had to concentrate on the task at hand. She sat on the floor and pulled Nicholas onto her lap, which, surprisingly, he didn't fight. His body was rigid with distress. The class looked at her expectantly. She cleared her throat and began the lesson. She told the story of Cain and Abel while holding Nicholas. The children watched with wide, attentive eyes, fearful that Nicholas might rise or scream again.

Mrs. Kless came and took the children to another class for craft. For some reason, Emily wasn't ready to relinquish Nicholas or Jason. The lost boys, as she now thought of them.

Nicholas's harsh look died, and she felt him relax in her arms, molding into her form. She looked up to see Darin's worried frown.

"Nicholas. You all right, buddy?"

The boy ran to Darin and allowed the big man to embrace him like a baby. Jason watched the whole situation without saying a word.

Emily raked her hand through her hair. "I'm sorry, Darin." Her lips quivered, and she fought a wave of emotion. She'd done the right thing and remained calm, but she didn't feel that way. Everything within her didn't want to let go of the boys, to send them back to the adult world they lived in.

"I—" Her voice broke.

"Emily, what's the matter? It's just a little fall. Kids take falls all the time."

She bristled. "Yes, you're right." After Nicholas quieted down, Emily pulled Darin away. "I just wish there was something more I could do."

"When kids climb, they sometimes fall."

Mrs. Kless came in and brought a first-aid kit and an accident report for the church office. Emily calmly filled out the paperwork, but she didn't feel soothed in her heart. She regretted sending Nicholas back home to whatever pain he clutched. His cries over a fall would haunt her like the cries of her next-door neighbor as a child. She excused herself.

Free of teaching second hour, she ran across the parking lot and found her car. Fumbling with her keys, she unlocked the door and clambered into the driver's seat. Images of the handsome Darin Black—and her inability to teach a simple Sunday school class in front of him—filled her mind. She closed her eyes and imagined herself touching the soft red stubble on his shaved head. Maybe her subconscious believed his dangerous side was enough to rescue her from her loneliness. She'd thought the same of Mike, but he'd seen through her gentle façade. He'd seen the real Emily for who she really was, and he'd run away like a frightened fawn. No knight in shining armor was coming to rescue her. She needed to get over that dream and continue loving the kids God had given her to help: her students.

She didn't know how long she sat in the car, but when she looked around, the parking lot was nearly empty. Darin rapped on her window, and she started at the sight of him with four young boys. Nicholas was one of them.

"We just wanted you to know that Nicholas was fine. He gave us a good scare, but he's a tough cookie. Aren't you, bud?"

"Better believe it," Nicholas said with all the bravado of a high school quarterback.

"We're going to get some lunch before we head back to EPA. You want to join us?" Darin lifted his light red eyebrows, and the motion captivated Emily. So much so, she forgot to answer.

"Emily?" he asked.

"Oh, I'm sorry. No, I've got to get my classroom ready for tomorrow."

"Working on a Sunday?" There was a hint of disappointment in his voice.

"I'm afraid a teacher's work is never done. I had to work the school fair yesterday, so I didn't get all my lesson plans finished."

"Em, this wasn't your fault, you know. Nicholas told me what happened and said he was sorry."

She just shook her head. "I know, but I was in charge and I feel badly that I let you down."

"Emily?"

She met his eyes and marveled again at their color—a slate gray-green that calmed the senses. It was the kind of color a hospital might use on the walls to lower blood pressure. It certainly lowered hers.

"Let me drive you home. Work can wait."

She still stared into his eyes, hoping for a little of the peace they seemed to emanate. How did someone who knew the Lord for such a short time possess such inner peace?

"I'm all right." But Emily longed to throw off all of her responsibilities for the day and enjoy a nice afternoon with Darin and the kids.

"Hang on a minute, Emily. I'm going to ask Pastor Fredericks to drive the boys home."

"No!" the kids whined in unison.

"No, Darin. I need to get to work. Really." But she was about as convincing as a two-year-old turning down candy. Darin laughed at her and crossed his arms at her lack of conviction.

She sat there, staring at the steering wheel, and soon Darin returned without his inner city boys' club.

He opened her door. "Get into the passenger seat. I'm driving."

Emily didn't argue.

Darin gazed at her. "Emily, what's wrong? You seem to be making an awfully big deal of a kid falling and having to work on a Sunday. Are you trying to avoid me?"

"No." *Quite the contrary.* "I was just reminded today of something that happened a long time ago. Something I thought I'd sorted out with God. I didn't know how to handle a child like Nicholas. It never occurred to me as a child to defy the rules. Maybe I'd be more exciting if I had."

"Is it so surprising that you couldn't handle Nicholas?"

"I'm a teacher."

"In the middle of Mansion Row, Emily. You're a teacher for spoiled rich kids. In contrast, these kids saw a slasher flick last night, and they were pretending to knife each other when I picked them up this morning. That something you're used to?" He fought off laughter.

Emily shuddered. "How can you protect them when you take them out?"

"I do my best. I keep a close eye on them, but ultimately the Lord has to care for them the rest of the week. Their mothers all work two jobs or more. Most of the kids don't know who their fathers are. I can only be a piece in God's puzzle for them. I can't be everything." He paused for a moment, looking deeply into her eyes. "And neither can you."

But she wondered about that. Wasn't being there for the kids exactly what she was called to do?

Darin started her car. He turned out of the parking lot and headed away from her home.

"Where are we going?"

"You need to get some food into you. You're happier when you're full; at least I am. There's a nice little breakfast place downtown."

As the car approached the city, Emily thought the restaurant was better described as a greasy spoon. Clearly, being a Christian wasn't the only definition they disagreed upon.

"This place has the best eggs Benedict you'll ever eat," Darin said as the hostess motioned toward a vinyl-covered booth.

Somehow I doubt that, Emily thought.

"The usual?" the waitress asked.

"Two, please. Emily, what do you want to drink?"

"Just iced water." Thinking better of her choice, she said, "Make that a Diet Pepsi." In Mexico, they always warned you not to drink the water. Somehow Emily thought that might be good advice for this restaurant.

The waitress grabbed the menus and left. Emily was grateful Darin had taken over for the moment. She found herself staring at him again. He was so beautiful. Not a word you'd use to describe a man, but it fit Darin to a tee. Movie-star gorgeous with a dash of danger.

"What are your parents like?" she asked, wondering what terrible stories he could tell of living with ungodly parents.

"They're good people. They don't know the Lord, but they gave me every opportunity to make something of myself. Albeit, without much guidance. I was pretty much free to do as I liked. I had a basketball scholarship to college, but I quickly squandered it when I discovered the college life could be so much fun."

Emily crossed her arms, sinking into the booth. "College was fun?"

"No." Darin laughed. "College wasn't fun, but all the extracurricular activities were. So much so, I flunked out. That's why I'm doing landscape work now. I was in a five-year program for architecture. I got enough engineering to design a great sprinkler and lawn system. But not much else, other than how to down a six-pack in six minutes."

Emily mentally calculated the strikes against Darin Black based on her mother's list of qualities to look for in a man. He was a college dropout, former street racer, and former drinker. There was the issue of the earring and the fact that he was comfortable in the inner city, not to mention this dive restaurant.

Staring at this gentle man across from her, it was hard to believe all she knew about him was true. She rubbed the back of her neck, wondering what she might say to keep normal conversation flowing. She didn't feel like conversing. She just wanted to go to the school and try harder to be the teacher she should be. And she wanted to ignore her growing feelings for a man who would not meet the approval of her parents.

"You're quiet, Emily." Darin lifted her chin slightly with his thumb. It was the first time he'd touched her, and her body betrayed her. She felt his touch to her toes. "It's okay if you don't feel like talking. Just sit back and enjoy breakfast. I'm content to look at the beautiful view." He winked at her. "I'm really sorry if the boys were too much for you."

Emily shook her head. "No, the boys weren't too much. They just reminded me of something Fireman Mike once told me." She paused for a moment. "He said I couldn't rescue the world. But I wonder if I could rescue anyone?"

Darin kept those green eyes upon her, and she felt the need to keep talking.

"I can try harder, but those words haunt me. If I'm not good at teaching, what's my purpose?"

He smiled. "I don't believe it for a second. What could haunt the zealous Miss Emily Jensen?"

She forced her eyes away to the baseball game that blared from a mounted TV set. A hit cracked on the television, and cheers from the restaurant patrons drowned out her answer. "What, indeed."

Chapter 3

D arin stared at Emily's apartment for a long time after dropping her off. They'd switched cars back at the church parking lot, but he had insisted on seeing her safely home. He wished he'd stayed in the classroom to help her with the boys. She loved children—that was obvious—and he certainly hadn't meant to overwhelm her with the boys. Her background must have been so free of troubles growing up with a strong Christian family. It wasn't like his, where he'd seen some terrible things on the street. Emily had been protected her whole life, and he just couldn't imagine what warranted her fears that she was an inadequate teacher. He scratched the back of his head and finally pulled away in his car.

His parents were expecting him for early supper, but he didn't feel up to it. Ever since he'd become a Christian, life with his parents had become strained. Darin wanted them in heaven with him, but his parents saw it as another crazy fad. Just like his sports cars and brief college stint. Darin sighed. It was up to God and beyond his control, but that didn't mean he'd stop telling them about Jesus. The name of Jesus was harsher than the word *God* in his parents' home. The holiness of it evoked strong responses.

As he pulled into their driveway, his stomach lurched. In front of the house sat Angel's flashy red convertible. His old girlfriend. A woman who knew how to pull his strings. Any man's strings, in fact. He thought about running. Didn't God say to flee dangerous situations? But how would that prove to his parents that he was different now? His mother obviously thought Angel could rescue him from what she called his "religious phase."

He took a minute to bathe himself in prayer before he approached the front door. Before his hand touched the knob, the door swung open, and Angel Mallory stood at the threshold. All five-feet-eight of her. He was surprised that her image didn't cause the usual response in him. What he felt now was more akin to disgust than lust.

She wore a too-tight T-shirt and form-fitting jeans that were cut low. Too low for decency's sake. Her smile was welcoming, inviting, and purposeful. Darin gulped.

"Angel," he said as calmly as possible.

"That's all you have to say to me?" She put a hand to her hip, then came toward him and wrapped him in a hug. He remained stiff and pulled away quickly.

"Nice to see you again." Darin walked right past her and kissed his mother on the cheek. "Hi, Mom. You didn't tell me you were having company."

"Honey, did you say hello to Angel properly?"

"I did." Darin flashed her an impromptu smile. "I hugged her." Actually, Angel had hugged him, but he wasn't splitting hairs now.

"Hey, Darin." His dad lifted a bottled beer toward him. "You want one? Giants are playing."

"How about a root beer instead?" A soda and baseball. That, he could handle. Not to mention that the game provided the necessary escape route.

He left Angel to help his mother without any semblance of guilt. She had invited Angel; she could entertain the woman. Darin had tried to speak with Angel about the changes in his life. He'd tried to get her to go to church, but she'd only laughed at him and called him weak, relying on religion to do his thinking for him. The sting still hurt. He was stronger now than he'd ever been.

Angel had paraded various men in front of him, to let him know she was still attractive. A man would have to be blind not to notice Angel's outer beauty, but Darin failed to see anything beautiful within her now. She was like a train wreck waiting to happen. He still prayed for her every day, asking for forgiveness if he'd done anything to initiate her fall. They'd only dated for two short months, but God started speaking to him in that time, and as God's light became more apparent, Angel's darkness became ever bleaker.

"The game's boring," his dad said.

"Baseball's always a little slow, Dad."

"You wouldn't think so if you didn't try all those extreme sports. Bungee jumping," his father said, shaking his head. "If man was meant to jump from a bridge, we would have been made with rubber feet. Or should I say heads."

Darin laughed. "Don't worry, Dad, my bungee jumping days are through. I'm moving to EPA now, and I don't want to set a bad example for the kids."

Ray Black clicked off the television set. "You are what?"

"I'm going to move with the ministry team there, Dad. I'm going to live in a house with some guys to work with the kids. I'll still be doing the landscaping during the day."

"Are you nuts? Those kids are someone else's problem, not yours. Sometimes I think you were born with rocks for brains." He kept shaking his head, his disapproval more than obvious. "Where did we go wrong with you? What did we do to make you think you have to live like a martyr? So you didn't get through college; that ain't no crime. I've done just fine without college. Got me a nice house, big-screen TV, a camper for long weekends. Why don't you set a goal instead of trying to save the world?"

"Dad, this has nothing to do with education. As a matter of fact, one of my new roommates graduated from Stanford, and the other has his master's degree from Princeton. This is about me doing what God is asking me to do."

The comment only set his father off. "If God is talking to you now, I'd rather have you bungee jumping than listening to voices!"

"Dinner's ready!" his mother called.

Darin sat on the sofa for a moment and was surprised where his thoughts went. Not to the kids, not to his new home, but to Emily. He saw her face and longed for her comfort and understanding in this situation. Could Emily deal with a man like him? Accept him with all his mistakes and wrong turns? When she'd stayed on the straight and narrow path, and Darin had done everything but follow the right road?

Angel stood in the doorway, her belly peeking out between her jeans and short tee. He wanted to ask her if that was supposed to be attractive, but he snapped his mouth shut. It was better if she thought he hadn't noticed.

"Let's eat," his father said.

Everyone gathered around the table, and Darin silently offered up a word of thanks and asked for help in getting through the uncomfortable meal. His father was now livid, his mother thought him incredibly rude to Angel, and Angel herself sat waiting for him to say something.

His mother took the opportunity to pass the green beans and elbow him in the process. "Talk to her."

"So your mom tells me you're still in that cult of Jesus freaks." Angel stifled a giggle.

Darin looked down at his plate, focusing on the mountain of mashed potatoes. He bit back a sarcastic comment and stuffed potatoes in his mouth instead. It wouldn't do him any good to attack. It would only reflect badly on him and his faith.

"Angel is trying out for the Raiderettes!" his mother announced brightly. Could she truly want a professional cheerleader for a daughter-in-law? The whole subject mystified him. What did his mother see in Angel that kept their friendship going long after Darin knew there was no point to a relationship? The only thing he and Angel had had in common was the club scene and their red sports cars. Now they had nothing in common. Nothing but this dinner table, anyway.

It was hard to see Angel as a person without seeing her as a symbol of all he had left behind. It wasn't that he felt above her, it was that he feared falling backwards into the life that had him by the throat for so long. Angel was like a beautiful casket, inviting him for a visit without escape. He actually shivered thinking about it.

"The Raiderettes, huh? A lot of my boys from the neighborhood are big fans of the Raiders. You'll have to let me know how it goes. Maybe I could bring the boys to a game."

"Maybe next week you could go watch the tryouts, Darin." His mother nodded her head briskly. "Angel is in the finals, so you won't have to watch all those amateurs."

"I'm kinda seeing someone, Mom. I don't think she'd appreciate me watching a bunch of professional cheerleaders." *Jesus wouldn't appreciate me watching a bunch of half-dressed aerobics instructors.* He looked at Angel. "No offense, of course. That's exciting news. I'm very proud of you."

The look on Angel's face was one of outrage. Darin wished he could take back his words, which she probably heard as judgmental and harsh. Her narrowed eyes made her motives painfully obvious. Angel didn't want him. She wanted him to want her. When his interest faltered, her desperation for his attention grew. Why else would she be sitting here over roast beef and mashed potatoes making small talk about professional cheerleading?

"Seeing someone?" Color drained from his mother's face. She lifted her plate from the table, throwing the silverware with a clang. She started to clear the dishes from the table, though no one was finished eating. "You never told me you were seeing someone."

"I just started seeing her, Mom. It's nothing serious yet. She's—" He started to say not like the other girls he'd dated but quickly refrained. "She's very special to me, and I just think it's something I want to follow through on."

"What does she do?" Angel smirked. "She's a model, I bet." Her eyes mere slits, Darin felt like a trapped rat in a gutter. Nothing about his relationship with Emily could be considered truly "seeing her" except what Darin felt in his heart. To explain that would have made his parents question his sanity even more.

"She teaches first grade."

Angel cackled out loud, and his mom joined her.

"You are dating a teacher? You, who never listened to a teacher in your life?"

"We're seeing each other, Mom. I don't know if we're at the dating stage yet." *But I want to be.*

His mother sat beside him and cupped his hand in hers. "I don't want you to be hurt. Does she know you're a college dropout? Is this one of those church girls? You know, church girls generally marry church boys."

Darin nodded.

"Oh, honey." She looked at his dad. "Talk to him, Ray. Won't you?"

"He's never listened to me, either, Mabel."

Angel stood. "I'd better go. I've got an aerobics class to teach." She shot Darin a lethal glance and exited quickly. His parents both sat back in their chairs, crossing their arms.

"Did you have to hurt her feelings like that?" his mother said.

"I wasn't trying to hurt her feelings, but I am seeing someone. You're the one who invited her here."

"Because I thought my son knew his manners. Honestly! Talking about another woman in Angel's presence. There will come a day when you regret that move. None of these church girls know who you really are, Darin Black. Angel loves the real Darin, just like we do."

Darin's thoughts drifted to Emily Jensen. Who was he kidding to think he was worthy of a woman like her? Angel's forced smile reminded him of all he'd been. And though Christ had washed away his sins, had He taken away the consequences that made him unworthy of Emily? He couldn't help but wonder.

~

Emily cleaned her apartment until she thought the paint would erode under the pressure. The work made her forget what a fool she'd been earlier in the day to thumb her nose at a nice breakfast with Darin. It certainly beat all the meals she ate alone, yet in her own judgmental way, she'd probably sent him a clear message. She ripped off the plastic glove and rubbed her forehead. She felt like she was back in high school. Darin Black was the popular kid, and she was still the gawky teen who didn't know what to say or how to dress. Being cool eluded her. Apparently, it was a lifetime legacy.

Why did she care if Darin thought she was crazy? He was a college dropout. He worked with his hands, she kept telling herself, trying to add disdain to the voice. But his heart. There was something so beckoning about a man who would minister in the ghetto, a man who would give up his own life to tell others about Jesus. Her Sunday school teaching felt pale in comparison. And then there was the small matter of what his appearance did to her heart.

She made herself an artichoke and plopped a big helping of mayonnaise beside it. Grabbing a bottled iced tea from the refrigerator, she settled down in front of the television. She killed a few channels before realizing she'd have to get something decent to watch. Placing a romantic video in the player, she settled back in when the phone rang.

"Hello," Emily answered.

"Emily, it's Darin."

Her stomach twisted, and she put the plate on the coffee table, as if he could see her eating an artichoke. Somehow the vegetable didn't feel very feminine, and she was instantly embarrassed. All her mother's prodding came back to her. "Don't let a man see you eat." She laughed at the Scarlett O'Hara advice, but, sadly, some of it stuck, and the artichoke seemed like eating barbecue at Twelve Oaks.

"Hi, Darin." She wanted to ask how his afternoon went, what his parents had to say, what he had for dinner, but she clamped her mouth shut for fear she'd babble.

"Have you eaten yet?" he asked.

Emily swallowed, looking at the half-decimated artichoke. "Yes, I have."

"How about dessert? Are you up for that? It's only six thirty."

She looked at her watch. Indeed, it was only six thirty, so why did it seem like such an eternity since she'd seen Darin?

"Dessert would be great." She vowed she wouldn't mess things up this time, as she had at breakfast.

"I'll pick you up in ten minutes."

Emily threw her plate in the kitchen sink and rushed to her bedroom to find something to wear. She shunned all the floral dresses that seemed to announce her lifetime in the church and found a pair of jeans and a baggy red T-shirt. Looking at her reflection, she felt disappointed. The jeans hung on her, as if she feared getting something that actually fit her, and the T-shirt covered her too-big jeans, making her look like a red potato with legs.

"I'm afraid this is as wild as it gets," she said to the mirror. "Scarlett, I'm not."

She put on her pearl earrings. Darin wore a cross in his ear. She giggled. She was dating a man with an earring. *Take that, Mom. We could share earrings. Well, earring.*

Emily knew exactly what her mother would say, and she didn't want to hear it. She already heard echoes of it in her mind. Fireman Mike had been so upstanding, a local hero who was handsome and a longtime believer. He was everything Nancy Jensen expected. Everything she'd wanted in a son-in-law. But there was no spark between Emily and Mike. She'd wanted there to be. It would have pleased her mother and helped both women to forget their tumultuous relationship.

God's will and true love proved stronger than Emily's desire to please everyone else. Mike had never made her heart thunder like this dangerous stranger. She wondered if this were her way of silently rebelling. If her brother could see her now. The thought brought a smile to her face.

"You'd love him, Kyle!" Emily looked toward the ceiling. "Just because Mom wouldn't."

Her doorbell rang, and Emily sprinted for the kitchen, rinsing her dish and disposing of the artichoke before answering the door. She sucked in a deep breath and opened the door. Then she forgot to breathe. Darin's sage green eyes smiled, and she could feel her stomach flipping.

"Hi." He winked.

"Hi."

"Is it too soon to see me again?"

Never, she thought. "No, I actually missed you. I wanted to apologize for my strange behavior this morning. I'm not usually so strange, but I had a trying morning. It seems to me you haven't seen my best side as yet."

Darin bit his lip and looked straight at her. The directness of his gaze almost knocked her over. "Then I'm not sure I could handle your best side. Because I like all the sides I've seen."

Emily thought about asking him in but wondered what he would think of her country decor. Did it make her look too simple? She closed the door behind her. Darin didn't need to see any more of her floral ways. "Where shall we go?"

"How about a coffeehouse downtown? I know a great one."

"I'd love that. How was your mom's house? Did you have a nice dinner?"

Darin snorted. "It was weird. Thanks for asking. Things aren't the same since I became a Christian. They don't talk to me the same. Maybe that's my fault, but it still makes dinner different." He shrugged. "I don't know. My mom and dad keep hoping I'll come back around. I think they'd rather have me driving sports cars and living the life I used to. At least they understood that. I was a rebel, and they accepted that. But this. . ." He held open his palms. "They don't understand this at all."

Emily surprised herself, but she took Darin's hand. "I'm sorry. I know what it's like to be different from your parents."

He grasped her hand back. "Do you mind if we walk to the coffee shop?"

"Not at all." *More time with him,* Emily thought.

"East Palo Alto is the only place I fit in. The church doesn't know what to make of me, my parents would just as soon disown my religious ways, and my old friends have nothing in common with me. Becoming a Christian can be a lonely place."

"Christians shouldn't judge," Emily said.

"Yeah, but what would your parents think of me?"

Emily looked away, unwilling to answer the question. She knew exactly what her parents would think of him. She was glad they'd retired out of town. She'd only have so long before a gossiping goose at church told her mother what she was up to. She could hear the whispers now: "I hate to be the one to tell you, but Emily is dating a boy with an earring. He's not the kind you'd approve of, Nancy. I think you might want to plan a visit." Her parents would probably move back without a second glance.

She held Darin's hand a bit tighter. "Maybe being a missionary will change people's minds. Do you have to wear the earring?" It was a fair question.

Darin shook his head. "No, but I got my ear pierced the day I became a Christian. With this same cross. I did it myself." He shrugged. "It means something to me, kind of a symbol of my new birth."

"I guess you do have to wear it then."

"The EPA kids accept it. I'm moving there this weekend with a couple of guys from the Bayshore House—that's a local ministry."

Her eyes widened. "You're serious." She clutched her stomach, wishing the butterflies would disappear. Darin was going to live in the inner city. She felt a small shiver down her spine. She certainly wasn't meant to live in the ghetto with a man who wore an earring. That wasn't the life for her. Her parents wouldn't be the only ones to tell her that. She slipped her hand from Darin's and focused on the sidewalk in front of her. Maybe her desire to annoy her mother was far too strong. But when she looked into Darin's eyes, her heart thundered all over again, and she sneaked her hand back into his. Sometimes the head and heart disagree. She'd heard that said before, and that it was time to rely on God in those times. *Well, God, here I am.*

Chapter 4

The dim lighting of the coffee shop created a soothing ambiance. An elegant, antique table stood in the center of the room on big black and white tiles, with smaller laminate tables placed elsewhere in true hodgepodge form. A huge metal roaster that resembled a wood-burning stove lifted to the ceiling and provided the focal point of the room. The machine announced the freshness of the beans, but the rich coffee scent overwhelmed the senses.

Emily drew in a deep breath. "That smell is just heavenly. Even if you don't like coffee, you have to love that smell."

"If you think it smells good, wait until you taste it." Darin winked, but then his eyebrows furrowed. "You do drink coffee, don't you?"

She bit her lower lip. "I like the kind with excessive amounts of sugar and chocolate poured into it, topped with whipped cream, of course."

He squeezed her hand. "I know just the thing. What do you want for dessert?" Pointing to the refrigerated glass cabinet, he motioned for Emily to look over the delicacies. Pies and chocolate concoctions beckoned her, and she looked to Darin with expectant eyes. She couldn't have said which looked more appetizing, the desserts or Darin's warm gaze. She looked away to settle her soda-fizzling stomach.

The shop's patrons consisted of tattooed, pierced youths, older couples reading papers, and everything in between. The sounds of a jazz clarinet filled the room, and Emily saw that, next to the roaster, a lone musician played his instrument. The coffeehouse was the kind of place Emily would never venture into alone. Once inside, though, she was mystified. The natural shyness within her evaporated. She wanted to talk to everyone and find out their story. How did they get here? What were they doing tomorrow? What were they typing on those laptops of theirs? So many people, so many questions. She looked at Darin in awe. She was braver with him, and she liked that feeling immensely.

"Emily? Did you decide?"

"Oh yes, I'll have the chocolate decadence cake."

Darin ordered their death-by-chocolate desserts, and they found a small table in the corner. "I'm so glad you came out with me tonight. I don't usually ask people out at the last minute, but somehow I thought it might be okay. You seemed to be having the kind of day I did."

"I'm so glad you called," Emily said. "I'm not usually bold enough to venture out on Sunday night. Ever since we stopped having evening service, I feel a little paralyzed at home. I usually do last-minute lesson plans and watch a video, but I can't get it out of my mind that it's church night. Maybe I should find something to do on a laptop and come here." She laughed.

"It's sad about Sunday evening service, though." Darin shrugged. "I guess in the Bay Area people just didn't show up, huh?"

"No, and I think it depressed Pastor. He took it as a personal failure. They tried doing communion on Sunday nights to get the members there, but it ended up that the members weren't taking communion, so they finally just stuck to church and Sunday school."

Darin stared at her. "You are so beautiful. Do you know your face just lights up when you talk about the church or teaching?"

"Well, since you prefaced that with my being beautiful, you could have added anything onto the end of that sentence. You know, 'You are beautiful, but your feet are the size of a large tanker.'"

Darin's eyes laughed, and he looked under their table at her shoes. "Well. . ."

She playfully slapped his hand. "Seriously, I see that joy in you when you talk about the boys in the city. How did you get started with them?"

"You probably don't want to know."

"Yes, I do."

"I did a talk on drinking and driving at the Bayshore House. That's how I met the guys and started teaching the Bible study. It just ballooned from there."

Emily felt weak. Maybe she didn't want to know after all. She thought about her mother's prejudices and how she might answer them. *He's a good friend of Fireman Mike's. They met in the gutter. Yeah, he was arrested for drunk driving, but that's in his past. Oh, the earring. That's just his way of announcing his form of Christianity, Mom. And he started college. He just didn't finish because of partying.* Emily thought about the verse on being a new creature in Christ and wondered if there were any further way she could test that scripture with her mother.

Darin must have sensed her discomfort. "I'm sorry, Emily. My testimony is not for the faint of heart."

All hints of a smile faded from his face, and she felt horrible she'd stopped him. "Do you think I'm faint of heart?"

He cupped her hand with his own. "I think you're sheltered, Emily. And that's a beautiful place to be. I don't ever want to take that from you. Innocence is a precious commodity. Cherish it. I wish I had."

A waiter in a studded leather jacket placed their order on a counter and yelled it out for all the patrons to hear.

"Excuse me." Darin got up, and Emily watched him as he crossed the room.

Except for the shaved head and the earring, one might never know he'd led anything but a respectable life. She wondered if she might make him more presentable if meeting her parents should ever come to pass. She chastised herself immediately for trying to change who Darin was. She should be so lucky that he would want to meet her parents.

"How did you find this place?" she asked when he got back to the table.

"I used to come here when I was studying for my contractor's license."

"You can study with all this activity?"

Darin looked around. "What activity?"

She crossed her arms. "You are so much like my brother. It makes me laugh."

"Your brother? I didn't know you had a brother."

"I don't anymore. Not that I know of, anyway. He'll always be in my heart. He's gone on to live a different life."

"I'm so sorry." Darin sat back in his chair, visibly shaken by her words.

"Me, too," Emily said. "He's the only one who ever really understood who I was on the inside, but my mother and he never saw eye to eye, and unfortunately it just got to be too much for him."

Darin leaned forward, his eyes meeting hers with such an intensity, Emily couldn't break from their power. "Who are you inside, Emily?" he asked. "You come across as 'what you see is what you get,' but I can tell by your interest in people that just isn't the case. Just by the fact that you showed up at that wedding when no one thought you had it in you. So who are you really? You're obviously stronger than you give yourself credit for."

Emily shoved a bite of cake in her mouth. That was a question for the ages. Since her brother, Kyle, left, she had no idea who she was anymore. For so long, she was Kyle Jensen's little sister, then for a while Fireman Mike's girlfriend, but now she was just Emily, first-grade teacher. Was there any more depth than that? She prayed so, but she sure couldn't summon it up if it was there. Teaching school was important, but when she saw how the boys looked up to Darin, she wondered if she'd have a lifelong impact on any of her kids. Since most of them were from wealthy two-parent homes, the needs just weren't as obvious. Darin looked at her expectantly.

"I don't know as yet, but when I find out, you'll be the first to know." She hoped that ended the conversation. In truth, she feared she was no deeper than a sidewalk puddle. That wasn't information one wanted to share with a missionary from the ghetto.

"Tell me about your brother. You said he was like me." Darin swigged his coffee.

Emily smiled at the thought. "He didn't like rules, either. Kyle lived by the spirit of the law rather than the letter. And in our house, that was a terrible thing because we dotted every *i*." She looked down at her cake. "How my heart grieved when that part of our family was torn away and only the rules were left. Nothing was ever the same." She felt a tear fall and quickly wiped it away with the back of her hand. "I'm sorry. Give me a forum and I blubber like a fool. I'm one of those commercial criers, I'm afraid. Today I'm even worse than usual."

Darin gazed at her gently. "How long ago did your brother leave?"

"It's been ten years now. It was his first year of college, and I was already lost with him being away." She stopped abruptly. "You didn't come out to coffee to hear me whine. Tell me about your ministry."

Darin paused. "Tomorrow night we're going to San Francisco to a crab dinner and a play."

Emily shook her head. "Tomorrow is Monday, a school night. You're taking the kids up to the city?"

Darin threw back his head and laughed. Emily loved how he did that, as though he relished joy and emanated it like a flashlight. He didn't seem to care if anyone looked at him or if his laughter was out of place. He just laughed.

"Emily, these kids are up until 1:00 a.m., regardless. They watch cable movies all night that aren't fit for adults, and I think a night in the city is much better than what they could be doing. The playwrights' association donated the tickets, and I got the meals donated. Want to come along? I can invite two more kids if you go. We'll take the Bayshore ministry van instead of my car."

"I don't know. Monday night usually means a lot of grading for me. That would be a bit irresponsible for me to take off to a play."

"Irresponsible or out of character?" His eyebrows arched.

"Both."

"Hey, D." A tattooed, leather-clad man holding a helmet stood over the table.

"Rich!" Darin stood and clasped the hand of this frightening person. "Meet Emily." He motioned toward her, and Emily swallowed hard before taking the hand of someone her mother would have warned her about. Rich was covered with tattoos, mostly of dragons and spiders. He even sported a black widow above his left eye.

"Hi," Emily forced.

"This guy," Rich said as he pointed toward Darin with his free hand, "this guy is such a trip. Do you know he base jumped in a parachute from El Capitan in Yosemite? Just like Bond in that one movie. Crazy, man. He was lucky to be alive when they arrested him. A sheer granite wall he could have blown into any second." Rich gave a low whistle of awe.

Emily tried to hide her shock, but she felt her eyes blinking rapidly. Darin had been arrested. Really arrested! Not for any pro-life rally or something she could identify with, but for parachuting off one of the highest peaks in California. Of course there was also the drunk-driving matter. She wondered if she could possibly handle a life with such a man.

Every time she heard something new, she took a step back mentally. If he wasn't so much like Kyle, she probably wouldn't be interested. But Kyle had been the same way. Gallant, good-looking, and fearless. It was hard for Emily to ignore what kind of heart lurked beneath Darin's history, and her own heart beat rapidly at the sight of him.

"It's not as shocking as it seems, Emily," Darin explained about the arrest. "That was a long time ago. I was young and stupid."

"Oh yeah, he's a church boy now, I hear. Not doing any of those crazy stunts anymore," Rich said.

Emily looked outside at the pink twilight sky. It was too late for her to walk home alone, but she felt the immediate desire to leave. It wasn't the jail stint; it was just that the more Emily learned about Darin's life, the more certain she knew she could never be a part of it. She wasn't a fun person by nature, and she didn't want Darin to know that the last chance she took was trying a new lesson plan. Kyle had found their mother's home too stifling. Would Darin find her the same way? If so, it was better to know now.

Suddenly she longed to get home, have a cup of chamomile tea, and go to bed. Sunday night outings were just reckless. If she furthered anything with Darin, it seemed her whole life would be that way. Out of control—irresponsible and frightening.

"Rich, I'd sure like it if you'd come to church with me one day. Jumping into faith was more exhilarating than any base jump I ever did." Darin started an easy sell job to Rich. It wasn't forced.

Rich put up a palm. "Not me, buddy. I ain't the churchgoing type."

"And I am?" Darin asked.

"Point taken." Rich laughed. "I'll tell you what. You come with me to Burning Man, and I'll come with you to church."

Emily watched Darin carefully. How far was he willing to go for this guy? Burning Man was a get-together of life's weirdos in the middle of the Nevada desert. From what Emily heard, there was a lot of nudity and strange art; then at the end, they ignited a man-shaped structure and screamed at it.

"No, I'll tell you what. You come to church with me first, and I'll go to Burning Man with you. How's that?"

Rich shook his head. "Always the negotiator. You're too fast for my blood, D."

Rich patted him on the back, and Darin sat back down. "Let's get together one of these days. Don't be a stranger. Emily, it was nice to meet you. You're too good for this guy." He winked and walked away with his helmet and gloves.

Emily swallowed hard. "Would you go to that event? Burning Man, I mean."

"Not in a million years." Darin rubbed his chin. "Unless God called me to it to preach there. Think about how many lost people are there looking for answers. Thinking they're going to find it in some invisible spiritual vortex like in a science fiction movie. It makes my stomach sick to think about it. I've been too close to death to think the afterlife is something to mess with."

Emily felt trapped in her chair, wondering how she came to be with such a divergent man. Right now, he seemed like a different species entirely. "You know, I'd really like to go home."

Darin ignored her plea. "Do you know what the life verse I've picked out for myself is?"

"Do I want to?" she asked.

He cleared his throat and continued. "When David danced before the Lord, he humiliated himself in front of people. His wife Michal was mortified and told him so. David replied, 'I will become even more undignified than this.' That's my life's verse. If God is calling me to something, I'm not going to worry about what society thinks, Emily. I'm going to listen and be undignified if necessary."

Emily could hear her own heart thundering in her ears. "But what about church society? If your life isn't held up in esteem, how do you earn respect? Being undignified is hardly godly behavior."

"There's a difference between being undignified and being undignified to praise the Lord. Are you afraid I'd embarrass you?"

She looked him straight in the eye and almost lied, but the truth came tumbling out. "Yes, I am."

He winced, and Emily felt her harshness to the core. Poor Kyle. Now she knew what he must have felt like when Mom couldn't accept him for who he was.

"I'm sorry. David cried out to the Lord so many times when he was humiliated, when he was downtrodden and beaten. What makes you call on the Lord?"

This date. "Just because I haven't had all these wild experiences doesn't mean I don't know what it is to need the Lord. I have endured tragedy multiple times, and I'm still standing." Emily scooted her seat back. "I think we should go."

Darin reached for her sweater on the back of the chair, but she grabbed it first. "Emily, are you afraid of me?"

She let the question fall unanswered.

Chapter 5

Once home, Emily dropped her purse and ran to answer the phone. "Hello," she said breathlessly. She was thankful for the ringing phone so that she and Darin didn't have an awkward good-bye at the door. He had just waved at her as she clumsily ran for the phone.

"Emily, where have you been? It's Sunday evening. Shouldn't you be doing your lesson plans?"

She sighed. "Mom, I was out with a friend." *What am I thinking? Why don't I just announce I had a date!*

"A friend? Where?"

"We just went for coffee. It was no big deal. It's eight forty-five and I'm home, okay? It's no later than I might have been home from Sunday night service. I just went out for a little fellowship."

"Are you dating someone?" Her voice rose with anticipation.

"No, Mom. It's just a friend that I met at Mike's wedding."

Nancy Jensen clicked her tongue in disgust. "Oh, that wedding. Why on earth did you go to that? Isn't it humiliating enough that he married someone else? You have to go and announce to all my friends that he married someone else?"

"I like Mike, Mom, and I like Grace, too. It would have been unkind for me to stay home. I want to support their marriage. Besides, everyone at church knows the story. It's not like I'm keeping any secrets. What kind of lesson would it have been for little Josh if I didn't go?"

Her mother clicked her tongue again, followed by a long exhale of breath. "Emily, you are never going to get married being everyone's buddy. Men need to think of you as a woman, not as a companion they'd take to the ball game. I wish your brother was still around. He'd find you a wonderful man to marry. You do know you're my only chance at grandchildren."

It pained Emily to hear her mother speak as though Kyle were dead and as though she herself had nothing to do with his disappearance. When Kyle was home, her mother didn't like anyone he brought around. Now that he was gone, Kyle was remembered as the salvation for Emily's singleness.

"Mom, you didn't even like parenting. What's with the sudden urge for grandparenting?"

"That's not true! Where do you get such wicked ideas? Mildred said she saw

390

you with some bald man. You're not dating an old man, are you? There are so many strange men around now. You've got to be careful."

"He's not bald. He shaved his head. It's kind of the style now. The youth pastor even did it."

"What? It's true then? Emily, that is not the style for Christians. That is the style for hoodlums. I thought you wanted to get married."

"I do want to get married, Mom."

"Then the first thing I would suggest is that you find a man who respects his hair."

Emily giggled. She couldn't help herself. Each time she tried to stop, she only giggled harder, thinking about a man who respected his hair.

"What are you laughing at, young lady?"

"Mom," she said through laughter, "where does a man who respects his hair hang out? So I know where to look next time."

"At church. That church has twelve hundred members in it. There are single men there, and most of them have hair."

"There's one less now since Mike and Grace got married." Now she was just being ornery, as her mother would say. But did any woman at thirty-two need to be reminded she wasn't married? "Besides, I met the bald guy at church."

"So you are dating him?"

"I didn't say that. I just said that I met this man at Mike's wedding."

"So he's a firefighter!" She emphasized the word *firefighter* as if Emily was about to be rescued from her spinsterhood.

"No. He's a landscape artist."

"A gardener? Oh, Emily, really! You're a teacher. Your father and I paid good money for your education."

Yes, he's a gardener, and he was involved in a drunk-driving accident where he totaled his car and met Mike as a firefighter. It took everything in Emily's will not to announce the earring or the base-jumping arrest. Kyle's defiance had taught her mother nothing, and Emily's certainly wouldn't change her mind, either.

"I'm friends with the man, Mom. Do you remember that Oprah show you sent me on videotape? It said to keep my options open and not to date a man based on his credentials."

Her mother stammered, "I didn't mean—"

"How's Dad doing?"

"He's fine. Maybe you should move up here with us. There are good teaching jobs in Oregon. The San Francisco area is known for. . .well, you know what it's known for."

"I have a good teaching job and I like California. We have sunshine."

"With your brother gone now, you're our only hope for grandchildren."

"And that lowers the odds quite a bit, doesn't it?"

"What is that supposed to mean?"

"Mom, Kyle had that kind of personality. People were attracted to him. They wanted to be around his magnetic presence. I'm not like that, and I never will be. I'm Emily Jensen, first-grade teacher. Let's just be happy with that, okay? That I'm not serving time in a mental hospital somewhere."

"I never meant I didn't think it was possible for you to be married. You're a beautiful, talented young woman. Surely. . .never mind. I suppose you're tired of hearing from me tonight. You always respected your brother's opinion. Do you think things will go anywhere with the gardener?"

"Tomorrow night we're taking a group of teens to San Francisco for a crab feast and a play." Emily surprised herself as much as her mother.

"To the city? On a school night?"

Help! I've become my mother. That's exactly what I said to him. "Darin says the kids stay up late regardless, so he's taking some of them to an African-American playhouse. They are doing a reprisal of the Brer Rabbit folk tales. I'll have to leave right when school gets out tomorrow."

"You're not going to lose your job for this, are you? First, you're out Sunday night, and now you're talking about leaving right after school. I don't want to tell you how to run your life, but it's sounding reckless."

Emily thought about the endless school nights of planning and how her social life had always taken a backseat to her job. Even her summers were filled with summer school and committees. "Yes, it probably does sound reckless, but I've given my life to teaching. They can give me two nights that should be mine, anyway."

"Does anyone know this man who can vouch for him? It sounds a bit dangerous to head into San Francisco with someone you barely know."

"Pastor Fredericks vouches for him," Emily said with satisfaction. "Mom, I'll call you Tuesday night. I need to call Darin and firm up plans."

"Very well, but have your cell phone on so I can reach you if necessary."

"I will for everything except the play, Mom. I love you."

"We love you, too, dear. I'll be praying God brings you the man of your heart. And that he has hair!"

"Thank you." Emily rolled her eyes. "Tell Dad I love him, too, and I'll see you both at Christmas. I'm planning to drive up there."

"We may see you before then. Your father and I just might show up on your doorstep for a surprise visit soon, so keep the furniture dusted," she mock-threatened. "Bye, honey."

Emily hung up the phone and stared at it for a minute. Before she lost her mettle, she dialed Darin's number, hoping he wasn't home yet. It was the first time she'd ever called a man, and it didn't feel right. He answered on the second ring. Emily gnawed on her lip before gaining the courage to speak.

"Darin, it's Emily."

"Emily!" He sounded pleased to hear from her, and she meditated on that for a moment. When had anyone been glad to hear from her within the last year?

"Darin, you said you could take two more kids with you if I went to San Francisco tomorrow."

"Yes! Tell me you're coming." His enthusiasm made her smile. How could anyone say no after that?

"I'm coming. I'll drive home right after school and meet you at the Bayshore House. I've tutored there before, so I know where it is."

"No, Emily. I don't want you there at night. I don't even want your car there. I'll pick you up before we get the van. Okay?"

"That would be great."

"I'll see you about four. And Emily?"

"Yeah?"

"Thanks so much for calling. I'm thrilled you're coming. It will make the whole night that much better."

"Bye, Darin." She drew in a deep breath. Darin made her feel important, just like her brother, Kyle, always did. There was a gift in that ability.

~

Darin hung up the phone and raised a fist to the sky. "Yes! Thank You, Lord! She doesn't hate me."

He scanned the room of his apartment; emptiness filled the place. Now that most of his belongings were boxed up and ready to move, he wondered if he were doing the right thing. Moving into the Bayshore House seemed like a great idea a week ago. Now he wondered. Emily was everything he wanted in a woman, but she obviously wouldn't be willing to live in the ghetto should their relationship continue. Would any woman worth having be willing to live there? He shook the thought. He had to rely on God for that.

Thinking back to their uncomfortable silence all the way home from the coffeehouse, he probably didn't need to worry about Emily and a future. She'd made it pretty clear that his past nixed him as a candidate for marriage after Rich's discussion of his arrest. It would probably nullify him with any woman worth her salt. He may have become a new creature, but the old one was still there lurking for other Christians to see like a scarlet letter upon his chest.

Images of Angel floated through his mind. There was a time when a beautiful woman like Angel was all he expected, all he could have hoped for. But now he wanted so much more. He wanted a woman whom he was proud of on his arm, a woman whose heart highlighted her beauty. Not a woman who would flaunt it at a football game for any old geezer to gawk over. His whole definition had changed, and for that alone he was deeply grateful.

Darin ignored the moving box mess and went to his Bible. He needed confirmation, not questions. When he opened his Bible, a picture of the boys from EPA fell out, and Darin grinned. Those boys needed him. Was there any more confirmation necessary? Wanting Emily was one thing, but it wasn't enough. He knew the boys were God's will. He had no idea if Emily was anything more than a fierce desire. Angel had tugged his heart that way once, too, and look how wrong that turned out to be.

"Hey!" Jack, Darin's roommate of four years, slammed the door. "Where you been? At your mom's this whole time?"

"Nah, I went out with a woman from church."

"Hope she's fine-looking, because Angel called while you were gone. She said she had some things of yours she wanted to return."

Darin sighed. "She's trying out for the Raiderettes. That's her big news."

Jack raised his eyebrows. "Is she now? I wish my dates looked as good as your castoffs."

Darin didn't know what to say to that. He remembered the day when all that mattered to him was how many men stared in awe at his date. It sickened him now to think how shallow he'd been. He was still a man, of course. He wanted a woman to be beautiful, but not in the same, showy way. Now he wanted a beautiful woman like Emily, whose dark hair and bright eyes shone with inner beauty. Emily didn't slather on makeup or cover up all her flaws professionally the way Angel did. There was an honesty to her beauty that stirred him like no woman had before her. Emily would give everything to the man she finally loved. How he wanted to be that man. He turned to face his roommate.

"Angel looks good on the outside, but you want more than that. Trust me."

"I'm not saying I want to get married or anything. I'm not looking for Mrs. Right. Just Miss Right Now." Jack laughed in his crude way, and Darin knew it was God's blessing that they were parting as roommates. Too much of Darin's past was tied up into this apartment, and Jack would never see the difference in him if he didn't do something drastic. Like move to EPA to work with troubled youths.

"I'm going out tomorrow night. I've met someone, and if you meet her, I'd really appreciate it if you didn't ramble on about Angel."

Jack cackled. "I'm no stooge. Since when do I ramble on about ex-girlfriends when the new one is in the house?"

"This isn't a girlfriend. This is something I take very seriously." He looked at Jack in frustration. "Never mind. Jack, have you noticed anything different about me in the past two years?"

"After your accident, you mean? Before or after the conversion?"

"After."

"Yeah, you never date. Angel was the last woman I ever saw you with, and she didn't last too long. You're not going completely choirboy on me, are you? It's like this religion thing scared away the chicks. That's enough to scare me away. Have you put a curse on this apartment or something? It seems like forever since either one of us had a date."

Darin rolled his eyes. "If you read what the Word has to say about how we treat women, how we as men are responsible for how we treat women, you'd flee from this horrible broken life you lead." He hated giving sermons, but Jack wasn't listening anyway. Darin could say whatever he wanted.

"Hey, at least I've had a few dates lately. It's not like I'm going to take advice from you."

Darin dropped his head and shook it back and forth. "I'm praying for you, dude." If he wanted confirmation, he had it and then some. These young kids he worked with still had a chance to lead their lives with conviction. He prayed God would show them how through him. Tomorrow night, he'd get to show them how to treat a date. He smiled at the reminder. Hope lived on. But definitely not in this apartment—after two years, Darin was tired of casting pearls before swine.

Chapter 6

On Monday afternoon, after a long day of landscaping at a luxury home site, Darin showered and slapped some aftershave on his face. He hadn't been this excited for a date since. . .well, he couldn't remember ever being this excited about a date. He checked his watch again, and time seemed to lumber. Only ten more minutes and he could leave to pick up Emily. The phone rang.

"Hello, Darin speaking."

"Darin, it's Mike. How are you doing?"

Darin gulped back his emotion. The unwritten guy rule was that you didn't date ex-girlfriends of buddies. Did Mike know he was seeing Emily? Would Mike offer his blessings? Or think Darin's history was too dark for the likes of Emily Jensen? "Doing great. How was the honeymoon?"

"The honeymoon was fantastic. Fastest two days we ever spent, but Josh has school, you know. Carmel was incredible. You ever been there?"

"Yeah. My boss sent me for a bonus last year. Heavenly place, but it lacks a little something when you're alone."

"I can see that. Listen, we're going to take a smashed-up car over to Los Altos High School next week, and I was wondering if you'd be willing to talk about your experience."

Darin paused for a moment. He'd never hesitated to talk about his accident before, since it led to such a radical life change, but now he wondered. What would Emily think of him in her school district? If everyone knew she was dating a former drunk, would that stop her? He hesitated.

"I don't know, Mike. Things are sort of busy right now. I'm working with the kids at Bayshore, getting ready to move and—" He let his voice trail off.

"I completely understand. Fortunately, we have a cache of speakers we can use. I just thought of you because of your testimony. Anytime we can work God into the program, we like that when someone gives proper credit for their life. I've got another guy who killed a high school student, but he has a hard time in the high schools for obvious reasons."

Darin's heart raced. All those kids, all of them thinking they were invincible, just like he used to think. "Of course I can do it."

"I didn't mean to guilt you into it." Mike laughed.

"Mike, I'm seeing Emily Jensen tonight. I met her this weekend at your wedding," Darin blurted.

"No kidding? Well, I'll be. You and Emily. Hey, Grace!" The phone became muffled. "Darin Black is seeing Emily Jensen tonight."

"That's wonderful!" Grace said from the background. "Josh would be so excited," she said, referring to her son.

"Don't tell Josh!" Darin said. "Emily's world has been so sheltered. I'm a bit worried about what she'll think of me being on the drunk-driving speakers' tour, you know? Do you think that will bother her?"

Mike paused for a long time. "It shouldn't matter what she thinks. I've never seen you care about what anyone thinks when it comes to sharing who you are. Besides, I think you should give Emily a little credit. She may come off as shallow sometimes, but still waters run deep, as they say. Emily's got a lot of heartache in her past. God has really grown her faith."

"Yes, she told me about her brother."

"Her brother, oh, right, that. Emily's a great gal, Darin. I hope things work out for the two of you."

"Just let me know the time on that talk, okay?"

"Will do. Grace and I will pray for you and Emily. I'm really happy to hear you're seeing her. She's a wonderful woman."

"I heard that!" Grace called out in mock jealousy.

"But of course not as wonderful as my wife," Mike said through laughter.

Darin heard a bit of wrestling with the phone, and Grace came on the other end. "I'm kidding, you know. I think Emily is just tops. Anyone who can teach kids all week long and find the energy to do Sunday school each week has to have sainthood written all over her. Grab her up, Darin!"

"Thanks, Grace. You looked stunning on your wedding day, and you can tell that lug I said so. He doesn't deserve you. Listen, I'm running late. I'll see you later." Darin dropped the phone back into its cradle and checked his tie, which hung crooked. He tried to fix the knot quickly, then grabbed his keys.

He dashed out the door, got into his car, and drove the familiar route to Emily's house. Once there, Darin asked God to be with them all evening. He prayed for safety and bonding between the kids and Emily and most of all for a fun time in San Francisco. He felt like he was going to his high school prom. For some reason, Emily felt more important than just a standard date. There was something about her eyes. In them, Darin saw a multitude of emotions, and somehow he felt God was actually pointing to her, saying, "This is the one."

Emily opened the door and looked radiant. Her skin glowed clean and pink. She appeared not a day over twenty-two, and he almost thought he was robbing the cradle. Her dark hair framed her face and highlighted her striking eyes.

Emily Jensen was a sight to behold. Rather than a simple floral dress, she wore a long pantsuit with a fitted jacket that cinched her small waist and strappy heels to match. Although she didn't show an inch of skin, other than her feet, Darin thought she was sexier than any woman he'd ever laid eyes upon.

He took her hand. "You look absolutely gorgeous."

She smiled and tossed his hand away. "My brother used to tell me that. I didn't buy it from him, either." She winked at him and picked up her purse.

He watched her for a moment, not relinquishing his direct gaze. Could she possibly be for real? Didn't she have any idea what her smile could do to a man? Melt him in his tracks, that's what. And leave him a pathetic puddle on the porch. His heart thumped wildly, and he wondered if he would have noticed Emily's quiet beauty before his conversion.

"I don't care if you're buying it or not, Miss Jensen. You are gorgeous! Do you have a coat? It will be cold up there tonight."

Emily laughed. "I grew up in the Bay Area. I know about San Francisco nights. Brrr." She pretended to shiver, then grabbed a coat. Darin took it from her and laid it over his arm, offering her the other one.

"You ready to meet the kids?"

"How many of them are going?"

"Well, eight are signed up. How many actually go depends on how many show up, and that could be none. I've learned not to depend too greatly on the kids."

"None?"

"One thing I've learned about working in EPA is that time means nothing. It's a very arbitrary thing, the clock."

Emily laughed. "You got those boys to church on time yesterday."

"Only because I went to their houses and honked very early in the morning. That bugged their mothers, so they were out in a flash. There's an old saying, if Mama ain't happy, ain't nobody happy. And Mama's sleep after a long week of working two jobs is pretty important."

"You're kidding me. You honked outside the house?"

"Like I said, I've learned a bit in the last year. Today they have to come to me, though. The tickets will be waiting at the door, and they'll give them away to someone else if the boys don't come."

"How did you get the restaurant to donate the meals?"

"I called and asked them. It's criminal that these boys should live so close to Fisherman's Wharf and never have eaten crab or San Franciscan sourdough. I told the manager that, and he agreed. I also told him we'd put an ad in the church bulletin for people who can afford the dinner. They usually say no, but once in a while. . ."

"I can hardly wait! I love crab season. I've been dreaming about it all day."

Once they arrived at the Bayshore House, Darin saw a few kids milling out front. "It looks like a few of them showed up."

Emily squinted to look at the boys. "These are all new kids from yesterday."

"These kids all have grandmothers who make them go to their own church. Bless their hearts. The boys I brought yesterday are on their own most of the time, and their mothers appreciate the break on Sunday mornings. I only invited African-American kids tonight because this play is in a theater that only does performances by black playwrights or plays that represent black history."

"How wonderful that they would think of those less fortunate kids in the audience."

"I think that's part of the reason they do it. Maybe it will inspire one of these kids to write someday, and these kids have had so much tragedy, yet they still have an unbreakable hope at the same time."

Darin got out and opened Emily's door. The boys laughed at him for his chivalry. "Hey, what are you all laughing at? Do you have a date tonight?"

The boys broke into laughter again. "Nah, man, we're white."

Darin pulled out one of his pockets and translated. "White means poor. You only have the whites of your pockets. Emily, meet Reggie, Lonnie, and Sean."

All of the boys went beyond his expectations and shook Emily's hand. She asked each one about their school and took an active interest in their answers. He couldn't hide his pleasure. The exchange made him think he and Emily weren't too far apart. She loved kids. He loved kids. Surely, everything else could be sorted out.

With all the formalities out of the way, Darin looked at the boys. "Are you all that's coming?"

"Yeah. Danny and Rock had football practice, and Damien's grandma wouldn't let him go." At the last information, all three boys broke into laughter. Rules were a comical thing in this town. And someone who adhered to them was absolute hilarity.

"All right then. We don't have to take the van. We can just take my car."

"Yeah! The grandpappy mobile," Reggie said to the amusement of his friends.

"The boys don't think my car is too cool."

"We liked the one he crashed. Not that we ever saw it." Sean crossed his arms. "But five liters of power and all those horses under the hood, and he has to go and total it before he gets here."

"You're lucky I'm here to talk about it. Now get in." Darin winked at Emily as he opened her door. "You don't mind riding in the grandpappy mobile, do you?"

Emily patted his Buick. "I'm a teacher in the San Francisco Bay Area. This is luxury to me. Everyone I know drives a compact of some sort, usually with a dent or two."

Darin thought he'd like to be in a compact tonight, with just the two of them, but his heart was full that she would come out with the boys. His joy felt complete.

Once in the car, the boys quickly commandeered his radio, and current rap tunes blared from the speakers. About halfway to the city, Reggie spoke up.

"Yo, we ain't eatin' none of that crab. Just sose you know."

Emily turned around and spoke for Darin, almost verbatim what he was thinking. "You boys can order a hamburger, but you have to at least try the crab. Otherwise, I'll have to tell the other guys you were too chicken." She shook her head and clicked her tongue. "That's gonna be embarrassing."

Darin could see Reggie's shock in the rearview mirror. "She's tough, huh?"

"Oh, man, that ain't right." Sean crossed his arms in mock disgust.

Once in San Francisco, Darin found parking fairly easily since it was Monday night. As he watched Emily and the boys climb from the car, his stomach twisted. This was how he wanted life to be. A beautiful woman and a ministry he loved. Life didn't get any better than this, and he hoped Emily saw it the same way.

Chapter 7

San Francisco's Fisherman's Wharf brought a certain excitement to Emily no matter how many times she visited. The steady tapping beat of the crab crackers, the caw of gulls, and the sour yeasty smell of French bread mingled to create the perfect outdoor ambiance. The evening was remarkably warm, absent of fog, and both Alcatraz and Angel Island could be seen from shore. The red Golden Gate rose nobly in the background, and although Emily had lived her entire life in the vicinity, she marveled all over again. San Francisco was truly a beautiful city, one of the most beautiful in the world. She breathed in all the sights and sounds, noticing the boys did the same. Even in their "coolness," they were awed. Nature and manmade architecture coexisted magnificently in San Francisco, and Emily wondered if anyone could see it for the first time without a dropped jaw.

Reggie put his hands in his coat. A coat made for a remote winter in Alaska, not a fog-free Indian summer evening in San Francisco. But one never knew with this city. The fog could roll in anytime, and they'd all be freezing as if they were on a polar island. There was something about San Francisco cold that was unlike snow cold; it seeped into your body subtly, not like a biting frosty cold.

"San Francisco is the most beautiful city on earth." Emily finally let her thoughts loose.

Reggie bobbed his head up and down. "It's pretty decent."

Sean scanned the sailboats. "Not bad."

The rigging of the boats clanked joyously, and the salty air filled with colorful sights and sounds. The blue of the bay, the stark contrast of Angel Island, and the pristine white of boats in the harbor—it all delighted Emily's senses just as it had when she'd come with her parents as a child.

"Just being here makes me crave food. I always thought it was the chill of the evenings that made me hungry, but there's something Pavlovian about being here. It makes me want to eat."

Darin laughed and took her hand in his. She shivered at his touch. The boys all seemed to notice the motion but said nothing. Their respect for Darin gleamed obvious as they smiled among themselves.

"I think you're right. It's more palatable without the sea lions here. Their bark takes away some of my appetite." Darin laughed. "Okay, their smell doesn't do much for me, either."

"They'll be back in January. We'd better eat while the season is right." Emily felt like a child in a wonderland. Being out on a Monday night, when she normally would have been correcting papers or working around the clock on lesson plans, overwhelmed her. She felt free.

Alioto's Restaurant had been on Fisherman's Wharf since Emily was a small child, and probably long before. She remembered her own parents forcing gooey clam chowder down her once a year. To this day, she couldn't stand the stuff, but she knew it was a delicacy to most. As the ragtag little group headed to the renowned restaurant, the setting brought warm emotions to the surface of her mind. Happy times—before her brother disappeared, before her mother had become so overwhelming.

"My mom and dad used to take me and my brother here at least once a year."

"Mine, too," Darin said.

"While you all is strolling memory lane, we be hungry," Sean quipped in bad English.

Darin laughed. "Y'all ought to be strolling grammar lane."

"Yeah, yeah," Sean answered. "You date a teacher, and we's supposed to talk like Shakespeare."

Emily bristled at the word usage but couldn't help her laughter, and she tried to put her teacher's voice to use. "Poor grammar makes people think you're stupid. And I've heard enough to know you're not stupid."

"Man, not in the hood it don't. We start talking like you, we get our—" Reggie snapped his mouth shut. "Never mind."

Emily listened to the banter with interest. She'd spent her whole life in the Bay Area, and she'd never known anyone from the "hood," as they called it. With a mixture of fascination and disbelief, she realized tonight was the first time she'd stepped out of her comfort zone and her own upscale city. Even if she was poorer than a church mouse while living there and educating the wealthy kids, she'd never know what it was like to be in the hood. Or so she hoped.

Her gaze traveled to Darin's muscular form, his set jaw. She knew she would be protected this evening. But how realistic was a date like this? And another? And another? Darin had his world, and she had hers. Barricaded and protected was the life she knew how to live. Darin lived his life without training wheels or brakes. She felt herself shiver.

Close to the restaurant, a homeless man shifted on the dock, and Emily jumped and clutched her chest. For a moment, she thought she imagined the movement, but the shifting continued. His clothes were an ashen gray that blended into the salt-worn wood of the building. The man's stench was horrible. His brown beard was covered with bits of food, and Emily felt sick to her stomach. It was hard to tell where his beard ended and his face began, so gray in tone was he.

Reggie approached the man, and Emily nearly pulled him back, but Reggie dwarfed the man. "Yo, man, you okay?" As the man rolled upwards, Reggie pulled back. "Whoa!" His nose twitched.

The man nodded that he was all right and started mumbling to himself. Why weren't people like this in proper facilities? Suddenly Emily felt alone in the bustling area. Everyone walked right past them, and she wondered why they weren't doing the same thing, moving on. Yes, they were Christians, but this man was beyond help—steeped in alcohol and his own world.

"You hungry, man?" Sean asked.

Darin just stood behind, taking it all in and not saying a word. Emily wanted to call the police. She kept her cell phone clutched tightly in her hand in case the man made a move, but she guessed he had some kind of right to be there. It was a public place, but he certainly was doing nothing for her appetite.

"Ch–change?" the man finally stammered. "You got any change?" He sat up when he noticed the group gathering around him, but his position looked precarious—as if he might fall at any moment.

"No, man, no change. You hungry?" Lonnie said.

"Yeah, I need money for food." The homeless man moved like a sea lion, bulky and slow. But when he moved, Emily automatically felt herself stepping backwards on the pier. The boys, however, stepped closer, and Darin still did nothing to stop them. He held up a palm, like he knew she was annoyed, but he wanted to see the scene played out. If they all ended up dead in the bay, she wondered if he'd chalk that up to experience, too. She'd been a teacher for too long to willingly allow kids to enter into danger.

"We ain't got no money, man. We'll get you some food if you's hungry."

The man just nodded slowly in resignation. Without checking with Darin first, Lonnie rushed across the street and dodged into a convenience store. Emily watched the whole thing in disbelief.

"You're just letting him go over there by himself?"

"He's 275 pounds! Who's going to mess with Lonnie?"

"He's a minor child. Alone in the city."

Darin looked at her. Then he looked deeper into her eyes, and the spirit of fire she carried for the moment left her like a torch drenched in water. Darin, though burly and broad in the shoulders, moved with the grace of a dancer. He stepped lightly toward her, his eyes gentle and concerned.

"Emily, you worry too much. Lonnie lives in East Palo Alto. Fisherman's Wharf has nothing on him. It's all right. I promise. I'm not going to let anything happen to the kids."

Emily felt her face flush red. "You're responsible to Lonnie's parents for his well-being tonight."

"I am concerned with his well-being, Emily, but God's ultimately responsible for it. I can't let a man go hungry because of fear." Darin whispered loudly and with enough force that Emily's angst returned with a vengeance. She was not heartless, but who knew what this man hid under his filthy jacket? Darin pulled her aside, away from the two boys, who hovered over the homeless lump.

"Lonnie has a heart as big as the Pacific Ocean. The boys are hungry, they said so themselves, but they cared more about that man getting some dinner because they know they aren't that hungry. So I've got time for that." Darin's tone was that of an angry principal, and Emily felt the hairs on the back of her neck prickle in her defiance. But he continued. "Lonnie has been given nothing in this lifetime and yet still has time for good character. So, yes, I'm responsible to Lonnie's mother, and tonight I'll tell her, if she happens to be home at midnight, that her son is a quality human being. Despite his pathetic upbringing."

Emily wanted to crawl into a discarded crab shell. She felt the sting of tears, the threat of them spilling, but she refused to give way to them. He saw her only as coldhearted and icy, but she just wanted to protect the children. Why didn't Darin see that?

"I'll wait over by the restaurant."

Darin grasped her arm gently. "Emily, I don't want you hanging out in the city by yourself. You're safe with me. I promise." He looked at the boys. "You're all safe with me, and most importantly, you're safe with Jesus." He turned and looked at Emily. "What are you so scared of?"

Afraid of, she wanted to correct him. She was reminded that the beauty of San Francisco was much darker in the company of Darin Black. Her parents had each grasped one of her hands, lifting her in elation as they walked the pier. Now she stood beside a homeless man who obviously hadn't seen a bath in weeks. She waited on a linebacker-sized kid from the hood while he did his good deed, and everyone was just fine with the situation but her. She was not callous. She was cautious.

It wasn't that she didn't have a heart, but they had missions for this. She gave her old coats and blankets every year to the local shelters. That didn't mean she wanted to stand in trembling fear with a crazy man who talked to himself and didn't bathe. She wasn't heartless; she was savvy and level-headed. And right now she wished Darin was the same way.

She pushed a few tendrils of hair over her ears. "I shouldn't have come. I suppose that's what you're thinking right now. I'm sorry if I'm ruining your fun."

Darin grimaced, obviously not wanting to discuss this in front of the boys. He pulled her to the fence that protected them from the water below. "On the contrary. I'm ecstatic you're here with me, but I want you to believe in me, Emily. I wouldn't put you in danger, and I'm not going to let anyone hurt you." The dinging of the sailboats clanged more insistently as a gust of wind blew forth.

Let anyone hurt me. Like thieves come up and ask for permission. As Emily opened her mouth to speak, Lonnie came darting across the street, a small carton of milk and a hot dog foil in his hand. He gave the food to the homeless man.

"Here, man, it's hot. Be careful," Lonnie said as the man devoured half the hot dog in one bite.

He sat up and smiled broadly at the boy. "You thought I'd use the money for drink."

Lonnie nodded. "Yeah, man. You don't smell like you need more drink."

The homeless man laughed, and Emily saw his humanity for the first time. She swallowed hard and turned away, unwilling to face her emotions. Fine, so he was human. She still wished she were inside the restaurant, away from the dark reminders of San Francisco's seedier side.

The man eliminated the rest of the hot dog and nodded. "Thank ya kindly, kid."

"It ain't nothing, man," Lonnie said. "You'd do the same for me if you could."

With that, the three boys headed toward the restaurant, and Emily followed with Darin at her side. He smoothed his shaved head. "Those boys have hearts of gold, huh?"

She pursed her mouth shut for fear of saying what she felt. She'd imagined a night of romantic bliss, not a night in the depths of humanity learning some kind of valuable social lesson. This wasn't *A Christmas Carol.* She wasn't Scrooge.

"You know, Darin, I don't mean to be rude. But I was taught that people like that man back there were dangerous. I was taught it's quite inane to give them anything because they become dependent on handouts. Give a man a fish and all that." She tried to keep her voice down so the boys didn't hear her chastising Darin. "I don't know that you've taught the boys anything of value here. You could have placed them in a dangerous situation."

Darin looked at the boys in front of them, then halted his steps. "Emily, there's about one thousand pounds of us and a homeless man in a heap on the dock. I guess I just fail to see the threat." He blinked, waiting for her answer.

"He could have had a gun," she suggested.

"He could have had a machete and a nine iron, too."

Emily looked away. "Now you're just making fun of me."

Darin brushed the back of his hand along her cheek. "I am not making fun of you, Emily. You're right. I should have taken you on a proper date. I just wanted the boys to meet you, and I guess I got a little ahead of myself." He cupped her hand in his. "For tonight, I ask one thing. That you would trust me for just this evening. I know I'm not your standard fare when it comes to dating. I just can't help myself when I see someone down on their luck. It's like something in me clicks. Two years ago that was me in the gutter, and Fireman Mike rescued me for Jesus. I feel indebted every day and I want to repay." He clasped her hand tighter. "I don't know how to put my gratitude into words, and actions just never seem enough."

"But no one said anything to that man about Jesus."

Darin shook his head. "We *were* Jesus to that man today. That's more important than handing him a tract, Emily."

She had never encountered this in her lifetime in the church, and she squirmed in her uneasiness. She was a good Christian. She lived a good life and set a good example for her students. She left the gutter-gathering to others. Was it so wrong that she hadn't been called to evangelize? She bit back tears.

"A good tract is an important item."

"Not without relationship and prayer. Only God can make a tract come to life."

Emily checked her watch. It was going to be a long night. She wanted to live a bold faith, but it wasn't in her. Looking into Darin's misty green eyes, she didn't think it would ever be. It was just like a young writer aspiring to be the Hemingway of his generation. One only had so much capacity for learning. Part of it had to come from God.

Chapter 8

According to the car's dashboard, it was 11:47 p.m. when Emily arrived home. After they'd dropped the boys in EPA, the ride to her home was nearly silent, and she didn't know how to break it. She wished for something to say, something that might let Darin know she wasn't proud of her actions, but that she'd been frightened, nonetheless. His silence spoke volumes. This evening had been like trying to force a puzzle piece that didn't fit into the puzzle. Darin and she shared a strong attraction, but little else. She didn't share his vibrant outgoing personality, and she certainly didn't share his lack of fear.

Emily supposed she'd sounded callous, judgmental, and unconcerned for her fellow man. She might have felt guilty if she hadn't legitimately panicked. Her thoughts drifted away at the sight of her lighted front porch.

Darin turned off the car and faced her. His handsome face was lit by a lone streetlight, and when he turned toward her, all ambiguity was gone. She wanted to forget the life he led. She wanted to follow Darin into the barrio and learn his ways, but she wasn't that type of person. She wasn't that type of Christian. Couldn't he see that? Some Christians were called to the mission field, and some were called to other pursuits, like children in the public school system.

Darin spoke, his voice forlorn. "I'm sorry, Emily. I really am. I had hopes tonight would be different. I had dreams of dining you over the San Francisco Bay and gazing at the sunset and the Golden Gate Bridge with the kids learning how to treat a woman. I guess I'm not the romantic I imagine."

"But you wouldn't change what happened tonight?" Her tone sounded so angry and clipped. She felt ashamed and almost astonished that she'd chastised him as easily as she did. Like he was one of her students.

"Wouldn't you have done the same thing? That man was hungry," Darin said. She could see his eyes blinking rapidly under the street light. It was obvious he didn't understand her at all.

Emily sat up straight, trying to maintain a sense of decorum. "You know, we're just obviously called to different ministries." Sadness enveloped her as she spoke.

"We both love children," he said.

"But it's different. You work with children I don't understand and teenagers." She crossed her arms, but inside, her heart withered a bit. She sounded remarkably like her mother. A woman who scared most children to the point they'd run from her at church. Would Emily grow old the same way? "I want to work where I'm comfortable."

Darin spoke quietly, reverently, and in a way that commanded attention. "You know, Emily, I run the risk of sounding judgmental here, but God didn't give you a spirit of fear. I don't know what you were so frightened of in San Francisco—that guy was an old man who needed something to eat. He obviously didn't have the strength to pursue us, much less the motive."

"No motive, you say? He's sleeping on the pier, and you think he has no motive to steal? I don't think you're judgmental, Darin. I think you just live in a world that's far too trusting and naive. We're obviously called to different arenas." She shrugged as if none of it mattered, but her heart pounded. The clipped voice continued as if it had a will of its own. "No harm done, I suppose. Thank you for an interesting evening." She started to grasp the door handle but turned back. In her own way, she was hoping Darin would stop her.

Darin clicked on the light in the car. "No, it's not okay. If you never see me again, that's your choice, but you can't live your life for Christ cowering behind the safety of your little created world, Emily. 'There is no fear in love.' " He quoted scripture, which only infuriated her more. Yet, in some strange way, she felt softened. She actually envied Darin's self-assuredness. "You fear because you don't trust God."

Her stomach roiled. "What? I have trusted God my whole life. So my faith isn't bright like a newly lit candle as yours is, but mine burns constant and true. Yours may prove to be a flicker in time." Just as she said it, her hand flew to her mouth. Darin's demeanor sparkled bright with the Holy Spirit. She didn't know where her tears came from, but she started to cry. Guilt mounted, and she had to face the truth, as ugly as it was. She controlled her world. God did not.

"The man was hungry," Darin said again, and this time Emily got it.

She swallowed her tears as if they were an acceptance of something hateful. Something she didn't want to own, yet must. "I didn't help him, and he was hungry," she repeated.

"Whatever you do for the least of these. . ."

"I do for Jesus." How many times had she taught that Sunday school lesson?

And then, as if showing her he forgave her, he added, "I'd like to bring you home for dinner to my parents' house. You're nothing like what they imagine I'd be interested in, and I admit I'm kind of excited to show you off."

"I don't imagine I'm anyone you would be interested in." Emily forced a laugh. She didn't want to put herself through this again. Her world may have been simple, but it was predictable and safe. She could learn to trust God more on her own terms.

"You're wrong there. I know this isn't easy, you and me. But I feel it with everything in my being that we're meant to do something great together." He paused before adding, "Are you busy Thursday night?"

"I have choir practice. For the kids' Christmas musical at church."

"Friday night then? Do you want to have dinner with me again? Or do you think of me as some kind of project?" He looked away when he asked, as if he was nervous for her answer.

Why did he care? It was obvious nothing serious could ever come from this awkward relationship. Why didn't Darin just move on? Like her brother had done, like Mike had done, and like all the men in between.

A crash suddenly broke the silence, and Emily felt shards of glass hit her arm. The passenger window had been broken, and drops of blood trickled down her arm. Darin lit from the car like a rocket, and she saw him chasing a man down her darkened street.

Emily looked to her feet in utter amazement. There was no purse at her ankles, only broken glass everywhere. When her mind stopped reeling, she heard herself call out to Jesus, begging for Darin's safety. She punched her cell phone and dialed 911, but her fingers shook, and she had to dial it three times before getting it right.

It was all so fresh, she could barely tell the operator what had happened.

"There was a man," she gasped.

"Where is the man?" the operator asked.

"Ran down the street. Darin chased him."

"Who's Darin, ma'am?"

"My friend." Emily exhaled deeply. "My purse is gone."

"I need your location, ma'am."

She hadn't even given her address. She did so, then blurted, "When will you be here?"

"We have an officer in the neighborhood. They'll be there soon. Which way did your friend head?"

"North, toward Cuesta Drive."

"Help is on the way. Are you hurt?"

Emily clutched her arm. She had a small cut. "I'm bleeding a little on my arm. Nothing serious."

She lost all sense of self and just wanted to know Darin was safe.

O Lord, bring him back to me.

GET OUT OF THE CAR!

Emily heard the voice as clear as day but had no idea where it came from. She didn't question it. Once out of the vehicle, she looked around, unsure what she should do next. She stood there in her apartment driveway, as if waiting for some miracle voice to tell her what to do, but nothing came. Nothing happened.

In her shortness of breath, Emily started to run in the direction Darin had gone. Soon she had a steady gait going, and she screamed out, "Darin!"

No one answered her.

She screamed again, "Darin, answer me!"

Again, only silence met her shaken voice. At the corner, she saw Darin's coat crumpled in a heap. She swooped to pick it up and stood for a moment, calling his name desperately. He moaned, and she saw him lying on his side.

"Darin!" Emily grasped his shoulders and turned him over. The dim streetlight lit his face, and she saw a gash in his forehead. "Darin, no! What happened?"

"Pipe," he mumbled. He reached to touch his forehead, but Emily grabbed his hand.

"No, don't touch it. Help will be here soon." The wail of sirens pierced through the late night, and she ran into the street to stop the policeman. She waved him down, standing directly in his path. To her relief, the vehicle slowed down.

"Help me! A man is hurt."

The policeman radioed for help and climbed out of the squad car, leaving it running. He bent over Darin's frame, shining a flashlight into those brilliant eyes that first caught her attention. Now the sight of those eyes, under a canopy of pain, wrenched her heart. She could still hear her heart beating, not from her own fear, but for Darin.

If he wasn't okay, she'd never forgive herself. Her cold words came back to haunt her, and she tried to force her own voice away, but the echo kept coming. *He could have had a knife.*

"Is he going to be okay?" Emily heard herself ask the officer.

"Paramedic's on the way. He's got a concussion. Has he been conscious at all since you saw this?"

"He spoke to me. He said the word *pipe*."

"Do you know if he's had a concussion before?"

"I think so. He was in a bad car accident once."

The officer nodded. "How'd this happen?"

Emily pointed behind her. "I live up the street. Darin and I were in the car, and someone broke in for my purse." Her voice trembled in her disbelief. She lived in a solid neighborhood with upstanding people. She'd just come from the inner city. "How could they have known where my purse was? Tell me he's going to be okay."

"Did you have a light on in the car?"

"Yes." Emily shrugged, not understanding the question.

"People on drugs are often attracted to light, like a moth to the flame. Do you know if the assailant hurt himself on the window?"

"I never even saw him until Darin chased him, then he was just a shadow." She let out a small sob.

"Ma'am, you need to calm down. He's been hit hard, but we'll get him help just as soon as we can. It's probably just a simple concussion, and he'll be back with us soon. I'm going to need a statement from you."

Emily shook her head. "No, I'm going to the hospital. I need to be there for Darin. I wouldn't feed the hungry."

The officer looked at her cockeyed but didn't question her babbling. "I'll get you there as soon as I have your statement. Do you want to find the guy who did this?"

"No—I mean, I don't care. I just want Darin to be okay."

The paramedics arrived and went straight for Darin. Emily stood idly wondering what she should do. She wanted to help, but when she stepped forward, the officer held her back. Seeing bold, muscular Darin lying helpless in a crumpled heap on the lawn brought chills to her spine. For her purse, he'd ended up this way. She thought about the twelve dollars in cash she carried and wanted to cry out. For twelve dollars and a few credit cards, someone had done this.

"Ma'am, please. I just need to get a statement from you."

Emily turned toward the officer and nodded. Silently she prayed, undone by the night's irony. She'd survived the San Francisco Embarcadero and Theater District, and the inner city of East Palo Alto, only to be mugged in her own safe-haven neighborhood. Someone had a wicked sense of humor, and she tried to force the thought from her head that it was God.

Emily told the police all she could remember, but it was so very little. All, except the voice that propelled her from the car. She didn't think hearing voices made for a very good witness. She heard Darin moan again, and she felt the sound to the soles of her feet. There is no fear in love. Shockingly, with all she'd witnessed tonight, she felt no fear. She knew with everything in her being that Darin would be fine. With amazing clarity, she realized she trembled from the cold. For once in her life, she wasn't in her comfort zone and she wasn't afraid. Her eyes narrowed at the sight of her pained friend. She felt only anger now. Life wasn't fair, and it really should be.

Chapter 9

Peacefully, Emily sat among the city's transients. She didn't even know Los Altos, home of the rich, had transients, but there they sat—smelling of liquor and in desperate need of clipping shears. She drew in deep breaths and let them out fully, the way she'd been taught at Pilates exercise class. Although she felt peace, she still felt thankful for the metal detector at the door. She feared sharp objects within the vicinity of these men. She focused on watching the cable news show and reading day-old newspapers in the emergency room waiting room.

Emily called Darin's parents, after guessing with the local phone book. Luckily, they were listed. His mother didn't sound pleased to hear from her, but who could blame the woman? It was the middle of the night, and she brought bad news. Hardly the way to ingratiate oneself into the family.

Not long after, an older couple rushed into the waiting room, heading straight for the triage nurse. Emily knew that must be them.

"Someone called us. Our son is here, Darin Black." The woman wore full makeup with dyed black hair and had the same striking green eyes as her son. Smile lines didn't frame her eyes the way they did Darin's. Rather, she had one deep crease in the center of her forehead. Emily got up to greet them.

"Only one of you may go in at a time," the nurse droned.

The mother exhaled. "Why? We're both his parents."

"Because those are the rules." The triage nurse crossed her arms, making it obvious the subject wasn't up for discussion.

"That's fine. We'll wait for his fiancée to get here. She's parking the car, and she'll want to see him.

Emily sat back down, her eyes darting about the room. She knew Darin didn't have a fiancée but couldn't imagine why his mother would make one up. It was the middle of the night. Where would they find an imaginary fiancée? Had Darin lied to her?

"Only family members allowed," the triage nurse repeated. "His fiancée doesn't count without a marriage license. See security when you're ready and decide which of you will go in." With that, the nurse sliced the window shut and went back to her paperwork.

The mother cursed, and Emily winced. Darin's mother was nothing like she imagined. Darin emanated joy, while his mother seemed angry at the world. His father just looked conquered, as if any means to speak up for himself had long since disappeared. His chin hung low, and he sat down in a chair, obviously waiting for his wife to make a decision for them both.

"I'll go in first," Mrs. Black stated.

Mr. Black acquiesced with a nod of his head.

Emily went toward the couple. "Excuse me, I'm Emily Jensen. I was with Darin tonight when he was hit. I mean, I was with him in the car before he chased the man."

Mrs. Black looked Emily up and down. She felt the scrutinizing glare and squared her shoulders against the laser-sharp stare. "What was he doing with you?"

"We went to the city tonight with some of his kids from East Palo Alto."

"This happened in the ghetto? I should have known." Mrs. Black couldn't hide her disgust at the mention of EPA. Her face puckered like a prune. With shame, Emily thought she and Mrs. Black weren't as far apart as she would have hoped.

"No, actually it happened on my street. In Los Altos."

"Los Altos? You must be kidding me. You're the one who called then?"

Emily nodded.

"Who are you?"

"I'm Emily Jensen," she repeated. "I teach first grade in Los Altos. I met your son at a wedding in our church."

Mrs. Black sighed loudly. "My son is not the type to go to church, missy. Whatever he told you, it's temporary. He's always into one phase or another, and right now I'm afraid he's into the tortured sinner role." She lowered her voice. "His future bride will be here any minute, and I don't think she'll like finding you here. But I do appreciate your phone call and concern. That was very sweet of you." She paused before adding with a smile, "Very Christian of you." Then she motioned with her hand for Emily to leave. "Thank you again."

Emily stumbled over her words, but confidence filled her. "Mrs. Black, your son is not engaged." She said the words gently, hoping that she was not offending. Mrs. Black had enough on her mind, but Emily hated to see Darin's reputation tainted by his mother's beliefs. "I feel quite sure our pastor would know about it if Darin were betrothed, and he was the one who set us up. I don't want anything from your son, ma'am, and I really want to stay until he's out. I feel responsible since he was at my home."

Mrs. Black's eyebrows shot up. *Oh, that didn't sound good! It implied something definitely not good,* Emily thought.

"My son is lying in there on a hospital bed, and I can guarantee you who he'll want to see when he wakes up. Darin and Angel have a long history together, dear, and I know you wouldn't want to stand in the way of that. Please just do him a favor and leave, being the good Christian girl I know you are."

For a moment Emily's legs gave way, and she turned toward the door before turning around again. "I beg your pardon, Mrs. Black, I didn't mean to be disrespectful, I only meant—" She stopped. What good would it do to argue with an upset mother? "I'll be leaving. Please be sure and let Darin know I was here and that I'll call him tomorrow."

"Of course we will." The way she said it in staccato implied a curse word.

She nodded at Mrs. Black, for Mr. Black never said a thing. He watched the television as if it had a laser beam pointed directly at him. As Emily was exiting, a young woman was entering. The woman demanded attention. Even in the middle of the night, she wore full makeup and her hair shone in dark silky waves. The contrast between her olive skin and red lipstick lit her complexion as though she were on stage. Even the drunks looked up.

"Angel!" Mrs. Black gripped the young woman's hands in her own, and Emily faltered. Angel, as she was called, looked like someone from a lingerie catalog. Her small frame was graced with long legs and a tiny waist. There was a synthetic appearance to Angel, and Emily felt weak. She stood in the electronic doorway, causing the doors to partially close, then open again.

"Can you step out of the door, please?" the triage nurse yelled from her guillotine window. The Blacks and Angel all turned toward her. Emily, against her better judgment, stepped back into the waiting room.

With all eyes upon her, she stepped forward and thrust out her hand to the gorgeous brunette. "Hello there. I'm Emily Jensen. I was with Darin tonight when he was hurt."

Angel stammered and didn't hold out a hand. Emily dropped her own and shrugged to let Angel know she wasn't intimidated. But of course she was. Angel possessed the kind of beauty that rendered men speechless, and she couldn't help but compare herself. She tried to remember Darin's words about fear. Being intimidated was not allowing God to work within her.

"Why was Darin with you?" Angel's eyes held contempt. She let her slender fingers trace down her long hair.

"We were up in San Francisco tonight with some of the kids he works with."

Angel's eyes lingered on Emily's comparatively shapeless figure, and subconsciously Emily crossed her hands over her waist, suddenly sure that Darin and she were futile. Darin garnered the kind of attention that frightened Emily. He possessed an invisible charm that emanated from him like a high beam, while she was the exact opposite: the mousy teacher who people tended to forget in the corner.

Out of the corner of her eye, Emily saw the triage nurse smile coyly and cock her head sweetly. She saw why almost immediately. Darin's broad frame stood by the triage door; he smiled and thanked her for the prompt attention. She giggled and bit her lip. Darin's face was pale, but his eyes shone with vitality.

"What kids?" Mrs. Black asked Emily since she didn't see Darin.

"From my ministry." Darin winked at Emily. He came toward her and put his arms around her.

"Darin," she breathed. "You're all right."

Darin closed his grasp around her. "They just wanted to observe me. Make sure I didn't have a complex concussion. I was ripe for one after my accident last year. Did you know once you get one, you're more likely to get another?" Darin looked at his family over Emily's shoulder. "If I'd known I'd get all this attention, I might have done worse to myself. It's kind of like attending my own funeral. Do you all want to say something nice about me now? I'll wait."

Mrs. Black came forward and pulled Darin toward her. She roughly moved his chin. "Let me see your eyes."

"Well, I still can't drive tonight if that's what you're worried about. Emily will take me home. My car's at her place, although the window's broken out."

"Angel came to drive you home," Mrs. Black said with authority. Emily could feel her fingers starting to tingle. Darin had all the charm in the world, but this was clearly a bad situation. He had a concussion and was expected to make a choice in the middle of the night. A choice that would clearly have reverberating results. Silently, she prayed that she could handle whatever his choice was.

"Angel, thank you." Darin reached for Angel's hand and shook it, never relinquishing his grip from Emily's waist. "It really was nice of you to think of me."

Angel looked as if she might catch fire. Her ample chest heaved, and her teeth remained clenched. She smiled through them tightly. "It was your mother who thought of you. I was asleep in the middle of fantastic dreams when she called. I thought with our history I owed you a visit."

"You'd better get your rest. Aren't your cheerleading tryouts coming up?"

A tinge of jealousy shot through Emily. If the game of chess had cheerleaders, she still wouldn't be qualified. With her small stature and conservative clothes, she looked more like Angel's mother. Certainly not her rival. She squeezed Darin's hand tighter for support. He turned his eyes to hers, and she swallowed at the strength in their gaze. He wore a bandage on his right temple, but it did nothing to diminish his good looks. It only made him appear more masculine.

"Darin, you can stop your games now. We all know a relationship with the schoolmarm isn't going to last." Angel looked down at Emily. "I'm sorry, honey, but he's not your type. Darin likes the wild side of life." She tossed her head back and laughed. "Do you remember when you drove us to Nevada on your Harley?" And to Emily, "This religious thing will pass, and you'll have an untamable stallion on your hands. I'm doing you both a favor. Darin can come home with me."

Emily saw Darin's jaw twitch, but he laughed lightly. "No one needed more grace than me, Emily. Angel can attest to that fact. So can my mother. But you know where my heart is now."

Emily forgot their audience. "I needed more grace than I ever knew. I found that out tonight on the pier. At least you knew it. I was living in ignorant bliss as a Pharisee."

"A what?" The corner of Angel's mouth lifted. "You two want to speak English here? For those of us not up on the current religion-speak of the day."

Darin kept his eyes glued to Emily but spoke to Angel, " 'For it is by grace you have been saved, through faith—and this not from yourselves, it is the gift of God—not by works so that no one can boast.' "

"Whatever," Angel said, putting up a palm in front of them. "Darin, when you're ready to come back to the real world, call me." She looked at Mrs. Black. "He's a freak now. When he's away from the moonies, call me."

"Son!" Mrs. Black said as Angel walked out the door. "Don't do this. You're not going to marry that little wallflower."

Emily felt the first sting of tears.

Darin's eyes thinned. "I'll marry whomever I please. Considering that Emily and I haven't completed our first date alone yet—"

"Look at her!" Mrs. Black motioned toward Angel's departing frame. "She's the most beautiful girl you've ever dated. She's sweet, and I can teach her to cook. You've only got so much time. Soon every man who sees her on national television will want her, and you can't exactly compete with a professional football player."

Darin reached down and kissed his mother. "I'm not trying to compete with a football player. I'll call you first thing in the morning, Mom."

"Should you sleep after your concussion?"

"The doctor said I'm fine. Dad, Mom, thank you for coming all the way down here."

Mr. Black grunted. Mrs. Black pulled Darin from Emily's side. "This is serious."

"There's more to beauty than the outside, Mom." Darin whispered the words, but they were like a dagger to Emily's soul.

He didn't think she was beautiful on the outside, and her insides felt ripped apart.

～

Emily grew quiet, and her swirling thoughts blossomed into full-fledged emotions. She didn't look like Angel. While she was comfortable with that fact, she wasn't comfortable with being thought beautiful only on the inside. Yes, the Bible may have called for that in Proverbs 31, but she'd read Song of Solomon, too, and she wanted the man she admired to desire her physically. It wasn't that she wanted to look like Angel, a woman who gave herself freely to anyone who would look;

she wanted Darin to understand that just because she didn't flaunt her figure did not mean she didn't have one.

"What's the matter, Emily? You haven't said anything since we left the hospital, and we're almost home." Darin pressed his hand to the bandage on his forehead.

"Nothing." Emily clamped her mouth tight in a straight line.

"I hope my mother didn't say anything to upset you."

"Nope."

"Angel?"

"Nope."

"Then what it is, Emily? Am I just too much trouble for you? I bet you've never had to work this hard a day in your life, huh?" He forced a laugh.

No, actually she hadn't had to work this hard. Dealing with Darin was like dealing with a foreign student in her classroom. She knew there was so much he was capable of, but they spoke different languages. God wouldn't make romance this difficult. Would He? Their evening date had stretched into the wee hours of the morning, and neither of them needed more drama right now.

"You've given me a lot to think about. Living in fear is not living at all."

"Wow, you got all that tonight?"

Emily nodded. "You would have been proud of me if you'd seen how I handled myself." *When your mother came on the scene.*

"I am proud of you. You came out with me on a Monday night, and look, I stretched it into Tuesday and you're still here. I'm impressed by that."

"Your mother wants you to marry that girl."

Darin laughed. "I bet your mother wants you to marry someone, too. Is it going to happen?"

Emily felt her stomach flutter. "The man my mother wanted? He got married to Grace on Friday, so it's not going to happen. Alas, I think her hopes for grandchildren are quickly dwindling."

Darin grabbed her hand and squeezed. She felt an electric pulse shoot down to her toes. "I certainly hope not. You'll make beautiful babies, Emily."

Chapter 10

The week passed like molasses, and Emily hadn't heard from Darin. Not a phone call. Not a note. Nothing. Countless times she'd picked up the phone to call him, only to have her mother's voice ring in her ear. "Good girls do not call men." So she'd place the phone back into its cradle and correct more papers or create another lesson plan. At this rate, she'd be ready for school in January.

She tried to think the best. She figured Darin was busy with his move, and she tried not to worry that the blow to his head had erased her from his mind. Even calling him to check on his head felt pushy, so she avoided it. Tomorrow was Sunday, and she was certain she'd see him at church. Then she could put her fears to rest. She climbed into bed and prayed to God that if He were to take Darin from her life forever, He would also take away any desires she had for a family.

Although she'd known Darin such a short time, she could already picture him as a father. What a good father he'd be. She'd also seen the possibility of her wearing white down an aisle—although her mother and his would heartily protest. Maybe that was part of the romance of it all. The forbidden love affair. She hoped that's all it was, because it was humiliating to wait for the absent phone call.

Once at church, Emily kept one eye on her Sunday school curriculum and one eye on the doorway, hoping Darin would bring the boys from EPA back to church. But service ended, and there was no sign of Darin or the boys. Despondent, she put her things into a bag and headed toward her car. Stepping out of the sanctuary, she saw Angel. Her stomach knotted. Was she here with Darin? *Please, God, no.*

Emily forced her chin to the sky and tried to walk right past Angel, who was much better covered than the last time they'd met. Her conservative shirt showed off her pretty facial features, and Emily couldn't help but wonder why Angel would force everyone's eyes toward her chest by dressing suggestively. Seeing the pain in Angel's eyes, she walked up to her.

"Hi, Angel."

"Darin's not here?" She blinked back tears.

Emily felt her knotted stomach clench tighter. "I haven't seen him this morning. Was he supposed to meet you?"

"No," Angel answered quietly. "I had just hoped to find him here. I don't know where he lives now that he's moved into the ghetto. I didn't want to call his mother. She gets so excited that we're getting back together. I figured you'd know where he was. Actually, I figured he'd be here."

"Did you try calling him?" She couldn't help the hope in her voice. She wanted to know desperately if everything were okay. Ugh. She wished her mother had told her sometimes it was okay to call men. She might not be living this turmoil if she'd known there was a time to break the rules, but rule breaking was just not in her character. And no matter how many times she'd pressed the buttons, she couldn't bring herself to push the final number.

Angel continued. "Yes, I called him. His old roommate doesn't know the new number. He asked for mine to give it to Darin when he called, but I just didn't trust him enough to give it to him. Darin knows my number."

Emily forced herself to breathe. "I haven't heard from him since that night in the hospital, so I'm afraid I can't help you." She felt so broken, admitting that Darin hadn't called her. Standing next to this striking brunette, Emily was ready to get herself to a nunnery—though she wasn't Catholic and she didn't exactly know what nuns did. She was chaste and loved the Lord, and she was never getting married. So she probably qualified for the nunnery—except for the Catholic part.

Angel looked truly worried. Her dark brown eyes glistened, and she wiped her reddened nose. "So you don't know where he is, either? Or you don't want to tell me?"

Emily smiled. "I don't know where he is." She wanted to feel for Angel, this lost ship looking so desperately for an anchor, but she felt her own pain too deeply, her own loss of Darin's whereabouts too keenly. Jealousy was an ugly emotion, an ungodly emotion, but she felt it just the same.

"I didn't make it as a Raiderette." Angel sniffed. "I don't know why I feel the need to tell Darin about the failure, but I do. So if you know where he is, I wish you'd tell me."

"I'm sorry." Emily's voice sounded cool, though she hadn't meant it to. What did one say to a woman who didn't make the professional cheerleading team? If Angel wanted to compare failures, Emily had been to three weddings in the last two years for men she'd once dated. That probably qualified in the loser hall of fame. "But God must have different plans for you, Angel. Better plans."

The woman's hard expression melted but returned almost as quickly as it disappeared. "Look, I know Darin is seeing you, and I'm sorry, but I can't help but feel you don't have the right to him. Darin and I were meant to be together. I knew that the day I met him, long before he got into this religious thing. Whenever something happens, good or bad, we call each other." She stopped and licked her lips. "There's some comfort in him that I just don't believe he'll ever have with someone else. So, excuse my rudeness, but I feel you're in our way, and I think you should just do the Christian thing and bow out gracefully."

Bow out. Emily didn't know she'd ever bowed in. "It might be the Holy Spirit," she said. "The Holy Spirit is a very attractive presence. Have you always felt this way about Darin? Or just in the last two years?"

"Are you crazy?" Angel's full red lips parted in disbelief. "I've seen him during these last two years. What does that tell you?"

"That you two should either get back together or not see one another. We've got more in common than you want to admit. I think we've both been enamored with Darin's natural charm and his fiery presence of the Holy Spirit."

"Whatever."

"Clearly, something else is more important than either one of us. I haven't heard from him this week, either." Emily shrugged her shoulders, trying to feel camaraderie with this pinup model.

"Do you have a point, or are you just messing with my mind?"

"My brother, Kyle, was like Darin. He had friends galore and girls calling at all hours of the night, and I really knew Kyle. I never saw him do a thing to really encourage the girls, except talk with his natural charm. But still they followed like he was the Pied Piper himself. Maybe we're both following Darin the same way."

"We?" Angel laughed.

"Yes, I say we. I'm not immune to him." Emily crossed her arms around her Bible. "And he's not immune to me, either, Angel. I may not be as beautiful as you, but Darin and I share a strong connection."

Angel's chin quivered, but she didn't answer.

"I can tell you one thing," Emily continued. "Darin knows the Lord, and he won't marry someone who doesn't." She offered one of the church student Bibles that were available for taking to Angel. "Start in the book of John."

Angel kept her hands tightly clenched. "You know, it's just like you Christians to talk in code. I have no idea what that means, to 'know the Lord,' and quite frankly it creeps me out. I came here to find Darin, not to get some pious speech from some freak. Darin will marry me. Just as soon as he gets away from people like you. You all remind me of those aliens in *Toy Story* who worshiped The Claw."

Emily winced at Angel's harsh words. She closed her eyes and prayed for peace, trying to see Angel for the hurt child she was within, but the taunts of her own childhood haunted her. While the other girls had cool jeans and stylish haircuts, Emily wore long dresses and had stringy hair. She was a freak, and the words still cut like a knife.

Pastor Fredericks emerged from the church, and Emily saw her escape.

"Pastor!" she called. "I'd like you to meet Angel. She's a friend of Darin Black's and is looking for him. Maybe you could help her." *I certainly can't.*

Angel looked like a trapped animal, but she smiled and held out a hand. Obviously, Darin's pastor might have some answers, and she wasn't willing to risk rudeness with a man of the cloth.

"Excuse me," Emily said. "It was nice to see you again, Angel."

This was one rejection she hadn't been prepared for. Darin had pursued her; Darin had asked her out. He'd actually said she would make cute babies—and now where was he? Long gone, like all the other men in her life. Only this one had left without a trace.

"Emily!" Grace waved at her from across the courtyard. The mere sight of Grace forced tears, as she was just another reminder that Emily had run another one off.

"Hi," Emily said, emotionless.

"What's the matter?"

"I'm short, among other things."

"What?" Grace's brow furrowed. Emily couldn't help but wonder what it was like to go through life looking like Grace. Or Angel. Emily was the kind of woman you walked right on by. She didn't grab attention or make men do double takes. She just was. Emily sighed.

"Emily, did you hear me?" Grace's voice jolted her.

"Do you see the leggy brunette over there? She's looking for Darin." *Just like you came looking for Mike.*

"I see her. So?" Grace shrugged.

"So it's time for a change, I think. I'll start with churches. I've been going to this one my whole life, and I'm quickly becoming known as a black widow, the kind of woman who swallows up men in her evil lair and spits them out a mere shell of themselves."

Grace's eyes twinkled. "You're kidding me, right? You do not possibly believe you have any such reputation. Everyone loves you here. You can't just leave because of what a few nasty people think. No one who knows you thinks anything like that. Darin called Mike, and he sounded very excited about you two seeing each other. You don't know that this woman means anything to him. You and Darin are still dating, right?"

Emily looked over toward Angel. "Not anymore apparently. I suppose I'll be attending his wedding next."

Grace was silent for a moment. "I'm sorry, Emily. I'm sorry things happened the way they did with Mike. I never meant to get in between you and him."

Emily shook her head, annoyed that she couldn't keep her negativity to herself.

"No, Grace. I didn't mean it that way. You know I didn't mean it that way. God made you two for each other. I'm not thinking I got left behind, trust me.

I'm just feeling sorry for myself today, a bit self-conscious. You were just the closest victim. I mean friend." She smiled slightly.

"I don't think you should be thinking about any major changes because of Darin. There is a place for you at this church, regardless of what happens with him."

The words of comfort didn't really register. She was like a broken record that her parents played when she was small, stuck in the same annoying groove. The only way to fix that was to knock the needle past the difficult spot, and that's what Emily felt she needed to do.

"My parents are up in Oregon. They've been trying to get me to move. I'm thinking now I might go. I could get a new job, a cute little place of my own—I could afford it up there, you know."

"You're going to change everything because of Darin?"

Emily laughed. "No, not because of Darin, just because I'm questioning what kind of person I have become. Do you see Angel over there? Well, Grace, she is at the exact same point you were when you met Mike. She doesn't know Jesus, doesn't seem to want to, and I can't see her broken heart. I don't like her because she's so hateful, but how would I expect her to act? I haven't learned the lesson, and I think I need to get over this wall before I'll ever be worthy of living for God. I know I'm redeemed, but I want to live that way. I saw you as a dangerous viper, a single mother who made an unforgivable mistake. I was totally wrong about you. I'm not the judge and jury, and yet I keep thinking that about other people."

"I think you're being hard on yourself, Emily. You were one of the first people to welcome me into this church. I'll admit you were cold when I started, but you were the first one to warm up to me, really. The first one to understand Josh was more than just a youthful mistake."

"I want to start again. I want to be a better Christian, a bolder Christian, and I don't know how to do that here. Looking at you is just a reminder of my failure."

"I'm shocked! I really feel you were responsible for changing Josh's heart—which eventually changed mine."

Emily blinked rapidly. "Really?"

"Ask Mike if you don't believe me. Emily, you were vital in Josh's life. You told him about God when you could have been fired for doing so. If you hadn't planted the seeds for Josh, you wouldn't have planted them for me, either. Don't ever deny God's power in you."

Emily pulled her hair into a makeshift ponytail, blinking back tears.

"Angel over there is a beautiful woman, but she's not half the woman you are. Not even close," Grace said.

"You know, I've heard that my whole life. You're a sweet girl, Emily. You're such a doll, Emily. What would the kids do without you, Emily? But I'm selfish underneath it all. Just once I want to hear I love you, Emily—and the man is there for me one week after he says it. Just once I want him to stick around, not walk off with someone who looks like you, Grace."

Grace had tears in her eyes. "The right man won't walk off. I promise you. And God will never leave you." She looked over at Angel. "She's very beautiful, but her heart is not. I can tell that from the scowl she wears. Look, Emily, there's Darin now. He didn't abandon you."

Emily's head snapped up, and she saw Darin walking toward her. His expression changed when he noticed Angel standing beside Pastor Fredericks. Whomever he chose was his choice. She swallowed hard and waited. He hesitated, standing on the curb for a moment before offering a warm smile and a nod to Emily. His long legs then strode purposefully toward Angel.

She tried to smile at Grace. "I guess we have our answer, don't we?"

"Don't think that. We don't know what is going on, Emily. It's unusual for Angel to be here. I'm sure Darin's just concerned."

"Excuse me." Emily jogged toward her car and climbed inside before her tears fell freely.

Chapter 11

Darin looked at Emily, and the knot in his stomach tightened. He could see the pain in her eyes. He wanted to run and gather her into an embrace. But then he saw Angel. Angel talking to a pastor. It was a sight he never thought he'd see, and his feet stood planted. He hesitated only a moment before he walked toward Angel and Pastor Fredericks. From the corner of his sight, he saw Emily run, but he had to rely on God to fix that. *Father, please be with her.*

"Angel, is everything okay?"

"Darin!" She burrowed herself into Darin's chest. He unwittingly wrapped his arms around her and questioned Pastor Fredericks with his expression.

"What happened?"

"Your friend Angel was just telling me she didn't get a job she was counting on," Pastor Fredericks said. "We were talking about God's will and disappointments."

"You didn't make the cheerleading team."

Angel shook her head and sniffled. Her dark brown eyes were rimmed with red, and her nose had a touch of pink at the tip. She'd clearly been crying heavily for some time.

"Do you want to get some lunch and talk about it?" Darin asked.

Angel sniffled again and nodded.

"Darin, can I speak with you first?" Pastor Fredericks said, his forehead wrinkled.

"Sure. Angel, here are my keys. I'll meet you in my car. It's right over there." Darin watched her walk away defeated, and his heart pained him. "What is it, Pastor?"

Pastor Fredericks rubbed his chin thoughtfully. "I wanted to warn you about 'missionary dating' and how that applies to Angel."

"I beg your pardon?" Darin had heard the term, but he hardly saw how it applied to them.

"A beautiful woman in trouble is a temptation that I'd be very cautious about, Darin. Angel is a nice girl, and I understand your friendship goes back a ways, but don't let her neediness translate into the fact that only you can help her. Pray for her."

"I'm not thinking I'm the only person." He stood a bit taller. He didn't like where this conversation was headed. He wasn't some mealy-mouthed wimp who couldn't handle talking to an ex-girlfriend. What was Pastor thinking? That Darin would be so overcome with lust he couldn't control himself? The notion angered him. He had a responsibility to share Christ with her.

As if Pastor read Darin's mind, he continued. "Maybe you should think about asking God to raise someone else up for Angel. Sometimes in our attempts to do God's will, we end up buckling under the pressure of the outside world."

"Pastor, I appreciate your concern, but I'm not sure you understand about Angel and me. We have a long history together, and I'm not interested in her that way."

"I just watched Emily Jensen run from here, and she looked upset to me. You can't straddle this fence, Darin. You've got to make a choice. Women don't like to share. Remember Rachel and Leah?"

"I'm not going to make a choice between Angel's salvation and dating Emily, if that's what you're saying. Emily will understand; she has a heart for people. You worry too much, Pastor." Darin winked. "I wouldn't do anything to hurt Emily."

Pastor Fredericks crossed his arms. "I'm not worried about Emily being hurt so much as I am about you getting in too deep. Emily has a lot of friends, and she can handle whatever comes her way. She won't wither away into a shell; that's not what I'm saying."

Darin shook his head. "I've been friends with Angel for two years. I'm not going to just abandon her when she's hurting and I've got an opening for the gospel."

"I'm not asking you to abandon her. I'm just asking you to be accountable. Being alone with a woman in that condition is a warning sign. That's all I'm saying."

Darin started to laugh again but saw that Pastor Fredericks was dead serious. He wasn't interested in Angel that way, and without his mother there prodding things along, he felt completely safe.

"Don't look at Angel as a project for faith, but as a woman God loves and will search for."

Emily's car exited the parking lot, and Darin hated the choices set before him. He knew that Pastor meant well, but he was obviously overreacting. Angel needed him right now, and what kind of Christian would he be if he just walked away?

"Thanks for the advice. Angel is waiting. I'll pray on it tonight."

Pastor lifted his brows. "I'd pray on it before I got to the car if I were you." Nodding his head, he turned his attention to another congregation member and left Darin alone.

Rather than praying, Darin mumbled all the way to the car about Emily.

What was going on? Didn't she understand how rare it was for Angel to show up at a church? Couldn't Emily see the blatant cry for help?

"Women!" Darin grumbled. "There's just no making them happy." He got to his car and saw that Angel had shed her conservative sweater. He swallowed hard at the sight of the tight pink T-shirt that hugged her curves and forced his eyes away.

"What took you so long?" she asked in a voice completely free of melancholy.

"Pastor had something to discuss with me." He cleared his throat. "You know, Angel, why don't we go talk with Pastor right now?"

Her tears started again. "I don't want to talk about my failures with a man I never met before. I came to my friend." The way she emphasized *friend* made his skin crawl, and suddenly he wished he'd heeded his pastor's advice.

"Angel, look. I don't want to hurt you, and I need you to know that God cares for you more than you can possibly imagine. But I can't make this hurt go away. I can't make things any better for you."

"No, you won't make it better. There was a time when you cared for me, and now that you're religious and I'm not, you are just abandoning me."

"That's not true, Angel. I'm here, aren't I?"

"Only in body. Not in spirit." She moved closer to him. "But if that's all you're willing to part with."

Darin backed away and hit his head on the window. "Ouch!" He rubbed his head, feeling like a child running from a scary stranger. "Angel, you're just trying to tick me off, and it isn't going to work."

"Then why don't you go find Miss Goody Two-Shoes? Clearly, she's all you can handle anyway."

Darin's heart caught in his throat. What was he doing? Angel didn't want anything to do with the Lord. She wanted to find a way into Darin's mind, and this was her way. The only way she knew. He looked at her with sympathy but knew he was not the man who could make a difference in her life. He was only endangering his. But a real man proved himself with self-control.

"Angel, you're right. I'm not enough man for you. I suggest you find one, preferably with the name of Jesus. I'll meet with you and Pastor Fredericks anytime. But I won't meet with you alone again. I'm going to find Emily and salvage what we have left. I love her, Angel. Nothing you do or say will change that. She's the one I want."

Angel let out a string of curses. "It's not enough that I have to lose my cheerleading status? You pick today to tell me we're through? You are coldhearted, Darin Black. Coldhearted. God has done nothing for you. You've only become more selfish and more heartless. You think only of yourself. As always."

Darin stared at her pert nose and angry eyes. "I'm sorry you feel that way. If you'll excuse me, my girlfriend is waiting for me."

"You wish she was. I saw her peel out of the parking lot. I may not have you, but you don't have her, either." She crossed her arms, and Darin could see she had no intention of getting out. He grabbed his keys and left the car without another word.

Outside the church, he saw Mike Kingston, the fireman who'd saved his life. "Mike!"

"Hey, Darin. What are you up to?"

"I need a ride to Emily's. Can you give me one?"

Grace came up beside her husband. "I don't think Emily wants to see you right now."

"You talked to her?" Darin asked.

"You walked over to your ex instead of Emily. Bad move. It's been a week since you've called her. I'd say you're in a bit of a pickle, Darin. We women do not like coming in second with a man we're interested in. Worse yet, to come in second to another woman, that's lethal."

"If that ain't the truth," Mike added, shaking his head.

Darin felt as though he was getting everything he deserved. "I didn't call her because I did that drunk-driving speech this week, and I didn't want her to have to explain to her colleagues that she knew me."

Grace gave him a look of disgust. "Why don't you let Emily make that choice? She's a big girl, and she doesn't need you deciding what's best for her."

Mike laughed. "You've heard about a woman scorned? What you haven't heard is how they stick together."

"I'm a terrible boyfriend. I admit that. This morning I had planned to make everything up to her, but one of my kids had a fire in his grandmother's house last week. I had to make sure everything was settled with them."

Mike kept shaking his head. "Darin. Darin. You have great excuses, but I can tell you from experience, they are all useless with a woman."

Grace slapped her husband on the shoulder. "We women just want to know what's going on. Emily just assumed you weren't seeing each other anymore. Lack of communication is deadly, you know."

"She said she didn't think we were seeing each other anymore?"

"It's been a week, Darin. What is she supposed to think?"

"We'll give you a ride, but then you're on your own. Don't say we didn't warn you." Mike laughed.

"Where's Josh?" Darin asked.

"He's with his grandparents this weekend. Come on." Mike led the way to his truck, and they all piled into the front seat. The ride to Emily's was quiet. All the way there, Darin rehearsed what he'd say to the woman he loved.

At Emily's house, he felt confident enough to wave Mike and Grace off. The last thing he needed was an audience for his groveling session. He rang the doorbell and waited. There was no answer. Sighing, he sat at the edge of her porch and waited for her return. *Mental note: Do not teach inner city boys about romance. It is not my gift.*

He watched each car pass expectantly and glanced at his watch. He'd wait one hour, and if she hadn't shown up yet, perhaps it wasn't meant to be. He kept thinking about Emily. About her enthusiastic smile that turned to a frown when he walked over to Angel. What could he have been thinking? Maybe he had more head injury than he gave himself credit for. As he mentally beat himself up, Emily pulled into the driveway. She got out of her car and looked at Darin. Then she walked around to the trunk and pulled out a few grocery bags.

It was worse than he thought. She felt like a stranger to him now.

Chapter 12

Emily blinked several times. Someone was sitting on her small porch. A big someone who resembled Darin, but she knew better. Darin was with Angel now. Still, her stomach flip-flopped at the possibility. She'd hoped Darin would be different. That he would tell her the truth rather than let her find out the hard way. The way she'd found out her brother was gone. Hope sprang eternal, but Emily thought of her pastor's words about mental illness: to do the same thing twice and expect a different result. What did three or four times make her? How she wished Kyle were still around to translate man-speak for her. Squaring her shoulders, she pledged that she was done playing the welcome mat and prayed for strength.

I will not fall victim to my feelings. I will not fall victim to my feelings. I will be strong.

It was high time Emily started spending more time with God rather than constantly looking for a man. That was a wasted effort. If God wanted her to be married, He could just have the guy knock on her door and sweep her away. Since that wasn't likely to happen, she unloaded her groceries from the trunk.

"Hi," Darin said, his voice tentative. He took the groceries from her. She nodded at him and unlocked her front door.

"So it is you. How's Angel?" she asked, unable to help herself.

"She's upset," Darin said, as though Emily really cared. It was hard to be overly concerned for the other woman. No matter how godly one was.

"Good, so am I. Thanks for asking."

"Emily."

She took the groceries back from him and put them down inside the foyer, then turned toward him. "Darin, I never asked to get involved with you. You were the one who kept asking me out. If you weren't over Angel, you shouldn't have strung me along."

With annoyance, she realized a tear had fallen. Darin wiped it away with his thumb.

Clearly, he hadn't expected her to stand up for herself. Doormat Emily never did, after all. He could just ask Mike Kingston if he didn't believe it for himself. But those days were over. She was far too old to be every man's buddy. If she ever hoped to be taken seriously as a woman, she needed to stop wasting her time with men who wanted a companion at baseball games. She needed to trust in God, not herself.

"I wasn't stringing you along." Darin's jaw set. "Angel lost out to the other women for cheerleader. She was upset."

"Well, then, that changes everything. Look, lest you think I'm jealous or envious or any of those things that bring out the green-eyed monster—maybe I am, but that's not all I am. I'm just sick of being taken for granted by men. I thought we had something between us. At least enough where you would give me the common courtesy of letting me know if you were really with her. I know that's what your family wants."

"Angel—"

"Angel had nothing to do with why you didn't call me all week when you said you would."

"No, she didn't."

Emily felt the first sting of tears in her nose. For someone who never had a serious boyfriend, her batting average with men was horrible. She supposed dashed expectations were to blame. It served her right for having any. Relying on people would get you nowhere; that's what her brother always said. Only God, Kyle used to say. That was an easy thing to say, but not easy to live. Relationships were a vital part of living.

"Emily, are you willing to hear why I didn't call you?"

Was she?

"I don't know. Is it going to hurt me? Because if it is, I think I'd rather remain blissfully ignorant for now."

He put his arm around her and led her to the sofa. "Do you remember Lonnie? The kid we took to San Francisco?"

"Of course I do. Big as a house with a heart to match." She grinned, thinking about the boy.

"That's him. Did you read about the arson fire in EPA in the paper? That was his grandmother's house. Lonnie's cousin suffered smoke inhalation and has been in Stanford Children's Hospital all week. I've been staying with Lonnie and his cousins so his grandmother could be at the hospital. I wanted to call you, but every time I did, someone needed me for something. And I figured that's why God called me there, so that was my priority at the time." He shook his head. "Looking at your face today, I don't know that it was the right choice."

He touched her face with his palm, and she saw the honesty in his eyes.

"How is Lonnie's cousin?"

"He's fine now. It was touch and go for the first couple of days." Darin shook his head again. "Emily, I'm terrible at this. I'm trying to court you the way a good Christian man should court a woman, but I'm at a loss. You're not like any of the women I've dated before."

"I've noticed."

"Angel doesn't mean anything to me. It's just that I can't stand to abandon someone who is so obviously looking for faith."

"Is she looking for faith, Darin? If she is, that's God's job. Not yours."

Darin raked his fingers through his hair. "No, she's not looking for faith. At least not yet. Pastor told me the same thing, that it was God's job, not mine. But I admit I'm struggling with the idea. What if no one else comes along? What if her time comes, and she doesn't get it? As it is, she's a death sentence waiting to happen."

It was a good question. What, indeed? She wondered if God weren't preparing a special ministry for her. Bringing women to God so her old boyfriends could marry them. Now there was a harsh thought. At the same time, the eternal life of a soul was so much more important than her pride. Or her marriage dreams.

"I'll talk with her. Do you want me to talk to her?" Emily asked.

"I would if you don't mind." Darin got up from the sofa. "Let me help you put these groceries away."

Emily watched him stride toward the kitchen carrying the brown bags as if they were cotton balls. He embraced a humility she didn't understand.

He came back into the living room, and Emily's heart clenched. He was so good-looking, inside and out, and her feelings toward him were like nothing she'd ever felt for any other man. There was an invisible attachment to him, a chain that held her heart and told her Darin was a gift from God. But how could he be? Everything about him was wrong. He lived in the ghetto. His parents hated her. Her parents would hate him! He wore an earring. Was it really worth going on? God didn't want her to bring all these differences to a marriage. Marriage was hard enough, wasn't it?

"Are you going to help me with the groceries?" His eyebrows rose. "Or are you going to make me do it myself as penance?"

Emily laughed. "I should make you do it. It's quite attractive to watch a man work in the kitchen. Go ahead."

He walked toward her and picked her up as easily as one of the grocery bags. "I'll give you working in the kitchen." The two of them collapsed on the couch in a flurry of laughter. And then Emily's smile died as Darin's eyes met her own. "I'm through playing around, Emily. I took you for granted because I thought you knew my heart. I won't make that mistake again. Grace read me the riot act."

His expression moved her heart. She loved this man. How could that be true so quickly? But she knew. "You haven't even kissed me."

431

"I can change that." Darin grasped her chin gently and pulled her toward him. They melted into a soft kiss, and Emily couldn't imagine ever kissing another man.

The doorbell broke the moment. They separated like two teenagers caught in a high school hallway.

"The door," Emily said.

Darin broke into laughter. "It is the door."

"I'm stating the obvious."

"You are." He pushed her up from the couch. "You should get the door."

She nodded and headed toward the door, but all she wanted to do was find her way back into Darin's arms. She smiled at Darin, searching his green eyes and forgetting what she was doing.

"The door," he reminded her.

"Oh, right." She opened the door, and her mouth dropped. "Mom! Dad!" Emily looked back at Darin, and all she could focus on was his shaved head. His earring.

Nancy Jensen stepped into the duplex while Emily's father waited on the stoop. "You've got a man here?"

Emily exhaled, trying to contain her own emotions of guilt. "Mom, Dad, this is Darin." Her dad, wearing his Sunday toupee, finally stepped into the foyer and stared at Darin—and his earring.

"I warned you we might drop in for a surprise visit," her mother said. "We didn't see you at church today."

"I was teaching, Mother. You know I teach on the second and third Sundays of the month."

"Emily, may I see you in the kitchen a moment?" Her mother stalked into the kitchen, and her long nervous fingers began fiddling with the coffeepot.

Emily ground some coffee beans, the whirring sound drowning out her mother's admonitions. When she finished, she poured the grounds into the coffeepot.

"Mom, before you say anything else, I like Darin. Please don't ruin this."

"I don't understand what you mean. Maybe this is your own guilt for having a man in your apartment. On a Sunday, no less. Besides, is there something to ruin? I thought you weren't seeing anyone."

"Mom, he's my friend. I've known him a short time, and we're not getting married at this point. Okay?"

"I heard he lives in the ghetto."

"As a lay minister, Mom."

"And that he's a gardener."

"A landscape artist. I told you so myself," Emily corrected. "He designs gardens."

"And a garbage man beautifies the neighborhood, too. Emily, you're a teacher. How do you expect to raise a family on a gardener's salary?"

"I guess the same way Jesus expected to find His food in the desert. I'm going to trust God that if Darin is the man for me, He will provide."

Silence. Ah, that beautiful sound when her mother was stopped cold in her harsh words.

Something about her not even giving Darin a chance infuriated Emily. She could feel the flame in her cheeks. Emily clenched her teeth to speak.

"Mom, Darin is a godly man. Please don't ruin this for me."

"You keep saying that. What am I ruining if there's nothing going on between you?"

"When you dated Dad, were you willing to announce your engagement in the first week? Or did you want to get to know him a bit before that?"

Her mother's mouth pursed. "I don't remember. I do know, however, that my parents approved."

"I am thirty-two years old! I'm old enough to approve my own boyfriends."

"I just heard from Lois that he brings all these hoodlums to church. That he wears an earring. And I see he doesn't respect his hair, just as I thought."

Emily felt the first prick of tears. Is this what she would become? It was how she treated Grace when Mike first brought her to church, like a throwaway person because she didn't act right, look right.

"Kyle didn't look right, either, Mom, and I never met someone who loved the Lord like my brother."

"Your brother couldn't play by the rules!" Nancy Jensen sniffed.

"Whose rules?"

The question hung between them as Darin entered the room. He smiled at her mother, and his natural charm forced a smile to Emily's face.

"Mrs. Jensen, it is so nice to meet you. You have raised a fabulous daughter. My compliments." Darin helped fill the creamer with milk. He'd obviously seen Emily's hands trembling, and when he was finished, he stilled her tremor by holding her hands.

"Where did you grow up, young man?"

"Right here in town."

"I heard you're a friend of Fireman Mike's." The small creases at her mother's eyes deepened. She was like a hawk looking for prey.

Emily felt her heart pound against her chest wall. Would Darin explain how he met Mike? Would her mother chase him away, too?

Chapter 13

Darin eyed Mrs. Jensen curiously. She was a strange woman, nothing like her daughter. Where Emily embraced fears and doubts, Mrs. Jensen appeared undaunted and on the offensive. Her eyes were fierce like a wolf's, and she had a spindly frame. To watch mother and daughter side by side, there was no obvious connection, nothing to show a bond or apparent love. Maybe he'd envied Emily's upbringing erroneously.

He cast a glance toward Emily, who was wide-eyed with fear that he would tell his drunk-driving story or, worse yet, his gutter-surviving testimony. She needn't have worried. If Darin had learned anything from his old life, it was when to staple his mouth. Too much information was sometimes the death knell in a conversation, and he had no desire to end this dialogue.

"Yes, I'm a friend of Fireman Mike's." He lifted his voice with enthusiasm. After all, who couldn't love Mike Kingston? "I met him on the job two years ago. And I owe him big thanks because I met your daughter at his wedding." Darin winked at Emily, and her shoulders visibly relaxed.

Mr. Jensen lumbered into the kitchen. Although large in stature, he kowtowed to his wife, but mostly avoided her. Still, Darin could see that Mr. Jensen had limits.

Emily's dad embraced his daughter, squeezing her with a growl. "We've missed you. You'd hate it there. All it does is rain." He pulled away and looked Darin straight in the eye. "What do you say we all go out to dinner?"

"Only if you let me treat. It isn't every day I get to meet my girlfriend's parents when they live so far away."

"Girlfriend?" Mrs. Jensen tapped her toe against the worn linoleum. "Emily, is this true? I thought you were only friends."

Open mouth, insert foot.

"No, Mother, we're not just friends. He's my boyfriend," Emily said. "To put it in his terms, he's courting me."

Darin stifled a smile at Emily's enjoyment of standing up to her mother. It was obvious that people didn't stand up to Nancy Jensen often. Most likely, it wasn't worth the battle in most instances.

"You're dating a gardener then," she said.

Without thinking, Darin stepped back. There was something both comical and sad about Mrs. Jensen's statement, all at once. Of the many things to disapprove of—his living in the ghetto, his drunk-driving history, even his earring—the vocation surprised him. Granted, he wasn't a Stanford MBA like so many in the Valley, but he made a good living and he had time to enjoy life. The time to mentor troubled youths when most men couldn't break free of their cell phones and constant meetings. As far as he was concerned, he led a pretty good life.

"A gardener who's in love with your daughter," Darin said, almost surprising himself.

Emily shook her head, silently urging him to avoid any confrontation.

Mr. Jensen laughed heartily, his big belly jiggling. "Well, that's the way to tell her. A gardener who's in love with my daughter." He nodded his head in approval. "How do you feel about that, Emily?"

Emily's eyes popped like two lightbulbs. "Um. . ."

Mr. Jensen laughed again. "He loves my daughter and he's paying for dinner. Darin is my kind of man." He slapped Darin on the back.

Nancy Jensen remained stiff. The wall between mother and daughter stood firm. Darin wished he could take Emily into his arms and rescue her from such fear. Now he knew why she possessed it. Everything she did was under the studied gaze of Mrs. Jensen.

"Let's go, then," he said loudly. "Mr. Jensen, since you're our aficionado, you can choose the restaurant."

"Since you're paying, I think we should do prime rib."

"Dad!" Emily squealed.

"I'm kidding, darling. Don't worry. I won't break his wallet before you do." Mr. Jensen's white hair highlighted his steely blue eyes. Every time the man opened his mouth, Darin wondered how he had remained so cheery after a lifetime of living with his wife. The woman emanated no joy at all, but she no doubt knew her Bible inside and out. *The modern-day Pharisee,* he thought.

"McDonald's is taking orders, Mr. Jensen. Do you want a Big Mac or a double cheeseburger?" Darin winked.

"Is that all you can afford?" Mrs. Jensen asked.

"Mom! He just told you he makes good money, and he lives in the ghetto, so costs are low."

"What? You think it's comical that you live in the ghetto? I don't understand you, young man. God would want you to be financially prepared before taking a wife."

Darin watched Emily's countenance falter. They hadn't discussed marriage—not even love. After all, they'd only known each other a week, but Darin felt this was how it must have been during WWII, when you found a bride and knew it. People today wasted too much time in his opinion. God had provided clarity.

Darin hadn't wanted to scare her off, of course, but he knew just as sure as he stood there that Emily was his wife-to-be. He knew the moment he laid eyes on her at Mike's wedding.

Mrs. Jensen was still mumbling something when Emily spoke again. "Mom, Darin is offering us dinner, not a lifetime." She winked at him.

He looked into her eyes and knew instinctively what her heart was saying, that she was apologizing for her mother. Emily wasn't coldhearted like some people at their church believed. She was stifled. She longed to break free of the emotions that bound her. Darin could feel it.

"I hate to be the voice of reason here," Mrs. Jensen said. "But we're a family, and I think our dinner should be reserved for family tonight. Mr. Black, should you hope to become family, I would expect you to respect our time. We've been traveling for two days now, and we'd like to have dinner with our daughter."

The linoleum was spinning. Darin would have respected Mrs. Jensen's wishes if he could not see Mr. Jensen and Emily struggling to protest. It was obvious the two of them would rather leave her behind, not him. The thought forced a nervous chuckle. Would he respect his potential mother-in-law or show his masculinity by standing up to her? It felt like a no-win situation. He prayed for God to show him the right direction.

"Mom, Darin and I get together now on Sunday evenings, and I didn't know you were coming," Emily said. "Besides, he's paying, so I know Dad wants him along."

Mr. Jensen put his arm around Emily. "That's my little girl. Always watching out for her daddy's pocketbook."

The three of them laughed, but Mrs. Jensen remained stoic. Darin's heart plunged at the sight of her. The woman had forfeited her son; what else would she lose in her unhappiness? He vowed then and there to pray for her every day.

Darin hesitated about going to dinner with the family. It was clear Mrs. Jensen didn't want him to attend, but he thought if he gave in to the woman now, he'd never be able to stand up to her. He wanted to respect her, but he also needed to protect Emily. That was his priority. She wanted him to come, and that was all that mattered to him at the moment. Chances were he would never win over Mrs. Jensen.

"Are we ready?" Mr. Jensen asked, a bright smile on his face.

"We are. I know a great place."

Emily's face contorted, and he stifled a laugh. "Don't worry, Emily, it's not my breakfast hole in the wall." He leaned over and whispered in her ear, "I can be classy, too."

Visible relief washed over her expression, and he delighted in her joy.

The odd threesome made their way out the door with Mrs. Jensen following behind. One thing Darin knew without question: Emily and her father would pay for their betrayal.

"Mrs. Jensen, is there something you feel like eating for dinner? I have a great restaurant in mind, but it's a steak place. Do you like steak?"

She kept her lips pursed, the angry wrinkles showing themselves easily.

"Steak would be great, don't you think, Dad?" Emily said.

"Any man that would buy me a steak is a good man. Earring and all." Mr. Jensen winked at his daughter.

While her expression spoke volumes, Mrs. Jensen remained quiet.

~

Sundance Steakhouse's neon lights lit up the afternoon sky. The bright blue and white western sky matched Darin's mood—joyous and filled with hope. They were seated right away, and Mrs. Jensen plopped down next to Emily, hoping to discourage him.

"What did you do before you retired, Mr. Jensen?" he asked.

"I sold insurance. I loved it, but it's not the same business nowadays. A man would rather buy a big-screen TV and DVD player than see to his family's long-term care. In my day, a man provided for his family."

"I don't own a TV," Darin said. "Nothing worth watching, I'm afraid."

"Not even football?"

"I'd rather be out playing. The guys and I can get a pick-up basketball game any day of the week. I want to do that while I'm young enough to enjoy it."

"You should take up golf. You can do that forever."

"I'm afraid golf is out of my price range." Darin laughed, but Mrs. Jensen coughed. He supposed he couldn't blame the woman. Who wanted a son-in-law who relied upon God to see to financial needs? One who risked losing his job every time he took a morning off to speak on drunk driving. He wished he could express how much he felt God's call to marry Emily. It was odd: There were so many chasms separating them, the least of which was their difference in education and backgrounds, but Darin was willing to fight for her. Mrs. Jensen may have set her jaw against him, but she had no idea the sheer amount of prayer power she was up against.

"I'm still a member of the club here. Let me take you out sometime this week," Mr. Jensen said.

"Mel, I don't think a beginner on the course is exactly what they expect at the country club," said Darin.

"Who cares what they expect? I've kept up my membership. I can bring anyone I care to. I just want to see if the boy likes the game."

"He just told you he can't afford to play it, so what does it matter?"

"Nancy, stay out of it," Mr. Jensen warned.

"What are you having, Mom?"

"I'm not hungry."

"So a salad, then?"

"Mel, I want to go home." It was a challenge, not a request, and Mr. Jensen squared his shoulders.

"Well, we're having dinner with our daughter." He turned back toward Darin. "So you think you can get a morning off this week?"

"Sure I can," Darin replied happily. "Who knows? Maybe I'm the next Tiger Woods. Mrs. Jensen, do you play?"

Again, rather than answer, Emily's mother just threw him a glance, as though he were a mere buzzing noise.

Emily excused herself to wash her hands, and Mr. Jensen decided to follow her lead. Mrs. Jensen looked like a hawk going in for the kill. She was obviously anxious to speak to him alone, and he shifted in his seat waiting for the on-slaught. Sure enough, as soon as father and daughter were out of sight, Mrs. Jensen spoke.

"It's very charming that you find my daughter so attractive. But she's not for you. She's been a good girl her whole life, and she deserves a man who's done the same for himself. I don't mean to be rude, but she's better than the likes of you. Do you understand that?"

"I don't mean to be disrespectful, Mrs. Jensen, but Emily's husband is God's choice. Not yours. I believe I'm that man and hope that someday Emily and you will see things that way as well."

"Over my dead body, you are."

Darin sat back in his chair. That statement made things abundantly clear. *Lord, make me sure of this. Because I feel certain Emily is who You have for my wife, and from the sound of things, it's going to be an uphill battle.*

Chapter 14

E mily changed the sheets on her bed so her parents could sleep comfortably in her room. She had already made up the sofa for herself. Her mother hovered, leaning against the doorjamb in the bedroom. Emily tried to ignore the piercing eyes and especially avoid the subject of Darin. Everything was happening so fast. He'd said he was in love with her. In love with her! They barely knew one another, and yet she couldn't help but think the feelings were reciprocal.

"You need to tuck the corners," her mother chided.

"Sorry, Mom, I forgot you liked it that way. I don't like to be stuck under the sheets at night. I feel like I'm in a straitjacket." Emily tucked the sheets, making the corners so tight a marine would be proud.

"You should do it for yourself. Someday a husband won't want to get into a sloppily made bed like that."

"With the right lingerie, I imagine he would."

"Emily Jensen, what a foul mouth!"

Emily bit her lip. "I'm sorry, Mother. I was just making a joke."

"Are you sleeping with that man?"

"Absolutely not! Mother, it was a joke. I just don't think most people care about a perfectly made bed like you do. Kyle never did." She stopped breathing. Had she really mentioned her long-lost brother's name? His name had been forbidden for years, but she suddenly felt empowered, and she searched her mother's face for a reaction.

Mrs. Jensen gasped and fell back onto the bed, her hand over her heart. "Where did we go wrong, Emily?"

"Oh, Mother, spare me the dramatics. I've seen that act before. It's amazing you never do it where a sofa or bed isn't there to catch you."

"We've told you not to mention your brother. He was dead to us when he joined that cult."

"He did not join a cult, Mother. He went into the mission field. You're the one who told him not to contact you if he made the choice. You left Kyle no options, and he was just doing what he was supposed to do."

"Kyle disrespected his parents' wishes. The Bible says to honor your mother and father."

"That doesn't mean doing whatever they say as an adult, Mom. Kyle was listening to a call from God. He wanted to share the Word with the people of the South American jungles. The Great Commission, Mother. Leave and cleave and all that."

"We supported plenty of missionaries in our day. There was no reason for a boy with his education and skills to go jaunting off into a third-world country. It's the same with that boy of yours. He could get himself an education and find a nice job, but he'd rather be traipsing about in the ghetto, talking to kids who don't listen to him. Dodging bullets all the while. Not getting a real job. You think I'm cruel, Emily." Her mother got up from the bed and helped finish with the bedspread. "But you mark my words, you were created for better than this. You'll be miserable if you marry that gardener."

Emily lowered herself slowly onto the bed. A revelation of sorts fell upon her. "Mother, are you happy?" The truth was, she had never met a more miserable person than her mother. "Are you?"

"Of course I am. I'm very well respected in the church. When I told Pastor something, he always listened. I have the gift of administration. You'd be wise to listen to me on matters of the heart such as this. It's not just an emotional decision. You must live with the consequences for the rest of your life."

"You never gave Kyle a choice in his consequences." Emily focused on a painting above her bed. "Will you give me one?" The phone rang. "I'm going to get that. Dad's watching the news. He'll be in later. Sleep tight, Mother."

"Tell your father not to keep you up too late. You've got work tomorrow." The phone continued to ring. "Who is calling you so late?"

Emily grabbed the portable phone. "I'm about to find out. Good night, Mother." Running from the room, she picked up the phone. "Hello."

"Hi," Darin's smooth baritone answered.

She felt a blush rise into her cheeks. "Hi, yourself." She shut herself in the utility room for some privacy. The blaring television set made it difficult to hear, but when she slid the door shut, quiet prevailed. "Did you survive dinner with my parents?"

"I did, and I plan to invite myself over later in the week, too. They're staying until Saturday, you know."

Emily scrunched up her nose. "No, I didn't hear that. Thanks for being the bearer of bad news. Rosencrantz and Gildenstern have a run for their money," she quipped, referring to Hamlet's messengers.

"Am I supposed to understand that? I know the difference between a dahlia and a tulip, you know. That's my area of expertise." Darin laughed. "So, as I was saying, I'm coming over sometime this week."

"You might just have to eat my cooking then."

"Is that a bad thing?"

"Depends on who you ask. It's not a great thing, that's for certain." She giggled. What a strange sound to hear. She couldn't remember the last time she really laughed, and her laughter was genuine, not a flirtatious act of cuteness, but real and heartfelt. "I make a mean pot roast and can boil up an excellent hot dog. If you're looking for a soufflé, you might want to head elsewhere."

"Pot roast and hot dogs? Well, what else does one need? We can throw some cabbage in the water, and voilà, dinner! Better a meal of vegetables with love than a fattened calf with hatred."

"Like tonight's steak dinner with my mother, you mean?"

"Your mother just wants what's best for you, Emily. You do deserve a man who can afford to golf if he wants. Your father was talking to me about the insurance business."

"Don't you dare!" she exclaimed.

Darin chuckled. "Don't worry, I could barely even get car insurance to drive with my history. Selling life insurance seems unwarranted to me at this point. I prefer the only kind of insurance that pays in full in every circumstance: the gospel."

"Promise me one thing."

"What's that?"

"If our relationship goes anywhere, we won't live within one hundred miles of my mother." Emily said it jokingly, but in her heart she meant every word.

"But your dad was just telling me the house next to them is for sale."

"You are not funny." She slid down the wall onto the floor of the utility room and sighed dreamily. "I miss you already."

"Right back atcha, babe. I have an idea," Darin said.

"What's that?"

"Let's introduce our mothers to one another and see who does a better job of thwarting this relationship faster. Mine or yours."

"I think there's little question in that. Are you really going golfing with my father?"

"Wouldn't miss it."

"This, from the same man who used to bungee jump? You're going to play a sport where the biggest excitement is a sand wedge shot?"

"Hey, I'm looking forward to wearing some plaid pants and white shoes. Jack Nicklaus is my hero."

"Tiger Woods wears Nike now. Why are you doing this?"

"Because I've met this incredible woman, and I will do whatever I have to. I want her father to know that I will care for his daughter, and my history is just that—my history."

"I don't think it's my father you have to convince. I think it's our mothers."

"So you agree that there's something more here than just friendship."

Emily paused. "I do."

"Now those are words I'm longing to hear. I know I'm coming on fast and furious. I don't mean to scare you, but—"

"Are you still planning to live in East Palo Alto? The former murder capital of the United States?"

"Now come on, that's not fair. EPA has a very small population, and it was a per capita figure. It's not a murder capital anymore."

"That makes all the difference in the world to me, Darin."

"Emily, dive in. The water's great. There are so many real dangers. Why worry about the fake ones?"

Her heart fluttered. How she wanted to dive in, to just seize what she most desired. What she most desired was an outlandish missionary she'd met a mere week ago. But loving him meant giving up all the security she'd known. And suffering her mother's wrath, not to mention his mother's. Was she strong enough to take the risk?

"Real and imagined dangers are a matter of perception."

"Need I remind you my head still throbs from being in your lovely Los Altos neighborhood?"

"Touché."

"There you go speaking in a different language again," Darin said. "Please speak slowly. And in English."

"You think you are so funny, Darin Black. Did you not get into Cal Poly's five-year architecture program?"

"Long enough to drop out. Yes, ma'am, that was me."

"But you know who Rosencrantz is. You did not pass Advanced English in high school without Shakespeare."

"I know who he is," Darin admitted. "But would you like me if I didn't?"

"Maybe even more so," Emily said. "So how's Tuesday night for dinner here?"

"Perfect. You're sure you don't want me to ask my parents?"

"Quite sure. One mother is enough for any dinner party."

"On a more serious note, would you pray for Angel? I'm going to have Pastor call her, and I've vowed to stay away, but don't write her off yet. God is speaking to her."

"Like God spoke to Grace? And my then-boyfriend married her? Like that?"

"Absolutely nothing like that. Just pray she finds God before she finds her next boyfriend. It's like a fix to her, having someone hanging on her arm."

Emily shifted uncomfortably. She wanted to have mercy on Angel, but hearing Darin talk so lovingly about the woman instilled a small seed of fear in her. She'd been in this position before. And it felt too close for comfort.

"See you Tuesday."

"Uh-huh," Emily answered absently. "See you then." Against her better judgment, she prayed with fervor for Angel.

Chapter 15

Darin splashed water on his face. Lonnie and some of the kids were over watching television, and the constant noise of the wrestling match was beginning to grate on him. It was after eleven, and he yawned with exhaustion. With the fire last week at Lonnie's grandma's house and his own head injury, his calendar had been filled up with emergencies. His laundry stood piled high in the closet, and roommates Pete and Travis worked overtime to unpack Darin's belongings while he selfishly went out to dinner with Emily's parents.

Moving to East Palo Alto became a full-time job in itself. The kids longed for stability and often hung out in the home all hours of the evening. Pete and Travis set hours, but enforcing them often fell to Darin, who was the only one awake late at night. Apparently, his roommates had learned to sleep through everything. Darin dried off his face and headed into the small living room with its secondhand furniture donated by the church.

"Hey, guys, it's time for us to hit the hay. I'm turning into a pumpkin now. Your grandmother's light is still on, Sean," Darin said while looking out the window.

"Dawg, you need to live a little. Going to bed at eleven like my toddler cousin," Lonnie joked.

The three boys laughed, and Darin joined in their friendly banter.

"Dawg, you need to turn in that homework you did tonight, and your slothful self isn't going to want to leave your bed in the morning. Bedtime is being responsible, lounging until ten, pathetic. Unless you're planning to work in a nightclub for a living."

"Hmmm," Sean said, as though thinking about it.

Darin and his roommates had two rules in their ministry home. It was open nearly every night of the week, but closed, unless there was an emergency, at 11:00 p.m. And there was no entrance until homework was produced and finished. Most of the boys had become A students just by doing the work given to them at school. Success bred success, because now it had become a way of life thanks to Pete and Travis's rules.

"You just want to get to bed early because you have a girlfriend," Sean said. The boys whistled. "Man, you ain't never gonna get married."

"I'm not?" Darin crossed his arms, anxious to hear their reasoning.

"Nah. What woman is gonna live in this dump?" The three boys broke into laughter.

"Hey!" Darin said. "This is a nice place. And Emily and I can get our own place. Do you really think my wife is going to want roommates and kids who eat her out of house and home?"

The boys laughed while crunching on a bag of chips.

"The schoolteacher is coming to the hood!" Lonnie clapped his hands in laughter.

Darin wiggled his eyebrows. "Maybe she is coming, and maybe she's given to tutoring slang English until midnight."

"Dude, we're outta here. We're outta here," Lonnie said. He gave Darin a high five and left. Darin watched the threesome until they entered the home next door. Then he peeked out again, just to make sure they stayed there. At that moment, he collapsed onto the couch and praised God. His life echoed rejoicing in every corner now. He loved gardening and being in the sun all day. He loved coming home to the boys and pick-up basketball, and he loved that Miss Emily Jensen had seen fit to date him. It was as though he were floating above everything that might harm him now. His mother, Emily's mother, their protests meant nothing to him now. God would work it out; Darin had no doubts. She was the woman for him.

Someone knocked at the door, and Darin checked the clock on the wall. It read 11:15. Looking out the peephole, he saw Angel standing there. He quickly opened the door.

"Angel, what on earth are you doing out at this time of night?" He pulled her in. This was the time of night people shot off guns for fun. It was no time to be out alone in a strange city.

Her eyes were red and puffy, and she wore no makeup. "I'm pregnant."

The words hit him with the force of a train. Bile rose in Darin's throat. "Come sit down, Angel." He led her to the sofa and helped her into her seat. This wasn't an act; she trembled, and her expression held true anxiety.

"Does the father know yet?"

She looked away. "He's a professional football player. He's going to think I set him up. He'll give me some money and want me to go away."

Darin paused for a moment. "Did you set him up?"

"No! I should have known you'd ask that. You preaching—"

"Look, I'm not trying to be cruel, but it's a fair question. You haven't mentioned any boyfriend, and you show up on my doorstep pregnant."

"It doesn't matter whose it is because I'm getting rid of it."

"It? You're calling your unborn child it? Angel, that's not like you. You always wanted to be a mother."

"Not now I don't. What am I supposed to do, settle down with a baby and give up my cheerleading career? Just because I didn't make the Raiderettes doesn't mean I won't get there next year, or even with the Sabercats in San Jose."

Darin's stomach lurched. Surely, no woman was bad enough to sacrifice a child for a job in cheerleading. He just couldn't believe it, and he didn't know how long he stood there with his mouth hanging open. He'd known Angel a long time. He'd seen countless scenarios where her selfishness surprised him. But even this was beneath her. This was something he wouldn't have expected.

"Angel, please. Promise me you won't do anything rash. This is something that's going to take a lot of thought and prayer."

She rose from her seat and sat in his lap. "This is why I came here," she purred.

Darin tried to wiggle free. He was really worried about Angel now.

"There is one condition under which I will keep this baby."

"What?" he asked, his heart hammering in his chest.

"Marry me, and we raise it as our own."

He pushed her off his legs. "I think you should leave."

"That's just what I thought. You're not willing to put your money where your mouth is on this God thing. You're the same hypocrite you always were."

"Me? Why on earth would you want to marry me if you think I'm such bad news, Angel? You come over here, attack me, tell me you'll kill a child if I won't marry you, then tell me I'm not worthy of being a husband. I don't get it."

"This is hard for me to say, but deep down I think you're the only man for me. I know if you'd search your heart, you'd think that, too. Yes, we have our issues, any couple does, but you would care for another man's baby as if it were your own. You know me, Darin. I can't do this alone, and that schoolmarm won't ever make you happy."

"Is everything all right?" Pete stuck his head out his bedroom door.

"Everything's fine," Angel snapped.

Seeing her and knowing her history with Darin, Pete didn't disappear into his room again. He went into the kitchen and noisily started to make a sandwich.

Angel exhaled a tornado-worthy sigh. "I can see we're going to be chaperoned. So I'll just leave you with this decision. How far are you willing to go for this so-called faith of yours, Darin?"

"This doesn't make any sense to me, Angel. Why would you want to marry someone who didn't want to marry you?"

"I don't want to marry someone who doesn't want to marry me. I just don't believe that's true. You loved me once, and even with all this goody-goody business going on in your heart, you will love me again." She stood and tried to kiss him on the lips. He dodged the motion and accepted her kiss on the cheek. "I'll be in touch."

"This is blackmail," he said.

"Your mother and I know the true you resides in there somewhere, Darin. We'll get him back. If it's the last thing we do."

Darin watched her safely to her car and came back into the house where Pete was waiting. Pete's lanky frame bent over a huge submarine sandwich he'd just created. "You want half?" he asked.

"Sure."

They sat together at the table.

"I didn't just hear what I thought I heard," Pete said.

"Angel's pregnant with some football player's baby. She wants to marry me to keep the child."

"Are you sure she's really pregnant?"

"How could I be? She's troubled, Pete. Deeply troubled. She thinks I can solve all her problems, but I can't begin to solve her problems. But if there is a baby, how could I live with myself if I knew I could stop her from. . ." He didn't want to think about it. Nor could he bring himself to say the word.

"When God calls you to ministry full-time, things happen," Pete said. "When I first came here to live, my fiancé wouldn't come with me. She loved the Lord, but she said she just wasn't called here, so I must not be the man for her. That day broke my heart, Darin, but I couldn't break God's. He wanted me here."

"I'm sorry."

"Following God always has a cost. Sometimes it feels too high, but it never is."

"I'm commanded not to marry an unbeliever, but if it costs a life—" Darin shook his head. "God doesn't give that one away in the Bible."

"Hosea married the prostitute."

"You're a big help, Pete, thanks a lot."

"It will cost you either way. Did you think about Emily in all this?"

"I haven't thought about anything. It's just too fresh, too unbelievable. I wonder if my mother knows anything about this."

"Wouldn't surprise me if Angel told your mother it was your baby," Pete said with his mouth full of sandwich.

Darin let his head fall to the table. "I hadn't thought of that," he mumbled. "I was planning to buy an engagement ring soon for Emily. I thought my life was finally falling into place, that I finally understood."

Pete stopped chewing. "You can't marry Angel, Darin. This is a temptation, and I don't believe temptation is sent by God. He can handle it. We just have to pray. In the meantime, you need to let Emily know what's going on. Before she finds out from someone else. Namely, Angel or your mother."

Darin downed the last of his sandwich. "Because that's just what Emily needs. Another reason to dump me." He got up to get a glass of milk.

Pete stood to his feet. "Angel knows you're working with the boys on responsible parenting, trying to keep them out of adult situations. She'll use this against you, Darin. You need to come clean right away and let people know this isn't your baby. A life of ministry is always rough to begin with. I think it's a testing period."

Darin slammed a hand on the table. "She's not going to win."

"Don't think of it as her; think of it as the enemy. And God is much more powerful."

Darin skulked to his bedroom. In two years of being a Christian, he'd never felt this low. *Lord, help me. I don't know where to turn.*

Chapter 16

Emily's mother prepared a gigantic breakfast before work, but the thought of food in the morning nauseated Emily. She'd never been a morning person, preferring food at ten, not six when she woke up. That time was reserved for coffee. She ate as much as she could stomach before making excuses to leave. She'd stop at the coffee shop on her way to school and purchase a tall latte.

At three dollars a pop, such java luxuries weren't everyday occurrences on her teacher's salary, but today, with her mother's constant nagging about Darin, it felt like an investment worth making for the mere escape. If she had any doubts about Darin and her future, her mother's incessant complaints against him made her feelings even stronger. Hearing her mother's fears expressed only made Emily realize that she loved Darin, despite the obvious differences between them.

For example, he was a gardener. There was such a purity about the fact that Darin worked with his hands, that he'd given up chasing the corporate dream like so many of the fathers she knew. Some of these men had forfeited their families for the opportunity to be a corporate vice president, while Darin made the kids of EPA his priority. Kids he hadn't even fathered. Her mother kept rehashing that Darin couldn't afford to play the game of golf. Well, then Darin also couldn't afford to spend every Saturday away from his family like her own father had always done. Emily hoped she'd be the kind of wife that Darin didn't want to avoid. Bitter memories boiled up. Did her father avoid their home, and thus her mother? She prayed she would never be that kind of wife.

"Bye, Dad, I'll see you this afternoon. Mom, thanks for the breakfast. It was terrific."

"You didn't eat a thing, Emily. Don't you teach your kids at school about a healthy breakfast? It's the most important meal of the day, they say."

"Sure I teach them. I just don't practice what I preach in that case." She giggled. "If I eat in the morning, I'm hungry all day." *But a latte, now that's a different matter altogether.*

"Leave her alone, Nancy. She's not a child," her dad said. "We're going to the beach today, Emily. Do you want to meet us over there for dinner? We can eat at the Chart House, your favorite."

"Oh, Dad, I'd love to, but I really need to catch up on lesson plans. I've been so social this weekend. I haven't finished my plans for the week. You know how it bothers me to be unprepared."

Her mother clanked a dish into the sink. "You certainly have been a bit too social. Don't give up your job for a man who might not be around in two weeks. I would think your short-lived relationship with that fireman would have taught you something."

"Mom, I was talking about you and Dad coming to California by surprise. I generally work on my stuff Sunday afternoons. While I love having you, it did throw a kink into my schedule."

"Hmmph." Her mother pursed her lips.

The phone rang, much to Emily's relief. She raced to get it before her mother answered and gave someone the third degree. Her phone rarely rang in the morning, and she couldn't help but throw up a prayer before answering.

"Hello."

"Emily, it's Darin."

"Darin, is everything okay? You don't sound so good."

"It's nothing for you to worry about, but I just called Pastor Fredericks's office and got an appointment with him today at four. It's usually his day off, but he's making an exception for me. Do you think you could meet me there? I want to tell both of you at the same time."

"Tell us what?" Emily's heart hammered against her chest. Was this where he told her he was already married? Or where he explained his life of crime back in Brazil or something?

"Emily, please trust me, and wait on this one. I can tell you it's not as bad as you're thinking."

"But you want me to meet you at the church? What's this about?"

"It's something I can't talk about on the phone, but I'd really love for you to be there. It concerns you in an off-hand way. It concerns our future." The seriousness in his voice alarmed her. She wasn't used to Darin being evasive with answers. Was there more to his ministry that she didn't understand? More than she would be able to handle?

"I'll meet you there at four o'clock." Emily decided she just had to trust God for the day. But within her heart, she prayed there was nothing more. Nothing she couldn't handle. She had quickly fallen in love with Darin. Would her heart be dashed as it had been so many times before? Would Darin leave like Kyle had? Like Fireman Mike had? She felt sick. A whole day of not knowing, just waiting for the other shoe to fall.

Emily offered her mother's questioning glances no satisfaction. "I'll see you both tonight. I take it I'm not cooking for you, then, you're eating out?"

"Do you really think we should waste the money, dear? I can get something for us all at the grocery today." Her mother grabbed her purse, as if ready to go.

"We'll eat over on the coast tonight, Nancy. That way Emily won't feel in any hurry to get home and entertain us. It sounds like she has enough going on today." Her father turned toward her. "We'll be home by about eight. That will give you time to get caught up on lessons."

"Before they fire you from that job," her mother added.

"Tenure, Mom. It's a beautiful thing."

After a peaceful latte and a morning newspaper at her local coffeehouse, Emily rushed into her classroom to find her principal waiting. She looked at the clock nervously, but she was on time. "Mr. Walker, is everything all right? What can I do for you?"

She hoped he hadn't noticed her absentmindedness lately. A mere two weeks ago, Emily had no social life, and her work could never be questioned, but lately she lived in her own little world. Going to the city on a weeknight, staying all hours at the local hospital, and filling out police reports. Dating Darin was certainly not for the faint of heart.

Mr. Walker cleared his throat and looked toward the white board with the morning's assignment written on it. Emily silently thanked God she'd been prepared on Friday. "Miss Jensen, one of your students was in an accident over the weekend."

Her throat caught and words tumbled from her mouth. "An accident? Who was it? May the Lord have watched over them!"

"I understand your religious beliefs, Miss Jensen, and, of course I tolerate your first-amendment rights, but I'll need to make sure this kind of speech doesn't come from you when you tell the rest of the class."

"Is someone hurt?" Emily asked, ignoring the admonition. One of her children's fate lay in the balance, and Mr. Walker could only worry about the liberal lawyers in California waiting to pounce.

"Not seriously. David Bronson's car was hit by a drunk driver this weekend. His whole family is fine, but David is in the hospital with a broken collarbone. You might want to have the class make him a card or an art project. I told his mother you would visit this afternoon and bring any homework."

Homework. Leave it to Mr. Walker to be concerned about the homework of a first-grader when the boy could have lost his life. Had the school administration lost all sense of decorum? Of rational behavior?

Mr. Walker ignored her shock. "I'm contacting MADD today. Apparently, they have a drunk driver with a history of this kind of criminal background. He's actually reformed and is supposed to be excellent talking with children. He has a way of bringing it home, they say."

"What's his name?" Emily asked tentatively.

"Not sure. It's that Fireman Mike's friend. Remember that trouble-making mother you had last year? That delinquent boy Josh of hers? This is a friend of her husband's. Oh, wait a minute, you used to date that fireman yourself, didn't you?"

"Briefly." *Mr. Tact. Briefly.*

"We'll have an assembly at the end of the week. Hopefully, David will be back to school by then, but if not, we can still emphasize the importance of seat belt safety. They said if David hadn't been in his booster seat, he wouldn't be coming back to us."

Emily clutched her heart. Her principal seemed to lack any feeling for children but loved edicts as if Robert's Rules of Order were written upon his heart. She suddenly realized he bore a striking resemblance to her mother. And for a moment, she seethed at the sight of him. With one more word, she couldn't trust herself. Rules first. People second. Would her life ever be spared of people who ordered their life so?

David Bronson exuded charm. He was the kind of kid who could get into trouble, smile, say something sweet, and make it all go away instantaneously. All the girls loved David, and he was the first boy Emily had ever seen dominate the first-grade love note competition. One day he'd be a grown-up Darin Black. Charming, confident, and in many ways free of life's consequences. It was as though the two of them, David and Darin, had a dozen angels on full-time watch helping to break any falls.

Mr. Walker broke her reverie. "I'm a little worried about bringing the drunk driver here. He is a felon, after all, but I think it will do more good than harm if we keep him chaperoned the entire time."

"I don't think it's something we need to worry about. Who knows? He might even be an upstanding citizen now."

"Phht, just like Charlie Manson is a reformed citizen now."

Emily clenched her teeth. "I'm dating that drunk driver. And do you know what? I might even see fit to marry him, so I'd appreciate it if you'd take your prejudices elsewhere. He's a Christian now, and he's changed." She stood with her mouth open, wondering if she'd really spoken her thoughts aloud. She watched Mr. Walker for an indication, but he said nothing. She scratched her chin, and like a gorilla in the zoo, the principal did the same thing.

"I don't know what's gotten into you, Emily, but I am watching you. Closely." His brows furrowed into an angry V. Mr. Walker was antagonistic toward religion of any sort. Well, that wasn't exactly true. If it reeked of tolerance and ethnic background, it was more than accepted. He despised talk of the Bible, however, and he'd tried to force Emily's Bible from her desk on countless occasions. She now kept it in her drawer.

She had no doubt that if Darin's faith was announced at his speech, he'd never be allowed to speak in the schools again. Mr. Walker would see to that.

Chapter 17

E mily watched the clock tick for what felt like an eternity. *Tick. Tick. Tick.* At 2:28, she practically cried out for the bell to ring. When it finally did, she called, "Class dismissed!"

She sighed, quickly planned for the next day's lesson, and headed to the church to meet Darin. Her stomach was in knots at the thought of seeing him. She could picture his face, and her heart did somersaults at the mere thought of his strong jaw.

Darin stood outside the office, a big bouquet of peach roses in his hand. She drew in a deep breath. How she loved that man. She loved that man! Was it even possible? She giggled like a kindergartner. She hadn't felt such joy since her college graduation, a time when she thought the world was fresh and full of promise. It held promise once again, and she closed her eyes. "Thank You, God. Thank You for this man."

When she opened her eyes, Darin stood in front of her, the roses perched under her nose. "They smell divine," she said. "Are they for me?"

"They'll never be for anyone else, but, Emily, things are going to get rough. I need to tell you about the dilemma I'm in, and I want Pastor there to speak truth to me because I'm in love with you. You and no one else. But life is so valuable to me, so precious. And I know you feel the same way about children."

Emily pushed the roses back toward him. "You have a child somewhere?"

He dropped his head, the light red stubble appearing. "I don't have a child, not one that's my own anyway. Promise me something, Emily. You'll hear the whole story before you run out."

She clutched her stomach. Why didn't anything come easily to her? Why did everything have to be strife-filled? "Darin, I don't know if I can handle any more bad news. I haven't told you the whole story of my brother."

"Now's a good time."

"We had a next-door neighbor. A little boy who was badly abused by his mother. We didn't call it that then; we just thought she was mean and spanked him too much." She fiddled with the collar on her shirt. "The little boy disappeared one day. We found out later he'd been taken to the hospital and eventually taken from his mother. My brother rebelled, vowing not to be hurt when my mother disciplined us harshly. But she never hurt us; it was just his reaction. So he left."

"Mike hinted there was something haunting about your history."

"I became a caretaker, baby-sitter for the neighborhood, one-time child psychology major, but I changed it to teacher. It was too hard for me to see how many children were hurt by people who should love them."

Darin shifted his weight, and just by his reaction, Emily realized she'd probably said too much. Whatever was on his mind, he didn't need her drumming up past hurts of her own.

"Darin, Emily, you're both here. Good." Pastor Fredericks greeted them each with a handshake and brought them into his office. "I've just been on hospital visits. Come on in and sit down." He waved a hand toward two red chairs before his desk. "Do you mind if I open us with prayer?" He bowed his head and dedicated the time to the Lord.

"Pastor, I have a big problem with an old friend from my past."

"The young woman named Angel?"

"Exactly."

Emily closed her eyes instinctively, as if she might not be able to hear by doing so. She knew Darin didn't love Angel, so what did any of this have to do with her? "Darin, maybe it's better if I wait outside."

"No, Emily," he said with force. "You're here because I love you, and I want you to know the truth. If I tell you in front of Pastor, you'll have no reason to doubt me."

So this was where she was told good-bye. Abandoned for the other woman, the other woman who needed him so much more. She braced herself.

Darin stood and walked the length of the office back and forth. "Pastor, Emily, Angel is pregnant, or so she says. It's not my baby. I swear to you that there's no way it could be my baby. But she's given me an ultimatum. I can either marry her and raise this child as my own, or she will take care of it in her own way."

Emily circled herself with her arms. A child's life hung in the balance. Just like when Josh needed Fireman Mike for a father, this baby would need Darin. She closed her eyes and nodded her head, trying to get her heart to accept the fact that Darin was going away, but for good reason. Kyle had gone away for good reasons, too, but she still felt her brother's absence acutely every single day.

"You're not going to like what I have to say, Darin." Pastor Fredericks stood.

"But I'm willing to listen. That's why I'm here."

"The Bible says you are not to marry an unbeliever. You know Angel is an unbeliever, am I right?"

"Yes, Pastor, but—"

"Darin, you have the heart of an evangelist, and just like all spiritual gifts, there's a downside to this gift. It's thinking you can do God's work for Him, if only you try hard enough. I take it you're willing to live a life of sacrifice for a woman who's made some terrible life choices and wants to pull you down with her."

Emily stood up. "I should go. I don't feel that I belong here."

"Sit down, Emily," Pastor Fredericks ordered, and she did so. "You've stepped back enough times and given away things that are rightfully yours. Now I don't know if you and Darin are meant to be married, but I will not have you back away from this because of a woman's schemes. You're both going to listen to me. You asked for my opinion, and you are more than going to get it."

Darin grabbed her hand and clenched it tightly. She squeezed back. *I love you,* she thought silently.

"What is it you want to do, Darin?"

"I want to marry Emily."

Her heart swelled. Hearing those words from such a man was more than she ever hoped for. All her years of teaching, all her love for family, nothing matched hearing those words from Darin Black.

"Then why would you go against the Bible, marry a woman you don't love, who may or may not be pregnant, and quit your ministry in East Palo Alto? Because I'm willing to bet this woman is not willing to live in the ghetto. Am I right?"

"You make it sound so simple, Pastor. But is it really? She's carrying a child she's threatening to destroy. Can I live with that my entire life?"

"I don't think you have a choice, Darin. This isn't yours. This is God's to handle. You cannot devote your entire life to the salvation of one person, which may or may not happen. And in the meantime, you would hurt the woman you do love and let her live alone? God wants authenticity, Darin. He doesn't want sacrifice to the point of sin. He's already been the sacrifice."

Darin raked through his stubbly hair, and relief flooded his face. He lowered himself onto the burgundy carpet and perched himself on one knee in front of Emily. She wanted to touch the soft red stubble on his head, and this time she didn't stop her hand.

"Emily Jensen, I love you. I've got issues; you can hear that as plain as the organ in church. Your mother hates me, I'm going to be poor as long as I can imagine, but I love you with my whole heart. I prayed like you can't believe that Pastor would tell me I owed Angel nothing. I don't love her. I never did, and I had such guilt over her bad choices. I wanted to fix her, like Jesus did for me."

"I understand." And she did.

"What I'm trying to do, very badly I must say, is ask you to be my wife. Emily, will you marry me?"

Tears of joy sprang forth, and Emily lowered herself onto the carpet and sobbed into his shoulder. "Yes, yes, I will marry you."

Pastor Fredericks coughed. "Now I think it's me who should leave." He stepped through the door and closed it behind him.

"Do you think if we offered to care for Angel's baby she might carry it?"

Darin's smile faded. "Emily, you would do that?"

"I told you, I've spent my entire life caring for other people's children. I thought I'd never have any of my own. Raising a child with you is what I want. Where it comes from is the least of my concerns."

"Praise God for you, Emily. Praise God. He has blessed me so."

Emily clutched her heart. "I'm still having trouble breathing. A minute ago, I thought you were marrying another woman. Now—"

"Now I'm doing what I'm truly called to do, not feeling guilty about something that only God can fix."

"We'll pray for Angel every day, Darin."

"We will," he agreed.

A quiet knock invaded their privacy. Pastor Fredericks poked his head in the door. "Are you two done with my office?" He winked.

Emily felt the heat rise into her face. "Thank you, Pastor, we are."

"Emily and I are engaged."

"Have you told her parents?"

A little bit of Emily's joy died within. "No, but we're on our way."

"First, we'd like to pray with you, Pastor. It seems the world is stacked against us, and yet I've never felt so within God's will. Not since I moved to East Palo Alto."

"East Palo Alto," Emily mumbled. "I'm going to live in East Palo Alto."

The corner of Darin's mouth turned up, and he reached his hand to her jaw. "You're going to live with me."

She exhaled. "I'm going to live with my husband." A few weeks ago, she thought she'd never get married. Now the man of her dreams was standing before her, professing his love. In front of their pastor, no less. If only her mother would understand, everything would be perfect.

Chapter 18

Nothing is ever perfect, Emily lamented. She paced her apartment. Her parents would understand; they just had to. She looked at the clock and watched the second-hand click away the minutes until Darin arrived. She knew she must tell her parents before he did, but every time she clutched the doorknob, the sick feeling in her stomach began. She squared her shoulders and reached one more time, this time opening the door.

"Dad," she yelled over the television set. "Can you turn that off for a moment? I have something to tell you both."

Her mother looked up at her from over her magazine. "This had better not be about that hoodlum."

"It is about Darin," Emily said. *I will not live in fear.*

"Surely, you're not thinking of anything serious with him."

"Nancy, be quiet and let your daughter speak," her dad said. "She's a grown woman."

"Mom, Dad, Darin and I are getting married. I'm going to live in East Palo Alto, but I'll still teach for the time being in Los Altos."

Nancy Jensen gasped and swooned as if she might pass out.

"I know this comes as a surprise to you both, but I just know this is God's plan for my life. I don't think it will be easy or even romantic at times, but I'm following His lead and Darin's, as well."

"I forbid it," her mother said. "I absolutely forbid you to throw your life away on a gardener who lives in the ghetto. He wears an earring, Emily. We raised you better than that."

Mel Jensen stood and placed his fists on his hips. "That's enough, Nancy. You will rejoice in your daughter's joy regardless of your opinions. I lost my son because of your constant nagging. I won't lose my daughter, too." His words came like daggers. The memories of the terrible battle before her brother left still haunted her. She couldn't let her own marriage break apart her parents.

"Please, don't fight. There's nothing to fight about. This isn't your decision. It's mine. Mom, I understand this is not the way you would have it. But I'm happy, and he's a strong Christian. He's just not the Christian we expected."

"I suppose you expect me to pay for this—oh, I can't even call it a wedding." She crossed her arms and practically spit her words.

"Nancy, I'm warning you."

"If you support her in this harebrained idea, I will leave right now."

Emily's father planted his feet on the carpet. "Do what you have to do."

"No, no. Please, don't do this!" Emily cried.

"Emily, if you back down on this, she will rule our lives forever. Is that what you want? Do you think her version of Christianity is what you want to live for the rest of your life? Because I've lived it for far too long, and I can testify it's like selling your very soul to please her. Do you want to please your mother or God?"

She choked back her emotion. "I want to please both."

"And if that isn't possible?" he asked.

Emily stared at her mother's hard expression. She would end up as Kyle had, coming from nowhere, her family legacy lost in one life choice. A choice for a man she barely knew. Yet she felt God calling her toward him as clearly as if He'd whispered the word *Darin* in her ear.

"I don't know," she admitted. She searched her mother's eyes. Eyes that wouldn't meet her own. "Please, Mother, look at me."

A look of disgust crossed her mother's expression. "You're not the daughter I raised."

"Yes, I am the daughter you raised, Mother. You just don't like it because I'm different from you, but God made me this way. I am His creation. Darin is His creation. We are in His image, not yours." She couldn't believe all that was tumbling from her mouth. She knew it might cost her a relationship with her mother. Something she swore she'd never let happen. But her father's encouragement spurred her onward. "Do you think that all Christians must look as you do?"

A knock at the door left the three of them looking at one another, each wondering who was going to open the door. Minutes passed, and finally the door opened on its own. Darin stood framed in the doorway.

"Is everything okay?" he asked.

"No. My mother will not be attending our wedding. Apparently, she is not happy about our news." Bitterness dripped from Emily's words.

Darin looked at the floor, then at Nancy Jensen. "I'm sorry to hear that. Your daughter will be a beautiful bride. We'll miss you."

Emily loved his firmness, yet her insides squirmed. She wanted it all. She wanted a husband and her family.

"Your father will be there to walk you down the aisle, Emily," her dad said.

"Thank you, Dad," she said huskily.

"This is the way it's going to be then?"

"It doesn't have to be, Mrs. Jensen." Darin walked away from Emily, looking her mother in the eyes. His expression gentle, he took her hand. "I'll spend my life proving I was right for your daughter. Whether or not you choose to

AN UNBREAKABLE HOPE

watch is your decision, but I will miss you greatly in our life. I will miss you as a grandmother to our future children and, most importantly, a mother to your wonderful daughter."

For the first time Emily could ever remember, she saw her mother's eyes fill with tears. Real tears. Not the kind that she often used with Emily's father for manipulation, but real tears.

"I don't ever want to hear about your mistake," she said to Emily.

"You won't."

"And you'd better keep my daughter safe in the ghetto, or I'll come after you personally."

"Yes, ma'am!" Darin saluted. "My parents are waiting in the car outside. Are you ready, Emily?"

"Ready as I'm going to be."

Darin went outside, and when he appeared again, his mother was with him, her black mascara running down her cheeks. His father came in behind her, looking at the television, most likely upset at missing some sports event. Emily headed toward him.

"Hi, Mr. Black. Mrs. Black, nice to see you under better circumstances."

"Let's just get this over with," Mrs. Black said. "You're marrying my son. None of us has any choice, so when's the date?"

Emily looked at Darin, who slapped his forehead. "Mom!"

"I think that guy hit you over the head harder than you're aware of," Mrs. Black snapped. "I'm hoping this wedding will at least be after the trial. It's not going to look good to have your wife testify against this guy."

"There is no trial, Mom. He was wanted on other charges, so he's just in jail for that now. If there is, I think her testimony is quite clear on the police report."

"You both plan to go through with this? You are aware my son is not a college graduate?" she asked Emily.

Emily nodded.

"And that he goes through phases that don't last very long. I'll admit this Jesus-thing has lasted awhile, but when he wants to race cars and parasail, where will you be?"

"I guess I'll be at his side." Emily's stomach felt like she'd just jumped from a cliff. Where would following Darin lead? It didn't matter.

Darin spoke up. "We know how you all feel about this wedding, and we're sorry you're not happier for us. It's happened fast. We still have so much to learn about each other, but I'm following my gut here. I love this woman. I can't explain how it happened so quickly. I only know it will never happen like this again. When I had my accident, I learned to grasp life for all it's worth."

Emily watched her mother wince, and she took a step closer to Darin, fitting her hand into his. Her heart pounded at the four worried expressions facing them. She'd never done anything like this, never dared to go against anyone else's wishes; but looking into Darin's green eyes, she couldn't defy what she felt in her heart.

"We'd like to take you all to dinner," Darin said. "I don't expect you to fall in love with the idea, but I hope you'll get more comfortable with our decision and get to know one another."

Emily's mother shook her head. "I'm not going to get comfortable with the decision because it's not going to happen."

Mel Jensen clenched his teeth. "It is going to happen all right. Get over it, or I'm done."

"What?"

"You heard me," he whispered. "I don't want to make a scene, but I'm not sitting for this. Mrs. Black, this goes for you, as well. No one is going to ruin my baby girl's happiness. She loves this man, and that's good enough for me."

Guilt welled up in Emily's chest. She felt so torn by the conflict all around her. But then she embraced the most comforting thought. Kyle would want her to stand up for her rights. This was not just for Darin and herself. This choice was for Kyle.

"Thank you, Daddy." She kissed him on the cheek, then kissed her mother. The elder woman went stone cold, her face rigid with anger. Emily squeezed Darin's hand for strength.

Epilogue

two years later

G randma Jensen put the baby boy down in his crib and offered a light kiss. "You are the most beautiful baby ever born. God shined His grace upon you, little one."

Emily nearly cried at the sight of her mother bent over the bassinet. Who would have imagined that such hard women as her mother and mother-in-law would melt at the warmth of a single, precious baby boy? She looked up when she heard Emily.

"I hope you and Darin will consider moving up by us, Emily. It's not fair for you to keep our grandchild from us. And to raise him in this neighborhood. It's unthinkable."

Emily laughed. "Are you kidding? With all the free baby-sitting I get in this neighborhood with Darin's Bible study kids? I'm not going anywhere. Besides, Grandma Black would wrestle you to the floor if you took her favorite little man."

Darin walked into the tiny house, and Emily met him in the hallway. "Hi, love. How was another day in paradise?" he asked.

"Perfect, as usual. Andrew started to roll over today. It won't be long now."

Darin sighed. "Did you get it on videotape?"

"Of course."

"It's a wonder anything in that child's life will ever happen without being caught on video," Grandma Jensen said. "Poor little thing. He needs his grandma just so his mother can carry the camera."

Darin laughed out loud. "He does need his grandma. You know, Mom, the house up the street is for sale."

Emily giggled. "Right, Darin. My mother is going to move to the ghetto, as she calls it."

Nancy Jensen pursed her lips. "I'll move anywhere for my grandchild, Emily. Don't be smart."

The doorbell broke their conversation, which Emily could only hope was a joke. She opened the door to see the most handsome face she'd ever seen besides her husband's. She couldn't breathe and had to find a chair when oxygen failed to creep into her nose.

"Can I help you?" Darin said threateningly.

"I heard I was an uncle."

Emily buried her face in her hands and soon felt her brother's arms wrap around her. "Is it really you?"

"I've been in South America. I got word from my supporters that my sister had a baby. I couldn't take a chance he'd grow up uncool. So I came to teach him."

She clutched her brother in her arms and held on for as long as he'd let her. When Kyle pulled away, she noticed he'd grown a beard, but other than that and a few wrinkles around the eyes, he was the same brother she'd last seen ten years before.

She looked to her mother, who blinked steadily to force her tears away. Then Nancy Jensen ran to the son who had left so long ago. "I'm sorry, Kyle. I'm so very sorry," she sobbed.

Emily looked into her husband's eyes. "I will become even more undignified than this," she said, quoting Darin's life scripture. And she would. Because fear had rendered her useless, but jumping off of life's precipice provided her with daily, unending joy.

A Letter to Our Readers

Dear Readers:

In order that we might better contribute to your reading enjoyment, we would appreciate your taking a few minutes to respond to the following questions. When completed, please return to the following: Fiction Editor, Barbour Publishing, Inc., P.O. Box 719, Uhrichsville, OH 44683.

1. Did you enjoy reading *San Francisco*?
   ❑ Very much—I would like to see more books like this.
   ❑ Moderately—I would have enjoyed it more if _____
   _____
   _____

2. What influenced your decision to purchase this book?
   (Check those that apply.)
   ❑ Cover   ❑ Back cover copy   ❑ Title   ❑ Price
   ❑ Friends   ❑ Publicity   ❑ Other

3. Which story was your favorite?
   ❑ *Grace in Action*   ❑ *Meet My Sister Tess*
   ❑ *The Landlord Takes a Bride*   ❑ *An Unbreakable Hope*

4. Please check your age range:
   ❑ Under 18   ❑ 18–24   ❑ 25–34
   ❑ 35–45   ❑ 46–55   ❑ Over 55

5. How many hours per week do you read? _____

Name _____

Occupation _____

Address _____

City _____ State _____ Zip _____

E-mail _____

_H_EARTSONG ♥ PRESENTS

Love Stories
Are Rated G!

That's for godly, gratifying, and of course, great! If you love a thrilling
love story but don't appreciate the sordidness of some popular paper-
back romances, **Heartsong Presents** is for you. In fact, **Heartsong
Presents** is the premiere inspirational romance book club featuring love
stories where Christian faith is the primary ingredient in a marriage
relationship.

Sign up today to receive your first set of four, never-before-published
Christian romances. Send no money now; you will receive a bill with the
first shipment. You may cancel at any time without obligation, and if you
aren't completely satisfied with any selection, you may return the books
for an immediate refund!

Imagine. . .four new romances every four weeks—two historical, two
contemporary—with men and women like you who long to meet the one
God has chosen as the love of their lives. . .all for the low price of $10.99
postpaid.

To join, simply complete the coupon below and mail to the address
provided. **Heartsong Presents** romances are rated G for another reason:
They'll arrive Godspeed!

YES! Sign me up for Hearts♥ng!

NEW MEMBERSHIPS WILL BE SHIPPED IMMEDIATELY!
Send no money now. We'll bill you only $10.99 postpaid with your
first shipment of four books. Or for faster action, call toll free 1-800-
847-8270.

NAME _____

ADDRESS _____

CITY _____ STATE _____ ZIP _____

MAIL TO: HEARTSONG PRESENTS, P.O. Box 721, Uhrichsville, Ohio 44683
or visit www.heartsongpresents.com